LIGHT
at
LAVELLE

LIGHT
at
LAVELLE

PAULLINA SIMONS

INTEGRATED MEDIA
NEW YORK

All rights reserved, including without limitation the right to reproduce this book or any portion thereof in any form or by any means, whether electronic or mechanical, now known or hereinafter invented, without the express written permission of the publisher.

This is a work of fiction. Names, characters, places, events, and incidents either are the product of the author's imagination or are used fictitiously. Any resemblance to actual persons, living or dead, businesses, companies, events, or locales is entirely coincidental.

Copyright © 2023 by Paullina Simons

ISBN: 978-1-5040-9646-1

This edition published in 2025 by Open Road Integrated Media, Inc.
180 Maiden Lane
New York, NY 10038
www.openroadmedia.com

LIGHT
at
LAVELLE

PAULLINA SIMONS

INTEGRATED MEDIA
NEW YORK

All rights reserved, including without limitation the right to reproduce this book or any portion thereof in any form or by any means, whether electronic or mechanical, now known or hereinafter invented, without the express written permission of the publisher.

This is a work of fiction. Names, characters, places, events, and incidents either are the product of the author's imagination or are used fictitiously. Any resemblance to actual persons, living or dead, businesses, companies, events, or locales is entirely coincidental.

Copyright © 2023 by Paullina Simons

ISBN: 978-1-5040-9646-1

This edition published in 2025 by Open Road Integrated Media, Inc.
180 Maiden Lane
New York, NY 10038
www.openroadmedia.com

For Alex Lloyd,
for his unwavering faith in me from the get-go.

LIGHT at LAVELLE

*Fate whispers to the warrior, "You cannot withstand the storm."
And the warrior whispers back, "I am the storm."*

Unknown

Fate whispers to the warrior, "You cannot withstand the storm."
And the warrior whispers back, "I am the storm."

Unknown

Prologue

One warm summer evening, in a tiny hamlet south of civilization, east of the wild mountains, west of the Black Sea, a beautiful young woman named Isabelle cooked and baked and decorated her house for the wedding of her friend Cici to her brother Roman Lazar. When she was done with the house, Isabelle decorated herself. She put on a red dress and five heavy strings of coral beads. She wove silk ribbons through her hair, pink and orange and yellow, and she made a flower wreath of mallow and magnolia and fitted it over her golden mane, the color of a Karabakh mare.

The large family had labored long, toiled from the first hour, and now the work was done, and soon it would be time for a well-earned banquet. The tables were fully laden for the high festival. The harvest had not been good that summer, but that didn't matter, for nothing was spared to honor the pair about to enter into holy matrimony.

Roman, a spectacular groom in an ultramarine blue shirt and black velvet trousers, rode in on Boyko, his beloved palomino stallion. And Cici, a beaming bride in embroidered white, adorned with peonies and roses, was swept up into Roman's saddle to circle the village church three times before they were crowned husband and wife.

The *korovai* had been baked, and the *gorilka* brew made with extra honey and peppers. The poppyseed cake, the *pamplushki*, the *kutia*, the shishkebobs, and the stuffed cabbage were all laid out like offerings.

Isabelle's husband was on the fiddle, her younger brother accompanied him on the accordion, and her mother played the balalaika. Isabelle's youngest brother was wrestling with her sons over in the dirt by the trees where the three of them must have thought Isabelle wouldn't notice.

They drank to life and rejoiced in their good fortune. They bestowed the newly married with their gifts and their pleasure. They danced the Ukrainian Wedding March, the fastest bridal polka in the world, they danced "the Kolomeyka" and "the Hopak." The music never stopped, and the homemade brew flowed freely. And Боже Мій, it was strong! It was a wonder they made it till morning. The wedding began at eleven and continued through the night and sunrise was like dusk, incandescent indigo and pink.

Four thousand miles away from the Lazars and their all-night worship of the power outside the physical world, separated from Isabelle by space but not by time, Finn Evans hired Paul Whiteman and his fifteen-man orchestra to play live on stage at the exclusive Somerset Club in Boston. Paul's band drove up from New York for one night only, to serenade Finn and Vanessa's seventh wedding anniversary. Everyone else in America listened to Whiteman through the little speaker on their living room radio, but here in *this* room, the king of jazz himself, in a white tux, stood on stage, the gold of his sax glistening, the gold from his sax floating through the air like tenor confetti, while Finn danced with Vanessa.

White linen and lilies covered the tables, and the handsome crowd wore their Friday night best, their hair immaculate, their silk dresses shimmering. The food was exquisite, from the cold lobster to the freshly made bread, from the clam chowder to the cod and scallops; all of it divine. The music drowned out hundreds of sober voices, sober because there was no wine, no moonshine, nothing but bloodless apple cider and virgin mint juleps coursing through the veins of the revelers.

A regretfully sober yet joyous Finn whirled in a waltz with Vanessa, his hand delicate on the small of her back, their guests looking on approvingly. Finn too was approving. His wife was a regal platinum vision, and the world he had built with her so concrete, it was as if he had hammered a perfect David out of a block of shapeless, unforgiving marble.

Such was life—measured by value, by time, by place, by space. It pressed upon them from all sides, and though Finn and Isabelle did not yet know it— feasting sumptuously in their corners of the vast world and spinning to the sax fandango and the fiddle—they were already at the precipice.

BOOK ONE

The Sword of Damocles

PART I

The Vanished

*"Conceal me what I am,
and be my aid
For such disguise as haply shall become
the form of my intent."*

William Shakespeare
(Twelfth Night, *Act 1, Scene 2*)

1

Cici Lazar and Her Stories

Ukraine, February 1929

"They killed them! They killed them all!"

Isabelle looked out the window to see the tiny Cici atop the massive Boyko, galloping up the sloping hill. High above her, a sedge of gray cranes, long-necked and mighty-winged, flew in a broken formation.

Jumping off the horse before the mount stopped moving, Cici ran into Isabelle's house. Not just ran but sprinted as if she had something great and important to announce that couldn't wait another second. Isabelle wanted to say, *tie up Roman's horse*, but before she could speak, Cici flung open the door, cried the words above, and bent over gasping.

Isabelle was almost twenty-nine years old, fair-haired, fair-eyed, fair-skinned. She was lean and strong in the way women are who live on a farm and work all day. There was only one mirror in her house, and she often went weeks without glancing in it. She brushed her teeth, washed her face, smoothed and braided her hair, got dressed, put on her boots, and began her day without once considering what she looked like. She knew. Only on Sundays did she put on a few airs and a pretty dress. Sometimes she left her hair down, in the summer put flowers in it. But often she didn't catch a glimpse of herself, even on Sundays.

And today was not a summer Sunday. It was a Tuesday in the dead of February.

Isabelle set down her wooden spoon; she had been frying potatoes and eggs. It was seven in the morning. Mirik had come in after loading the milk canisters into the dray. In the winter they made their deliveries right after sunrise. The light was still low, the sky a hulking gray.

Until Cici burst in, the cottage had been quiet. Isabelle's boisterous boys were down in the barn with Isabelle's mother. Talk about the blind leading the blind. Oksana was a good teacher, engaging and level-headed, but a terrible dairy farmer. However, Isabelle's children weren't allowed in the stables with Roman anymore, not after he allowed the boys to ride two untamed foals without a saddle! Now only the inefficient but safe grandmother was allowed to supervise them.

Isabelle's husband came to stand next to her as they stared at Cici panting. Mirik Kovalenko was seven years older, a serious man with a stern nose, kind brown eyes and a composed manner. He wasn't much taller than Isabelle or much bigger than her in build. His light brown hair was thinning, and he needed glasses, but wouldn't admit it.

Cici was still gasping, but not because she was out of breath.

"Killed who?" asked Isabelle.

"Who is *they*?" asked Mirik. "And who is *them*? Cici, speak sense."

"Stan and Vitaly!" Cici said. Stan and Vitaly Babich were Cici's cousins.

"Someone killed Stan and Vitaly?!"

"No!" cried Cici. "Stan and Vitya ambushed a squadron of Soviets coming down the road and shot them. I don't know if they were council members or OGPU. Stan is convinced they were *chekists*." OGPU were the Soviet internal security forces. Colloquially they were referred to by their post-Revolution name, *chekists*, from when the secret police was called CHEKA. "But either way, they killed them all. Maybe four dozen men."

Isabelle and Mirik half-relaxed. Cici was known Ispas over for her fantastical and far-fetched embellishment of facts. And Stan and Vitaly were not exactly famous for their intrepid military ingenuity. They were potato farmers who liked to drink and get into stupid trouble.

"Our Stan and Vitya shot four *dozen* soldiers?" Mirik said in his slowest, most skeptical voice.

"That's *right*, Mirik." Cici was adamant.

"And they were walking, these fifty officers?" Mirik said. "Not riding in military vans with loaded automatics?"

"They were walking, yes."

"In the middle of the night." It wasn't a question.

"Yes!" said Cici. "I am witness."

"You were up in the middle of the night in the middle of the woods and saw Stan and Vitya shoot a company of Soviets?" It was Isabelle's turn to sound incredulous.

"No! By the time I heard about it and got to the woods, it was over."

"Ah," said Mirik.

"I saw the last of them being thrown into a mass grave," said Cici.

Isabelle and Mirik exchanged a glance, less relaxed but still skeptical.

"What do you mean, by the time you *heard* about it?" Isabelle said. "How could you possibly hear about it? Weren't you next door with Roman, sleeping together like husband and wife? I just left Roman at the stables. He mentioned nothing about this."

Cici waved dismissively at Isabelle, as if to say *don't bother me with nonsense.* "Roman slept at home, if you must know everything, and I was at Tamara's."

"Why?"

"Why, why. Who cares. We had a fight."

"About this?"

"Isa, did you not hear what I just told you?"

"Oh, I heard." Isabelle really hoped Cici was exaggerating because otherwise, their simple life was about to get a lot less simple. When she first saw Cici racing up the hill, the girl had looked so much as if she was bringing good news! Isabelle thought maybe she was pregnant. Now Isabelle knew the truth—not only *not* pregnant but burying Communists in ditches, apparently.

"Cici, this story of yours is getting more and more marvelous," said Mirik. He was always calm. "Please—tell us more," he said. "We have *all* the time in the world. It's not like we have work to do or milk to deliver."

Isabelle elbowed her husband. She was *not* always calm, but she remained calm now because she didn't want to believe Cici.

"It's fine, Isa," Mirik said. "It didn't happen, so there's nothing to worry about. Is my food ready?"

"You don't believe me?" Cici said. "Go see for yourselves. On the other side of Ispas, on the road to Kammenets, just past the gray rock." Kammenets was the closest city to their hamlet.

"Now, why would all those Soviets be coming to Ispas all of a sudden?" Mirik said.

"You *know* why," Cici said, her voice laden with meaning. The rumbling through the countryside was getting hard to ignore. The Soviet food procurement units had been sent out into the Ukrainian villages since December. The cities didn't have enough to eat. It had been a fallow summer and an empty winter.

"Look, let's all pipe down," said Isabelle. "We don't know who they were—"

"Or even *if* they were," said Mirik.

"We don't know what they were—soldiers or requisitionists or just propagandists," Isabelle said. "We don't know if it was forty men or three."

"It was zero," said Mirik.

"It was four dozen!" said Cici. "You don't think I know the difference between three soldiers and fifty? I saw the bodies with my own eyes!"

"Cici is right about one thing, Mirik," said Isabelle. "Whoever it was, and however many, if they were walking down the road in darkness, before dawn, that's not a good sign. No one creeping into a village in the middle of the night can be up to anything good." But Isabelle knew and didn't want to say—if Cici was telling the truth and Stan and Vitya actually killed Soviet men, that was even worse.

"The Ukrainian loves a good story," said Mirik. "Isabelle, is my breakfast burning? Because there's work to do. The milk will go off before Cici is finished speaking."

"Please say you're making it up, Cici," said Isabelle, peering outside her kitchen window for a glimpse of she didn't know what.

"I'm not! I know sometimes I like to tell a tall tale or two, but trust me, Isa, this is not one of those times. Look at me. You know I'm telling the truth." Raven-haired, raven-eyed Cici was a minute, slightly rounded girl, but she carried herself high and mighty, as if on a plinth. Cici had always been a raging ball of fire. Part Romanian, her heart all Gypsy, she was impulse and flame. "Still don't believe me? Ask my husband. He knows."

"Oh, *now* he's your husband," Isabelle said. "A minute ago, you weren't even sleeping in the same bed."

"Don't humor her, Isa," said Mirik at the stove, spooning his own potatoes from the cast iron pan onto a pewter plate.

Cici shook her fists. "Both of you—get your heads out of the ground!"

"Oh, I would," Isabelle said, "if only the Soviets weren't supposedly in that ground, rotting in a shallow grave."

"Who said anything about shallow?" said Cici. "Our boys dug practically to Australia! They dug that hole like it was the most important hole of their lives!"

"And the ground looks freshly dug, like a grave?" asked Isabelle.

"They're not idiots. They covered it with twigs and leaves."

"No, of course," said Mirik. "Not idiots." He wolfed down his potatoes.

"Mirik, you heard what that *kramar* from Shatava told us who ran through here last week," Cici said. "The Soviets arrived uninvited and unannounced, upended his store, and took nearly all his provisions. He had to abandon the village and flee! That's why Stan and Vitya reacted as they did."

"If that's the case, what's their considered plan?" said Mirik. "To lie in wait every night waiting for more Soviets? That's the problem with Ispas. Too far out in the *glyxi doki* to have any sense. We have a village full of cavalier clowns with a few rifles and even fewer bullets. We can't fight the OGPU or the Red Army, Cici. We couldn't beat them ten years ago when we were better organized and better armed and we're not going to beat them now. We'll give them some milk—we've done it before—and they'll be on their way."

Cici got quite worked up. "Mirik, they're not coming for just your milk this time," she said. "They're coming for your cow. They're coming for Roman's horse."

"Yeah, good luck with *that*," muttered Isabelle.

Mirik, who didn't get worked up about much, turned red in the face. He waved his dirty spoon at the two women. "So, what are you going to do, follow Stan and Vitaly's lead?"

"They want to come here? Let them," said Isabelle. "This is Lazar land. We have my three brothers, we have Yana, who's worth ten men, even though she's expecting a baby. We have me, we even have you, Mirik."

"Thanks a lot, wife."

"And me," said Cici.

Yana was a warrior, Cici a wannabe warrior. "A Lazar by marriage lies in the same bed as her husband," Isabelle said, adding, "but fine. And you, too." She turned back to Mirik. "We have rifles, we have shotguns. We have horses. That's a cavalry, husband. And Roman even kept some grenade sticks from the war as souvenirs." The *war* was the Civil War of 1918–1921 between Bolshevik Russia and Ukraine.

"Yes, and you know what else we have?" said Mirik, wiping his mouth. "Because you seem to have forgotten. Two small sons and our feeble mothers. We can't be waging another war with the Soviets."

"Who are you calling feeble?" said Isabelle's mother Oksana, who had just walked inside.

"And who are you calling small?" said nine-year-old Slava, Isabelle's first-born son, black curly-haired and round-faced. Slava was the word for *glory* in Ukrainian. As in *Slava Bohu*, Glory to God.

"Yeah, Papa, who?" said Maxim, Isabelle's second son, who was a blade of long grass like his mother. They called him Max. He was eight.

"Decade-old grenades and two enormous boys," Mirik said, his hands on his children's diminutive heads. "Yes, Mama, we're unbeatable."

2

The Banker

On a sweltering evening at the end of August 1929, an evening Finn thought was like any other, he left Adams Bank and Trust on the corner of Washington and Winter and began to amble home. As he passed Jordan Marsh, the luxury department store, purveyors of silk, wool, and finery, he allowed himself a satisfied glance at his reflection in the glass windows. He was pleased with himself, though his mind was distracted.

The bank's quarterly profits, to be released to the investors at the end of September, had been made available to him that afternoon, and they exceeded his most optimistic expectations. He had increased quarterly revenues by 70 percent over the year before, contained operating costs at last year's levels and kept the default rates at a minuscule 2.2 percent—the lowest of all the banks in Boston. Finn invested heavily, diversified the bank's holdings, spread wide the nearly non-existent risk, and greatly increased his capital, both personal and professional. The returns had been phenomenal. So much so that for the last twelve months, Finn had been investing the bank's deposits chiefly on margin. Buying stock on margin allowed him to multiply the bank's profits not just exponentially but geometrically. Because of this, Finn was able to offer his depositors the highest savings rate in Boston, which in turn attracted more customers. When Finn started at the bank in 1921, they had barely five hundred depositors. Not even a decade later, they were about to break five thousand, and their total deposits were nearing seventeen million dollars! Walter Adams, his father-in-law, who owned the bank, was as pleased with Finn as Finn was with himself.

Thus occupied with his successes, Finn strolled languidly past City Hall. The walk home was a favorite part of his day, especially on these waning Fridays, when everyone in Boston knew the winter freeze was just around the corner and took advantage of the balmy weather. Finn and Vanessa planned on taking the girls to their cottage on Cape Cod, to prolong for one more weekend what had already been a mostly blissful summer.

Finn liked seeing himself as he appeared to other people. He had just turned thirty-one. He was refined, groomed, tailored, not a wrinkle on him. His dark blond, thick, naturally unruly mop of hair was brushed all the way back and kept under strict barber discipline. He had a glint to his blue-green eyes and a humorous bend to his expressive mouth. The humor he also tried to keep under control, as his wife was often not amused by his teasing. He was over six feet tall, which he liked, and broad, which he liked less—more demolition man than jockey—but one could only do so much with the card one had been dealt at birth. His custom-made suits slimmed him, made him appear every bit the elegant businessman he aspired to be. He kept his large frame in trim shape by walking up and down the steepest hills of Boston, admiring himself in the welcoming glass and assessing his life.

And life was good.

Finn had made it so.

He had made it what he wanted it to be, made himself into the man he wanted to be. Well raised, immaculately educated, beautifully mannered, bespoke, smooth-faced—though that five o'clock shadow was never far. He had a wife. Two girls. All four parents still living. His mouth twisted at that last thought, but one would've had to look really close to notice.

Catching his long stride, his imposing size, the drape of his light gray coat, the straight back that had never bent over wheat or needle, Finn turned his gaze from the window and walked on, counting his blessings.

3

Lemonade

The first time Vanessa Evans née Adams began to suspect there might be something wrong with her, she was eight years old and feared she might be allergic to lemons. This made her melancholy because she loved all things lemon: lemonade, lemon meringue pie, lemon bars, lemon ices.

She loved lemons so much that the mere possibility of being unable to enjoy the food she loved best made her distraught. This in turn made her determined to prove that she was not allergic to her favorite thing. So she continued eating lemons and distracted herself from feeling unwell by thinking about something else so she wouldn't have to acknowledge the gnawing pain in the middle of her body. First, she tried thinking about something else, and then she began doing something else. When she was eight, she systematically and fastidiously pulled the petals off all the daisies in their garden.

That's how it began.

That was twenty-two years ago.

Now there was no going back. For the most part, she had led an idyllic, charmed, protected life. Which was appropriate for someone who looked like her. She was the ideal of female beauty. She wore clothes well, had a pleasing smile, slight hands, a kind demeanor, and a great sense of fashion. There was nothing wrong. All her life, her mother and father told her so: the perfect child with perfect manners, the perfect daughter, sister, student, friend, and dancer, Vanessa deserved nothing less than to make someone a perfect wife and continue to live a perfect life.

She met Finn when she was eighteen and he was nineteen. He was in his junior year at Harvard. They had a whirl of a summer together, but in November 1917, he went off to war. He was gone eighteen months, and when he came back, he was a different man. Vanessa didn't know how or why. But the silly happy romantic boy she had danced with and walked through the Public Garden with was no longer present in the wounded and decorated serious man who returned to her. Some secret burden cast a shadow on Finn's every smile and every stride.

Their previous talk of marriage stopped. He wanted to take his time, focus on his education. If they were going to be married, he wanted to make sure he could provide for his family. That was the most important thing to him, he said. Not to let her down.

The happiest day of Vanessa's life was when Finn finally proposed. The second happiest was their wedding day.

Vanessa gave him two girls, one after the other, born a year apart. Afterward, she had a little trouble coping. There was nothing specific she struggled with, just an acidic malaise, a little burning in the gut that made it difficult to get things done.

Finn never questioned it. When Vanessa said to him, dear one, I could use a little help, he sprang to action, finding her Edith, a professional and conscientious governess, if slightly long in her years.

This Friday evening, while Vanessa waited for Finn to come home, she was washing all the sponges in the house. Also all the rags, towels, and cloth napkins she could find in the cupboards. She set them into the tub of hot water and washed them all, scrubbing them with her soft milk-white hands.

On the surface, it was a good and proper thing for the woman of the house to do. It meant she liked to keep things clean.

But just under the surface was the plain truth that Vanessa had a full-time staff to perform these tasks. What no one else could do was be a proper hostess to her family, most of whom were sitting out on her balcony at that very moment, waiting for her to join them. What she *needed* to do was her hair and makeup, what she *needed* to do was put on a summer dress, and join her family for canapés.

Vanessa needed to be on top of different things today.

Instead she was exhaustively washing the rags in the scrub room off the kitchen on the lowest level of their multi-level manse.

Everything was fine. There was nothing to worry about.

But Vanessa couldn't stop washing the rags.

Not only couldn't stop, but didn't want to.

She was thinking about their eighth anniversary celebration last week.

First the blessings: Finn had such a way of smiling at her, such an open way of showing his frank affection. Also: Finn's occasional salty word, his occasional saucy way with her. Much to be thankful for there.

More blessings: the girls looked like her, flaxen-haired and slight, and not like Finn, who was handsome and shaggy-haired but had a broadness of body and ruggedness of face that served men much better than it served women.

There were two tiny black marks on Vanessa's otherwise shiny existence. The first was the continued consequence of the long-ago suspected allergy to lemons. It had seemed so insignificant once, especially from a child's point of view: to quiet your mind by focusing on something else.

And the second blemish: Finn wanted to have another baby. He wanted a boy. As if he cared nothing for her two difficult pregnancies or for her subsequent miscarriage. The specter of the baby they had lost cast a pall over the Elysian Fields that was their life.

"But Finn," Vanessa said to him the night of their celebration last week. It was late when they got home, and they sat in their drawing room before turning in after a fantastic evening. Then he had to go and ruin things by bringing it up again. "You're not serious about having another baby, are you? If we have one more, why, that will make three."

"Yes," he said in his resonant male voice. Usually, Vanessa loved his voice. It was so protective and comforting. But not that night. She wished she didn't need to explain the starkly obvious. But he sipped his tea in their state-of-the-art drawing room with the fire burning and the candles flickering, as if he were waiting for just such an explanation.

"Finn, what if it's another girl?"

He beamed. "How lucky—three girls."

"And then?"

"Perhaps we can try for a boy after that."

Vanessa wanted to faint. Then *and* now as she was remembering it, her hands immersed in the cooled soapy water, scrubbing, scrubbing, scrubbing.

"Try for a boy *after* a third baby?" The tips of her nails quivered with the impossibilities. "Finn, no one we know has even three children," Vanessa whispered. "Try for another? What are we, Catholics?"

She watched him take an almost imperceptible breath.

"I know many people," Finn said, "who have more than three children."

"Not people on the hill," Vanessa said. "Maybe people you lend money to. Not *our* people." Two children is what civilized human beings had, the kind of people who attended Park Street Church on Sundays. Two children at most. Sometimes Vanessa wished her parents had stopped with her and not gone on to have Eleanor. Her sister is what happened when parents unwisely decided to have more children.

"It's late," he said. "I'm turning in." That's all he said. But he didn't kiss her head and didn't smile at her as he bade her goodnight.

"You're an only child, Finn," Vanessa said to him before he went upstairs. "What do you know about having many children? If we were meant to have a boy, we would have." Neither looked at the other when she spoke these words.

"We have our precious girls. In so many ways, the hand we've been dealt has been a royal flush. No use complaining."

"I'm not complaining," Finn said. "I know better than anyone what I've been dealt." That odd faint bitterness crept into his voice. "But if we don't at least try again, my life will eventually feel to me less like a royal flush and more like a handful of queens."

This, after their night at the Somerset Club when Mildred Bailey sang "The Man I Love," and they danced with such abandon that Vanessa was certain that penumbras of lost and not yet created children were far from his heart.

Showed you what she knew.

4

The Borrowed Avtomats

Ukraine, February 1929

Isabelle stood in the black mud, her coat buttoned up to her ears, and stared grimly at the clearing off the side of the main road from Kammenets into Ispas. There, a little way into the bare woods, a visible dell had been dug out, filled with bodies, and covered back up with dirt and broken branches. Mirik stood to the right of her, Stan and Vitaly to the left.

Cici did not exaggerate. She barely embellished. It may not have been four dozen Russians, but it was more than three. And it was certainly more than zero, which is the number Isabelle's placid, professorial husband had tossed into the jar of guesses. But the awful point about Cici's story was that the core of it was entirely true. Yesterday, the ditch did not exist, and today it did, and there was a platoon of dead Soviets in it.

For the life of her, Isabelle couldn't understand why Stan and Vitaly thought it was a good idea to kill a horde of men when the hard ground required so much disturbing. To dig a grave in February! Ispas didn't even bury their own in February. They waited until the spring thaw. Stan and Vitaly were impetuous fools, and now the whole village would pay.

"What do you think?" Stan said with a proud grin. "Pretty good, right?"

"Only a newborn who'd never seen a grave would look at this giant mound and not call it what it is," said Isabelle. "Stan, every fresh grave in our cemetery looks like this. But, of course, *smaller*. If someone was looking for burial grounds—and you can be sure someone will be—what do you think they'd be looking for?"

"No way," Stan said. "You're wrong." How he'd managed to survive into his mid-twenties, Isabelle had no idea.

"Who knows about this?" she asked.

"No one," Stan said.

"Stan, promise me on your mother you didn't get the rifles from Roman, or I will—"

"Promise, absolutely not. Never."

Vitaly piped in. "Well, we asked, but Roman said no."

Stan elbowed Vitaly hard. Isabelle groaned.

"Who else knows?"

"No one!"

"You mean you didn't boast about it to everyone?"

"I didn't boast!" Stan said. "I got help digging the hole, that's all."

"Who helped you?"

"Vitaly."

"Who else?"

"Lots of people came to help. Don't worry. Everyone knows how to keep a secret."

"It's only a secret when one person knows, Stan," said Mirik. "When two people know, it's not a secret anymore. It's common knowledge. And in your case, the entire village knows. A handful of your so-called friends will be the first to hand you over when a fresh death squad, now armed to the teeth, is sent to Ispas in search of their fallen paper pushers." He tugged on Isabelle's sleeve. "Let's go, Isa. We're so late with the last of our deliveries. It's almost nine."

"They were *not* paper pushers!" Stan sounded indignant. "They were definitely soldiers."

"Oh? Where are their weapons, Stan?" said Isabelle.

Stan was stumped.

"You better pray it snows between now and when the Soviets come," Isabelle said to the two men, walking away in disgust and climbing into the wagon. "Pray real hard. Because the earth rises with the truth."

It remained too cold to snow, and in the meantime, discord brewed in the normally tranquil Ispas. Most of it was in Isabelle's own house. The evening after the discovery of the shooting, the family collected for a chaotic, homemade-vodka-fueled confrontation, with Stan and Vitaly in their cross sights.

Isabelle and Mirik were there, of course, along with Isabelle's three brothers and Mirik's brother, Petka. Isabelle's mother was on the sidelines. Isabelle's children were being watched by Yana in another hut.

Though increasingly anxious throughout the scolding, Stan and Vitya remained adamant they had done right. The trader from Shatava was the canary in the coalmine, they said. He had warned the farmers in Ispas that Soviet operatives were being sent en masse to the outlying villages on orders from the Central Committee of the Communist Party. Some came to requisition wheat and beets. Others came to try again to collectivize the farms. The Shatava *kramar* said *chekists* came into his village in the middle of the night and evicted the farmer who lived in the largest house and commandeered it for their operational headquarters—"All before daybreak!"

"So when we saw Soviets marching down the road also in the middle of the night, headed for our village, what were we supposed to think?"

"You were supposed to think nothing," said Petka, who suffered no one gladly and fools least gladly of all. "You were supposed to be sleeping in your beds like all decent people who get up at dawn to make their living." Mirik's brother was a stiff, utterly humorless man, with a gray beard, a large angular nose, and cold small eyes. A dairy farmer his whole life, he was ten years older than Mirik. He had married late, had his children late, and carried himself like a man who spent his days regretting most of his choices, especially tonight.

"And now you've ensured the Soviets will come here not just for bread but for bloodlust," said Roman to Stan and Vitaly, clearly pained about agreeing with Petka. There was *no* love lost between the brothers-in-law.

At twenty-eight, Roman Lazar was a year younger than Isabelle but often acted like he was the firstborn child—because he was the firstborn son. Roman was of medium height and wiry like a jockey. He was wild-haired, wild-bearded, and wild-eyed. His hair, his beard, and his eyes were coal black. When he tied up his hair in a ponytail he looked like an Old Rus priest, like the unfrocked monk the Ukrainian Cossacks helped put on the throne of Moscow many centuries earlier. Roman called himself "blameless and wicked," quite a combination for a native son of Ukraine who loved horses and his family and Cici, though as Cici liked to frequently point out, he loved Cici last.

Stan and Vitaly disclosed that since last week they had been on night watch in the woods, anticipating the Soviet appearance. They borrowed two Fedorov avtomats, the selectively repeating semi-automatic Great War rifles, from Oleg Tretyak, Ispas's cobbler. A decade earlier, Oleg had confiscated them from fallen Red Army soldiers. He lent the weapons to Stan and Vitaly in exchange for a week's worth of potatoes. Stan and Vitya had gone to Roman first, but Roman said he smelled trouble and refused.

"They were walking in a formation," Stan said, explaining *again*, "and we just picked them off one by one. Our rifles were fitted with two cartridges of twenty-five rounds each."

"And we had two extra clips," said Vitaly.

"As one fell, we got the next one," Stan said. "It was over in less than a minute. We got some cash from them, too."

"Pretty good, right?" said Vitaly.

"You killed them *and* robbed them?" said Isabelle. "Great work, Stan. Good job, Vitya."

Isabelle and her brothers stood against the wall with their arms crossed. Ostap was twenty-six and Nikora twenty-two. All three Lazar men looked like their father, tar-haired, compact, broody, intense. And Isabelle looked like her mother. Except her mother was sitting in a chair in the corner away from the ruckus, reading a book. That was definitely not Isabelle. She didn't know how to sit.

The family warred and smoked and drank, fiercely divided over what to do.

"Why does anything have to be done?" Stan said. "Even if they send more men—and they'd be fool to—we'll keep it quiet. They ask, we deny. We say we don't know what happened."

"Are you sure you don't want to just keep killing them, Stan?" Roman said.

"Don't joke, Roman," said Petka. "This is not the time." He stood on the opposite wall from the Lazars, next to Mirik.

"We won't say anything!" Stan said, no longer in a joking mood.

Vitaly agreed with his brother. "They're not going to find them, and we are not going to tell them. You can't drain blood from a stone."

"But you're not a stone, Vitya," said Nikora. "Inside you is foolish blood that *can* be drained. What will you say when they string you up by your ankles and interrogate you?"

"Can't be worse than what's happening tonight," Stan muttered. He and Vitaly sat at the table, surrounded.

"You really don't think so?" said Isabelle.

"String us up by the ankles?" Vitaly squealed. "Stop teasing!"

"Do we look like we're teasing?" said Nikora.

That the killing was impulsive, no one disputed. "Just think of the trouble that will now fall on *you*, who dared raise your voice in meek protest," said Ostap. "And on us by association."

"Shooting two dozen Communist apparatchiks and trying to hide their bodies is not meek protest, Ostap," said Mirik. "It's a declaration of war."

Ostap was mild, with the diplomatic mannerisms of a middle child—until he was provoked. Ostap was married to the warrior princess Yana, who was banned from these meetings because of the volatility of her temper. *Meek* was not a word Yana used or understood, unlike her soft-spoken husband.

Meek was also not a word Roman used or understood. "If Stan and Vitya are right," Roman said, twirling his enormous curlicue mustache, "and the Soviets are coming to take what's ours, is that not also a declaration of war, Mirik?" Roman had abstained from getting involved in the ambush, but he bowed down to no one, especially not the Russians. His hatred was generational, genetic, ingrained, pervasive, abiding—and deeply personal. Everyone knew it, which is why Stan and Vitaly had come to him first.

"I would like to not declare war on anyone," Mirik said.

"I second that," said Petka.

"We're going to reason with them, Roman." Mirik was a reasonable man. Isabelle had swum all her years in the deep waters of tempestuous, impulsive, temperamental Lazars, each one more ferocious than the next. Isabelle needed the cool, still water of her level-headed husband.

Roman raised an eyebrow. "How I would like to be a fly on the wall of the hall where *you*, Mirik, explain to the Soviet official how much milk he can take from you and Petka."

"How much milk could they possibly take, Roman?" Mirik said with a shrug. "They can only take what won't go off in two days."

"Mirik," Cici said, "Roman told you, and I told you and the Shatava *kramar* told you, and all the latest from the Kiev papers told you—they're not coming for your milk. They're coming for your cow."

"Even there I'm safe," Mirik said. "They don't know how to milk a cow."

"Everything will be fine," Stan repeated. "They won't find the bodies."

"It's not about the bodies, you fools," Isabelle said. "Or the milk. Or even the cow. Don't you understand? It's about the *grain*."

From her corner, Oksana nodded and nodded, without looking up.

The family fell quiet.

A bad harvest in the fall meant a food shortage the following winter. That was now. There was no way out of that. The hundred million people living and working in Russian cities, far away from Stan and Vitaly's potatoes and Mirik's milk, had to eat. Where would their bread come from if not Ukraine and Ispas and the Lazars?

And if Ispas had no grain, then what?

And if the Lazars had no grain, then what?

After everyone had gone, Isabelle and Mirik checked on their sleeping children. The youngest boy woke up, and while Mirik went to lock up, Isabelle lay down between her sons in their bed for a few minutes and cradled Max in her arms to calm him.

"You were all talking so loud, Mama," he said. "I got scared."

"Sorry, *malenky*, sorry my *sonechko*," she whispered. "Adults sometimes talk loud when stressful things are happening."

"You and Papa don't."

"Your papa is tough to rile, that's why we love him."

"What did Stan and Vitya do? You sounded so mad at them."

"Nothing, nothing." Isabelle pressed her lips to Maxim's silky head. "They're just foolish. They did a foolish thing, and we're mad because we're all afraid they'll be punished for it."

"Punished how?"

"Go to sleep, Maxi, go to sleep, *milyy*."

"Mama, sometimes I do foolish things."

"Not like that."

"Slava does. He's always terrible, you say so yourself."

"Shh. Like you, your brother is a glorious boy." A terrible boy, but glorious.

Maxim hugged her with his thin arms, burying himself near her heart. "I'm not going to do anything foolish, Mamochka, I promise you," he whispered. "Because I don't want you to yell at me. I want you to yell only at Slava. Because he is very terrible."

After she and Mirik undressed in their own room and fitted in next to each other under the heavy covers, Mirik tried to joke Isabelle out of her gloom, tried to laugh away her nerves. "We'll be fine, Isa, why are you worried? We've overcome problems before. Ispas is too small and out of the way for them to care about us. The God who has given us the life we are meant to live will not abandon his creation."

Isabelle wasn't so sure. Not abandon maybe—more like cast off into the steppes, get busy with other things.

"In any case," Mirik said in a whisper, "there is nowhere to go. We are farmers, this is all we know. There is no way out of this life."

"That's what I'm afraid of," said Isabelle.

"Don't be afraid. We are blessed. Sleep well, my wife. You'll see. It will snow tomorrow."

But it didn't snow tomorrow.

The Soviets came tomorrow.

5

The Tailor's Request

Finn was almost at Charles Street, lost in the reverie of his pervasive contentment, when he remembered his promise to Vanessa. He had told her he'd pick up her dresses from Schumann for their upcoming weekend away.

Swearing under his breath, he turned back. Now he was going to be late getting home. He'd been so busy congratulating himself, he'd forgotten to behave in a way worthy of congratulation. If he came home without the dresses, Vanessa might cancel the trip because she'd have nothing to wear. If he arrived late, but with the dresses, she would also be out of sorts. One measure of me as a man, Finn thought, is that I don't forget what I'm supposed to do.

Less composed, Finn hurried back uphill.

When he got to the elevated train separating Boston proper from the immigrant enclave of Boston improper, known as North End, he slowed down, evened out his stride and took deep breaths to calm his lungs.

But though Finn walked more slowly as he crossed under the clanging trains, shadowed in the artificial darkness of the elevated track and the tall buildings packed around the narrow winding alleys, he didn't search for a glimpse of his reflection in the sooty North End windows. He already knew what the looking-glass would reveal: that his shoulders were slumped and his head was lowered. On the corner of Salem and Prince, Finn walked into Schumann's tailor shop not as a conqueror but as the great unwashed, which was the truest measure of who he felt he was, in the deepest deep from which his soul sprang.

Finn liked coming to see Schumann. His shop was unlike other places Finn frequented, and in that lay some of its appeal. The bank was spacious, gleaming, full of glass, and Schumann's place was dark and narrow, with only two windows and a front door for light. Schumann's bell never stopped ringing. The tailor was somewhat of a celebrity in the North End. When Vanessa would ask Finn why he insisted on going "all the way there" when there was a perfectly good tailor right around the corner on Myrtle, he would tell her it was because Schumann was the best.

He was also inordinately fast. Need the shirts starched and pressed by five this evening? Not a problem. I'll have them ready for you. You want your wife's dress taken in four inches in the waist and the length hemmed and biased? Give me till 6:15 tonight.

It wasn't just for Finn that Schumann worked like this, it was for all people, even those who hadn't lent him the money to start his business. Schumann was the man who got it done, no matter what *it* was.

But Finn knew—Schumann worked for Finn the fastest of all.

Finn watched the tall, thin tailor discuss various holes, fadings, and stains with the customers ahead of him. Schumann was soft-spoken and polite. He treated everyone with the same level of courtesy, be they chimney sweeps or vice-presidents. Occasionally he wore a yarmulke, but not today, and he sported a beard that he often shaved clean off, as if he wasn't particularly attached to it either. His gray hair was still impressively thick. He was in his late fifties. His back was stooped from bending over the looms, and this made him appear shorter, but in fact he was taller than Finn, though half as wide. There was something calming about the man, his mouth full of thread, his sharp eyes smiling. Maybe that's why Finn liked coming to him. And not just Finn. Schumann's clients regaled him with more than just the rips in their fabric. They also plied him with minute details of their aches and pains, their inflammations and congestions. And Schumann, courteous to the last, listened to them all.

Schumann's face always lit up when Finn walked through his door, but today, he looked even brighter than usual. His voice pitched louder. "Finn, hello there! Just a moment, sir, just one moment." His finger flew up, beseeching Finn to wait. The tailor remained polite with his other customers but became less patient.

Finn watched him approvingly. There was nothing that Schumann wouldn't or couldn't do. Finn had tried. He'd tested the man.

Schumann, I have a silver button missing off my suit jacket.

Not a problem, Finn. I'll replace it for you.

But it was custom-made in Brookline!

When do you need it by, tomorrow morning?

Schumann, my girls got purple paint on my favorite shirt.

Not a problem; leave it with me. The tailor would smile. Unless you want me to dye the whole shirt purple color? I can do that, too. Purple can be quite fetching.

A purple shirt, for a *man*, Schumann? Are you being funny?

Yes, sir, a little bit.

And so it went.

He had found Schumann by accident years ago, even before he got married. Back then, it was just the tailor, his iron, a sewing machine, and a steam hose. And to be perfectly accurate, Finn didn't find Schumann. Schumann found Finn. One day when Finn was walking up Salem Street, a man had stopped at the corner to let the produce carts pass. The man said to Finn in heavy English, "You have rip in back of your suit, sir. Very big. Yes, afraid so. Would you like me to fix for you?"

"I can't just take off my jacket and give it to you," said Finn. Gentlemen didn't take off their coats in public!

"Of course not, sir. Step right here with me. Right here, into doorway. Now, take jacket off. I fix." Like a magician, from the depths of his seemingly bottomless pocket, Schumann produced a spool, a thread, and a small pair of scissors. In a minute or less he had repaired the damage. "All done," the tailor said. "Good like new."

"Where are you from?" an impressed Finn had asked.

"Right here, on Salem Street, sir."

"They taught you well in the old country."

"I wasn't tailor in old country. That was my, how you say—relaxation."

Finn thought Schumann had a wife who helped with the sewing. He never indicated one way or another if he had any children. But then the woman vanished and was replaced by another woman at the sewing machine. After a while, she too disappeared and was replaced by someone else.

"Everything good, Schumann?" Finn asked this evening when the tailor was finally free.

"Very," Schumann replied. "Thank you for asking."

Finn glanced at the new girl sitting at the table, stitching. "Where do you get them from?" Finn smiled. Was Schumann an old dog?

"They come from the old country." Schumann didn't rise to the bait.

Finn smiled. "Not quite what I was asking, but okay. Listen, I have a question for you."

"And I have something to ask of *you*," Schumann said. "But you go first."

"I meant to mention it the last couple of months," Finn said, casually tapping his fingers on the counter. "I've been looking through the weekly business, and I noticed odd activity in your business account."

"Odd?"

"Yes, you've been withdrawing your money."

"Is that strange to manager of a bank?" Schumann asked. "When people withdraw their own money from their own accounts? What kind of activity do bankers find normal?" His eyes twinkled teasingly.

Finn continued drumming. "Here's the odd thing," he said. "While you're withdrawing your money, everyone else is depositing theirs."

The tailor shrugged.

"Why are you taking your money *out*, Schumann?" Finn asked. "We're all booming, sky high. What do you know that I don't? You can tell me. I'm like your financial doctor." Finn smiled.

"Very good. Like I'm your clothing doctor." Schumann smiled back and stroked his beard, watching Finn thoughtfully. "There is nothing to tell. I have some money left in the accounts, no?"

"Ten percent of what you had in the spring. Why did you withdraw 90 percent of your savings?"

Schumann leaned forward and lowered his voice. "Because, Finn, the price of thread has gone *up*."

Finn was silent, his brain assessing.

"Thread," Schumann repeated. "It's gone *up* in price."

"Oh, I heard you. So?"

"That's a big deal to a tailor. Thread, you see. Vital to my business."

"What about U.S. Steel? Is that not vital to your business?"

"It is, sir! My needles are very important. Steel has also gone up."

"You don't mean the price of steel shares," said Finn. "You mean the price of actual steel?"

"Well, I suppose both," said Schumann. "But I am more concerned with the price of actual steel."

Finn straightened the sleeves of his suit jacket. "You wouldn't think rising prices are a bad thing if you had invested in the company that produces the steel for your sewing needles, as I have been advising you to do for years."

"Let's see how the year ends for steel, and then we can revisit."

Finn was still mulling. "If thread has gone up, Schumann, just increase your own prices to cover it."

"I can't."

"Why?"

"I will lose customers. Wages have not gone up."

"Okay, but coal and gasoline have also not gone up," said Finn. "Or rents. Or taxes."

"No, Finn. Just thread," said Schumann. "And it's gone up in price because Coats and Clark is producing less of it. Now why would *that* be?"

"That's not possible." Finn frowned. "Schumann, for the love of God, stop speaking in riddles."

"You asked. I'm telling you."

"There must have been a bad cotton crop."

"No, record crop," the tailor said. "Three years in a row."

"Maybe the looms broke."

Schumann shook his head. "Nothing's broke. Harvest is excellent, nothing's broke. C and C simply have too much inventory."

"There's your answer. They've been making too much thread."

"No." The tailor lowered his voice for emphasis. "*People have stopped buying thread.*"

Finn frowned again. "If that's the case, then the cost of thread should come down, to level out the surplus."

An animated Schumann slapped the counter. "Exactly!" he exclaimed. "Prices should have come down. And yet—they went up instead." The tailor looked anxious but self-satisfied. "*That's* why I'm taking my money. When strange things happen around me, I become like the keeper of light." He lifted his hand to his brow. "Watching out for my ships at sea." He paused, glancing over to the silent girl by the sewing machine, then coughed his angst into a handkerchief.

"And now all your ships are under your mattress," Finn said. "I thought you were stepping out on me." He smiled. "Giving your business to someone else."

"Never, sir. But perhaps you can step outside with me for a moment?"

"Outside?"

"For a moment."

This was unprecedented. Schumann had never asked Finn to step outside. Hanging a sign on the door that said he would be back in five minutes, Schumann led Finn by the elbow out into the street.

"I have a big favor to ask of you, Finn."

"You want me to lend you money to buy a bigger mattress?"

But Schumann didn't smile, and he didn't hem and haw. "Would you please hire the girl in my shop? I need to find her a situation as soon as possible."

Finn was not expecting this. For a moment he was too stunned to speak. He stammered. "You want me—what—you want—I—to hire your sewing girl? But, Schumann, I don't need any sewing done at my house."

"That's good," Schumann said, "because she can't sew to save her life."

"Is that why you're trying to get rid of her?"

"I'm not getting rid of her," Schumann said tensely. "Just the opposite. I want to find her a good position. But also, I do have some others who need my help. I can't find them adequate employment. Nate brought too many. Even though the ship crashed, and some of them died. Despite the deaths, still too many."

"Um—who is Nate?"

"Least important detail, Finn."

"What ship?"

"Also not vital."

"Why did the ship crash?"

"Why do ships crash, Finn? Bad luck? Ill will? Dark omens?"

Finn's head was spinning around the merry-go-round of startling details. "Who *is* she?"

"Now we're getting somewhere," said Schumann. "Someone who needs my help." He paused. "And yours."

"Is that the real reason you've been withdrawing your money?"

"So I can *what*? No." Schumann coughed. "Though Nate does need to find a new ship now."

"Because his ship crashed?"

"Exactly!" Schumann frowned. "Or are you being ironic?"

"Exactly." Finn ran his hand through his hair. He was stupefied. "What am I supposed to do with a refugee who doesn't speak English? How can she help me?"

"I didn't say she speaks no English," Schumann said. "She is very good with languages, and she is a quick learner. In everything but sewing. She speaks Ukrainian, Romanian, Polish. Russian." The tailor said the last word like he was spitting it.

"Less helpful than you think to have a polyglot in the house who knows Romanian."

"She will learn, I promise. And it's just her."

"As opposed to what?"

"There could have been a whole family. There could have been another person." Schumann looked wrecked when he said it.

Finn stepped away, defeated as always by the magnitude of things he didn't understand. "What you're asking is not a favor, Schumann."

"I know, Finn," Schumann said. "What I'm asking for is an act of service." He pressed his fists to his heart and stared pleadingly into Finn's face. "It's not lending money or writing a letter. It's much bigger than that. I understand. But she is very important to me. I know she will be safe with you and your family. And I will not forget it. I will never forget it."

Finn was still reeling. "Who is Nate?"

"A young man who thinks he knows everything, and who doesn't listen. I've got serious problems, Finn. I don't ask you to help with all of them. Just this one."

"Schumann, what is this woman going to do in my house?"

"She can assist your wife with your daughters. Don't you say your wife needs help sometimes?"

Finn blinked. "We have a governess."

"She can clean."

"We have a housekeeper. And a maid. Two maids."

"She can cook. To be honest, I don't know if she can cook."

"I have a cook. And a cook's assistant."

"Maybe she can work for you at the bank?"

"Maybe she can work for me at the *bank*?" Finn repeated incredulously.

"Why not? She will do whatever you need. She can drive, she can make deliveries. Uh—actually, I don't know if she can drive. She can ride a horse."

"Aye," Finn said, nodding. "And there you have it. There's the rub. The bank doesn't make deliveries by horse." Finn narrowed his eyes, realization dawning. "But you don't want me to just give her a job. You want me to take her home and give her a place to live."

"Yes," the tailor said, his lip trembling. "But just her. Not a family. Not another person." He looked as if he were about to cry.

Finn rocked back on his heels. He knew how hard it was for a proud man to ask a favor. It had been a long time since he himself had asked anyone for anything. What a watershed life he led.

"When do you need me to do this?" Finn said in a resigned voice. No sooner had the words left his mouth than the young woman was out of the shop and by his side, all three of them warily looking up and down Salem Street.

Finn watched them say goodbye, Schumann embracing her like one of them was going off to war. His shoulders were shaking. The young anesthetized woman patted his back, but her expression read, *you foolish soul, if only you knew all the things to weep about.* The tailor wiped his face and said something to her in a foreign language, brushing away from her cheek some loose cotton thread. The only part Finn understood was, "Come on, chin up. You're in America now."

What had Finn done? What was he going to tell Vanessa? And their families, who were sitting in his lush garden, relaxing, waiting for him to come home. It was barely acceptable that an Evans should cross the uncrossable divide, head into the fetid square mile—the walled Irish-Italian-Jewish ghetto that was North End—into a hovel owned by a runaway Jew to drop off and pick up his own suits and his wife's dresses. Maids did this. Servants! His old friend John Collins from Harvard would never live down the doggerel his father the poet had written about this very thing: "*This was good old Boston, the home of the bean and the cod, where the Lowells talk only to Cabots, and the Cabots only to God.*" The Evanses and the Adamses did not bring home fresh-off-the-boat refugees, gaunt, pale, emaciated, in clean but squalid dress, nothing but eyes and mouth and barely breath.

Finn Evans was about to. He hadn't thought it through. Except . . .

She was so numb and haunted, her eyes the color of Boston Harbor in a storm, some indefinable green slate. She wore a maroon-colored head scarf, wrapped around her head and tied in a large knot at the front over her prominent forehead. "What's your name, anyway?" he asked, unable to keep the sigh out of his voice, expecting no response or perhaps just some guttural croak.

But the young woman raised her granite eyes to him, straightened her spine, and with a proud air of old-world grandeur said in a deep, strong, androgynous alto, "Isabelle Martyn Lazar." Her lip trembled slightly.

They stood, facing each other.

"I'm Finn," he said.

6

Lucas

Despite being handsome and tailored, even with his five o'clock shadow—or maybe because of it; despite his brushed-back dark blond hair slightly at sixes and sevens—or maybe because of it; the big, well-appointed man who had agreed to take her home with him rubbed Isabelle the wrong way. This was for two reasons. One was his suit. It reminded her most unpleasantly of the other people in her life who had worn suits, though none as crisp and fitted as this one.

But the main reason was the palpable reluctance with which this Finn person agreed to do a favor for Schumann. Isabelle didn't understand much English, but she understood human nature, and she knew she was being foisted on an unwilling partaker, on someone who didn't want to be foisted upon. This was a most inauspicious start to her new life.

They walked through the foreign city streets. It was muddy and dusty and noisy. It was altogether disagreeable until they crossed into another part of town where it was suddenly less crowded and there were some trees. She didn't know what was wrong with the man's gait; he seemed a young enough man, around her age, but he moved slower than the lame seventy-year-olds in Ispas. She tried to slow down to accommodate him, but the slower she walked, the slower he walked! Was this perhaps some aberrant form of chivalry? In Ukraine, all men moved like they were running to a fire, their women be damned.

While Isabelle was preoccupied with the American man's struggle with the simple act of walking, he was talking to her in a language as foreign as the city. There were some words she understood. *No car. No park. Walk.* Maybe he was apologizing they had to walk instead of taking a car? She wished she could tell him she had never been inside a car, so there was nothing to apologize for.

As they neared an expansive hilly park, a man approached them. Finn took Isabelle by the elbow and tried to move past him. But this man was having none of it. He was good-looking—and drunk. Isabelle could smell his breath from two meters away. He was trying to engage Finn in conversation, slap him on the back, beseech him. Finn barely responded. "Lucas," he kept saying, "Lucas, stop it."

The man named Lucas lumbered toward Isabelle and stuck out his hand, bowing—part mocking, part flirtatious, mostly drunk. "My name is Lucas," he said. "And what is *your* name, young miss?"

"*My* name," said Isabelle, emphasizing the same pronoun as he, "is Isabelle Martyn Lazar."

Lucas bent and kissed her hand. "Very nice to meet you, Isabelle," he said, drawing out her name in a way she hadn't heard before. *Eeeezabellllle.*

"Enough," Finn said, pulling Isabelle away.

After they were past him, Finn said, "He is no one. Don't worry about him."

Isabelle scoffed lightly. As if a drunken fool was even on a list of things she was worried about.

But one thing she knew: Finn was lying. Lucas wasn't no one. Lucas's expression as he implored Finn was one of familiarity, misery, apology. And Finn's return gaze, as he coldly tried to ignore the man, was abrim with hostility and injury.

7

Hampton Farm

His parents and Vanessa's parents were relaxing on the patio overflowing with blooming potted flowers and drinking virgin mint juleps when Finn arrived home, unacceptably late.

"Finn, where have you been?" bellowed the semi-retired Walter Adams, the president of the bank Finn ran and his father-in-law. His wife, Lucy, smiled critically from her chair, holding a glass of grape juice. Actual blasted grape juice, not a euphemism for wine, unfortunately.

"I like to keep my hands in it, sir, you know that." Finn smiled tensely.

"Walter is being unduly impatient, Esmond," said Lucy, beige perfection with a cruel streak. Lucy was the only person he knew who insisted on calling him by his middle name, Finn *Esmond* Evans. She handed him a glass of sparkling water and he downed it like a peasant; he was so thirsty. Finn had come in on talk of repeal, as always. Repeal and the stock market was all anyone talked about for ten years.

"Vanessa still not downstairs?" he asked. "Hello, Mother."

"Hello, darling, and no, we haven't seen her," said Olivia, sitting under a large umbrella with a lemonade and a book in her hands.

His father, Earl Evans, was by her side, reading the paper. "Hello, son, everything in tip-top shape at the bank?" The paper was not lowered.

"Hello, sir, and yes, both tip and top."

"Walter, are you going to talk to Esmond about John Reade's request," Lucy said, "or are you going to wait forever?"

"Not forever, Luce, just till dinner," said Walter.

Anxiously, Finn spun toward the house. He had led Isabelle into the parlor room and asked her to wait there until he could inform his wife of the sudden, previously undiscussed new hire. But Vanessa was still not ready.

"Finn, sit down, take a load off," Walter said. "I want to talk to you."

"Let's wait till dinner, Walter," Finn said. "I've got—"

"John Reade needs more money to finish renovating the Hampton farm," Lucy blurted.

"Thanks, Luce," mumbled Walter. "And you have it backwards. He doesn't want to renovate it, he wants to sell it. He's found a motivated buyer, so time is of the essence. It needs some final sprucing."

Finn raised his eyebrows. "Sprucing" was a term usually attached to a dollar sign. Sometimes three. "And what farm would this be, Walter?" said Finn, refusing to sit down.

"Precisely, dear boy, even *we* had forgotten about it," Lucy said. "I don't think we've been there once since we got married thirty-three years ago."

"It *was* my father's," Walter said, as if no further explanation were required. "And my father's father's. And my father's father's father's before that. John Reade is a good friend, and we need to give him an extension of credit on his construction loan to cover this and also a few other projects he and I are developing. You can make that happen, can't you? Maybe under your Business Expansion Program?"

"First I'm hearing of the Hampton place and John Reade, and his loan needs," said Finn. "Let's talk about it at dinner, shall we? I need—"

"Don't worry about any of that," Walter said, waving his hand. "Like I said, John wants to roll our other joint ventures into the loan, four or five things in the pipeline. He needs an additional three million dollars."

Finn whistled, grounded into the conversation by the inordinate sum. "How badly in need of repair is this property I've never heard of, Walter?"

"Just some sprucing, I told you. A final coat of paint, some doorknobs."

"Three million dollars' worth of doorknobs?" Finn said. He almost said, *that's a fuckload of doorknobs*. "Are they cast in gold like the ones at the Louvre?"

"The bulk of the money is for other developments in Amesbury and Newburyport. It's an umbrella loan, that's all."

Finn shrugged noncommittally. "The housing market is in a slight downturn."

"We have a buyer! It's a done deal."

"It's the other projects I'm curious about. Monday, okay?"

Thankfully, Vanessa finally walked through the French doors and onto the patio, as always the epitome of poise, coiffed, understated, smiling—and unrushed.

"Vanessa, there you are, my darling. Aren't you a sight!" Lucy said. "We've been waiting for you."

"I know, I . . ." said Vanessa, and Finn wondered if she had prepared something to finish that sentence with. Lucy saved her daughter the trouble of explaining by handing her a tray of canapés.

Finn kissed his wife on the cheek and took the tray from her hands. "Hello, darling. No, no, don't sit, come with me for a moment. I need to show you something."

But inside, before he could just come out with it, Vanessa said, "Where have you been? You're so late. Were you with that awful Lucas again, drinking?" She tiptoed up to smell his breath.

"No, Vee, I told you, I don't see him anymore." He decided to omit his impromptu encounter by the Boston Common, where Lucas often lay in wait. "I picked up your dresses from Schumann's. But I have good news." Finn smiled, his teeth on edge. "I got you some extra help for the house."

"I'm fine, darling. I have all the help I need." She reached for his hand.

"Hear me out." They were standing in the dusky hall just inside the open French doors. "I think you and the house could use an assistant."

"I'm fine, we're all fine." A frown swept over Vanessa's face. "What do you mean you *got* me some help? As in, we're not just talking about it?"

"Come with me, Vee," Finn said, taking his wife by the hand. "I want you to meet someone."

8

Lavelle

Vanessa watched in disbelief as her husband prodded forward a young woman in poverty rags and ugly man-boots, a woman with a maroon turban over her head, her face gray and plain. She was from a world Vanessa had never seen. Vanessa couldn't tell if the woman was or could be attractive, and didn't care. She was too shocked by the appearance of this fragile, frightened being inside her house.

"This is Isabelle," Finn said. "Isabelle, meet my wife, Vanessa." He had a smile on his face, like he was introducing his good friends to each other!

Vanessa stood, speechless.

Finally, she remembered herself and said, "How do you do?" She glared at her husband.

The woman mimicked her precisely. In a Slavic-sounding accent and a hard voice, she said, "*How do you do?*" But she did not glare at Vanessa's husband.

"Where are you from . . . Isabelle, is it?"

"Isabelle Martyn Lazar," the woman said, her head high, her thin shoulders squared. "*Ukraina.*"

"We say Ukraine in America," Vanessa said.

After the slightest pause, Isabelle said, "*Ukraine in America.*" The words were spoken in a perfect imitation of Vanessa's soprano.

"You speak English?" Vanessa asked, grimacing in confusion.

"I speak English now, no?" The accent and the gritty voice were back.

"Will you excuse us, please?"

In the hallway, Vanessa whirled to Finn, her face distorted. "Finn, *no!*"

"Vanessa, I'm sorry, darling." He squeezed her shoulders. "I had no time to think. Schumann ambushed me. He asked me to hire her as a favor. I couldn't say no."

"I'm saying no now. Take her back. Please."

"Listen, let's give her a chance for a month or two. It's an extra pair of hands, we can always use those, right?"

"Finn!"

"Sweetheart, just the other day you were saying how you were feeling slightly overwhelmed." Finn looked her over. "And I can't help but notice that you barely got yourself together for our evening with the family."

"I am perfectly together," she said. "And you weren't here either."

"I was at work. And then halfway across town. But you were right here, darling. And you're still not ready..."

"I'm *entirely* ready."

"You look wonderful," he said. "No question about *that*. But the pins in your hair are from this morning. You're wearing almost no makeup—"

"I'm wearing neutral makeup, appropriate for a summer night."

"Only on one eye, darling. You forgot to neutrally make up your other lovely eye." Finn smiled.

"What does that have to do with *anything*?"

"Perhaps she can help you so you don't have to do everything in such a rush. Get the girls ready, play with them, take them to the park, that sort of thing."

Vanessa blinked. "We have Edith for that, thank you very much."

"Edith is not as young as she used to be. She has trouble with the stairs and navigating the turns on our landings. Doesn't like to go up and down hills. Junie told me they didn't go to the park at all last week! It's summer, darling, the best time in Boston. Yet the girls are cooped up in the house."

"Finn, we have a patio and a garden, and—oh, what am I saying, this isn't about the girls or the park!"

"Isn't it?"

"You brought a strange woman into our home to live with us without talking to me first!"

"I'm talking to you now."

"That's just a formality, Finn."

Finn peered earnestly into her face. Vanessa knew the expression well. It was his tireless persuasion face. Calm, good-natured, full of reasoned argument, her husband persisted until Vanessa became okay with whatever it was he needed her to be okay with. A third child? Sure. A wanderer from a foreign land? Certainly.

Vanessa marched back into the parlor room. "How did you get here, Isabelle?"

"We walk," she said. "We walk from Schumann."

"Where did you come from?"

"Schumann," Isabelle repeated.

"Oh, my goodness! Why can't I make myself understood? Do you have immigration clearance to live here in America, to work here? Finn, can you help? Can you make her understand what I'm asking her?"

"Our boat sink in night," Isabelle said. "Big shtorm. Many people die. Not me." But she didn't say it like she was blessed. She said it like she was cursed.

"What boat?"

"I don't know name of boat."

"Your ship sank?"

"Yes. Ship crash at Lavelle."

"Where?"

Finn interjected. "I recall reading something a month or so ago about a merchant ship accident at the east end of Boston Harbor. It hit some rocks and capsized. That's probably what she's talking about."

"Why would she be on a merchant ship?" She turned to Isabelle. "Why were you on a merchant ship?"

"I don't know what merchant is. My ship crash."

"I'm very sorry to hear that," said Vanessa. "But that's not our fault, is it? We are not responsible for the shipwreck, are we? You haven't answered any of my other questions. You did, however, answer a question I wasn't asking."

"I want to answer, but I really don't know name of boat," said Isabelle.

Vanessa turned on her heels and stormed out. Finn followed her.

9

Truro

Finn realized with shame that Isabelle had probably picked up on his wife's hostility. It was hard to miss. He had mishandled the whole situation. He didn't properly prepare Vanessa—couldn't properly prepare her, but that was beside the point. It was disrespectful to both women. He trapped one and offended the other.

After Vanessa blustered outside, Finn sheepishly returned to the parlor room, where Isabelle stood waiting. But she wasn't alone. Finn's little girls were standing by her side, curiously looking up at her. She was looking at his two children with an expression Finn couldn't decipher. There was something bottomless in it.

"Who is this, Daddy?"

"This is Isabelle," Finn said. "She'll be staying with us for a while. She'll be helping Wicker in the kitchen, and Loretta and Martha and Edith, and Mommy, too. These are my children," he said to the woman. "Mae and Junie."

"How many ages," Isabelle said in stilted English.

"How old they are? Mae is seven and Junie six."

Isabelle stood looking at them. "They babies," she whispered.

"We're not a baby, you a baby," said Junie.

"Junie! Your manners!" said Finn.

"Sorry, Daddy."

"Not to me."

"Sorry, Isabelle."

She said something in Ukrainian that sounded like *sonechka*.

The girls began peppering Isabelle with questions. Finn had to explain about the language barrier. "But maybe when she takes you to the park, you can teach her some English?"

"We can be *her* teachers!" said Mae with delight.

"Precisely." And to Isabelle, Finn said, "Don't worry. Everything is going to be okay."

Isabelle blinked, her haunted eyes deepening. "*Don't worry,*" Isabelle repeated. "*Everything is going to be okay.*"

With his girls tagging along, Finn took Isabelle downstairs to the kitchen and asked Wicker to give her something to eat, and Martha the housekeeper to prepare a room for her in the servants' quarters.

"I've never heard of this Lavelle," Finn said to Isabelle as he was leaving to rejoin his family. "I know all the islands in the harbor."

"Lavelle," Isabelle said. "Two lights same."

"Twin lights . . ." Finn almost smiled. "You mean *Lov*ell's Island."

"No, Lavelle," Isabelle said. "I know where I crash."

"It's pronounced LUV-el," Finn corrected her.

"It's pronounced Luh-VELLE," said the woman.

Outside, a bombardment of questions awaited him.

"What's going on, Esmond?" Lucy said. "Vanessa tells me you brought some woman home."

"Not a woman . . ."

"She's not a woman?" Vanessa said.

"Technically, but . . . I didn't bring a *woman* home. I brought home a worker."

"You don't need her," Lucy said. "Vanessa keeps a beautiful home."

"Absolutely," Finn said. "But even perfect wives need help once in a while." Finn didn't look at Vanessa, and Vanessa didn't move a muscle on her face.

"But she speaks no English?" Walter said.

Finn shrugged, feigning nonchalance.

"She's from Ukraine?" Lucy said. "How in the world did she get here? Does she have family with her?"

"I don't know."

"I wonder if I can ask her a few questions," said Walter. "National Shawmut keeps lending tens of millions of dollars to the Soviet Union. I'd love to find out how it's going over there."

"Walter, I doubt she'll be able to help you with that level of geopolitical information," said Finn. "Unless you know Ukrainian."

"Does she know how to read and write?"

"Did she even go to school?"

"Where in Ukraine is she from?" Walter asked. "The region is mostly agricultural. Is she from a city, from Kiev, maybe?"

Finn opened his hands to the questions.

"Well, bring her out here so we can ask her."

"You know what," Finn said mildly, "we're going to let her get settled before we inquisition her."

"Not an inquisition." Walter was huffy. "We're just curious."

"We certainly are, Daddy," said Vanessa. "For example, *I* am curious how a mute thing who doesn't speak English or understand simple instructions is going to help me around the house and with our children."

"I don't know," said Finn, sounding testy because he was getting testy. "Can mute things peel potatoes? Slice onions? Clean floors? Weed a garden? Take children to the park? We have a large home and much to do. I'm sure we can occupy her somehow." For once, Finn didn't care to hide his irritation. "If you really feel she can't help you here, I'll take her to the bank and have her help me there."

"Don't be ridiculous," said Walter.

"Don't be ridiculous," Vanessa echoed, but with a tremble in her voice.

It was Finn's mother who intervened. "Leave Finn alone," Olivia said. "A good man who's been his tailor for a decade asked him for a favor. My son was in the fortunate position to be able to say yes. A friend was in need, this woman is in need, and Finn answered the call. Only good is being done, no harm. Why are you acting as if he started a war?"

"Olivia, you are so right," Earl said. "It's good to help people in need if you're able to. It's an act of charity."

"Thank you, darling," Olivia said. "But really, it's a spiritual lift to both sides—the giver and the given."

Why did Finn feel that the support from his parents came with a dull blade between the words? Were those remarks pointed at him? And if so, why?

"When she gets more comfortable, son," Earl said, "we would like to meet her. Not to interrogate her, merely to welcome her to the family."

"With all due respect, Earl," Vanessa said to her father-in-law, "if we are paying her, which I assume we will be, she is a servant. She is not family."

"We show common courtesy to the people we share our home with," Olivia said, and even Lucy had to make a grudging noise of agreement with her counterpart. The Bostonians living on Beacon Hill treated their staff with utmost respect. "And darling," Finn's mother added, "tell Isabelle to listen to the radio and read the newspapers. It's a marvelous way to learn a new language."

"He'll have to find another way to communicate this to her, Olivia," said Vanessa, "because right now she doesn't understand a lick of English."

They found the woman wandering the rooms of their house, touching the toggle switches, the marble hearths and the mirrors, running her fingertips over the fresh flowers, the ceramic vases, the polished silver, gliding her hands across the smooth parquet floors, opening and closing the lid of the washing machine, bending over to peer into the drum. And in every movement she was shadowed by Mae and Junie, who followed in their bare feet, imitating her. She touched, they touched. She glided, they glided. She opened the cabinets, they opened the cabinets.

"Light switch," they would say, as she flipped it on and off.

"Light switch," she would repeat. "Chandelier." "Ice box."

She picked up Junie and put her inside the washing machine, right into the empty drum. "Washing Junie," she said.

"Oh, yes, please!" said Junie.

And Mae, who was usually the more cautious of the two, jumped up and down next to them, squealing, "Me next, me next!"

And Isabelle said, "You next. Washing Mae."

"Why was she rubbing my children's heads with her palms the same way she was touching the washing machine?" Vanessa said gruffly. "They don't have children where she came from?"

They took Isabelle with them to Cape Cod for the weekend, to Truro. Finn drove in his brand new Packard Eight sedan, bought just a month earlier, a spacious, plush, meticulously designed automobile. Isabelle, who sat with the girls in the back, spent the three-hour ride staring out the window and occasionally repeating the words Mae and June barraged her with.

Nestled in the expansive dunes near the tip of the Outermost Harbor, Truro was a laid-back coastal town of clapboard houses with cedar shingled roofs. Finn's weekend retreat was a large white cottage landscaped with verdant greens and bright flowers. It sat on a knoll that overlooked miles of unspoiled beach and marshes on Cape Cod Bay. A private pathway with wooden steps led to the water. Finn had bought the house as a present for his family when Mae was born in 1922, and it was everyone's favorite place to spend summer weekends and breaks, except maybe Vanessa's, because she was a city girl at heart. Truro had no pace. It just was. That's what Finn liked most about it.

There was plenty of room for everyone, even a new arrival. Isabelle stayed in the cook's room. Adder and Eleanor arrived later in the afternoon with their obnoxious son Monty. Adder, a small man with a large head, kept calling Isabelle over to ask her things. Her silence in response would divert him briefly, but then he was right back at it, wanting to know how she got to Boston, how long it took, where she had sailed from, if she had any family, and where they were. Isabelle stood like a pillar with no expression as she repeated, "I not understand," over and over.

"Do you have a mother, father, husband, children?" Adder persisted, pointing to the children, the husbands, the mothers.

"I not understand," said Isabelle, not blinking.

The girls asked Isabelle to go to the water with them. Vanessa said she probably didn't know how to swim. "Isn't Ukraine landlocked?"

Isabelle responded by walking down to the waterline, taking off her leather boots, which she wore even on the sandy beach, wading into the sea in her dress and head scarf and diving in.

"Maybe they have rivers in landlocked Ukraine," said Finn. "Also the Black Sea."

"Maybe she understands more than she lets on," said Adder.

"Maybe she wants you to leave her alone, Adder," said Finn.

She swam back and forth for a long time, with Mae and Junie shouting at her from the shore.

"How does she plan to dry herself?" Adder said as the couples sat on the veranda, drinking peach soda and watching.

"Please get her a towel, Vanessa," said Finn. "I would do it myself, but how is that going to look?"

"Oh, it's warm," said Eleanor. "She's fine, she'll dry without one."

Good old Eleanor, always coming to the rescue. As soon as her sister told her not to, Vanessa rushed off to fetch two towels for Isabelle.

"Does she have other clothes?" asked Adder. "She should probably change into something dry."

When Isabelle finally came out of the water, her head scarf had fallen off, and Finn saw that she was indeed bald. They must have shaved her head when she was processed through immigration. She sat on a log near the water while Mae and Junie oohed and aahed over her hairless scalp, rubbing it like they were polishing the furniture.

"Poor woman," Adder said. "She is soaked in that long thing that's clinging to her. Vanessa, give her a bathing suit. She'll be more comfortable in one."

"Nothing I have will fit her. She's too tall."

"They don't make bathing suits for tall people?" Finn asked. "And you're not swimming."

"I'm planning to, darling," she said. "Maybe later if it's still hot."

It remained hot, but Vanessa did not go swimming.

Vanessa *never* went swimming. She talked about the water and the heat, but she never went in, not with Finn, or her children, or her sister.

On Sunday afternoon, Finn watched Isabelle standing near the water, her now dry, ankle-length purple dress waving, her scarf tied around her head. She stood for a long time, her arms crossed in front of her chest in a guarded position, staring at the glass-like sea. Both she and the sea were motionless. Finn watched her in puzzlement, in bafflement. Junie ran up to her, and he almost wanted to shout, *No, no, don't disturb her, let her be. Let her be where she wants to be.* But Isabelle came out of her reverie, bent to Junie and smiled, reaching out to place a tender hand on the child's shoulder. Junie showed her a seashell and led Isabelle away to find more treasures.

It was an unsettling though mostly uneventful weekend, marred by Adder's inexplicable injury, sustained sometime before breakfast on Sunday, when he arrived at the table sporting a swollen nose and an impressive black eye. His lip was cut. He barely ate. He said he had walked into a door, had been careless and wasn't looking. Eleanor was horrified. She wanted to know which door and whether it was a danger to "my darling Monty." She demanded to know why Vanessa had doors that could injure an adult man. Adder told Eleanor she was making a fuss and to forget about it. He didn't talk during the meal, didn't ask Isabelle any more questions, didn't even look at the woman, and after breakfast he and Eleanor packed up and left immediately.

It was a serene beautiful Sunday, and no one else wanted to leave. Finn and Vanessa finally set out for Boston well after nightfall. The exhausted children were asleep in the back of their Packard, while in the front, Finn and Vanessa talked quietly about Adder's injury. They could not figure out how a man could walk into a door so hard as to cause himself a split lip, a black eye, and a nearly broken nose.

From the rear seat, Isabelle spoke. "That man no good," she said.

Finn didn't wait until the following Friday to see Schumann. He brought the repairs to him on Tuesday and took Isabelle. Schumann had mentioned he might have some clothes for her. Finn also really needed Schumann to translate between them.

Isabelle's work boots were irking Vanessa. She wanted the new hire to have decent shoes to wear to take her girls to the park. Because in addition to wanting to shave their heads "just like Isabelle," Mae and Junie started requesting leather boots like Isabelle's, for Christmas. Schumann told Finn the boots were a treasured possession. They were well made and expensive.

"I get it," said Finn, "I'm not telling her to throw them out. But maybe you can find her a pair of regular shoes, Schumann. To help her assimilate."

He told Schumann about a small misunderstanding he'd had with Isabelle and asked for clarification. At the Cape, he had come up behind her sitting by the window and asked if she wanted some dinner. She didn't react, as if she hadn't heard him. Only when he called her name did she acknowledge his presence. "Isabelle," he said. And then she turned around. He apologized for startling her. "For a moment, I thought you were deaf," he said.

"What?" she said.

"I thought you were deaf," Finn had repeated, louder and slower.

"What?" she said.

He pointed to his ears, then to her ears, and said, "I thought you couldn't hear!"

"What?" said Isabelle.

Finn waited while Schumann explained this to her.

"She says to tell you she is not deaf," said the tailor.

"Then why did she keep repeating the word *what* over and over?"

Schumann and Isabelle had another brief exchange. "She says she was joking."

After the briefest of pauses, Finn blinked and said, "What?"

"*Tochno*," Isabelle said in Ukrainian. She didn't smile.

"She said *exactly*." Schumann didn't smile either.

"Okay, Schumann," said Finn, "I need you to tell her that the language barrier between us at the moment is too great for her to make jokes."

"You want me to tell her she cannot joke?" Schumann said.

"*Tochno*," Finn said. "I want you to tell her she cannot joke."

Isabelle lifted her hand to stop Schumann from translating further. "I understand what you say. *The barrier between us is too great to make jokes*." She didn't say this in her alto voice, with her usual accent. She said it in Finn's baritone, with his Boston inflection, and no Ukrainian accent. She simply repeated his own words back to him, like a recording.

"I thought I made it clear there is to be no joking," Finn said.

"*You made it clear there is to be no joking*," said Isabelle.

Finn turned to Schumann. "How does she do that?"

Schumann shrugged. "She's always been a remarkable mimic. Humans, horses, birds, you name it. Frankly, I'd rather she sewed."

Finn was thoughtful. "Schumann, ask her about Adder, my brother-in-law. I want to know if something happened between them."

By the time Schumann turned to Isabelle, she was already speaking in rapid-fire Ukrainian as if she had understood Finn's question.

Schumann cleared his throat and said, "I wouldn't ask her a question you don't want an answer to, Finn. She won't mince words."

"I want an answer to my question."

Isabelle said something.

Schumann sighed. "She said no one touches her unless she wants to be touched. And the man tried to touch her."

Finn shook his head, disgusted. The snake! "Maybe it was a misunderstanding?"

"*Ni*," said Isabelle.

"So she gave him a black eye?"

"Trust me," said Schumann, "he got away lucky."

Finn whistled. He couldn't hide that he was a little bit impressed. Isabelle stood next to Schumann impassive, leaf-thin, most unintimidating.

"Finn, can you give me and her a few minutes?" Schumann said, reaching into his cabinet for something. "But no more than a few—the customers are circling. Do you hear them banging? They're going to break down my door like it's a run on the banks back in 1921."

10

Efros and Zhuk

Ukraine, February 1929

A week after the shootings, Isabelle and Mirik were finishing their milk deliveries, the metal cans rattling in the back of their cart, when they passed by the side of the road where Stan and Vitaly had buried the Soviets. It was just after sunrise and in the dim overcast light it was hard to see. Isabelle squinted into the woods and gasped, grabbing on to Mirik's arm. "Mirik," she whispered. "Stop the cart."

"No," Mirik said, his hands shaking as he gripped the reins. "Let's keep going."

"Stop the cart, Mirik!"

"No, Isa, don't look. Please. Don't look." He spurred the horse to go faster, attempting to outrun what they had just seen. But Isabelle knew: you couldn't outrun the ineradicable image of your own doom.

Swinging upside down from the bare trees, strung up by their ankles, were Stan and Vitaly's naked, mutilated bodies.

"We told you in Shatava, we told you in Proskuriv, we told you in Kammenets. We told you in Russian and Ukrainian, as loudly as our voices could carry. Let it be known to one and all that no one is to raise a hand to any operative, worker, or representative of the Communist Party or an official of the Soviet Government. There will be no other warnings but this one. Anyone who ignores us will face certain death."

Standing in a dark blue uniform covered with military insignia, calf-high boots, and a fur-trimmed hat, Yefim Efros, the bespectacled OGPU junior lieutenant assigned to Ispas, delivered the grim message to a community hall of equally grim village parishioners. Flanking him were his armed *operativniks*.

Finn whistled. He couldn't hide that he was a little bit impressed. Isabelle stood next to Schumann impassive, leaf-thin, most unintimidating.

"Finn, can you give me and her a few minutes?" Schumann said, reaching into his cabinet for something. "But no more than a few—the customers are circling. Do you hear them banging? They're going to break down my door like it's a run on the banks back in 1921."

10

Efros and Zhuk

Ukraine, February 1929

A week after the shootings, Isabelle and Mirik were finishing their milk deliveries, the metal cans rattling in the back of their cart, when they passed by the side of the road where Stan and Vitaly had buried the Soviets. It was just after sunrise and in the dim overcast light it was hard to see. Isabelle squinted into the woods and gasped, grabbing on to Mirik's arm. "Mirik," she whispered. "Stop the cart."

"No," Mirik said, his hands shaking as he gripped the reins. "Let's keep going."

"Stop the cart, Mirik!"

"No, Isa, don't look. Please. Don't look." He spurred the horse to go faster, attempting to outrun what they had just seen. But Isabelle knew: you couldn't outrun the ineradicable image of your own doom.

Swinging upside down from the bare trees, strung up by their ankles, were Stan and Vitaly's naked, mutilated bodies.

"We told you in Shatava, we told you in Proskuriv, we told you in Kammenets. We told you in Russian and Ukrainian, as loudly as our voices could carry. Let it be known to one and all that no one is to raise a hand to any operative, worker, or representative of the Communist Party or an official of the Soviet Government. There will be no other warnings but this one. Anyone who ignores us will face certain death."

Standing in a dark blue uniform covered with military insignia, calf-high boots, and a fur-trimmed hat, Yefim Efros, the bespectacled OGPU junior lieutenant assigned to Ispas, delivered the grim message to a community hall of equally grim village parishioners. Flanking him were his armed *operativniks*.

It had taken Efros and his men barely ninety minutes of questioning a fistful of people before Oleg Tretyak, whom Isabelle had always hated, served up Stan and Vitaly, lying to the Soviets that the boys had stolen his weapons and beaten him. Tretyak led Efros straight to the burial grounds. Old man Tretyak had always been venal, and he thought that by giving up the Babich brothers, he could save his own hide. But within a day, the OGPU shot him anyway— for aiding and abetting mass murder and for conspiracy to cover it up. They strung him up next to Stan and Vitaly over the grave of thirteen Soviets and forbade the villagers to take down the three bodies. They would hang until they were nothing but skeletons. Taking them down for burial would also be punishable by death.

Within a few days of Efros's arrival, Ispas was overrun with Soviet internal security *chekists*, agitation supervisors, administrators, councilmen, and collectivization activists sent by the Secretary of the Central Committee for Propaganda in Ukraine.

Cici and Yana were planning all kinds of payback destruction, but Roman and Isabelle forbade them to do anything that would bring more attention to their family, especially Cici who was related to Stan and Vitaly by blood—their mothers were sisters.

At first, Cici wouldn't listen. She said she would divorce Roman before she left Stan and Vitaly unavenged. Yana wholeheartedly agreed. But before Cici could file for divorce and the pregnant Yana could take matters into her own hands, Efros arrested Myron Koval, Ispas's wealthiest grain merchant, and evicted his family from their large house next to the village square, just as the trader from Shatava had foretold. The Bolsheviks took over the house, knocked down the walls, made the first floor one big cold room, and called another hastily assembled meeting about next steps.

Next steps included two things: requisition and collectivization.

Requisition was taking food from the farmers' own supplies first by demand, and then by force if necessary.

Collectivization was the massive Soviet effort since 1928 to consolidate the small Ukrainian private farms into larger farms under Soviet control. Mirik said he hated to be right. "We have a hundred Communists invading," he said, "armed, hungry, angry, and ready for war. If Stan and Vitya, God rest their souls, had kept to themselves, we might still have a hundred Communists, but they would just be hungry."

"And there I was thinking just the opposite, Mirik," said Roman. "If they planned to run roughshod over us no matter what, then Stan and Vitya didn't shoot enough of them." He turned to his sister. "What do you think, Isa?"

"Leave me out of it," said Isabelle. She didn't want to contradict her husband in front of her brothers.

When the villagers in Ispas remained unenthusiastic about next steps and refused to attend, the Soviets made the meetings mandatory. Any family who didn't send a representative to Bolshevik headquarters was subject to arrest and deportation to "re-education facilities" in Russia itself. When attendance remained spotty, the Soviets started sending delegates to individual farms to spread their message more directly. Each morning, a propaganda operative, armed with flowery rhetoric and a loaded rifle, would visit a homestead right around breakfast time to extol the benefits of collectivizing. Much too soon, they arrived at the Lazars'.

Ispas, a landlocked village, was home to a thousand people, a mere two hundred households, spread over the limitless rolling plains and sparse woods of southwest Ukraine. Every farm in Ispas specialized in one thing or another. The villagers bartered their goods among themselves, and there was almost no need for currency unless they went to the market in Chervona, where they sold their surplus crops to buy boots or housewares. In exchange for their milk, the Kovalenkos received bread and bacon, and it was usually enough, even during hard winters like this one, which was almost ending, yet seemed neverending.

The Lazar land was three kilometers west of the village center. They had fifteen mostly flat acres, with seven homes built on a hillock overlooking the valley. The houses were comfortable, two of them quite large, all with thatched roofs, multi-colored clay walls, and troweled floors. There were two barns for Mirik's cows and a twenty-stall stable for Roman's horses. Nearby streams were used for watering and fishing, but the closest proper river was the Dniester, thirty kilometers south, snaking through the border between Ukraine and Romania. The nearest city was Kammenets, twelve kilometers east. The distances were great between villages and towns, and news traveled slow; newspapers were sometimes weeks behind, mail almost non-existent.

The farmers worked hard, but there was much joy in their good life. There were woods nearby to pick mushrooms after rain. In the summer, blueberry and raspberry bushes abounded for pies and moonshine. The black soil would disappear under a sea of golden wheat in the summer and then go gray in the winter, as if the earth itself was in mourning while waiting for the next crop to seed.

And in Isabelle's house now, as the earth mourned, sat two men, one in a suit, one in uniform. They ate her food, but they wanted more than a few potatoes from her. One man was the OGPU lackey Yefim Efros. The other was Kondraty Zhuk. He was the Communist Party activist in charge of collectivization.

Zhuk said he wanted to speak to Roman Lazar, "man to man." Roman stepped forward, but Isabelle pushed back her chair and gestured to her brother to stay put. "I am Isabelle Kovalenko," she said. "The land belongs to me. I am my father's oldest child."

Zhuk clucked his lips while he appraised her. He was a rotund yet oddly stiff man, intense and sweaty, with a pronounced crow nose and stringy hair. He was probably thirty, but fanatical zeal had aged him. "I thought the Cossacks were all about male supremacy," he said appreciatively.

"We are not Cossacks," said Isabelle without even a blink at Roman. When the enemy came inside your house, it was important to hide what you were until you knew what he wanted, and she was glad Roman remembered that lesson from their father and stayed silent.

"No?" said Zhuk. "I must have heard wrong, then. Aren't you the children of the notorious *Kazak* Martyn Lazar? Well, no matter. Water under the bridge. War, and all that. Fine, I will talk to you. We will begin by addressing your first inaccuracy. But, do you have more bacon and potatoes? How well you eat around these parts!"

She brought him more bacon; he tore into it, and continued. "What were we discussing? Oh, yes, your inaccuracies. Yefim, would you educate Comrade Kovalenko on my behalf while I finish her delectable meal?"

Efros, sitting at the table, also gorging on Isabelle's food, spoke with his mouth full, potatoes and onions sliding out. "This land is not your land," he said, chewing. "This land, as all other land in the Soviet Union, belongs to the Communist Party. This was made law in 1917, right after the Glorious October Revolution. All land in Russia and its republics was nationalized twelve years ago. Were you not aware? You are being made aware now. This land is our land. We generously allow you to live on it and work on it." Efros had a red bulbous nose. He was an alcoholic clown in military dress. He panted as he ate and panted as he spoke.

"And here lies our problem," Zhuk said. He took another forkful of food and without wiping his mouth, continued. "You have fifteen acres, which is a tremendous estate with unlimited potential."

"Its potential is limited to fifteen acres," said Roman.

Zhuk raised his hand without glancing Roman's way. "The potential of this land is going entirely uncultivated."

No one spoke in response. In the room were Isabelle, her brothers, and Mirik. She had sent her sons to the barn with her mother, and Cici and Yana weren't allowed inside because it wasn't time for war.

"Very well," Zhuk went on, "I will continue. First and foremost, you are not growing wheat on your land. You are not growing beets. You are not growing potatoes. Sounds like a waste of fifteen acres, especially when hard-working people in the cities are going hungry."

"We breed horses," said Isabelle.

"And cows," said Mirik.

"Those other things you mention are not our business," said Isabelle.

"We are here to tell you to make them your business," Zhuk said.

"Our business is ranching and dairy farming," said Isabelle. "If you want potatoes, you should speak to Stan and Vitaly Babich. They are the potato producers in Ispas. Well . . . they *were*," she added. Hate was in her voice.

"We are talking about *your* farm, Comrade Kovalenko," said Efros, "not the murderous criminal Babiches who have been duly punished. Do you *really* need fifteen acres to make a few gallons of milk?"

"We do," said Isabelle. "The cows need pasture. Horses too. They need even more grazing and riding land than the cows. Fifteen acres is very little when you consider the needs of the animals."

"What about the needs of the poor Soviet people breaking their backs for Mother Russia even as we sit here chatting?"

"All people need milk," Isabelle said. "Soviets and Ukrainians alike."

"Because from milk you make butter and cheese," explained Roman, as if he were speaking to the village idiot.

Zhuk barked at him to shut up, but seemed flummoxed by Roman's aside, as if he didn't know where butter and cheese came from.

"My brothers," said Isabelle, "breed, raise, train, and supply much of southwest Ukraine with the horses required for all agricultural needs."

"Ah! This brings me to another important point, Comrade Kovalenko," Zhuk said, recovering his arrogance.

"Seems like a *lot* of important points," Roman said. "Any chance we can prioritize them?"

"I'll prioritize them for you," said Zhuk. "Horses are the past! Horses will soon be extinct—like the dinosaurs. They are a useless vestige of imperialism—and they need to be fed to boot!" One stirring propagandist and one rifled Bolshevik requisitionist, sitting, smoking, and drinking Mirik's milk. Isabelle, who sat directly across from Zhuk, had to shield her eyes by focusing on the tablecloth. She knew how to control herself, but it was impossible for her to keep from her expression how she really felt about an insect like Zhuk coming into her home uninvited and then maligning the most noble kingly indestructible animals like their Karabakh horses. She knew Zhuk would see the black contempt in her gaze. And perhaps more ominous things. She kept her gaze lowered, while Zhuk continued.

"In five minutes, you Lazars will be out of business," Zhuk said. "No matter what Ukrainian farmers want and feel and believe, the entire Soviet Union will be brought into the modern world. Including Ukraine. Horses will be obsolete, even in your backward Ispas. And good riddance! The tractor is coming, the thresher! The harvester! The winnower! Your agriculture will be mechanized and you will be industrialized. To get the machinery, we must buy it on the export market. But we buy it with crops, with the very wheat you are currently not growing."

When neither Roman nor Isabelle replied, Zhuk continued.

"Last summer, Ispas had a quota. Each household was to contribute to the total number of bushels of grain we required. Did you meet it?"

"No one met it," Isabelle said. "Not just the Lazars, not just Ispas. Ukraine didn't meet it. The quota was set too high. There were serious problems with the harvest. That's the nature of weather, comrade. Sometimes it's unpredictable. We delivered as much dairy to make butter and cheese as was required of us."

"We do not ask you to explain your failures, Comrade Kovalenko," said Zhuk. "Comrade Stalin decreed, and we must follow."

Isabelle raised her hand at him. "I wasn't finished," she said. "Aside from weather considerations, the reason the Lazars didn't meet your grain quota is because we are not wheat growers. We cannot reap what we do not sow, Comrade Zhuk. We cannot be penalized for not delivering grain or sugar beets. That would make as much sense as a bread maker being penalized for not delivering to you the required number of bullets."

Zhuk swelled red like a boiled beet. "We tell you your business, you do not tell us ours!" He was breathless with affront and embarrassment. What Isabelle was saying was so reasonable that he had no recourse but to bluster and bellow. "But you make a good point, Comrade Kovalenko. That's why we are here talking to you today. This coming fall we will require from you a wheat harvest. And collectivization is the best method of preventing the disruptions of which you speak."

"I heard that the grain quota is set even higher for this fall than last," said Mirik.

"Of course it is!" Zhuk said, slapping the wood table. "It must be—to make up for the unforgivable shortfall of your last harvest."

"Did you hear what I said, comrade?" said Isabelle.

"Yes, yes," he snapped impatiently. "I don't want to hear your Ukrainian excuses anymore. You will become wheat growers. You will collectivize and become the modernized, efficient, wheat-growing socialists the Party requires you to be."

"You want us to start growing wheat which you will then sell to buy equipment to get rid of our horses?" said Roman. "No, thank you."

"We require you to start growing wheat because the Soviet people need to eat!" said Efros.

"You poor simpletons," Zhuk said with a sneer. "You seem to be under the impression this is a conversation." He scoffed. "We are not asking."

Roman had had enough. "You're not listening to my sister," he said. "You're not listening to me. I'm going to explain it to you as simply as I can. You cannot go from pasture to wheat-bearing ground in one year."

"We can and we will," said Zhuk.

"Would you like to walk the property with us now that you've eaten?" said Roman. "I will show you that the ground is tamped down. It has never been tilled or fertilized, it has never received a seed or grown a crop. We have half an acre of cultivated soil, on which we grow food to feed our family. But the rest of our land is flattened steppe-like earth."

"It's the famous black soil of Ukraine, is it not?" Zhuk said. "Everything can and will be planted in it."

"Go out into the road," Roman said, "which horses and wagons have trampled for decades. Go out there and dig a hole and plant your seed in the clay and see how well it grows, comrade." Roman almost spat.

"Sign over your farm to the newly formed Ispas collective, and we will send you labor and plows to till your steppe-like soil."

Isabelle saw her brother was getting hot under the collar. He too couldn't hide what he felt. "City men like you came to Ukraine two years ago," Roman said. "There was another food shortage then—there seem to be so many of them in your socialist paradise—and you tried the same tactic. Tell us, were your efforts to take our farms by force successful in 1927?"

Zhuk sneered. "In 1927, we didn't come to Ispas, did we? We had bigger fish to fry. This is how you know times have changed, because this year, even an insignificant common shiner like you is being called to action for the glory of the Soviet Union."

"Even a common shiner like me can read," Roman said. "Can you read, Comrade Zhuk?" From a small cabinet, Roman retrieved a yellowed *Kievskaya Pravda*. "It says here, in plain language, '*All collectivization must be of your own free will*.' Roman threw the paper on the table in front of Zhuk. "That's direct from Comrade Stalin. He wrote this letter to all the citizens of the Soviet Union including, I assume, the citizens of Ukraine. Who are we to argue with our great teacher and leader?"

Zhuk stood up. "That was last month. This month things have changed."

"We know better than you what our dear leader's letter says," Efros barked. "We're not here to compel you. We are here to persuade you."

"This is where you're incorrect, Efros," Zhuk said to his OGPU colleague. "If persuasion doesn't work, you *will* compel them."

Efros told Isabelle that by new decree she was required to hand over one half of her provisions. "One half of whatever you've been hoarding for yourselves. Half your onions, potatoes, beets, wheat, rye, carrots."

In response, Roman, Ostap, and Nikora stepped forward. Isabelle's brothers were younger, taller, and more robust than the Bolsheviks. Their physical proximity and the squaring of their shoulders must have alerted the city men to the precariousness of their situation. Zhuk and Efros had no immediate method by which to requisition the family's food supply, or even to protect themselves. Efros fumbled for his revolver, which lay on the table by the dirty plates, but Roman got there first. Grabbing the revolver, he spun the chamber a few times before handing it to the junior lieutenant.

"We're going to need a day or two to get the supplies together, comrades," Roman said. "Come back and we'll have them ready for you."

"When we come back," Efros said, "we will bring ten militia men."

"Won't be necessary."

"Tonight there's a mandatory meeting at the village hall," Zhuk told them. "You're required to be present, including your wives and children. Comrade Kovalenko cannot be the only woman attending these meetings, even if she *is* nominally the landowner. We do not trust her to get the message across to the other women who run these homesteads."

Efros approached Isabelle, who was already by the flung-open door. "Can we trust you, Comrade Kovalenko?"

"You should trust me least of all," said Isabelle. "Get out."

11

The Devil's Advocate

On Fridays, Finn started coming home first instead of going straight to Schumann's, and taking Isabelle with him to visit the tailor. Vanessa, who had been momentarily excited to see Finn home so early, balked and said, "What are the girls going to do without her?"

As gently as he could, Finn ventured the obvious. "Couldn't they make do with their actual governess . . . or their mother for an hour?"

On the way, Isabelle said only two words to him. One was "Truro?" That one word was filled with such longing, it tugged at him.

Finn told her no, they weren't going back to the Cape because he had to work on Saturday, and because it had gotten considerably colder. Isabelle looked so crestfallen, Finn didn't have the heart to tell her there would probably be no more visits to Truro until next spring.

The second word she said to him was, "Lucas."

And sure enough, across the street, winding his way through the paths of Boston Common was Lucas, trailing but not trailing. When he saw Finn notice him, he gesticulated like a wild man. Finn walked faster, ignoring both the wave and Isabelle's questioning gaze.

"Is she doing all right, Schumann?" Finn asked when they had a moment alone, after the tailor showed Isabelle a tabletop of separates in the back of the shop and told her to pick out some warm pieces for the coming fall. Finn listened to them talking to each other in Ukrainian, noting the cadence of it, trying to understand the words, the meanings, hoping to catch something that would answer his million curiosities.

"Of course. Why wouldn't she be?"

"I don't know. She is quiet. The language barrier is a real obstacle."

"I think you've just answered for yourself why she is so quiet. But she was the only girl in a family of three brothers. Believe me, she is full of verve. And she is tough. Don't worry about her. She is fine."

"Does she want to come to church with us?" Finn said. "Or is she Jewish like you?"

"She is not Jewish," Schumann said. "Her father was Eastern Orthodox, her mother a Polish Catholic. But does it matter? All the lines are crossed when the Orthodox, Catholics, and Jews live side by side. That's how we lived. As for church, if you can, give her Sunday mornings off. That way she can find her own place of worship and come visit me afterwards."

Finn said he'd talk to Vanessa about it. "Is she family?"

"Family by association." Schumann's voice barely registered. "I've known Isabelle since she was four years old. Her father was one of my closest friends. And Cici, the daughter of the woman I was with for fifteen years, married Isa's brother." Schumann looked ready to cry.

There were many things a discomfited Finn didn't understand. Why didn't the mother and daughter escape with Schumann? Finn didn't feel it was his place to ask. "Cici wasn't *your* daughter?"

"I've known Cici since she was born," Schumann said. "So she was mine, but not mine, you understand?"

What happened to Isabelle's family? Finn wanted to ask but didn't know how to. They weren't with her, that much was obvious, and she looked hollowed out. Finn's face must have shown his struggle because Schumann said, "Finn, if you want to know about her life, ask her. She'll tell you."

"She can barely tell me if she is thirsty."

"Patience is its own reward," Schumann said. He blew his nose. "What a sweet kid she once was."

"Yes, weren't we all. But you just said she was tough. Define tough."

Schumann stared at Finn for a few moments before he replied. "Tough as in, she will do whatever needs to be done."

"You don't say." Finn was even more intrigued. She did get herself to America all the way from Ukraine, so he supposed toughness was a prerequisite for accomplishing something like that.

"Isa! Come here," Schumann called. He pronounced Isa not *Issa* but *Eeza*, with a long *e* and a *z*. Inaudibly, Finn mouthed it to himself.

She came out carrying a bundle of cardigans like they were small children. "I found nice yellow sweater for Yunie," she said. "And blue for Mae. They will like."

"I said find warm things for yourself," Schumann said with an eye roll.

"Yes, my children have three closets of clothes," Finn said. "But it's true, they will like these, thank you." *Eeza*.

"Would you like to have a drink with us, Finn?" The tailor brought out a flask from behind a secret compartment in the cabinet and set out three glasses. "I must be quick because the evening rush is about to be upon me."

"It would be rude to refuse," Finn said, his mouth watering, "seeing as you already took out a glass for me."

"And poured it for you, too. I can't explain to her what Prohibition is," Schumann added. "She doesn't understand even in Ukrainian."

"It's inexplicable in any language," Finn said, raising a glass to them both.

"To life," said Schumann.

"To life," said Finn.

"*L'Chaim*," said Isabelle.

If only Vanessa knew that Finn had stopped drinking with the no-good Lucas only to take up drinking with the tailor and the Lavelle girl instead.

At the end of September, during one of their weekly family get-togethers, Walter and Adder Day had a boisterous discussion about the pros and cons of aggressive investing. Adder ran the Massachusetts Insurance and Investments brokerage, and he kept trying to wheedle Finn into giving him some of the Adams Bank's investment business. But Finn dealt with Lionel Morris's firm instead, much to Adder's chagrin. Lionel and Finn had been good friends since their Harvard years, while Adder was someone Finn barely tolerated even before the sordid business with Isabelle.

Adder was a devil's advocate and a naysayer. His main activity in life was taking the opposite of whatever position Finn held. If Finn liked a utility company, Adder found something wrong with it. If Finn was cautious on a stock, Adder went in on it full cocked. If Finn liked Coolidge, Adder hated him. If Finn said the weather was pleasant, Adder forecast three weeks of rain. Finn had long recognized this pattern. In his dealings with Adder, he tried to follow his father's example and keep his mouth shut. It wasn't easy because Finn generally didn't like to keep his mouth shut and because Adder aggravated him like a canker sore. But the main reason Finn avoided doing business with Adder was because he simply didn't trust him, and you couldn't give your father-in-law's money to someone you didn't trust.

Adder, his eye still bloodshot and bearing the yellowing marks of his alleged encounter with a door, was particularly vexing that Sunday afternoon. Even Walter was getting steamed. "Adder, why do you keep arguing?" Walter said while Finn pretended to read the paper. "Trust me—everything is better than it's ever been. Didn't Finn tell you? Our quarterly earnings came in." He smiled proudly at Finn. "The average growth for Boston banks was 31 percent. Ours was seventy-three! We've outperformed the outperformers by double, Adder. All thanks to Finn. We are tremendously well positioned, and our revenue streams are diverse. There's nothing to worry about, right, Finn?"

Finn grunted, wary of being sucked into an unwanted discussion. "When is lunch? Wicker, are you there?" he called down to the cook. "And where are the girls?"

"They're getting your immigrant ready for her first family viewing," said Vanessa, her eyes shielded behind a pair of sunglasses.

Adder rolled his eyes, though whether at Walter's pride parade or at Isabelle's imminent appearance, Finn wasn't sure. Walter was always bragging about Finn, and Finn particularly enjoyed how much it ticked off Adder. Eleanor's husband ran his investment firm cautiously, and his earnings were correspondingly cautious. Last quarter Adder barely broke even, and this was clearly incensing him.

Trying not to sound sour, Adder resumed harassing Walter into limiting the bank's risk exposure, what with the bank's "sky-high liabilities and dynamic (read 'uncertain') liquidity." The market had been off its highs lately. "Buying more stock only makes sense if the market doesn't keep going down," Adder said.

"Why in the world would the market keep going down?" Walter shouted. "For goodness' sake, Adder. We had some profit-taking. Inevitable when the market's been at record highs. We took some ourselves."

To support his position, Adder gleefully recited the latest construction figures for August 1929. They were down. Manufacturing figures were down too. "Even Finn said the other week that the real estate market was flattening," Adder said. "Many companies on the market are overpriced and overvalued."

"Who's overvalued?" asked Walter. "Finn, do you hear this? Is General Motors overvalued?"

Finn grunted.

"Maybe Steel? Is *that* overvalued?"

The mere mention of U.S. Steel prickled Finn because of his recent conversation with Schumann about it. The tailor was also not impressed with America's largest publicly traded company. Finn had had enough.

"Adder is right about one thing, Walter," Finn said to his father-in-law. "You can't maintain an inflationary boom indefinitely."

"Who said?" boomed Walter. "Money is so cheap to borrow, to lend, to invest!"

"Yes, but money is not as cheap as it was," Finn said. "The Fed just raised its lending rate. I think we *are* going to proceed more conservatively."

"Oh, bollywocks," said Adder. "The Federal Reserve is always doing too little too late to control the market." He turned to Walter. "It's fine," he said. "No need to be cautious. The market is inching back up to 400. Mark my words, Walter, October 1929 is when we'll make a real killing."

There it was. As expected, Adder had switched sides midstream and was now vigorously defending more aggressive investing! Smiling, Finn went back to pretending to read the paper.

"Enough bank talk," said Olivia, putting down her book. "It's time for us to meet this girl of yours, Finn. Where is she?"

"She's not my girl, Mother," Finn said.

"Just a figure of speech, dear."

Flanked by a beaming Mae and Junie, Isabelle emerged in a new blue dress Schumann had made for her. It was pressed and well made and fitted around her long, slender form. On her feet were her leather boots. A light blue silk scarf was tied around her head. The girls had found a string of orange beads their mother had given them and wrapped it around her neck and dabbed some pink lipstick on her generous mouth.

She approached the family gracefully, without fidgeting. With her little support birds flanking her, she cleared her throat and said, "How do you do, Lucy, Walter, very nice to meet you." She turned to Finn's parents. "How do you do, Olivia . . . Earl . . ." Mae and Junie clapped, delighted with the success of their student. Isabelle had trouble getting the word *Earl* out of her mouth, so she had to resort to an imitation of Mae, who had taught her to say it. She could say *Earl* in Mae's voice, but not her own.

"The girl is much too thin," declared Lucy. "She's not eating?"

"Nonstop, Mother," Vanessa said. "Eating us out of house and home."

"I eat white bread and tomatoes, Lucy," Isabelle said. "Very delicious."

"Well, the girl seems perfectly adequate," Lucy said. "I don't know what you were complaining about, Eleanor."

"I wasn't complaining, Mother," Eleanor said. "In Truro, we did not find her very approachable, did we, Vanessa?"

Still standing tall, Isabelle glanced coldly at Adder. "*In Truro,*" she said in Eleanor's voice, "*I was not very approachable.*"

"How in the world does she do that?" Olivia exclaimed. "That's quite remarkable. Does she know what she's saying?"

"Oh, no, not at all." Vanessa studied her nails.

Finn asked the girls to take Isabelle back inside. He had noticed the way she stared down Adder, and he didn't want a confrontation to mar their agreeable afternoon. Finn had not told Vanessa what transpired between Adder and Isabelle, because he knew it would become a thing (another thing) between his wife and her sister, and in any case Adder would simply deny it. Finn feared that Vanessa, not knowing whom to believe, might challenge Isabelle about it. Finn had no intention of injuring Isabelle further when she couldn't defend herself—not with words, anyway.

"Finn, darling, did you hear what I said?"

"Sorry, Mother, lost in thought. Come again?"

"Has the girl been out and about?"

"I think so," he said. "Vanessa would know more about it."

Vanessa shrugged. "She *has* been out and about. My husband takes her on promenades throughout Boston."

"Yes," Finn said. "I promenade her to North End so she can visit with the one person she can speak Ukrainian to."

"I think it's unseemly for the vice-president of a respected Boston bank to be walking the streets with the hired help, that's all," Vanessa said.

To which Finn responded after a laden pause, "Who am *I* of so high a station? What do *I* have, that I have not received?"

12

The Towels

Vanessa hovered at the door of the nursery and eavesdropped on her children as they listened to Isabelle's stories, which she herself interpreted as lies. Vanessa wanted to march in and order Isabelle to take her fanciful fibs downstairs, far from her precious girls, to the lower floors where she belonged.

"It is true your ship sank?" Mae asked.

"Yes. Ship crash."

"Tell us the story, Isabelle. Please!" said Junie.

"Okay, I tell. We were at sea long time. Boat shake and bob, many waves, couple shtorms. We cross Black Sea on ship, then Greek Sea on other ship, then wait and wait. We wait in Italy, city called Brindisi. Can you say Brindisi?"

They could, but not as well as Isabelle with an Italian roll of the tongue.

"They had good grapes in Italy," she said. "Green and sweet. But then ship crash."

"In Italy?"

"No. In sea near Boston. It was shtorm and dark and rain. Captain said not worry, but definitely time to worry. Ship go this way and that way." With her hands and body she must have been making the motions of being thrown back and forth. "And then boom. Crash on big rocks. Turn over on side and sink."

"And then what happened?"

Isabelle was quiet, as if gathering her voice to speak. "People go under, swallow water. Some people die."

"Not you."

"No. Not me. Terrible man named Nate save me. Can you say terrible?"

Vanessa jealously wished she had incredible stories to tell her children, so she could make them ooh and ahh.

Vanessa needed someone to talk to. She could never confide in her mother, or God forbid her sister. And confide what, exactly? When Vanessa had tried to express her reservations about hiring Isabelle, Finn's mother shut her down, as if she weren't being a good wife. As if she was dense and couldn't understand why her husband felt obligated to bring home outcasts, and she, Vanessa Adams, was duty-bound to approve of it! Well, she did *not* approve of it, but she could never admit that. She could never reveal a hint of anything in her marriage that wasn't perfect, wasn't the very epitome of what marriage was supposed to be.

Her friend Dorothy had stopped coming around some months back. She said she was offended that she was always the one to call on Vanessa. Besides, what could Vanessa articulate even to Dorothy?

Isabelle was a hard worker; there was nothing wrong with that. She helped the cook, the housekeeper, the governess. Edith couldn't be happier, because Isabelle was doing the things Edith didn't want to do. Really, the person Vanessa should be upset with was Edith!

So what was it?

While Vanessa twisted and churned over the matter, she spent arduous weeks arranging and rearranging the towels and sheets in the house. She made the housekeeper launder them and Isabelle iron them, all thirty-five sets, five for each bedroom, and thirty-five sets of towels, too. Vanessa emptied out and cleaned the sideboards where the sheets resided—there was one in every bedroom—dusting every nook and cranny thoroughly. Vanessa emptied and cleaned out the shelves in every bathroom where the towels were kept.

The true source of Vanessa's unyielding anxiety was this: she was afraid Finn had hired the woman because he sensed that Vanessa needed help, that she wasn't managing. And the more industrious and diligent Isabelle was, the more anxious Vanessa became, not only that Finn suspected she wasn't coping, but also that Finn was right.

But she was fine, had been fine, was going to be fine.

However, there was no question that the towels and sheets needed to be washed and ironed *again*. They had spent so long outside the cupboards that Vanessa was certain they had gotten quite dusty. And no one wanted to sleep on dusty sheets and dry themselves off with dusty towels. It was a kindness to everyone in the house to empty the shelves and launder the towels one more time, just in case, and to do it herself so it would be done right.

Finn couldn't sleep. Quietly he went downstairs in the middle of the night as was his nocturnal habit and rummaged in the cupboards for something to eat and drink. He was barefoot, in pajama bottoms and a T-shirt. After he found himself a scone and some cheese and washed it down with juice—cursing the absence of anything stronger—he remembered that he had left the quarterly asset and liability report he'd been working on in his study. Perhaps that was why he couldn't sleep. Walter was coming into the bank tomorrow to go over it, and Finn didn't want to forget it at home. Taking the stairs two at a time—for a little exercise at one in the morning—he ascended the rear staircase to the first floor and then the main staircase to the third floor where his study was located. He was out of breath and pleased with himself for keeping up a good pace when he turned the corner on the landing and crashed into Isabelle, who was dripping wet and naked.

They both gasped. She teetered as if about to lose her balance, voicing some choice words in Ukrainian. His hands flew out instinctively—to catch someone about to fall—never mind that he grabbed her by her wet slippery upper arms or that she had knocked into him with the full-frontal force of her soft hurrying body.

"Close eyes," she said.

"Excuse me," he said, stumbling away.

Her arm crossed over her breasts. The other hand lowered to cover her modesty.

Finn closed his eyes and grabbed on to the landing rail.

"Your wife wash towels," Isabelle said. "No towel in tub room, not one. Zero. *Nul.*"

"My apologies." Finn turned away from her. "Let me go grab you one."

She waited at the top of the stairs while he raced down to the second-floor bathroom. There were no towels there either!

He found all the towels in the laundry room on the lower level. Carrying a stack of them in his arms like brides, he stopped at the foot of the third staircase, looking at his feet and averting his eyes. "Do you want me to throw—"

She had already descended the stairs and took them out of his hands.

"Thank you," she said. "You can open eye."

He opened his eyes but did not look at her standing in front of him damp and wrapped in an inadequate towel. What a muddle.

"Why didn't you use the bath on the lower floor?" he said.

"*Vanna gryazna* downstairs," Isabelle said. "How you say. . . ?"

"Tub is disgusting?"

"*Disgusting.*" She used his voice to repeat it.

"Sorry."

"Sorry too." She used her own voice to say it.

"Goodnight."

"Goodnight."

The next afternoon, after his successful meeting with Walter about the status of the bank's business, Finn walked across the street to Jordan Marsh department store and bought a luxe, cream-colored, extra-long silk robe. Upon his return home, he left it on Isabelle's narrow bed, still in the shopping bag with tissue paper around it, almost like a present. She didn't mention it, and he most certainly never mentioned it. It was terrible manners for the man of the house to slam into a wet naked woman at night—any woman, really, but especially one who was not his wife—and then to ever ever *ever* remark on it. That it happened at all was awkward enough. Finn tried to put it out of his mind.

Except every once in a while, he wished he had caught one more glimpse of her glistening naked body before closing his eyes and never seeing it again.

13

The Importance of Radio and Milk

Fully dressed from her neck to her stockinged feet, Isabelle took the center of the parlor room as if on a stage, with Mae and Junie splayed at her feet as her admiring audience. Isabelle was listening to the weather report on the radio, which she would repeat syllable for syllable, in the exact voice and dialect of the male newscaster.

"*And Sunday promises to be a cold one! We have a front coming in from Canada—now what else have the Canadians ever given us besides icy weather, Norm? Oh, maple syrup, you say. So right. But we can get maple syrup from Vermont. Every bit as good. What* else *have the Canadians ever given us?*" Norm said something, there was giggling, chortling, and Isabelle giggled and chortled, too. "*Well, Norm, we're not going to mention* that *on the air during family hour. It's against the law, our Constitution now says so.*"

And on and on.

Finn asked his children about it.

"She does it all the time, Daddy." He regretted he wasn't home early enough during the week to hear it more often.

"Only with the weather?"

"With everything. The best is when she repeats the jokes on the comedy hour."

"Jokes, no kidding."

"Daddy, Isabelle is so much more fun than Edith," Junie said.

"Edith is a very nice lady," Mae said, shushing her sister. "But she can't run or play tag or hide-and-seek like Isabelle. Or make jokes."

"Well, Edith teaches you more serious things." But Finn bought two more radios for the house.

"She should be paying *us* for buying her radios," said Vanessa. "Finn, I need you to talk to her. She keeps taking the children downstairs! Say something to her. Tell her to stop."

"Why?"

"Why are our girls spending time with the servants?" Vanessa said.

"Edith is a servant."

"You know what I mean. It's inappropriate."

"What are they doing down there?"

"Getting up to no good. The other night, they made cookies!"

"They *what*?"

"Don't joke, Finn, it's not funny."

"The cookies they fed their father?"

"That's not the point. They shouldn't be in the cellar."

"But the oven is in the cellar."

"They shouldn't be using the oven!"

"Are they having fun?"

"Not the point."

"Are they learning something new?"

"They're learning useless things."

Finn shrugged. "I don't know. Baking seems all right. Who doesn't like cookies?"

Vanessa, apparently. "Finn, are you going to talk to her, or should I?"

Finn kissed Vanessa on the head. "I think you should do it, cupcake. I'd like to listen in from the other room, though. I want to hear how you carry it off. I told her to stop joking once. It didn't go well."

"How could she possibly joke in English, Finn?"

From downstairs came the sound of a loud piano. Finn had bought the piano because all fine homes in Beacon Hill had one. The girls had been taking lessons, but they were reluctant learners at best and still very much beginners. But this piano playing was discordant and joyous and had hints of a real though unfamiliar melody.

In the drawing room, the girls and Isabelle were pounding the keys in cacophony and unison.

"I teach them 'Kolomeyka,'" Isabelle said. "Very good Ukrainian song. I play on *akordeon*. Not same, but almost . . ."

Vanessa was cross and exasperated. "Girls, stop that. You'll ruin the action. Isabelle, please don't do that anymore. One at a time, please. And don't play anything that hurts our ears. The piano makes beautiful music, not—"

"Vanessa," Finn said in a quiet, chiding voice.

Vanessa clicked her heels and her tongue. "You know, it *really* bothers me," she said, "that the idiot savants are allowed to make a disharmony of our evenings, and I'm supposed to just say thank you."

"Who are you calling idiot savants? Not our girls, I hope."

Vanessa continued. "Yes, what a show-stopping party trick this so-called piano playing is going to be when Mother and Daddy come for tea. I'm sure Adder and Eleanor would like nothing more than to hear it. Why, it's a veritable Beethoven."

"*Why, it's a veritable Beethoven!*" echoed Isabelle in the same irritable tone.

Finn laughed.

Vanessa didn't.

It was hard to deny that for Finn—even without accidental nighttime run-ins with wet naked Ukrainians—the house had become more fun since the arrival of this mysterious creature, all woman, part naiad, part dryad, part siren, singing, swinging from trees, telling stories in other tongues, baking melt-in-your-mouth delights, and making music. Work was growing increasingly stressful, but at night, if he managed to get home in time to catch it, there was laughter. Sometimes there was dancing, too. With Isabelle's help, the girls put on skits for them after dinner. Vanessa wasn't impressed, but it was all Finn could do not to break up when his babies tried to imitate Isabelle imitating Will Rogers in her own version of his comedy routine. "*Write to your congressman,*" Isabelle would say, sounding more Will Rogers than the man himself. "*Even if he can't read, write to your congressman!*"

Vanessa leaned close to Finn. "Do you think she knows what a congressman is?"

"*Get some laughs and do the best you can,*" said Will Rogers to Vanessa, standing with her hands akimbo on her slim hips in the middle of the parlor room. Isabelle switched gears into a high nasal twang and instantly became Jack Benny, shuffling the two-step. "*Now remember, ladies—a smile is the second-best thing you can do with your lips.*"

"Does she have *any* idea what she's saying?" said Vanessa. "Any at all?"

Isabelle flashed a beguiling grin.

Finn rocked back, trying to conceal his own beguiled smile from both women. "I don't know, Vee," he said. "Ask her what the first thing is."

Many nights, along with the entertainment, there were little cakes, and one time even lemon bars, which for some reason upset Vanessa so much, even Finn couldn't joke her out of her mood.

Isabelle seemed to adjust to her new situation better than Vanessa to the same old situation with the addition of a helping hand. Finn found it inexplicable that the woman who had escaped her homeland, presumably under some duress, who had been shipwrecked and was now alone, was adjusting better to her circumstances than the woman who had lived her life wrapped in cotton, slept on a bed of silk, had servants for every job in the house, and whose single nervous malady seemed to be an overzealous need for organization and a slight antipathy to keeping time.

However you weighed it, one woman played with the children and mimicked jokes, and the other woman grumbled. There was nothing so small that Vanessa could not blow it out of proportion.

"Oh, you want to know why I'm slightly churlish tonight, my darling?" Vanessa exclaimed to Finn when he inquired about the cause of Vanessa's sour disposition. "Come with me. I want you to hear with your own ears what the girls told me earlier." She led Finn to the nursery. "Girls," she said, "will you please tell your father what you asked me this morning. About milk."

"Oh yeah, Daddy," said Mae, "we want to know why we only drink milk once a week."

"Milk is for babies, darlings," said Finn. "Not for big girls."

"But Daddy," said Junie, "we want to drink milk every day."

"Twice a day," Mae said. "Morning and night."

"Isabelle says we can have our milk delivered to our door. Can we?"

"We could." Finn was unsure where this was going, but judging by Vanessa's expression he knew it couldn't be anywhere good. "Nothing wrong with a little more milk, I guess. But why such a keen interest?"

"We asked Isabelle why her boobies were so big, and she told us it was because the Ukrainian girls drank milk every day since childhood," said Mae.

"And she said many boobies in Ukraine were bigger than hers," said Junie. "Me and Mae want to have big boobies like Isabelle."

"Mae and *I*, Junie," Vanessa corrected.

"Mae and *I* want to have big boobies like Isabelle," said Junie.

"Very good darling," said a deadpan Vanessa.

"We need milk twice a day, Daddy," said Mae. "Please can we have it, starting tomorrow?"

To keep a straight face with Vanessa giving him a side-eye glare took all the powers in Finn's possession. Even her crossed arms glared at him.

Finn crossed his own arms. "Oh yeah, Vanessa, that reminds me," he said. "If you're going to launder all the towels in the house, please make sure you leave a few clean dry ones in every washroom. The other night, there was not a single towel to be found in either of the bathrooms upstairs."

Vanessa became flustered and unsettled. "I don't know what you're talking about, darling," she said, stammering slightly. "But I will most certainly speak to the servants about it. It's inexcusable." She paused a moment. "Our conversation about *milk* reminded you of the towels?"

"What can I tell you, the human man works in mysterious ways," said Finn. "I meant mind."

* * *

There was something about her. On the surface she was capable, quiet, even-tempered. She wasn't flashy or showy. She acquitted herself well with his parents and in-laws. She was patient and polite to Vanessa, even though his otherwise courteous wife sometimes forgot her manners when she spoke to or about Isabelle. She tended to his children with such an aching tenderness that it made Finn's own heart ache, for his children *and* for Isabelle.

Finn didn't want to observe the woman too closely; he didn't want to study her as if she were a painting or a subject desirous of being painted, but he had to confess to a certain magnetizing unfamiliarity about her that made him sometimes want to stare.

She had strong, developed hands with pronounced knuckles and trimmed, unpolished nails, uncommon for Boston women. Many things about her were singular: the high exposed forehead, the crescent-moon unplucked brows, the penetrating eyes of indeterminate color, half-sea, half-concrete, the defined bones of her oval face, her artist's mouth. She wore no makeup, as if by design, and always had a scarf covering her head as if she was embarrassed by her choppy tufts of hair. Her face was a good face, and her gaze didn't waver. When you spoke to her, she looked right at you; she wasn't shy. There was an exotic confidence about her, merited or misplaced? He didn't know and couldn't tell.

There were other things too.

Late one night Finn came downstairs to get himself a drink and a bite to eat. Everything was quiet, but just as he was about to rummage in the ice box, he heard a noise in the pantry just off the kitchen. When he moved to investigate, he saw Isabelle, down on her knees, prostrate, her head flattened into the cold floor. She was motionless except for her heaving shoulders, and the racked weeping coming from her was the sound of a living beast tearing apart the heart of a human being.

Finn staggered back. He felt he had walked in on something he wasn't meant to see, something she was giving only to God. Quietly he left the kitchen and after that night stopped wandering around his own house, lest he be confronted again with unfathomable things he didn't understand and was afraid to.

Isabelle may have shown the world a defiant, self-assured hardness, but now Finn knew. Just below her surface was the floodline of a shallow grave.

14

Definitions of Words

Ukraine, February 1929

"Comrade—"

"Don't call me comrade. Do you know the definition of the word? A comrade is a friend, a compatriot, a brother in arms."

"Then I will call you citizen."

"Reluctantly, I will agree to being called citizen."

"Your reluctance is noted, Citizen Lazar. I've written it down in your file."

"Please also note in my file that I'm asking for clarification on the word *voluntary*. I have a feeling we may be at odds on the difference between that and the word *compulsory*."

"I was about to explain to you the meaning of the words *enemy of the people*."

"You haven't answered my first question. I'd like us to conclude one topic before moving on to the next."

"Enemy of the people! Also the meaning of the word *kulak*."

"Fine, we shall move on without a clear definition of the term *voluntary*. Let *that* be noted. And as for *kulak*, the word is *kurkul* in our language."

"Your language is Russian, citizen!"

"Do the Armenians speak Armenian? Do the Tadjiks speak Tadjik? Do the Georgians speak Georgian, like our leader and teacher, Comrade Stalin? They do. Therefore the Ukrainians also speak their own language. That language is called Ukrainian. So please, Citizen Zhuk, explain to me in my language what a *kurkul* is."

That was the testy exchange that took place between Roman and Kondraty Zhuk in the village hall, in front of three hundred people. The meeting had been going on for four hours, as if no one was a farmer, no one had to be up at dawn, no one had any work to do other than discuss the meaning of *collectivization*, *enemy of the people*, and *compulsory*.

Isabelle wished her brother would stop poking the foul bear, but she understood how Roman felt. After two hours of numbing speechifying, repeating the same propaganda points over and over, who wouldn't be testy, who wouldn't be tearing out their hair?

The party officials droned on and on. In their words:

The poor farmers had had enough.

The rich farmers, the *kulaks* or *kurkuls*, were making all the money and taking all the profit.

The *kurkuls* were making themselves richer, while the less fortunate villagers starved.

It was the *kurkuls'* fault the poor villagers were starving, because the *kurkuls* weren't sharing their abundant harvest.

"The time has come to put an end to this disparity, to this criminal inequity," Zhuk declared. "The time has come to redress the wrongs of such imbalances.

"Collectivization is the only way. The poor farmers should have no mercy on the *kurkuls*. Killing them, destroying them is the only way the average Ukrainian farmer might rise above his pauper station and attain a prosperous future."

Collectivization, the officials proclaimed, would not only achieve the goal of liquidating the rich farmers, but it would make every poor farmer's life better. The farms would no longer be privately owned by *kurkuls*, they would be owned by the Soviet state.

The farmers working on the collective farms would work less and produce more. They would no longer be exploited. And they would be protected from both the caprices of rich farmers and Mother Nature.

And, most importantly, collectivization was the best course forward for the Soviet Union.

"And what is best for the Soviet Union is, by definition, what's best for the farmers."

Repeat. Over and over.

After two hours, Zhuk asked who wanted to sign over their homes to join the Ispas collective, and a chillingly large number of farmers came forward. After two more hours, almost a third of the homesteads had agreed to organize into the collective—a full third!

"They were simply bored into an agreement!" hissed a fed-up Cici. "They'll sign anything as long as it brings this meeting to an end."

But after the initial surge of signatures, enthusiasm waned. To force the numbers higher, Zhuk declared that anyone who refused to voluntarily collectivize was, by definition (again, that definition!), "an enemy of the people" and a "*kurkul*." Which is where they were now. Cici raised her hand, wanting to know if Zhuk was being paid by the signature, if he was being "incentivized" with vodka and a kilo of bacon into raising the sign-up numbers. "Perhaps he can incentivize us to work for him," Cici said. "Say, pay us more for delivering more grain—almost like a profit, you know?"

"Shh!" Mirik said.

"Zhuk is not leaving here tonight until he achieves 100 percent collectivization," Cici said, indifferent to Mirik's shushing.

"Well, it will be 100 percent minus one," said Roman, pulling down his irate wife's raised arm and stepping forward again. He had not sat down for the entire four hours.

Mirik leaned over to Isabelle, who was seated. She had stood for the first two hours; that was enough. This wasn't church; this wasn't the Easter vigil. She wasn't going to stand in front of Communists the way she stood before Christ. "Don't let your brother speak for you, Isabelle," Mirik whispered. "Don't let him put words into your mouth."

"He has not said a single thing with which I disagree," Isabelle said.

"He'll only get us into more trouble," Mirik said.

"Is that even possible? Enemy of the people, Mirik. *Kurkul*. That's you."

"That's not me," Mirik said, leaning slightly away. "The Kovalenkos don't own any land."

"Nice, husband, commendable," Isabelle said. "But your wife does. Are you washing your hands of me and our half-Lazar children?"

"I don't understand why you must be so antagonistic. For our boys' sake, tell your brother to pipe down."

"Observe how your children are looking at Roman," said Isabelle. It was true; Slava and Maxim gaped at their uncle worshipfully.

"They're babies, they don't know any better," Mirik said, yanking on his sons to close their mouths.

Roman had one of the Soviet propaganda pamphlets open and read from it, his voice carrying across the hall. "Right here, in the brochure titled 'Every day of labor is a step toward Communism,' you define a *kurkul*. I'm going to read from the pamphlet now, Citizen Zhuk. This is the official Soviet classification. *One: A kurkul is someone who hires outside labor to work for him on his farm.* That is not the Lazars or the Kovalenkos. Only our families work the Lazar ranch. *Two: A kurkul is someone who possesses heavy machinery.* That is definitely not us. We have the horse and the plow, that is all. *Three: A kurkul is someone who rents out this machinery for others to use.* Also not us, as explained in two. *Four: A kurkul is someone who leases his own land for industrial purposes.* Again, not us. We have never used our land for any purpose other than our own activities, and we certainly don't intend to start now."

"You strongly misunderstand the definition of *kurkul*, citizen," said Zhuk. "You are trying to hide behind false information, and I won't have it."

"Are you saying that the words written in this exciting pamphlet produced by the Communist Party are false information?"

"I'm saying it's not the only definition!" said Zhuk. "A *kurkul*, in his very essence, is a farmer who disagrees with the agricultural policy position of the Soviet Union."

"You mean, anyone who disagrees with you about a policy position is automatically defined as an enemy of the people?"

"Correct."

"What happens to the enemies of the people, citizen?"

"You will be arrested. You and your families and your children will be deported to 'corrective camps' in other parts of the Soviet Union, where you will be made to work as part of your rehabilitation."

"And who will work the farms that the relocated have left behind?"

"Not the *kurkul*, that's the only important thing," said Zhuk. "Other farmers not motivated by profit will reap the fruits of their labors for the Soviet Union."

"But after they reap the fruits of their labors," Roman said, "won't these poor farmers prosper and grow wealthy through the work of their hands, and won't that make them, by virtue of all that fruit reaping, *kurkuls*? In other words, the very thing we are trying to define and liquidate?"

"I have had enough of your insolence, Comrade Lazar," Zhuk said. "Sit down and let someone else ask the questions."

"Please, answer my very first question," said Roman. "What is the meaning of the word *voluntary*?"

"Voluntary means of your own choice. We cannot force you to collectivize against your will. But that doesn't mean there will not be consequences."

"So, if we don't voluntarily collectivize, we will be labeled enemies of the people and arrested and deported, and our farms will be taken from us and given to others who will collectivize?"

"Yes!" Zhuk said happily, as if pleased that Roman was finally getting it—and in a public forum too, for the benefit of many others.

"So by your logic," said Roman, "a pauper farmer can become a *kurkul* by gaining property, but a successful farmer cannot stop being a *kurkul* by losing his."

"Finally, I've led the horse to water," said Zhuk.

"Oh, that you have," said Roman, laying the propaganda pamphlet down on the chair. The expression under his knitted brows was one of hardness and darkness. "The horse has finally understood."

***

"There is no escape. Ispas is going to be ruined and depopulated," Roman said when the families returned to the ranch well after midnight, tied up the horses, and piled into Isabelle's cottage, exhausted and dispirited. Isabelle's children had long since fallen asleep in the dray. Roman and Mirik carried the boys inside and laid them in their bed and were now talking intensely but quietly in the common area so as not to wake them.

"We're going to be arrested and sent to Solovki or outer Siberia to mine ore and coal for their revolution," Roman said. "Or we'll be shot. We will vanish. Our civilization gone, our way of life. Is that what you want, Mirik?"

"Is that what I *want*?" Mirik said. "No, it's not what I want, you fool. But what I *do* want, what *is* my imperative, is to protect my children. Why are you so intent on leaving your new wife a widow?"

Roman stared at Cici. Cici stared back. There was love in the exchanged glance, but something else too.

"Once Ukraine is lost and our farm is gone, what will it matter if Roman and I are married?" said Cici. "What will it matter if I'm a widow?"

"Cici, shush," said Isabelle. She wasn't as cautious as her husband, but she wasn't willing to risk everything for a principle. "What are we doing then, Roman," she asked, "if we're doomed to fail no matter what?"

"Counting the steps to the guillotine," said Roman. "Wondering if we can make a run for it before our head is fitted into the lunette."

"Before our heads are on the block," said Mirik, "perhaps we can put them together to come up with a workable compromise."

"Oh, I have a compromise," said Roman. "They can have my farm. But not without a fight to the death."

"A fight you will lose," said Mirik.

"At least I'll die fighting," said Roman.

"All I hear is that you'll die," said Mirik. "Everything else is just words."

15

The Lost Hat

Isabelle didn't know how to put it into words, even Ukrainian words, but something was wrong with the mistress of the house. At first it was an odd thing or two, a peculiarity Isabelle wasn't used to—like the towels—which she attributed to a different way of living. Then she thought maybe Vanessa was sick. She spent so much time upstairs in her bedroom. But if she was sick, where were the doctors?

For some weeks Isabelle suspected heavy drinking was involved. But Isabelle knew that drinking to such a degree was hard to hide. It was accompanied by strong odors, slurred speech, by loud irrational arguments. None of these things were present between the withdrawn Vanessa and her unfailingly courteous, slightly secretive husband. She and Finn never spoke a cross word to each other. Everything was yes, darling, please, darling, thank you, dear. What kind of married people talked like that? Only people who were keeping things from one another, each reining in their secrets with impeccable manners.

"Junie," Isabelle said one day when she was at the park with the girls, though it sounded more like "Yunie"—she had trouble with the J sound when she used her regular voice. "Junie," she repeated, in Finn's voice, and that came out correctly. She continued: "Why your mama not like to take you to park? It's nice fall day."

"Oh, she likes to," said Junie. "But she lost her hat."

"It was her favorite hat," Mae chimed in, lest Isabelle misunderstand the hat's importance. "It was gray cashmere."

"And Mommy had it since she was a girl," Junie added.

"She was taking us for a walk and got too hot for cashmere, so Mommy put it in her coat pocket, and when we got home it was gone."

"Gone!" said Junie.

"She went back to look for the hat..."

"She was gone like three days," said Junie.

"She was gone like three hours," corrected Mae. "She left us with the cook, and when Daddy came home late, the cook quit."

"Daddy said the cook quit because he had to mind children and couldn't make chicken."

"Very upsetting, yes," said Isabelle. "You sure he not say he quit because he had to mind chicken and couldn't make children?"

The girls giggled. "We like Wicker better anyway," said Junie.

"Mommy searched for the hat," Mae said. "Like a thousand times."

"A million times," said Junie. "It was dark out, and she was still looking."

"The hat was never found!" said Mae with a dramatic flourish.

"Mommy was so upset, a doctor had to come and check on her! After he left, she still cried." The girls fell quiet.

Isabelle waited. "End of story?" she said. "Mama stopped going to park because she lost hat? Why not get new hat?"

"Mommy said the hat was . . ." Mae struggled to recall the word. "Irreplaceable."

"The *hat* was irreplaceable?" Isabelle stared at the two girls.

The girls shrugged. "Mommy is funny sometimes," Mae said.

"When ago this?"

"Long time," said seven-year-old Mae. "Junie was still a baby."

"I'm not a baby, you a baby," said Junie.

Isabelle wasn't sure how to help Vanessa. Instinctively she felt that Finn, at least in part, had agreed to let her live with his family so she could help his wife in some way. The problem was, Isabelle had never seen the things that plagued Vanessa. Isabelle had lived through a lot. But not this.

Instead of dressing, Vanessa rearranged the furniture. Instead of taking the girls for a walk or playing with them, she took all the china out of the cabinets to search for cracks or scuffs, then put it all back when she didn't find any. Instead of overseeing the management of the household, she involved the entire household in searching for one of the children's many socks, which had gone missing on the way from the laundry room to the dresser. Isabelle couldn't fathom it.

Carefully, Isabelle would knock on Vanessa's door to ask if she wanted to come for a walk with her and the girls. Isabelle would hear an array of excuses in reply. There was some chaos somewhere that needed to be attended to, or Vanessa wasn't dressed to go out, or she was about to engage in some task that couldn't wait even an hour, or she was under the weather. Whatever the reason, Vanessa avoided setting foot outside the house.

How Vanessa kept this from Finn was a mystery. They did go to Truro when Isabelle first came to live with them. But Vanessa was jittery and tense the entire weekend, and never went down to the sea, never left the veranda.

Vanessa had no interest in strolling in the Public Garden where the rest of Boston turned out en masse every Sunday. Finn would take the girls by himself and act as if it was the most normal thing in the world, his wife not on his arm ambling down the crowded canopied paths on sunny afternoons. "Go with your children, darling," Isabelle would hear Vanessa say to Finn. "I'm with them all week, and they sure do miss you and want a little time with you."

But Isabelle knew: Vanessa was with the girls all week by virtue of geography only. Spiritually, mother and daughters might as well have been on different continents.

It was none of her business, Isabelle told herself, keeping her head down. Boy, was Tolstoy right. Every unhappy family was unhappy in its own way. She thought about asking Schumann for advice but decided against it. She didn't want to be a gossipmonger. This seemed like a private matter, and she didn't want it to get back to Finn that she was blabbing intimate details about his marriage to an outsider. She would hate to offend the gracious man who had given her a place to live and a salary.

Isabelle redoubled her efforts at learning English, hoping to become confident enough to approach Finn herself about the best way to support his wife. She was slightly intimidated by him. And Isabelle did not say this about many men. Any men. Not only was his physical size and presence imposing, but in his dapper suits, shined patent leather shoes, with his constant talk about peculiar financial things she didn't understand, and in his utter outward indifference toward her, Finn truly seemed like a man from another world.

But toward the end of October 1929, just as Isabelle thought she was ready to start contemplating a possible conversation with him, her halting English be damned, bizarre and troubling things began happening at the house—*other* bizarre and troubling things—that made the planned dialog all the more imperative and at the same time, all the more impossible.

PART II
Unto the Breach

"All changed, changed utterly:
A terrible beauty is born."

William Butler Yeats

16

The Pad Shover

On Monday, October 28, as soon as Finn got to work, Barney Levine was on the phone from New York. "They're at it again," Barney said.

By *they* he meant the brokers on Wall Street. By *at it*, he meant gnashing their teeth and rending their clothes at another market correction. This pattern of a few sharp falls followed by more gradual rises had been happening for the past month. Finn acted untroubled and was, for the most part. At the start of September, the market had reached its highest level in history. Finn had anticipated a "taking profits" correction, just as many experts smarter than him did. Thus far, every downward session was accompanied by days of buying, of enthusiasm, of rises.

It was true, the market *had* been slightly saggy in October, reaching for the heights and at every closing bell failing to achieve them. It was a slow downward trickle of a bear market, and Finn was not unduly worried. Every bear market was a buying opportunity; every banker and savvy investor knew this. Staying calm was key.

Barney was a former exchange clerk, a pad shover who ran the bid orders to the traders at their posts, and who was now employed by Finn full-time to report on the goings-on from the floor of the New York Stock Exchange. He was more efficient than the ticker tape, which tended to run behind, even on light volume days. Barney rented a one-room office on Wall Street across from the stock exchange, and literally ran from the trading floor to the office to call Finn and report on the direction and trading volume of Finn's most important stocks, like U.S. Steel, Standard Oil, Consolidated Gas, and General Electric. The ticker tape machine at Adams Bank confirmed the information a half-hour later.

But three days ago, on Thursday, October 24, 1929, even the hard-to-rile Finn had to admit some unusual stuff was happening. Not only was there wave after wave and hour after hour of irrational selling, but the sheer number of shares traded during the interminable five-hour day was unprecedented. Nearly thirteen million shares changed hands!

For two hundred minutes it was admittedly hair-raising, but after a day of catastrophic selling, the market somehow managed to rally, and finished trading only a few points down. It started at 305 and finished at 299. To someone looking in from the outside, everything would appear almost normal, as if the market had barely moved, as if the earth had not temporarily slipped off its axis during the previous five hours of relentless dumping of stock. However, many small investors at Finn's bank were wiped out before the late rally, and their accounts unfortunately had to be liquidated and closed. Even Finn had a couple of margin calls—a few hundred dollars here and there—that he was able to satisfy without difficulty.

The ticker tape didn't catch up with the actual bids until after seven at night, some four hours after close of trading. But thanks to Barney, Finn already knew they had weathered the storm, and he acted accordingly, remaining calm, at least on the outside. The worst had passed, he told Walter, and Adder, and even his barely interested wife.

And he almost believed it.

The niggling concern that Finn had was the sheer volume of sell orders. It was as if selling had become a mob contagion. Was the small-time investor spent and sold out of the market all over the United States, not just at Adams Bank? The newspapers, the Federal Reserve, President Hoover all tried to calm nerves.

Despite Thursday's insanity, Friday was steady and Saturday nearly normal and so, on Monday, Finn came into work expecting a regular day.

"Oh, there's going to be *nothing* regular about today, Mr. Evans," Barney told him. "The pit brokers are screaming like banshees. Do you hear them? I called you from a phone near the floor so you could hear."

"What are you talking about, banshees?" Finn said. "The market doesn't open for another hour."

"They have so many sell orders from Saturday, they're collapsing on the floor," Barney said. "I mean literally collapsing. Shrieking like hyenas."

Barney didn't have to tell Finn again. Finn could hear it down the phone line. Grown men were hollering, bawling. Finn's hand began to tremble as he gripped the receiver.

"They're clawing at each other, Mr. Evans!" Barney said. "They're grabbing each other by the lapels and screaming and flinging themselves on the floor."

"Sell! Sell! Sell! Sell!" Finn heard as he hung up.

By the time the market opened at ten, things had gotten worse.

Light at Lavelle

* * *

At 11:30, there was a sharp knock on Finn's barricaded office door. Finn didn't want to see anyone, and he didn't want anyone to see him. He had taken off his tie, his jacket, his vest. He'd undone the top buttons on his white shirt. He was so hot; he couldn't stop sweating.

"Myrtle!" Finn was uncharacteristically loud. "I told you, I don't want to be disturbed!" Myrtle was his secretary, with him since 1921.

The door was pushed open and Walter Adams barreled in, panting and sweating himself, looking as if he, and not Barney, had been running back and forth across Wall Street.

"Finn, what in the name of hell is going on?" Walter bellowed. He had to sit down before he continued speaking. Walter had had two heart attacks in the last three years, which was why he was semi-retired. He gave his son-in-law the run of the bank and in return got peace of mind and weekly reports.

"Walter, calm down," Finn said. "Everything will be fine. But I can't get distracted even for a second."

The phone rang.

"Pick it up!" said Walter.

But Finn didn't want to pick up the phone, not in front of his weakened father-in-law. What if it was Barney with more bad news? Last Finn heard, the floor was out from under U.S. Steel. The brokers were trying to keep it above $200 and failing. It had opened at $202, and the center could not hold.

The phone stopped ringing for a moment and resumed instantly and insistently.

What if it was Lionel? Finn wanted to hear from Lionel *least of all*. Lionel Morris was Finn's broker, business partner, and one of his closest friends, but Finn knew he would not enjoy their conversation today.

"You don't want to pick it up in front of me," Walter said. "I thought you said everything was fine?"

"I didn't say that. I said everything will be fine," Finn said, crushing his hands together. "Walter, I beg of you, go home. Smoke a cigar, lie down, turn off the radio. Let me take care of this. I really need to be—"

"Why is everybody selling fucking everything?" Walter exclaimed.

"Because it's contagious," Finn said. "Everyone thinks everyone else knows something they don't, and they're all panicking together."

"This is not just a little sell-off," Walter said. "Not like you pretended it was on Thursday."

"I didn't pretend. On Thursday, the ship was listing, but it righted itself."

"What about today?"

"We're still in the middle of today," Finn said, trying not to hyperventilate.

The phone didn't stop its demanding trill.

"Why is the ticker not running?" Walter said, gesturing to the outside of Finn's office. Through the open door, across the hall, in its own small, dark-paneled, oakwood room, the black ticker tape machine rested proudly and prominently on a walnut table. The machine printed out NYSE stock market prices on a long white ribbon—what fell, what rose—during trading hours. The ticker tape machine was the heartbeat of the bank for five hours every day but Sunday. But at that moment, on Monday, October 28, it stood completely silent.

"We ran out of tape," Finn said. "Lionel's boy is bringing more shortly."

"You ran out of tape?" His father-in-law was right to be surprised. This had never happened. But after Thursday's record volume, all the machines in Boston were low.

"Walter, nearly thirteen million shares changed hands on Thursday," Finn said. "No one has any tape."

"So how do you know what in holy heavens is going on if you don't have a ticker?"

The phone kept ringing. Finn thought he might go mad if Walter didn't leave.

"Through Barney." He and Walter both stared at the ringing phone.

"Pick it up," Walter said. "I have a right to know what's happening at my own bank."

"Please," Finn said, almost begging. "Go home. Let me do my job."

Walter struggled to his feet. "Fucking Rockefeller," he said. "He told us on Thursday the fundamental conditions of the country are sound."

"He's not wrong," said Finn.

"What a crock of shit," said Walter. "Listen, ride it out," he told Finn. "Don't *you* panic."

"I know."

"The bank can't panic."

"I know."

"Don't sell because you're afraid. A wise man doesn't sell at the first sign of trouble."

What about at the tenth sign, or the twentieth, Finn wanted to ask, but of course, did not.

"I know," Finn said. Very carefully, as if preparing his father-in-law for what was to come, he added, "We may need to sell one or two things to cover our margins."

"Only sell what you absolutely must. Get yourself an iron gut," Walter said.

"Grit your teeth. That's what I told Adder. He was at my house this morning, crying! A grown man!"

"Thank God he's not here with me," Finn said.

"This is a battle, Finn," Walter said. "And you are a soldier, unlike him. You stay and fight. When all the fools sell, that's when we buy. Buy, buy, buy at low, low prices."

Finn couldn't speak. Walter was a shrewd financier, but he had no idea of the scale of the deluge. And better he didn't. Finn saluted his father-in-law, his body a taut coil, until Walter Adams shut the door behind him, and Finn ripped the receiver off the stand.

"Barney?"

"Oh, Mr. Evans . . ."

"Tell me."

"Where have you been?"

"Tell me!"

"Police cars have blocked Wall Street from Broadway," Barney said. "So no one can enter."

"Why?"

"Because the crowds are threatening to make a run on the trading floor."

"What else?"

"The market is a cyclone."

"Volume high?"

"You could say that."

"Not as high as Thursday, though, right?"

"No, not as high as Thursday," Barney said slowly. "But the drop in the market is much greater."

"How much?"

"Twenty points so far, Mr. Evans."

"Don't exaggerate, Barney! I need facts. None of your hyperbole. You're not writing a book, for fuck's sake. Tell it to me straight."

"At least twenty points," Barney said, his voice both intense and dead. "People are screaming. Traders can't answer their phones. They've taken off half their clothes, they're dripping wet. After saying fuck for five minutes straight, the industrials trader passed out and had to be carried off the floor."

"It's against the Exchange's rules to run, curse or go coatless," said Finn in his own flat, disbelieving voice.

"I fear a number of rules are being disregarded today, Mr. Evans," said Barney.

"The trading, is it back and forth or—"

"Sell orders only."

"They'll rally, Barney. They will. Like on Thursday. Buyers waited till the end of the day."

"Mr. Evans, remember I told you about Steel? It lost a dollar a share after a single sell order of fifty thousand units at two dollars below market price."

Finn went cold, then hot. "It's just one order, right . . ."

"A thousand sell orders came after it. For GM, too. Billy Durant is going to go broke." Durant was one of the founders of General Motors, and owned a hefty chunk of the company's 107 million shares. "GM has already lost $200 million of its value and it's barely noon."

"You know who else owns a hefty chunk of GM?" Finn said. "Me. This bank. Lionel. Adder."

"Your brother-in-law has been calling me all morning," Barney said. "I'm afraid to pick up my own phone. He keeps crying."

"Dear God." Finn heard the ticker tape through the receiver. "You still have tape?" For some reason this encouraged Finn. He had to look for hope somewhere.

"My third spool this morning."

They usually went through a roll a week. Finn went hot and cold again. There wasn't a single moment of respite.

The events Barney was describing were nothing short of a catastrophe. Even as Finn was living it, he knew he was living through something that had never been and might never be again.

Five minutes later, Myrtle poked her head in. "Lionel is on the phone, Mr. Evans."

"Tell him I'm not in."

Myrtle tilted her head. "I can't tell him that."

"Why not? It's your job. Tell him I'm not in."

"I can't tell him that," Myrtle said, "because I've already told him that four times today. He told me if you don't pick up the phone, he will walk over here personally in five minutes."

Lionel Morris was the VP of Commonwealth Capital Partners, the brokerage firm Finn and Lionel had started together seven years ago, which now handled all of Finn's bank's trading business.

"Hey there, Lionel," Finn said into the receiver, affecting his typical tone. "What's up?"

"You're not taking my calls anymore?"

"Nonsense. 'Course I am. Just a tad busy." Finn closed his eyes.

"Do you want the bad news or the worse news?"

"Can we talk after three?" Finn looked at the clock. It was only 1:45. Another interminable seventy-five minutes of trading left.

"We can talk after three as well. But we must talk now."

Finn was silent.

"You know what I'm about to say."

Finn remained silent.

"Your accounts are under margin, Finn."

Finn pulled the receiver away from his ear.

"Which accounts?"

With Lionel's next words, Finn realized that maybe he wouldn't be able to get out of this.

"All of them," said Lionel.

"That's impossible."

"I know."

Finn said nothing for a few moments, then forced himself to ask. "How far under margin?"

"All together, $778,000."

Finn made a noise like he was in physical pain.

"How much is my total liability to you?"

"All portfolios, bank and personal?"

"Yes."

"A little under six million."

The receiver dropped from Finn's hands.

"Finn, Finn!" He heard Lionel dimly.

A margin account was a collateralized loan with stocks as the collateral. When the value of the stocks stayed steady or went up, it was a great way to maximize profits, and Finn had, both for himself and for Walter's bank. Instead of using only the bank's money to buy shares, Finn borrowed funds from Lionel and invested double (or triple or quintuple) the amount the bank was investing. When the stocks doubled in value, instead of merely doubling the bank's profit, Finn quadrupled it. He repaid Lionel the money he borrowed, and on a million-dollar investment made four million dollars in profit.

For years, Finn had engaged in some version of this, making money for the bank, for Walter, for Lionel, for himself, and for his father. He was Lionel's biggest customer, and together they rode the unstoppable wave, reinvested their earnings, and grew their fortune vertically like the California sequoias, all the way to the sky.

The only wrinkle in the margin plan was when stocks fell. Then, instead of losing only your own money, you also lost what you had borrowed. If you had simply invested your own million bucks, and the stock fell 50 percent, you would lose half a million dollars. But if on top of that, you also invested the four million dollars you borrowed from Lionel, then, when the stock halved in value, you lost your half million, plus an additional two million dollars of the money you borrowed.

And no matter what happened to the price of the shares, Lionel had to be repaid in full and with interest on the entire amount he had lent Finn—and he had lent Finn millions of dollars.

A little under six million, to be exact.

In normal trading, you had a few months to repay the colossal loans. The real bad news came when the value of your stocks crashed below the line of the agreed-upon ratio between what you invested and what you borrowed. If you invested a million and borrowed four million, that 25–75 ratio had to be maintained no matter what. That line—the margin—had to be met or exceeded before any business could continue in your portfolio. The collateral that underpinned the four-million-dollar loan had to be maintained even if the actual collateral was now worth only three million. Or two. Or one.

When the broker called in the margins on your accounts, you had twenty-four hours to satisfy the call. You could add funds by depositing cash. You could sell some or all of the stock in that account. You could sell some or all of the stock in your other accounts. Or you could borrow the money from somewhere else. Whatever you had to do, you did, to meet your margin.

And here was Lionel, telling Finn he had to come up with $778,000 by tomorrow at noon.

"Finn, I waited as long as I could," Lionel said.

"Last Thursday, we managed to pull out with only minimal damage," Finn said. "Why are you panicking today? Wait till the end of trading."

"The ticker tape is hours behind."

"As it was last Thursday. Just wait."

Lionel groaned. "This isn't a little rain, Finn. It's the Flood."

The two men remained on the phone in pained silence.

Finn pressed the receiver to his head. *This can't be happening.*

"Call in your own margins," Lionel said. "You've got two thousand investors left, all underwater. Call them in."

"And how much is their total margin call, Lionel?" It was a rhetorical question. Finn knew.

"Just over $300,000, I think."

"So what are we talking about here?"

"It's better than nothing."

Finn's customers' savings were his bank's savings, his father-in-law's savings, his family's savings, his savings. There was no us and them. There was only us.

"What about my personal portfolio?" Finn asked.

"You told me to give you the total amount you owe. I did."

"What about Walter's personal investment?"

"Are you not listening to me?"

"What about my father's?" Finn nearly yelled.

"I told you," said Lionel. "Total margin, $778,000. That amount is rising every minute we're not satisfying it. Stocks are in the ninth circle of hell."

Finn hung up. For ten minutes, he sat and looked at his hands.

He called Lionel back. "How much is my total equity in all accounts as of right now?" he asked. "Not just margin, all of them." He had so many investments! Utilities, oil companies, retail, banks.

"If you sold every single share at current prices, met your margins and paid off all your loans, you would still owe me nearly a quarter of a million dollars."

Finn felt sick. His hands were numb.

"Finn, it's impossible to overstate how many billions the market is losing today."

"You don't have to tell *me*."

"You've been wheeling and dealing nearly at your September levels, thinking any moment we'll have a rebound. Selling this, buying that."

"Yes, Lionel," said Finn. "When the Dow was climbing to 400, I could afford to float the risk of my margin accounts because the only way was up."

"No one expected this," Lionel said. "But Finn, I built my business on your business. If you fail, I fail. If we wait, and you are wrong . . ."

"I won't be wrong."

"Fucking Federal Reserve," Lionel said. "They told us there was nothing to worry about."

"We'll get out of it. Just give me till the end of the day."

"Finn."

Silence.

"Finn, what if prices continue to sink like they're sinking now?"

"We don't know what's happening now. There could be a huge rally going on already."

"Is that what your heart is telling you?"

"The market rallied last Thursday." Finn could barely get the words out. They were the words of a desperate man, and he knew it.

"Fuck last Thursday. Today the sell orders are outnumbering buys ten to one. Call Barney."

"We have another hour of trading to go." Seventy-three unforgiving minutes.

"People are throwing themselves out of windows on Wall Street," Lionel said. "They're walking in front of cars. No one, *no one*, thinks this is going to end in a rally."

"It must! The speculators will buy up stock after this crazy sell-off. That's what they do. It's what always happens. Give it a minute. Tomorrow is going to be huge. People will be champing at the bit to get Standard Oil at pennies on the dollar. Please. Just wait till tomorrow."

Lionel was heavily silent.

"I'll figure it out," Finn said. "We just need the market to rally a few percent, a few points. Five, ten . . ."

"Won't get you to $800,000, Finn," Lionel said in a low voice. It was the first time Finn had ever heard him sound afraid.

It was the longest seventy minutes of Finn's life. Or so he thought. At three o'clock he called Barney. It took four tries to get him.

"Don't tell me anything unless it's good news."

Barney panted into the phone.

"Aren't you going to say something?"

"You told me to say nothing."

"Barney!"

"It's ruin, Mr. Evans," Barney said. "There's no other word for it."

Finn could think of several other words for it.

"Westinghouse is down twenty dollars a share. General Electric down twenty-five." Barney's voice shook. "Steel is down seventeen today, and forty-nine dollars from when you bought it in September." His teeth were chattering. "There is no bottom yet."

"Okay, Barney, just—"

"You might want to tell Mr. Morris to sell, Mr. Evans, because—"

"Barney! I don't need advice! Facts only!"

"Montgomery Ward down nearly a hundred dollars from its high! From 156 to 59."

Finn groaned.

"Standard Gas down over 120."

"Down or at?"

"Down, sir. From a high of 243 four weeks ago, currently trading at 110, down 40 for the day."

Finn hung up.

Finn did not go home on Monday. Lionel's errand boy brought Finn new tape, and Finn sat at the walnut desk in a deserted bank, listening to the machine rat-tat-tat its destruction of arrows and numbers. He forced himself not to look at the prices until it stopped typing, some hours later. Somehow, Finn had managed to convince himself Barney did not have the latest numbers. After all, the rally wouldn't happen until the last minutes of trading, and what would be the point of looking at the prices before then?

Everything would work out, Finn reasoned, chain-smoking and pacing. It had to. Nothing else could be considered. Nothing else was possible. Because last Thursday, when everyone around him was dashing their heads on the rocks, Finn told Lionel and Barney it would be fine. The market would rally.

And last Thursday it did.

The market had been good for so long, for so long! Since 1921, it had been a steady, unstoppable climb. The Dow Jones Industrial Average started the 1920s at 60 and at the end of the decade had reached 381! Okay, so there was a little selling. How could there not be after years of such inconceivable gains? Everyone was a winner. And the gains weren't based on nothing. The economy was sound. The companies on the stock exchange had real value. They made things, they built cars, they sold steel to the companies that made the cars, they sold fuel that powered those cars, and they dressed the men and ladies who drove those cars to Cape Cod on the weekends. The companies Finn invested in provided electricity and natural gas to cities, they sold groceries to feed families. They built submarines for the U.S. Navy. He didn't invest in speculative stocks. He had his money and his bank's money, and his father-in-law's money, and his father's money—oh good God, his *father's* money! In U.S. Steel, in Sears, Roebuck & Co., GM, Atlantic and Pacific, Standard Oil, Woolworth, Philip Morris. These were highly valued, highly capitalized giants of American industry. Finn's entire future and the bank's future depended on what the paper ticker, running hours behind, drummed out in its letters, arrows, and numbers.

Their stocks would recover. And with them, Finn would recover.

There was no other way.

17

Sell at Market

On Monday, October 28, 1929, in the final few minutes before the market closed, three million shares were traded, most of them sell orders. The greatest losses to Finn's extensive and varied investments occurred in those last few minutes of trading. The damage was staggering. The market fell 13 percent on Monday, the largest single-day fall in Wall Street's history. American companies lost some $14 billion of their value in one disastrous day of panic selling.

The high for industrials as a block had been 469.49 on September 19. Finn soared on that like a bird in flight. He viewed the small correction that followed as a massive buying opportunity and leveraged an enormous amount of his investment accounts to buy thousands of shares of industrial stock on margin at $430 a share.

Yesterday, the block closed at 315, a collapse of 154 points overall, and 49 points in one day.

At eight o'clock on Tuesday morning, having managed only a few hours' sleep with his head on his desk, Finn tried to get in touch with Barney, but no one picked up. Finally, at 9:30, half an hour before the market opened, someone answered the phone. That person was not Barney, but Terrence, who worked in the office next door. Terrence told Finn that Barney was not in yet.

"That's impossible."

"A lot of things are impossible these days," said Terrence. "Are you Finn?"

"Yes, why?"

"There is a note for you on Barney's desk," Terrence said. "In large block letters it says: 'FINN—SELL EVERYTHING AT WHATEVER PRICE YOU CAN GET.' The word 'everything' is underlined five times."

"But the market hasn't opened," muttered a stunned Finn. "Why would he say this? Terrence!"

"Don't shoot me," Terrence said before he hung up. "I'm just the messenger."

* * *

Herbert Hoover, the President of the United States, announced that he wasn't going to be at the White House on Tuesday. How serious could the market crash be if Hoover isn't even at his desk, Finn thought with a tiny bit of hope. Then he heard the president was attending a funeral, and knew that his hope had been misplaced.

A minute after the ticker machine began printing, Radio was down to 40. It had been 114 in September. Finn bought it at 110. He didn't want to sell Westinghouse yesterday, when it was 140, because he had paid 180 for it. Now it was at 120. It was only 10:05 am. The market had been open five minutes.

No one thought they would see the day when Steel would drop below 200. Yesterday it closed at 186. Today, ten minutes after the opening bell, it was at 180.

Barney called. "No one is interested in Steel, even at 179," he said dully. "Did you sell?"

"No."

"Mr. Evans!"

"Where have you been?"

"Buying a bus ticket to Chicago. I'm giving my notice," said Barney. "I thought I would impress my mother with my fancy job, but I've lost her life savings instead. I'm getting out while I can still afford a bus ticket."

Finn wanted to argue, but couldn't. He almost wished he himself could buy a ticket to another state and steal off unnoticed.

"Before you ask me, I'll tell you," Barney said. "Yesterday's volume at this time was 800,000 shares. Today, it's three million."

"I wasn't going to ask you." Finn felt like he was being physically beaten.

"Radio is at 30."

"It was at—"

"It doesn't matter where it was." Barney's voice was emotionless. "That's where it is now. Get off the phone, Mr. Evans, and call Lionel. The longer you wait, the worse it will be for you and your bank. You can't get out of this. No one is getting out of this."

"Wait, I have something—"

"This morning at 10:03, more than 650,000 Steel shares were dumped on the market," Barney said. "No one wanted to buy them."

All Finn could say to this was, "It's still morning."

"Really? Because it feels like the middle of the darkest night," said Barney. He described the funereal silence that hovered over the trading floor. Yesterday they were howling wolves. Today they were mute.

"Are there any bright spots?" Finn asked. "Any at all? Can you give me one thing?" *Please*, he almost added.

"A broker was screaming so loud earlier while hammering Radio down at Post 12, he lost his dentures on the trading floor," Barney said.

"That's your bright spot?"

"He found them again," said Barney. "But while we are talking, Radio has fallen to 26."

"Barney..."

"How much did you pay for IBM two years ago?" Barney asked.

"Back then, I paid 95 or 96 for it. Why?"

"There's your bright spot. Today it's 125. I mean, it's down from 241 in September, but you didn't lose everything."

"Barney," said Finn, "is that the best you got? Because I bought fifty thousand IBM at 237, and another thirty at 200."

"How many at 95?" said Barney.

"Fifty thousand."

"You see?" Barney said. "You *can* crawl out of it. But while we're sitting here chatting, IBM has dropped to 120. And Radio is now at 25. Spit-spot, Mr. Evans. Westinghouse is losing two dollars a minute. At this rate it will be worthless by the time you call Lionel. How many Westinghouse do you have?"

"Twenty fucking thousand," said Finn, hanging up.

An hour later, Finn finally called Lionel. The ticker tape was already ninety minutes behind. It still had Steel at 185. Finn sat down at his desk with the door shut. And not just his office door. At 11:15, Finn was forced to close the bank. He had eight hundred customers trying to take money out of their accounts. One by one, then two by two, and then in groups of ten, he had to explain to his tense, superficially calm depositors how it wasn't in their best interest to take their money, and then he had to explain why he didn't have their money. They became less calm. He tried to explain that he kept only a small portion of their deposits in the vaults. This was how the business of the bank was run, he told them. Of any bank. The rest of the deposits he lent out to others, or invested. "Invested so I could give you that great interest rate you've been getting all these years on your savings accounts. Where do you think that savings rate comes from?"

They didn't care. They wanted their money.

He tried to explain that many of those clamoring at his doors owed *him* money. For some reason, this was difficult for him to explain and difficult for them to understand.

"Mr. Harris, I don't see what you don't see." Finn didn't shout, he didn't raise his voice. He knew his raised voice could easily trigger a cascade to mass hysteria. So he kept his tone carefully modulated, even though inside, he was anything but. "Mr. Harris, please don't shout, sir. Let me try again. You have two thousand dollars in your savings account, correct, which you're trying to withdraw. But at the same time, you have three loans with the bank, totaling seven thousand and seven hundred dollars. One of those loans is a secured loan with stocks as your collateral. This morning, the five hundred shares you have securing that loan have lost nearly 90 percent of their value. So you must now either pay the difference on that collateral, or the loan will be in default."

Mr. Harris shrugged. "What's it to me? So, my loan is in default. Sell my shares."

"Selling them will only cover about 20 percent of what you owe me."

"How much could they have possibly dropped by?"

"It's hard to tell, Mr. Harris, because this morning the Dow Jones ticker is already more than an hour behind." Finn spoke in measured tones, but he felt his legs going numb. He wasn't thinking about Mr. Harris's sinking stocks. He was thinking about his bank's. And his own.

Harris shrugged again. "You're a good man, Mr. Evans. But who's to say you're going to meet your own margins today? By the pallor on your face, I reckon you have some looming. How do I know you won't take my few measly thousand to save your own hide? I know I would. Just give me my money, and I'll be on my way."

Thus, at 11:15, Finn had to close the bank. His cash reserves were dangerously low. He kept about a million dollars on hand. Half of it had already vanished to the likes of Mr. Harris.

When Lionel answered the phone, he sounded half dead.

"Nothing is good in the world, Lionel," Finn said, failing to keep the terror out of his voice.

"Finn, that is most certainly fucking true."

They were quiet.

"Steel has fallen to 175," Finn said, trying to be matter-of-fact, but his voice was hoarse. "As soon as the market saw that, the bottom dropped out of everything. Steel is an avalanche. It's taking everything down with it."

"Oh, Finn, if only Steel were at 175," said Lionel. "Ten minutes ago it was at 166."

To keep himself from groaning, Finn squeezed the receiver. Any harder and either it would break or his fingers would.

"What did we buy it at?"

"Our average price was 220."

"Sell it, Lionel," Finn said. "Or we will have to close my bank and your brokerage. It'll take us down with it too."

"You think I haven't tried?" Lionel said. "I can't find buyers at any price anymore! Forget sell at market. Hah! Would that I could sell at market. I would be a lucky man. I can't make a bid low enough for anyone to take anything!"

"Find a price someone will buy it at."

"Not today. No one will buy anything today."

Finn said nothing.

"It's hard to believe I'm saying this, but Steel is not your biggest problem," Lionel said. "Standard Oil, which you bought at an average of 210, yesterday was at 105, and you told me not to sell, to wait, that the market would rally, oh to buy Standard Oil for pennies on the dollar, remember? Well, last price for Standard is 79 and one-half. Don't forget that half."

"Sell it."

"If I sell every single share of Standard Oil you own, it won't be enough to satisfy your margin, forget about paying back your actual loan."

"Sell everything else."

"Hershey is at 86. You bought it at 150. Last Thursday you told me not to sell it when it was at 135."

"Sell it at 86."

"Westinghouse we could've sold yesterday at 140. Today it's at 100."

Finn had bought it at 200.

"Macy's?"

"Bought at 190, could've sold yesterday at 160. Today, 120 if I can get it."

"Get it. Sell it."

"You have half a million dollars in DuPont," Lionel said. "You bought that at 115. Yesterday you could've sold it at 150, and actually made some money. Today it's at 80."

"Purity Bakery?"

"Bought at 100, now at 55."

"General Electric?"

"Bought at 220. Yesterday's low was 250, today it's at 210."

"Sell it." Finn kept himself from exhaling.

"Everything? Even your personal accounts?"

"Everything."

"Your father's? Your father-in-law's?"

"Everything."

"Your father has ten thousand shares of Montgomery Ward. He bought it at 90. Its high was 150 in September, when I told him to sell some of it, and you and he decided not to. It's at 22 now."

"Sell it." They both groaned. "Sell it all," Finn said, "before we are completely wiped out. Let's see what's left."

"Nothing, my friend," said a drained, weakened Lionel. "There will be nothing left."

18

Gray Ice Over the Charles

It was after eight at night before Finn received the brutal tally from the black ticker tape machine on the walnut desk, got a printout of lows on Thursday, lows on Monday, and lows for today, Tuesday, October 29, 1929.

For an hour he sat at his desk in the tomblike darkness, simply stunned.

Finally, he got up and walked four blocks to Commonwealth Commercial Partners.

The first thing Lionel did was pull out a bottle of his finest whisky.

"I was saving it for the day my daughter got married," Lionel said. His girl was three. "I thought I was saving it for the best day. Now I know I was saving it for the worst."

If ever there was a time for drinking, it was tonight.

"No clinking though," said Finn. "It's a funeral, not a celebration."

"I'm sorry, Finn," Lionel said after three glasses of whisky.

"I'm the one who is sorry," Finn said. "Why did you listen to me?"

"Because you've always been right."

Finn stared grimly into his empty glass. "We have to figure it out, Lionel. I can't keep my bank doors closed. I can't steal my customers' money."

"You're not stealing it," Lionel said. "You don't have it."

"A thief who spends the money is still a thief," Finn said.

"You didn't spend it. You lost it."

"I spent it," said Finn, sounding as dejected as he had ever felt in his life. "I took it, I invested it, smartly or so I thought, and I lost it. Investing is also spending, Lionel. Spending what isn't yours."

"You're not buying a railroad with it, Finn!"

"Apparently not even one fucking share of a railroad," said Finn.

No matter how you looked at it, Black Tuesday was the most ruinous day in Wall Street's history. Sixteen million shares were traded in that single day, another record, dwarfing Monday's nine million and the thirteen million traded the previous Thursday.

The Dow Jones began that Thursday at 305. It finished Monday at 260 and Tuesday at 230. Since the high of 381 on September 3, the NYSE industrials lost 40 percent of their total value. More than $30 billion was wiped off the companies' worth in just two days.

There was a rally at the end of trading on Tuesday, as if the sellers were drained by the frenzy, and the bargain basement prices were finally attractive, just as Finn had said—but it was too little and much, much too late. The collapse was so sudden and extreme, it washed fortunes away. It crippled people and institutions. The good and the bad went down together.

Finn, Lionel, Walter, and Finn's father, the honorable Judge Earl Evans, all went down with them.

Lionel managed to sell Earl's Montgomery Ward stock for $22 a share, garnering $220,000 in total. Half of the shares had been bought with money borrowed from Lionel, the other half with Earl and Olivia's life savings. But Earl Evans borrowed $450,000 to buy the shares, and now had a grand total of $220,000 with which to pay it back. Earl still owed Lionel $230,000, and he didn't even know it. There had been no chance for Finn to speak to his father.

And so it also went across the bank's accounts, across Finn's accounts, and across Walter's. By the time the liquidation was complete, and nearly every single share had been sold and every Adams Bank investment account closed, Finn managed to cover the margins and pay off some of the underlying debt. But just like Earl Evans, he had a red balance and no money left to satisfy it. And at the end of the day, he was still over a million dollars short to Lionel.

"You have to talk to Walter, Finn," Lionel said at two in the morning, when they had analyzed the numbers for the thousandth time, checking and re-checking their arduous, mind-numbing math. "There's no way around it."

"I *can't* talk to him. Vanessa told me he had a heart incident yesterday."

"I don't mean to be insensitive," Lionel said, "but is he still breathing? If the answer is yes, you must tell him what's happened. Because his name is on the title of the bank and the title to his house. What about your brother-in-law Adder? As I recall, he lives in a house that's also in Walter's name."

"My brother-in-law has his own problems," Finn said. "Last I heard, he was ready to jump into the Charles."

"Perhaps it's good then, that there's gray ice over the Charles," said Lionel. "I thought you told me he was conservative with his investments?"

"Apparently that was a pile of bullshit," said Finn. "I can't solve Adder right now. But why are you talking about our residential properties?"

"Because they must be sold or mortgaged, Finn," said Lionel. "There is no other way out of this unholy mess. Even if you hock your house and every last one of Walter's properties, you probably still won't get to what you need. A million dollars is a lot of scratch. You'll come close. The bank is an asset. You still have some depositors left, some outstanding loans? I see here on your books there's a loan of three million dollars to some John Reade, secured with real estate. Is he good for it? As long as your customers keep paying you, the bank won't lose value." Lionel raised his eyes to the ceiling, mouthing *please, Jesus*. "And then you can keep paying me."

"You want me to go to my father-in-law, who's just had a heart attack, and tell him I need to mortgage his house, my house, and his bank for the stellar return of *not* breaking even?"

"You have another plan? I'm all ears, my friend."

Finn slept on one of the couches in Lionel's office in the same clothes he'd worn since Monday. Lionel found a dull razor for him in one of the washrooms, and Finn shaved, erratically. He looked worse now, all cut up with patches of facial growth peppering his ashen face as he shook hands with Lionel and left to go speak with Walter in person. He decided to walk to Back Bay—to clear his head, to prepare his words, to steel himself for Walter's reaction when his father-in-law, in poor health, would learn of the hull of his family's ship sinking beneath the sea.

It was gray out, cold and drizzly. Massachusetts Avenue in Back Bay was a long way from Congress and State. The leaves were almost gone, and the taupe-colored oaks waved the last of their brown flakes off the branches. Finn's coat hung open. He wished it was colder. He wanted to sever his emotions, like limbs from frostbite. He desperately didn't want to have this discussion with Walter. And afterward, Finn would have to face his own father to tell him that not only were his life savings gone but that he needed to mortgage his house to pay back the money he still owed to Lionel's firm. Finn shuddered. It was hard to overstate how much he did not want to have this conversation with his terse and exacting father. He would rather face Walter twice, and he didn't want to face Walter at all.

19

The Adams Bank

His mother-in-law opened the door, barely made up. "He's resting, Finn," Lucy said. "He's not feeling well. He can't be disturbed." She was so anxious about Walter, she couldn't even be bothered to needle Finn by calling him Esmond.

"Unfortunately," Finn said, walking in, "this is no time for resting. Is he upstairs?"

"No, he's in his study. But Finn!"

"But Lucy."

She grabbed his arm, but he pulled away and strode through the house, without even bothering to take off his coat. Finn knocked on the door of Walter's study and entered, with Lucy fretting behind him.

"I'm sorry, darling," she cried. "I told him no, but he wouldn't listen."

"Lucy, leave us please," Finn said, pulling a chair over to the couch on which Walter lay.

"Leave us, darling," Walter said, his eyes closed.

Sighing, she shut the door. The two men were left alone in the silent study.

"I can't have this conversation, Finn," Walter said. "I mean, I physically can't." He looked so depleted lying on his sofa covered by a blanket.

"I understand. I don't want to either. We are going to have to do a lot of things we don't want to do," Finn said. "Talking is probably the least of it."

When Walter didn't reply, Finn continued. "I haven't been home since Monday morning. God knows what your daughter must think. But I need to make it right for her and for all of us. I need to make it as right as I can. I want to come home and tell her there's nothing to worry about."

"That can't be true, can it?" A brief flash of what looked like hope crossed Walter's face, as though he seriously believed it might be.

"Of *course* it's not true, Walter," Finn said, frowning. For a moment he wondered if his father-in-law was in his right mind.

"Did you come to tell me how bad it is? Because I can't bear to hear it."

"I won't tell you how bad it is," said Finn. "But we need to find a way to come up with $1.15 million, because Commonwealth Capital will fold if we don't pay them, and we will go under when they sue us to recover their money. We won't be able to stay in business."

"What business?" Walter said.

What Finn heard was, *You, Finn, destroyed my business.*

"Walter, we had record growth, record profits, a record decade," Finn said. "When I started, your bank was capitalized at less than a million dollars. Last week it was valued at $20 million."

"Not this week."

"No business can lose 100 percent of a large part of its assets and not be where we are."

"The market is up today," Walter said. "I called Barney myself a few minutes ago."

"Barney is gone," Finn said. "He is on a bus to Chicago. You spoke to Terrence, who knows nothing."

"The market is up," Walter repeated stubbornly. "We should have ridden this out like I told you—"

"Walter." Finn said his father-in-law's name quietly. He didn't yell it, though he felt like screaming. He clasped his hands, tried not to clench his fists. "It doesn't matter anymore if the market is up, or down, or sideways. It's somebody else's market. It doesn't concern us anymore." He paused, trying to get more oxygen into his lungs. "We have no securities left to ride anything out with. We had to fire-sale them all."

Walter cried out. "Why all? They weren't all on margin!"

"No, they weren't, which is the only reason why after total liquidation we owe one million and not six. You told me to ride it out and I did. I rode it all the way to the bottom, to yesterday when the market had no bottom. All it had was a vertical death spiral."

"*Now* you decide to listen to me? What about our personal portfolios?"

Finn made a swirling motion with his hands. "All in the same pot, Walter. All gone to pay the piper."

Walter gasped. "Lionel sold *all* our stocks?"

"Everything."

Walter put a hand to his chest, and for a few minutes there was nothing but the sound of his death-rattle breathing.

"And we're still over a million short?"

"Yes."

"What about Adder? Call him! He'll help us. For God's sake, he'll help us."

"Adder is in worse shape than us," Finn said. "And I didn't think that was possible. Apparently—and entirely against the rules set by his brokerage house—Adder loaned out his accounts at a 90 percent debt to equity ratio, and three-quarters of them defaulted."

"He has his own investments. Three million dollars. I know he does. He talked to me about it last week. Call him!"

"Yes, he told me. They're all under margin." Finn shook his head. "But unlike us, instead of selling his stock to meet the call, Adder borrowed against his commercial accounts and naked-short-sold three million dollars' worth of securities, hoping to make back his losses."

"Oh, my God." Walter covered his face and then stared at Finn in horror. "Naked short selling is illegal," he whispered.

"You don't have to tell me," Finn said. "Your other son-in-law contracted other people's money, money he knew wasn't there, to short-sell thousands of shares in Steel, Standard, and Radio. Also GM and GE. But the shares really had nowhere to go but up. So up they went. The market rallied 14 points this morning."

Walter wailed. "Poor Adder! What's he going to do?"

"Poor Adder? Well, he asked me for funds to buy back the shares he sold short." Finn almost smirked. "He asked me for $3.5 million. I told him I didn't have ten thousand dollars. He said he was coming here to ask you for it."

Walter gasped for air.

"The stocks are gone," Finn said. "We can't change that. But our bank is not gone. We can salvage it. And we still have our houses."

"My house, your house, Eleanor's house, your cottage in Truro, my few other properties are not worth a million dollars in total! If we sold them all, we wouldn't get it. And who'd buy it now, anyway?"

"No one. We're not selling our homes," Finn said. "We have to live somewhere."

"Mortgaging them will bring in even less."

"True," Finn said, "but mortgaging them, plus the bank, will get us close. The bank is an appreciating asset, despite the last few days."

Walter spoke, his eyes closed, his mouth barely moving. "You've never had a mortgage on anything in your life, Finn."

"That's true, Walter. I have been very fortunate." Finn just echoed the words. He did not feel fortunate today.

"Everything has been given to you, paid for you, handed to you. I know you understand what a mortgage is. It's a loan. The bank that is fool enough to lend you money will need to get paid, every month. And if you don't pay them, they will take our homes, and our cars, and your summer place on the Cape. They will take the bank that has been my family's legacy for a hundred years." Walter sounded like a broken man.

"Why would we not be able to pay the mortgage?"

"On a million dollars? I'll tell you why. Because a monthly payment on such a sum would be somewhere between ten and fifteen thousand. Maybe more, depending on the interest rate."

"That's a lot," Finn said, trying not to sound broken himself. "But we'll make it. The Federal Reserve may be able to lend us some money to stay afloat until the market recovers."

"They lend to their member banks," Walter said. "We're not a member bank, Finn."

"I know," Finn said, "but Lionel thinks the Fed will loosen the rules to help the banking industry in light of what's happened. In any case, we're talking about just a few months of battening down the hatches, and then—"

"You want to ride it out with *borrowed* money, Finn?" Walter said with quiet bitterness. "That's what got us into this stew of incontinence in the first place."

Finn folded and unfolded his hands. "You've been in this business a lot longer than I have. You know we're living through a once-in-a-lifetime debacle."

"It's going to get worse before it gets better," Walter said. "You don't think what's happened is going to bounce right down the line to your tailor in North End and to every person who works for us?"

Finn shook his head. "I hope you're wrong. But about the mortgages..."

Walter waved Finn away, covering his face with the crook of his elbow. "Go ahead," he said. "Sign away what crumbs are left."

"Your bank is not a crumb," Finn said. "Our homes are not crumbs."

Walter spoke again. "Before you put our historic mansions on the auction block," he said, "I want to tell you something."

Finn lowered his head. Walter sat up and threw the blanket off his lap, color and passion suffusing his face.

"My great-grandfather, born in 1800, was a poor man," Walter said. "He was a tenant farmer; he didn't own his farm, he worked for someone else. But he knew how to do two things. He worked hard, and he saved money. Before others were up, he was already working. After others had left, he was still working. And he spent nothing. He lived long enough to buy the farm after its owner died.

"Years earlier, his wife had given birth to their only child, my grandfather. As he grew up, Grandfather worked the farm the way his father had taught him, but he was not a farmer by nature or temperament. He was not a man of many skills, but he knew how to do two things. He knew how to save money, and he knew how to count money. And he did those two things better than anyone else. His neighbor needed help, and my grandfather loaned him a few dollars. It took the neighbor over a year to pay back the money, but as long as the money was repaid, Grandfather didn't care how long it took. He took a little interest for his trouble. Not much, but a little.

"The neighbor told others of my grandfather's generosity. And another neighbor came to ask for help. My grandfather was happy to oblige. Other people in the area, who were not good savers and not good counters, started coming to my grandfather to borrow money for their rakes, their plows, and even their horses. Once word got around that he was willing and able to help, there was no stopping the line of people at his door. My grandfather knew that most people occasionally needed assistance, and that most could not save money. His reputation in the area grew, especially when he partnered with a friend who wanted to be a horse breeder. Grandfather lent his friend money to buy a young mare and a stallion, and they were off. Out of that pairing grew the banking business you are trying to save now.

"Because just as they got going, the Civil War broke out. Grandfather and his friend sold horses to the Union Army, and Grandfather lent money to the local towns for the war effort—operating from one of the stalls inside the stables. While his friend bred horses, Grandfather sat at his desk, set right over the hay, and lent out money. He maintained all accounts payable and receivable by hand and kept his own books. The profits rolled in from the horses, the muskets, and the loans. War was very good for business, my grandfather was sorry to say. After the war, he rented out a small office in Amesbury so his customers didn't have to traipse through the mud of the farm. He soon realized what he had was not an office but a bank. So he called it the Adams Family Bank for Savings and Investments, got a charter, got registered, and continued working. His little bank had one teller window and one desk, and my grandfather was both the teller and the loan officer. He was the CEO, the CFO, the president, and the general manager. He worked at that desk until the day he died, in the middle of filling out another loan application.

"My father grew up under Grandfather's desk at the stables, listening to every loan interview, to every request for money. But when my father was nineteen, he went to war. After he returned in 1865, he realized he could do two things well, but neither of them was running a bank. My father could fight, and he could work.

"So after the war, he worked as security for my grandfather. He carried two rifles and two revolvers and made sure his father's business was protected. When Grandfather died, he left the bank to my father. But just as Grandfather didn't like the farm life, my father didn't like the small-town life. He wanted the excitement of a vibrant and growing city. During the Reconstruction, there was nowhere else to be or make money than in the cities.

"So my father moved my grandfather's bank to Boston, bought the building on Winter Street, renamed the bank Adams Bank and Trust—he wanted to get the word Trust in there—and continued in Grandfather's name. Except my father was a fighter. He wasn't born or bred for sitting behind desks and working with numbers. He did it to honor his father, but it wasn't the joy of his life. And when you do something half-hearted, your work can't help but reflect it.

"The business fell into disrepair, despite the golden location, despite the wealthier clientele. That's the business he passed on to me, in 1889. I was not the smartest in my class, nor was I a fighter in the strict sense. But I knew how to do two things. I knew how to count money, and I knew how to talk to people. With those two skills, I revived the business and competed with the largest commercial banks in Boston. I got married and had two daughters. I didn't know what was going to happen to the bank, because my daughters had absolutely no interest in and no head for business.

"Your future wife did two things well. She was an organizer non-pareil, and she was remarkably beautiful. She took care of herself. I knew she would make someone a fine wife. And that someone was you, Finn. I didn't realize how much I had wanted a son until you entered our lives. You were a fighter, like my father, and you were very good with people from all walks of life, like me, and these two things made me like you tremendously.

"And you could do two other things remarkably well. You had a gift for taking a lemon and making it five. And very much like my grandfather, you knew that the little guy needed financial help even more than the big guy and on this principle, you rebuilt my business. You transformed it into the institution Grandfather had always envisioned in his dreams. You renovated and modernized the bank and made it appealing to visit. You grew our customer base in ways no one imagined. You took a hundred-year-old sapling and made it into a mighty oak. And you did it all in my family's name, not in yours. For ten years you enriched my life and my family's life and my daughter's life. I don't know if I've ever told you how proud I have been of what you've accomplished."

"You're making me feel worse, Walter," Finn said, his head hung.

"No, just the opposite. As you go forth, I want you to remember what you are saving. You are saving my great-grandfather's deepest desire to work for himself, to be dependent on no one, to make his own money, to stand on his own two feet. That small dream my great-grandfather had and my grandfather after him is what you are trying to salvage now, with limited tools and a depleted arsenal. I'm not going to pretend it doesn't matter to me whether you succeed or fail. My family's entire legacy depends on your efforts. So go out there, son, and see if you can find some new skills you didn't know you had, and save my horse bank."

20

OONK

Ukraine, March 1929

Roman started an organization called OONK. By hand, with thick pencils, he and Ostap made their own flyers and distributed them all over town, nailing them to the doors and walls. When he was stopped on the street by one of Efros's OGPU men who asked him what he was doing, Roman replied, "I'm serving the Revolution, comrade. What are you doing?"

The brothers were brought in front of Efros and Zhuk in the requisitioned house on the village square. Zhuk asked if Roman wanted to be exiled to Murmansk. Roman said no. He explained that there were no ostensible *kulaks* left in Ispas after the concerted weeding of the last six weeks. So Roman and Ostap decided to start an organization that anyone was free to join, and they were having their first meeting next week. The organization was called OONK, and it stood for Organization of Not Kulaks. "I even made the despised word in Russian, in national solidarity with you and your comrades, Comrade Zhuk," Roman said. "It's an organization of *un*wealthy peasants, which includes the entire remaining population of Ispas. One of the difficulties in perpetuating the class war in Ukraine between the successful farmer and the less successful farmer is that the classification shifts from harvest to harvest. Last harvest's *kulak* is this harvest's pauper. And because the harvest has been so dire and because of your commendable efforts, of course, there don't seem to be any *kulaks* left in our village. So we were unsure how to conduct the class struggle of which you spoke so eloquently some weeks ago." Roman smiled amiably at Zhuk. "We are very committed to clearing out the last of the anti-Communist elements. Therefore—OONK."

"If you are really serious, you will collectivize," Zhuk said.

"I understand your point about the small-scale farm being inefficient, comrade," said Roman. "I hear what you're saying. But hear me out. Our Lazar property is too far from other farms to be easily collectivized and to provide the kind of economies of scale and cooperation you desire. So our proposal is this: My family and I will agree to meet your quota without collectivization. Let us show you how we work—with your help, of course. Perhaps you could lend us a steel plow as a gesture of our new understanding and partnership? I'm sure it will work so much better than our old-fashioned wooden plows. Provide us the seed, the plow, and we will do the rest. We will till our soil now, plant your wheat in April and harvest in August. We will serve the Soviet state the only way we know how—by working tirelessly for the cause and delivering to you the grain you require—at whatever price you set. We will not haggle or negotiate. We will not ask for more."

"And in return?"

"Nothing," said Roman. "In return, we continue to breed our horses and our cows in peace."

"Are you going to pay other people to help cultivate your wheat fields, Comrade Lazar?" Zhuk said with oily smarm.

"Of course not," said Roman. "I know that if I own as little as three horses and pay even two people to work for me, it will make me a fat lazy *kulak*, a less than human swine. And then I will have to exterminate myself as a founding member of OONK. So the answer is no. I will not pay anyone to work for me. Anyone who works the fields will work for free, as all Ukrainians must, correct? As you told us we must, if we are to be considered truly patriotic."

Zhuk paled. "Mock, if you will," he said. "But if you and your band of thieves fail to meet the compulsory procurements, you will be labeled a *kulak*."

"I fear we are losing the definition of what a *kulak* is, Comrade Zhuk," said Roman. "Never mind. Our goals are the same. We want to use our land to serve the Bolsheviks, and I'm certain you don't want anarchy in the southwest. We don't wish to rise up against you in arms and flames. We don't want you, our honored guests, to feel that the All-Russian Extraordinary Commission for Combating Counter-Revolution and Sabotage—or the State Political Directorate, or the Unified State Political Administration, or whatever it is you call yourselves now—can't control the luckless, unarmed Ukrainian farmer."

"When did we ever say we couldn't control you?" Yefim Efros in his OGPU uniform turned white, then red, then white. He stepped forward.

"That's what *I'm* saying," Roman said pleasantly. "I don't want you to feel the CHEKA or the OGPU or militia or the Red Army can't rule the land or hold the enraged Ukrainian to order." His tone was light, but his expression was fire and concrete.

"Who is enraged?" Efros shrieked.

"I'm hoping that the categories you've imposed on us are more flexible than your quotas." Roman smiled. "The free people of Ukraine, the farmers and the ranchers will work ceaselessly to give you what you need for your Revolution, your Five-Year Plans, your industrialization, your cities, and your people. Who do you think is going to work harder, the unpaid Ukrainian farmer, or the demagogue and loafer you have brought with you from Moscow who cannot even get up with the sun? Is he going to plant the wheat for you at noon, Comrade Zhuk, Comrade Efros? Or will you let us work our own land at daybreak?"

"Or *what*?" Zhuk said, trembling. "Or you will rise up against us in arms and flames?"

"I don't want you to feel you *ever* have to worry about that, dear comrades," said Roman Lazar.

21

Secret Mission

Isabelle didn't understand what was happening. Jarring commotion was everywhere, in the house and on the streets. The servants who had worked for the family for years all said they had never seen Vanessa like this. Martha the housekeeper said something must have happened to Walter Adams because Vanessa kept exclaiming in agitation while talking to her mother on the phone.

Isabelle thought nothing too serious could have happened to Walter because Vanessa didn't leave the house to see her father. She did, however, disappear upstairs. Sometimes Vanessa didn't emerge until it was dark outside.

But the most jarring thing was that Finn left the house on Monday morning, October 28, and here it was, Tuesday night, October 29, and no one had seen him. Isabelle knew Vanessa heard from him because she sprinted out of her bedroom when the phone rang. She flew downstairs and tore the receiver off the stand. Isabelle heard how hard Vanessa tried to control her voice on the phone. "Yes, Finn, darling, of course, I hope everything is all right, yes, the girls are fine. Take care of yourself, my love."

After she hung up the phone, Vanessa called Isabelle upstairs, and in the privacy of her bedroom, stammering as if she were the one learning a foreign language, asked Isabelle to walk across town and "just glance in," to see if Finn was really at the bank.

"He has an office right in front, from which he greets his customers," Vanessa said. "But there's also one in the back where he does actual work. He mustn't see you, Isabelle, do you understand? Just peek in covertly."

"Like *shpion*? You want to shpy?"

"Not spy! Just . . . check. Confirm. Make sure. Oh, you *don't* understand," said Vanessa.

"I understand little bit." Poor woman, Isabelle thought.

"It's just not like him not to come home!"

"Maybe bad things happen like radio says."

With indifference, Vanessa waved off Isabelle's words. "What possible calamity could happen that he should not come home?" she said. "That he should still be at work at nine at night. The bank closes at five!"

Isabelle tilted her head. She didn't know. They didn't have banks where she was from. They had other things in her village that were calamitous.

"Please don't misunderstand," Vanessa said. "I trust my husband. But sometimes he likes to have a drink, and it's against the law, and sometimes he hangs around with some bad elements when he drinks, and I don't want him to get in trouble. I'm looking out for him."

"If he drink, won't you smell?" said Isabelle.

"Yes, yes, but . . ." Vanessa broke off. "Are you going to do it or not?"

"What if he see me?"

"Why would he? Our servants are invisible to him," Vanessa added. "You could bump into him and he wouldn't notice."

Isabelle put on her coat and left through the back gate. The streets weren't empty, not that Isabelle had been out much at night. By nine, the city of Boston was asleep. But on this Tuesday, there was upheaval in the square. Cars were in the road, people raced down Beacon Street, there was noise, yelling, distant histrionics. Isabelle didn't want to walk through the park, so she went uphill and around Boston Common. It was a twenty-minute walk, and the night was seasonably brisk, but Isabelle was sweating by the time she got to Winter Street. Adams Bank and Trust was dark. The stores around the bank were closed including a fancy-looking big store called Jordan Marsh. Isabelle did a double take at Jordan Marsh. That's where her gorgeous silk robe was from.

Isabelle didn't want Vanessa to be right in her suspicions about Finn. But it didn't feel to Isabelle that Finn was lying. It felt, judging by the agitation in the streets, that the truth was even less pleasant than a secret drink with some rogues. It felt as if, when Vanessa found out what was really keeping Finn away from home, she'd *wish* he were drinking.

The bank was terraced by shops on both sides, but there was a narrow alley at the rear service entrance, and that's where a circumspect Isabelle headed. In the back, there was a small fenced-in yard. Quietly, she opened the wrought-iron gate, walked through, and peeked in the only window with a light on.

Finn was there. Vanessa would be pleased. But he was in a state Isabelle had not seen him in. It was as if he had become a different person.

Isabelle wondered if perhaps this was the real Finn, and the buttoned-up, formal Finn was the pretender. This Finn had his jacket off, his vest off, his tie off, his shirt unbuttoned at the collar, his sleeves rolled up. This Finn smoked three cigarettes in the few minutes Isabelle watched him. He was frantic and manic. He paced his office, smoking and muttering. Every few seconds he ran across the hall to another room and returned with fistfuls of long, ribbon-like paper. He would stub out his cigarette, lean against the corner of the desk and study this paper like a divine scroll, threading it through his fingers, analyzing some invisible facts, facts that were so upsetting he would drop the spool on the floor, where it would fall next to other crumpled-up rolls. He would storm around his desk, light another cigarette, jump up again, and pace. Every ninety seconds or so—however long it took him to smoke one down—he would run across the hall and return with more white ribbon, which he again scrutinized like Moses did the tablets.

The phone rang. Finn lunged for it, grabbed it, spoke both animatedly and dejectedly to someone and then, after he replaced the receiver, sat slumped at the desk, not moving.

But something in a deadened Isabelle was moving. Something inside her was churning and roiling. On the surface it felt like the wind of compassion, of sympathy, a recognition of another person's suffering. But underneath, there were other things, too. Her acute awareness of Finn's misfortune joined her to him in a way she hadn't foreseen. The unexpected yet ordinary connection swept away some of the stones from her heart.

Her trance was disturbed by a noise behind her. A man's voice said, "Isabelle?"

If Isabelle had been a different person, a person who was easily spooked, she might have howled. Not only was she not alone, at night, in the dark, but the man who called out to her knew her name! Her first thought as she turned around wasn't for herself or her safety. It was for Finn and Vanessa. If there was any kind of trouble, Finn would hear it, and then Isabelle would have to explain what she was doing lurking in the back alley, peeping at him in the dark. And Vanessa might have to explain a few things too.

Her mind racing, she spun to see who addressed her from the darkness.

It was Lucas.

The drunken fool!

"What are you doing here?" he asked. He was inebriated, of course, but he still managed to also be perplexed *and* flirtatious.

"What *you* doing here?" asked Isabelle, not hiding her irritation.

"I'm looking out for . . . for Finn," he said. "You?"

Isabelle opened her mouth to say something asinine and false and then snapped her jaws shut. She didn't owe this man an explanation in any language.

It suddenly got dark in the garden, and it took Isabelle a moment to realize that Finn had turned off his office lights and left. There was a good chance he was headed home.

"Look what you did," she said to Lucas. "Now he gone."

"He went to Lionel's." Lucas was slurring his words. "Lionel Morris from CCP. Want me to take you there? It's not far."

"No, thank you."

Lucas came closer with a big smile. Isabelle put up her hands with no smile at all. "Stay way, Lucas."

"Why you have to be so hard, girly girl?" he said. "Come on, soften up."

Shoving him away, Isabelle turned and ran. Lucas pursued her. But in what world could a sloshed American man catch a Ukrainian prairie filly?

Not in this world. Before Isabelle crossed the street, Lucas had already stopped giving chase, plaintively calling after her, "Isabelle, come back! Why do you gotta be that way?"

Isabelle didn't know whether to tell Vanessa about Lucas. She sensed she shouldn't. The first time she met Vanessa, Isabelle had heard sharp sounds from her directed at Finn, and some of those sounds carried the name Lucas on them. Perhaps he was the scoundrel Vanessa didn't want Finn drinking with.

"Yes," she said to Vanessa when she returned home. "He was at office."

Isabelle told Vanessa what Finn had been doing, how agitated he was. Isabelle didn't tell Vanessa he had gone to Lionel's—for how could Isabelle know that?—and obviously she didn't tell Vanessa what she felt upon seeing Finn with his costume off, his mask off, alone and in despair.

As the troubling week continued, matters were not resolved by one stealth mission. Finn continued to be absent from home, and Vanessa continued to send Isabelle to the bank. Isabelle didn't know what to do. She didn't want another run-in with Lucas. She found another alley that led to the bank's rear yard, which meant another way out for her. Not only was Finn at his desk again, calculating numbers, smoking, talking on the phone, but Lucas was there too, and this time, he barred Isabelle's exit. A good thing Isabelle had another way out. It was always good to have another way out.

Who was this Lucas, whom Vanessa didn't like, whom Finn didn't want to speak to, yet who loitered near Finn at night, indifferent to the cold and to how Finn felt about him?

Isabelle stopped going to the bank every night. She pretended to go, but often she walked around the neighborhood instead, gawking at the townhouses. When she grew cold, she quietly returned home through the back gate, always with the same cheerful report. But she wished she knew English well enough to say to Finn and Vanessa the words her mother had taught her in Ukrainian that went something like, *Be sure your heart is brave; you can take much.*

22

Food for Finn

Finn was gone from the house for nearly two weeks. When he returned on Sunday morning, November 11, he looked five years older.

On the radio, the announcers talked nonstop about things that made no sense to Isabelle. Stocks, securities, the Dow Jones—whatever that was—brokers, bankruptcies, bulls, and bears. Why animals were brought into the conversation, Isabelle had no idea. The whole thing was baffling. Whatever had happened or was still happening was so drastic it made Finn Evans, an amiable and sunny man, behave like a hardened convict. Like someone who'd come back from Solovki, the Soviet death camps, and couldn't talk about the things he'd seen there.

He was cold and gray. He could barely fake-smile at his children; he could barely fake-talk to his wife. Maybe he talked to her behind closed doors, but Isabelle didn't think so, judging by the intensity of Vanessa's cleaning regimen. The breadth and depth of it was astonishing.

Isabelle blamed herself for lagging in her English studies, aggrieved at her inability to understand the cataclysmic things happening around her.

After the Absence, Finn resumed coming home, but invariably late. And every night he came home late, he looked older than the day before. The man was thirty-one but was beginning to look as old as Schumann.

Finn stopped going to Schumann's to have Vanessa's dresses repaired, or even to have the tailor clean and press his suits and shirts. He asked Loretta to launder and iron the shirts without starch, and he wore his suits crumpled one day into the next. Vanessa used to call Finn a "regular Joe Brooks," which Isabelle suspected meant a man who dressed to perfection, but now the wife teased (chided?) the husband about his frayed attire.

Another week passed. Never was Vanessa more distressed than when she talked to her mother or sister on the phone. The mask would slip from her voice and she sounded both shrill and overwhelmed in her responses. "I don't know what you want me to do, Mother," she kept saying. "I don't see how *that's* going to help." Or, "What could I possibly say to Eleanor that would make her feel better?" and then, "Daddy is resting, how would seeing me help him? He needs rest, not visitation!"

Everyone in the family stopped coming to the house, except Finn's mother, Olivia, who visited regularly to take her grandchildren either to the park or the stores. One time she asked Isabelle to accompany them, to help carry some packages back. Olivia was grim, but pretended she wasn't. Isabelle respected that.

"Whatever Vanessa needs, help her, Isabelle," Olivia said.

"Yes, of course." Isabelle walked, chewing her lip. She didn't know how to say the next thing but she needed to try. "Your son barely eating."

"Oh, don't I know it," Olivia said. "I saw him at the bank last week, and the poor thing looked like he'd lost thirty pounds!"

"He says he not hungry," Isabelle said. "At night he come home, I ask if he hungry, and he say no. I think midnight too late to eat."

"He comes home at midnight?" Olivia exclaimed. "Oh, that won't do. That's *much* too late."

"He need to have dinner at seven or eight."

"Agreed. How do we make that happen?"

Isabelle weighed her words. "Maybe Vanessa bring hot food to bank?"

Olivia smiled with a tiny shake of her head. "Problematic," she said. "But actually, that's a wonderful idea. Perhaps *you* could bring him some supper. You don't mind taking a walk in the evening, do you?"

"I do anything you need." Well done, Isabelle.

"Excellent," Olivia said. "Prepare him a plate, and walk it over to him. Wait for him to finish eating and then bring the dishware back."

"Okay," Isabelle said. "But . . . I don't know if he like . . . people anymore."

"I'm not saying he's going to be a chatterbox, entertaining you," Olivia said. "But he'll work better if he has food in him."

"Like everyone," said Isabelle. "But you tell Vanessa I do this?"

"Oh, can we go with Isabelle, Grandma?" Mae asked.

"It will be too late for you, my darlings," Olivia said. "Precious girls shouldn't be walking around Boston late in the evening. But perhaps on Saturday afternoons, you could go with Isabelle and bring Daddy some lunch, and maybe help him at the bank. He would like that."

When they returned home, Olivia shouted up for Vanessa, who descended the stairs wearing her smartest suit dress, her hair coiffed, and her face ready for a photoshoot.

"Vanessa," Olivia said, "I told Isabelle she needs to start making Finn a dinner plate and bringing it to him at the bank on nights he works late."

"Grandma said we could go too!" Junie said.

"Only on Saturdays!" Mae said sternly to her sister.

"I don't know how that's going to work, Olivia," Vanessa said, casting a worried glance at Isabelle. "Finn works late every night."

"Even more important that the family he is working so hard for should prepare him some supper to give him strength," said Olivia.

"He eats when he comes home," Vanessa said.

Olivia turned to Isabelle. "Does he?"

Isabelle hated to be put on the spot. "Many night, no, he no eat," she said.

"Well, if Isabelle doesn't have anything else to do during dinner hour," Vanessa said. "But often she is busy."

"That's fine," Olivia said. "If Isabelle is busy, then you can walk or drive to the bank and bring your husband some dinner yourself. Agreed?"

Vanessa could only grunt. It was clear she'd been outplayed.

"Vanessa," Isabelle said after Olivia left and they were alone, "this is good. If I bring him food, then I can check on him without secret, yes?"

"I suppose so," Vanessa said. "But can I count on you to be discreet? You didn't say anything to Olivia, did you? About your nighttime walks?"

"Never word," Isabelle said.

Vanessa visibly relaxed. Isabelle found it fascinating that when Olivia suggested that Vanessa bring dinner to Finn herself, everyone in earshot knew it was something Vanessa could never do. Olivia, who proposed the idea knew it, the two children knew it, Isabelle knew it, and, most important, Vanessa herself knew it.

23

Thanksgiving

Toward the end of November, Vanessa announced that for something called Thanksgiving, Schumann's services were required. Several buttons had fallen off Finn's best suit, and Vanessa's cardigans had become worn at the sleeves. Finn did not say yes or no. Instead, he said nothing, as if he were debating *what* to say. Both Vanessa and Isabelle watched him warily, the latter from the corner of the library, where she was dusting and pretending not to understand English.

In the end, Finn acquiesced and he and Isabelle walked to Schumann's. It was the first time they were out together in nearly a month. It was cold and windy. It wasn't a pleasant walk, and the wind made it hard to talk. Still, Isabelle tried. "Finn, is everything all right?"

"Not really, no," Finn said.

"You want to say?"

"Not really, no."

Isabelle pressed on. "You cannot say?"

"I don't want to say. If Vanessa asks, tell her everything is fine."

"But everything not fine?"

"No, but you say everything is fine."

Isabelle wished she knew the words to say more.

Schumann himself didn't look happy. "Business is down," he told Finn as he handed him the clothes that had been waiting since October.

Isabelle didn't have a moment alone with Schumann to explain what was going on. Nate was there. Isabelle could not be courteous to Nate. She barely looked his way or responded when he walked out from the back to say hello and ask how things were. Schumann introduced Nate to Finn.

"Oh, this is the famous Nate," Finn said.

"Oh, this is the famous Finn," Nate said.

They commiserated by having a quick mute drink. Finn wasn't done with the last swallow before Isabelle set down her glass sharply and said it was time to go.

"You don't like Nate?" Finn said as they began down Salem Street.

"*Not, really no,*" Isabelle said in Finn's voice. "*And I don't want to say.*"

Finn was about to respond when his gaze hardened. Swearing under his breath, he ushered Isabelle onward. Lucas was calling for them.

"Finn, why that man Lucas follow you all time?"

"I don't know, Isabelle. Pay no attention."

"Hard not to pay attention. He always there. Why?"

"Who can say."

"Maybe you?"

"No."

"Also don't want to?"

"Also don't want to," said Finn.

"If you talk to him, maybe he stay away."

"He won't."

This time Lucas did not stay away. He stopped in front of them on Salem Street, panting and wounded. "Finn, please."

"You're fried already," Finn said. "Get out of our way."

Lucas wouldn't move. "It's fine if you don't want to go drinking again. I just want to talk to you."

"Move, Lucas."

"I don't know why you're so sore with me. Can you just tell me? Whatever it was, I was drunk. I louse everything up."

"You're drunk all the time, Lucas."

"I didn't know, Finn," Lucas said regretfully, mournfully. "Honest to Christ, I didn't know!"

"Didn't know what—no, stop—I don't want to talk about it."

They stared at one another, one accusingly, the other apologetically. Finn shoved him out of the way, taking Isabelle by the arm. "Stop loitering around me, Lucas," he said. "Leave me alone."

"Why is it okay for her to follow you around but not me?" Lucas yelled after them. "I don't see you being all steamed at her!"

They crossed under the clanging elevated trains and kept walking. As they neared Beacon Hill, Finn said, "What did he mean by that?"

Isabelle, using her immigration status as an all-powerful crutch, spoke her standard. "I not understand."

"Why did he say you follow me around?"

"Follow you where?"

"I don't know. That's why I'm asking."

"I don't know what he mean," said Isabelle. "You said yourself. He fried."

From the corner of her eye, Isabelle watched Finn as they walked. She was not impervious to his ongoing distress, obviously, even though she didn't understand it. But she couldn't help being sympathetic to Lucas because she understood him better. Had Finn not been so mired in his own miseries, he might have been more understanding too. There lay an unhappy truth. Empathy and sympathy were first to fall victim to everyone everywhere being consumed by their own sufferings, other people becoming ghosts by comparison.

"I don't know if Lucas follow you or something else," she said to Finn when they were almost home. "Maybe keep eye on you."

"What's the difference?"

"One way he want something from you. One way he don't."

"He *doesn't*."

"So, if you know he doesn't want anything from you, why you ask me what is difference?"

"No, I was correcting you," Finn said. "One way he *doesn't*, not one way he *don't*."

"If you ask my opinion," Isabelle said, pretending she had no idea what Finn was saying, "I think Lucas all right. He not a wolf in, how you say, cheap clothing."

Finn bit his lip. "I know better than anyone that Lucas is not a wolf in . . ." Isabelle watched him struggling with himself, trying not to smile, ". . . cheap clothing," he finished as they reached Louisburg Square and their front door.

24

The Naked Short

Vanessa wanted everything to be normal for Thanksgiving, insisted on it, but Finn didn't see how that was possible. No one was feeling thankful or celebratory or normal.

And then—finally something to be thankful for! Wretched weather descended upon Boston, making it icy and dangerous to use the roads. Walter and Lucy stayed home in Back Bay with Eleanor and Monty, "for health and safety reasons." Earl and Olivia walked to Finn's from their home a few blocks away on Hancock Street. Finn had not seen his father since three weeks earlier when he had to tell Earl that his savings had been wiped out.

Earl and Olivia ate, chatted politely, played with the children, and then begged off early, citing increasing cold and thickening ice on the roads and pathways. Earl and Finn did not have a private word alone. That was for the best. Finn walked his parents home, his mother clutching his and his father's arms to stop herself from slipping on the steep and icy Beacon Hill streets.

"Are you eating better?" Olivia asked. "You're still dropping weight."

"I'm fine, Mother."

"He's fine, Olivia," Earl said. "He's a grown man. He can decide for himself how much he eats."

Olivia persisted as if her husband the judge hadn't spoken. "Has Isabelle started bringing you your dinner?"

"Yes! How did you—"

"Who do you think arranged that? Well, she suggested it, but I thought it was a splendid idea."

"Huh," said Finn, tightening his hold on his mother's arm, and staring straight ahead.

On Saturday morning after Thanksgiving, Eleanor came crashing into Vanessa's house, wailing and wringing her hands.

Adder had vanished.

In the middle of the night, already up and dressed, he had pulled out a packed suitcase and said to Eleanor, "I'm leaving you two thousand dollars in cash on the counter. If anyone asks, you don't know where I went."

"But I *don't* know!" said Eleanor. "Where are you going?"

"I can't tell you," said Adder. "For your safety I can't."

"My safety or yours?"

"Tell them nothing."

"But I know nothing!" she cried.

"Better that way." And Adder fled, leaving behind his wife and son.

Finn didn't know where Adder had gone, but he well knew why. Adder had naked shorted millions of dollars at the end of Black Tuesday, betting his clients' money—without their permission—that the market would continue to slide, and he would make a fortune. But the market rallied 30 points, and Adder had until October 31 to pay back three and a half million dollars.

Instead—with the Feds breathing down his throat for the multiple felonies he had committed—Adder Day became a ghost on Halloween. For nearly a month, he never left the house, didn't answer the phone, didn't open his mail, didn't talk to Finn or Walter, didn't go with his wife to Back Bay for Thanksgiving. He brooded and packed. And then up and left.

Vanessa stood frozen. She didn't know how to comfort her sister, Finn saw that. But it was her utter non-response to Eleanor's crisis that baffled him. All Vanessa said was, "Would you like a cup of tea, Ellie, or something to eat? You look famished."

This was Vanessa's way, even with Finn—composed but silent. He kept waiting for her to ask him about his work, about Lionel or his wife Babs, with whom she had been moderately good friends once, or to talk to him about what was happening in their country, the sudden wreck followed by a slow-motion derailment. It wasn't like the radio and the papers weren't on full throttle about the Crash and Mellon and Hoover and railroad stocks. Not Vanessa. And because the families no longer visited for a pleasant parlay in the parlor room on Sunday afternoons, Vanessa couldn't overhear even accidentally the disaster that was unfolding outside her well-appointed home.

She was always amiable, loving, solicitous, just as she was now with overwrought Eleanor. Vanessa would ask if Finn was all right, or hungry or tired. But she never said, "Finn, my love, the Earth's Holocaust has swept over our nation but tell me, I implore you, has it passed by my daddy's livelihood, has it spared our small happy life on Beacon Hill?"

Only in the expression of the young Ukrainian woman who brought him dinner at night did Finn catch a fleeting glimpse of the thing he ached for:

some understanding of his condition, some commiseration. Pity, maybe. He reckoned that must have been projection on his part. For how could she understand? What could she know about the plague of fear and hopelessness that infected Finn like a maiming sickness?

But sometimes when Isabelle sat in the corner of his darkened office, barely animate, listening to his heavy breathing, a curled-up body of formless compassion, Finn believed with all his heart that words were unnecessary to convey to her what it felt like to have the only life you knew vanish before your disbelieving eyes, a smokeless vapor.

On New Year's Eve, 1929, Herbert Hoover's Treasury Secretary, Andrew Mellon, gave an interview to the *New York Times* after returning from a Christmas holiday spent sunning himself on his yacht in the Bahamas. In the interview, he lauded the country's swift recovery, its continued emphasis on employment, the purchasing power of the middle class, and retail sales holding up through December. He prophesied a rosy outlook for 1930. Interest rates for new business endeavors remained low. Credit was ample and readily available. Oh, sure, he said, there might be some *small pockets* of sectional unemployment in the winter months, but come spring, he foresaw prosperity and revival. "The nation has made steady progress!" Nothing ahead but blue skies and sunny days.

The American Federation of Labor seconded Mellon's rosy sentiments. Obviously, there had been *some* slackening of demand for new vehicles. Thus, automobile production was downgraded. Detroit was forecast to build a million fewer cars in 1930 than in 1929. This would inevitably result in less demand for steel, and therefore a decrease in steel production. And sure, employment might be a little low (not unemployment high but employment low), but it would improve as the year continued. The main thing in avoiding a recession, both Mellon and the AFL concurred, was to maintain wages and employment. "To reduce expense, companies might need to look elsewhere than wage reduction and redundancies." And yes, stock prices remained low, but continued demand for new products would stimulate production and increase the companies' value, thus increasing share prices. Confidence is at a high, echoed the president of the largest labor union in America and the Secretary of the United States Treasury. Not at an all-time high. But definitely a high.

And then, the hedge.

"Of course, predicting the future," Mellon said, "cannot be done with any certainty." Complex forces were at work. "But there is no reason for pessimism," he added. "No reason at all."

25

Assets and Liabilities

Commonwealth Capital Partners closed its doors at the beginning of 1930. Lionel had been hoping for a recovery, a buying spree—prices so low, who could resist?

Buyers resisted. They weren't going to be snookered twice. The market stagnated. No wildly optimistic rallies materialized. The balance sheet of CCP was no assets and all liabilities. The firm was so in the red, it couldn't be bought even at pennies on the dollar by any of Boston's other banks, not even by Massachusetts National, which had allowed Finn to borrow half a million dollars with his homes and the bank as collateral. The rest of the money Finn owed CCP, he and Lionel negotiated away. Adams Bank held a mortgage in the commercial property that headquartered CCP. Lionel could not repay it, and Finn wrote it off. In return, Lionel wrote off Finn's remaining unpaid margin accounts. They drank half a bottle of whisky, shook hands, and called it even.

Lionel and Babs had to fire-sale their spacious Back Bay home. They moved to a two-room flat in South Boston. Lionel came to Finn looking for work. But Finn, fraying at the edges, didn't have a job for him. He was trying to stave off firing his most loyal personnel, including Myrtle, without whom Finn didn't think he could function.

Finn was about to let go his branch manager, his credit analyst, two of his loan officers, five of his tellers, all his customer service staff and *definitely* his risk manager. Talk about a job redundancy. He had to let them go if the bank was to have a chance at survival. Finn would be wearing many of those hats himself until he got the bank above water. He would keep Grover, his operations manager, who paid the bills and kept the lights on, four bank tellers, and one senior account executive. He promised Lionel he would hire him in a year if the bank was still standing and Lionel said, "In a year, will *I* still be standing?"

Finn suggested applying for a position at Shawmut or Old Colony. "You think I didn't go to them first?" Lionel said. "I've been to all nine Boston banks.

They wouldn't hire me. They said my previous work experience made me a high-risk employee. Apparently, the millions of dollars in profit I brought CCP over the last decade counts for nothing. Ten years against four days," Lionel added bitterly. "That's how I'm being evaluated."

"I'm sorry, Lionel," Finn said to his friend. That was how he was being evaluated too.

With his cash reserves depleted and the cost of his day-to-day operations vastly outpacing the money coming in, Finn expended effort on only two things. One was keeping the bank open. And the second one was keeping the fact that their life was falling apart hidden from Vanessa.

Finn tried to explain to his anxious customers that their profits of the last few months or few years were paper profits and, except for the margin accounts, many of their current losses were paper losses only. The good companies they invested in did not lose value. The companies didn't stop making telephones or boats or cars. They continued to sell their products and employ people and make money and pay dividends on their shares.

But few paid him any attention. The senseless liquidation continued. The worse the stock market continued to perform, the more people were laid off by the struggling companies, the less those companies produced as a result, the less weight Finn's argument held for the average Bostonian.

There was no way around it. The American consumer had stopped consuming. As a result, companies could not move the surplus of unsold inventory they had accumulated. They had been producing at a breakneck pace to keep up with demand, and suddenly there wasn't any. No one was buying new cars. They were driving their perfectly adequate Model Ts from 1927. GM also cut production. Cutting production meant laying off thousands of workers.

Herbert Hoover made it his business to help the wage worker by demanding an increase in his hourly pay. GM agreed to the wage hike, just as Ford had, but slashed their staff even more to make up for the increased labor costs. Other companies cut workers' hours from six days a week to three. The pay remained the same, even rose in some cases, but now, fewer people were working only three days a week. Before long, the cut in hours was followed by a cut in pay, Hoover's directives be damned. Either you worked reduced hours at a reduced pay or you didn't work. People chose work.

As the workforce dropped, prices dropped. People stopped buying homes, going on vacations, buying dresses. They spent less on gasoline because they drove less.

Finn's business suffered more than most. An unemployed worker couldn't pay his mortgage or his loans, collateralized or not. And if they had a choice, they paid their mortgage first because families had to live somewhere. But increasingly, it wasn't even a choice. They couldn't pay either. Finn could raise the interest rate all he wanted, on his loans and his savings deposits and his mortgages, it didn't matter. 1930 was a year of defaults, one after another, month after month. People couldn't pay their business loans, their personal loans. Few trusted the banks, and even fewer came in to open new accounts. What Finn got was desperate jobless people applying to borrow money. Money he knew they would never be able to repay.

Finn saw it snowballing the wrong way, and was powerless to stop it.

A full inventory of assets and liabilities had to be undertaken. And not just at the bank. At home too. And at home the charade was harder. At the bank, everyone knew what was going on and acted accordingly. They turned off the lights, they used the front and back of all papers to write on, they used the pens and pencils until the last bit of ink and graphite was spent. Despite this, Finn's indispensable Myrtle still had to be let go.

At home, on the other hand, Finn had to work hard to maintain the farce for Vanessa. At home he continued to employ a staff of six and maintain the exorbitant cost of running a 7000-square-foot house in which ten people lived. He had to maintain these expenses during a blizzardy winter with record low temperatures. The family's coal costs tripled. The women in his life became cranky, everyone except Isabelle, who was Marcus Aurelius in her stoic forbearance. But neither Edith nor Loretta appreciated the colder rooms, the economizing on coal, the paucity of food in the pantries. Edith complained, then resigned in protest. Vanessa didn't say a word to Finn.

Finn found out only because Isabelle told him.

"Edith left," Isabelle said to him in March from her corner of his office, where he placed a more comfortable chair for her to wait in while he ate.

"Left where?"

"Iowa."

Finn looked up from his food and his ledger. "What?"

Isabelle opened her hands. "What is Iowa?"

"Are you joking?"

"I do not joke," said Isabelle. "She say house too cold."

"When did this happen?"

"February."

"*What?*"

"Why you keep saying *what*? You joke or you deaf?"

Finn said nothing. Vanessa had not said a word to him about it! How could that be?

"Vanessa said she tell you," said Isabelle.

Finn said nothing.

"I think maybe she want you home little bit."

Finn opened his hands to his desk, to his bank, to the heavens. He knew Vanessa was flailing, but what could he do? He was only one man. How could he fix here *and* there?

Isabelle cleared her throat and said, "I think you should hire Mr. Morose to help you here," she said. "You need him. And home needs *you*."

"Mr. Morose?"

"Your old friend, Lionel Morose."

Finn shook his head. "Lionel *Morris*."

"That's what I say. Morose. Hire him."

"I can't afford him."

"He work for half what you think you can't pay him," Isabelle said. "He take care your paper, your money . . ." She waved her own hands over Finn's desk. "He cash your till. He add your numbers. And you can go home for dinner, and, how you say, inventory situation."

Go home for dinner? Finn wanted to say. Why would I want to do that when you bring it to me here, where it's dark and warm, and you sit in the corner and look at me, and talk to me and understand without understanding. "What could you possibly know about Lionel?"

"Nothing," Isabelle said. "Except I see him by Park Street Church when I come here. He stand on corner of Park and Tremont and he shout." Isabelle affected a voice precisely like Lionel's, yet not Lionel's. "*You want more margarine? You can't have more margarine! You want more margarine? You can't have more margarine!*"

"Wait, what?" Finn leaned forward at his desk. Did he mishear her? Was Lionel shouting in the streets?

"Yes. He shout lot. Every night in freeze for two weeks."

"Do you mean *margin*? Does he say, you want more *margin*?"

"No," Isabelle said. "Definitely he say margarine. I don't know what margin is."

"To whom is he shouting about this . . . margarine?"

"To no one. It freezing, I told you." Isabelle cleared her throat. "Once in while, he shout at Lucas. Lucas tries to get him somewhere warm, but Mr. Morose doesn't want to and they, how you say, shuffle?"

"*Scuffle*." Finn collected his dishes and grabbed his coat. "So Lucas and Lionel *and* you are now gallivanting in the streets at night?"

"Who gallivanting?" said Isabelle. "I'm here. Also, what is gallivanting?"

"Let's go and see what's what." As they were leaving, Finn said, "I'm asking again, how do you know who Lionel is?"

"I see him with you."

"When did you *ever* see him with me?"

"What?" said Isabelle.

Lionel had a nervous breakdown in the beginning of January when CCP closed. He began behaving erratically, waking up in the middle of the night, putting on a suit as if he were heading out to work. At home he would sit at his desk, sifting through invisible tape, muttering to himself. He began to speak of uselessness, of the unnecessary length of life, of the whole world being better off without him. Babs got so worried, she had Lionel committed to a sanatorium in Rhode Island. How she was going to pay that bill, she didn't know. Lionel escaped three days into his stay, and made his way back to Boston, which is when Isabelle found him. He was living on the streets, sleeping during the day in the basement of Park Street Church, Lucas told Isabelle, and wandering at night, shouting on corners.

Finn and Isabelle learned this when they brought a filthy-smelling Lionel back home to his terrified and furious wife. While Babs was running through the gamut of her emotions, Finn was trying to figure things out.

"What to think about," whispered Isabelle. "Give him job."

"You think he's in any state to put on a suit and come into the office?" Finn whispered back.

"Why not? He put on nice suit and stand on corner to yell about margarine," said Isabelle. "He can put on suit to come work for you. Then he feel better."

"Doesn't he need to feel better first?"

"No. He need job first. *Then* he feel better," said Isabelle.

"Would you like me to hire your new friend Lucas too?" Finn said. "Does he need a job?"

"He definitely need job," said Isabelle. "But you don't look like you want to hire him."

"You *think*?"

"Yes," Isabelle said seriously. "But Lucas work for you for cheap. Maybe he can be your bank cashier."

"You want me to put Lucas in charge of handling *cash*?"

"Maybe not best idea."

"You *think*?"

"Yes," Isabelle said. She paused. "Oh, was that you try to be funny?"

"Yes."

She shook her head. "Not very good, Finn," she said.

* * *

Finn didn't know how he would continue to pay his own mortgage. But he hired Lionel, who showed up a few days later grim but clean and almost composed except for an occasional glassy-eyed twitch. Finn reluctantly let go the rest of his skeletal staff, and just like Walter Adams Jr. presiding over the birth of his business a hundred years earlier, but in reverse, Finn and Lionel toiled over the remains of Adams Bank and Trust.

26

The Teacher

With Edith gone and private school out of reach, Isabelle was the only one left to teach Mae and Junie. Vanessa could, but Vanessa remained indisposed.

During the day Isabelle told stories to the girls, and by night, when they had supper with their newly present father, the girls regaled both their parents with what they had learned during the day.

"We learned so much today, Daddy! We learned that Ukraine is a very big country, almost as big as France, and it has forty million people, which is less than one half what we have in America."

"Very good, what else?"

"We learned that Ukraine is bordered by Russia in the north and east, Poland in the west, and Romania in the south. We learned that Poland is a very nice country that has beautiful girls. Isabelle's mother was Polish and a beautiful girl."

"Anything else?"

"We learned that the Soviets are . . . wait, I memorized it . . . the Soviets are petty, destructive, remorseless, stupid, and brutal."

Finn and Vanessa were mute.

"Mae, you forgot thieves and plunderers," said Junie, turning to Finn. "Daddy, what's a plunderer?"

"Finn," Vanessa said to him after the girls were asleep, "please ask Isabelle not to teach our children anything else about Ukraine."

"I think she is teaching them what she knows," Finn said.

"Maybe she can read up on American history," said Vanessa. "Heaven forfend the children should spout this to their friends at the park. Or to our parents. Do you want your father to learn that the Bolsheviks used famine as a political tool to starve the Ukrainians during the Civil War? Because this is what the children are repeating to me. I didn't even know the Russians fought a civil war!"

"Perhaps the girls aren't the only ones who need Isabelle's lessons," said Finn. "But this teaching thing reminds me, Vee, um, why didn't you tell me Edith left?"

First Vanessa was startled. Then she was indignant.

"Well, darling, you said it yourself. Should I bother you with nonsense about why Edith left? I told her to put on a sweater! You are working so hard for this family, I would never bother you with such trifles! Isabelle shouldn't have bothered you either. Look how agitated you are."

Finn almost bought it. "In the future, darling," he said, "if the servants are resigning or it's too cold for you and the children, promise you will tell me."

And Vanessa promised him she would. But Finn duly noted that she did not ask him to reciprocate in kind with some much-needed honesty.

On Saturdays, if Finn got home early enough, he would stand at the slightly ajar door of the girls' nursery and listen to Isabelle's strong, unwavering voice speak of bloodshed in a sing-song, like a nightmare lullaby.

"Girls, do you know what perfidy is?"

"No! What is perfidy?"

"Deceit, lying, betrayal. Like when you count on someone and instead of being your friend, they steal from you and then kill you and hang you upside down by the side of the road."

"Isn't that like murder?" said Mae.

"Yes," Isabelle said. "And also perfidy."

Later that night, downstairs in the kitchen, Finn asked Isabelle to teach the children some subjects other than history.

"I also teach them geography," said Isabelle. "Your girls know where Romania is, where Romanian ports on Black Sea are, where Italy is, where Atlantic Ocean is, where Lavelle is."

"It's *Lovell*," Finn said.

"I also teach them English vocabulary," Isabelle continued. "Also animal lessons about horses and cows. I teach them art of telling stories. I teach them music and dancing and athletics. We do jumping jacks, we run in park. I teach them how to play football. They are very good. I teach them gardening. Just last week, we planted some . . . how you say . . . hyacinth? Junie say it her favorite flower."

"All of that is excellent, Isabelle," Finn said. "But how about some arithmetic, to replace one or two of the history lessons?"

"Good idea," said Isabelle.

After a few days passed the girls informed Finn and Vanessa they had learned how to add and divide.

"Hm," Finn said. "Why not subtraction first, I wonder?"

"Isabelle says division is like subtraction but faster," Mae said.

"Let's hear what you've learned."

"We learned that every Ukrainian village is divided into many units of Communists," Mae said. "It's simple, Daddy, even Junie knows it now."

"Let me tell it!" said Junie, who was going to be seven soon and wanted to be a big girl. She took a breath and began to recite what she had learned. "In Isabelle's village called Ispas there lived a thousand people who were *divided* into two hundred households."

"That's about five people per household," said Mae. "Though in Isabelle's household there were nineteen."

"Big household," said Finn. "Did she tell you who the nineteen were?"

"That's not really arithmetic, Finn," said Vanessa.

"She did tell us!" said Mae. "There was Isabelle, her three brothers, their three wives, her mother, her husband, her husband's brother, her husband's brother's wife, her husband's brother's four children, her husband's parents, and her two children."

"Isabelle has *children*?" said Vanessa, exchanging a stunned glance with Finn.

"Two sons," said Junie. "Our age. A little older."

Finn said nothing. So she was married. She had children. In her muteness on the subject he sensed a heavy accounting, a bitter story. There must be pain there that would never be done with, Finn thought. "Tell me more about the arithmetic, Junie," he said.

"Her village got divided by hundreds, tens, and fives," Junie said. "This means, Daddy, that there was one Soviet official like a Papa Bear keeping an eye on one hundred families."

"Keeping an eye on them for what purpose, Junie?" said Vanessa.

"That's also not part of arithmetic, Mommy," Mae said. "But in Ispas there were two big Papa Bears. One for every hundred families."

"I'm gonna tell it!" said Junie. "After the two Papa Bears, there were ten Mama Bears who kept more eyes on them. So, ten into two hundred is twenty!"

"Okay," Finn said, uncertain where this was going. It couldn't be anywhere good.

"And then, each of the two hundred families were divided one last time into forty Baby Bears, and two hundred divided by forty is five," said Junie. "One Baby Bear kept his eye on five families. That's what hundreds, tens, and fives means."

"Forty times five is two hundred," Mae said. "Multiplication and division are the same backward and forward."

"Very good, dear," Vanessa said.

"We're not done, Mommy," Junie said.

"Don't forget to add now, June," Mae said. "It's addition time."

"I know, shh, don't rush me!" Junie's lips were moving as she counted. "So, two Papa Bears, twenty Mama Bears, and forty Baby Bears adds up to sixty-two Soviet Communists in one Ispas village, keeping an eye on two hundred families like Isabelle's."

"You can't divide two hundred by sixty-two, June," said Mae. "It's not an even number."

"Isabelle told us it's around three," said Junie, glaring at her older sister. "Which means that there were three Soviet officials keeping an eye on each one of the village families. But because Isabelle's family was nineteen people, she said they had thirteen Communists keeping an eye on them."

"How many?" Finn said. He hoped his girls had misheard.

"Whatever for?" said Vanessa.

"Isabelle told us," Junie said, screwing up her face in concentration. "She said they needed more than thirteen Communists to guard nineteen Lazars." She stuck out her tongue at her sister. "See, Daddy?" the proud girl said. "We learned arithmetic, just like Isabelle said you wanted us to."

27

Increasing the Productivity of Cows

Ukraine, April 1929

"I'm going to hang myself," Roman said. Every night there was another mandatory meeting. Everyone was at their wits' end. The Lazars had requested and received a steel plow. To accommodate Zhuk's demands, they turned over ten acres of their land to cultivate wheat and some sugar beets. They used their horses, their plows, and all available manpower to prepare the land and plant in April.

But every morning, a member of the Communist brigade arrived at the farm—either an old man or a rude Ukrainian youth hungry for power who decided to become a Komsomol, a young Communist—and walked around the fields and the stables. He took notes and reported on the Lazars' daily progress. Roman got so tired of it that he was about to send Ostap to puncture the tires on the Soviet trucks, except someone had beaten him to it. Efros took fifteen people into custody before the saboteur came forward and confessed. It turned out to be a middle-aged beet farmer named Andreyus, whose family was arrested two weeks prior and put on trains out of Ukraine. When they arrested him, he threw a bottle at Efros's head and was promptly taken out to the square and shot in full view of everyone. Andreyus's sabotage provided a brief respite—the tires had been slashed, and for a few days until the trucks were fitted with new tires there was relative peace on the farm. It didn't last.

Despite Roman's pledge to work together, Soviet apparatchiks, be they *AgitProp* activists or political instructors, could not walk the village roads alone or unarmed. They were constantly being dragged into the bushes and beaten. And every time there was an incident, Efros drove out to the farm reinforced with a half-dozen *chekists* to interrogate Roman.

In the middle of April all nineteen Lazars and Kovalenkos, even the pregnant and furious Yana, were dragged to an especially galling meeting.

Zhuk wanted to discuss ways to boost productivity. Not of the farmers, but of the chickens, cows, and horses. The mandatory meeting was poorly attended. Barely fifty fed-up people showed up, one-third of them Lazars. There were more Bolsheviks at this meeting than villagers. The Lazars came because they had been compelled to.

"We are going to solve the chicken problem once and for all," said Zhuk. "Please meet Comrade Potapov, who is here from Moscow. He is an expert on animal husbandry, and he is going to provide helpful guidance and suggestions, especially regarding horses."

"Excuse me for the interruption, Comrade Potapov," Roman said, standing up, even though both Cici and Isabelle were pulling on him to sit the hell down. "What do you mean *regarding* horses? Comrade Zhuk himself told me some months back that horses were a Tsarist remnant. Horses were obsolete, he said, they could not help us on the farm. We had tractors and threshers; we no longer needed horses. Why do we have to make more productive an animal we don't need?"

"Sit down, Comrade Lazar," Potapov said in a shrill, reedy voice. "Because this month there is a new directive from Moscow."

"*This month there is a new directive from Moscow,*" mimicked Isabelle, in an impression so spot-on it bordered on professional. She yanked on her brother. "*Sit down, Comrade Lazar,*" she said in Potapov's voice.

"Tonight," Potapov said, his pointed nose quivering above his thin lips, "we resolve to adopt a new resolution, not just for Ispas but for all villages in the region. From this moment forward, until further notice, every horse farmer, like you, Comrade Lazar, will strive, no, not strive—*achieve!*—yes, achieve, 100 percent pregnancy rate of all women horses!"

When the fifty people in the hall remained speechless, Potapov pressed on. "Is that clear? Is anything I said not clear?"

"*Is anything I said not clear?*" repeated Isabelle.

"Um, yes, Comrade Potapov," said Roman. "A number of things are not clear." Both Isabelle and Cici pinched him, Isabelle continuing to whisper in Potapov's unpleasant tenor, "*One hundred percent pregnancy rate of all women horses!*" Cici nearly laughed out loud.

Roman pushed away from his wife and sister, and walked out into the aisle where he could speak undisturbed by them.

"Did you say you are the animal breeding expert from Moscow?" Roman said. "Please instruct us on how we achieve such extraordinary results."

Ostap stood up—Ostap, who never spoke at these meetings! Even Yana was shocked; especially Yana. "Excuse me," Ostap said, his expression one of disbelief at his own audacity, "but is this what they call female horses in Moscow, *women* horses? Because here in Ukraine we call them mares."

"Whatever," said Potapov.

"And the mares are not *pregnant*," Ostap continued, his black eyes blazing with hatred, his voice low with contempt, "the mares are *with foal*."

"Fine—with foal." Potapov pointed at the Lazar family sitting together with Mirik and Petka. "Comrade Zhuk told me about you Lazars," Potapov said. Petka immediately got up and moved to a different seat. Mirik, too, slid his chair away—only a few centimeters, but still! He moved away, lest he be lumped in with those troublemaker Lazars, Isabelle thought. Unbelievable. Troublemakers like his own wife.

"We believe," Potapov said, "you are using your horses as a means of sabotage against the Soviet state."

"And how are we accomplishing this?" asked Roman, standing next to his brother.

"By having your female horses give birth only once a year!"

"The gestation period for a mare is eleven months," Roman said. "I do not create a horse, Comrade Potapov, I merely breed it."

"You must do better! Why are your horses, which you are supposedly so famous for, giving birth to only one calf each?" Potapov said. "Why is their pregnancy so long? Nearly a *year*? That is unacceptable! Couldn't you induce labor earlier and mate them again? Or you could see if there are ways to stimulate the horse to carry two calves instead of one? Now that would be very productive!"

The Lazars looked straight ahead and not at each other, lest they be arrested for undermining the Soviet Union with their visible disdain. You could not respect what you held in contempt, Christ was right about that, Isabelle thought, willing Roman to stay quiet. Poor Stan and Vitaly, Oleg Tretyak, the evicted Koval, and the recent Andreyus were witnesses and victims to Stalin's slavish devotion to the rule by terror. All pretense about the rule of law was about to be abandoned.

Yana struggled to her feet, holding on to the back of the chair. "I need to leave this meeting," she said. "As you can see, I'm a pregnant female about to give birth. But the experts from Moscow may wish to spend some time around a stable during foaling season before they start making their recommendations." Yana nodded at Roman, at Ostap, and waddled out. Isabelle thought Yana was exaggerating the slowness of her gait for the benefit of Potapov. Just hours ago she had been hopping on and off a horse with no help and no effort.

Potapov paid barely any attention to Yana's words or her departure. "We need to solve the horse problem!" he said to the men. "The horses must produce more than one calf."

"You mean *foal*?" said Roman.

"Whatever. And cows too—more than one foal."

"You mean *calf*," said Ostap.

"Foal, calf, whatever fucking thing!" said Potapov. "But also, it's imperative that chickens make more than one egg a day."

"*Lay* more than one egg a day?" said Roman.

"*More* than one egg a day?" said Ostap.

"You mean to tell me with all your great expertise and technique, you have not found a way to make your farm animals more productive, comrade?" said Potapov. "This is why Comrade Zhuk and I believe you are actively sabotaging the Soviet efforts with your antiquated methods of animal reproduction!"

"Could the expert from Moscow please instruct us how to achieve these results?" Roman said. "For the entirety of human stewardship over animals, chickens have laid one egg a day, mares foaled once a year, and cows calved once a year."

"The capitalist infiltration is everywhere," Potapov said. "Even in animals. The Motherland reveres horses. We need more horses, more cows, more eggs. We must solve the horse problem, the chicken problem, and the cow problem. To help the Motherland, we must!"

"So do we revere the horses or are they an imperial artifact?" Roman said. "I can never be sure."

"Horses are the future!" said Potapov.

Roman stared hard at Zhuk. "Tractors and threshers are no longer the future?"

"Comrade Lazar," Zhuk said, standing next to Potapov, "don't tell us you are not partly responsible for the terrible horse attrition in Ukraine. In 1927, there were 130,000 horses counted in your region. Last year, that number was only 40,000. I dread to think what the number will be this year—15,000? Lower? Why is this happening if it's not intentional disruption?"

"Are you asking me about the socio-political situation in Ukraine, Comrade Zhuk?" said Roman. "All I know is that last year I had thirty horses, and this year, I have nineteen."

"You see!" cried Zhuk and Potapov in unison.

"I should have had thirty-eight horses this year," Roman continued. "But many of my horses died over the winter."

"Because you killed them, Comrade Lazar!"

"Because they were starving, Comrade Potapov," Roman said. "Because there wasn't enough to eat, and a weakened mare is not going to let a stallion near her when she knows she cannot carry a foal."

"You must force him!" Potapov cried.

"I hope this is one of the questions before us on the agenda tonight," Roman said. "What do we do about the problem of the vital role that men horses—or, as we like to call them on the farm, *stallions*—play in making pregnant our revered women horses? The stallions are starving, you see, comrade, and when the animal is hungry, it's simply not going be in as amorous a mood. So how do we, in a Communist utopia, force a six-hundred-kilo male horse to mount an unwilling, hungry, infertile woman horse and make her pregnant so that she can have two or three calf babies after about five or six months of pregnancy? We must figure this out," Roman said, "so I can do more for my part in the Revolution. But since it's after midnight, and we all must be up at sunrise to tend our farms, perhaps we can continue discussing this fascinating problem on the morrow?"

The discussion did not continue on the morrow. That night Oleg Potapov was beaten to death. He'd had vodka by himself at the village center and was drunkenly meandering down the street toward his boarding house when he was dragged into a side alley and killed with a blunt object that cracked his skull. The only reason Roman was not summarily executed was because he had an alibi. He had been taken into custody right after his performance at the meeting and kept overnight in the village prison, which had been constructed by the OGPU in February in the back of the Koval house they had appropriated. Before then, Ispas didn't have a need for a prison.

28

The Order of the Books

Vanessa couldn't bring herself to ask Finn what the matter was over the last few months. She was never one to pry, to push, to force an unwanted conversation. She figured that once everything was back to normal, if Finn wanted to tell her, he would tell her. If they didn't talk about it, whatever it was would resolve itself on its own, as it usually did, and she would feel less anxious. One stressed person in the house was plenty.

But not addressing what felt like disaster meant that Vanessa had to reach new levels of coping. It became shocking to her, for example, that the house, which she kept such a careful eye on, still devolved into chaos in every room, every closet, every cupboard, and every cranny. Large pots mixed in with medium pots, sharp knives with butter knives, and what was happening with the spoons was nearly criminal. How was anyone supposed to find a teaspoon, when serving spoons and soup spoons were in the same drawer? Don't get her started on Mae and Junie's books. No matter how many times she tried, the children stuffed the books anywhere they pleased. It was unacceptable.

"Isabelle," Vanessa said, "where you came from, did they have the same alphabet as us?"

"No, alphabet have more letters, also some different letters."

"But you are familiar with our alphabet, are you not?"

"Of course. Yours very easy. Only twenty-six letters."

"So when you recite the alphabet, you do know that V comes after S and T?"

"Yes."

"So, why is Jules Verne placed before Jonathan Swift? And look, Robert Stevenson is placed *after Sw*ift. What comes first, a W or a T?"

Vanessa thought she had made herself clear, but a few days later, she walked into the nursery and all the books had been rearranged! They weren't just out of alphabetical order; they were in no order at all! And the girls, instead of being remorseful, were jumping with delight. Isabelle stood in the corner, smiling.

"What did you do?" Vanessa said.

"We organized the books, Mommy!" Mae said.

"I don't think so."

"We did, we did. Look how beautiful they are—we arranged them by color! All the pink books are with other pink books, and the blue books with blue, and the white with white, and yukky brown with brown. Isn't it pretty? It looks like a flower garden!"

Vanessa staggered out of the nursery. Was this deliberate sabotage? Who would do such a thing unless they were out to destroy her? She took to her bed. When Finn came home, she said, "Finn, I have to talk to you about something very important."

"Please, let's," said Finn. "We need to talk about important things."

Vanessa spoke at length, with emotion and passion, her voice rising and falling with umbrage, frustration, outrage.

After she was done, Finn sat quietly on the bed.

"Aren't you going to say something?"

"Vanessa, I don't know *what* to say."

"Why am I being subjected to such indignity from my own children and the person who is paid to look after them? The girls know better than anyone how important books are to me." Vanessa closed her eyes so she wouldn't have to look at Finn's sunken body, weighed down by struggles she couldn't and didn't want to acknowledge.

"Why don't you talk to Isabelle, explain to her how you'd like things to be done?" he said, patting her leg gently.

"I did talk to her, and this was the result! Besides, it's degrading. And she barely understands English. I won't be able to make myself plain when I'm this upset."

"Her English is excellent," Finn said.

"She clearly doesn't understand how to alphabetize books!"

"What would you like?" Finn said. "Would you like *me* to talk to her?"

"God, yes, please," Vanessa said.

"Okay," said Finn. "I will talk to her on the weekend."

But the weekend brought another crisis, and Finn was gone until Sunday night. When Vanessa reminded him what he had promised her, he walked into the girls' room and returned with a puzzled look. "Sorry, what's wrong with the books in the girls' room again? They seem fine to me."

29

Fact and Fiction

Oh, the fiction Finn wove to keep the truth from the one he loved. Was it cruelty or kindness? Was it that he didn't want his wife to worry? Or was he afraid her reaction would make it harder for him to hold it together? Was it for himself or for her that he kept pretending everything was all right?

Although summer had come, Vanessa didn't even ask if they could go to Truro, as they had every summer weekend for so many years.

Isabelle asked, though. To her, Finn replied that he had rented out the Truro cottage for some additional income. But even with Isabelle he didn't share the complete truth—that he had bartered the summer-long Cape rental to Jeremy Carlyle, the president of the bank that held his mortgages, in exchange for three months of interest payments he couldn't make. Come September, Finn didn't know what he was going to do.

But why had Vanessa not asked to go to Truro?

Isabelle provided him with an incomplete answer when she replied, "It's probably for best. Vanessa gets little bit anxious when she thinks she must leave house."

"Not *every* time, right? Just . . . sometimes?"

Isabelle shrugged. "She doesn't leave house."

"You mean, like ever?" said Finn.

"I mean, like ever," said Isabelle.

To help them cope without Cape Cod, the summer was terrible. It was cold and it rained. Sometime in July, when the weather abated for a weekend, the family got together, for the first time since Christmas. It was almost like old times, except Walter walked with a cane, looked older and talked slower. They sat out on the balcony; Walter had a hard time going down the stairs into the garden. Loretta brought them some finger sandwiches, and the only thing Lucy said was, "You still have a maid?"

"Of course. Why wouldn't we?" said Vanessa.

Lucy, without even a hint of side-eye at either her husband or Finn, said, "Yes, yes, it's a big house."

Eleanor hadn't heard from Adder. Vanessa, sipping a mint julep, said it was great the way they were making small talk; she missed it. A frowning Eleanor said, "Vanessa, talking about my husband vanishing off the earth and abandoning me and my son is not small talk. What's *wrong* with you?"

Vanessa apologized for her poor choice of words, but Finn could tell that she was struggling to remember why Adder had run off in the first place.

"Poor Monty. It must be terrible for him to live without a father," Vanessa said in commiseration. It was hard to tell how Monty felt. He was still throwing temper tantrums. Eleanor was still jumping up at his every whine. Little had changed.

"How is your Ukrainian girl?" Walter asked. "Is she still with you?"

"Oh, yes," Vanessa said. "Wreaking havoc on books but still with us."

"And her English?"

"Improving," Vanessa said, her lips tight. "Could be a lot better, frankly. She hasn't learned the alphabet."

"Where is she? We'd like to say hello."

"She's with the children, Daddy, I don't want to—"

"Well, ask her to come outside. We'd like to see our grandchildren, too."

Isabelle and the girls came out on the balcony all dressed and smiling, like it was just another summer Sunday in Beacon Hill, and the lantanas were blooming.

"Hello, Isabelle," said Olivia. "Aren't you looking lovely today." Finn's mother frequently came to visit the grandchildren, so she was well aware what Isabelle looked like.

"Yes, yes," Walter said, unable to hide his surprise at the serene, graceful statuesque beauty standing in front of him. He glanced at Earl and then at Finn, who watched his father-in-law with amusement. "Very nice to see you again, Isabelle. You've been well, then? You look, um, well."

"Thank you, Mr. Adams."

"Oh, please, my dear, call me Walter." He cleared his throat and grabbed his drink, turning to Finn. "Isabelle is so reserved. Is something wrong?"

"What could be wrong?" Vanessa said. "She's got it made in the shade."

"She is always reserved," Finn said. "Keeps herself in check. But, Walter, ask her if something is wrong. She's standing right in front of you."

Isabelle wore a bright cornflower-blue dress, and her growing-out honey hair was arranged in a bob pinned together with colorful ribbons.

"She has gained weight," Eleanor said critically.

"You mean she doesn't look half starved?" said Finn, his narrowed eyes studying Isabelle approvingly over the rim of his delicious mint julep. She had poured in a little bit of extra goodness for him from the flask she got from Schumann. It made the get-together so much more bearable. Isabelle indeed looked quite healthy lately, even though the summer had been awful. The summer dresses flattered her with their soft, pliant fabric.

"Is everything all right, Isabelle?" Walter said.

"You heard Vanessa," Isabelle replied. "*I have it made in the shade.*"

Walter smiled. "I see you're still a good mimic. You're speaking English wonderfully. What an improvement."

"Thank you, Walter," said Isabelle. "I'm sure if you lived in Ukraine for year, you would speak my language well, too."

"Oh, I don't think so," said Walter. "I'm terrible at languages."

"So, you're with the children full-time now?" Lucy asked.

"Yes," Isabelle said. "Except when I help Finn at bank."

"She helps you at the bank, Finn?"

"Yes, she's my girl Friday," Finn said.

"And that makes you Robinson Crusoe, darling?" said Vanessa, cheerful and smiling.

"That's me," Finn said. "Shipwrecked."

Vanessa stopped smiling.

So did Isabelle.

"What does she do for you, Finn?" Eleanor asked.

"Anything Finn needs, I do," Isabelle replied. "I bring food, I clean up, I file. I replace ticket tape."

"*Ticker*," said Finn. "Yes, Isabelle files, but in Ukrainian, so Lionel and I can never find anything."

"That might explain why my books are not alphabetized either," said Vanessa.

"You don't have anyone else to do your filing, Finn?" Walter asked. "What happened to Myrtle?"

Finn stretched out a smile. "Just trying to maximize efficiency, Walter."

"Finn, and . . . how *are* things . . . going," Walter asked, "at the bank?" He asked so tentatively, as if the last thing he wanted to hear was the truth.

And Finn obliged. He told Walter what he wanted to hear. "Can't complain. Things are improving, Walter."

"Just like Secretary Mellon said they would!" a relieved-looking Walter exclaimed.

"Yes," Finn said, purposely keeping his gaze away from Isabelle's. "Just like Secretary Mellon said they would."

30

The Black Beast

Ukraine, April 1929

"You are being indicted," Zhuk said to Roman, sitting behind a desk as if he were a one-man tribunal, while Roman stood in front of him, feet apart, arms locked behind his back.

"Indicted for what?"

"Agitation against the Soviet Government," Zhuk said. "For your ceaseless though unsuccessful efforts to undermine the Communist Party. And, most importantly, for your insufferable campaign in advancement of Ukrainian nationalism."

"But what did I actually *do*?" Roman said. "What specific crime am I being charged with?"

"I just told you."

"No, you gave me party slogans," Roman said. "You haven't cited a single specific instance of my wrongdoing. I have given you most of my farm to cultivate. I have agreed to work for you, nearly for free. I have begun an organization specifically to eliminate the very elements of our Ukrainian agricultural life you find most abhorrent—the successful farmer you call *kulak*. Unlike most other farmers, my family and I show up at your meetings to support your goals. We even started to develop chickens that might produce more than one egg a day. I mean, the project is still in the egg phase, but there's hope for next year."

"Next year will be too late for you, Comrade Lazar."

"Yes, too late seems to come rather early these days," Roman said. "But as with all farm life—the grain, the planting, the tilling, the breeding, the milking—the raising of new, more productive Soviet chicks requires patience, Comrade Zhuk. It requires perseverance. Are my efforts to help you achieve your aims considered sabotage just because we have not waited the necessary time to see results?"

Roman managed to talk himself out of arrest and indictment, despite Potapov's murder. He bought himself and his family some time. Perhaps it was because he'd been in custody when Potapov was killed; even Zhuk could not pin on Roman what Roman clearly could not have done.

"We're just giving you rope to hang yourself with, comrade," said Efros when he released him. "One way or another, we will determine if you had anything to do with Comrade Potapov's unfortunate demise."

Roman mock-saluted him. "As always, my full support for *all* your endeavors, Comrade Efros."

"Roman," Petka said when Isabelle's brother returned home, and the family gathered to assess their situation, "this is insane. You know the farm can't deliver what you promised Zhuk."

"I know," said Roman. "They also know what they're asking for is impossible. The private farm can't deliver it, and the collective won't deliver it either. You think just because you work on a farm owned by the state that you'll escape punishment when you fail to deliver their grain? We're all just buying time, Petka."

Petka disagreed. He thought the collective would offer them more security.

"Shame you forgot the meeting where they ordered me to find a way to foal my mares more than once a year," Roman said. "If they can demand this, they can demand anything. And punish me for anything."

Petka continued to insist on his preference for Soviet protection, not Roman's. "Collectivization is inevitable," he said. "There is no use fighting it."

"Said only by a man who doesn't own his land," said Roman. "Collectivization will come at too high a cost for Ukraine, for Ispas, and for us. And that includes you too, Petka, you *and* your family. And the quota will still be unmet. It wasn't met during the Civil War. Famine, burning farms, slaughtered livestock, murdered farmers." Roman ground his teeth. "It's not going to be met now."

"Said only by a man who refuses to grow up," Petka said. "There is no way out. Stalin is not going to let you keep your private farm. It's anathema to everything he believes. A Communist country created specifically to live under socialist ideals cannot be fed by large, privately owned, economically efficient, successful farms! Who is being naïve here? That's an impossibility Stalin will never allow. He will take the farm from you. Why fight it?"

Roman leaned forward across the table. "Why are you doing their bidding for them, Petka?" he asked, omens of evil in his voice.

"Why are you fighting a battle you can't win?" said Petka.

Roman threaded his hands behind his head. "So, off you go. Go join their collective. What's stopping you? Oh yes, that's right. You have nothing but your cow to yield to them. So, what you're really saying is you want *me* to join their collective."

"Yes! Of course that's what I'm saying. Do it for all of us."

"Petka, your childlike gullibility would be endearing if it weren't so dangerous," Roman said. "Over and over you keep proving to me that it's easier to fool a man than to prove to him he has been fooled. You think Zhuk will take care of you? You're adorable. Two months ago Efros took half of what little provisions we had. He seized our grain and didn't pay us for the theft! Zhuk promised my sister he would pay us. Where is our money?"

Petka, omens of evil in his own voice, said, "They didn't take even half of our provisions, did they, Roman?"

After last summer's poor harvest, when everyone in Ispas knew there wouldn't be enough to feed their families for the winter, much less to give to the likes of Efros and Zhuk, the Lazars dug graves for their few bushels of grain, wrapped them in plastic to protect against moisture, the killer of sown crops, and buried them underground. They buried their potatoes and radishes and carrots, too, in root clamps: holes in the earth, covered with hay. They couldn't bury their chickens or horses. But they buried everything else.

Every person on the farm helped hide the provisions. Including Petka.

Roman sat back in his chair and leveled a piercing stare at Petka, tall, jittery, self-righteous, and said nothing.

But after Petka retreated to his hut, Roman confronted Mirik and Isabelle.

"I'm going to give you my prognosis on your brother," Roman told Mirik. "It's bleak. It's bleaker than my prognosis on the harvest because the danger from Petka is more immediate."

"It's going to be fine," said Mirik. "You Lazars love to overreact. It's what got us into this mess to begin with."

"Yes, blame the Tsar for getting his family slaughtered," said Roman, his tone disgusted and scornful. "But tell me, Mirik, the husband of my sister, the father of my sister's children, what are we going to do when your brother turns informer and betrays us because he thinks it will save his hide?"

"I don't know, Roman," said Mirik, disgusted himself. "I suppose you'll try to deal with it like a Lazar, and I'll deal with it like a Kovalenko."

"I can't wait to see how a Kovalenko handles the exposed heart of a black beast," said Roman.

31

Black Days

Finn's customer base was shrinking month by month, week by week, day by day. In October 1929, Adams Bank had boasted 4980 accounts. They had been so close to 5000! They'd been planning to celebrate with a $25 bonus to all their customers. But then October happened. And by January 1930, the number of accounts dropped below 2700. By March, they were down to 1540, and by July to 982. Most of their small depositors were gone. The very people Finn had tried to help when he first started out in 1921 had closed their accounts. The bank's larger commercial accounts were constantly late on their payments, which meant Finn couldn't make his own payments. John Reade was never heard from again after he took what remained of the three-million-dollar line of credit for his property developments. Perhaps he was in Argentina with Adder, living it up.

Last year, Adams Bank had owned thirty commercial buildings and warehouses around Boston. They sold most of them to pay their debts and were now down to four. But the leases on the last four kept getting cancelled or broken or behind on payments. Before the Crash, they had four hundred personal home mortgages in their inventory. By the summer of 1930, half of those had defaulted. Half of the rest were over three months in arrears. The uncollateralized loans were in default almost to the one. There were a few new mortgages for small private homes, and a handful of new accounts each month, most of them checking, not savings, and all by people who immediately applied for overdraft lines in return. Every week Finn's dwindling customers kept applying for an unsecured loan or a refinancing on their house. Every week someone needed money for a funeral or medical expenses.

Nearly all the people who were applying for loans were themselves out of work, or had their hours cut, or their wages halved. In other words, all of them were a bad risk. Finn could lend them money, and sometimes did, but he knew there was a good chance it would not be repaid.

As the average American, one by one, hundred by hundred, million by million, kept losing his job, his car, his home, and sliding into default, so the bank's assets, one by one, dozen by dozen, hundred by hundred, kept sliding into default also. Finn and Lionel sat together and tried to wade through the debts and liabilities. How could Finn make any money if he was afraid to risk even a dollar on a dubious loan? How could he service the bank's debt if he couldn't get paid on the money he had lent out? These were the nightly questions they faced as he and Lionel desperately sought a way to stave off the inevitable sinking of the *Titanic*, not over one night, but over two hundred nights like a shallow drowning.

"Lionel," Finn said dejectedly as they commiserated one evening, licking their wounds, lamenting the cratering of their business, "did you hear that Joe Smith offered my father-in-law two hundred dollars for his horse?"

"But, Finn, Joe Smith don't have two hundred dollars!"

"I know, but ain't it a good offer?"

They almost laughed as they drank the last of their whisky, tipping the bottle over to drain every last drop.

32

Red Lantern

In September 1930, facing another enormous interest payment he couldn't make and six months in arrears on all the rest, Finn went to see Sullivan Murphy, the one-eyed chap who ran the Red Lantern in an alley off Hanover Street. Sully had more than just that one juice joint. He owned dozens of saloons from New Hampshire to Connecticut, most of them close to the water for easier transportation and delivery. Finn had been coming to the Red Lantern for nearly a decade, and he used to drink here with Lucas. It caused a rift in his marriage. Vanessa didn't care for either the drinking or for Lucas, but mostly she didn't care for how it would look if a vice-president of her father's bank was seen or, God forbid, arrested in one of those places.

In the summer of 1929, when Finn broke his friendship with Lucas, he stopped showing his face at the Red Lantern. It was a shame, because Finn liked spending an hour inside, and he liked Sully. In 1926, he extended to Sully an emergency infusion of cash. Sully said he would never forget the favor.

Finn hated to do it, but it was time to call on old Sully to see if the bootlegger was a man of his word.

"Finn! How have you been?" The man was happy to see him.

"I've been all right, Sully. How have *you* been? Business percolating?"

"Uh-oh. Things must *really* be in the soup if the great Finn Evans is telling me he is just all right. Cormac! Two doubles for me and my troubled friend."

They sat together at a corner table, clinked, and swallowed their whisky. They ordered more, drank again, chewed the fat for a while. "I'm glad to see you here, Finn," Sully said, "but I know you didn't come to shoot the breeze with me. What brings you?" He paused, a beaten but undefeated man with a bulbous nose and a black patch over his missing eye that was shot out in 1926 during a rum delivery gone wrong. "You need help?"

"Desperately," Finn said.

"How much?"

Finn told him. Sully didn't bat an eyelash on his one eye. He didn't even whistle.

"Look," Sully said, "it's not about the money."

"It is about the money, Sully."

"I can give it to you right now. You can walk out with what you need. That's not my problem. But how do you intend to pay me back?"

"The bank is not going to be in dire straits forever," Finn said.

"No? Look around you," said Sully. "Walk down the street. Have you seen the soup lines? Have you seen the Hoovervilles? And it's getting cold again. People are struggling mightily, and soon they're gonna freeze. Where's relief gonna come from? Unless something changes, nothing's gonna change."

Finn cracked his knuckles. "How long can this possibly continue?"

Sully shrugged. "Till we get a new president? Till we get another war? All the signs point to nothing but more misery." He lit a cigarette and offered one to Finn. "As long as Prohibition continues, it's no nevermind to me. But the rest of you poor bastards out there?" Sully clicked his tongue, clearly not optimistic about the poor bastards' chances.

Finn stared into his empty drink.

"You're a banker," Sully said. "I know you understand."

Finn did.

"If I loan you money, how will you repay me? Tell me. I don't want to send my collectors after you, Finn. I like you too much for that. I want no bad blood between us. You did me a solid when I was down, and I ain't gonna forget it when times are tough for you. But you see my predicament, don't you?"

Finn didn't answer. He didn't have an answer. Sully was right.

Now it was Sully's turn to study Finn. "I got an idea," the bootlegger said. "I need a job done. A job that requires a man like you. But it requires some of your other skills too, the ones you put away after you went to work for your wife's father the banker. Remember those skills? I need them."

"Sully, no."

"It's not bad. Nothing too stressful. A little time, a little muscle."

"I can't drive a rumrunner boat for you again, Sully."

"Can you drive a truck?" said Sully. "I got a thousand cases of hooch on the Vermont–Canada border and I've been waiting six months for a reliable set of hands to get it down to me. Someone I can trust. Like you. Now, contingent on what else you get going as cover for the booze in whatever truck you find, I'd say a minimum of four trips will be required. You can't get a truck close to the booze; it's stashed in a house in the middle of the woods. You'll have to carry the cases to the truck. So it's not a small job. I figure you'll need at least three of you. I leave the execution part to you. You bring me my thousand cases, I pay you fifty grand. A hundred cases at a time? I give you five thousand per load. Divide and conquer how you see best. Drive up, assess the situation, bring me what you can, I pay you for what you deliver, and we go from there."

"Are you suggesting I take Lucas for this?"

"I leave that part also to you," said Sully. "I like that boy, but . . ." The bootlegger shook his head. "He's been begging me for driving work, but that child cannot drive a truck filled with rum. He can barely ride a bicycle. I feel bad for the fella. What else am I going to give him to do? He can't be my enforcer. He can't be my barback. He can't be added muscle—he can't kill a fly. I've been giving him a few pennies here and there, but Lord, talk about chasing your losses! He can't repay nothing ever. He means well, I give him that. What are you shaking your head for?"

Finn looked down into his glass. "I'm gonna need more of this."

Sully motioned to Cormac, asked him to leave the bottle of whisky on the table. Finn poured and drank, poured and drank.

"I'm going to be honest," Sully said. "Lucas is entirely unreliable. He can be bought with a bottle, and no man who can be bought with a bottle can be counted on in any situation."

"Do you want me to take him?"

"You do what you want. I just want my liquor."

"There's no way this ends well, Sully," Finn said.

"You're telling me like I don't know," Sully said. "But I'm not a banker or a bricklayer. I got no other jobs for that man-child—or for you, Finn—other than rum-related work."

"I need to save my father-in-law's bank, Sully," Finn said.

"With bootleg cash?"

"Whichever way I can." Finn rolled the idea around in his head. A thousand cases of whisky! From Canada to Boston!

"I need a hundred percent success rate on this," Sully said. "It's been tough out there. If I tell you I'll accept five hundred cases, you can be sure I'm going to get only half of that. And that ain't a good return on investment for me. So, what do you say, will you help me out, like before?"

Back in '21, Finn was finishing his degree and gambling a bit. He'd lost more money on poker than he cared to admit and agreed to help Sully by padding the muscle numbers during a rum run. The difference was, in 1921, the Feds were still years away from fully understanding what it was they had unleashed with their Volstead Act. They didn't have the men or the funds or the breadth or the width of their current enforcement operation. There had been no one on the water to stop Finn and his men or to search the boat. To pay off his gambling debt, Finn went on five runs up to Nova Scotia. He brought weapons, but there wasn't a hint of trouble for a hundred miles. It was the easiest eight grand he ever made, but after he repaid it, he swore off gambling for good. He chose a different path for himself, married Vanessa, had children, put on a three-piece suit and went to work like the respectable man his father the judge raised him to be.

"Different times back then," Finn said. "Different men. Different needs."

"No, the needs are the same," Sully said. "Nothing's changed."

Why did that make Finn feel even worse? Ten years of life and nothing had changed.

He agreed to Sully's terms. When you had only one option, you took it.

33

Four Trips and One Dream

Lucas was inappropriately overjoyed when Finn reached out to him.

"I'm doing this to help myself, Lucas," Finn said.

"Okay, mate," Lucas said. "But to help me, too, a little bit, right?"

"I need you to get us keys to the coal truck you sometimes drive," Finn said. "Can you do that?"

"Of course. Anything for you, mate, anything."

"Just the truck, Lucas."

"And to come with you and help you, right? That too?"

"I guess so."

Finn asked Lionel if he wanted to make a little bit on the side. He told Lionel about the job, and he said yes instantly. Babs was pregnant, and they needed a bigger apartment. "But what do you plan to do about Isabelle?" Lionel said.

"Isabelle?" exclaimed Lucas. "Oh, she can come, too! We need a fourth."

"Don't be insane," Finn said. "What the hell is wrong with you?"

"She can handle herself, Finn, don't be deceived by her fragile exterior," Lucas said.

"I don't want to discuss it." Finn turned to Lionel. "What do you mean, what's my plan about Isabelle?"

"She brings you dinner every night," Lionel said. "How are you going to explain your absence to her?"

"Well, since we're going to be gone overnight, I'm going to have to explain a lot more to my wife than to Isabelle."

Lionel and Lucas both shrugged. "You can make your wife believe anything," Lionel said. "Isabelle is another story."

"If you tell her what's going on," said Lucas, "you won't have to lie, and she can cover for you with the missus."

"I swear to Christ," Finn said. "We haven't set a foot out of North End, and I'm already fed up to the gills with the both of you!"

***

Finn told Vanessa he had to be away for a few days to deal with a flooding problem at their Truro property. He said one of the neighbors had telephoned him at the bank to tell him there'd been some damage to the house. He needed to fix the problem immediately, and he was bringing Lionel to help with repairs. This was the story they told Babs also.

All the women believed it except Isabelle. Downstairs in the kitchen, she stood by the prep table with her arms crossed while Finn got himself some ginger ale and a slice of pound cake.

"Well, it's late," he said, brassing it out like it was any other evening.

"You off to Truro tomorrow, are you?" Isabelle said. No one, literally no one, could have sounded more skeptical.

"Yes," he said. "So don't bring dinner."

"Right," she said. "Because you in Truro."

He chewed silently.

"To fix house that has big flood."

He continued eating without a word.

"How you plan to get to this Cape Cod," she asked. "Lionel have car?"

Not a syllable from Finn.

"I know it can't be in your Packard," she continued, "because you sell that beautiful car."

The pound cake was really getting stuck in his throat. He washed it down with the soda pop.

"And it can't even be *your* house in Truro," said Isabelle, "because you sell that house few weeks ago to some man named Jeremy Carlyle."

"What can you *possibly* know about that!" Finn exclaimed.

"I see transfer of ownership papers on your desk when I clean."

He put his plate and glass into the sink and wiped his mouth.

"So where you Three Stooges really going?" said Isabelle.

"Goodnight, Isabelle."

It was a five-hour drive to the spot on the border of Vermont and Canada where the abandoned cabin was located, deep in the woods a few miles off-road from a tiny town called North Troy. The directions Sully had given him were as obscure as a tangram. *At the village, take the third road on the left after the second large rock near a half-dead pine tree. Count the roads only after the second rock near a half-dead tree, not the first. The first is there to throw the agents off the scent if you're being followed. Take the third road, which has no name, it's just wide enough for one truck. Take that road four miles north, then make a quick zigzag to the right, and take that road three miles farther north. By this time, you will have crossed the border, but you'll be in the woods, and there won't be any roads or markers. There'll be nothing to guide you but precise counting. After three miles, make a left. Don't worry if there is no visible path. Just count three miles and make that left. Unless it's raining or has rained in the last twenty-four hours. If yes, then you must make a right not a left and go two miles around, or you'll get stuck in the swamp and won't be able to get out until the mud either dries or freezes. Let's pray for perfect weather. If weather is dry, make that left and drive another three-quarters of a mile. Park your truck in the woods, there should be a clearing, but either way, park after three-quarters of a mile and walk north through the forest, forty yards, and you will see the cabin. Bring flashlights, because it's pitch black at night if there's no moon and you won't see a thing. The whisky has been sitting in the house for months awaiting pick-up. Gird your loins because you'll have to carry it through the woods, case by case.*

"You want us to carry a thousand cases of liquor forty yards through the woods?" Finn said to Sully.

"I told you, you'll have to make the trip a few times," Sully said. "A big truck won't fit in the clearing. Lucas's coal truck will fit two hundred cases at most."

"More trips increase our chances of being stopped," said Finn.

"Yes, and if you lose my liquor, you won't get paid. So don't get stopped is my suggestion," said Sully.

They couldn't decide if they should drive at night or during the day. On the one hand, the agents manning the roads were likely asleep at night. On the other, a truck barreling down the road at four in the morning when all God-fearing people should be in their beds would raise nothing but suspicion in any state trooper who just happened to be passing by.

It stank every way you looked at it; Finn felt it in his gut.

"Sully, I can't imagine you've had success not getting caught," Finn said. "Where are the guys who usually do this for you?"

"In jail," Sully said. "Rumrunning is a dangerous business, Evans. But it has many rewards. Like fifty thousand dollars, plus another ten for your friends. The liquor that's been collecting dust in the woods is worth half a million to me."

Sully advanced Finn a few thousand off the first run, and Finn paid Lionel two and a half thousand dollars before they left—half of his total share—so Babs had at least some of the money, no matter what happened. Finn didn't give Lucas any because he'd never see Lucas again if he did.

"Before we go," Lucas said, "can we talk about the thing between us?"

"Nope," said Finn.

"It's my name, isn't it? You're upset by my Irish name."
"Remember I just said I didn't want to talk about it? Literally just now."
"You and I were such good friends . . ."
"Go home, Lucas. We have a big day tomorrow." They were borrowing the truck from the depot of the Coal and Coke company. Finn didn't want to talk about anything, didn't even want to look at Lucas. Couldn't look at him.

"You haven't spoke to me. Ever since that night in July we was leaving the Red Lantern and Rodney called out to me."

"No, Lucas."

"I didn't keep it from you, Finn. Honest, I just . . ."

"Go, Lucas."

Rodney had said nothing important. It was so trivial, yet the earth had shifted under Finn's feet, and nothing had been all right since. Just after that, Isabelle had come into his life. And two months later, the bottom fell out from under him—he feared for good.

"What up, McBride!" Rodney had shouted to Lucas. "Don't tell me they let the likes of you inside the Red Lantern!"

What up, McBride!

Finn had turned to Lucas that hot July evening. He stared into Lucas's jolly, inebriated face. "You're Lucas *McBride*?" Finn said in a dull voice.

"Yeah, what of it?" But something had clicked in Lucas, some forgotten instruction perhaps, the realization that he was admitting something he wasn't supposed to. He frowned and clammed up. Finn saw it all.

"Are you related by any chance to a Travis?" Finn swallowed. "Travis *McBride*?"

"I don't know no Travis," Lucas mumbled. "There's so many of us McBrides around. I know at least twenty."

"All related to you?"

"No, none is my family."

"Not even your mother or father?"

"I don't know my dear old dad from the hobo over there. Tadhg McBride's been missing since before I was born. And I don't know no Travis." Even as Lucas was saying it, drunken tears sprang to his eyes.

"Are you *sure* you don't know him?" Finn said.

No man tried harder to suppress his emotion than Lucas did at that moment. "I don't know no Travis," he repeated with a sob, and ran off as fast as his sloshed feet could carry him.

The following evening at five, Finn, Lionel, and Lucas met at the Coal and Coke truck depot. The lot was in East Boston, a dot in the spread of warehouses and yards that littered the industrial and commercial waterfront in that part of town. It was a cold October night. Finn drove without stopping to North Troy. By the time they got to northern Vermont, it was nearing ten.

They made their way down the roads, past the rocks and the half-dead trees, through the woods and on foot for the last forty yards, and got to the hut by eleven. It was time to lie down and sleep, not haul 250 cases of whisky through a dense forest at night. The hand truck they'd brought was inadequate to wheel through the brush. The wheels kept getting stuck and the cases kept falling over. They ended up using the coal cart, and awkwardly fitting two or three cases at a time, with two men rolling it through the woods while the third man lit the way.

It took them five arduous debilitating hours to load 230 cases into the truck. They could've loaded more but they would've had to leave the coal cart. Finn didn't want to do that. If the coal cart was found missing, Lucas would be blamed, and Lucas had enough trouble.

They finally started back at five in the morning, just as the sky was turning blue. There was no one on the country roads, and by the time they got to Massachusetts around ten in the morning, they got mixed in with other traffic and no one paid them any attention.

After they left the truck heavy at the coal depot, parked next to a hundred other trucks exactly like it, they went their separate ways.

Everything on Finn's body hurt like he'd been moving cases of liquor all night. He couldn't bend or straighten. He also couldn't go home; Vanessa would go into cardiac arrest seeing him in his inexplicable condition. Finn went to the bank, put up a sign on the door that said, CLOSED FOR A BANK HOLIDAY, lay down on the cot in the back, pulled a thin blanket over himself, and was asleep instantly.

And when he slept he dreamed.

He is in Jordan Marsh picking out a silk robe on a table full of silk robes in the middle of the women's lingerie department. Shoppers are everywhere. It's daytime and lunch hour. There are so many robes, wine, red, maroon, burgundy. He is looking for a cream one, a light one, and there is one underneath all the others, at the very bottom. He's happy to find it. He clears away the rest, and under them finds not a robe but Isabelle, naked, and on her back, splayed out in front of him. She whispers something in a foreign language that sounds like my kohanyi *and he leans over her because he can't hear her and doesn't understand. He kisses her. His hand travels up her colt-like legs. She pushes his head down to her stomach.* Laska, *she murmurs. She is dripping wet like she has just gotten out of the bath, her body reflecting light from Jordan Marsh's high ceilings.*

"Right here?" he says, gripping her hips with his hands.

"Tak."

He lowers his head to her and she moans. Tak tak tak. He unbuckles his suit pants, takes off his jacket, unbuttons his waistcoat.

Sliding her hips toward him, he enters her, and he makes a sound and she makes a sound.

The shopping floor is filled with people, milling milling milling, but no one pays him any attention except her. Someone is near his elbow, but Finn can't look away from her face and her breasts, can't look away from what he is doing, what he can see, he can't stop moving and doesn't want to, can't finish and doesn't want to.

Excuse me, a shopper next to him says, I need the robe underneath her. Do you mind? I need a pink medium.

He ignores her. Isabelle pulls him toward her, over her.

Isabelle, he whispers, is it good? He gets more and more insistent.

Tak, tak, tak. She moans. And he moans.

But the shopper by his elbow won't stop tugging the pink silk robe from under them!

Excuse me, she keeps saying as she taps on Finn's arm like an aggravating woodpecker, excuse me . . .

"Fuck!" Finn exclaimed—and opened his eyes. Isabelle was over him, tapping on his arm.

"Excuse me?" she said.

He sat up, mortified, confused, half-asleep—and intensely unfinished in his waking state. He wouldn't look at her. He couldn't look at her! What was happening? That wasn't fair, that wasn't nice.

Yet so nice.

But so not fair.

"*What?*" He rubbed his eyes. "I mean, yes?"

"I have questions," she said.

Don't we all. "What do you need?"

"You sound like you had bad dream," she said. "You were thrashing side to side, groaning."

He grunted without reply.

"Why you sleeping middle of day?" she said, appraising his muddy boots by the door, studying his dirt-covered shirt, the twigs in the winter coat hanging over the back of the chair. His dinner was in her hands.

"What time is it?" he asked, still trying to shake himself awake, sadly, to rid himself of the traces of the dream, sadly. His body was sore—and throbbing.

"After seven," she said. "I brought food. You want?"

He ate sluggishly while she watched him.

"Lucas is outside," she said.

"Great."

"And why sign in window say bank closed?"

"We didn't get back till this morning."

"Working all night on flood in Truro?" Isabelle said. "Well, what other time to fix water damages, right?"

He set down the half-finished plate. Everything was only half-finished. "Please send in Lucas. You go on home. Tell Vanessa everything is fine."

"You cannot lift spoon to your mouth," said Isabelle. "You bending your face to bowl like horse to water. Is that fine?"

The image of bending his face to her bare stomach was still vivid in his eyes and in his loins.

"You want me to feed you?" she said. "Bring spoon to your mouth?"

"Take your bowl and spoon and go. Tell Vanessa I'll be back soon."

"How you gonna explain you paralyzed all of sudden?" she said. "Yesterday morning you normal, today evening you can't move your body."

He could move his body. He moved it quite successfully in Jordan Marsh. "Let's not keep Lucas waiting, shall we?" Finn said.

"You ignore that man for year, now you don't want him to wait five minutes while you explain things?"

"That is *tochno* correct. Because there's nothing to explain."

"Then why you not looking at me when you speak to me?"

"I don't know what you mean."

"You talk to me like you guilty." She folded her arms.

He forced himself to meet her questioning gaze. "See?" he said. "It's fine. Go get Lucas."

Shaking her head, Isabelle left and returned with Lucas who limped inside and slowly lowered himself into a chair, creaking and groaning.

"How was Truro, Lucas?" she asked.

"Where—"

"*Isabelle!*" Finn cut in. "That'll be all, thank you. Wait—one more thing." She turned around.

"How do you say yes in your language?"

"*Tak*," said Isabelle. "Why?"

He stared at her. She stared at him. "No reason," said Finn. *I had a dream that you were mine.* "Goodnight."

Sully was the happiest bootlegger in North End when his men unloaded the truck later that evening. Sully paid out Lionel and Lucas, and gave Finn an extra two and a half grand as a bonus, making Finn's total take for one trip an even twenty thousand dollars. That was an astonishing amount of money for less than two days' work. After Finn paid off just enough to keep the lights on and prevent his loans from sliding into default, he wondered if perhaps he wasn't in the wrong business.

A week later, after telling Vanessa he'd found some extra work doing the graveyard shift on the loading docks ("Nothing to worry about, darling, just for the holidays"), Finn, Lucas, and Lionel returned to North Troy. This time, things went a little faster. Their bodies were less sore; they left at four pm instead of five, and got to the cabin just after nine. They loaded and unloaded in five hours, got back on the road by three and were back at the depot in East Boston by eight. Finn brought a change of clothes, and only needed to sleep until noon—without flagrantly inappropriate though exquisite dreams.

Together with Lionel, he called in a few delinquent loans, wrote off some others, paid a few bills, checked the ailing stock market, and closed by five. Sully gave Finn another fifteen thousand dollars. Finn paid Lionel, gave a few hundred dollars to Lucas, they all had a double whisky, and Finn was home for dinner, shocking his wife and children, who were not only startled by his early arrival but also by his jubilant mood. He couldn't explain it except to say that a little extra money for the holidays was going to make all the difference. Vanessa said, how much could you possibly make working as a dockhand, and Finn almost said sixty thousand dollars but didn't.

Four days later, the men drove north for the third time, this time on a Saturday night. Finn reasoned and Lionel agreed that it was better for the bank to stay open as much as possible during their busiest holiday season. On the way to North Troy, they discussed hiring a few extra tellers for December and taking out some ads for the bank, hoping to attract new business. They talked about rolling over some of the bank's depleted assets into new investment opportunities and applying again for a Federal Reserve loan to pay down some of their enormous liabilities so they could make a fresh start in the new year. The five-hour drive flew by amid their hopeful chatter.

But in North Troy it snowed.

The boys didn't recognize the town. All the markers were covered in white. The half-dead pines looked just like the alive pines, no rocks of any size were visible, and none of the roads had been plowed. There was no way to get the truck into the woods until the snow melted. And it was still snowing!

They pulled into a lot at a roadside cafe and sat glumly in the truck deciding what to do. A sheriff's patrol car pulled alongside them, and an overeager young officer stepped up, wanting to know why a coal truck with Massachusetts plates had been idling for over an hour. He asked Finn what address they were delivering coal to. Finn had no good answers. The cop asked to see his bill of lading. When Finn couldn't produce it, he ordered him to get going. "If I see your truck on the road again without a destination point, I'm going to assume you gentlemen are up to no good."

Finn had no choice but to drive back to Boston. His triumphant mood had evaporated. He told Sully they couldn't risk borrowing the same Coke and Coal truck again. In North Troy, a town of barely fifteen hundred people, it was now too recognizable.

After Thanksgiving, Sully managed to finagle from a friend an innocent-looking Vermont Maple Syrup Company truck with a bill of lading and even a few cases of Vermont's finest as decoy. Finn, Lucas, and Lionel set out for the fourth time.

But they didn't want to make the mistake again of not checking on the weather before they left. Finn first made Isabelle promise she wouldn't ask him any follow-up questions and then had her call the North Troy Village Hall to inquire about the snow conditions. In a Southern drawl, she said to the clerk who picked up the phone, "Hi there, I'm plannin' to visit my sick mama who live in North Troy just off Pike Booleyvard, but she don't have no phone, and I's wonderin' how the weather's up there before I commit to a thirty-hour drive north." The woman on the phone assured Isabelle the snow had melted, and though it was freezing, the roads were clear. She said, "Hey, if you give me your mother's address I can check on her for you on my way home. I don't live too far from there, I can tell her you're on your way."

Isabelle had to hang up quick. "Aww, that nice lady was going to check on my mama," she said to Finn. "What's in North Troy?"

"Nope," he said. "You promised."

In North Troy, it had gotten much colder over the course of November, and Finn's hands were nearly frostbitten, even in his work gloves, as they carried the 250 cases to the truck. Lamenting the absence of the coal cart, they had to use a smaller hand cart, and the job took eight hours instead of five.

By the time they left North Troy, it was mid-morning. Lucas and Lionel needed to take over driving for an hour or two so that Finn, who had driven all the way north, could sleep. But instead, Lucas broke open a bottle of whisky, and he and Lionel drank themselves into a stupor. They told Finn to pull over if he needed a nap. But Finn, unwilling to take the risk of being confronted by police again, decided to plow on through.

Three hours in, as they entered Massachusetts, Finn fell asleep at the wheel. The truck veered off the road and crashed into some snowy bushes.

No one was hurt, but all three men were needed to push the truck out. Instead, Lionel and Lucas were stewed to the gills. Finn closed his eyes, cursing alcohol, Sully, the stock market, Lionel, and especially Lucas.

He was roused by state troopers. The cases of maple syrup passed muster during a routine inspection of the cargo, and the cops were about to help Finn push the truck out into the road when they glanced inside the cab. They saw Lucas passed out drunk and Lionel slumped next to him, muttering, "It wasn't me, it wasn't me, it wasn't me." They both reeked of alcohol, and it was difficult to convince the Massachusetts highway police that Finn's compatriots were hopped up on maple syrup.

This time, the cops searched the truck a little more thoroughly. Finn tried to claim he had no idea the Vermont Maple Syrup Company was putting him in such jeopardy by having him transport whisky instead of maple syrup. Unfortunately, the bill of lading for the syrup didn't stand up to even the most cursory scrutiny. For one, it was from 1927.

The three men were arrested, two of them not fully sober. In handcuffs, they were driven to Boston and booked. All the liquor was impounded, along with the borrowed truck. They spent the night in jail, with Lionel, now terrified and sober, apologizing over and over to an outraged Finn and praying loudly to God that if he got out of it, he would never *ever* touch alcohol again as long as he lived, which Finn thought was more than God would want from mortal man, especially in the current circumstances.

In the morning they were assigned a public defender and went before Finn's father, the Honorable Judge Earl Edward Evans on charges of transportation and possession of contraband liquor, of bootlegging, and of distribution and sale of illegal substances. The amount found in the truck was so excessive, it precluded any defense that the men were in possession of such quantities purely for personal use.

Earl set bail for his son and Lionel at $250, one dollar for each case of whisky, but for Lucas—who had several priors, including arrests for alcohol-related activity—the bail was a thousand dollars. Sully paid their bail but was furious that he'd not only lost a quarter of his liquor but also a truck that didn't belong to him.

"Why didn't you open fire?" Sully said to Finn. "Why'd you bring weapons if you weren't going to use them?"

"You wanted me to kill two Good Samaritan troopers for twelve thousand dollars?"

"For you it's twelve grand, but for me it's a hundred and fifty thousand," said Sully. "Now we're both in deep gin."

"You think *you're* in deep gin? I have to face my father!"

"You poor bastard," said Sully. "Listen, if you can figure out a way to get me the rest of it, I'll pay you. Round it up to an unlucky thirteen."

"Forget it, Sully," Finn said as he left. "We've run the last of the rumrunner's gauntlet."

Sully opened his hands. "Tough business we're in," the bootlegger called after him. "You're dead broke, and I need my fuckin' liquor."

34

Father and Son

Finn sat in his father's study on Hancock Street, glum like a scolded child.
"Finn, what were you thinking?" Earl said.
"I was thinking I needed the money."
"This isn't the worst of it," Earl said. "The DA wants to make an example of you three, even of you, who has no prior infractions! You know they're bearing down on the booze trade harder than ever."
"Ironic, since people need work more than ever," Finn said.
"Not illegal work."
"Any work they can get."
"Is this your plan for life now?"
"No, Father. It's my plan for November."
"Charges of bootlegging, and right before Christmas. Finn, you're a banker!"
Finn couldn't look at his father in his shame and his anger.
"You have so much to be thankful for," Earl went on. "Why would you want to throw it all away?"
Finn slumped in a chair next to the sofa where his father sat.
"Say something."
"Are you going to help me or not? It's just a misdemeanor."
"It's 250 cases of whisky! They want to fine each of you a hundred dollars per case and give you a week in jail times two fifty."
"Al Capone is still running loose in Chicago and they want to give me five years in jail?" Finn laughed.
"I'm going to do what I can," Earl said. "But that's not—"
"I'm not the only one who needs help. Lionel and Lucas too."
Earl's rigid body was disappointed, his limbs downcast. *Welcome to the club,* Finn wanted to say.
"Did Lucas get you into this mess?"
"No," Finn said. "I got *him* into it. I couldn't go alone, and I asked him and Lionel to come with me. I can't repay them with prison."

"Lucas has been courting prison for the better part of a decade."

"Not because of me."

Father and son stared at each other.

"It's not your fault he's got a record," Earl said.

"Or yours," said Finn.

"Mostly drunk and benign," Earl continued quickly, "but there've been fights, some ugly brawls; there's been stealing. There's been this too."

"I know."

"I'm going to have to stick my neck out," Earl said. "The DA is not going to be happy with me." Finn and Earl appraised each other for a pained moment. "Son, you have to consider the whole weight of your importance to your family. It's not just to overcome the present crisis, which I'm not denying is real and exists. But there's also the future. It can't be overlooked."

"Father, if I don't deal with my present crisis, there won't *be* a future."

"There won't be a future as you had once imagined, true."

"I read that in New York," Finn said, "eleven hundred men waiting in the soup line ambushed two bakery trucks and made off with their bread. That's one way to feed your family."

"Yes, but that way you will only feed them once. What about next week? And the next?"

"That's for future Finn to worry about," said Finn.

"Much like your present situation, eh?" When Finn didn't deny it, his father spoke again. "You didn't let me finish my earlier point," Earl said. "Your value to your family is based on three things. One is all the years you've already put in. Two is the things you are doing right now. And three is the things you are yet to do, the things you will do in the years to come. Your value to your family, who need you and love you and depend on you, is determined by all these factors. And if you get yourself into trouble that I can't get you out of and get sent to prison, you will have taken from your family both their present *and* their future. I'm begging you to consider your role in your life and to refrain from activities that will deprive you of the opportunity for renewal and rebirth."

"Father, you know that bootlegging and coming to you afterwards are both measures of last resort," Finn said. "That's how you know what terrible trouble I'm in. Because I'm here."

"I know, son," Earl said. "Last time you came to see me at home, your mother and I had to mortgage our house."

"I wish that selfless act on your part would have done us more good."

"It bought you a little time before you had to resort to crime," Earl said. "That's a measurable good."

Finn had nothing to say. Nothing positive, anyway.

"I worry that you didn't listen to me the last time we spoke about this," Earl said, "so I'm asking you to please listen to me now. Last October you came merely for my residence. But now you're coming for my livelihood, Finn. If I don't help you, you and your friends will face prison. But if I help you, I will damage my career. Defense counsel has filed ten motions today demanding my recusal on all matters of similar crimes, which make up 50 percent of the current cases in my court, and the DA, fearing I'm hurting his chances for convictions, is seconding those motions! I haven't even asked the DA to drop your charges yet and already, simply by your actions, you are making it difficult, if not impossible, for me to continue my work. Which I need to do to feed *my* family. Your mother needs to eat, no? Would you like me to join you on these bootlegging runs to Canada? I'm seventy-two, Finn; I don't think I'll be of much use."

Finn could not bring himself to respond.

"Son, listen to me," Earl said, reaching across and cupping his palm over Finn's lowered head. "You've always been a boy who's held himself responsible for everything. And I know you feel the weight of the entire catastrophe on your shoulders. I would agree with you if we were the only ones to suffer in last year's collapse. But since I personally know many families who have been made destitute, bankrupt, broke, and since I'm a man who can read the papers and thus can attest that millions of other families are suffering the same hardships as you, I can't blame you entirely for what happened. Could you have been more prudent? Maybe. But what you're doing now is compounding the misery. You might as well rob banks like Dillinger; what would be the difference?"

"Oh, I would in a flash," said Finn, "but there's hardly any point. All the banks are bust, too." He nearly broke down. "I don't know what to do, Dad," he said, putting his face into his hands. "I just can't keep it going."

"Keep what going?" Earl asked gently, his parental hand on Finn's back.

"All of it," Finn said, struggling to his feet. "Any of it."

35

Crocodile

Just after New Year 1931, Finn sat in the dining room of his house, his hands palms down on the polished table, and stared at the darkness outside. Isabelle came up from the kitchen to bring him a cup of tea and a sweet roll with butter. He ate while she perched nearby. She was already dressed and ready for the day, as was he, though it was still so early the sun hadn't come up. The rest of the house was asleep.

Finn was shaved, in his best suit.

"We don't have much coal left," Isabelle said. "There hasn't been delivery since Christmas and we almost out."

"Use less," Finn told her. He would get more soon.

"It's cold," she said. "And we still need to wash clothes. Wash children."

"How dirty do these children get?" he said, carefully replacing his cup on the saucer so it didn't clang.

"Yesterday your wife told me she doesn't know where you going so early and staying out so late. She worry you drinking again."

"Tell her not to worry," Finn said. "Though I'll admit, few things sound better right now than a drink. Let's see what the number one issue will be in the next campaign for president, joblessness or the lack of legal liquor."

He and Isabelle stared at each other. "All those poor people, out of work," she said.

"Yeah. Those poor people." Finn walked to the front hall. She followed him. He put on his coat, took his hat and an umbrella from the stand. He wondered how much they could get if they sold the Duchess grandfather clock that had been in Vanessa's family since 1800.

"Vanessa said to ask you to pick up her dresses from Schumann. She says you had six of her finest with him since November."

"Soon." He didn't look at Isabelle. "Oh, but that reminds me," he said.

"Vanessa asked *me* to ask *you* to please re-order the books the way they used to be, instead of the way they are now."

"What?"

Finn explained again.

"*This* is what you want to tell me?"

"That's what Vanessa wants done."

"Why didn't Vanessa say herself?" asked Isabelle. "She says things all time. Tell Finn this, tell Finn that."

"I don't know why. Just take care of it"—he rubbed the bridge of his nose—"so I don't have to."

Isabelle shook her head, clasped her hands together, and hardened her gaze. "No."

"Excuse me?"

"You heard me. *Ni*. You stand here drooping because you have too much to say, and real things, big things going on, and this is what you say? Are you hearing your own ears?"

"It doesn't matter to me," said Finn. "I couldn't care less."

"Then don't talk to me about it," said Isabelle. "Or to her. It's too small."

"I don't want her to be upset by petty things, can you understand that?"

"It is up to Vanessa not to get upset by books, not up to you—"

"It's not your place to say."

"I wasn't finished."

"Yes," he said, impatient and irritated, "and if she's upset by books, do you see how much harder it is for me to talk to her about important things?"

"You speaking to her about important things, are you?"

"Okay, enough."

Isabelle shook her head. "Since we talking so honest, Finn—"

"We're not talking that honest, Isabelle," Finn said. "And I'm done." He glanced at the clock behind her. "I have to go."

"Again, not finished." She looked up at him, her tone direct. "I think Vanessa getting upset by little things stops her addressing big things. Like when Adder leave Eleanor, that whole day Vanessa upset because Junie lost one pair of shoelace. Or when Mr. Adams get attack of heart, she spent two days questioning servants about crack in one of her dishes. How it happen, when it happen, why she wasn't told. Walter has attack of heart, and his daughter upset about ding in dish. Do you see what I'm saying?"

"No! Plus I don't want to hear it."

They were in the vestibule by the front door. No room to move apart or away, no room to put distance between them.

"Books is excuse," she said.

"You think I don't know that?"

"I don't think you do," she said. "And you not listening. You either ignore everything or you discuss big thing, but what you *don't* do is humor her when she on and on and *on* about books on shelves when it's January and books happen last June! Because your way, you just feeding crocodile."

"What?" He blinked. "You have crocodiles in Ukraine?"

"You understand meaning, right?"

"No," Finn said. "And I don't want to."

It was only 6:40 am.

Nothing is happy for him over whom terror looms. Isabelle knew this as bitter truth, and she saw it in all the people living in the mansion on Beacon Hill. Especially Finn. When she first came to live with them, it seemed to her as if nothing could ever be wrong here; or rather, nothing could ever be so wrong that it could not be made right. But there was no question—there were things happening that could not be made right, even here in this gorgeous palace made of hardwood and stone that used to have fresh flowers in every room and candles and paintings abounding.

36

Bullfinch's Last Church

It was cold and windy the morning of the pointless argument over the crocodiles. Finn walked down the cobbles of Avery Street and made a left at the Commons. He walked on, staring at nothing but his doggedly moving feet. Long gone were the days when he sought out his reflection in any glass.

It had rained and snowed and sleeted steadily since Thanksgiving, and the icy mist clung stubbornly to the Boston air. Finn's face was freezing. But still, this would be the easiest part of his day. Asking for help.

He crossed under the elevated trains to North End and hurried up grimy and slushy Hanover Street to St. Stephen's. The seven o'clock service was about to start. This wasn't the Park Street Church Finn and his family used to attend on Sundays, on the tree-lined corner of Tremont and Park with its shops and restaurants and beautiful people alighting on the common square, long before Lionel started shouting on its steps about margarine.

There wasn't a tree to be found in the entire North End, and the church was wedged deep in the ethnic neighborhood, a block from Union Wharf. St. Stephen's was out of the way of everything but the prayer of supplication. When he needed to thank God, he went to Park Street. When he needed to beg God for help, he went to St. Stephen's.

On the corner was a small coffee and smokes shop called Our Lady of Victories, behind which used to be a superb speakeasy named Our Lady of Vicetories, now tragically out of business. It was probably just as well. Seven in the morning was too early to long for a speakeasy. Frankly, it was too early for mass. But after receiving the holy wafer, a newly braced Finn could go out in search of work. If he found some, all the better. If he didn't, he'd go back to the bank and open it for a few hours, hoping for a customer or two. The sign CLOSED FOR A BANK HOLIDAY was always up now just in case he got some actual work and couldn't open.

He was a few minutes late; the service had already started. The pews were packed. He noticed that; lately, the benches had been getting fuller. He found a seat a few rows from the altar. The church was dark and always smelled of incense. The balcony choir, though a bit ragtag, still sang like angels. Stained-glass windows adorned both sides of the altar, in the center of which was a seventy-foot icon of Christ the Pantocrator. Finn never liked to look at it directly because the eyes on that icon were so deeply unsettling. Alive and profound, it seemed to Finn that at any second Christ's eyes might blink. Keeping his own less profound, less divine, though just as alive eyes on the pew in front of him, he listened to Father Umberto recite the litany of supplication. But Finn had his own.

Please God, help me support my family. Please help me find something, *anything*, that will bring in some money. Please help me save Walter's bank. Please turn something around for me, for us. It's slipping out of my fingers, no matter what I do.

Please help me maintain a calm face, a soothing demeanor for my wife. She is so worried, and I don't want her to know the desperate trouble we're in. Please help me stay strong for her and the girls.

Please help me deal with Sully, with the problem I created. I can't go to Vermont again, yet I need that money. Without it, there's not enough to go around. There's nothing.

Please keep my father healthy, my mother. Please let my father forgive me for costing him his lifelong job. He helped me at a true cost to himself. Please let me make it up to him.

It may be out of even Your power, but please keep Lucas sober. And help Lionel in his new life. I will miss my friend. Now that Lionel has pulled up anchor and skipped town, I've got no one to help me, and the crisis at the bank seems all the more final.

And after you help everyone else, please don't forget about me. Help me with my life, in whatever way pleases You.

Oh, and one more thing. I beg You, please—help me shut my soulsick being to the presence in my house of a woman who is a threat to my entire existence. She can upend it all. Please make me strong and not weak, make me blind, make me deaf, to her and myself. Please make me not break. Send me a sign, O Lord, any sign that You hear me.

When Finn opened his damp eyes, Father was lamenting the loss of hope he had been witnessing in some of his parishioners. He said he wished that the lack of material things wouldn't make people forget the other things they still had that no joblessness could take away. "Those are the things we must think of when the daily grind gets us down."

But this was what Finn was *most* afraid of: that there had appeared something in his life which even the lack of everything else could not subdue.

"Ask yourselves," the priest said, "is there something *else* in my life worth living for? Is there something *else* worth waking up for? Is there *something* I can still open my heart to, lift my eyes to?"

You're not helping, Father, Finn thought, standing in the Communion line. Not helping at all.

After receiving the Eucharist, Finn hurried to the exit; it was nearly 7:40. He had to get in the job line at Faneuil Hall by 8:00 with the rest or he'd get no work today. Lost in the waters of his anxiety, Finn dipped his fingers inside the bowl of holy water, crossed himself, turned to rush out through the narthex, and barreled full steam into Isabelle.

His hat fell out of his hands.

He lifted his eyes to the ceiling of the church in silent rebuke. Is this a cosmic joke? I beg you for strength, for a sign, and you send her to me in the place I creep to hide?

"You do this lot, don't you," said Isabelle. "You really need to watch where you going."

He let go of her as if scalded; he almost pushed her away. "Excuse me," he said, grabbing his hat off the floor, dodging her and vaulting outdoors.

She raced after him. "Finn!"

What could he do? "I'm late," he said, barely turning to her.

"What are you doing here?"

"What are *you* doing here?"

"I go to Catholic church like my mother," she said. "Because I can't find my Orthodox one. What about you?"

Not only could Finn *not* explain, he didn't want to. And now other vital things were threatened. What if she said something to Vanessa, innocently enough, the way she pretended to say all things? How could Finn explain to Vanessa why he was receiving the Eucharist at a Catholic church? And how could he explain it to Isabelle? But to *ask* her to keep a secret was beneath him.

Finn wished to God he hadn't run into her. With regret, he realized he wouldn't be able to return to his favorite church, and this made him hostile toward her and resentful she wasn't where she was supposed to be—at the house with his wife and children—instead of rambling around Boston's houses of worship at daybreak.

He didn't even say goodbye to her before hurrying away. She was making him forget his manners, him, the politest of men!

Why did she always make him feel so out of sorts? What was she accusing him of? He felt such anger at her and became even more upset because she had made him angry in church, of all places—and right after receiving

Communion! That's why you need God, Finn thought, buttoning his coat and pulling his hat low over his forehead. Because you can't get away from sin, no matter where you turn, no matter how hard you try. Grace is the only thing that can get you through it.

37

Hard Truths

It took Isabelle a day to bring it up.

"Why you were at St. Stephen's?" she said as she handed him his coffee and buttered bun the next morning.

"I don't owe you an explanation for anything."

"Are you Catholic, Finn?"

"What part of *I don't want to talk about it* is not clear? How do you say that in Ukrainian?"

She watched him with her intense gray eyes, blinking, assessing—understanding? God, he hoped it wasn't understanding!

"Leave me alone," he said. "Stop studying me. I just want to sit in silence before I go out. For just one minute!"

"Are you going to church? Let's go together," she said quietly.

"Oh, my God, stop it!"

"Let's go. We both need it." She stretched out her hand to him.

He didn't know where she got the nerve to speak to him like this. "Absolutely not," he said through his teeth, pulling his hands away from the table, from her. "I need to find work. I'm trying to earn a living."

She sat back. "A living, huh?" She smirked. "You banker, Finn. You have living. What do you mean?"

"I can't—I'm not going to discuss it with you," he said. "It's not possible for us to talk about it."

"Oh, yes," she said with irony. "I'm sure you talk to your *wife* about it."

"I am not," he repeated very slowly, "going to talk to *you* about it."

"You should," Isabelle said. "Just for advice."

"Do I look to you like I need advice?" he barked.

"Desperately," said Isabelle.

This was Finn's penance. She didn't mention the church to Vanessa and hadn't said a word to his wife about Lucas or North Troy. In return for keeping some of his secrets, she was torturing him.

They were in the dining room. Everyone else was asleep. All the lights were off to save on electricity, only a single candle was burning between them; even the furnace was off. It was cold and dark.

"Can you tell me why—" she began, before Finn interrupted her.

"Isabelle, would you please go put some coal in the furnace. I want the house warmer for when the girls wake up."

"Can you tell me why your bank is not open during weekdays? I know Lionel left, but where do *you* go?"

Would this nightmare never end? Finn wanted to slam the table, but he needed to stay quiet to fake indifference. He didn't say anything, and she didn't say anything else. Finn knew what she was about to say, and he didn't want to hear it. But he also knew that if he raised his voice, Vanessa might overhear. He was trapped.

"Are you closing your bank forever, Finn?"

"No!"

"Is that yes?"

"Isabelle!" Finn nearly hissed out her name.

"Finn!" she said. "You so upset all the time. I see it. But don't worry. Even if bank close, it's all right." She nodded. "You find another way. Other work. Don't be upset. It's just money. How you say, *easy come, easy go.*"

Finn's teeth ground together. He stood up. He didn't raise his voice, but the heat with which his words left his mouth, he may as well have been screaming. "You think it's just money?" he said. He threw his arms behind his back so she wouldn't see his fists clench. "You know nothing, *nothing!* I don't know where you come from, but it's not about the fucking money. I can't feed my family. I can't pay for this house. I can't save—no—don't speak," he said, when she opened her mouth to refute some part of what he was saying. "I've heard enough. You think it's nothing that I'm losing my wife's father's bank, the business that sustained four generations of their family? His great-grandfather lent merchants money during the war of 1812, and here I am single-handedly destroying his business."

"Not single-handedly," she said before he could shush her.

"Don't shake your head. My family depends on me, and I failed them."

"You have not. Somebody needs to help you."

"Be quiet! My own father trusted me with his life's savings, and I flushed them down the toilet."

"You did not."

"My family's life savings wiped out. My father-in-law ruined. My father left penniless. I can't feed my children. Soon I won't be able to keep them in this house. All that is nothing to you?"

"I agree, it's not nothing," she said, undaunted by his anger. "This house very beautiful. Takes lot of your money. Too much money. But it is not your big problem."

"Oh, my God, Isabelle, if you dare tell me what my problem is—"

"Your most big problem," Isabelle said, "is that you fake to your wife that everything is still good, still same. This is terrible unjust burden. Because everything is not same. You need to let her help you. Wife helps husband. Like Barbara helped Lionel. He didn't keep her in dark, saying everything was hunk-dory. No. First they move to smaller place, and now they left Boston for Indiana to live with her mother until Barbara has baby. Like them, you and Vanessa must glue your heads and together solve life. You need each other. *Your* problem is—you trying to live every day like nothing changed." She lowered her head. "I don't know banks and loans and stock exchange, whatever, but I do know something about *that*."

"It's difficult to put into words how *much* I don't want to talk about this—with you of all people."

"Finn, you can't keep paying your servants money because you afraid to talk to your wife!" said Isabelle. "It's crazy. You have to do what you did at bank. Let them go."

"And how is that working out at the bank?" Finn said through his teeth.

"You need to talk to Vanessa," Isabelle repeated.

"No!"

"To which part?"

Finn groaned in barely stifled outrage.

"*I* will talk to her," Isabelle said. "Even about stupid books if you want. But about this first. I will tell her things you afraid to."

"I am *not* afraid," he said, too loudly, "and *no!*" But there was a moment when he almost wished he could say yes. *Yes, please, oh God, yes, talk to her.*

From the top of the stairs, Finn heard Vanessa's voice. "Finn, darling? Is everything all right?"

"Of course, darling," he called out to her. "Everything's fine. Go back to bed. I was just leaving."

"Everything is very long far from fine," said Isabelle. "Tell her, Finn. Wife deserves to know what's happening to her own life."

It was all he could do not to slam his hands over his ears, not to run from her and the house and his life and the continent, from the whole earth entire.

"I'm sorry you ever learned English," he said. "I'm sorry I ever helped you in the first place. You have brought nothing but strife and conflict into my house."

"You think *I* brought strife into your house?" Isabelle laid her hands on the table. "You don't think it's your secrets that drive your wife into crazy bin? Lucas, bootleg, bank, broke, Holy Communion—who knows what else."

That was it. Finn had had enough.

38

Cici's Map

Ukraine, April 1929

As soon as Cici spread out a creased, yellowed map on the stump of a tree, deep in the woods, Isabelle knew it was trouble. More trouble.

"Cici, no." She put up her hands.

"First you will listen to me, then you will say no."

"I want to save you the trouble."

"You are going to listen to me. I don't want to talk anywhere where Petka might hear."

"I don't want you to talk at all."

"Roman is going to get himself killed," Cici said. "He is baiting them, goading them, provoking them, he is so sick of them, but he'll die for nothing. It's not like we will then get to keep our land. He will lose his life and we will still lose everything else. His death will be pointless and meaningless. So please—I beg you. Listen to me."

"I don't want to."

"Escape is the only recourse we have," Cici said. "Look at my map. I want to show you the same way Schumann once showed me."

Cici's finger moved over the topographical lines of rivers and wetlands, across boundaries between countries and the seas. Isabelle didn't look at the map. She stared at Cici's face and listened to her voice.

Cici talked for fifteen minutes.

She was proposing that the family flee in the middle of the night and make their way through the woods to the Dniester River, the natural boundary between Ukraine and Romania. She was proposing they cross the Dniester into Romania, and travel south to a port on the Black Sea. There, they would buy passage on a ship via Italy to Boston, where Schumann would be waiting for them. There were some breaking points in this plan, some complications that even Cici acknowledged. The Dniester was difficult to cross, and to get to the Dniester pass was thirty kilometers. The road in and out of Ispas was blocked by multiple checkpoints and the river was manned by armed security forces. If they managed to get out of Ukraine, on the other side were hundreds of kilometers of precarious travel through the Danube wetlands that led to the Black Sea.

"Am I allowed to speak now?" Isabelle said when Cici was finished.

"Only if you say, 'Great idea, Cici.'"

Isabelle was silent.

"I thought you wanted to speak?" Cici said.

"You just told me not to."

"Isabelle . . ."

"First of all, I wish you would run your lunatic plans by your husband first, instead of coming to me."

"I came to you first because I know you can talk Roman into anything," Cici said. "He always listens to you."

"I can't talk him into crazy because he is not crazy. What you're proposing is madness, Cici."

"It's the only way."

"It is *not* the only way!"

"You have a better way?"

"What trait is this, Cici, that lets you come up with these things?"

"I didn't come up with this. Schumann did."

"You have no idea he got out," said Isabelle.

"You know I do. You know he did. He sent me a package of silk scarves."

"That's your proof?"

"Of course!" Cici said. "He told me and my mama before he left."

"I don't remember you getting a package."

From the pocket of her skirt, Cici pulled out a deep red silk scarf and unfurled it.

"So now it's one scarf?" Isabelle said. "You just said a package!"

"He told me: if you get even one scarf, unmarked, without a letter, know that it's from me, and that I'm waiting for you."

"When did you get this? How did you get this?"

"Seven years ago. The Civil War ended and soldiers and stragglers were crisscrossing these parts from Romania to Poland. A trader left it in the Ispas village hall. *For Kasia and Cici*, it read on the brown paper. He didn't know Mama had died. And here it is. That's how you know there's hope."

"That's how I know there's a cracked dumb head in these woods."

"Let me hear *your* plan, Comrade Lazar," Cici said, mimicking Efros. "Does it include Communists sleeping in your *izba* and pillaging your fields?"

"Cici, don't do this."

"Does it include exile to Murmansk, to Solovki, to Siberia? Does it include prison and hard labor? Someone has to mine their coal for free in their corrective colonies, Isa! Does it include you being wrenched from your family, from your sons?"

Isabelle lifted her eyes to the sky.

"Does it include Stan and Vitya's fate?" Cici spoke through tears. "Tell me your way out!"

Cici was part Romanian, that must be why she was always thinking up these schemes, these wild dreams.

"I can't leave my mother," said Isabelle.

"You won't be," Cici said in a thrilled voice. "Oksana comes with us."

"My mother is going to come with us," Isabelle repeated, disbelieving.

"Your mother, your brothers, their wives."

"My children?"

"Of course your children!"

Isabelle groaned. "So half a village is going to travel by stealth on foot many kilometers through a dark forest to a river. Nineteen people!"

"Not half a village. Just the Lazars. Maybe some Kovalenkos."

"Roman won't come with you."

"He will if you tell him to."

"He is not my child! He will never!"

"Roman," said Cici, "loves two things. He loves his father, and he loves his father's horses. Everything else, even me, is a distant third. Possibly fourth if you include you, your mother, and your brothers as one thing. Otherwise, I'm even farther down the list. If you tell Roman that in America, he can have his horses, and no one will take them from him, he will come."

"Cici . . ." Isabelle squeezed her hands in abject prayer. "I beg of you, listen to yourself. My small children!"

"They're not small. They're nine and eight."

"They're babies, Cici," Isabelle whispered. "They can't do it. *I* can't do it."

"Do you remember what Roman asked your husband?" Cici said. "Are you going to yield up your life and theirs without a fight?"

Isabelle shook her head. "The cost is too high. Mirik is right." Suddenly, seeing her options in stark relief, she jumped the fence to her husband's side, where she should have been all along. "We'll collectivize. I've decided Petka is right. We'll do what they want. They'll have to feed us to farm their crops, won't they? We'll have something. And we'll get to stay."

"You think they're going to let you live?"

"Someone has to! How can they feed the workers in their factories if all the farmers are dead?"

Although they were having this conversation alone, in the woods, they spoke quietly. Isabelle didn't want even the trees to hear.

"You're going to stay on your farm, with the Bolsheviks and the propagandists and the *chekist* killers sleeping in your house?" Cici said. "Sleeping in *my* house with Roman, to keep watch over us?"

"Yes, Cici! Because there's no other choice!"

"There is a choice. Live or die."

"Live!" cried Isabelle, her voice fading into her terrified chest.

"That's not the choice," said Cici.

"You just said live or die was the choice!"

"Life or death you can't control. You have no power over it. Stay or go is your only choice."

"We can't stay," Roman said to Isabelle. "Unfortunately, Cici is right, just this once. Don't tell her—she's already insufferable. But she is right."

This is what her own brother said when Isabelle relayed to him what Cici was proposing. She was counting on Roman to react as she had reacted. It was absurd! Impossible! Instead, Roman listened carefully, twirling his moustache, was quiet for five minutes as he assessed further, repeated the plan back to her to make sure he understood and then said, "Yes, let's do it."

"Roman! You're not serious."

Roman shrugged. "I don't know what you plan to tell Petka. Ah, hell, tell him nothing. The man is a nuisance. But perhaps they'll let him stay on the farm after we're gone."

That was when Isabelle knew that Roman was lying; that whatever his ultimate plan was, he had no intention of actually escaping with them. Because if he was truly agreeing to Cici's entire plan, including the America part, he knew the Soviets would never let Petka live after they learned the Lazars had fled. Petka and his family would be destroyed. Roman might care nothing for Petka, but he was not a slayer of children. And they both knew that Petka would never come with them. Escape was not for the faint of heart.

Life was not for the faint of heart.

Be sure your heart is brave. You can take much.

"I know what you're thinking," Roman said quietly. "Petka may have already betrayed us. I don't think so. Not yet. But in any case, I'm not hanging my family's destiny on the narrow shoulders of a craven weakling."

"What about Yana?" Isabelle said. Yana who was having a baby in less than a month!

"Yes, Ostap has a real problem," Roman said, standing up to face her. "But it's not *your* problem. I know you think I have other plans. But believe me, escape is the only road left to you. We did not make this, or build this, or cause this. We are not to blame. We have been invaded, and the parasite is going to suck us dry and end us. Our father raised us to ride our horses and to love our land. Zhuk said a radical solution to our current troubles would be required. This is the Lazar solution. The flames will have it."

Mirik wouldn't *hear* of it. Wouldn't allow Isabelle to speak, wouldn't allow her to finish her sentence. "What you're proposing is out of the question!" he said. "*Out of the question*. I won't discuss it. I won't consider it. I won't listen to it. I won't engage in any way with you or your family about it. But most of all, I won't allow you to take my children."

"They're my children, too, Mirik," said an ashen Isabelle.

"You and the mule-headed Cossack blood that runs through this farm," said Mirik. "Why oh why did I agree to marry you, pressured for months by your mother and my father?" He leaned into her face. "Your beauty swayed me. Your incomparable body seduced me. But that was then. We were ten years younger, and I hadn't borne the struggle with you yet. All I wanted was to live like a Kovalenko, not a Lazar, and look where it got me."

"Yes, Mirik," said Isabelle. "Better to live as a Lazar."

"Run if you want. But you will not take my sons."

"You come with me," she whispered. "You all come with me..."

"If we come with you, we die," said Mirik.

"If we stay, we die," said Isabelle.

"No. We might be forced to live as Soviets. Give up our Ukrainian pretensions. But we will live."

"Mirik, I beg you, please don't do this. Mothers don't leave their children," she said hoarsely, her tongue numb from terror, squeezed as she was on all sides by the iron vise of unresolvable conflict.

"Mothers don't kill their children," said Mirik.

39

Say Goodbye

"Where we going?" Isabelle kept asking, trying to keep up with Finn as he hurried along Beacon Street. It was wet and miserable and too cold for conversation. "Finn, where we going?" He was down to his last drop. He would send on her things later. He needed her out of his house, at once.

"Are you taking me to Schumann's?"

He didn't reply.

"Are you getting rid of me?"

He didn't reply, he just kept walking.

Isabelle stopped walking. He had to turn around. He had to reply.

"I'm taking your advice, Isabelle," Finn said. "You told me I can't keep employing all the help in my house. Very well. But I'm starting with you."

"You are fool."

"I'm not going to stand in the middle of the street and argue with you."

"Why not? You certainly can't argue with me in your house in case your wife hear some hard truths."

"Enough!" he said. "I can't take it anymore. You're not my family, you're not my responsibility. I helped you as long as I could—"

"You think *you* helped *me*?"

"You don't think I helped you, Isabelle?"

"Okay, you help little bit. But don't joke yourself, who do you think is going to take care of your children once I'm gone? Who do you think is going to shovel coal into your furnace to keep your children warm? Who is going to dress them, bathe them? Loretta? Martha? Wicker? Vanessa?" She was derisive at first but then lowered her voice, beseeching him with her eyes. "Who is going to help *you*?" she said emotionally, taking a step to him.

"You think you're helping me?" He leaned his face into hers. "All you do is cause me pain."

"The pain part I can't help," she said. She didn't back away from him. "But you got it all messed up, Finn. All messed up. Your thinking is . . ." She struggled for the word. "Kerflooey. And I can see why. You got no person to talk to." She paused. "Nobody but me."

"I don't want to talk to you," Finn said. "I don't want to explain to you, I don't want to pay you, or see you, or have anything to do with you. You can be Schumann's problem now, the way you should've been from the beginning."

"Oh, my God, will you stop it!" she cried, her composed demeanor finally cracking. "What you saying is tomfoolishly! You don't fire *me*! You fire everyone else and keep me! Let them all go, and I take care of you and your wife and your children and your house. I do it for you." She pressed her hand to her heart. "I do it for *you*."

"I don't want you to do anything for me!"

She shook her head. "You don't mean it."

"With all my heart," Finn said, his fist on his chest.

She grabbed him by the coat sleeves. "You drowning in burden," she said.

"Unless you got a million bucks under your pillow, you can't help me." He yanked away from her.

"Your mother and father, and Vanessa's parents, and her sister, they all living in separate homes, yes?"

"What's it to you?"

"Answer me."

"It's raining, and we're in the middle of the street."

"Let's go back to house and talk."

"No!"

"Answer me!"

"Okay, yes—so what?" Finn was panting. He couldn't believe he was fighting with a woman who was not his wife in a public place. Good thing it was raining and there was no one around.

"And you paying house loan or mortgage on these houses?"

"So?"

Isabelle laughed with scorn. "And you think *I'm* insane? You think *I* don't understand things? Too simple to figure things, poor village idiot Isabelle. I mean—that's *craziest* thing I ever hear, and I heard woman tell me to cross two countries on foot with small children looking for some port somewhere. Finn, you live in house size of small castle. You have five floors, plus lower level, with seven, eight bedrooms? Plus attic space, plus libraries, office—my God, you could fit all of Ispas into your house! But whatever, not my problem. But you keep saying you have no money. You sell your car, how much you get, few thousand? Money gone five minutes. You sell your Truro house in secret, how much time you buy? Two months, three? Why don't you sell all those other houses and have your family come live with you in your big empty house? You save money. You live under one roof, everybody does little bit for house, live cheaper, and you don't need all your servants."

"That's your advice?" Finn was mirthless. "That I live with my mother-in-law, and Vanessa live with hers? And you think *I'm* crazy?"

"To save money until job chances improve, why not? It's not forever, just little while."

"I'm not going to discuss this with you, Isabelle. You are not my wife."

She folded her arms. "So go back home and discuss with your wife."

"Oh, to be sure, I will, but first I'm going to say goodbye to *you*."

"You want to say *goodbye* to me, do you?" said Isabelle, the balloon of her beseeching enthusiasm popping. "After all I just say?"

"Especially after that."

"Great and dandy," she said, waving her hand. She wouldn't look at him. She shoved him, pushed him down Beacon Hill. "You going wrong way, Finn Evans. Home is that way. Vanessa that way too. Me, I'm opposite way. You getting rid of me? Bye-bye. I don't need you to walk me to Schumann's. You can get rid of me on street. You don't have to return me like dog you don't want anymore. Leave me. Go head, say goodbye to me."

Finn was silent. Isabelle was panting. With open eyes he stared into her angry, upset face for a few frozen moments in the falling rain, for the first time realizing something he didn't want to realize or understand or acknowledge. He resumed walking uphill in the direction of Schumann's store, dogged but determined. "I can't do that," he said. "It is an impolite thing to do."

"Oh, and we all know you so polite," Isabelle said. "*Yes, dear, everything is fine, dear, nothing to worry about, dear.*" She was mimicking his voice as he talked to Vanessa.

"I owe you a paycheck for the last four weeks."

"You haven't paid me for eight weeks, polite man," said Isabelle. "But who's counting."

"I want to talk it over with Schumann. Out of respect. I owe him that."

"*Him* you owe things?" Isabelle said. She walked next to him, but so quickly he could barely keep up. "Yes, bring back cur he tried to hand off to you and ask if he want me back, that's great."

"You have nowhere else to go but Schumann's," Finn said. "So that's where I'm taking you."

"What do you care where I go after you done with me?"

* * *

Schumann sat at his tailor's desk near the window, stitching on his sewing machine. He took one look at Finn, at Isabelle, at their frantic, frenzied expressions and said, "Uh-oh." He took his foot off the pedal and the machine stopped.

"And how is everything this morning with you two?" Schumann asked.

Isabelle rolled her eyes.

"Not good," Finn said. "About the dresses I left with you last month... you said you might find a buyer for them?"

"Ah, yes. Someone in Chestnut Hill was interested." Schumann opened his register and pulled out an envelope from under the change tray. "I managed to get twenty each for them. So, a hundred and twenty altogether." With a longing sigh, Finn glanced at the money, peeling off a twenty for himself and thrusting the remaining hundred dollars at Isabelle. She refused to take it. Finn dropped the envelope on the counter.

"If you need twenty dollars so bad," she said, "you need rest even more."

"Fine, take everything." He stuffed the twenty back into the envelope and thrust it toward her.

"Not penny," she said.

"And what is happening?" Schumann cut in, fake-brightly.

"I'm so sorry to do this, Schumann, but..."

"Don't be sorry—but whatever you're thinking, the answer is no."

"You don't know what I'm about to say."

"I do. It's still no."

"Schumann, please. I can't pay her anymore."

"He hasn't paid me two months," said Isabelle. "I don't know why he care about it all of sudden."

"I just offered you a hundred dollars and you refused to take it."

"I need room to sleep," Isabelle said. "Food. I don't need money. You take money Schumann give you for your wife's dresses and pay your five house loans. Maybe you can sell your children's dresses next."

Finn whirled to Schumann. "Do you see?"

"Frankly, I don't," Schumann said. "She is right."

"She is wrong! Isabelle, can you wait in the back for a minute, so Schumann and I can talk?"

"No," said Isabelle.

"Excuse me?"

"You heard me. I don't work for you anymore. You fire me, but also you don't pay me. So you don't tell me what to do. Whatever you want to say, you say in front of me."

"There's nothing *to* say," Schumann said. "I can't take her. Business is bad, money is tight, problems are everywhere."

"Schumann, I can't keep her!"

"Me neither."

"Thanks, gentlemen," said an unfazed Isabelle, as if they hadn't just been horse trading over the fate of her life. "Please continue, this is fastening."

"Schumann, you have no idea what I'm dealing with," said Finn.

"But *I* do," Isabelle said, "and you refuse to let me help."

"I advise you not to reject her help," Schumann said. "But also"—and here, Schumann folded his hands before he continued—"none of us has any idea what anyone is dealing with," he said. "If we knew even a fraction of it, we would all be kinder to each other. So why don't you be a little kinder to Isabelle, Finn, and be on your way."

"I've kept her with me for a year and a half! That wasn't kind?"

"This isn't."

"Schumann, I need to fire my cook," Finn said in supplication. "I need to fire my housekeeper and my maids. I've already let go my gardener, and we've cut our milk delivery. Any minute I'm going to start carrying the coal from the shed to the furnace myself."

"Why not? I do," said Isabelle.

"Yes, but *I* won't be able to afford the coal."

"Oh, but by all means, pay five loans for five houses," said Isabelle.

"It's not five houses!" He breathed deeply. "It's four houses and a bank."

"Sounds like five to me," said Isabelle.

"Sounds like more reason you need her," Schumann said, "not less."

"That's what I say!" said Isabelle.

"I can't!" said Finn.

"That's the trouble with the new country, Isabelle," Schumann said. "They don't know the trouble in the old country that brought us here."

"Oh, he knows," Isabelle said. "I told him."

"There is no trouble like our trouble," Finn said, and at that moment he sincerely meant it.

Schumann and Isabelle stared at each other, and then both of them stared at Finn. Unplumbed depths were in Schumann's and Isabelle's gazes, realities Finn couldn't comprehend. Finn adjusted his hat to cover his eyes. He was filled with shame. "Okay, you're right, I know nothing," he said quietly. "I'm too busy watching my own life being snuffed out."

"Are we alive?" Schumann said. "Are you both standing in front of me, diminished but breathing? Am I standing in front of you, business slow, not making ends meet, but still open? We have no money. We don't have much work. I *know*. But I still have two dozen people a month coming by ship. Why do they come? I told Nate don't put anyone else on the ships! I told him there is no more money! But they keep coming to Constanta, and he keeps buying passage for them, paying for their visas somehow, sending them on. Why? Because they're all mad optimists. Even now, they think America can help them."

"This isn't the twenties," Finn said. "We can't help anyone anymore."

"No, not with *that* attitude."

Finn struggled for breath. "Why can't you hear what I'm telling you? I can't even help my family. And she's not my family."

Schumann said nothing.

"I'm going to lose my bank, Schumann," Finn said in a gutted voice.

"I'm sorry. I hope you don't. But times are hard."

"She," said Finn, "*she* is making my life harder."

"I don't see how that's possible," Schumann said. "She is the daughter of Martyn Lazar, the most capable man in all of Ukraine. Martyn Lazar risked his life for a Jew during the war when the Red Army and the White Guard and the Poles were all hellbent on snuffing out every Jew in Ukraine. That Jew he helped was me. And she is his daughter. Ask her to do anything. She'll do it."

"I don't need capable," Finn said, losing the fight inside himself and with himself. "I need fewer mouths to feed."

"You can barely feed mouths you have because you pay five loans for five houses," said Isabelle.

"Oh my God," Finn said. "I'm going to smash my head against the rocks. She and you both, like a chorus. This is not how we do things in Boston, not how *I* do them. Why can't she work for you here for free?"

"That's not how we do things in North End or Ukraine," Schumann said. "Not how I do them."

They were speaking quietly, blistering, hissing. Isabelle was standing behind Finn. Behind her, through the wet glass, was freezing January drizzle.

"Schumann, please," whispered Finn.

"Finn, please," said Schumann.

Schumann put his palms down on the counter. Finn's palms were already down. The two men stood for several long moments.

Finn grabbed his hat and turned to Isabelle. "Are you really refusing to leave me?" he said.

"Honestly now, I don't know," she said. "You deserve leaving."

"Goodbye, you two!" Schumann called after them, smiling and waving.

Outside in the rain, they stood motionless.

"Let's go, I guess," Finn said, as cast off as he had ever felt. "We'll stop at the soup kitchen on the way, see how long the line is."

"What about rest of your job with Lucas and Lionel?"

"I don't want you to bring it up again. I don't have a job with Lucas and Lionel. Lionel took his share and moved to Indiana with his pregnant wife. And Lucas is probably sleeping off a two-week binge somewhere."

"He is not," said Isabelle. "I see him last week, he fine. More or less. He said you didn't complete full job, so you didn't get full money."

"Isabelle, I asked you before and I'm telling you again. I'm holding on to my sanity by a thread, a thin fragile *thread*! Don't talk to me anymore about it."

"I heard Lucas say some man named Sully still owe you thousands of dollars for liquor cases."

"How do you hear everything you're not supposed to and nothing you *are* supposed to? How on earth could you possibly hear Lucas say this?"

"What you mean?" she said calmly. "I asked him, and he told me."

"Why would you ask him!"

"I wanted to know what you were up to with secrecy and truck and that cock-maiming story about flooding at Truro in house you no longer own."

"Secrecy being the main part of that *cockamamie* story! Why would Lucas tell you?"

"Don't you listen? Because I asked him."

A maddened Finn didn't know where to look or how to get out of this absurd conversation. There was nowhere to look except Isabelle's open, composed, serene face.

"A lot to be mad about, Finn, I know," she said. "I'd be mad too if man named Sully owed me money. You need to get it. It's not hundred bucks for dresses. It's thousands of dollars. It will pay loans on your half-dozen houses. It will feed your family. Why such discussion about it?"

"I can't get the liquor, I don't want to explain why."

"Take Lucas and drive."

How did she always get him to divulge what he had zero desire to divulge? "Lucas is part of what got me into this diabolical mess to begin with. The three of us got arrested because of Lucas and his uncontrollable drinking, and my father had to get me out of it without jail time. For that, he is now being forced into retirement. And it's my fault! But I have no one to get me out of a jam when I get caught again."

"Don't get caught again."

"I barely kept it from Vanessa. I almost went to prison. It's not worth it."

"It's more than thirteen *thousand* dollars!" said Isabelle. "It's worth it."

"I don't have a fucking truck!"

"Ah," she said with a nod, "now you talking. Wait out here. I be back." She disappeared inside, leaving him standing in the rain. Finn watched her talking to Schumann, pointing to Finn, explaining things. Nate popped his head in, and she thrust her finger at him, gesturing to the rear, and he lowered his head and slunk away. Five minutes later she walked outside. Her face was relaxed, smiling, as if she were full of good news.

"I found you truck," she said. "Schumann has truck to borrow. Tomorrow. We need to bring it back in three days though because Nate need it. You see, you tell me problem and I find solution."

"It's like speaking to a deaf-mute," Finn said. "I can't go alone. Lionel is gone, and Lucas is drunk! And I got no one else."

"Not true," said Isabelle. "You got me. And I come with you."

"You're going to come with me? On a bootleg run to Vermont?"

"How hard can it be?" she said. "You three boys did it. Nate has weapons. We bring them. For just in case. If we bring them, we won't need them. But if we don't bring them, you can be sure, we will need them."

"We're going to bring weapons," Finn echoed.

"Yes," she said. "You fight in war, no? You know how to handle weapon? That makes two of us."

"What do you plan to do with these weapons?"

"Let's hope you never get to find out."

PART III
Troy Has Fallen

"What though the field be lost?
... And what is else not to be overcome?"

John Milton, Paradise Lost, Book X

40

Pride of the Sea

Finn and Isabelle set out early one cold January morning in 1931.

At the tailor's shop, Isabelle, Schumann, and Nate discussed Finn's lack of believability as a truck driver. "You look like banker," Isabelle said.

"I am a banker."

"Okay, but you need to dress for job you have, Finn Evans."

Schumann lent Finn the shabbiest clothes he could find. The shoes, they could do nothing about. Schumann found Finn a current bill of lading for the crates of cotton thread, linen, and tobacco that were in the truck awaiting transfer to a sea carrier. "If you get stopped," Schumann said, "show them the bill of lading and hope they don't count the total number of cases."

When they were ready to leave, Nate offered to come, but was rebuffed by Isabelle. Finn did accept Nate's rifle and Colt pistol.

Schumann's truck was parked near one of the warehouses on Lewis Wharf, just a few minutes' walk from his store. The truck was metal and painted white, with the sides of the cab featuring the logo for American Trucking and Transportation. Schumann rented the truck from AT&T on a semi-permanent basis to transport goods from North Carolina to Boston.

Isabelle also borrowed a hand cart with large wheels from Schumann. "I'm not carrying two hundred fifty cases of liquor through woods in my naked hands," she said. "We be there two days doing that."

Finn noted her use of *naked*.

"We also didn't carry them with our *bare* hands," he said. "We're not idiots."

"No, of course not," said Isabelle.

She was wearing oversized relaxed-fit cotton canvas work pants and a big boxy jacket, and her hair was completely covered by a woolen hat. "Are you trying to hide that you're a woman?" Finn said when he noticed. "Because..."

"Yes, like you trying to hide you banker," she said, pointing at his shiny black shoes. They set off.

"Isabelle," Finn said, "we have five hours ahead of us."

"You want to play road games?" she said. "When we deliver milk in horse cart, sometimes we play games."

"No."

"Sing songs?"

"Maybe you can tell me things to keep me awake while I drive."

"I can teach you Ukrainian alphabet. Or say little jokes."

"We agreed no jokes," Finn said.

"I did not agree to this," said Isabelle. "You should teach me how to drive truck. Then you can sleep and I drive."

No way was he sleeping in front of her; he didn't dare. "You want to drive a truck on the highway while I sleep?"

"What you doing that's so special?" she said. "You are sitting. I'm sitting. Your hands on wheel. Mine on my lap. Your foot is on pedal. Well, mine is on floor, but I could put it on pedal."

They drove.

"I crashed the truck last time because it took us over eight hours to load after six hours of driving, and I fell asleep," he said by way of an explanation she wasn't asking for.

"I'm not worried," she said. "But eight hours and three of you. It might take us longer, just two of us. On way back, you probably be tired again."

"I won't be tired. I'm not taking any chances this time. On cops, I mean." But he meant sleep.

She took off her hat, fluffed up her hair, and sat back comfortably with her legs tucked under her.

"Do you want to listen to the radio?"

"No," she said. "I listen to radio all day long. I'm *tick and sired* of radio." She said *tick and sired* in Eddie Cantor's voice.

"So, talk to me," Finn said. "Tell me about Nate."

"I'd rather listen to radio," she said, opening the map and pretending to check Sully's directions.

"Why don't you like him? Is it a long story? We got time." For once, they had more than just fractions of moments when she would bring him food, or when Lionel was there, or when they walked to Schumann's—a twenty-minute walk, half of it spent dodging cars and people. They had 220 miles to go. Massachusetts, New Hampshire, Twin Mountains, Littleton, Lancaster. North Troy. They had *time*.

"Not long story. Short story," said Isabelle. "I don't like him because Nate is lying skunk. End story. And look at that, we still in Boston. Route 1 take long way to get to Route 3, like fifty miles. How much that is in kilometers?"

"Like a thousand," Finn said. "Come on."

"I don't know what *come on* mean."

"It means don't be like that."

Isabelle put down the map. "Okay, we will do take and give. I tell you about Nate," she said. "If you say why you not nice to Lucas."

"Probably the same reason," he said.

"Very good. And now we done!"

Finn persisted. "A few months ago, Mae and Junie said you told them a man named Nate saved your life."

Isabelle made a throaty sound of displeasure.

"*Did* he save your life?"

She scoffed. "He think that entangle him to something."

"*Entitle*. Who is he?"

She peered at Finn. "Are you being funny? I can't tell because you often . . . well, you know. Not funny. But you know who he is. You just talk to him."

"I mean . . . how does Schumann know him?"

Isabelle did a double take. "Schumann know him," she said with a bemused smirk, "because Nate is Schumann's son."

"He is?" Finn was astonished.

"How you not know this?"

"Schumann kept it well hidden. You Ukrainians are full of secrets."

"He no hide it at all. Look how he look at that child, with nothing but adoration." The way Isabelle said it, though . . . like on the one hand she was judging Schumann for loving a person like Nate, and on the other, knew it was the only way to look upon your flesh and blood.

"Schumann and Nate escaped in 1919," Isabelle said. "Father and son tried very hard to get fifteen-year-old Cici and Cici's mother Kasia Babich to run with them. Schumann was with Kasia many years. Nate was his son from early wife who died giving childbirth, I think. Schumann left Cici maps and money and told her Nate would be waiting for them in Port Constanta in Romania. He and Nate planned for year; they thought they were so smart. A good way to get to Boston and beautiful way too, down the Danube and across southern seas instead of cold hard way through Poland and ice and Baltic Sea and Liverpool, because you always have to depend on weather northern way, while south route you have warm and sun, and it's nice. They not wrong. Sun part was nice. Especially Brindisi. Your girls like when I tell them about Brindisi because that port is like magician, if you like beauty and water and sun and food.

"When Schumann and Nate get to America, they work hard and buy cotton from company in North Carolina they do business with, Clark Coats."

"Coats and Clark," Finn said.

"Also tobacco from Nate Sherman. Like fools they pick Nate Sherman for simpleton reason: because name Nate and because it sound like Nate Schumann. It took them much time to save money, maybe whole year. Nate bought passage on merchant ship for himself and his crates of cotton and tobacco, and he sail back to Romania, and in Constanta he sell goods to local traders, and he wait and wait for Cici and Kasia, and they didn't come, but some other people wanted passage, so he took them. They pay him, and he pay captain, and he bring six people to America. Nate made good friendship with one captain, Florin, and with cotton and tobacco they make money for Clark Coats. He and Nate make partners and together buy old ship. For six years, Nate and Florin sail back and forth from Boston to Constanta and he would wait for Cici. One way with cotton and tobacco, reverse way with Ukrainian or Polish or Romanian people who wanted to go to America. Nate got himself big reputation. Everyone knew him in Constanta. He sold them American goods cheap. He did it so when Cici finally escape and come to port town, and say one word, *Nate*, anyone could tell her where to find him."

Finn listened intently as he drove. "Is that the ship that crashed at Lovell's Island?"

"Yes," said Isabelle. "Merchant vessel *Mândria Marie. Pride of Sea*."

"You told Vanessa you didn't know the name of the ship!"

"Yes." She brushed some lint off her jacket. "I didn't care for your wife's tone."

Finn almost laughed. "I bet. What has Nate been doing of late?"

"Fighting with Florin. Selling tobacco. Sailing on other ships, renting cargo space. But now Nate coming back with more immigrants than Schumann can support. It's not good."

When Finn didn't say anything, Isabelle said, "I know, many problems here, but problems there, too. More and more people come southern way. Families." Isabelle touched the cold window of the truck. "*Other* families."

Finn glanced at her watching the fields and trees whizz by. He didn't know how to ask the next thing. "Did Cici die at Lavelle?"

"No," said Isabelle, gazing at the passing countryside. "I tell you so much, but you tell me nothing about Lucas."

"There is nothing to tell about Lucas," Finn said, stepping on the gas.

"Yes, sure," she said. "You mean you just realized how much you don't want to talk about it?"

"*Tochno*," said Finn.

"You think I want to talk about Nate?"

"Forget Nate for a sec," Finn said. "Tell me what happened to Cici."

"*Roman doesn't love me like I love him*," Cici wrote in a letter to Isabelle. "*You know what I say to that? So what? That's right. Because who could ever love anyone* like I love him? That's the gift I've been given. Maybe he wasn't given it because he'd been given so much else. I have been granted the grace of my love for him, and my love is not dependent on his reception or its return. And if I leave without him—"

But Cici *was* leaving without him. Wasn't she?

The ship was already out of Constanta Harbor, on her way through the Dardanelles. The water carried Isabelle away, Cici receding, invisible, gone. Cici didn't stand on the shore and wave goodbye. She had already vanished before Isabelle stumbled on deck and said, "Nate, where is Cici?"

Nate told her Cici had decided to return to the land that didn't want her, to find the husband who was lost. He didn't tell it to her easy. He cried when he spoke. Cici and Nate had pretended just long enough to get Isabelle aboard and settled into a cabin.

Isabelle stared glassily through the windshield. The ship cast off, and Cici flew away. When Isabelle came on deck, Nate handed her the letter Cici had written to her. Oh, the betrayal, the outrage.

"*Roman's love is not required for my heart,*" Cici wrote. "*That he allows me to love him is everything. And if I abandon him—what am I? If I leave him behind, run to a better life without him, what does love even mean? I don't want to be a wife of empty words, Isa. I love you, my closest friend, my sister, my family. I love you, but I love Roman more. I want to be worthy of the gift that God has laid upon my soul.*"

"How could you do it to me, Nate?" said Isabelle when she could move her mouth without her teeth chattering.

"I didn't do it to you," he said. "I'm torn on all sides. Think how my father will feel. I did it for Cici."

Isabelle tried to throw herself overboard. "You can't stop me," she said to Nate, who stopped her. "Let me go. I can't do this without Cici, without my family, can't and don't want to. Let me go, like you let her go. I must find my husband, my—"

"Your family is gone, Isa," Nate said.

"You're a liar. It's not *true.*"

"What is it to me to lie?" said Nate. "I don't love you. I don't want you for myself. I'm just trying to help you, Isabelle. I'm trying to help you for Cici."

Isabelle was mute in Brindisi, a golden seaport, hot dusty salty mute. The wordless woman stared at the neon water without any idea what to do.

And then in Boston, an epiphany—a disaster!

"*We split, we split, to prayers, to prayers!*" Prospero was wrong. All was not lost. God sent Cici love but Isabelle a shipwreck!

And when Florin's *Pride of the Sea* spilled over like a great wet carton of human cargo, all flailing limbs, raging winds, bobbing heads and screaming,

screaming, Isabelle didn't even bother to hold herself above water. As the ship slammed against the rocks in its death throes at Lavelle, Isabelle closed her eyes and sank into the darkness.

She felt not one but two male arms pulling her up, holding her afloat, offering her a life ring. And she fought, pushed it away, pushed the arms away.

"Hold on, Isabelle!" cried Nate, one arm around her, the other windmilling them both to shore.

Let me go, Nate, this is my fate. Can't you see I don't want it? I have nothing left, you said so yourself.

"They're alive!" he cried, holding her even tighter. "Your husband and your sons. Cici told me. They're alive, and they're going to find their way to you. I promise you, I *swear* to you, I will do everything I can to make that happen. What do you want my father to tell them when they come to Boston, looking for you? That you gave up? Gave up right at the light to the harbor? Live, Isabelle! Live because they live. Save yourself, and they will save themselves. Fight, hold on, and they will come back to you."

That's why Isabelle didn't talk to Nate anymore. In Constanta he told her her family was gone. In Boston he told her they were alive. One of those was the truth, and one wasn't. And nothing Nate could say would make her believe one or the other.

"But Isabelle," Finn said, "Nate himself doesn't know the truth."

"This is good why? So, he is man who will say *anything* to get you to do what he wants. You cannot trust person who manipulates you this way."

"Didn't he say it to save your life?"

Isabelle clammed up.

They didn't speak for a while.

"I know something about this," Finn said at last, his words heavy like his hands on the wheel. "A long time ago, I was friends with an Irish guy from North End named Travis. After America entered the war, we signed up together, went to basic training at Camp Devens, were part of the 332nd Infantry Regiment. We sailed to Liverpool and were deployed to Northern Italy, where our job from July 1918 almost to Armistice Day was to pad the Italian numbers to scare the shit out of—excuse me."

"You fine," said Isabelle. "I grow up with three brothers. You fine."

"We were supposed to intimidate the Austro-Hungarian army. For three months near the Piave River, at the foot of the Alps, we had a great time." Finn half-smiled, remembering. "You don't usually say this about a war, but we really did. There was frolic and tomfoolery among the doughboys. We fought in only one battle." Finn stopped smiling. "The Battle of Vittorio Veneto. It lasted ten days, from the end of October till November 3. Everything in my life seems to happen at the end of October," he added ruefully. "We lost thousands of men, the Italians many more thousands, but Austria most of all. After they lost the battle, they surrendered. And a week later, the war was over. That was it. Three months of camaraderie followed by ten days of bloodshed. That was my Great War." Finn gripped the wheel, wishing it was night and she couldn't see his face. But she was watching him the way she always did—vigilantly.

"One big battle, and you escape," she echoed.

"Yes," Finn said. "A wound to the head, shrapnel, a broken rib. But I only escaped because Travis took the fire that was meant for me. He died so I could live."

Isabelle made a rasping sound.

"What?" he said, slightly alarmed.

"Nothing," she said, her voice dim. "Continue."

"It was November 2, the day before the ceasefire," Finn said. "We were so close! But I was sure I was a goner. I was bleeding so much from the head I thought I was dying. And with shrapnel in my legs I couldn't get up and run. I was lying in a ditch, and the Austrians were advancing through the field. But Travis wouldn't leave me. I kept saying, just go, I'm not going to make it." Finn's mouth twisted. "And Travis responded with a version of what your Nate said to you."

"He not my Nate," said Isabelle. "Nate nobody."

"Okay. But Travis wasn't a nobody. Travis," said Finn, "was my Cici. He said get up because if you don't get up, we both die. And I can't leave you."

"I guess you got up."

"He pulled me up." It was hard for Finn to continue. "At least, I think he did. Soldiers sometimes lose their memory around a catastrophic event. The shock makes them forget what happened right before and right after."

Isabelle's breath was shallow, her expression blank.

"I'd known Travis since we were ten," Finn said. "We met in the park. We went to different schools but stayed close. All the shenanigans I ever got up to—and I was the son of a judge, so it wasn't many—it was always Travis and Finn, Finn and Travis."

Isabelle stayed silent, letting him find the words he needed. And he really needed to find the words.

"When I came to, we were at the tree line. He was wrapping his scarf around my bleeding head. Somehow, he got me to my feet. Run, he said to me. Run, and I'm behind you."

In the corner of the cab, Isabelle pressed herself against the passenger door with a dry sob. "Go on," she said. "Did he tell you no matter what, not to turn around?"

"Yes. But I did. And he was on the ground."

She didn't nod.

"I went back. I don't know how, I thought I had nothing left in me, but I picked him up and carried him into the woods. He was hit, and now he was telling *me* to leave him!"

"He got some nerve," said Isabelle.

"My sentiments exactly. What about all the things you just said to me, Travis. But he was shot bad, in the back through the stomach."

Isabelle sat squeezed into herself, rigid with empathy.

"Travis whispered, '*You're my brother, Finn.*' I know, buddy, I said. Just hang on. And Travis, who I assume was moments away from death, gripped my sleeve, his mouth filling with blood, and said, 'You are my *brother*.'"

Isabelle assessed him quietly. "Why you say assume?"

"Because I have no memory after that. When I woke up, I was in a field hospital. The battle was over. They told me Travis had died. His body had been sent back home for burial. I felt like I was going mad, like maybe I dreamed his injury, because when I was bent over him, my tunic and my hands were soaked in his blood. And when I woke up, it made no sense that my shirt should be clean. For many months I would wake up and stare at my hands, wondering where his blood had gone."

"What was Travis full name?"

Finn didn't want to say. But it was the whole point. "Travis McBride."

"McBride, like *Lucas*?" Isabelle said, widening her eyes.

"Yes," Finn said. "Like Lucas."

"Travis was Lucas's *brother*?"

"Yes."

"And Travis said to you, you were *his* brother?"

"Yes."

They were silent for the next fifty miles, all the way into New Hampshire.

"There are things I don't understand," she said.

"Welcome to my world."

"Thank you. What did you do?"

"I was wounded, and the war was over," Finn said. "I spent until March 1919 recuperating in an Italian hospital. I was in no rush to come back stateside. Nominally I remained part of the peacekeeping force. The last of us sailed home that April."

"Did you find Travis parents after you come back?"

"Of course not. Am I crazy?"

"So you never met Travis mother and father?"

"No, Isabelle!" Finn said. "Why would I?"

"Did you speak to your parents?"

"Eventually. It wasn't easy. I mean, they were my parents! I held them in the highest esteem, especially my father. I revered him."

"He very good man."

"I relayed to them what I told you."

"What they say?"

"My father nothing, as usual."

"He man of few words," said Isabelle.

"Very few. But my mother asked the most incongruous thing. Like you, she asked what Travis's last name was."

"Aha."

"She didn't say, oh, darling, the man was delirious. She didn't say, how wonderful that someone cared for you, my boy. She asked for Travis's name."

"I said to her, 'Travis *McBride*, Mother.' She flinched. You know how someone flinches when they hear an unexpected thing?"

"Yes."

"That's how Mother flinched. When I saw that, I found the nerve to ask the most outrageous question. I mean, I was twenty-one at the time. My entire identity was that I was Finn Esmond Evans, only son of Earl and Olivia. But I asked if it was true. '*Is* Travis my brother?'" Finn smirked. "I almost asked them a demented follow-up. I had become a dunce. I almost asked my mother and father if they had had another child before me—Travis—and given him up for some unexplainable reason."

"That not demented," said Isabelle. "That reasonable."

"Before I could embarrass myself, Mother said of course it wasn't true. I turned to my father. He and Mother exchanged a glance, a short silence, and he said, 'You heard your mother, son. She already told you what's what. Are you corroborating with me to prove your mother a liar?'"

"He didn't answer your question."

"He did not."

They were almost in Vermont. Another twenty miles of road.

"Did Nate answer yours?" Finn asked.

"In ocean, at Lavelle, I was drowning, so no time for questions," said Isabelle. "But in Constanta, yes. He looked at me with his wounded rabbit eyes and said, I'm sorry, Isabelle, but it's true, they're gone."

Finn was skeptical. "But he gave no details, either in Romania or Boston."

"*Tochno!* And I couldn't ask Cici. Her letter said many things about love and vengeance but not word about them."

Another hour and they would be at the cabin. Something pinched in Finn's chest, tightened, expanded, hurt. He slowed the truck.

"What do you think?" he asked her. "About Travis?"

"I want to know why dying man, who could say anything, say *that*, when he knew they might be his last words."

Nodding, Finn emitted a pained sigh.

"Clearly your heart tell you that Travis telling truth," Isabelle said.

"Why do you say that?"

"Because you go to St. Stephen's for Communion," Isabelle said. "You believe you are Catholic."

Finn shrugged in reluctant admission. "I went for the first time in 1920. I thought it would be like a foreign language to me, but it wasn't. I justified it by telling myself I was going for comfort."

"Park Street Church wasn't comfort?"

"Guess not," Finn said. "But what I did most of all was get on with my life. I buried it. I graduated from Harvard, got married, went to work for Walter. I forced myself to live the life I'd been given, not the life I suspected I was born with, whatever that life was. I know Travis was desperately poor, and his father was gone."

"But Finn, Lucas can tell you."

"Lucas doesn't know anything. Besides, you don't think Lucas is a little bit like Nate, Isabelle? Someone who'll tell you what you need or want to hear?"

Isabelle shook her head. "Unlike Nate, Lucas doesn't have secret door in his total body. He not manipulator."

Finn shook his head. "Lucas may not have a secret *bone* in his entire body, but now that I'm thirty-two and my life is falling apart, I don't want to hear it. Whatever the truth is, it's twenty years too late."

"Maybe like me, you want to know for sure."

"Here's the thing," said Finn. "Thirteen years ago, my mother showed me my birth certificate. It looked official enough. It had a raised seal, was generated by the Boston Office of Public Records. It had my name on it, Finn Esmond Evans. It had my date of birth, July 23, 1898. My parents' names. It was beyond a reasonable doubt. Until I heard that Lucas's last name was McBride and everything got connected, I almost believed it."

"Except for going to Catholic church," she said.

"I guess except for that." He sighed.

"Mother McBride probably never—how you say—register your birth," said Isabelle. "You say Travis come from poor family."

"So poor they couldn't afford a free birth certificate?"

"So poor it wasn't important," said Isabelle. "Finn, there is no question that Lucas your *brat*."

"Don't say that."

"In your heart you know it's true. He follow you around like baby brother."

She lowered her head. "All my brothers were younger than me. They followed me like Lucas you."

"I didn't know he was a McBride until 1929," Finn said. "We were drinking buddies, that's all. We met by accident—or so I thought—at the Red Lantern in '24. We drank and had fun together."

"That's why Vanessa doesn't like him?"

"Yes, Vanessa doesn't like me to have fun," Finn said, and quickly realizing how that sounded, smiled to put a smile on it. "Vanessa doesn't like him for many reasons." He gave his wife a little bit of truth, riding through the open country with another woman. "The main reason is that a few years ago I was out with Lucas one night when she really needed me, and I don't think she's forgiven either one of us for that." Finn wanted to close his eyes as he drove. He wanted never to think about it.

Isabelle was full of thoughts about Lucas and didn't follow up on Vanessa. "When I ask Lucas how he manage to get out of jail so easy, he tell me whenever he get in trouble, he always ask public defender to get hearing in Judge Evans courtroom because he said Earl always more nice to him than other judges, more lenient. He gave him probation, hit on wrist, no jail time."

Finn tightened his grip on the wheel.

"Why would your father help Lucas McBride, Finn? Maybe because he know who Lucas is?"

"No," Finn said. "He just has a soft spot for souses."

"Is that what your heart tell you?"

"I'm going to beat the crap out of my heart if it doesn't stop speaking to me," Finn said.

They were nearing North Troy; only fifteen more minutes. A walk to Schumann's was what was left of their time together.

"What does *your* heart tell you about Nate's words?" Finn asked.

"Nothing good," Isabelle said. "I swing from believing him in Constanta, which I don't want to, to believing him in tempest in Boston, which I do want to. On bad days I'm on Black Sea. On good days I see light at Lavelle. But on all days I have fury for fabricator of fabricators."

"He was trying to save you, Isab—"

"What if I didn't want to be saved? He didn't let me go back; why? He let Cici go back! What, he didn't want to save *her*? She was his family."

"Maybe Cici would not be stopped."

"And I could be?"

"Doesn't seem right to be mad at a man who saved your life."

"I'm not mad for that," said Isabelle. "I'm mad because I live afraid I will never know truth, will never know what happened to my husband and children." She brought her fists to her chest and pressed inward so hard, it was as if she wanted to stop her heart from beating.

They drove the rest of the way in silence, past the half-dead trees and the telltale stones.

41

Slayer of Peasants

Ukraine, April 1929

"Do you feel sometimes like we're not going to make it?"

Who said that? Isabelle? Mirik? Definitely not Cici. The girl was a wild optimist. Everything was going to work out, according to her.

But sometimes, when Isabelle looked forward, she couldn't see a tomorrow. She couldn't see them staying, not unless the Bolsheviks fled from power and crawled away to the taiga of Siberia. She couldn't see them being left alone by Zhuk. She couldn't see them working on the farm after it was given over to and run by Zhuk.

Most certainly Isabelle couldn't see them going. Practically speaking, to leave Ukraine was inconceivable, despite Cici's rosiness. Isabelle had only the vaguest notion of where anything was beyond Ispas.

Kiev? Somewhere northeast. Warsaw? Perhaps northwest. Odessa? On the Black Sea. But Romania? The Danube delta? Five hundred kilometers on foot or by boat in alien terrain, with only the dimmest notion of what would happen when they got to Constanta? Unimaginable. And Constanta wasn't America! There were still three seas to cross and a mighty ocean. What if Nate wasn't there? What if Nate couldn't help them? What if Nate or Schumann had died during the last decade, red silk scarves notwithstanding?

It didn't help that Mirik, after declaring he would *never* go with her or let her take their sons, kept trying to prove to her mathematically why they couldn't go.

"That's how you know he'll come with you, Isa," said Cici. "Because he keeps yakking on and on about it."

More professorial than ever, Mirik kept drawing diagrams for Isabelle, concentric circles, overlapping squares. His persuasion was numbers, his comfort was math. Kilometers they must cross, kilos of food they must carry, the daily ration needed by an adult to sustain life, Cici's tiny stash of cash that must be divided into multiples of bribes and fees and family members.

Isabelle was a toy boat thrown against the stormy will of others. Some who longed to leave, some who never could, baby boys who knew no better, an overprotective husband, a volatile brother, a violent sister-in-law, a gutless brother-in-law, and a mother who watched it all in agonized silence.

Mirik was right. There was a lot to be anxious about.

Take Nikora's child-like bride, for example. Twenty-year-old Zoya was a barely literate woman. She was a terrible rider, worse even than any Kovalenko. Nikora married her for her beauty. Oh, the men who were ruled by passion and not reason—as Mirik now attested. "Ukrainian women are the most beautiful in the world," Nikora said on the day of his wedding. "And Zoya is the most beautiful of all."

Zoya was a wonderful girl, no question. Her family was in textiles. Zoya embroidered sleeves and necklines and hems of dresses. All the Lazar and Kovalenko women looked more attractive and fashionable because of Zoya's skills. But those skills were useless when fleeing your country in the middle of the night.

Mirik's parents were well over seventy. Escape was for the young and the willing and they were neither.

Petka was spineless though argumentative, with a shrewish wife and four teenage children. Lydia the wife wasn't in good health, and one of their sons had lost his leg four years ago when a cow had a stroke during labor and died, pinning the boy to the ground for several hours.

And Yana, who was a rider and a fighter, was heavily pregnant. They either escaped before she had her baby or waited till after. Both options presented obstacles that set Isabelle's nerves on fire.

A pregnant Yana could ride a horse, she could run, she could swim, and obviously she could break someone's skull with a pipe in an alley, if need be. But what could she do with a babe in her arms?

Isabelle bit her nails to blood and spent her days outside, worrying the ground under her feet into a trench. She busied her hands, she worked nonstop from sun-up to sundown. None of it made any difference. All her anxieties thrived unabated—unlike the wheat and the sugar beets.

"It's not *just* about the grain, Petka," said Roman in April when it hadn't rained in days and the wheat hadn't germinated. "It's about the soul of Ukraine. Stalin wants to break us because he connects our bond with our farms to Ukrainian nationalism." The once-happy family was gathered together in one room again, wretched and confrontational.

"He wants to break us because your farm—still in your private hands—cannot deliver him the grain he requires," Petka said. "It can deliver it in his name, but not in ours. I, for one, do not wish to have this fight with Comrade Stalin. I don't want to be at the bottom of his boot."

"What's going to stop you from being at the bottom of it?" asked Roman. "The Kazakhs have already been stamped out. No revolt there anymore."

"Roman is right, Petka," said Isabelle, sitting next to her brother across from Mirik and his brother. Her mother was behind her, her younger brothers nearby. "What's happening here is a deliberate effort to crush us, to cement the Soviet stranglehold over our black earth."

"Of course!" said Petka. "Because we are not Ukraine anymore! What about this don't you two understand? We are a Soviet republic. We fought a war to keep our country, and we lost. We lost Ukraine. The Communists won. We are not our own. We are theirs and our farms are theirs."

"I don't see you having a farm, old man," Roman said. "I don't see you living anywhere but on *our* land."

"That's right," Petka said. "I'm a tenant farmer on your land, and I will be a tenant farmer on theirs. But it's *their* land, Roman! Their grain, their cattle, even their steel plow. At least if we are on their side, we're not going to lose our lives," he added. "They need us—to work their fields or in Siberia. Someone's got to mine that iron ore."

"Are you proposing being sent to Siberia as a way *out*?" said an incredulous Roman.

"Better than what you're proposing. To flee Ukraine! What drivel!"

"Better to leave. To start new."

"It's madness!" said Petka. "It's suicide. It's certain death, and I won't be part of it, not me or my children or my parents or my brother and his family."

Isabelle sucked in her breath. It was about to go from bad to worse.

"*His* family?" Roman said quietly. "You mean *my* sister and her children?" He stared at Mirik.

"Roman, it's no secret how I feel," Mirik said. "I'm with Petka on this. I also don't want to be part of it."

Isabelle shook her head in reproach and disappointment.

Roman couldn't sit anymore. He pushed away from the table. Isabelle pushed away with him, but she couldn't lift her gaze off her brown boots.

Petka and Mirik continued to sit.

Roman focused on Mirik. "Are you putting a dividing line between what's ours and what's yours, *brother-in-law*?"

"As *you* are doing!" Mirik said.

"Blood does not turn against blood!"

"I am not your blood," said Mirik.

In disbelief, Roman spun to Isabelle.

"Mama thought marrying him was a good idea, blame her," said a trembling Isabelle.

Oksana got up from her chair and came forward, leaning her arms on the table and facing Mirik. "You are afraid, I understand, but you're not thinking straight. Your children—who *are* your blood—are Roman's blood. You are *all* bound by blood on this farm. So stop talking fear and rubbish. Talk like family. Solve like family." She stepped away from a chastised though no more converted Mirik.

"Petka," Roman said, "here's my solution for you. Because I see that nothing here is going to come to any good. Take your family, take your parents, and go visit relatives in Proskuriv."

Petka blustered. "Are you kicking us out?"

"I'm advising you in the *strongest* possible terms," said Roman, "to leave my farm and go spend a few months somewhere else. Somewhere *safe*."

"Summer is coming! Two of our cows are about to calve."

"You can take them or leave them," said Ostap. "We'll manage."

"Are you kicking Mirik out, too?" Petka said.

"That's up to Isabelle."

"It's up to Mirik," said Isabelle, grimly folding her arms.

"You Lazars are out of your minds!" Mirik cried.

"We don't need hyperbole right now, Mirik, especially from you," Oksana said.

"Hyperbole from *me*?"

"We need level-headedness. We need calm to prevail. Isn't that why you married my daughter, to be the voice of reason?"

"Yes, and I found out from bitter experience," said Mirik, "that level sands are washed away by the raging seas." When no one responded, he gasped and said, "Fine, but if I go to Proskuriv, Isabelle comes with me."

"Does she now." Roman spoke the words with scorn.

"Yes, she does. She's a Kovalenko," Mirik said. "She is not a Lazar."

"You think a piece of paper changes her essential nature?" said Roman. "She is forever a Lazar. I don't even know if there is a record of this name change." He scoffed. "Isa, have you signed a single piece of paper as a Kovalenko?"

Cursing under her breath, Isabelle glared at Roman without replying.

"Our marriage certificate names her as a Kovalenko!" said Mirik.

"It probably names *you* as a Kovalenko," Roman said.

"It's not even worth arguing about," Mirik said.

"Oh, I heartily disagree," said Roman. "I know of only two pieces of paper that have my sister's name on them. One is her birth certificate. The other is the deed to this land. And neither mentions a Kovalenko anywhere."

"That's *not* the point I'm making!" Mirik said, frayed in face and tone.

"I get the fucking point you're making, Mirik," said Roman, Isabelle's brother, her father's son, her mother's son. "You think that in a life and death crisis, my sister is going to side with the Kovalenkos. Fine. Straight to the horse's mouth, so to speak. Isabelle, what say you?" They all turned their eyes to her.

"Yes, Isabelle," said Mirik, her husband, the father of her Kovalenko children. "What say you?"

Isabelle raised her hands in surrender.

"Roman is right, sister, you can't straddle the fence anymore," Ostap said and Nikora quietly seconded. "You must decide. Are we paper tigers, fighting only with our words? Or are we what our father raised us to be—free men with swords and on horses who will not be subdued?"

"It's up to you, Isabelle," Roman said.

A desperate, frightened, anguished Isabelle frantically looked from one face to the next, pleading to each of them for an answer that wasn't in one way or another an unimaginable, unendurable wrong.

Unable to ride the power inside herself, Isabelle spun to her mother. "Mama!" she cried. *Where in here is the act that is right?*

Oksana stepped to the table, her gait and hands unsteady. "You should read the papers and the poets more as you fight with each other and bear down on my daughter," said Oksana. "Osip Mandelstam called Stalin the destroyer of life. *Ten paces away, and our voices cannot be heard*, he wrote. But he is a poet. He's born to artistic license. Why don't you read what Stalin himself said about Ukraine in his speech at the annual All-Party meeting in January. *It's either Ukrainian peasants or our cities*, he said. *It's them or our army, our party, our economy, our country. It's either them or us.* He didn't mince words. *We are Bolsheviks*, he said. *We do not turn away from difficult matters. Without taking the grain and the farms from the peasants, our country will not survive.* These are his words, not mine. He said, *the Ukrainian farmer must be sacrificed if we are to industrialize the Soviet Union and make it into a modern power.*" Bleakly, Oksana looked over her warring family. "Stalin is about to become the *slayer of peasants*. Daughter, sons, family, ask yourselves if it's better to have death or live in tyranny. And then act according to your answer. My children's father Martyn Lazar answered it for himself before he died, and his voice was silenced."

42

A Hut in the Woods

Almost as soon as they parked the truck in the clearing, Finn felt that something wasn't right. He couldn't quite put his finger on it.

"What?" Isabelle said, catching a glimpse of Finn's unblinking gaze.

"I don't know," he said. "Let's take the weapons, just in case."

He took the rifle. She grabbed the pistol. "What about hand cart?"

"Leave it for now. We'll come back for it. But switch your safety off, Isabelle. Just in case."

"It's off," she said. "It's first thing I do when I pick up any weapon. I switch safety off."

Quietly, they made their way through the woods, single file, Isabelle in the rear. Finn got a strong sense memory of Travis being behind him in battle. Viscerally he heard the gunshots as if the battle were raging at that very moment. "Isabelle, get in front of me," he whispered. They stopped to listen. The woods were quiet. It was cold. The forest had remnants of old snow covering the underbrush. He turned off the flashlight, and they stood close together. All he could hear was her shallow breath, and his own.

"What is it?" she whispered.

"I don't know."

They kept walking. Why did it feel to Finn that they had parked in the wrong place and instead of forty yards, they were trudging three thousand yards in the blacked-out snow?

The cabin was dark. Putting the flashlight between his teeth, he raised his rifle. Before they moved forward, they listened for anything that might warn them of trouble ahead.

"What is that sound?"

"Thumping?" she said. "That's my heart."

"It's too loud."

"Okay, Finn," she said. "I'll try to have my heart beat less loud."

The half-moon in the sky floated behind clouds. It allowed only the shapes and shadows of objects to be caught by the eye. Finn didn't want to open the door to the cabin.

"If someone is there, they would hear us by now," Isabelle said. "They would see our light." She moved to the right.

He caught her arm. "Where you going?"

"Turn off your flashlight," she said. "I'm going to peek through window."

"If someone is there, they'll take your head off."

"I said peek, not put my head in window for target practice," she said. He had his rifle pointed at the door, ready to fire, as she stepped toward the glass. Isabelle was so stealthy, you couldn't hear a footstep from her. She glanced in, yanked her head away, waited, glanced in again, this time a second longer before pulling back behind the window frame. The third time she continued staring inside the cabin and didn't pull back.

"Finn," she said, and she wasn't whispering, "it's one-room cabin, right? No secret rooms?"

"Shh. Yes. Why?"

"Come here."

"I'm manning the door."

"I know. But put rifle down and come here."

Moving much more loudly than she had, Finn crunched in the pine needles and twigs to the small front window just outside the porch and glanced in. "I can't see anything," he said.

"Finn," she said, "you can't see nothing, because nothing is there. Give me flashlight." She shone the light inside the window.

The cabin was empty. The remaining 250 cases of whisky, which had covered the floor, were gone.

43

Razorblade

Finn kicked open the door and raged in.

The hut was stark and bare. In the far corner, a single lonely crate stood with a piece of paper nailed to the top.

"*Sully*," the note read in large sloppy handwriting, "*thanks for the liquid gold. Cross me again, and your Lantern turns to ashes.*" It was signed *Vinnie the Blade*.

"Fuck," said Finn. "Fuck, fuck, fuck, fuck." He dropped the note and his weapon and kicked the wood walls, the fireplace mantle, and the crate with the liquor. He kicked everything in his path, he yelled and cursed, while Isabelle stood nearby in silent disappointment.

Afterward, Finn became a pillar of salt near the window with his back to Isabelle, as he stared out into the night, into nothingness. All hope was gone. He had been so close! He needed just a few months of expenses, both personal and professional, before things turned around, before business picked up in the spring. Clearly a different way was meant for him, but he didn't want to go that way! He was a banker who lived in a corner townhouse on Louisburg Square in Beacon Hill. That's who he was. He didn't want to be the other thing, a destitute man with no name and no work who struggled for his every meal. He had fought so hard all his life not to be that man.

He felt her come up behind him and place her soothing palm between his shoulders. "I'm sorry, Finn," she said. "It's okay. It will be okay. We figure out different way. But who is this thief Vinnie?"

"Vincent Moretti," Finn said. "Sully's current distiller and distributor from Canada used to be exclusively Vinnie's. Sully wanted in, and they fought a war over it back in '26. Moretti is why Sully lost an eye."

"Lost an eye but won the fight?"

"Yes. Afterward, Sully worked out this convoluted system of transfer to hide his booze from Moretti."

"How did Vinnie find it?"

"Who knows," Finn said. "He could've paid off the delivery guys or someone at the distillers. A thousand ways this operation can go wrong." Finn's shoulders were weighed down by black ruin. "What are we going to do now?" he whispered.

"First thing we do," she said, "is leave. You don't know when they come back. We didn't bring enough munition for proper fight."

They took the note and the case of whisky. She carried the note and the rifle. He carried the whisky.

After they'd been on the road for a while, still in Vermont, she asked how he knew that something wasn't right.

"The brush was cleared," Finn said. "Someone cut a swathe through the woods with an axe, like they didn't care that they were leaving a trail to the cabin because they knew they were going to leave nothing in it."

"Sully gonna be mad," Isabelle said.

"*Sully?*" said Finn. "*I'm* not going to get paid."

"Maybe he has another job for you? We can do another job. This can't be only liquor cabin he has. Border with Canada long. Maybe other cabins?"

"You're something else." Finn smirked. "You want to traipse through two thousand miles of border looking for liquor in the woods?"

"Just offering ideas. Your shoulders too big to be slumped."

"We're finished," Finn said. "If there had been someone waiting for us in that house, we'd be cooked. The two of us couldn't fight Moretti's goons even if we were armed to the gills with automatics."

"If you say so," said Isabelle, aiming the revolver at the windshield and the night road beyond and pulling a phantom trigger.

"I say so because it is so. Put that down. We have a rifle and a handgun to scare off accidental burglars. We can't have a cage match against the toughest mobsters in the Northeast."

"How tough can this Moretti be?" said an unperturbed Isabelle, the gun still aimed at the darkness. "He left note for Sully. Now Sully will find him and bring revenge. Moretti making danger for himself and his men for few bottles of whisky. That's man who doesn't respect his life *or* his business."

"Yes, and you and I are not going to risk *our* lives for a few pieces of silver."

Isabelle looked disappointed as she lowered the weapon, though Finn suspected it was less about the few pieces of silver and more about the firefight that wasn't to be.

He didn't ask her about it. Most of the drive back to Boston was brutal. The optimism Finn had felt on the drive north was demolished by the realization that he wasn't going to earn, find, steal, or borrow the money he needed to barely break even. He still had a bit left from the second November trip; he felt grateful for the prescience that had told him not to pay *all* his past debts, keeping a few bucks in reserve for the just in case.

Isabelle was speaking to him.

"Finn," she was saying. "Finn."

He came out of it, refocused on her.

"Finn, I'm sorry it went so poor. This isn't what we wanted."

"No kidding."

"But I wasn't joking what I said to you before we went to Schumann when you tried to fire me," said Isabelle. "You will save much money if your parents sell their house, and Walter and Lucy theirs, and Eleanor and that son of hers theirs, and everybody come live with you."

"Oh, I definitely thought you were joking," Finn said. "When you are saying this, are you thinking of how my wife is going to take it?"

"No, Finn," said Isabelle. "Because what you need to do, you need to do, and you can't not do it just because Vanessa won't like it. You need to let your people go, cooks and maids. It's too many dollars. Sell all houses, everyone live together, like one big family, and see what you see. You may get new job soon. There are banks in Boston, other job chances. But no more Sully. No Vinnie the razor either."

"Vinnie 'the Blade,'" said Finn.

"That's what I say, razorblade."

"Just bl—never mind."

New Hampshire passed like this, in sadness and snow.

"How do you think Sully is going to react when he finds out someone stole a hundred and fifty grand of his liquor?" Finn said, somewhat rhetorically.

"Not someone," said Isabelle. "Dumb mobber Moretti. There's going to be war. Stay away from North End until things calm down."

"I'll have to find another place to drink."

"We can make our own."

He laughed.

"I'm not funny," she said.

"Oh, most definitely not funny, Isabelle," said Finn, but for some reason felt better, a little lighter.

"I teach you," she said. "It's not hard. I can make it very delicious."

"In my house? Tell me, will this brewing and distilling be before or after I have all my relatives move in? I assume there will be some distilling?"

"If you want delicious moonshine, then of course much de-stilling. But fine, you want to make fun instead of make liquor, go head. But you can't make money from funny, Finn. Especially not you."

"Perhaps we can open not just a brewery but a speakeasy in my kitchen?"

"Certainly can't open comedy show in your kitchen," she returned.

"Do I want to keep my house or don't I?"

"You make so much money with my moonshine, you keep your house and get more houses."

"Do I want to keep my family?" For a second that sounded like a rhetorical question, and he regretted it as soon as the words left his throat. "I do, *and* I don't want to go to prison."

He wanted to add that he was a banker, not a bootlegger. But now that he had confessed to Isabelle the secret of the McBride brothers, lies became the truth, doubt became certainty, nightmare a reality. The hopelessness he felt at his doubt over who he was, coupled with the loss of his self-made self, was doubly unmooring him. What was better, to be a fake Finn Evans, the once well-respected businessman, born and raised in Beacon Hill, pretend son of a judge and a teacher, or a true Moses-basket baby McBride, born in the North End to the kind of woman who abandoned her children? And not all her children, obviously.

Just Finn.

"It can't continue," Isabelle was saying. "People can't be out of work *and* not drink too. It can only be one or other. Both together is, how you say . . ."

"Unsustainable."

"Right, unassailable."

"That's not what I—" He waved it off. "I don't know if I can face Walter," Finn said. "How am I going to talk to him about this?"

"Is there any way you can keep bank open?"

He shook his head.

"Then I don't know how thirteen thousand dollars would help you keep it open," Isabelle said. "I'm not saying it's not big money. But it's limited money. It goes away. To keep bank open, you need continuing money."

"That's really the crux of it, isn't it, Isa?" said Finn, and coughed quickly, as if he'd misspoken. It was the first time he'd called her anything but Isabelle.

She smiled and went on almost as if she hadn't noticed. "Can you borrow more money?" She clicked her tongue. "I'm not advising it. My mother said if you can't afford it, you shouldn't have it."

"What could you possibly need in Ispas?" he said.

"What you mean? A new saddle. Some beads. Cici and I wear them on our wrists and necks, many beads, they look pretty. And dresses. Sometimes nice to dress up. We bought ice skates and sleds. I bought toys for my . . ." She broke off. "You know, everybody likes nice things, even simple farm girls. These boots I wear, for example," Isabelle said. "I save for two years to buy them. I never borrow money. I save and save, because they so expensive, they cost like half horse. But they last me look how long."

"Half a horse or half a house?"

"Half horse. House so cheap in Ukraine. Made of mud. But horse expensive."

He was quiet. "So many things have happened to you and to me in such a short time, haven't they?"

"Feels like someone else's life," she said, blinking away memory. "I know you feel terrible, Finn. Vanessa is going to not react good. But if you realize you have no choice, if you know this is what you must do, it's easier to talk to people about hard things. Because you have no option."

When they stopped somewhere in Massachusetts to have a smoke and some food, she asked what he planned to do with their one case of whisky.

"Give it back to Sully, of course," Finn said. "It's his liquor."

She shrugged. "There is his, and there is his," she said. "Is he going to pay you for this trip, your time, Schumann's truck?"

"Well, no . . ."

"Exactly," said Isabelle. "He should pay something. He man of business."

"Man of crime business."

"Even men of crime business have honor. He not Communist. You show him note from Razorblade. Whisky can be your payment for your trouble. Then you can have drink or two right at home."

"Keep the entire case?"

"One bottle to Schumann. Rest to us."

"I don't know about that, Izzzabelle . . ."

"Finn, you gonna be out of work soon," she said. "Remember I tell you, country can take your job or your liquor. Not both."

Finn laughed. And then, because he couldn't help it, he opened his arms and hugged her. They were outside a roadside cafe in the hard dust and cold. He was in his big coat and she was in some borrowed lumberjacky cape, and the embrace was awkward and bear-like—two large paws wrapped around a slender girl inside layered winter garb. "Thank you," he whispered, pressing his cheek to her covered head. Her hands patted his sides, clutched his coat.

"You just happy I say you hide eleven bottles of liquor in your house."

"Am I that transparent?"

"Well, don't thank me yet," she said into his chest, her head pressed against him, not moving away. "You got crap of stuff left to do before you can raise glass of Sully's delicious whisky." She squeezed him. "Like retailing your wife with stories of your life of crime."

"I can't wait to retail her about that," said Finn.

44

Walter

Finn and Walter sat in the drawing room with the doors closed.

"I know why you're here," Walter said in a low, sad voice. "I've been dreading this conversation for months."

"Me too. I'm sorry, Walter."

"I know you are." He sat. Finn sat. "Did you do everything you could?"

"And some things I didn't want to. And some I can't believe I did. We just can't claw our way out of it."

Walter lowered his head. Finn lowered his.

"When I came to you that morning in October," Finn said, "neither you nor I imagined that fifteen months later, everything would continue to slip into the abyss."

Walter offered straws to a drowning man. "Did you try approaching some of your bootlegger friends? I know you have a few of those. Did you try asking them to launder money through our bank?"

"I did," Finn said. "They refused. They can't trust paupers with their king's ransoms."

"They're right," Walter said. "I wouldn't." What about selling the bank's commercial properties? All sold, Finn said. Calling in commercial mortgages more than three months in arrears? All called in. Liquidating personal mortgages more than six months in arrears? All liquidated. How about reinvesting the bank's meager cash reserves back into the devalued market, buying stocks on the cheap, getting dividend payments while waiting for the upturn?

"Insufficient cash reserves for that, Walter. Large investment for small return. The dividends aren't enough to keep us going, even operationally, forget profitably. The market is still falling."

Walter carried the look of a shellshocked man. "It was at 160 last week, *160!*" he said in disbelief. "Remember on Black Tuesday it was 260 and we wrung our hands at the collapse? How could it continue falling? It's unthinkable, and I've been in finance all my life."

"Companies aren't making what people aren't buying," Finn said. "Why in the world would anyone invest in the stock market when they can't pay their rent? Did you see the unemployment rate in January?" It had doubled from the previous month to nearly *16 percent*. And that didn't account for people who were working a reduced week for reduced pay. Which was probably half the country. And it didn't include people like Finn, who were technically working but miserably wretchedly desperately dead broke.

"I know, my boy," Walter said, appraising Finn with affection and pity. "It's so vicious."

"The wheat crop last year was one of the worst on record," Finn said, "yet the price of wheat is at a historic low. That makes no logical or economic sense. It's a market that doesn't know which way is up, that can't be counted on for anything. We can't invest our precious remaining dollars in a market we can't predict with even a child's degree of accuracy. What if 160 is *not* the bottom? What if the Dow Jones continues to fall?"

"That's *impossible*, Finn! Andrew Mellon . . ."

"Fuck Andrew Mellon," Finn said.

45

A Bad Day on Beacon Hill

Finn couldn't put off the conversation with Vanessa any longer.

As he was leaving, Walter had shaken his hand and said, "How's my daughter taking this?" And when Finn didn't have a response, Walter said with an astonished exhale, "You haven't told her? You poor bastard."

And now it was weeks later. He had to do it. There was no way out. After he came home from a twelve-hour day at the docks, he first went upstairs to his girls' room and lay down on the floor with them for a few minutes, letting them climb all over him. Then he went downstairs to the kitchen to get the plate Isabelle had prepared for him, which was waiting for him warm on the stove. He ate silently, exchanged a grunt, a nod, a shake, and a double Sully whisky with her, and finally trudged upstairs, where Vanessa, already in her nightclothes, was diligently wiping the bottoms of her perfume bottles.

"Hello there, darling," she said, offering her cheek to him. "Your day was so long. You must be tired. Ready for bed? You go on while I finish up here." When he kissed her, she frowned slightly. "Is that liquor on your breath?" She studied him.

"Of course not," Finn said, moving away. "It's Coca-Cola and a throat lozenge." Without undressing, Finn sat down on the long ottoman at the foot of their bed. "I need to talk to you, Vee."

She glanced at his face and shook her head vigorously. "Oh, no, no. I'm *so* tired. I too have had a long day. Maybe tomorrow."

"No, Vanessa," Finn said. "It can't wait."

"I'm not up to a conversation right now, Finn."

"I'm getting up at six tomorrow," he said. "Do you want me to wake you, and we can talk then?"

"How about tomorrow night after you come home?"

"Are we haggling about when we can speak?" He shook his head.

"Well, I can't talk when it's convenient only for you, Finn," Vanessa said, peevishly. "It must also be convenient for me."

"Right now is convenient."

"Right now I'm tired."

Finn was done negotiating future communications. Besides, he knew it was a ruse; it was Vanessa's way of not talking about it. Tomorrow morning she wouldn't wake up, or she would wake up with a headache or stomachache. Tomorrow night, she would complain of another hard day. On and on.

"Vanessa, we lost the bank," Finn said, taking a page out of Isabelle's book and just coming out with it.

"What do you mean, lost it?"

"Sixteen months ago we lost our money in the Crash. I mortgaged our properties, hoping to stave off foreclosure. Many people, me included, believed investors would come back to the market to buy at record low prices. But it didn't happen. The opposite happened. We lost almost all our customers. They took their money and left. And the rest have been struggling and out of work and unable to repay their loans. The rainy day has turned into a rainy year—and then some. Our customers did not come back, and the market didn't come back because the economy didn't come back—and it doesn't look like it's coming back any time soon."

Vanessa interrupted him. "What do you mean we *lost* the bank?"

"I mean we lost our business. The bank has stopped making money and we had to close our doors. We had too few customers. We have no assets, only liabilities. Massachusetts National is going to auction it for parts or absorb it into their own business." It was painful to put it in terms so stark.

Vanessa kept shaking and shaking her blonde head. "It can't be," she said. "You can't close my father's bank. He has money. He can lend us . . ."

Finn stared at Vanessa with sympathy. "I know it's hard to deal with."

"Does Daddy know anything about what you're saying?" she cried out.

"You think I could close your father's bank without talking to him? Of course he knows—everything."

She fiddled with her hands, driving the nails into her fingertips. "Shawmut didn't close."

"Different clients, different lending practices, different business model, different outcome. Four other banks closed in Boston before Christmas, not just us."

"Christmas?" Vanessa said. "But it's February."

"That's true."

"So where have you been, if you weren't going to work?"

"I *have* been going to work. I've been doing other things."

"Like what?"

"Driving a truck," Finn said. "Making deliveries. Working the docks, loading and unloading merchant ships. All of it has brought in a few dollars, but nothing even close to what we need to pay the expenses on four homes." He didn't want to tell her how hard it was to find even inadequate work on the pitiless streets.

"Why can't you get a job at another bank?"

"Because there are ten thousand bankers looking for work and two hundred positions. Because no one is quitting, and no one is hiring. And they don't want to hire me, when they think—rightly or wrongly—I couldn't manage the bank I had."

"Is there no *other* work you can do?" she cried.

"I've done that work," said Finn. "It floated us for months."

Vanessa looked faint. "It's that Lucas . . ."

"It's not Lucas's fault we're broke, no matter how much I'd like it to be. But Vanessa . . ." He didn't know how to say the next part, she already looked so white. "There's more."

"Darling, this is about all I can handle."

Finn plowed on. "My father said he will sell his house, and he and my mother will come to live with us here."

Vanessa made a strangled sound, like a trapped animal. "Absolutely not," she said.

"*And*," Finn continued, because there was no point in stopping now, "your father and mother have sold their house and are also going to be staying with us."

Vanessa jerked against the dresser, and the bottles of perfume she'd been cleaning crashed to the carpet.

"Eleanor and Monty too." Finn bent down to pick up the fallen bottles. Vanessa staggered to the bench. Now it was his turn to stand at the dresser with the perfumes in his hands. "I don't like it any more than you do."

"Finn, we can't!"

"It's the only way, Vee," Finn said, deciding it wasn't a good time to admit to his wife that even all that would not be enough unless he got some real paying work. What were they going to do when the money ran out? All too soon, a whole new kind of bottomless reckoning might come, one that would make four families living under one roof seem like heaven.

"*Your* father is still working, isn't he?" Vanessa said in a shrill sharp voice. "Why can't he help us? You bought him his house!"

"Yes, and we mortgaged it to help us, and now we sold it to help us." Finn turned his ashamed face away. "And he's no longer working. He's had to retire."

"It's not your fault your father's decided to retire at a time like this!"

"It *is* my fault."

"Finn, I can't do it, I'm serious," Vanessa said. "I can't live with my parents and my sister and your parents."

"Why?"

"I just *can't*." Her voice was barely audible.

"You got somewhere else to go, Vee?" Finn said. "Let's pack up the girls and get there in a hurry. But barring that, there's only one way out, and that's through it."

"Why can't you borrow from the central bank like you did in the past?"

Vanessa knew just enough not to understand the most fundamental things. "Vanessa, please listen to me. I have always tried to protect you from the ups and downs of my work. We can't save the bank. It's finished. I'm not coming to you to discuss what's already happened. I'm coming to you to tell you what's going to happen."

"But things will pick up, right?" she said. "Remember 1921 when we first got married? There was a panic then too."

"You are right, darling," Finn said, sounding like he was sure things would never pick up again, "but right now we're still in the thick of it."

"There must be something *else* we can do!" she cried.

"I've done it." Finn squeezed his hands together.

"They can't come here!"

"Vanessa, I can't pay four mortgages and four sets of property taxes. I can't pay the electric, water, coal, the phone bills, the Beacon Hill and Back Bay garbage collection on four homes! We don't have a business anymore. If we don't sell the other three homes, soon I won't be able to pay for the little food we do eat." Finn breathed heavily for both of them because he saw that Vanessa was barely breathing at all.

"What about our car?"

"Sold long ago."

"You sold our car?"

"Why do you sound upset? You never went anywhere in it."

"Ah—what about our house in Truro?" Vanessa said in the self-satisfied tone of someone who thought she'd solved things.

"Sold back in September, Vanessa."

"You sold our house in Truro? And never told me?"

"I didn't want you to worry," Finn said.

Husband and wife stared at each other.

"What about my father's ski lodge in Vermont?"

"We sold it."

"What about his mews in Lothbury?"

"We sold it."

In a weak voice she said, "So what's left?"

"We've sold everything we have and everything we own," said Finn. "Their homes are next. And our home is next after that."

"We don't need that much heating! We have our fireplaces."

"Unless I'm going out to the Boston Common and chopping down trees, firewood also costs money."

"What about our staff? They cost money too, don't they?"

Finn took a breath. "I've had to let them all go, Vee," he said.

"You didn't! What about Isabelle?"

"We can't afford her either," said Finn. "I let her go too . . ."

"No!" Vanessa screeched in a near-hysterical voice.

Finn raised his hands to comfort her. "Isabelle refused to go. She said she would work for us for free, for room and board."

"Isabelle will work for free?"

"Has been, since last October."

They eyed each other despairingly from across the room.

"What do you want me to say, Finn?"

"What do you want to say?"

"Absolutely nothing."

"Then say absolutely nothing," Finn said. "Now that you know what's happening, it will be easier for me."

"Anything to make it easier for *you*, darling."

Finn was quiet. "Why the tone?"

"I can't modulate every single word out of my mouth." She sounded like a wounded bird. "Oh, goodness! Isn't there *something* you can do so everybody in Boston doesn't have to come live in my house?"

He saw her graceful face twisted with anxiety, her shoulders narrowed, her arms knotted at her chest. Finn did what he always did when he saw she couldn't handle the stress and was on the verge of a nervous episode that could last for weeks. He backed off and tried to soothe her.

"Don't worry, Vee," he said. "Please don't worry, darling. Come here." When she didn't, he went to her and embraced her. She shook with emotion. Her arms stayed at her sides. "I'll take care of it," he said, kissing her head. "We just need to live in the foxhole for a few months. It's a new year, business will pick up. I'll get a new job that pays well, and everything will be fine."

In the smallest voice he'd ever heard from her, Vanessa said, "And what if business won't pick up? Will it still be fine?"

46

How Time Flies

"Isabelle," Vanessa said the following day, confronting Isabelle because she was the only person Vanessa had the courage to confront, "why didn't you tell me my husband fired you?"

"He tried," Isabelle said. "He didn't succeed. There was nothing to tell."

"Why didn't you tell me about the bank?"

"It wasn't my place."

"But why didn't you say *anything*?"

"It wasn't my place," Isabelle repeated.

"So what has he been up to if not working at the bank?"

"He been working very hard to help his family," Isabelle said.

"Clearly not! If Finn wants something done, it always gets done. If he was doing what he was supposed to, we wouldn't be on the brink of having a house full of people!"

"Not people," Isabelle said. "Family."

"*Same* difference," spat a threadbare Vanessa. "Who is going to cook? Who is going to clean? Who is going to look after the girls?"

"We all will. We muddle by. Make some judgments."

"Do you mean *adjustments*?"

"That too." Isabelle stared at Vanessa with a hard expression.

"We need a different plan," Vanessa said, looking away. "Because this is *not* going to work for me."

"Oh sure, definitely talk to Finn about *that*," said Isabelle.

But when Vanessa brought this up with Finn, he was downright impatient with her, almost as if Isabelle had been ironic with her advice. "We all have to pitch in, Vanessa," he said. "Our troubles are not over just because we're combining our households."

"I agree, darling. Our troubles are just beginning."

"Our troubles have been beginning for some time, Vee," said Finn. "But now we'll be a house full of men and women. We have arms, legs, brains. We will figure it out."

"Isabelle wants *your* children to help cook for the family!"

"Wonderful," Finn said. "They're industrious girls capable of anything."

"She said I should clean my own house!"

"She's not wrong, Vee. You are a very accomplished cleaner."

"I don't clean the whole house! I clean some things."

"If you feel you can't do it, ask your mother and sister to help."

"I'm going to ask my *mother* to help me keep my own home?" Vanessa's voice rose in pitch. "Yes, humiliate me more, why don't you? No," she said firmly. "Isabelle can clean it."

"Isabelle *can't* clean it," Finn said quietly but no less firmly. "Unless you and your mother and sister agree to do all the shopping and the cooking and the heating. Then she can clean it." He softened his tone but only slightly. "My mother said she will look after our girls. She said she will school her grandchildren herself. So that's one less thing to worry about."

"Frankly, it sounds like one *more* thing to worry about."

"Then you're welcome to do it. Or we can send them to public school."

Vanessa gasped. "Why can't Isabelle do it?" she said. "You said she would help with whatever I needed. That's what you said when you brought her home to me, remember?"

"I brought her home for *us*," Finn said. "Not just you. And I was paying her then. But our life has changed, can't you see that?"

Vanessa's life certainly changed. Within a month, three moving trucks of other people's things—other people's dirt, chaos, dust—and other people barged into her quiet house. The commotion was unbearable. Eleanor and Monty moved to the attic rooms. Olivia and Earl and Walter and Lucy took over the entire third floor, which used to be Finn's study, library, and game room. Isabelle had the run of the lower floor.

Vanessa confined herself to her room—to give everyone time to settle in without her intrusion, she said. But even after the messy ruckus had died down, there was no avoiding the daily cries of, "Vanessa, are you coming downstairs for morning coffee?" "Vanessa, we're going to the park, are you coming?" "Vanessa, what would you like for dinner?"

As the days, weeks, and months dragged on and flew by, Vanessa went into a fugue state. She was living, yet not living, functioning, yet not functioning, awake, yet not awake. The only room in the house that stayed spotless was her bedroom. That was where she could lock herself in and clean, scrub, scrape, dust, and polish nonstop. She didn't attend to the rest of the house because the only way she knew how to clean was room by room. That's what she told her family. When one room was clean, she moved on to the next. It was no use leaving a place until it was flawless. Best to finish one job well instead of having the whole house half-done.

And that one room was *never* clean enough.

Dust kept falling, windows kept getting smudged, the birds kept dirtying her window ledges. The bedspreads were wrinkled, water spots dried all over the cabinets near the washbasins because her husband cared nothing for such things and would leave the water where it fell without wiping it away. The cornices, floorboards, and corners of every single man-made thing were hosts for crud. In nature there were no corners; everything was rounded. If only they could build Vanessa a house with rounded walls and doors and windows, rounded furniture, everything round, nowhere for dirt and bugs to hide. Just circles and circles of order.

Sometimes, when she was in her room, Vanessa didn't get to any cleaning at all, busy as she was assiduously sanding down the infernal corners of her extra-large dressers with emery paper. She spent countless hours smoothing out every enormous sharp point in her furniture, edges that jutted out just like those Lovell's Island rocks Isabelle's ship had thrown itself against in the violent harbor.

Vanessa couldn't say for sure how long she continued this way. It was cold, then less cold, then cold again. It rained, there was wind. She was always cold. She wore her sweaters in layers. Sometimes she took off one of the layers. Sometimes she cracked open a window to let in some fresh air. During family dinners, Vanessa paid no attention to talk of politics or the economy or Prohibition or markets—as always. It was easy to tune out. She sat there, nodding like a marquee star, pretending she was listening.

Finn was out all hours working. The only one Vanessa had regular contact with was Isabelle. She came in every day to air out the room, to bring fresh water and sometimes even fresh flowers. She said Ukrainians loved flowers because they brought a smile to every face. She brought Vanessa books, and she turned on the radio that Vanessa turned off as soon as Isabelle left.

To Vanessa, this non-existent existence seemed to continue for infinity.

But one Saturday morning, there was an insistent, loud knock on the door that alerted even Vanessa to her external circumstances. She cursed herself for leaving her room and sneaking downstairs to get a cup of tea. Finn was either out or with his parents upstairs. Isabelle was down on the lower level. There was no longer a maid or a housekeeper to open the door for visitors. Vanessa was forced to answer it herself.

She regretted it as soon as the door inched open because there on her top step stood Lucas. She had seen Lucas only once, five years ago when he brought her husband back home to her, late and unforgivably drunk. She never forgot his stupid good-looking face or forgave him.

Vanessa made to shut the door quickly, but Lucas threw his foot forward to stop her. "Wait," he said. "I'm sorry to intrude, but I really need to speak to your husband. It's an emergency. Please."

"What kind of emergency could *you* possibly have that you need my husband for?" said Vanessa. "You're not in the drunk tank. I see no police with you. You're not bleeding."

"My mother is sick," Lucas said, and his wretched face bore witness to the truth of his struggle. "I think she's dying."

"What does that have to do with my *husband*?" said Vanessa. "He's not a doctor."

"Please can I talk to him." It wasn't a question.

"No, you cannot," Vanessa said superciliously. "Please leave—"

A voice sounded behind her. "Vanessa." It was Isabelle.

"This is none of your concern, Isabelle," Vanessa said. "Step away."

"Hello, Isabelle," said Lucas and started to cry.

"Finn is coming, Lucas," Isabelle said. "Wait."

"You know Lucas?" said Vanessa. Why didn't you ever tell me about him, she wanted to ask. But she wasn't entirely certain she had ever mentioned the lowly Lucas to Isabelle, had ever made clear how much she despised him.

A moment later, Finn was at the door. "I'll take it from here, Vee," he said, from behind her. Vanessa didn't move. "Will you excuse me?"

"Finn, you promised me," Vanessa said. "You promised you would never see him again."

"Vanessa, will you excuse me," Finn repeated, pushing past her and shutting the door behind him.

Vanessa stood with the closed door between them, struggling for breath. When she turned around, Isabelle had her coat on and was carrying Finn's coat in her hands. "Forgive him, Vanessa," said Isabelle. "His mother must be very sick."

"Forgive *who*? And whose mother?" Vanessa muttered, flummoxed off her axis.

"Will you excuse me, Vanessa," said Isabelle, repeating Finn's words but in her own voice, not his. "The girls are upstairs. They'll probably need some breakfast soon." Opening the door, she slipped outside.

Vanessa was motionless for a few moments. Slowly, she turned around and, grasping the railing tightly, went to her bedroom without addressing her family or checking on her daughters.

47

Oksana

Ukraine, May 1929

Isabelle left her house at five in the morning and walked down to the fields. The ground was hard. It hadn't rained in seventeen days, a historical record for April and May in Ukraine.

When she told Mirik this, he laughed it off, because he bred and milked cows, and as long as there was enough forage, rain meant nothing to him. But Isabelle knew: the seedling crops couldn't last much longer in the dry earth without water. The crops needed relief from the skies, and none came, *for seventeen days*. The desperate earth needed rain. The skies were silent.

"Isa, don't you have enough to worry about?" Mirik said.

"No," she said. "This is it. This is all fate and all hope."

"Say the prayer words," Mirik said. "Say them like your mother taught you, from Agamemnon."

"*Rain rain beloved Zeus,*" said Isabelle, "*rain on the cornfields and the plains of Attica.*" She crossed herself and made the sign of the cross on Mirik too.

Over a decade ago, famine came during the Civil War between the Bolsheviks and everyone else, wiping out half the farms. Many left to fight; some escaped the country altogether, like Schumann. Though all sides in the conflict were starving, they still had enough energy to blame the Jews for the entirety of their ills: for the Revolution, for the famine, for the war, for the carnage. The countryside was ravaged, a hundred thousand Jews destroyed, Martyn Lazar murdered, and then came a few years of a fragile truce, when they were left more or less alone to grow what they wanted, to live as they wished.

Ispas was so far southwest that had Kaiser Wilhelm and the Germans been more demanding and Lenin more accommodating during their separate peace talks in 1918, Ispas could have easily been handed to Austria-Hungary instead of remaining in Russian hands. What would that have been like, Isabelle wondered, to be a Ukrainian in Austria?

For one, her father would not have been at the forefront of the Peasant Rebellion of 1919. To be a Ukrainian in Austria might have meant her father would still be alive—though who could say for how long? As soon as Austria lost the war in November 1918, Russia grabbed back what they had ceded to Germany six months earlier. Isabelle would've been in the same place, dreading each step of the dry ground as she walked with the jug to bring milk to the gestating Yana, who was weeks away from giving birth.

Isabelle's worry about the drought was confirmed by Cici, who upon seeing her all glum said that maybe Mirik was right. "Soon, the milk from his cows will be the only food left for us to eat."

"Stop, Cici, why do you say this?"

"Because it's time for us to go. Look at our poor potatoes." They were shriveled in the parched earth, the roots barely sprouting. "Two of our chickens have died," Cici said. "Forget about Soviet chickens laying six eggs a day. We can't even keep alive our mangy Ukrainian chickens, who are so hungry they've stopped laying eggs."

"How many chickens do we have left?"

"Four. Maybe we should eat the chickens, Isa?"

Slowed by the chilling grip of her fear of the rising sun and the future, Isabelle trudged back down to the barn, the empty canister heavy on her shoulder.

"What are we going to do, Mama?" Isabelle said to her mother in the covered shed.

"Stop wringing your hands like you're a child," Oksana said. "You know what you must do." Her back was turned. She reeked of petroleum. She was filling dozens of small containers with kerosene from the spout of one of their 200-liter drums. Every year, Roman traded one of his horses to Ilya Petrov in Kammenets for a giant cask of kerosene. This year, Roman traded for two casks.

"Mama, what are you doing?"

"God's work. What are *you* doing? Stop interrogating me and go oil the saddles, make sure they're in working order."

"I have to make breakfast."

"Fine. Go do that. Anything, really. Go do it."

"Mama, it hasn't rained."

"You don't have to tell me about it. We have almost no well water left. Ration it carefully. Tell the boys not to play in the mud."

"What mud? There's no water."

"In the dust, then. You don't want grimy children. It reflects poorly on you." Straightening up, Oksana wiped her brow with her dirty field gloves.

"You're going to need a bath yourself, Mama," Isabelle said. "Does a filthy mother reflect poorly on her daughter?"

"Stop being sassy," Oksana said. "Send the boys to the brook with two buckets each. If it hasn't dried up."

"It has dried up," said Isabelle, "and you didn't answer my question."

"You can't stay, Isa," Oksana said. "For many reasons all of which you know. Seventeen days of no rain is God telling you for the final time."

Isabelle had walked her fields.

She knew.

You could not reap what you didn't sow.

"And when Zhuk sees nothing growing in our fields in May, he will know it too," said Oksana. "What do you think he'll do then?"

"Him taking our farm isn't going to produce more grain," said Isabelle.

"It doesn't matter. They've already decided on a course for us. The rest is pretense." The dust-soiled woman gazed at her daughter with love and sadness. "Ten years ago, your father died because they tried to make him into what he wasn't."

"What was that, a Russian?"

"A slave," said Oksana.

"Oh, Mama."

"So much blather out here," Oksana said softly. "I thought your children needed breakfast?"

"If we run, what are we going to do with all our things?"

"Leave them behind," said Oksana.

"What, everything? The things you collected for three decades with Papa? The priceless precious things you brought with you from Krakow? Your mother's linens and tablecloths? The pewter silverware and drinkware? The art you painted, the books you read, that I read, that my children are reading now? All our embroidered blankets, our silk shawls, passed from generation to generation—you can't be serious! Are you really suggesting we leave it all behind?"

"Yes," said Oksana. "You carry your sons on your horse and your life on your back. Every last scrap of life will be ripped from your fingers. Especially anything that looks Ukrainian. The Soviet purpose is to stamp out our nation, Isabelle, not to preserve it through family heirlooms."

On the *twentieth* day of no rain, in the middle of the night, Yefim Efros, with a posse of armed OGPU *chekists*, drove up in a military truck and arrested Oksana and Bogda, who was Mirik and Petka's mother.

Roman and Cici, Ostap with a livid Yana by his side, Nikora, Petka, Isabelle, and Mirik could do nothing but stand helplessly as they watched the guards drag their mothers in their nightgowns across the clearing.

But even as they pulled a struggling Oksana away, they were pulling her away unbowed. "Isa, don't you dare give them your father's farm!" she cried. "Forget me, I don't matter! Only the land matters!"

A guard hit her over the head with the butt of his rifle to silence her and then stuffed her unconscious into the back of the wagon.

"Don't move, Roman," Isabelle said, grabbing her brother's arm and yanking him behind her. "Don't talk. Please. Let me handle it." She stepped forward. "Why are you taking them?" she said to Efros, not even bothering to address him. "What have they done?"

"You are hiding food from us," Efros replied. "The nation is starving, and you are hoarding what's not yours."

"It's not hoarding," she said. "It's called storing."

"It's against the law!"

"You want to take our wrinkled potatoes, comrade?" said Isabelle. "Be my guest. They're right in the pantry. But what would I fry up for you when you came to visit me?"

"Next time we come, we're not coming to eat, I promise you," Efros said.

"We are starving like everyone else, I promise *you*," Isabelle said. "After a poor harvest, spring is the most difficult time. We are buying what meager food we can find on the market. The few fresh potatoes we have, we dug up from Stan and Vitaly's potato farm. There is no hoarding."

"And we see the future! The ten acres you've allotted us are not enough. We need all fifteen from you. It's been decreed."

"The future will have a very good harvest," said Isabelle. "Why are you really taking my mother?"

"Because Comrade Zhuk has been too generous with you. He is soft-hearted."

"You gave us a requirement," Isabelle said. "We planted what we agreed to. You inspect our fields every day. You know this to be true."

"Fifteen acres will grow more than ten acres, we also know *that* to be true," Efros said.

"That's not what we agreed to," said Isabelle, elbowing her brother to stay back and stay silent but failing to keep the loathing out of her own voice.

"We are done negotiating with you, Lazars," Efros said, sliding into the passenger seat of the truck and slamming the door. "It's simple. Sign over your farm to the collective and you will save your mothers."

***

Petka stood crying, flailing his arms, pulling on his beard, ripping out tufts of his hair.

"You are my wife," Mirik said to Isabelle, as she listened to the departing truck huff down the hill. "I am *ordering* you to sign over the farm. This has gone far enough. Petka! Calm down, come on."

"Mirik," Isabelle said, "you should really start to worry when you sound like them and not like us." But she was drained of bravery. While the rest of the family dispersed, she and her brothers stayed outside in the clearing between their houses, pacing and arguing, shouting even, planning for their vanishing future. Afterward, she didn't lie down with Mirik in their bed but instead squeezed between her two little boys in theirs, where she tossed and turned until sunrise when Maxim woke up and snuggled against her.

In big city prisons, the Bolsheviks fed the incarcerated, which was one of the reasons that when times were hard, the farmers strived to get arrested—because they knew they'd at least be fed. But in the villages, the prisoners' families had to bring them their daily meal; otherwise, they wouldn't eat.

Isabelle brought food for her mother and the frail shivering Bogda. The two women were being kept in a single dwarf-sized cell in the hastily constructed jail. To get extra time with her mother, Isabelle brought some low-quality homemade rotgut for the guards. She almost had no decent *zapivka* left. The Communists were consuming copious amounts of liquor whenever they came to assess her fields, draining her supplies of alcohol just as they drained her of everything else.

Isabelle doubted Efros had informed Oksana or Mirik's wheezing, rheumatic mother Bogda of the charges against them, but he had. They were being accused of criminal hoarding, sympathizing with saboteurs, sabotage of collectivization efforts, and collaborating with anti-Soviet elements.

As Isabelle sat despairingly on a low stool by the metal bars of her mother's cell, Oksana said to her, "Isa, *sonechka, milaya, dochenka,* kiss my hand and leave me. For your sake, not mine. Stop behaving like I mean anything to you. Act the opposite."

"You're my mother," said Isabelle, kissing Oksana's fingers through the bars. "No matter how I act, Efros knows what that means."

"How are your brothers? Yana?"

"Not great." That was an understatement. Especially Yana. The blood of fury spurted from that woman's eyes.

"Do your best to calm Yana down. They took me to provoke a reaction from my children," Oksana said. "Tell your brothers to be smart, not foolish. Tell them to keep their heads. Yana especially."

"She's deaf to my pleas for reason." Isabelle leaned forward so her mother could caress her lowered head through the bars.

"Tell her to think of Zhuk and Efros as scavengers. The carrion birds see only the outside of your body. If you act like I'm nothing, they won't know I'm an alive thing, a significant thing. They are vultures."

"Yana is not thinking about fooling them, Mama," said Isabelle. "She is more of a pregnant lord of war with a sword."

"Hide or act, Isa," said Oksana. "Or they'll take something else you love."

Isabelle paled, already translucent from hunger and worry.

"My precious girl, my beautiful bravest girl, your fate has been decided," Oksana said. "Remember you asked Roman who our enemy was? I'll tell you. It's me. It's your husband. It's your sons. The heavens have blackened over Ukraine. You're part of Russia's descent into hell. Famine is only the first weapon of evil. Terror is another. The slave caravans are to follow. I'm gone, forget me. Poor Bogda, too. The life is gone. Your father's farm and *everything in it*," Oksana said meaningfully, "is what you've got left. It's your only remaining leverage. The sooner you realize it, the greater your chance is of salvaging a fragment of yourself to find another life."

48

Cora

"Let's go!" Isabelle barked at Finn, interrupting Finn's open-handed refusals to help his brother.

"Why did you come here?" Finn was saying. "What do you think I can do about it? I'm going to catch hell for this. My wife—you've caused me so much trouble already, Lucas—"

"Finn! Shame on you," Isabelle said. "Let's go!" Her words were so sharp and final, Finn and Lucas were halfway down Acorn Street before Finn ventured to ask where they were going.

"To Schumann's," she said, walking like running. The men could barely keep up.

"Why are we going to Schumann?" Finn asked, panting. "We don't need anything tailored or cleaned."

"We're going to Schumann's because he can help us," said Isabelle. "If anyone can, it's him."

"By stitching a torn sleeve?"

"By tending to your"—she stopped herself and regrouped—"to Lucas's mother."

Finn's eyes were to the ground. "How can Schumann tend to the sick all of a sudden?"

"Not all of sudden," said Isabelle. "Continuously. Why do you think he's got so many customers who come to him with their problems? In Ukraine, Schumann used to be village doctor. He is still doctor. Everybody knows."

"*I* didn't know," said an astonished and anxious Finn.

"Lot you don't know," said Isabelle. "You didn't need him before. You were lucky."

The first thing Schumann said when Isabelle told him about Lucas's mother was, "What's wrong with her?"

"I don't know," Lucas said. "She collapsed this morning at the sink and couldn't get up."

"Did she faint?"

"Maybe. Then she started babbling." Tears sprang to Lucas's eyes. "She kept saying *Finn Finn Finn* over and over."

It was all Finn could do to stand straight.

"What's your mother's name, Lucas?"

"Cora," Lucas said. "Cora McBride."

"Is your father with her?"

Lucas shook his head. "No one's seen Tadhg McBride in ages. Ma thinks he's back in Ireland. Or dead. Hardly a difference between the two."

Schumann disappeared into the back, emerging in a white coat and carrying a black doctor's bag. "Lead the way, Lucas," said Schumann.

With Isabelle bringing up the rear, Finn doggedly followed Lucas through the narrowing streets of upper North End, winding here, ending there, past tenements of such decrepit poverty it hurt Finn's eyes. They stopped at a slight ramshackle house, squeezed as if in a vise between two tall apartment buildings. The stoopless front door was level with the sidewalk. Lucas opened the door, calling out, "Ma, I'm home!" and showed them into the rundown parlor room, where a white-haired woman lay on a brown sofa, her head thrown back. "Ma, look, I brought a doctor." Lucas knelt by her side and kissed her hands. "And look, Ma, I brought Finn. Remember you was asking for Finn? Well, here he is, look, Ma, look."

It was then that the woman, who had appeared to be in a dead faint, opened her eyes, turned her head, and stared into Finn's oppressed, aggrieved face.

Schumann stepped up, taking out his stethoscope. "Excuse me, boys," he said. "I need to listen to her heart."

The woman shooed Schumann away and motioned for Finn. "Come here, my boy." Her voice was gravelly, tinged with Irish brogue, crackling with emotion.

No one could've been more reluctant than Finn to step forward. But now he stood, towering like a mute hulking presence over the woman on the sofa. Isabelle found him a chair, and he fell into it.

"I'm Cora McBride," she said.

"I'm Finn," he said.

"I know who you are," she whispered. "I know it well."

"Her pulse is weak and irregular," Schumann said, holding Cora's wrist. "Very weak. She may have had a heart attack."

"I've been having them heart attacks for the last ten years," Cora said, pulling her hand away from Schumann. "It's nothing. I'll be all right. Lucas, being the last child and the only one in the house with me, is as always overreacting. I fainted is all. Get me some soup and a sandwich, doc, I'll be good as new." All of this was spoken weakly but firmly, as if brooking no argument.

"Is there any food in kitchen I can make you?" Isabelle said.

"Who is this?" said Cora. "If there was food in the kitchen, would I be faint on the floor? I'd be eating that food, wouldn't I? You think I need you to go into me own kitchen to make me a sandwich? I need you to go out there"—the woman gestured to the front door—"and find me something."

Schumann didn't think that was a bad idea. "If she eats a little, she might feel better. Let's go, Isa."

Finn couldn't explain to Schumann or to Lucas or to the ailing woman on the couch, or to Isabelle, or even to himself, how much he didn't want Isabelle to leave. For reasons innumerable, he needed to feel her presence behind him, needed her not to leave him alone with what he didn't want to face.

"Isabelle and I will go together," Finn said.

"No," Cora said from the couch. "You stay, *Finn.*" She said his name with such emphasis, such intensity, such meaning. He nearly groaned.

Behind him, Isabelle said, "It's fine, I go by myself."

Finn whirled around, imploring her with his eyes.

She blinked in silent understanding. "You know what? Why don't we wait," Isabelle said. "Or perhaps Lucas can go?"

"I got no money," said Lucas.

"I don't want Lucas to leave my side," said Cora. "He already left once to fetch you, Finn. That's plenty of fetching for one day."

"Cora, let Schumann examine you," Isabelle said. "He's doctor."

Cora wouldn't let Schumann touch her. "I can't be helped no more," she said. "But I can be comforted."

Reaching out, she grabbed Finn's sleeve and pulled him closer. Her hand slowly traveled up to his face; she rested her palm against his cheek. She rubbed his stubble and ruffled his hair and caressed his face, her blue eyes oozing love and sadness and regret, her entire long imperfect life sliding out of her tear ducts. Finn could barely look at her.

"Oh, my boy," she kept whispering. "Oh, my boy."

No one said anything else. For long minutes, Cora's agonized sniffling and Finn's agonized breathing were the only sounds in the room.

"Finn, I know you must be smeck with me for what I done," Cora said. "Lucas tells me how awful you are to him."

"No, I don't, Ma! I don't say awful, never!"

"I don't blame ya," Cora said. "But you know what Lucas says to me? He says why didn't you give me up, Ma, instead of him? Lucas says all you want is to be back with me, and all he wants is to be where you are. Your brother keeps telling me I gave up the wrong son."

"Ma, I never said this in my whole wasted life," Lucas said. "Those words never come out of my mouth. Why you saying this?"

"You wanted to, though, son," Cora said to Lucas. "You been thinking it for thirty years." She turned her eyes to Finn. "Finn," Cora said, "I birthed you, and I named you, and I fed you with my own milk. For five months you were my bonny baby boy, such a good, sweet baby. It broke my heart to give you up, but your brother Travis was sick, Finn! He had tuberculosis, and to fix him was going to cost me a thousand dollars! And if I didn't fix him, he was gonna die!" Cora almost laughed. "I had eight kiddos back then. It was Christmas 1898, your father away on one of his binges I thought, but he was already in the wind, my Travis eighteen months and dying, you five months, and I was pregnant with Lucas! Now there's only you, me and Lucas left." Cora's voice was barely a whisper. "And soon there'll be only you and Lucas. I couldn't give up the dying boy. And your older brothers and sister wouldn't have fetched a quarter of what we got for you."

A dry sob left Finn's throat.

"Your new mother and father gave me *two thousand dollars!*" Cora said. "They'd been trying to have a baby fifteen years. I knew your mother well. She was a teacher here in North End. Every Saturday she stayed hours to tutor your brothers and sister who, don't mind my saying so, were not the sharpest tacks in her drawer. She was a remarkable woman who wasn't given the gift of childbirth. And my Travis was gonna die. What could I do, Finn? Olivia said I changed her life by giving you to her. And you saved your brother's life, and me and all the kids lived off the money I got for you for nearly three years. Lucas was more than two when that money dried up."

Finn hadn't raised his sunken head once, looking nowhere but at his feet, at his knotted hands. He couldn't speak about Travis, couldn't tell Cora about the existential injustice perpetrated on Travis McBride in Northern Italy on November 2, 1918. *Finn, you are my brother.*

"I know you think I sold you, son . . ."

"I don't *think* this," Finn said. "You did. You sold me."

"You never come to me, though you knew I was here all them years," Cora said, tears down her face. "I would've begged forgiveness from you. I didn't give you away to a slave master. I gave you to a lovely, serious couple mourning their barrenness. I knew you'd be in good hands. And you were. Look at you, look how you turned out. Your one life made so many other lives better. At this late hour, this eleventh hour, please don't be cross with me. Please forgive your dear old desperate ma and rejoice in the pride I feel for you, in the love I've had for you my whole life."

Finn didn't know how he was ever going to look up or face her or Lucas or himself. *O Lord, hear my prayer, help me.*

And help bent to him from above in the form of a refugee fleeing all her days from her own sordid griefs. Finn felt a strong, warm hand around his shoulder, an open palm full of tenderness and compassion, clasping him, holding him, and Isabelle bending to him, to his deeply lowered head, and whispering in his ear, "Finn, it's your *mother*. She is dying, and she is begging you for mercy and forgiveness. Don't leave her this way. Please, Finn. Lift your eyes. Look at her."

Finn wiped his face, raised his suffering gaze, leaned forward, and very carefully laid his head into the crook of his mother's neck.

Lightly sobbing, Cora gratefully wrapped her arms around him. "There, there," she whispered. "There, there, my golden boy, my beloved baby, my sweetest son, my divine angel. There, there." One of her arms continued to hold Finn, and the other hand lowered to Lucas's head.

Isabelle didn't have a chance to bring Cora McBride soup and a sandwich. She died that morning, with Finn's head cradled under her chin and Lucas's resting on her stomach.

49

The Four Passions

Ukraine, May 1929

The split in the family was bitter, blackening every word and darkening every soul.

No one could put forth a persuasive enough case for what was best. They were all like vile Zhuk, relying on the power of useless words to affect a change in their circumstances, and failing. No one knew what combination of words they could use to persuade the others.

Fear was a ruler.

Anger was a ruler too.

So was pride.

And so was despair.

And each one dictated a different response to the matter of Efros and Zhuk and the Communist Party of the Soviet Union.

Fear said, do nothing, keep quiet, work, they'll leave you alone. Give them what they want, feed them; give them the land, the milk, the horses. Do anything to stay alive. Anything to save the children.

But Anger said never. Never! To all those things.

And Pride echoed Anger's words. *Never*, to any of those things. They already took from us almost everything. They cannot have what's left.

While Despair said, do whatever you must, anything, everything, to live.

The crisis made the family behave in starkly different ways. Even Petka understood that when you arrested the mother of a Cossack you were not mending fences. And after his own mother was taken, Petka—who was most definitely not a Cossack—wanted no part of the war to come.

To save his hide, Petka made a separate peace with Roman. He swore to him on the blood of the covenant that he would never say a word about anything to anyone in exchange for one of Roman's older horses. Petka decided to take Roman's wise advice and go visit family in Proskuriv. Roman agreed, though he later told Isabelle he didn't know how Petka would answer even the most basic questions at the roadblocks out of Ispas without disclosing almost immediately that he was a tenant farmer on the Lazar ranch and was, inexplicably—in the middle of the farm's busiest season—leaving with his entire family and all his belongings. "Our time is drawing short," Roman said to Isabelle, "and not just because of Petka."

Petka loaded the milk cart with essentials, which included his wife, children, and his ailing father, harnessed the nag, and took off before sunrise. The day before they left, Mirik asked Petka to take Slava and Maxim.

Petka refused. "I can't be responsible for Lazar children, brother," he said. "They can't be controlled. You tell them one thing, they nod their heads and do what they want."

"They're your blood," Mirik said.

"Maybe, but look at them," said Petka. In the dusty clearing, Slava and Maxim were fencing with two of Martyn Lazar's old swords. "Open your eyes. They're not remotely Kovalenkos."

Isabelle came up behind the brothers and stared at her sons through their backs. "Are you giving away my children without speaking to me, Mirik?"

"Why not?" he said. "You're planning to declare war on the Soviet Union without speaking to me."

"Slava, Maxim, come here, boys," Isabelle called to her sons.

They ran up, swords up.

"Darlings," she said, her hands on their shoulders. "First of all, don't run with your swords up; it's not safe. Second, your Uncle Petka is going to visit relatives in Proskuriv. Would you like to go with him for a little visit? Just a few weeks. Mama and Papa will join you soon."

In unison the boys refused. They did everything together.

Isabelle took a deep breath. "What about if your father comes with you?"

"Isabelle!" said Mirik. "Don't—don't do that. Don't speak for me."

They took a few steps back to speak privately. "You believe there's danger here," she said. "I'm offering this to you. You want to go? Go."

"Only if you come with me," Mirik replied, just as quietly.

"You know I can't," said Isabelle.

"Is Uncle Roman going to come?" Slava said, whooshing his sword. "Is Mama going to come? Because if they're not going, we're not going."

"If they're not going, we're not going," echoed Maxim.

"Case in point, dear brother," Petka said to Mirik. "And probably for the best. There's no room in the milk cart for you and your sons."

* * *

The day after Petka fled, Oksana and Bogda disappeared by train to parts unknown. Isabelle went to bring her mother her daily meal, and Oksana was gone. In their cell were two new women stretching out their hands to Isabelle's plate of potatoes. Neither Efros nor Zhuk, nor anyone else would say a word about where they'd been taken. In exchange for half a bottle of vodka, a guard at the jail told Isabelle about a Kammenets train that took the mothers in the night.

A day after Oksana vanished, Yana, who was by then nearly at term, showed everyone what it was like to be ruled by all four passions—fear, anger, pride, and despair. While Ispas slept, she walked three kilometers to the village, climbed to the second floor of Efros's requisitioned house, crept through his window, suffocated him with his own dirty socks lying on the floor, and then dragged him and hanged him by the neck off a thick branch of the beech tree she had just climbed. The socks were still stuffed in his mouth.

Yana took his revolvers and walked three kilometers back home. Day was almost breaking, but she didn't go to bed. Instead, she proceeded down into the valley, past the fallow fields, to the far end of their property by the brook, and induced labor by breaking her waters with a thin piece of metal wire, inserted just so. Alone in the woods, Yana gave birth and smothered her infant in the earth. She buried him and then shot herself with Efros's revolver, falling over the little grave. Isabelle and Cici heard the thundering gunshot echo through the cold morning. Screaming, the newborn cranes flapped up into the sky and flew away without a formation.

Yana spoke of her plan to no one; she asked no one for help. She must have believed it was the only way to help her fearless Ostap fight the way he was meant to, the way Yana would have, had she not felt herself to be a burden to him.

Ostap wept for a day and then hardened into granite.

The grim and mute family was still burying Yana when Zhuk and the OGPU men arrived, armed and furious, set to arrest and execute the pregnant blonde woman four witnesses saw stringing up Efros near the public square.

After what happened to Efros, Zhuk and the *chekists* didn't leave Isabelle's farm. During the day, the OGPU guards shadowed the Lazars on their daily tasks or pointed rifles at Isabelle's children for sport, and at night they smoked and drank and played cards and ate the meager rations Isabelle prepared for them.

Zhuk forbade the family to meet or speak privately. His guards upended their pantries in search of food and rifled through the homes looking for weapons.

Roman allowed Zhuk's men to do what they wished and said nothing, stopping his sister and brothers from raising their voices in complaint. "The time has not yet come," said Roman.

The only way Isabelle and Mirik spoke to each other was out in the fields or in bed at night and only in the softest tones because the sentry sat either right below their open window or at the table in their living room. But even before the incursion, Isabelle had nothing to say to her husband lately, even in bed. The cleft between the Lazars and Kovalenkos had grown unbridgeable.

After her mother had vanished and Yana died, Isabelle had even less to say to Mirik.

A few nights after Zhuk came, it was Mirik who reached out to Isabelle.

"Isa," he whispered, lying behind her. His arm went around her. He nuzzled into her hair.

"Shh."

"Isa, I'm sorry."

"Still shh, but for what?"

"For thinking we could do it my way. I really believed they'd leave us alone."

"Not very likely now, after Yana. Or even then."

"You and your brothers terrify me," Mirik said. "Can I just say this before I say anything else?"

"Say it quick," Isabelle said. "He's going to hear you in a minute."

And right on cue, Gregor the sentry yelled outside their open window. "Hey, you two, enough! Fuck or sleep but shut the hell up!"

Grinding her teeth, Isabelle breathed to calm down, to settle in, to sleep for a few hours before another hard hungry day would begin. They waited for Gregor to step away to piss in the grass before they spoke again.

"They tore all goodwill out of my chest when they took my mother," Mirik whispered.

"I had no goodwill left before they took mine," whispered Isabelle.

"I didn't think I would feel this heavy with my anger."

"We are mocked by them," Isabelle whispered back. "They drip poison upon our earth. But we have not been beaten yet, Mirik, and we have not been dishonored."

"Not yet," Mirik said. "But it's coming. I can tell by Zhuk's demeanor. Something bad is coming."

Isabelle's unblinking eyes were focused on a splintered crack in the plank wall. "Oh, I agree," she said. "Something bad is coming."

"I'm so scared for our sons," Mirik whispered.

"No matter what we do," she said, "our sons have been disinherited from this land. The question is, can we promise them a place of their own? A place free from grief and pain."

"I don't know if such a place exists," Mirik said, sounding as down as he had ever sounded. "But let's try to find it. I'm with you. The time has come for us to act against those who act against us."

Turning, Isabelle embraced him. "It's long past time," she whispered.

"How would it even work?" Mirik asked.

"That part you leave to me."

"Don't they have to leave first before we can ride away?"

"One way or another," said Isabelle, "those men will leave my land."

"Why do I fear it's going to be another?" said Mirik.

It didn't look as if Zhuk was leaving voluntarily. "The murderess may be beyond our punishment," Zhuk told Isabelle, "but her family is not." He was waiting for reinforcements from Kammenets, he said. "Whether by chance or design, your labor force seems to have gotten quite depleted, comrades," he told the Lazars. "You barely have a handful of Lazars left on your farm. That's another reason we don't believe you can work these fields and animals yourselves. There are too few of you."

"Are you here to help us?" Roman said, looking over the dozen indolent men lounging around his clearing.

"We are here to keep you singularly focused on the pledge you made to me and my dear fallen colleague Yefim Efros," Zhuk said, "that you would deliver to us *two hundred bushels* or six metric tonnes of grain by September and produce two cows and five horses by June. You seem to be too distracted with murder and sudden trips to visit distant relatives to remember your quota requirements."

Poor Petka, Isabelle thought, pitying Mirik's brother and his innocent family.

"The cows will calve, Comrade Zhuk," Roman said. "The horses will foal. And six tonnes of grain will be delivered to you on time and in full."

It helped that neither Zhuk nor his Soviet guards had any idea what wheat stalks were supposed to look like in late May. The shoots should have been dense and over a meter tall, but instead they were sparse and barely out of the ground. Drought and torrential rains had done them in. It had rained only once in twenty-three days—the day Yana died.

And it hadn't stopped raining since.

Roman's pledge to Zhuk of a bountiful harvest may have been singed by drought and drowned by mud, but it was out of this sludge of earth and rain, with the armed Bolsheviks ten meters away on dry ground, that the plan took final shape in reedy piecemeal. The time to strategize was in the mire of the blighted fields.

They named it *Operation Enay*—Operation Aeneas—in tribute to their mother, Oksana Malita, a classical scholar at the University of Krakow, one of the few women who had studied there and taught there. Prince Aeneas was a mythical warrior, one of Troy's sole survivors who, after the destruction of his city, fashioned a boat out of wood and, with his father and son, set off into the great unknown through warm and treacherous waters to find a new homeland and build a new civilization.

After the rains, there were fish in the stream. Cici and Isabelle went fishing together. Next to them sat an OGPU soldier and a runt trainee from the Youth Brigade, one armed Communist for each unarmed farm woman, always watching, always listening.

"Your brother asks when," Cici said to Isabelle in Romanian, their fishing lines in the brook. "He's at breaking point."

"Tell him the time is near," Isabelle said. "*Enay* is a go."

"What are you saying?" screeched the nearby *chekist*, almost dropping his weapon.

"We caught a trout," Cici said, showing him.

In Romanian, Isabelle said, "Tell Roman to practice his *hoot-hoots* like a *bufnitsa*."

"I said Russian," screamed the guard.

"I said we need more worms," said Cici. "We don't have enough."

"In Russian!"

"How do you say worm in Russian? Maybe *you* know?" Cici asked.

"*Chervey*," replied the *chekist*.

"We dig for *treisprezece* black worms *when the moon is full*," said Isabelle to Cici, mostly in Russian so the Soviet guard could understand.

50

Husband and Wife

It was late when Finn returned home after that late-October day. As soon as she heard the front door close, Vanessa flew downstairs, disheveled and wild-eyed.

"She's been beside herself, Finn," said Lucy. "I've hardly ever seen her in such a state. What's wrong with her? Where were you today?"

"Lucas is not here, Vee," Finn said to his wife, falling into the armchair. Schumann had a supply of Tennessee whiskey, of which Finn and Isabelle and Schumann and Lucas had partaken most excessively before Finn and Isabelle left Cora's house and staggered home. Finn could not have faced the end of this terrible day without a drink, but now that he'd had it, he still didn't want to face anything, especially not Vanessa.

"Where have you been, Finn?" Vanessa said. "You've been gone all day . . . darling." He could see she forced herself to add *darling*. "And you smell of alcohol most strongly. Have you been drinking?"

"Exorbitantly," Finn said. "And with Lucas, too."

"Finn!"

Finn turned to his parents. "Lucas's mother, Cora McBride, died today," he said, and turned away from their gasping reaction. They tried to recover, but Olivia burst into tears.

"I'm very sorry for Lucas, son," said Earl, comforting his wife. "Now, now, darling. Oh, that poor boy."

"I'm sorry, Finn," said Olivia. "*My* poor boy."

"Who is Cora McBride, Earl?" said Walter. "If you don't mind me asking."

"Cora is—was—Lucas's mother," Olivia said, blowing her nose and wiping her eyes and sparing her husband a response.

"But who is Lucas?" asked Eleanor.

"You don't want to know, Ellie," said Vanessa, crossing her arms. "Just look at the state of my husband. That's the kind of person Lucas is."

Finn remained in the chair, his arms and legs stretched out, his eyes closing from drink and sorrow. His head bobbed back. Through the haze, he heard his father's voice. "We're sorry to hear about Cora, son," Earl said. "She was a big-hearted, kind, loving woman."

"Would that I'd had a chance to discover her attributes for myself," said Finn, raising his head and fixing his father with a scolding stare.

"That was not Cora's wish," Earl said. "And it was not our wish. This was the way the three of us chose to handle the situation. To the best of our abilities. You know something about that, don't you, Finn? Dealing with things to the best of your abilities, even when others might judge you for your actions?" Earl turned to the rest of his family. "I suppose there is something you all should know, even though it's really none of anyone's business," he said. "We adopted Finn when he was five months old. He was our Christmas miracle in 1898. Cora McBride was our son's real mother."

Earl began to say more, but before he could speak, Vanessa fainted.

After Vanessa came to and was settled in Finn's chair near the fireplace, she said to Finn, "Darling, forgive me, I thought I had misheard. Last thing I remember was Earl saying that Lucas's mother is also your mother." She chuckled. "But I know that couldn't be, my love, because that would mean that Lucas was your brother, and that would be just unbearable."

In the heavy silence that followed, Finn squeezed Vanessa's hand. "I'm afraid it's true. He's not a brother like Eleanor is your sister, in the fullest sense of that word, but biologically, yes, Lucas and I were born to the same mother and father."

Earl piped in. "Vanessa, sweetheart, there is nothing to be upset about other than this is a terribly sad day because a good woman has died. Not a single other thing is changed with the knowledge."

"Oh, Earl, now I *know* you're joking," said Vanessa. "Thank goodness! Because if it *were* true, it would mean that my precious girls are related to Lucas McBride, whom I consider to be one of the worst people on earth. It would mean my beloved sinless children are as closely related to a detestable man as they are to my own sister. Related to a man who has been in jail, who's been arrested for stealing to pay for drink, for begging to pay for drink, and heaven knows what else he has done to pay for his drink. Related to a man who has been an awful influence on the father of my children. If it were true, it would mean my family and I have been duped into believing one thing when the ugly truth has been quite another. I'm glad it's just a joke, and I wasn't led to believe I was marrying an upstanding member of Boston society, a dependable, trustworthy man, deserving of my hand, who would not let me down, who would provide for me and our children, who would raise them with dignity and respect for the law. I'm delighted to hear that my husband did not marry me under false pretenses and sire children who are genetic spawns of the most downtrodden elements of our Boston society. Phew!"

Earl's expression, filled with concern and sympathy only moments earlier, now acquired the concrete edges of a man who was being held in contempt to his face.

"Dad . . . wait . . ." Finn tried to say, swaying. The gavel was about to come down. His father wasn't wrong. There was no order in this house.

"I'm not sure I want to get your meaning, Vanessa," said Earl, extricating himself from his wife's imploring hand and standing up, because some things could not be said while sitting. "Aside from maligning our son, I don't see how this news affects your marriage or your family. It's not open to public scrutiny, but if you must know, my wife and I were childless and deeply mournful about it. We had been married many years and had a wonderful life, but there was a hole in the middle of it that no amount of busyness could replace. Suddenly, as if by divine grace, we were given an opportunity to change our fate. My wife, who taught Cora's children, knew what a wonderful soul Cora was and how deeply troubled her life had been. She was trying to take care of eight children almost entirely on her own, while her husband was either unable or unwilling to meet his most basic responsibilities as a father and provider. She asked us to adopt her baby boy, knowing it was our heart's desire. Cora asked from us two things. One was to keep the name she had given her son who would now be our son, and the second was not to tell him the truth about where he came from. She wanted to give him a full chance at a new life, and she was afraid if he knew that his real mother had given him up, his life would be tainted, would be forever lived with one foot in one world and one foot in the other."

A tormented Finn begged off from further conversation, feeling all the wrong words swirling through barrels of whisky in his head. He helped Vanessa to their bedroom, though he himself could've used a little help up the stairs. He was done speaking to everyone, including his wife.

Unfortunately, Vanessa wasn't finished with him.

"You deceived me," she said. "Tell me the truth, how long did you suspect? Maybe even know it for a fact?"

"I'm not capable of discussing this, Vanessa. Let's try again tomorrow."

"That's what *I* said to you!" she cried. "And you said it can't wait, we must talk now, the business of our life, blah blah, blather blather."

"You weren't drunk."

"I was tired!"

"Not the same."

"Oh my God!" Vanessa exclaimed, putting a hand on her heart. "Your friend, Travis *McBride*! He was your brother, too? How many of you McBrides are there?"

"Uh—I assume that's a rhetorical question?"

"You were friends before the war," Vanessa said. "And then you went off to Italy. You came back and he didn't—but you came back a different man. Did you know, all the way back then?" Vanessa rolled her head. "Did you learn in the war he was your brother? Why didn't you tell me, Finn!"

"I can see I'm not getting out of this conversation, not even on the day the woman who gave birth to me died," Finn said. Just once in his life, he wished he could get a pebble of sympathy from his wife. He felt an intense desire, almost a physical ache, to be down in the cellar of his house, where another woman, one who offered him nothing but compassion, sat at his table.

"I asked my mother and father about it when I was back stateside," Finn said, "and they denied it most strongly. I had no choice but to believe them. If you recall, I still spent years battling my doubts about starting a life with you. Nonetheless, on *this* day of all days"—his voice broke—"I want to confess to you the full force of what my parents' deception meant in my life. Had they told me the truth," Finn said, "I never would have married you—"

"I never would have married *you*!" she cried.

". . . because I would have believed—and clearly correctly," Finn went on, his body stiff with liquid exhaustion, "that I wasn't worthy of your hand. I held you in the highest esteem, Vanessa. I had the utmost respect for you. But I would have gone my own way and never gotten involved with your father's bank. And then I wouldn't be where I am today, right now, in this awful moment with you. You want the *truth*? Every God-given day I feel I'm letting you down," Finn said. "That's a terrible way for a man to feel and to live, especially a proud man like me. I feel so knocked down sometimes that I can barely get up and carry on. But you know what?" Finn clenched his fists. "I do. I still do."

"Do *what*?" she said rudely.

"Get up. Carry on. I don't wallow in bed all day, wringing my hands. I get up for you, for our girls, for your father and mother, and for my own parents, who went to immeasurable lengths to keep me from failing. So when I see you recline on your down pillows and cry of what ifs, I—who have spent my whole adult life running away from those what ifs and remaking myself into a man worthy of your love—feel that I've failed even there, in the most intimate aspect of myself. So now that you and I both know the truth—yes, I'm adopted, yes, I came from the deepest well of Irish poverty, yes, I have one living brother who's a drunk and a petty thief—I'm asking you: what do you want to do?" Finn was standing at the foot of the bed, and she was sitting against her pillows.

"What are my options?"

"If you can't live with me because of who I am and where I came from, let me know now, before I spend another *second* trying to right this sinking ship," Finn said. "If you feel you can't bond with my children because they carry the genes you despise, as you've just told my father, tell me that too, because the girls deserve better than a mother who is absent from them the way you've been absent from them."

"I always suspected there was something wrong," Vanessa cried. "I always feared you carried a dark secret that would one day ruin me."

"Here's your chance to right your own sinking ship, my wife."

"Why are you provoking me?" said Vanessa. "What would you do if I took you up on what you're proposing?"

"My children and I know where the door is," Finn said. "Do you?"

"I'm not rising to your bait, and it's ridiculous for you to suggest that I should part with my babies!"

"Would you even know they were gone?"

"Finn!" Vanessa cried. "Stop yourself before you say something you'll regret."

"Too late," Finn said, his heart aching and his teeth gritted. "I wouldn't have married you, and you wouldn't have married me. What a marital pledge! Take *that* into our bed, lie back with *that* to sustain you, while I go out and shovel coal for a pittance, and you can cry to your mother and sister, my darling, how I'm failing to deliver you the perfect fucking life your perfect self so perfectly deserves."

51

Four Children

Ukraine, May 1929

The sun was coming up. It was cold and gray at the end of May, the morning fog so thick, Isabelle couldn't see to the end of the woods where they had buried Yana. Isabelle couldn't see to the end of the world. Her whole small world, the tiny part that was visible, was steel blue and vanishing in the haze. Somewhere up above the clouds, the cranes were crying, crying, their floating choir echoing in the hulking sky.

Isabelle sat outside on the bench, having a smoke before she started her day, and stared out over the unseen land where she was born and raised, where she was married, where her babies were born and raised. When she was a little girl, she and her brothers would sled down the hill to the grazing lands. The four of them would frolic in the snow, long ago, before the Revolution, before the Civil War, before the last famine, before this.

Isabelle was cemented into the bench with sorrow so heavy, she didn't know how she would get up. It was as if she glimpsed the future and saw it drained of the love that had sustained her life for three decades, saw the hollow future where she was bereft and alone.

She wasn't a crier, and she tried hard not to be one now. For a long while, she was by herself, but one by one, her brothers joined her and for a few minutes the four of them sat on the bench, looking out into the fog, trying to make out the familiar details. Isabelle, Roman, Ostap, and Nikora—together but in solitude, silent, each lost inside their own sorrows—gazed out onto the valley that gave them their lives and their livelihood, that bore their horses and Isabelle's children.

"But horses first, right, Isa," she heard Roman say, and she wanted to reply, horses first when you have no children, but she didn't, because Ostap was next to her, struck down from the loss of his wife and child. She put her arm around Ostap, and Roman put his arm around her and Nikora.

"We were ecstatic children in these gentle hills," Nikora said.

"Even as adults we were," said Isabelle.

"We're bringing it home to them, Isa," said Roman. "What do we say?"

"You reap what you sow," the four of them echoed.

"It's going to be a long night," Roman said.

"Call out like I taught you," Isabelle said to her brothers. "A quail, a corncrake, an owl—not a human. The quail loud enough for me to hear. My house and bedroom window are all the way at the end."

Two guards standing nearby shouted, pointing to the fields with their rifles. "Hey! Enough yammering and smoking. There's work to do."

Rising from the bench, the four Lazar children stood shoulder to shoulder. In unison, they threw down their cigarettes, tamped them out with their boots, and looked up at the dawning sky.

The fading moon was full.

52

Mother of Exiles

On Thanksgiving 1931 Olivia said they weren't gathering at the half-laden table until Isabelle joined them. Vanessa objected, saying Isabelle did not join them in the formal dining room for celebrations. She wasn't family.

"That's not right," Olivia said, shaking her head. "Finn?"

Finn sided with his mother. He had bigger concerns at the moment than coddling Vanessa. Than even agreeing with Vanessa. Besides, he didn't agree. Of course Isabelle must sit at his table.

"It's my house," Vanessa muttered. "I can do as I please."

"It's Thanksgiving," Olivia said. "What happened to the spirit of unity between tribes? If ever there was a time for the tempest-tossed refugee to sit by our side, it's tonight."

"It's because you're a McBride, not an Evans," Vanessa whispered to Finn as the family was gathering. "You care nothing for propriety."

"My mother is an Evans." Finn wasn't whispering. "What's her excuse?"

Isabelle came to the table in her Sunday best, a chestnut velvet dress to match her honey-colored hair tied in red velvet ribbons, her face flushed and pink, her eyes shining. She even had on some lipstick! No matter how grim Finn felt, he couldn't help but smile at the sight of her.

Finn and Vanessa took their seats at opposite sides of the long dining table, the family arranged all around—Isabelle of course between their two daughters—and they broke bread. The feast wasn't as full as in other years. Finn thought they were lucky to have what they had. The turkey was smaller and the stuffing bigger. All the side dishes—the yams, the sweet potato casserole, the string beans—were plentiful, as were the pickled beets, but there were no oysters on the half-shell as had been customary in the past. Oysters were expensive.

But onions were cheap and the bowl of creamed onions overflowing. They had cider to drink, Coca-Cola, and a new lemon-lime soda called 7-UP. There was coffee and tea and pumpkin pie. The conversation didn't flow as well as in other years. Finn, who was usually the life of the party, sat silent and rigid, listening to others, nodding, but contributing little. He had things on his mind tonight he could not turn away from.

An hour into the meal, Olivia addressed her son. "Finn, darling, you're awfully quiet. And you've barely touched your food. You're just moving the turkey around on your plate."

"Leave him alone, Olivia," Earl said. "He's a grown man."

Finn patted his mother's arm and took a bite of his turkey. "We should've invited Lucas, Mother."

"Oh, my goodness!" Olivia exclaimed. "How thoughtless of us!"

"Lucas is not alone," said Isabelle. "He is having dinner with Schumann and Schumann's son, Nate. Though after seeing what Ukrainians eat for Thanksgiving, Lucas probably wishes he was alone."

A relieved Olivia chuckled. "Oh, no, what do they eat?"

"Herring," said Isabelle. "Beets. Pickled onions. Maybe some tongue."

Finn put down his barely dirtied fork and folded his hands. "Family," he said, taking a deep breath. "We need to talk. I didn't want to do it on Thanksgiving, but we are all together and I can't put it off any longer."

"Finn, *darling*!" Vanessa exclaimed, her thin voice trembling with nerves. "Whatever it is can wait. Let's have a wonderful evening."

"It's too late to have a truly wonderful evening, Vanessa," Finn said, "because we didn't invite my brother to our house."

"Fine, but we can talk about serious things another time. Not in front of the children. Or Isabelle."

"Nonsense," Earl said, cooler toward Vanessa than he'd ever been. "The children benefit from being treated with respect, and Isabelle is part of the family as far as we're concerned. No reason to exclude her any more than there's reason to exclude your sister."

"Why would that even be a consideration, Your Honor?" Eleanor exclaimed. "Why would *I* be excluded?"

"Enough, Ellie!" Walter said. "Finn, go on, tell us what you need to."

For a few moments Finn was silent, weighing his words. "We are at the end of the road, I'm afraid," he said. "We have to leave this house."

Only Vanessa's hands flew to her mouth.

"We've been luckier than most," Finn said. "But our luck has run out. We lost the bank, sold our other homes, budgeted, cut corners. But there's almost no work out there with unemployment at nearly 25 percent." He couldn't look at anyone, staring at his clasped hands as he spoke, his matter-of-fact tone belying his true torment. "I have no money to pay the mortgage on this house and haven't had any for six months. I've been negotiating for a future that's just not coming—not with the Dow Jones at 80."

All the men at the table groaned at the shock of that number.

"And the property taxes are due for 1931. They were due in June. I can't pay the arrears, and I can't pay our monthly bills. There is no more equity in this house to borrow against. I can't even pay the small sum I owe on the chattel mortgage for the movable personal property inside our home. I can't find work of any kind. This is where we are."

Even Walter and Earl who knew how bad things were didn't know how bad they really were.

"Maybe we should sell the house, darling," Vanessa said. "Move to a smaller place?"

"I've tried to sell it for a year. It's not that we have no offers. We don't have offers for what the house is worth."

"But we do have some offers?" said Vanessa with hope.

"We have one offer, yes, that's 20 percent less than the amount we owe the bank on our house."

"We mustn't be greedy, darling, especially not in hard times like these."

"It's not about greed, Vanessa," Finn said. "The bank which has a lien on our home won't let us sell it unless we first pay back what we borrowed."

"So let's pay them back with proceeds from the sale."

"But the sale would be a fifth less than the amount of our loan," said Finn. "We would owe the bank forty thousand dollars."

"Vee, quiet down," Walter said. "Financial things are hard."

"So, if we can't sell it, what do we do?" Vanessa said.

"We need to move out by the end of December. Five weeks from now."

"Move out *where*?"

"What will it take for us to stay here, Finn?" Walter said. "The bank must have given you a figure."

"Yes, Jeremy Carlyle himself gave me a figure—last June," said Finn. "I thought we could catch a break eventually. But every month has been worse than the last, and it hasn't happened. In September he asked us to leave. In October he told me if I didn't either pay or leave by November, he would be forced to call the city marshals to physically remove us from the property. And here we are. He gave me one month to pack up our clothes, our books, and our beds. The furniture, china, housewares, and window coverings are all part of the chattel. They stay. We don't."

"Oh, son," said Earl, his head in his hands.

"Oh, Finn," said Walter.

"Finn, answer my question!" said Vanessa. "Leave and go *where*?"

"That, Vanessa, is an excellent question," Finn said.

"Lucas said we can stay with him in Cora's house," said Isabelle. "Four years ago, her house was paid for, he said. He didn't know how. And her tiny life insurance policy is giving him monthly income."

"Isabelle! Excuse me, please," Vanessa said in an end-of-tether voice. "No one asked for your opinion. I was asking my husband a question. Finn?"

"Lucas says we can stay with him in Cora's house," said Finn. "Four years ago, her house was paid for, he said. He didn't know how." He glanced at his father, and away. "And her tiny life insurance policy is giving him a monthly income."

"Finn!"

"What would you like me to do, Vanessa?"

"Fix it! Fix it like you always do." She looked ready to cry.

"Like millions of others, I can't find work, and we're out of money," said Finn. "I've borrowed all I can borrow, and I've sold all I can sell."

"What about my jewelry? Sell that!"

Mournfully, Finn stared at Vanessa. "Maybe that'll feed us for a month. And then what?"

"Mother! Daddy!" cried Eleanor. "We are not going to move to that ghastly North End! Please say we're not!"

"No, dear, of course not," a shaken Lucy assured her daughter.

Everyone else stayed appalled and silent.

"I will never move into that man's house," Vanessa said, clenching her glass of cider. "Mother!"

"Girls, what do you want Mommy to do!" cried Lucy. "Walter, come up with something!"

"What do you want *me* to do, woman?" Walter said. "I have nothing left of my entire 130-year Adams legacy. *Nothing!* Nothing but that cursed useless farm in Hampton."

"If only we hadn't lent John Reade millions of dollars right before the market crashed that he never repaid," Finn said. "And what the *hell* happened to his supposed buyer—excuse Daddy's language, girls," he said to Mae and Junie.

"The market cratered and the buyer crapped out," Walter said.

"How much do you think the Hampton place is worth now?" Finn asked.

Walter shrugged. "A few thousand. Ten at most."

"Sell it, Walter, it's better than nothing," Finn said. "It'll get us settled somewhere else, keep us going for a bit."

"You think I haven't been trying to sell it for two years?" Walter was gruff. "Who wants a Revolutionary War farm in the middle of nowhere?"

Isabelle, who had been staring at her plate, averting her gaze from the anguished family, suddenly perked up. Her body straightened like an unwound string. "What you say, Walter? *Farm*? What farm?"

"Forget selling it, Walter," said Finn. "Mortgage it."

"No bank will give me a mortgage," Walter said. "I can't pay it."

"Tell me about farm," Isabelle said. "Is it just land or is there house too?"

"There's a house," Walter said, barely paying attention. "No one's been there since the turn of the century. Except John Reade."

"How much land?"

"How much is the land worth?"

"*No*," Isabelle said. "How much land is there?"

"I don't know, Isabelle, maybe five acres," Walter said. "What does it matter?"

"And you have paper to it? Like belonging paper? Farm belong to you?"

"The deed, you mean? Yes, unfortunately."

Isabelle sat back and smiled. "Family, we going to be okay," she said. "We thought we had nowhere. But we have farmhouse." She raised her Coke glass in salute. "*L'Chaim*. Life always find way."

"Isabelle, can you please stop talking?" said Vanessa. "*Please*. This doesn't concern you, and frankly we don't need folly. We need a real solution."

Isabelle picked up her knife and fork. "Farm is solution."

"No, it's *not*, Isabelle. Finn, can you please talk to her? I *can't*. I just *can't*."

"So go ahead and solution things," Isabelle said before Finn had a chance to cut in. "I eat." Heartily, she returned to her cold food.

No one spoke. No one had anything else to say.

"Vanessa," said Isabelle, wiping her mouth when she was done eating, "do you want to move to Lucas?"

"Impossible," said Vanessa.

"Okay, and you don't want to move to Hampton—where Hampton, by way?"

"New Hampshire," said Finn, watching her. He was perplexed by her sudden serenity. Just moments earlier, she had been as tense as the rest.

"So no Lucas, no farm," said Isabelle. "What's your proposal, Vanessa?"

"Pardon me," Vanessa said, "for not instantly having a solution to a problem I didn't create."

"Farmhouse is answer," said Isabelle. "To everything. Including work."

"With all due respect, Isabelle," Walter said, "you're preaching to the wrong choir here. You're talking to bankers and judges and teachers and homemaking women. We are city dwellers. Born and raised. None of us has ever lived on a farm. Vanessa, unfortunately, is right for once."

"Vanessa right many times," said Isabelle. "But not about this."

"Isabelle, can you please stop talking. Finn!"

"When Schumann came to America," Isabelle said, "he knew only to be doctor. He was doctor his whole life in Ukraine, and when he came to Boston he was fifty. But he didn't have American degree, and he didn't have money to get degree. So he became tailor. Because he didn't need degree for that. He built his customers, and then small by small he started taking care of his North End neighborhood, and people started paying him because he was doctor and he helped them. He was successful as tailor, but after Crash, his tailor business *pfft*. But that didn't matter, you know why? Because his doctor business was boomerang. So, even without degree, Schumann now makes his living as doctor in North End."

Eleanor chimed in. "Fascinating story about a man we don't know, but what does it have to do with us?"

"Because he expected one thing," said Isabelle, "and he had to make his life with another thing. I know you can't imagine farm, but I'm telling you, if house is big plenty for us, we will be good. And even if not big plenty, we can build more house later to add rooms. Finn can help build," she said. "He is not only head. He can be hands too, no?" She turned her gaze to Finn and smiled. He watched her intently but did not smile back. He couldn't figure out if this was a real thing or a make-believe thing.

"There is no work on the farm!" Eleanor cried.

"Very mistakenly incorrect there, Eleanor," Isabelle said. "All work in whole world is on farm." She nodded. "I promise you, you will work so hard on farm, you won't make it to your bed at night before you fall subconscious."

"Woman, what the crikey are you going on about?" exclaimed Walter. "I can't work the farm! I am nearly seventy years old. Earl here is edging toward eighty!"

"Bite your tongue, old man, I'm seventy-three," said Earl.

"Work on farm for all skills, all ages, all men and women and children," said Isabelle, ruffling Junie and Mae's heads. "You be my little helpers, girls?"

"I'm not doing anything," said Monty, as grumpy as the rest. "I'm going to Harvard when I grow up."

"But until Harvard, you help me feed your mother, right, Monty?"

"There's no food there, dear," Lucy said to Isabelle with exquisite condescension. "It's not a stand by the side of the road where we buy strawberries on our way to the Cape. It's not a farmer's market at Faneuil Hall."

"It's better than that," said Isabelle. "It's land that will grow infinite food for us. And it's house to live in. You just said you have no house. But you *do*."

"What kind of food?" said Finn. It was the first time he'd spoken since the farm was mentioned.

Isabelle looked so self-satisfied, Finn couldn't help but smile, but when he glanced across, Vanessa looked ready to scream or vomit. She was green.

"You name food, it grow in earth," Isabelle said. "Potatoes. Onions. Beets. Everything you see on this table, farm will grow."

"Bread?" Vanessa said with as much sarcasm as she could muster.

"Bread most of all," said Isabelle. "Earth grow wheat." As she spoke the words, her smile fell, and she shuddered and keeled forward. She went from pink to pale, from triumphant to defeated. Finn frowned as he watched her, but before he could ask if she was all right, the children chimed in enthusiastically.

"And corn, Isa!" exclaimed Junie. "Don't forget the corn!"

"I didn't grow corn," Isabelle said, forcing out a smile for Junie. "But we can try, Junebug. You and I can see if we can grow this corn."

"June! Mae!" Vanessa cried, as if just remembering her girls were still at the table. "What a debacle. Please excuse yourselves and go upstairs immediately. This isn't for children's ears. You too, Monty. Isabelle, go with them, please."

"No." That was Finn. "Isabelle stays. Our discussion is not over."

"But the children, darling!"

"We'll be fine, Mommy! You'll see." After the girls ran upstairs, a frazzled Vanessa faced down an unperturbed Isabelle.

"Isabelle, I *really* need you to stop talking," Vanessa said. "I'm going to have to insist. You're upsetting the entire table."

Isabelle did not stop talking. "Sometimes truth upsetting," she said. "I *know*. Think on it little bit. You will see there is no other way."

"Finn!" Vanessa cried. "Mother! Daddy!"

No one answered the call, each in their own wordless contemplation.

It was Finn who finally spoke. "Not a single person at this table," he said to Isabelle, "except for you, has been near a field. We have never plucked a flower, nor put a foot or a rake onto a hard ground. I don't know what you think we can do here."

"I agree, better if you were tillers and plowers and growers of crop," said Isabelle. "But we have Bible story in my country. It's called '*pritcha pro talanty*.'"

"Parable of the Talents," said Olivia.

"Sometimes we given five talents. Sometimes only one," Isabelle said. "And we must do what we can with what we be given. We must multiply according to our gifts. We thought we had nothing, but we are given farm and we are given land. That's *lot*. Rest is *mekhanika*."

"Mechanics," said Olivia.

"Mechanics," echoed Isabelle. "Which I will teach you."

"I see logistical problems I can't get my head around," Finn said.

Isabelle nodded cheerfully. "Logic very difficult for man," she said, twinkling at him. "But give me sample, maybe I can help."

"I mean *operations* of things." He tried not to twinkle back. "How things would work. For example, how would we get there?"

"Schumann will lend us truck," Isabelle said. "That's such small logic."

"*Logistic*. Can Nate drive us?"

"No, Nate going back to Romania next week," she said. "You will drive. What else? Lucas can help. He help you pack, move heavy things into house."

"I don't want Lucas to help us in any way!" Vanessa said.

"We need help," Isabelle said. "Better to make peace with husband's brother. You never know when you going to need brother." She swirled the pumpkin filling around her plate, making large orange circles with her fork.

"So your idea for my family, Isabelle, is that we should hippity-hop to this farm in the boonies, miles from our hometown, in another state? *That's* your plan?" Vanessa was red in the face. "We are going to leave our warm house in the dead of winter to go to an open field?" She was pulsing with anxiety, an unsteady prism of tics and itching.

"Vanessa has a point," Finn said. "I don't see how moving to an ancient farm in wintertime is going to help us when we have no money. I assume there's nothing growing in the ground at the moment?"

"Of course not," said Isabelle. "To grow in ground you need to plant in ground."

"Which brings me to my other point," Finn said. "How are we going to get this *something to plant*? Doesn't that literally require seed money?"

Isabelle smiled. "That part you leave to me," she said. "When time come, I get us things to plant. But even before receiving seed, soil needs to get ready for seed. What do you call it, it need to be, um, *plodorodnaya* soil? Like fruity soil? Fruitful soil?"

"*Fertile* soil?" Finn said.

"Yes! Fertile soil receives seed. Much to do before planting time. And you are right, Finn. We have to live on something before that." Isabelle turned to Vanessa. "You said you have family jewels to sell?"

"I was joking," Vanessa said.

"Oh, funny," said Isabelle. "Haha. But very good idea. Family jewels will have important purpose. Much better than wearing. Jewels will feed family while we get back on feet. We need few months. We plant in April. When August come we will have so much food. All extra we can sell. Or change it. *Ex*change it?"

"Barter it," said Olivia. She smiled.

"Yes! Barter it," said Isabelle. "We barter wheat for things we need. Once we have wheat and corn like Junie want, we can barter for ten chickens." Isabelle counted around the table and lifted her finger to the upstairs, where the three children were. "One egg each every day. We barter for milk, for cheese, for sugar..."

"Yes, Isabelle, we all see you can use *barter* in a sentence," said Vanessa.

"If there's apple tree, we will bake apple pie," Isabelle said, undaunted. "Very delicious. With fresh cream from milk."

Around the table the Adamses and Evanses were silent. Silent or speechless. Finn was the latter. It was as if a creature from Mars had descended on their planet and told them they could grow wings and fly themselves into space, maybe fly to the moon—or Venus.

"All I hear is gobbledygook," Vanessa said. "Eleanor, what about you?"

"Gobbledygook."

"Well done, Isabelle," said Lucy. "You got my girls to agree. Those two haven't agreed on anything since they were toddlers."

"If the sale of my paltry jewelry can feed us on a farm till the carrots come," said Vanessa, "why can't it feed us in this house?"

"Because in this house there are no carrots, *obviously*," Isabelle replied. "Come June, family jewels will be gone, and not single carrot in sight. And then what?"

"The economy will pick up. Finn will get a better job."

"And if it doesn't?" said Isabelle. "And if he doesn't?"

"But if it does, we will have moved to New Hampshire for nothing!" said Vanessa.

Finn cut in. "We're missing the larger point here. Come January 1st, we have nowhere to live. All of us will be homeless."

"We *not* homeless," Isabelle said. "We have farm."

"Isabelle," said Walter, "you're not taking into consideration that four people at this table are over sixty. That's very old."

"My mother was near sixty," Isabelle said. "She never stopped working. After she married my father, she left her job as professor at University of Krakow and moved to horse ranch with him. She took care of growing food and horses and children and grandchildren. She schooled us, taught us all to read and write, she milked cows, cleaned, bartered for food. She did everything." Isabelle stared into her hands.

"My back is bad," Lucy said. "I can't be picking cotton at my age."

"Okay, Lucy, we won't grow cotton," Isabelle said. "But maybe you can rake. Or cook or clean or care for chicken. Many jobs on farm."

"It's going to be freezing cold," Eleanor said. "A farm that has not been opened for thirty years will be uninhabitably cold."

"There might be a fireplace or two," Walter said. Walter!

Earl slapped the table twice. Once a judge, always a judge. "What do we think of Isabelle's idea? Let's vote. Yea or nay. But if it's nay, we can't just give a no vote. We must propose something else. I'll go first. I say yea."

"I second that yea," said Olivia.

"I have a weak heart," Walter said. "I get winded getting out of bed. I say yea, but only if no one expects anything of me."

"And I," said Lucy, "say yea, but only if Isabelle promises to leave me alone to take care of my husband. He needs me."

"No, I don't," Walter said. "Go out and till the land, woman. I've been working my whole life. I'll sit on the porch, drink lemonade, and watch you."

All eyes turned to Vanessa. She was having trouble opening her mouth. "I say no," she said. "I'd rather live in Lucas's house than have any part in this farce. At least Lucas's house is still in Boston, near familiar things. What Isabelle is proposing is untenable. Eleanor?"

"I want to agree with you, sister, I do," Eleanor said, "but I really, *really* don't want to live in North End!"

Finn turned his head to Isabelle. "We all know what *you* think."

"What about you, Finn?" said Isabelle. "What do *you* think?"

With only slight regret, Finn stared at Vanessa across the stretch of the long table. "I don't want to leave our home," he said. "I agree with Vanessa. Many things have happened to us that I have a hard time accepting. Since October 24, 1929, I've had to learn to live with a lot I didn't think I could ever bear. Previously impossible things have become a fact of life. This farm idea seems like another one of those. I can't imagine it—and yet . . ." He took a breath. "I say yes. Because at least for now, it feels like a way out. Not the way I would've liked. But it's better than being homeless, workless, and penniless. So, the yeses have it. The farm it is."

Soon the evening ended. Everyone retreated to their rooms while Isabelle and Olivia cleaned up. Upstairs, Finn approached Vanessa, but she cut him short. "Finn, it's been one of the longest days of my life. And one of the worst Thanksgiving dinners, thanks to you bringing up such an awful topic during what's supposed to be a convivial evening. I can't talk anymore."

"I just wanted to check on you, Vee, see how you're feeling."

"Fine and dandy," said Vanessa, hiding her shaking hands under the quilt. "But tonight's not the night."

"Right," Finn said. "Of course, darling. Tonight is never the night. Except when my mother dies. Then it's the only night."

He turned and walked out without waiting for or wanting a reply.

53

Roman's Last Advice

Ukraine, May 1929

Later that day at the end of May before dinner, when Roman and Isabelle were cleaning the stables and feeding the horses, Roman called over Slava and Maxim. "Come forward, my little men," he said. "Time to help me and your mama change the straw and pour fresh water for the horses. And other important things, too. Come." The two boys walked into the stall with Roman and Boyko. Three OGPU men moved forward after the children and stood too close to the rear of the horse. Roman exchanged a look with his nephews, with Isabelle, and sighed. "It would be so easy," he said quietly. "If only all of them could stand behind Boyko, right?" Before Boyko could get spooked, he grabbed the stallion's mane.

"Comrades," Roman said to the guards, "for your own safety, I implore you not to stand in a blind spot behind a horse. When the horse senses a presence it can't see, it assumes a predator, a natural enemy, and gets frightened. And when they get frightened, they kick their hindquarters. You don't want to be kicked in the head by a thousand-pound animal. We are all within your earshot. Just move back two meters—and observe us from the walkway." Not wanting to meet death by horse, the Communists stepped away and took out their cigarettes.

"No, no, no. Absolutely no smoking inside the stable, comrades," Roman said. "The hay is kindling. You will go up in flames."

"A lot of rules you have, Lazar," said Orlov, one of the OGPU men, and the one who usually guarded Zhuk.

"The animals have rules," said Roman. "I'm merely their steward. But not to smoke inside a wooden stable full of dry grass, that's common sense, no?"

The men stepped outside for a smoke. Roman drew his nephews near.

"Now, listen to me," Roman said to Slava. "You too," he said to Maxim.

Descending on one knee in front of the boys, he enveloped them in his arms, embraced them, kissed them, and continued speaking, all the while rummaging under the hay, searching for something. "Do you remember how you asked me what a Cossack was, and how you would know if you were a true Cossack?"

"You didn't tell us," said Slava.

"You said we were too little," said Maxim.

"You're little men now," Roman said, "so I will tell you. When I was a boy, my father—your grandfather—told this to me, and when he was a boy, his father told it to him. The Cossack is born of Ukraine, which means the borderlands. Ukraine is the frontier between warring tribes, and the Cossack is the only native son of this volatile land. He is the ultimate horseman and swordsman. He is defiant and bold. He will not be ruled by other nations. He will barely be ruled by Ukraine. Many centuries ago, he rode out into the wilderness, away from the conflicts of men, to find freedom, and has lived in an uneasy truce with other men ever since.

"And what makes one Cossack rise above the rest, succeed where others have failed, survive when others have fallen? In combat or a long journey or a war—or one final monstrous bitter battle—it's not the strongest who makes it out. The big he-man who can tame a bull?" Roman shook his head. "It's not him. And it's not the one who can ride the longest, though that does help. And it's not the one who thinks he's the leader of men, nor is it the one who is quickest with the draw or swiftest with the sword. It's not any of those things that help a man overcome the toughest odds, to triumph in the hardest endeavor of his life. The truest wild warrior of the steppes is the one who, when there is nothing left in him, when he's got no horse, no weapons, no endurance, no strength, when he's got no fight left, who thinks he's been beaten and all is lost, still somehow finds the will inside himself to pull to his feet and keep going. The one who, where there's nothing left, can turn to his right and help the fellow next to him who is down. He is the one who makes it out, the one who finds the divine inside himself. Do you understand?"

"Yes, Uncle," said Slava.

"Yes, Uncle," said Maxim.

"Very good. Go on now," Roman said. "And remember what I told you. You must look out for each other." He glanced up at the standing Isabelle. "And promise me you will watch over your precious mama."

"Mama can take care of herself," Mirik said, walking into the stall and pulling his sons away from Roman. Isabelle stood aside to let him. "Enough of this. Time for dinner and bed." Mirik's hands were shaking. "Mother, did you make food for your family?"

"Yes, fish soup with two trouts," Isabelle said. "And rabbit stew for Zhuk. Boys, don't touch a drop of the stew, understood?"

"Uncle Roman said it's tonight, Papa," Slava said, as he was being led away, closing his jacket and motioning Maxim to do the same.

"It is, son," Mirik said, his shoulders down. "The moon is full."

Slava took his younger brother's hand as they walked uphill to their house. "Finally, Maxim!" he said. "Tonight we find out if we are true Cossacks."

"You are not Cossacks!" Mirik said, yanking on his older son. "You are Kovalenkos."

"Tonight, Slava," said Maxim in a child's exhilarated voice, squeezing his brother's hand, "we learn if we are the wildest warriors of the steppes."

54

The Mustard Seed

Isabelle knocked on Vanessa's door.

"Please, no," said Vanessa. Isabelle knocked again. "I said, please no."

Isabelle didn't knock a third time. She opened the door and came in.

"I don't want to talk to you," Vanessa said, the covers up to her neck. "I don't want to talk to anybody."

"Vanessa . . ." Isabelle sat at the foot of the bed and soothingly rubbed Vanessa's leg. Isabelle knew that if Vanessa didn't yank her leg away, there was a possibility of conversation. Vanessa didn't yank her leg away.

"I know you're upset," Isabelle said.

"No, you don't. This is nothing to you. What do you care where you live, in my beautiful home or a hovel. But it matters to me."

"Your husband did everything," Isabelle said. "He didn't want this, and he doesn't want this now—no more than you do. Who would want to leave this place? It's *home*."

"You don't understand. No one does."

"You don't think *I* understand? My home was Ukraine and now I'm in your house."

"Okay, whatever, but no one appreciates how hard this is for *me*."

"I do," said Isabelle.

"I can't get out of bed," whispered Vanessa. "The more imperative it is that I get up, the more I can't do it. I can't explain it."

"You don't have to explain to me," Isabelle said, her voice full of sorrow and sympathy. "There was time not long ago when I was where you are right now. I knew there was no choice for me, yet I couldn't get out of bed. I simply couldn't take one step toward my future. My sons were waiting. My husband was waiting. My brothers were waiting. I was making danger for everyone by not moving. I knew I had to move, but I couldn't."

"But you moved."

"I got out of bed, Vanessa, because if I didn't, everyone I knew was going to die," Isabelle said. Her head was deeply lowered. She squeezed Vanessa's leg and raised her eyes to the tearful, pitying, pitiful yet terrified woman. "Your children, your father, your mother and sister, Finn's parents cannot be made homeless. You cannot live in Hooverburg. You cannot beg on streets. Finn cannot keep turning to life of crime to feed his family."

"What do you mean . . . what do you mean *keep* turning?"

"My English not so good, I mis-speak, use wrong word," said Isabelle. "But you know what I try to say, yes? Once you accept you cannot stay, then you must look for best solutions. Homeless is bad. Hoover-tents bad. Lucas house not very good—because it's only five rooms and Lucas can't feed your whole family on his poor dead mother's insurance tiny money sum."

Vanessa shook her head. "I'm so scared, Isabelle."

"I know," Isabelle said, rubbing Vanessa's leg. "You think you weak, but you not. You strong. You don't know what strength you have. You will only learn when you get out of bed."

Vanessa sat up and the two women embraced. Isabelle was comforting Vanessa, but Vanessa's hands were on her back, patting her. She thought she was comforting Isabelle! "Where are your children now, dearest Isabelle?" Vanessa whispered into Isabelle's stiffening shoulder.

"With my husband, I hope, I pray," Isabelle said, pulling away gently but unequivocally. "I don't talk about that. Talking about it makes me want to crawl into hole in your basement and never come out."

Vanessa began to apologize, but Isabelle cut her off there too.

"It's okay," Isabelle said. "I would like to never use my voice to speak of them except to say that how I made it to America—against many deprivations? destitutions? devastations? what is word? like miracle—I hope my husband and sons will make it one day same as me. But without shipwreck. I don't wish for them shipwreck."

Vanessa swallowed. "A few years ago, I had a miscarriage," she said haltingly. "No, no, it's fine, it was a long time ago. But at first, I was feeling quite low about it, as you might imagine. My doctor, to make me feel better, told me the story of Kisa Gotami and the Buddha. Do you know it?"

Isabelle shook her head.

"Kisa was a young mother in Japan whose baby was—sick. Dying," Vanessa said. "Desperate to save her child, Kisa went to the Buddha for help. He said he would heal her baby if Kisa would bring him back a single mustard seed. But the condition was, the mustard seed had to be given to her by a family that had not suffered a death." Vanessa fell quiet.

Isabelle waited. "There is more? I hope that's not end of story?"

"It is."

"How possibly did *that* help heal dying baby?" Isabelle exclaimed, skeptical and dissatisfied.

"I suppose it helped Kisa to know that there was suffering everywhere."

"Does that ever help?" Isabelle was upset. "Kisa's child was sick," she said. "So what is story about? Is it story about having sympathy for others, or is it story about mother trying to save baby? Because doctor's Buddha story fail bad both ways."

"Maybe it's a story about how death is universal."

"We need *story* for that?"

"I think her baby was already dead, and she couldn't cope," said Vanessa, her eyes vacant, her lips pale. "When she didn't find the mustard seed, Kisa realized she had to learn to let go of her grief."

"Aha," said Isabelle, scrutinizing the blonde, weary woman. "And *did* Kisa's story help you—to let go?"

"Still working on it, I suppose," Vanessa said, her nails jabbing into the pads of her fingers.

"Indeed," said Isabelle. "So let me get straight. Story is, Kisa goes to Buddha because she desperately needs help, and Buddha with zero sympathy for her universal condition says, leave me alone, dumb mother, don't bother me, everybody got trouble."

Vanessa chuckled.

"My advice is to find yourself new doctor, Vanessa," said Isabelle. "If his medicine anything like his advice, you may be in great danger."

"Isabelle, it's time to go. You know it is. Please get up.

"Isabelle, if you don't get up, we're ruined.

"Please. I know you're afraid.

"Isa? I've dressed the boys. Gotten our supplies together. Just get out of bed.

"You're pretending to sleep, Isabelle. I know you're awake and can hear me."

"No," Isabelle said. "I can't hear you. Can't, and don't want to."

"This was your idea," said Mirik. "Yours and Roman's and your damn Cici's. You can't be getting cold feet! I should be getting cold feet. I didn't want to do it, but now that we are here, we have no choice but to see it through, no matter the outcome, no matter the cost."

That's where the paralysis came from. The uncertainty of the outcome. The immensity of the cost.

To run, to flee, to leave the old country.

And when things went belly up, as things inevitably must, who was going to be blamed?

*If there was one thing Isabelle hated, it was to be blamed for anything. Yet she also wanted, no, needed, to make all the decisions. Quite a pickle she found herself in. Her whole life, this was so. I'm the one who did this.
The blame is mine.*

55

Isabelle and Finn

After everyone had gone to bed, Isabelle was sitting at the table, winding down from her own long day, when she heard the familiar footsteps down the back stairs.

Finn came into the kitchen, looked around. It was dark, and all the lights were off, except for the candle on the table in front of Isabelle. The darkness and the quiet soothed her. She knew it soothed him too.

He pulled up a chair, and she stood and walked over to the cabinet behind her. From behind the containers of beans and pasta, she pulled out a dark bottle and retrieved two glasses. She poured them each two fingers. He tapped on his glass, and she poured him a third finger, thought about it, and poured herself a third also. They clinked and drank, she half of hers, he all of his. He pulled out two cigarettes from his pack, gave one to her and lit it for her. She cupped his hand. They each took a long deep drag in synchrony and fell back against their chairs, sitting in the smoke, in the dark, in the silence. It was a full ten minutes before they spoke.

"What a day," he said.

"Yeah."

"How do you think it went?"

"Not bad," she said. "Until your father-in-law mentioned farm, I honestly thought you were going to have to persuade your wife to move in with man she hates most."

"Yeah, poor Lucas is going to be real disappointed. He was looking forward to sharing his small living space with Vanessa."

"I'm sure," she said. "He should have come tonight, Finn."

He looked away with his guilt. "I tried."

"You should have insisted."

"I *know*, Isa. I didn't want to have another episode like we had when Cora died. Suddenly it became all about Vanessa and her fainting. Yes, she apologized later, but real harm was done. Tonight, there was too much to discuss and decide."

Isabelle nodded, with respect and affirmation. "You did right. You made best decision you could."

Finn bobbed his head back and forth. "Do you really think the farm can work? Be honest with me. I can't have you telling me what you think I want to hear. Just give it to me straight. I don't want to do it, put my wife through it, if it's nothing but a charade."

"We will make it," Isabelle said. "All things I said were real. I relax as soon as I hear about farm. I breathe happy. My fears for your family—for *you*— they *poof*. I was so relieved." But she wasn't smiling. "Finn," she said carefully, "there is no easy way to make your wife feel better. Vanessa is not going to like moving out of her home to field in woods."

Finn opened his hands to say there was nothing to be done about it.

"She's afraid," Isabelle said. "She is terrified."

When Finn didn't speak, Isabelle prodded him with her stare. He shrugged. "I must admit, I'm less patient these days."

"It's because you always get things done. Vanessa thinks you can do your magic again. Somehow you make it fine, and she never has to think about it. Big strong husband fix it." She looked away from big strong husband.

"I tried to fix it," Finn said.

"Sometimes," said Isabelle, "man need help. Not lot. Just little help." Reaching over, she patted his hand gently.

"Man got help. Man asked and was answered." He placed his hand on hers. They stared at each other for a moment in the flickering flame. "Tell me the rest of it," he said, easing his hand away and sitting back against the chair. He pulled out two more cigarettes. "Where did strong, though not very big Isabelle get help? It's my turn to listen."

"You always listen," she said. "We need more drink for this part."

"Leave the bottle on the table," Finn said. "Next to the light." With the single burning candle, the ashtray, the shimmering bottle, the half-full glasses between them, they clinked and knocked it back.

"*Budmo*," said Isabelle. "That's what the Cossacks say when they drink."

"*Budmo*," Finn echoed. "What does it mean?"

"It means *let us be*."

"Let's have one more," he said. "And then you begin."

They had one more.

"You said the hour came at the end of May, in the night."

"Yes. I lay in bed, and I couldn't rise."

For nearly seventy kilometers, the Dniester River dividing Romania and Ukraine was flanked by steep white cliffs, ragged vertical stone, or ragged vertical forest. There was a narrow pass through the cliffs, thirty kilometers south of Ispas, between two large towns with their own border checkpoints and security towers. That's where the Lazars planned to cross.

But to get to the river, they first had to leave the farm, and they couldn't leave the farm without arousing the mini-army at their tables and in their stables. Before they could mount their horses, the Lazars needed to solve the Bolshevik problem. They were never alone. Someone was always awake and on guard. One side of the battlefield was lined with thirteen OGPU men plus Zhuk, all with automatic weapons, and on the other stood three Lazar brothers, one Lazar sister, two tiny Lazar boys, their terrified Kovalenko father, and Cici.

They each had a critical part to play in their liberation. Like mercury divided, the Lazars had to be ready to act separately but together at precisely the moment the clock struck the hour of no turning back.

Zhuk had kidney issues and a finicky bladder. He was often up in the night taking a leak all around the clearing. But for Operation Aeneas to succeed, Zhuk needed to develop an intestinal malady and disappear to the outhouse for a few minutes. To facilitate that, Isabelle prepared for him a tasty meal of stew and cabbage, made from rabbit that had been caught and killed weeks ago and left out in the sun. The Lazars sipped the meager fish soup, while Zhuk ate the rabbit enthusiastically, not noticing that his prisoners weren't touching the stew.

Zhuk's guard noticed. Orlov stood in the open doorway of Isabelle's house, half-drunk and half-suspicious. Wiping his mouth on his sleeve, he said, "Hey, why you Lazars not eating the stew?"

"Leave them alone, Orlov," Zhuk said. "More for us." He sat at Isabelle's table until nearly eleven. The Russians could really put away their liquor. It was no use counting on Zhuk to get drunk on a full bottle of vodka. Still in possession of his faculties but with a looser tongue as the night was ending, he decided to toy with Roman, to engage in some banter. Roman had been so quiet, Zhuk said, since Oksana's arrest. "Where is the fiery repartee, Comrade Lazar, that I've come to expect and, frankly, enjoy from you?" he said with a malevolent smile. "Where are your clever ripostes?"

"On the train with my mother," Roman said. "In the earth with Yana."

Even Ostap elbowed him to stop. But Zhuk was in a good mood. "He speaks!" the Communist said with a smile. "Finally. But let's just agree that Yana deserves to be in the earth. The woman committed murder."

Ostap elbowed Roman again, but harder. Roman said nothing, his black eyes boring into Zhuk, who threw down his napkin and got up. "Well, time waits for no man," he said. "But—one more thing, Comrade Lazar." Zhuk watched the proud man's face closely as he spoke. "Do you recall how some weeks ago, you and I were having one of our sparkling conversations, and I reminded you again that your farm was ours? By chance, do you remember what you said to me by way of your snappy reply?"

Roman didn't speak.

"*Do* you remember or don't you, comrade? When I told you your farm was ours, what did you say?"

Roman's wrought iron gaze didn't leave Zhuk's face. He barely blinked. "I agreed with you," he said. "I told you the farm was yours."

"*But*, you said?"

"But," said Roman, "you would have to come and take it from me."

Zhuk clapped and laughed. "That's right! How wonderful. That's precisely what you said." He stopped smiling and took a step toward Roman, leaning into his intense, bearded face. "Guess what, comrade? Tomorrow, first thing in the morning, that is exactly what my men and I are going to do. My supervisor in Kammenets is finally sending me some sorely needed reinforcements and field workers. Twenty more soldiers are arriving here, and together with them, I will take your farm."

Roman said nothing.

"Have you got nothing to say, Comrade Lazar? No pithy wisecrack?"

"Are you sure it's going to be *first* thing in the morning, comrade?" said Roman. "And not like second or third thing, at *10 am*?"

Zhuk blanched, as if that was precisely the time his fortifications were arriving. "Enough chitter-chatter," he said. "Enjoy the last evening on your farm, comrades, and maybe dwell on the answer to the question of why, though you Ukrainians always strive for independence, for some reason you are never able to achieve it. A very good night to you." Zhuk sauntered out through the door past Orlov, and he and his guard disappeared into the night.

Eleven pm was not the hour for the Lazars to act. They cleaned up in silence under Gregor's watchful eye, and dispersed into their separate houses, saying goodnight as usual, teasing each other as usual. Nothing could be different or out of place tonight.

The May night was damp and cool. Isabelle sat at her window to let some fresh air into her lungs. Her throat was hot and closed as if she was choking on smoke. Everything was quiet in the countryside except for the usual night sounds of fields and forests. Everything was as it had always been.

Except the full moon was under cloud cover, and it was hard to make out the shapes of the sentries in the clearing.

The six homes on the Lazar farm weren't built in a straight line or a semi-circle because they weren't built at the same time, but added on randomly as the need arose. Isabelle and Mirik's cottage had been the first to be built for Martyn, Oksana, and their four children. It was the largest of the houses and stood on its own, apart from the others, on one side of the leveled glade, next to the pantries and the sheds. Twenty meters away, in the center of the clearing, stood the small house where Oksana moved to after Isabelle married Mirik. Next to it—closest to the path that led to the stables—was an *izba* for Roman and Cici, and next to that, the second-largest house, for Petka and his family. At the very end, almost off the dell, stood the two huts that belonged to Ostap and Nikora.

When Zhuk commandeered the houses, he took Oksana's for himself because from her front windows, he could see all the other houses. His men took Petka's commodious home; that way Roman's house was sandwiched between them, and Roman was guarded on all sides.

At night, one OGPU was placed on Isabelle detail, another on Ostap and Nikora, and three watched Zhuk and Roman. Zhuk ordered everyone in the compound to sleep with their windows open, so any conversation or movement could be heard.

Tonight when Isabelle came to bed, she found Mirik on his knees, his mouth mutely moving. He curled up on the floor, his back to her. She couldn't tell if he'd fallen asleep. He was motionless. Isabelle had hours to lie awake in the black night, as she listened for the sound of the quail and convulsed with terror. She wasn't afraid for herself, nor was she afraid for her brothers or even her husband. She was afraid for her children. There was no way out except on horses, but it was one thing to ride a horse in the paddock under the protective eye of a loving uncle, and quite another for small boys to mount an adult horse and ride it blind through unfamiliar countryside long kilometers to a phantom river. Mirik could take one of the children in the saddle with him but not both. And Isabelle couldn't take even one, because if another rider was in the saddle with her, she wouldn't be able to fire her rifle or wield her sword, should firing her rifle or wielding her sword become required.

Weeks ago, near the seedling sugar beets, Mirik asked her how they would ride at night. He suggested taking Zhuk's trucks instead. She put her hand on his face. A tenderness still remained. "Dearest Mirik," she said to him, "besides the obvious—that none of us can drive—the trucks can't be driven at night without lights, on rough terrain, through the woods. And the main road to the river is filled with checkpoints."

He didn't look convinced.

"But also," Isabelle said, "trucks can't cross the Dniester."

"And horses can?"

"Of course."

"They can see at night?"

"Very well."

"You better hope the Dniester is shallow at the crossing," said Mirik. "Because what's your horse going to do when it can't touch bottom?"

"It's going to swim."

"Horses can swim?"

Incredulously, Isabelle stared. "Mirik, how is it that you've been part of my family for more than ten years and yet don't know this?"

"I'm a dairy farmer," he grumbled. "Can Roman milk a cow?"

"He knows what a cow does," said Isabelle. "But yes, horses are very good swimmers. They can see at night, they can ride through forest. They were bred to handle the most difficult terrain. Our horses are a mix of the Karabakh and the Cossack Don. It's an endurance thoroughbred juggernaut of a horse. It's the king of horses. It can run eighty kilometers an hour for short distances and ride all day without stopping."

He gazed at her with love and regret. "You're going to be sorry to let them go."

"I'm sorry for many things," said Isabelle. The horses were Roman's life. Of all the valuables to leave behind, they were the absolute toughest, and the main reason her brother was filled with such white-hot loathing for Zhuk and Efros and the rest of the tyrants that stomped upon Ukraine's black earth and refused to leave them alone to live out their quiet working life in peace and joy. Boyko was their father's horse. Fifteen-year-old Roman was present when the broodmare foaled him. Seventeen-year-old Roman held the reins as he walked next to Boyko, who pulled the carriage, in which their father's body lay, through the streets of Ispas, to the church, to the cemetery. And tonight, twenty-eight-year-old Roman was counting on Boyko to get his wife out of Ukraine.

With one ear listening for the quail, Isabelle had hours to think about Roman and his horses, about poor Yana, and about Nikora's wife Zoya, who'd sneaked out a week ago, by herself and on foot, just after Yana died. Zoya's instructions were to head west, to travel only by night, to swim across the narrow Zbruch into Poland, to stop in a village called Kivka, just inside the Polish border, and to wait there for Nikora. She couldn't remain on the farm because she couldn't fight, and Nikora couldn't go with her because he could.

Before Zoya left, she begged Isabelle to let her take the children. She *begged* her. "If *I'm* safe, they will be safe," said Zoya.

"It's you not being safe that worries me," said Isabelle. Poland was two nights away on foot. Well-meaning Zoya was a navigator of moderate skills. Just weeks ago, she had to be taught how to use a compass. And this was the woman who pleaded with Isabelle to hand over her small sons.

That Isabelle refused was a given, but the hours she had to consider the wisdom of that refusal were not. It was an object lesson in how to poorly cope with irreducible agony. What if Slava and Maxim were meant to go with Zoya? Or what if Isabelle sent them and they got captured, or lost, or other horrors befell them when their mother wasn't there?

But what if *this* way was the wrong way? What if *this* path was the incorrect choice?

Whatever it was, it was too late now.

Senseless hours in the dead of night while waiting for the apocalypse was too long to lie awake and think about the unthinkables.

And when it was finally time, when the hour had come with the first quail call from Ostap, she couldn't move from her bed. She had such a short window in which to act. He called out to her again. And again.

"Isabelle, woman, wife!" Mirik cried soundlessly, only his lips moving, his frantic eyes boring into her. "You will doom us all. Please, get up. Can't you hear the call? The hour has come."

Isabelle, woman, wife.

Isabelle, sister, daughter, farmer, friend, are you being cast headlong into destruction the way of your father? Through death or abandonment, you are being driven from your motherland, and soon you will be left without any hope to avenge him, and all your hate will have turned further inward. You must pray there won't be other, more current, more compelling reasons for you to shake your fists at the silent skies.

Creeping out of bed, she fell to her knees.

Don't be pitiful. Don't weep. They broke your house, your trade, your marriage, don't let them break you too. They are corrupt, but you are famished. They have made of your country an open grave. Go find another Eden to reap your harvest, to tend your young, but before you go, on your knees, plead to the God who blessed you that if there's any blood to be shed, it won't be innocent blood.

Isabelle, woman, warrior, wife.

Isabelle, mother.

She barely kept herself from crying out.

Still on her knees but now prostrate, her head to the floor, she reached deep under her bed and from against the far wall pulled out a Mark I military trench knife, with a double-edged blade and a dagger point, and a Cossack dragoon sword, sheathed in an ornate red and violet scabbard—a curved-blade Imperial-issue *shashka* with a gold-plated grip wrapped in leather.

She fastened the leather sash with the shield securely to her body and then fitted the fingers of her left hand through the holes in the brass knuckle handle of the knife, gripping it like she wanted to become the blade. *US 1918* was carved into the cast bronze. She wanted her soul to be carved in it.

"Oh, no! Gregor's in the house!" Mirik was sibilating, barely audible. "I peeked out, and he's armed and awake and at our table! What are we going to do? Why did he come back inside? He's supposed to be *out*side! How am I going to get the children out? Should we abort? What if he heard something? What's the signal to abort? Isabelle, can you hear me?"

From the floor, she rose to her feet and drew her sword. She stood erect, a black-clad angel of vengeance, gripping the Mark I knife in one hand and with her other lifting her father's Cossack saber across her chest.

Isabelle!

The gates of life or the gates of hell are opening.

Go, and take your fate.

BOOK TWO
The Crane Wife

Past Is Prologue

Mama, Mama.

Did Isabelle hear her sons murmuring for her, or was it the sound of the quail in the night that begged her reply?

"But the children!" Mirik mutely cried.

Isabelle pressed the brass handle of the military knife to her lips, commanding him to stay silent, and without another word, opened the door to her bedroom and strode five long steps to the dinner table where Gregor the OGPU man sat, his legs stretched out, machine gun resting on his lap. He was smoking a cigarette and looking straight at her coming for him in the dark, the swooshing metal in her hands catching the reflection of the dim blue moon.

He didn't have time to drop his cigarette or lift his weapon or make a sound aside from an aspirating *Oh*. She sliced his throat with the sword from left to right and with the knife from right to left, *one two*, and sidestepped to avoid his spurting blood.

Lunging forward, she steadied his gun with her elbow before it could slide off his knee and hit the floor. She lay down her sword and his gun and pushed in his chair, forcing him to the table so he wouldn't tumble over and make noise. Gregor's head dangled and faltered and finally tipped forward on his chest, attached to his body by a flap of skin at the back of his neck.

Calmly she wiped off her two blades on the embroidered kitchen towels, replaced the saber in its sheath, slung Gregor's machine gun over her shoulder and returned to the bedroom, where a white-faced Mirik sat panting. He looked ready to faint.

"Mirik, control your breath," she whispered, stepping to the window and piping the low-pitched note of the common quail to let her brothers know that the first part of her mission had been accomplished. She didn't hear a response.

"Mirik, please! Keep quiet."

"Is Gregor still out there?"

"Yes," said Isabelle. "But he's been rendered ineffective. Close your eyes if you don't want to see. I'll guide you to the boys' room."

She thought Mirik might argue, insist he was fine, but he didn't. Maybe that was best; Gregor looked a real mess. Grabbing her arm, Mirik closed his eyes, and she led him into Slava and Maxim's bedroom. The boys were sitting tensely on the bed, dressed and ready.

"Sons, husband, tell me what you do now. Quickly. Mama must hurry."

"I take the children down to the stables and wait for you," said Mirik.

"No, Papa," said Slava. "We don't move from this room until either Mama or Cici comes to get us."

Isabelle kissed his head. "I don't have to worry about you boys, I see."

"Mama, I didn't know you had your own sword!" said Maxim, touching the scabbard attached to Isabelle's belt.

"There's a lot you don't know," Isabelle said. "Now, stay quiet. I'll see you in a few minutes."

She nodded to Mirik and noiselessly climbed out of her children's window. With the machine gun on her shoulder, she crept around the house. Silence was paramount. If any of the remaining four sentries made noise while being dealt with, it would alert the others and give them time to draw their weapons. A single cry in the night would awaken the men in Petka's house. A sword, no matter how sharp, could not do combat with a machine gun. And one dead guard's weapon could not do battle against fifteen automatics.

At night on the farm, every sound was amplified and refracted, every sound carried down the hills and over the fields. At all costs, the five sentries had to be killed in silence and fall in silence. Zhuk's customary nocturnal urinations did not give the Lazars enough time to accomplish their task. They were counting on his distressed stomach to detain him in the long drop.

"It's better like this," Roman said when they were talking it through a few days earlier. "I need that man awake to see what's coming his way."

The Lazars had taken many precautions, but they hadn't counted on the incessant racket made by the actual birds around their homes. The real corncrake and the true common quail didn't shut up, and neither did the bubububu owl, making the human calls nearly impossible to differentiate.

Operation Aeneas was set into motion by Zhuk himself. As soon as he walked to the outhouse, either Cici or Roman, whoever could see him clearly, would sound the warble of the quail to let everyone know to begin.

Isabelle couldn't figure out where the plan had gone off kilter. It was fairly straightforward. Zhuk would walk to the outhouse. Quail would chirp. Ostap and Nikora would kill the guard near their house and Isabelle would kill Gregor. Corncrake was second, the unmistakable *krek-krek* of grinding gears, to signal the next move: the three of them flanking the three guards in the center of the cluster, preferably all at once. When they were done, they would hoot the owl signal to Roman to let him know it was his time to move. Everything before the owl call had to be done in the brief minutes Zhuk was using the privy.

Zhuk was supposed to be in the outhouse—but he wasn't. The privy was dark. Had Isabelle commenced her part too early—or too late? She edged around the front of her house and caught a glimpse of Orlov across the clearing. So, it wasn't too late. He was spread out on the bench at the back of her mother's house, guarding Zhuk, his cigarette a pinpoint orange glow. Past Orlov, she made out the dark shapes of the two sentries outside Roman's hut.

The quail had called, or so she thought, Isabelle had done her part—finally—but there was no lamp in the outhouse. Zhuk was still in his bed. The three sentries were alive, and her two youngest brothers nowhere to be seen.

The elaborate system of call and response had backfired. Either Isabelle had missed a sign, or Ostap and Nikora had. She took a breath and emitted the grating *krek-krek* of the corncrake. Come on, Ostap, come on, Nikora.

Before she heard her brothers' response, the back door to her mother's house opened and a cursing, grumbling Zhuk stumbled out in his skivvies and unlaced boots past Orlov. "Don't know what's wrong with me," he mumbled. "Stomach is inside out. Third time tonight."

"Fourth," said Orlov.

Carrying the kerosene lamp, Zhuk walked briskly to the outhouse. The privy door closed.

Louder this time, Isabelle called out again, "*Krek-krek!*" like metal being sawed—and heard a quieter but definite "*krek-krek*" in return, all the way from Ostap and Nikora's houses. *Thank God.* It was a go.

Soundlessly, nothing but a rushing shadow, Isabelle dropped the machine gun and the knife and bounded across the clearing. She didn't draw her sword until she turned the corner and smelled Orlov's burning cigarette. He had been leaning forward, resting his elbows on his knees. The blade flashed, catching Orlov's eye. He was quicker than Gregor. Before he turned his head, he reached for the gun that lay next to him on the bench. If he had been truly prepared to fight a war with Ukrainian ranchers who once were Cossacks, he never would have laid his weapon down in the first place. Because in three leaps Isabelle was at his side, a panther, her sword raised with both hands above his head like an executioner's axe. With all her strength, she brought it down across Orlov's neck, severing his jugular, carotid, and trachea, slicing his head off his shoulders. It wobbled at the last moment and would have fallen into the dust had she not dived forward and caught it by its hair. She set the dripping head on the bench, half a burning cigarette still clamped between its teeth.

Wiping her blade against Orlov's tunic, she replaced the sword in the scabbard and grabbed his Degtyaryov. With the weapon in her hands, she called out a deep *"hoo-hoo"* to Roman to let him know her part was done. Moments later, her brothers signaled their own *"hoo-hoo."* The two men guarding Roman and Cici were no longer a threat.

Before Ostap even finished his owl call, Roman had flung open the door and was tearing down the path to the outhouse.

He kicked away a rock and pulled up a double-barreled shotgun that lay buried shallowly underneath. From the hole in the ground, he filled his pockets with buckshot, felt in the dark through the action housing to make sure two of the shells were in position, and, hoisting the weapon to his shoulder, pulled open the privy door. The kerosene lamp swung from a hook, the light casting eerie shadows across Roman's face. Zhuk sat on the toilet—a hole cut in the center of a slat bench. Next to him lay his pistol.

"Hey!" Zhuk said. "Close the fucking door."

Roman didn't reply—and didn't close the door.

The light of the lamp was in Zhuk's eyes; he saw only a looming shadow. "Who is it?" Zhuk said. "Who *is* it?" He tried to pull up his lowered skivvies, then reached across his body for the weapon but fumbled it. The gun fell out of his hand. Kicking the pistol out of Zhuk's reach, Roman grabbed the lamp off the hook and set it on the ground.

A silent paladin, Roman stood, his feet apart, both barrels of the shotgun pointed at the man on the privy. Now Zhuk could see who it was. He gasped.

"Revolution breeds revolution, Comrade Zhuk," Roman said. He pulled back the hammer. "You forgot whose country you are in."

"Have you lost your mind?" Zhuk tried to screech but his voice failed him, his throat dry from shock.

"Too much power makes out of small men even smaller men," said Roman. "I can hardly make you out, you are so tiny on your throne."

"Orlov," Zhuk croaked feebly, trying to yell. "Orlov!"

"Orlov is not available, he's lost his head," said Roman, his weapon trained on Zhuk's heaving chest. "And you are *nothing*. If I turned you inside out and split you with my axe, I would find nothing. I can't even bury you, or burn you, or scatter your dust to the wind, because you cannot bury or burn or scatter nothing."

"Think about what you're doing!"

"I've been thinking about little else, *comrade*," said Roman, placing bitter emphasis on the corrupted word. His finger hooked around the front trigger. "And I'm about to show you as harshly as I can how many things in this world you don't understand."

"Roman! You are making a very big—"

Roman fired, emptying the right barrel into Zhuk's disbelieving face. The sound of the shotgun in the silent night was like thunder overhead. It fluttered the bats from their perches and the quails from their marshes and the owls from their nests. It shocked the horses into high-pitched whinnying. It echoed for kilometers downwind. Before another half-second passed, Roman fired the second barrel into the slumped, unrecognizable mass that was Kondraty Zhuk.

As soon as the first blast came, Isabelle, Nikora, Ostap, and Cici kicked open the doors of Petka's house. Barely awake Soviet men, scattered throughout the common room, scrambled for their revolvers.

"Comrades, think!" Nikora said, a machine gun pointed at the men in the open space. "In our hands are *your* automatic weapons. You know what they do. Each of us has 47 rounds before the drum is spent. Don't be foolish. Put your weapons down."

But in the bedrooms, some of the men fought against two women. One threw a knife, aimed for Isabelle's face. It missed, lodging in the wall behind her. Isabelle raised her weapon, but Roman was already in the room. Moving Isabelle out of the way, he shot the knife thrower with the pump-action shotgun, then pointed the barrels at the second man. "Where is my mother?" said Roman in a loud terrifying voice.

"How the fuck should I know—"

Roman didn't let him finish before he shot him.

Passing Isabelle the gun, Roman took the machine gun from her and strode into the adjoining room where Cici and Ostap held two more men at gunpoint.

"Wife, move out of the way," Roman said, raising the Degtyaryov. "Where is my mother?" he said to one of them.

"I don't know who she—!"

Roman didn't listen further. He shot him. The second man, his hands in front of his face, said, "No, no, no, no, no."

"I'm only going to ask you once," Roman said.

"I don't know where your mother is!" the man screamed.

Roman shot him.

Out in the living room, Nikora held four men pinned against the wall. Trying to prevent the inevitable, these Soviets tried a different tack.

"I know where your mother is," one of them said. "Zhuk told me."

"Where is she?"

"I want my life in exchange for—"

Roman shot him before he was finished speaking.

"Where is my mother?" he repeated to the three men left.

"In Kastropol," said one enterprising Soviet. "I make one phone call—"

It was Isabelle who pushed Roman aside and fired the reloaded shotgun. She aimed and fired again. The dispersing buckshot from the second barrel killed the two who hadn't spoken yet.

"I had a good feeling about that last one," Roman said. "I think he knew something."

"We need to leave, Roman," Isabelle said. "The gunfire probably carried all the way to the Dniester. They'll be coming for us soon. Ostap, Nikora, give me your weapons and run, go help Cici with the kerosene. Meet us at the stables. And send Mirik and the boys down. Hurry!"

Their arms full of weapons and ammo drums, Isabelle and Roman ran downhill to their spooked horses.

While Isabelle headed to the stables, Roman entered the barn and shot Mirik's last two cows.

In the back of Boyko's stall, Isabelle swept away the thick hay and yanked open a metal trapdoor that led to a shallow brick bunker filled top to bottom with weapons and ammunition. If they remained on their farm, they had enough to fight off a small army, but it was too much to carry away on horses.

Isabelle and Roman worked silently. With speed and proficiency, they saddled and bridled their horses. They strapped loaded rifles, revolvers, and Soviet automatics onto the mounts. They stuffed extra cartridges into their pockets and saddlebags and grabbed the few remaining Russian stick grenades they had saved from the Civil War. "Three grenades is all we have left?" Isabelle asked.

"Three is all we have left," Roman replied. Carefully they replaced the trapdoor and covered it with hay. Outside the stable, it wasn't dark anymore. A warm amber glow was blowing upwind and into the trees, carrying with it a strong odor of kerosene.

They loaded the saddlebags with a few provisions they had hidden around the stalls: bandages, bread, mink oil paste for their boots and their tack. For a few moments before the rest of the family joined them in the stable, Isabelle and Roman faced each other. "Please come with us," Isabelle said, her voice breaking. "I beg you. Please don't stay behind. I know you're planning something stupid. No good will come of it."

"Oh, that is most definitely true, sister," Roman said. "No good will come of it. I promise you, if I can come with you, I will. But I won't leave unfinished business here."

Isabelle couldn't say anything more because Mirik entered the stable, clutching Slava and Max. Roman and Isabelle moved apart. Roman kneeled down to embrace his nephews. "You two are good riders, my little beloved men," he said. "Don't forget the things I told you. Now, mount your horses and head out. You have a very important job. And listen to your father. He will tell you where to go."

"We know where to go," Slava said.

"Yes," said Maxim. "To the river."

"Yes. And do you remember what to do if you get there before us?"

"We wait," Mirik said.

"No," said Roman in his firmest voice. "You do *not* wait. You cross the river to Romania where you will be safe. *Then* you wait. The horses will take you on their backs. What do you do, boys?"

"We cross the river," said Slava.

"Then we wait," said Maxim.

"Be good and be brave. You have what you need?"

"We have what we need," said Slava.

"You know the way," Isabelle said to Mirik, laying her hand on his arm. "Lead the horses south and west. Stay in the woods, off the main road. Don't worry about anyone but yourself and the boys."

"Ride as fast as you can, Mirik," said Roman. "We're right behind you. Whatever happens, we'll catch up."

Mirik cast an agonized glance at Isabelle.

"Slava, Max, keep your horses close to your father." She kissed their heads. "And keep riding."

"We know, Mama."

"They need to leave, Isabelle," Roman said.

Something in Roman's tone must have set Mirik off, for the fear on his face grew stark.

"Go, Mirik," Isabelle said.

"I don't know where to go," Mirik blurted, in a panicked voice. "I thought I knew, but it's too dark out, and the moon is covered by clouds. I can't remember which way to turn when I reach the pine forest."

"Go east, Mirik! Take a slight left at the pines, head into the woods, and ride all the way south. It's not even thirty kilometers. There's a narrow path by the edge of the forest that runs to the steep hill by the river. Keep to the path. If there's any trouble, duck into the woods. Use your compass if you're not sure. Remember, you need to get to the river crossing between Okopy and Zhvanets. If you can see the castle, you've gone too far east."

Mirik looked like a man who had never heard Ukrainian before, let alone the things Isabelle was repeating for him, even though they had talked it through a dozen times and Mirik knew the directions by heart.

Cici stepped into the stable, rifle in one hand, can of kerosene in the other. "Mirik," she said, "get yourself and the boys to the tree line on the other side of the woods. Wait for me there. The three of you can follow me."

"Cici, no," said Roman.

"Roman, I know it's not the plan," said Cici, "but we can't follow them if they don't know where they're going. And if they get lost, we won't be able to cross into Romania without them. It's fine. We'll be at the Dniester before dawn, but we must hurry. You four Lazars can hold up the rear without me. Let's go."

Nodding her approval, Isabelle pressed her husband and sons to herself one last time. "Don't shake, Mirik," she whispered. "Be steady for our boys. Follow Cici. And remember Orpheus." She patted his chest and stepped away. "No matter what you hear, just keep riding. *Do not look back.*"

"We'll meet you across the river, Mama," said the intrepid Slava, already on his horse, the reins in his hands.

"Yes, my darling child," said Isabelle. "Godspeed." She couldn't bear to look at Maxim, her baby boy, the gentlest, most loving of children. She didn't want the divine angel to see the terror in his mortal mother's eyes. With her shaking hand, she blew them a kiss, she made the sign of the cross on them, she watched them go, two tiny figures and their lanky, quaking father. She thought she might break.

Nikora and Ostap ran into the stable, reeking of kerosene. "They left?" Ostap said. "Good." He swore. "If I'm not careful I'm going to self-immolate. But everything's drenched and lit—the houses, the sheds, the barn."

Outside, the air was flickering orange and gold, the smell of burning wood strong. Up on the hill their homes were on fire. "I opened the valves on the tanks," Ostap told Roman. "What's left of the kerosene is running down the hill into the fields. Light it when you're ready. We have three jugs left. Let's get the horses out before we douse the stable." But Isabelle and Cici were already splashing kerosene into the stalls. They were out of time.

The brothers tied the horses they weren't riding in a single file hitch, and draped themselves with rifles, machine guns, and extra ammunition drums. Nikora jumped on the lead horse; Ostap on the tail. Roman turned away. He couldn't bear to abandon his horses and so had agreed to let his brothers take them. They would let them loose, away from the property. Other farmers might identify the wandering animals and keep them; that was Roman's hope. His name was branded into their shoes.

Pressing his Cossack saber to his heart, Nikora saluted his brother and sister and led the seven horses out of the stable. Roman, his head bent, touched every one of them as they passed. As Ostap rode by, Roman squeezed his brother's boot. "Be careful out there," he said. "Watch out for your little brother."

"I will," said Ostap, reins in one hand, rifle in the other. "You too, Isa, watch out for *your* little brother." He pointed to Roman and was off.

"What horse for me, Roman?" said Cici, "Lytsar?" Lytsar meant *knight* in Ukrainian.

"Take Boyko," he said. "Isabelle will take Lytsar."

"No," Cici said. "Boyko is your horse."

"Take him," Roman said. "If I'm not there, he will protect you."

Cici swung into the saddle. Roman touched her hand with his sword. "I will never leave you or forsake you," said Cici. "You are my life. I'll see you on the other side." She bent down, nearly sliding off, kissed him deeply, and raced away to find Mirik.

"I'm hoping she's being melodramatic and will do both, leave me *and* forsake me," said Roman. "Ready, Isa?"

"Ready."

Fiercely they embraced, like a brother and sister who had shared a good but hard life, like soldiers at war, and mounted their horses, kerosene jugs in hand. With swords at their sides and rifles on their backs, Isabelle and Roman rode out of the stable and into the fields, where they soaked the emerging wheat with kerosene. Lighting their matches, they threw them into the rows of greening earth, igniting the stalks in pathways of flame. The rivulet of fire traveled up the hill to where the giant drums were still emptying. The tanks exploded like giant bombs.

They took one last look at their engulfed homes on the gentle sloping hill, at their stable, their barn, all scorched earth.

"The flames will have it," said Roman.

"But *they* won't have it," said Isabelle.

They galloped away.

It was less than fifteen minutes from Isabelle's takedown of Gregor to the last match she threw. From the deafening shotgun blast that ended Zhuk's life to the gallop off their land was no more than ten. Ten minutes to blow up one life and begin another. They needed those minutes to get a head start because Isabelle knew that the barrage of gunfire, followed by the tank explosions and the sight and smell of a blaze in the blue night would not and could not go unnoticed by the Bolsheviks that quartered in Ispas. She knew they would be followed. From the farm to the river was about an hour's ride on horses, but less by truck. Haste was imperative.

She and Roman met up with Ostap and Nikora and raced to catch Cici, Mirik, and the boys. The barely visible forest path too often ended in open fields and sometimes in wild steppe. The grass, the grain, the pebbles, the rough terrain lodged in the horses' hooves and slowed them down. Only Cici on the indomitable Boyko rode on unhindered, with her young charges behind her. The four of them were in a foggy grassland far ahead of Isabelle and her brothers.

It was just after four in the morning. The pre-dawn sky was turning a shade of gravestone granite. Dense haze fell into the fields. As Isabelle rode in near darkness, her head lowered against Lytsar's mane, she hoped her children and Mirik kept pace with Cici. Horses were herd animals. When the lead horse galloped, the rest galloped, too.

They were less than four kilometers from the hill before the river, riding the narrow way between the fields and the forest, when Isabelle heard engines behind her. Her heart fell. They were so close! In the distance, trucks barreled through a gap in the trees, one after the other. The Lazars spurred on their horses, but the animals were already at full gallop. The trucks were narrowing the gap.

Roman surged up to Isabelle. Slowing down, brother and sister stared at each other darkly across their mounts. Nikora and Ostap caught up. They all circled up.

"We can't outrun them," Roman said, panting. "Form a frontline. We'll blast what we can. Then me and the boys will lure the rest away." He waved over yonder, away from Dniester and Romania, away from Isabelle and Cici. "We'll take care of them. But you ride on, Isa. Ride on like the wind."

When she wavered, Roman yelled at her. "There's no other way! You want them to catch your sons? *Never*. The fucking bastards will never have them." He blew her a kiss and motioned to Nikora and Ostap, who without a word lined up with their brother and sister, four horsemen separating life from death.

"Ready? On one!" shouted Roman.

Pulling up on the reins, all four Lazars dropped the bridles, took their feet out of the stirrups and spun around in their saddles, facing the approaching vehicles. "*Urrah!*" they yelled as they threw the weapons off their shoulders, pointed and fired. Isabelle and Roman used rifles, Ostap and Nikora machine guns. The trucks weaved and sputtered, the men inside scrambling to aim their own rifles. Scattered shots rang out in the field. The Lazars aimed and fired again. And again.

"Go, Isa!" yelled Roman. The brothers continued to fire.

"*Davai!*" Isabelle yelled to Lytsar, the spurs on her boots hurling him forward into a run while she continued to face the rear and fire at the trucks. She shot out the wheels of one of the vehicles and shot the driver. The truck crashed to a stop. But the other was still zigzagging, the men shooting wildly, their pistols aimed low—at the horses, not the riders.

Roman yelled a war cry to his brothers, pointing away into the distance.

The men whirled around in their saddles and faced forward. Isabelle watched them gallop away into the field of fog.

The Soviets decided that three Cossacks were better than one, just as Roman had hoped, and set off in pursuit, firing erratically through the dark and dewy air. The truck dropped out of sight. Rat-a-tat shots rang out, piercing the mist. There was a fusillade of fire.

Astride her knight, Isabelle, with the rifle in her hands, faced forward herself and charged to the edge of the dawn field. But before she could reach her family, she heard a man's voice shouting from the truck behind her, "Over there, to the right! Stop, woman! Stop, we order you!"

A single blast rang out. Isabelle had no chance to turn around or aim her rifle. They shot her horse.

Lytsar stumbled over his front legs, the force of his thousand-pound body propelling him headlong another twenty meters. Isabelle threw herself off before the massive animal crushed her with his falling frame. Lytsar crashed to his side, his body pulsing and heaving. Isabelle had no time to think. Yanking the machine gun off her shoulder, she opened fire at the approaching truck. The additional drum was still on Lytsar and unreachable, so she fired selectively, a burst of shots, followed instantly by another—and then she ran. Every few meters, she turned, fired off another burst, and ran again. They returned fire, but their truck had stopped moving. Three men got out and chased her on foot, their pistols out in front, firing every which way. She knew they couldn't see her well in the fog because she couldn't see them.

But they were closing the gap, gaining on her. A steppe-raised Lazar thoroughbred like Isabelle couldn't outrun three fat Soviet drunks? Impossible! But they were barely ten meters behind her. Still running, she pitched away the machine gun, pulled the rifle off her shoulder, turned, aimed, and fired. One of the men dropped to the ground. The other two stayed in frantic pursuit.

Isabelle heard the clopping of hooves and for a moment thought, *hoped*, it was Roman. Instead, out of the fog, on Roman's mighty horse, appeared Cici, the reins at her sides, a rifle in her hands. She shot one of the *chekists*, but the last man leaped toward Isabelle, who yanked out her sword, spun around, and slashed through the air. Isabelle just missed the man's abdomen but nearly severed his hand. Screaming, his wrist dangling, he toppled her. Cici vaulted off Boyko, lunged, and stabbed the crazed man in the back of the neck with her bayonet. Isabelle cried out. Cici had thrust the blade so far through the man's throat, it pierced Isabelle's own neck above her clavicle.

"Is that his blood or yours?" Cici said as she heaved his body away and helped Isabelle to her feet.

"Were you trying to kill me too? Forget it, let's go." Isabelle pressed her tunic into the wound to stop the bleeding. "Hurry, Cici!"

"Why? They're all dead."

"You don't hear that?" said Isabelle. The faint but unmistakable sound of a sputtering, gear-shifting engine came from within the fog, where a battle had raged minutes earlier between the men in the truck and her brothers. "Quick," she said, grabbing her sword and her rifle. She abandoned everything else, all their carefully curated supplies. "You ride, I'll hop on behind you."

They mounted Boyko, back to back.

"You're facing the tail?" Cici said.

"How else am I going to shoot them?"

"There's no one there. Where's Roman?"

Isabelle waved to the fields of Ukraine. "Where's Mirik?"

"I told him to hide in the forest up ahead and wait for us," Cici said. "Over that hill is the river. We are *so* close."

The hill didn't look that close. It was still a field away.

"Cici! We told them to cross! Why did you change the plan?"

"Isa, you were about to be slaughtered! They shot your horse!"

"Answer me! Why did you change the plan?"

"I just answered you! I came back for you."

"Why!" yelled Isabelle.

"*Why*?"

"Cici, you shouldn't have done that," Isabelle said with dark desperation. "To get the boys across the river was your only imperative. You and I can run, we can fight, swim if need be. Let's go. *Davai!*" Boyko broke into a trot.

"Did Roman say he would follow you?" asked Cici.

"He said if he could, he would." Isabelle raised her rifle. "Do you see my children?"

"They're over there. Don't worry. Across the field, in the trees, they're waiting for you."

Mirik, Slava, and Maxim may have been waiting, just over there, across the field, in the trees. But Isabelle lost the rest of her story. She lost it at the precise moment she and Cici, galloping on the indefatigable, indestructible magic Boyko, the king of horses, reached the place where her children were supposed to be waiting. The very center of God's majestic earth, full of stones and wet grass, was empty of the divine weight of three bodies, two of them fragile and borne by her.

Where is your flock, Isabelle? Where is your tortured husband? Where is your blameless brood? Wake me, wake me, bloodied and battered, so the eyes of my soul can see. No, don't wake me, please—so they can never see.

"This is where I left them," said Cici, pulling up on Boyko's reins.

Isabelle called for them. "Mirik! Slava! Maxim!"

"They must have crossed," said Cici.

"But you told them to wait."

"We also told them to cross."

"But then you told them to wait."

"Yes, but they're not here!" Cici said. "So they must have continued on." Intently the two women listened for any man-made sound. They heard nothing. Cici spurred Boyko forward.

"Wait," said Isabelle. "Is there a chance they could have heard the gunfire and gone back for us?"

"Why would they do a crazy thing like that?" said Cici.

"*You* did!"

"Mirik's instructions were clear," said Cici.

"He is not here," Isabelle repeated in a trembling voice. "So clearly his instructions were not clear."

"We have to go. We can't stay here, Isa."

"Let's go back a little bit. *Please.*" Isabelle was going numb with fear.

"They're not behind us," Cici said. "We would have seen them. And if by chance they are behind us, then Roman will find them and bring them. You did tell me Roman is right behind you. Face front."

Gripping the rifle, Isabelle slowly turned forward in the saddle. But she found it difficult to stay upright on the horse. Her rifle grew heavy. Her body turned to stone. She grabbed the saddle, listing, losing her strength and her footing, the weight of a concealed wrong too heavy to bear. "Go slower, Cici."

"Do we want to live or do we want to die?" said Cici.

Isabelle didn't know if she wanted to live. Dawn hadn't broken. Isabelle kept calling out for her family. *Mirik. Slava. Maxim.*

The fog was heavy upon the earth.

"Wait, Cici! Do you hear that?"

"Hear what?"

Isabelle didn't know what. This was where her memory stopped. It fell through a black hole and a metal trapdoor shut over it.

The next thing she remembered, she was wet and draped over a horse. Cici walked next to her, holding the reins, maybe crying. *I didn't want to cross without Roman*, said Cici. Then, riding, riding, her body hitched to the horse by rope. Being at the bottom of a pontoon boat, leaning against Cici, lying in her lap, smelling fresh water, burning wood, fish, hay, oak, mud, swamp. There were no thoughts, just images, the visual remains of a shattered world.

Later, Cici offered some pieces of the broken whole. Isabelle had fallen off Boyko, Cici said.

But why?

Isabelle had never fallen off a horse in her life.

Was it her neck wound? She did lose a lot of blood.

Though the memory of the last darkness was gone, this much was true: single-handedly, Cici got the two of them across the Dniester. In Romania, they continued on Boyko a long way south. When the Danube delta got too muddy and marshy, and traveling by horse became impossible, they parted with the hero stallion, selling him to a pike farmer. "Wait for me," Cici told the man. Why did she say this?

Cici secured them passage on a trawler down to the mouth of the great Danube. From there, they caught a ride to Constanta in a two-horse wagon full of onions. Isabelle, who never cried, cried all forty kilometers to the seaport. Cici said it was the onions.

The story wasn't hers because Isabelle couldn't fill the gaps to make it hers. She kept hearing her own voice calling for her husband and sons, she kept hearing Cici cry in return, *Roman will find them.*

Alone and together, she and Cici made it to Constanta and found Nate. Isabelle had never in her life seen anyone as happy as Nate was when he saw Cici. They cried in each other's arms while Isabelle sat hollowed out on a nearby bench. *Papa will weep from joy*, she heard Nate whisper to Cici.

As they were filling out the paperwork before boarding *Pride of the Sea*, it was Nate who advised the two women to write down the same last name— Lazar—because two visas were more likely to be granted to sisters than to friends.

And then Cici went and abandoned her sister in despair and against her will. "*If I leave him behind, run to a better life without him, what does love even mean? I love you, my closest friend, my family, but I love Roman more. We are held together by an unconditional bond even if there be blood at our feet. If he stayed behind for Judgment Day, then he is not going to face it without me.*"

A mute and mutilated phantom that once was Isabelle sailed alone to Brindisi and then to Lavelle. Everything she brought with her sank to the bottom of Boston Harbor, except for her. She walked through immigration barefoot holding nothing but the damp leather boots in her hands.

Isabelle's story lingered, unconcluded and incomplete. She was on Boyko, and then she wasn't. She had a family, and then she didn't.

Do you hear that?

Hear what?

In the core of the concrete weight inside her, she had a sense that *something* made her fall off the horse. In the rupture, she was ground to dust and driven underground. There was a fracture in her lifeline, a break in her timeline. Like Orpheus, her story stopped the moment she looked back. She fell off the kingly stallion and lost her children forever. One moment she was Isabelle Kovalenko and the next she hung passed out and upside down on her horse, a fragile solitary ghost.

But Isabelle refused to accept this fate, refused to accept a long life of nothing but a weeping heart. She was determined to find the missing threads to the tapestry of the story that was hers and hers alone. She continued to live as most exiles do—feeding on empty dreams of hope that she would see her family again. She chose to believe that down the length of days, *Mirik! Slava! Maxim!* would return to her, the way she chose to believe that in the other, vanished life, Cici was reunited with Roman, and together with Ostap and Nikora, the four of them searched for her husband and sons.

And the only thing complicating Isabelle's crystal dreams of reclaiming her old life was the small but vital truth that when she wasn't looking and wasn't careful, by night and in broad daylight, she had allowed another love to enter her wretched grieving heart. She had neglected to construct an elaborate barricade around that part of herself. A new magic surged within her life, lighting her up like all the stars of night, like power. Isabelle thought she had used up all the good she ever felt or would feel, but there, in the hard dry bitterness, a vigorous seed had planted itself, unnoticed and unwatered, and by God's unfaltering grace grew into divine love that to her shame could neither be ignored nor denied.

PART IV

Harvest

"And then you came with those red mournful lips,
And with you came the whole of the world's tears,
And all the sorrows of her labouring ships,
And all the burden of her myriad years."

William Butler Yeats

56

Loving Lane

It wasn't easy to move eleven people and four households sixty miles north in the wintertime. It wasn't as easy as crossing a field, and Isabelle knew *that* wasn't easy. Packing up without servants, deciding what to take and what to leave behind, the limited energy and resources were taking a toll on everyone, especially Vanessa.

At Isabelle's insistence, she and Finn borrowed Schumann's truck in the middle of December 1931 and drove out to New Hampshire. They loaded the truck with boxes of books and general knick-knacks. Isabelle said it was essential they assess the new residence so that come moving day, on December 31st, there would be fewer surprises. Especially for Vanessa. "We need to do some, how you say that thing you do in war?" Isabelle screwed up her face. "Renaissance?"

"*Reconnaissance*."

"Your family not being very realistic, Finn." Isabelle sat in the cold truck, bundled up in her coat and hat as Finn navigated the unfamiliar roads.

"They'd disagree with you," he said. "This is too much reality for them."

"Your mother fine intelligent woman, but she wants to bring her books."

"Books are a good idea."

"Four libraries of books? Farms are small. They have no libraries."

"Have you ever been to an American farm?"

"Farm is farm. Maybe in America bigger. There will be one big room, kitchen, fireplace, hopefully some bedrooms. But not always."

"No bedrooms?" Finn said. "Where do the beds go?"

"In bed boxes next to stove and dining table."

"You've seen farms *without* bedrooms?"

"Don't get stuck on that," she said. "Of course I have. We lived on farm with six cottages. Mine was biggest, it had only two bedrooms. My mother's had one bedroom. Roman's had none. He and Cici had platform bed behind curtain. Ostap was building extension on his hut for when he and Yana had baby." Isabelle squeezed and unsqueezed her hands.

"We don't have to talk about it," Finn said.

"We *do* have to. I'm telling you something important. Not about Yana. About size of farm. Farmhouse usually has one floor."

"Maybe two floors, if we're lucky?" Finn's eyes were twinkling.

"Maybe, but not five floors like you have now. I'm saying, if we sell stuff we don't need, we can buy stuff we do, like farm clothes. We don't need your froufrou shirts and flapper dresses."

"I promise you, I have no flapper dresses."

"Real clothes to work in," Isabelle continued. "We need boots. Well, not me. But rest of you, bad in need of boots. We need work gloves. No one can work in fields without them. You damage your hands."

"I wouldn't want to do *that*. What would I hold my books with?"

"Go ahead, make fun."

"Okay. You mean *more* fun?"

"Are you going to speak to Lucy? She wants to bring all art from her old house! And her china. She says it's from her wedding."

"You want me to talk to my mother-in-law about leaving her wedding dishes behind when the house we're moving to belongs to her and Walter? Isabelle, *please*."

"China on farm," muttered Isabelle with a slightly irritated shrug. "Fine. *Nie mój cyrk, nie moje małpy*, as my mother used to say in Polish."

"Meaning?"

"Not my circus, not my monkeys."

The road north got narrower and snowier the closer they got to the New Hampshire border. "It's like North Pole here," Isabelle said.

"Close your eyes and see nothing. Wait, before you close your eyes, look at the map and tell me where to go."

"What is address again?"

"Lovering Road. Off Winnicutt. I thought you found it already."

"I found it but then I lost it. Loving Lane, Loving Lane . . ." Isabelle traced the map with her finger.

"*Lovering Road*," Finn said.

"That's what I say. Loving."

"No wonder you can't find it."

"It's tiny road. Many small lines on map. Hard to see little Loving Lane."

"You won't find it if you keep looking for the wrong thing," Finn said.

"Turn here!" she said. "This might be Winnicutt Road."

"Oh, boy."

It took them longer than they would have liked to go the last few miles. The icy road was poorly plowed, and the truck kept sliding. All the trees and houses and fences and barns were buried under overhanging snow.

"Turn here," Isabelle said. "This is Loving Lane."

"*Lovering Lane*—I mean road, damn it."

"We here, damn it."

It was hard to tell where *here* was.

"I hope you brought boots," she said when he stopped the truck by sliding it into a snowbank.

"You know I didn't," Finn said, "because I have no boots. But this is it." The house loomed in the distance, a lonely abode in a sea of white, set back far from the road. "Walter told me it was down a long lane."

"Where are farm keys?"

"Isabelle, look around you," Finn said. "We can't get out."

Ignoring him, Isabelle hopped out. The fluffy snow came up to her knees. It was crisply cold outside and sunny. She was pleased to see the farm was decidedly not a hut. It was a sprawling expansive farmhouse. It looked majestic, standing splendid in the middle of white fields, framed by distant, snow-covered forests. She looked up at Finn, still behind the wheel, and beamed, her excited breath circling in the air.

Finn's sturdy, square-jawed, freshly shaved face was that of a man who was being forced to eat pig slops. "I don't know what the hell you're smiling about," he said. "Snow's up to your eyeballs, there's not a soul around, and I don't see a single electric post near the property."

"We might need to dig little bit."

"Did you hear what I said?"

"Something about electric," said Isabelle. "On farm, when it's dark, you sleep. When sun comes up you rise. What you need post for?"

"Um, to read?"

"Who has time to read? It's not even proper farm yet. It's just earth. It's not going to sow itself, Finn Evans." She walked around to his rolled-down window and tried to gaze up at him with gentle sympathy only—no affection, no amusement, no anything else. His deep-set eyes were so full of woe under his furrowed brows that she tried hard not to tease. "Do you want to shovel road so we can carry your precious books into house?"

"Can't," he said. "I ain't got the shoes for it." He opened the cab door to show her the dress shoes he had worn to the bank for a decade.

Isabelle got back inside the truck. "Maybe when we move here in two weeks, you can ask Mae and Junie to shovel," she said. "Or Eleanor. She *definitely* seems like person who enjoys physical labor." So much for gentle sympathy only.

"I told you the farm was a terrible idea," said Finn.

Isabelle folded her arms. "Better we learn now about this thing called snow," she said, "than when your wife is on train and all her candlesticks are in back of truck. Because if it's still like this then, you won't be able to get anything inside house. She will have to sleep in truck. Which is good because that's where her books and candles will be." She gestured to the road. "Drive, Finn. Chop-chop. Back to Boston."

Finn cast his eyes heavenward. "Why, *why* is everyone in my life so melodramatic all the time?"

"Who melodramatic?" said Isabelle. "I'm unflappable like moose."

"Yes, you and moose are practically twins," said Finn.

The engine of the truck was sputtering. Everything else was crackling quiet. It was around nine in the morning. They had set out early to give themselves a whole day in case things needed to be done, but Isabelle could plainly see that no one wanted to do the things that needed to be done, not even the capable, clever, can-do man next to her, who for the last two years had done all kinds of unprecedented things.

Apparently, shoveling snow would not be one of them. She tried again. "Finn," she said, "why the hangnail expression?"

He almost smiled. "*Hangdog.*"

"You carried 250 crates of illegal liquor through thick woods in black of night. And you did it three times. What's easier, that or this?"

"Clearly *that*. But let me ask you," Finn said dryly, "does the place seem like a hovel to you? Will you admit that it's much larger than you expected?"

Isabelle squinted her eyes, brought an invisible cigar to her mouth, and murmured in a low, sultry voice, "*That's what the actress said to the bishop.*"

Finn tried not to laugh. "Where'd you hear *that*?"

"Mae West," said Isabelle. "She says it all time on radio."

"She says a lot of things you can't repeat in polite company."

"*Yes, and you're pineapple of politeness.*" Still smoky and sultry.

"*Pinnacle*! All righty, Miss West." He folded his arms. "I don't remember asking for jokes. You know when I could have used a joke? At Thanksgiving, when you told me the worst story I ever heard."

"My mistake," Isabelle said. "Next time I will be sure to prepare good joke to crackle between story of murder and arson."

"*Crack*, not crackle." They sat in the truck, staring at the silent house.

"I know you worried." Reaching over, she patted his arm, like a bear thumping another bear. "But your children ready for anything. Your father smart, he knows what's going on. Your mother, she more of thinker than doer. We gonna work on her. Walter, poor guy, we will give break to. Lucy is feisty.

She can work. Eleanor doesn't want to work but can and will. Eleanor's son is not good boy, but he is bored boy, and boys need activity. So, by my logistical brain deducements, only one really on your mind is Vanessa."

"You're like Sherlock Holmes with your logistical deducements."

"Vanessa is not going to be easy," Isabelle admitted. "But now we deal with snow. We shovel. Make path, get inside house, then do more decisions."

"I couldn't even save a bank. You think I can fix this?" Although Finn pointed to the fifty yards of snow, Isabelle suspected he was talking about Vanessa. "Also we don't have shovels. What are we going to use, our hands?"

"Schumann lent me two shovels, one for me, one for you." Smiling, she made the sound of a corncrake. "*Krek-krek,*" she piped in perfect imitation. "Ready for some action?"

Finn laughed.

It took the two of them till noon to dig out a path to the steps of the porch and up to the front door. After they carried the thirty boxes of books into the house, they were hungry and exhausted. "Let's go to Hampton," Finn said, "get something to eat and stop by town hall."

"What are you going to ask this town hall," she said, "if we don't look inside house and see what we need?"

"What I need is food."

"Let's go inside and maybe I give you something to eat."

"Are you going to grow it between now and five minutes from now?"

"I have tricks in my sleeves," she said.

"Isabelle, it's a deserted farmhouse," said Finn. "Vacant since last century. If you didn't bring it, you ain't gonna find it."

"Who says I didn't bring it?" said Isabelle, her flushed face turned up to him, her bright eyes sparkling. She opened her backpack to reveal a thermos full of hot chicken broth, hard-boiled eggs, a wad of cheese, salami, and half a loaf of bread. She'd brought some leftover cake and two bottles of beer. Isabelle knew the beer would change Finn's mood from whatever it was to 100 percent better.

And from the way he smiled at the beer and then at her, she knew she'd done well. The expression on his face—impressed and delighted—was exactly what she had hoped for. And she didn't even tell him about the little flask she had hidden in one of the backpack pockets. She didn't want to hit him with all her home runs in one inning, as they said in America. She wanted to spread them out in case he needed cheering up later.

The farmhouse was only moderately cold, insulated by the mounds of snow piled against the walls and windows. It was dusky, with blinding sunlight streaking through the wood shutters.

The house differed from Isabelle's previous experience in many ways. It had been extensively renovated since its humble 1800 beginnings. The floors were wide planks, well-made, sanded, polished. The walls were painted, the large windows set in intricate white glossy frames and covered with something Finn called plantation shutters. The house was well built, with deep window ledges perfect for flowers and keeping food cold in the winter.

On the left, through the open main areas, was a hallway with three bedrooms and an enormous bathroom, larger than Ostap's entire hut. It had a wall-to-wall counter into which two sinks were set, with oval mirrors above them like paintings framed in white wood. It had a sandstone floor that would probably be cold for bare feet but looked classy and pretty. There was a claw-foot tub placed under its own window, a wood-burning stove next to the tub for warmth, shelves galore for towels and linens, and a small lavatory with its own door. The privy had a toilet with a high tank and a flushing chain. It was a long way from the outhouse in Ispas. Isabelle yanked the chain. "There's even water in the tank!" she exclaimed.

"Well, not anymore," said Finn.

Water was piped in from a cistern at the rear of the house. The tank stood under its own awning and was partially buried to prevent freezing. Isabelle had never been on a farm that had such fancy indoor facilities.

The entire right side of the house was given over to the cooking, food prep, and family congregating area—from the long dining room and butler's pantry in the front to the enormous kitchen in the back. It was set off with carved wood entryways and had two fireplaces. There were smooth-stone countertops, painted white cabinets, and a colossal, waist-high center table that served as a butcher block prep area, cold stone bake area and meeting center all in one. There was a massive multi-level stove with two ovens and a cast-iron surface that looked like it was eight feet long. And to top it off, the kitchen had one of Isabelle's favorite things: a window in the back over the sinks so the woman of the house could glance outside and watch her children play as she prepared them dinner.

Swaying on her feet, Isabelle stepped away from the sinks. Finn leaned in to her with a puzzled expression. "You okay?"

"Very good." But the tremors in her legs took a while to subside.

"What did you see?" He peered outside.

"Nothing. I thought you were hungry. You want to eat or talk?"

She divided their food on the white wax paper she had wrapped everything in. They stood over the center counter and broke bread.

"Finn," she said, touching the cold stone, "what is this marvelous gray rock?"

"Carrara marble," he said. "Pretty swanky for a hut, eh?"

She tried to appear unimpressed. "Will be good to bake on."

She opened their beers, they clinked, said "*Budmo!*" and drank and ate with gusto. "What does *Budmo* mean again?" Finn asked.

"*Let us be.*"

Afterward, they checked out the rest of the house. Down a step off the kitchen stood two massive pantries, a canning shed, and a furnace room. Beyond the shed in the side yard were lean-tos for wood and kindling and a half-buried root cellar for winter storage of food and grain.

"Root cellar is very good," Isabelle said.

"I don't know what a root cellar is," Finn said.

Upstairs were four more rooms and a common area between them.

"Are you eating your hat right now?" Finn said. "Because I'm counting seven bedrooms in this shack with Italian marble countertops."

"I'm not eating hat because I'm full," said Isabelle.

They pushed open the back door, shoveled out a small square area on the long covered patio and stood next to each other in the cold, having a smoke.

"What are you thinking?" he asked.

"Just looking," she said, gazing at the fields. "What about you?"

"That we should get a bench for the side yard where we can sit and have a cigarette."

She smiled. "We should."

"Let's go. Clearly we need to get many more candles."

"Candles good," she said. "Kerosene lamps better."

"Are they?" Finn nudged her lightly for emphasis.

As if Isabelle needed emphasis to understand things. "Yes, kerosene super," she replied, throwing out her cigarette. "Especially for setting fires."

They headed to town, Isabelle doing her best to get them there with her inadequate navigational powers. One couldn't be good at everything, she told herself philosophically. The clerk at the village hall provided them with some useful information. Because of Herbert Hoover's public works projects after the crash of 1929, even a hamlet like Hampton was making headway into electrifying all the homes in the town and running water mains to the neighboring farms. "Progress is slow, but work continues," the woman said, opening her atlas of area coverage. "Where do you two live again?"

"Loving Lane," replied Isabelle.

"*Lovering Road*," Finn clarified.

The clerk confirmed that their street was within the utility coverage area but said that no one would be able to get to the house until the snow melted.

"My advice?" the woman said. "Wait till spring to begin your new life."

"We move in two weeks," Finn said.

"Aww, look at you two." The woman smiled. "Can't wait to start your family, can you?" Slamming the atlas shut, she nodded approvingly. "You'll have to start that family by candlelight," she said. "No electricity till spring."

Back in the truck, Finn sat and brooded.

"What is worry now?" Isabelle asked.

"Where do I begin?"

"Begin at first worry."

When he didn't reply, she suppressed an exhale. "You did see gorgeous farm, right?" she said. "I'm not only one with eyes?"

"No electricity, no heat, no running water," he said. "The cisterns frozen, no way to get the truck closer to the house when we move, and God forbid it should snow again like you said—then we'll really be up shit's creek."

Isabelle watched his soft, sullen mouth laying out all the reasons why it would never work. "You are absolutely right, Finn," she said. "It's not easy changing life in dead of winter. Maybe we should wait until end of May. I hear it's easier then."

After an amplified sigh, he said, "Fine. We'll do what you want."

"I want so many things—which one?"

"We'll go buy me boots with money we can't afford to spend. We'll get bags of sand or salt or whatever and shovel out the rest of the drive." He shifted into reverse. "But you know, Isabelle, you can't keep comparing every single thing with the worst thing that has ever happened or is ever likely to happen. Just because this is not as bad doesn't mean it's good."

"That is true," Isabelle said. "But doesn't it help, little bit, to know how much worse it could be?"

57

Mrs. Rochester

Vanessa didn't think it could be worse, and no tales of tragedies in ravaged borderlands would convince her otherwise.

The sheer chaos of what was happening around her would drive anyone to breakdown, not just the ill-equipped. Vanessa couldn't even be left alone to pack at her own pace. Every time she put things into a wooden box, out of nowhere would appear a Ukrainian gypsy, a foreign dervish, all purposeful and single-minded. She would glance at Vanessa's beautifully packed items, shake her head or her finger and say, "Vanessa, we don't have seven tables which require seven changes of linens for each day of week. We have one and require one." Or, "You're bringing flapper dresses to snowed-in farm in middle of nowhere? You have no closets in your bedroom and one wardrobe to share with husband. Think about things you need and pack only those. And high-heeled shoes—beautiful, but again, *farm*, Vanessa."

Why did Vanessa allow this impetuous waif to talk to her this way! She had a good mind to fire her. If only Isabelle wasn't completely indispensable. If only she weren't working for free. How do you fire someone you're not paying? "Don't you have someone else to go torture?" Vanessa said. "Isn't Finn doing something you can berate him for?"

"Always," said Isabelle, chipper as a toddler. "Man wore his best dress shoes to shovel long road. That required heavy berating."

It took four trips over four days to load the truck with the family's things and drive to Hampton. Finn and, unfortunately, Lucas took care of that while the family finished packing. Before, Vanessa could make her displeasure about Lucas known—and did—but what could she say now when she knew he was her husband's brother?

On December 31, 1931, Vanessa said goodbye to her beloved manse with plush seating, decorative rugs, and ornate lighting fixtures, the house where two of her children were born and where one had died, the home that was her marriage and her refuge. Finn, along with Lucas and Nate—who was staying with his father for the winter—drove to Hampton with the last of the family's belongings. All others, including Vanessa, boarded a train from Union Station.

On the train, Earl and Walter chatted easily with Schumann as men from all walks of life often can in stressful situations. Mae and June chirped nonstop because they knew no better. Pressed against the window, Isabelle sat by herself, looking the grimmest Vanessa had ever seen her. It was almost like the days of old when she spoke no English and stared at them as if she didn't recognize the human species.

Vanessa, sardined between the dual-channel complaining of her grousing mother and griping sister, was also mute. Curled inward to brace herself against the tension of being on a locomotive chugging through the open countryside, she couldn't calm her fidgeting hands. She couldn't respond to the excited banter of her children. It was as if her anxiety had thrown her into a concrete chamber in which normal sounds could only dimly be heard.

Olivia sat between her granddaughters while they regaled her with all the fabulous things they would do on a farm. "There is going to be ice skating, and sledding, and songs by the fire on cold winter nights, and card games, and cooking, and long walks, and building snowmen, and skiing, just like Isabelle told us there was on her farm!"

"It sounds magical, girls," Olivia said. "Is that true, Isabelle?"

"Once there were those things, it is true," Isabelle said.

"Oh yes," said Monty, Eleanor's rotund eleven-year-old son, himself in a gloom cloud. "Mae, Junie, you're going to fall through the ice and drown. You're going to break your legs skiing and then freeze to death. You're going to hit a tree with your dumb heads. Let's see how magical that will be."

Why did Monty's words mirror her own thoughts, Vanessa wondered. Was there something wrong with her or something wrong with Monty?

"Isabelle, darling," Olivia said, "why are you so quiet?"

"Nothing," Isabelle said. "I've never been on train before."

"Neither have I," said Vanessa. "No one is asking *me* what the matter is."

"I'm wondering if this is kind of train my mother was on when Soviets took her in middle of night and vanished her into land unknown," said Isabelle. "Probably not. They used cattle trains, I think."

Vanessa tutted in black despair.

Isabelle turned back to the window.

Finn was late picking them up, and they had to wait for him inside the brick station—for twenty minutes! Vanessa's nerves were on fire.

When they finally arrived at the snowed-in farm, her little girls were elated, like they were going to an amusement fair on Revere Beach. Their thrilled faces and voices contrasted sharply with Vanessa's constricted stare. She clung to her mother's arm as they got out of the truck, and squeezed her eyes shut to block out the vastness of the snow-covered fields and the joy of her children.

"Thank God for small favors, I suppose," Olivia said, taking in the unfamiliar rural surroundings. "But I must admit, the dense forests lining the fields contribute to my sense of Thoreau-like isolation."

Olivia, please stop speaking, Vanessa wanted to say. *You're making things worse.*

"It's not good here," Lucy said. "No use putting lipstick on a pig, Olivia. Ouch, Vanessa, you're hurting me! Why must you squeeze me so tightly, my darling? My bones are brittle."

"Vee, are you seeing this?" said Eleanor as she and Lucy helped Vanessa tread through the snow. "Everything's frozen!"

"I hope the water pipes aren't frozen too," Vanessa said to Finn on the porch. "Or we won't have running water."

"Why don't you come inside, Vee," Finn said, "get out of the cold, get yourself comfortable. All else in good time."

"Oh, but where to get comfortable, darling," Vanessa said. "There's barely any furniture."

"You only need one chair, and here it is." Finn set her down like a plant in the corner next to the fireplace and away from the commotion of the open door. He had built a fire so the farm would be nice and warm when they arrived. Of course, leaving the front door wide open while they unloaded rendered his thoughtful gesture somewhat pointless. Vanessa slumped while the rest of the family carried chaos into the horrifyingly open new space.

To make matters worse—as if anything could—the charmless Lucas was not only carrying Vanessa's things but flirting with her sister and joking with her children! And Eleanor, ever eager for male attention, was giggling as if she actually found his charm-free charm offensive charming!

At four, when it started to get dark, Eleanor said, "Finn, I'm trying to turn on the lights but I can't find them."

"Isabelle!" Finn yelled. "Bring the kerosene lamps!"

Isabelle emerged with three lamps.

"No, no," Lucy said. "Put those away at once. Kerosene is disgusting and dirty. I won't have it in my house. Please put proper lights on."

"Light by kerosene or candle, Lucy," said Isabelle.

"I have one candle," said Junie.

"Good girl, Junebug," said Isabelle. "Bring it to your grandmother and light it for her please."

"Where are the actual lights?" Lucy was strident. "Finn?"

"Finn, you didn't tell your family?" Isabelle shook her head. "There are no lights, Lucy. Not yet."

"I didn't want you to worry, that's why I didn't say anything," Finn said to his mother-in-law. "It's going to be fine, but for the time being there is no post on the main road."

There was an uprising.

"Oh, pipe down, Luce," Walter said to his wife. "You were born and raised in a world without electricity. Somehow you managed."

"When will the post be installed?" Lucy said, ignoring her husband.

"When snow melts," Isabelle replied.

"When is *that* going to be?" yelled Lucy.

Isabelle shrugged. "June? July?"

All the women shrieked.

"I'm joking," Isabelle said. "March, maybe?"

"That's not funny, Isabelle!" said Lucy.

"I keep telling her she's not funny," said Finn, "but she won't listen."

"I told you to tell family about lights," Isabelle said. "Did *you* listen?"

"Isabelle," cut in Vanessa, "could you make up my bed? I need to lie down." There was light from the crackling fireplace, but outside, no Beacon Hill gas lights dimly sparkled, no brights from passing cars rushed by, no reflection of civilization in the harbor or the Charles glimmered anywhere. Better to keep her eyes shut. There was nothing to see. Nothing good, anyway.

The family had kept their beds and mattresses, Walter and Lucy's old couch, their old dining table and chairs, Olivia and Earl's favorite reading chairs and their Tiffany lamps. They kept Lucy's wedding china and Olivia's silverware. They kept the silver candlesticks and all their books. Everything else they either sold or relinquished in mortgage default. Most of Vanessa's exquisite furniture and rugs and paintings went on the auction block.

After Isabelle made up Vanessa's large bed with fresh sheets and pillows, Vanessa fell into it, covered up to her ears with blankets. Mae and Junie crawled all over the bed. "Mommy needs a little rest and she'll be as good as new," said Vanessa. "Go play somewhere else, pumpkins."

"Do you want us to leave a candle in your room?" asked Mae.

"No," Vanessa said. "I'd like it to be black, angels." *Like my fucking future*, she almost said to her innocent children.

A few hours later, Eleanor came in to ask if she wanted to join the family for a small New Year's Eve repast. Vanessa declined.

"Everyone's out there, Vee, but you," Eleanor said. "We're talking and figuring things out. We're eating potato salad on Mommy's best china!"

"Great."

"My Monty is helping Finn and Lucas unpack!"

"Good for him."

"Listen, I don't like it any more than you do, Vee," said Eleanor. "None of us do. But it's not so bad, right?"

"Oh, it is."

"It could be a lot worse," Eleanor said, "and that's *me* saying it."

"It really can't, Ellie."

"Yes, it can. Come on. Try to make the best of it."

"Me lying here in the dark so I don't have to see the mess, the crates, the boxes, the disaster *is* me making the best of it."

"Don't be like that," Eleanor said cajolingly. "There's apple cider and cake. Come out and ring in 1932 with us. Isabelle promised to tell Daddy and Earl the story of her last night in Ukraine."

"Nothing she could say could be worse than this."

Sometime later, Isabelle came in and perched on the corner of the bed.

"Vanessa, remember Kisa and Buddha story you told me on Thanksgiving?" she said. "Now is good time to think about it."

"And remember what you told *me*?"

"Please get up," said Isabelle. "It's important to mark special occasions with people who love you." She rubbed Vanessa's legs.

Vanessa yanked them away. "I'm sick."

"You're not sick." Isabelle sighed.

"I am in here." Vanessa pointed to her chest. "And in here." She pointed to her head.

"Nothing will be different if you stay in bed or be with us for hour," Isabelle said. "You'll still be sick in head, but your family won't feel bad."

"They need to worry a little less about me and a little more about what's going on here." Did anyone else see where they all were? Madness!

"Every person is worried about many things," Isabelle said. "But candles are burning, it's warm, and we all together."

"Lucas is still out there."

"You mean your husband's brother? Yes. You know who else is out there? Your father. Your mother. Your husband. Your *children*." Isabelle breathed heavier than she wished to, Vanessa could tell, even in her diminished state.

From the kitchen came the happy noises of her family talking, laughing.

"Doesn't sound like they need me at all," Vanessa said.

"You don't think your husband needs you? Or your daughters?"

"They can't do without me for one night?"

"*One* night?"

Exhaling, Vanessa said nothing.

"What do you want me to tell them?"

"Anything you like," Vanessa said. "Tell them I'm Mr. Rochester's crazy wife, and my husband keeps me locked away in a dark part of the house."

"Hmm," Isabelle said. "In your nice picture who am I, then—Jane Eyre?"

That startled Vanessa into a sitting position. Fidgeting mercilessly with the blanket between her stiff fingers, she tried to pivot away from the ridiculous metaphor. "The girls should be in bed!" Vanessa said. "It's too late for them to be up."

Behind Isabelle, Vanessa heard Finn. "Leave her alone," he said, placing his hands on Isabelle's shoulders. "Junie is about to beat me in Go Fish and finish all the cake. Come. Show me how to beat her. She's a killer."

"Only one way to beat your daughter in cards, Finn," Isabelle said, getting off the bed. "You cheat. I learned hard way." She stretched out her hand to Vanessa. "Please come. Your family is waiting."

Finn pulled Isabelle away.

Vanessa gave them the back of her head. In a moment, she heard the door shut behind them as they left, thank God.

"I don't know why you keep trying so hard," Finn said to Isabelle outside the bedroom door.

"I want her to be better," Isabelle replied. "For her own sake, for your children's sake." She paused. "And yours."

"Sometimes we don't get what we want," Finn said. "And don't you dare tell me you know this well, Miss Eyre."

"I know this well, Mr. Rochester."

"I said don't you dare tell me!"

Their chuckling low voices faded from Vanessa's earshot.

58

Memory

Upstairs, temporarily sharing a room with Mae and Junie until the family figured out where everyone was staying, Isabelle spent her first night on this farm curled up on the floor in the corner, covered by blankets. The room was cold, but she didn't feel the chill. She felt the black abyss of the Lavelle water the night she almost drowned.

The last time Isabelle slept on a farm, her family was near. She saw her brothers, her husband; she touched her sons. In her new life, Isabelle tried very hard not to think of them, of her last night with them under the dim moon in the foggy fields.

And by and large she succeeded.

The key was to constantly keep moving, stay occupied, not be by herself. When she first heard about the Hampton farm, it energized her because Isabelle knew she would be able to help—truly help—the one she loved, the one who needed help so desperately. It was only now, in the cold dark room, that the dredge of old things washed over her.

She tried to comfort herself with thoughts of a more distant past, before she married Mirik, before her own children came. In 1913, the last New Year's Eve before the war, they had themselves quite a celebration. It was the only time she saw her mother and father seriously intoxicated. Martyn played the balalaika and Oksana danced and their four young children, one girl and three boys, whooped and hollered when they saw their parents kissing in the corner by the stove. Isabelle danced, while Roman locked swords with Ostap, and Nikora jumped up and down, shouting, "Me next, me next," and Oksana yelled, "Boys, no swordplay in the house! How many times do I have to tell you? Martyn, say something!" And their father, gazing at his sons with naked adoration, mock-furrowed his brow and said, "Boys, you heard your mother, put your sabers down."

Even *that* happy memory morphed for Isabelle into all the later New Year's Eves with Mirik and her own sons. The players had changed, but the words were still the same, the love was still the same. "Slava, Max," Mirik would yell, "how many times must we tell you? No swordplay in the house! Isabelle, say something!"

O Lord hear my prayer. Don't cast aside the unworthy mother who has orphaned her children. Bring the beloved lives back to me. What if Mirik has fallen and can't protect them, and they are alone? What if they're in the hands of deadly vipers? I left them behind and he lost them. Where do they hide? Who will look after them? What penalty have I paid, what suffering have I been punished with for abandoning my blood?

Isabelle needed to do better. She needed to work harder, to move faster—and not have energy left over to think—to set the dead woman back on her feet again.

She spent the icy night forming and reforming herself, burning down, sweeping away, and then, in the morning, got up, cleaned herself up, fixed herself up, and got going. She fired up the stove, ground some beans, boiled water, made a pot of coffee for the family. Soon the smell of coffee woke Finn, and they had a few minutes alone in the kitchen until Walter and Earl joined them. Isabelle chatted to the men and searched the crates for some bread and a pan to fry it in, hoping that when you glanced at her from the outside, self-possessed, graceful, good-humored, smiling, you'd never suspect that anything inside had ever been broken.

59

Waiting

No one promised it was going to be easy.

But whereas in Boston, Finn could flee the house—and often did—in Hampton, there was nowhere for him to go.

They spent a long time debating who was going to take which bedroom. Seven bedrooms, eleven people, much argument, heated discussion. It seemed to go on forever, but when Finn checked what day it was, it was still January 1st!

Finn and Vanessa took the master bedroom on the first floor in the back, but who would take the two adjacent rooms? They had been built for children, but the children wanted to share one of the large rectangular bedrooms upstairs with a view of the fields and the faraway river.

Walter settled the issue. He didn't want to walk up the stairs, so he and Lucy took the two downstairs bedrooms, since they slept separately.

Upstairs, Finn's girls took the large room in the back and Finn's parents took the large room in the front, which left three people for the two remaining smaller rooms: Eleanor, Monty, and Isabelle. Monty said under no circumstances would he share a room with his mother.

Finn said, "Who asked you?"

Junie said, "Monty, would you prefer to share a room with Isabelle?"

Monty turned tomato red and hid in a different part of the house.

Eleanor wanted her son to have what he wanted. Finn said that was Monty's biggest problem: irrespective of other people's needs, Monty got what he wanted. Eleanor said it was her father's house. Walter told Eleanor not to be a prig or he would make her sleep in the canning shed. Isabelle, peacemaker as ever, said she didn't mind sharing a room with someone.

"Who, Isabelle?" Finn said. "My father and mother? Walter, maybe? Lucy? Or would you and Eleanor like to be roommates?"

Eleanor said she wouldn't mind that. Eleanor!

"Daddy, Isabelle should share a room with you and Mommy," Junie said. And she and Isabelle laughed like clowns in a circus.

"Some things are worth argument, but not this," Isabelle said to Finn who stood with his arms crossed, waiting for her to finish the hilarity with his daughter. "Monty takes one room, Eleanor other, and I sleep next to furnace. I found myself secret room." She beamed. "Want to see?"

The family, minus Vanessa, piled out past the pantries, the canning room, and the shed. In the shoveled-out side yard, near the coal bins and across from the root cellar, was a door that led to a walled-in intimate space. It had an alcove big enough for a full-size bed and a raised, built-in platform with deep drawers and a mattress. There was a round table in the corner by the window, a narrow wardrobe, a counter with a wash-basin and a mirror over it as if for shaving. There was even a tiny bookshelf. It looked lived in, as if this might have been where John Reade stayed when he renovated the farm. It had hooks in the plaster walls, a mud grate for boots, set into the bluestone floor, a rug, and even curtains! As soon as the children saw it, they jumped onto the high bed and shrieked in protest. They all wanted to live in the secret room—even Finn.

Because in Finn's new life, he now shared a wall with Lucy Adams, the mother of the woman Finn occasionally claimed marital privilege with. Talk about a flue dragged shut on the weak-tea fire of his under-siege passion.

"Seven bedrooms plus secret cave and still not enough?" Isabelle said when he was sulking as they unpacked their dry goods in the pantry.

"I wonder how you would feel if your mother slept next door to you and Mirik," Finn said. "Or worse—*his* mother."

"My mother did sleep next room to me and Mirik," said Isabelle. "Until 1924 when we built her separate house. After you build me smoking bench, maybe you should build house for Walter and Lucy. How are you with hammer and nails?"

"This is why I can't talk to you," Finn said. "You're always teasing."

"Look at my face—do I look teasing?"

He left the pantry.

The next day, a blizzard dumped two more feet of snow on the farm. Finn longed for the snow to melt, for the earth to show itself, for spring to come, for life to begin. To him every January day felt as long as a year.

John Reade had done a good job with the renovation. But the water in the cisterns was frozen, and consequently there was no water inside the house except for what they could melt on the stove. There was barely any water to wash with, and all the heat came from the fireplace and the woodburning oven, which Isabelle fed nearly around the clock, until they came dangerously close to running out of wood.

Finn had to wade through the snow with her to the tree line to chop down a tree. When they were out by themselves, Finn confessed to her that he had never held an axe in his life and had no idea how to chop down anything. Isabelle teased him for five minutes and then showed him how to hold and swing an axe. She kept correcting his hold on the handle, but he got the job done. The tree came down, he fumbled with the saw, managed to cut the wood and then split it.

"I did well, right?" he said, admiring the pile in the snow.

"Very good," she said. "But you keep putting thumb in wrong place. Like you never grip wooden shaft before."

"Um—"

"I keep showing you. Thumb under and around, not over and on top. That's proper hold. See? Do you want me to show you again?"

Finn could think of nothing polite to offer in reply. "No, thank you," he managed, keeping a straight face. "I got it."

The girls and Monty joined them in the forest and were duly punished for their boredom when Isabelle directed them to carry logs to the lean-to and to collect small branches for kindling. After that day, while most of the adults sat in the house and read, the three children went outside with Finn and Isabelle, to shovel snow, carry wood, build snowmen. One afternoon, they slogged all the way to Cornelius Brook at the back of the property. Isabelle used a pickaxe to break a hole in the ice and taught the kids how to ice fish. They caught six small river perches! Finn thought Vanessa would require hospitalization when Mae and Junie returned, boasting that Isabelle had shown them how to gut and clean fish.

Restless and impatient, Finn and Isabelle cleared the snow that kept falling, organized the rusted farm tools and guns in the barn, searched for ammunition, discussed hunting rabbits, inspected the stables and the outer buildings, and made a running list of all the things they needed to get when spring came. Meanwhile, when Walter and Earl got tired of sitting around, they painstakingly melted the ice inside the cistern and the furnace tank. Finally, they bled the radiators and threw coal into the combustion chamber. The radiators hissed to the family's applause, the house became cozy and warm, and everyone took turns having a bath.

But January was a long month to live inside a snowed-in house, no matter how cozy it was. There was little wood, a shrinking supply of food and candles, dwindling coal, one deck of cards, and a mother- and sister-in-law whose main preoccupation was fretful agitation, salted by negative griping and petty grievances.

There were plenty of books, though. Like, *all* of them.

For entertainment, Finn's children unpacked the books and spent days arranging them by color in tall stacks on the floor. When they got tired of that, they reordered them by subject, and when they got tired of *that*, they arranged them by thickness. The one thing the girls did not do was alphabetize them, almost as if they wanted to provoke their mother.

The family had no access to radio or newspapers. Another war could have started. Jobs could have come back. The stock market could have rebounded. Prohibition could have been repealed. Isabelle's family could have arrived by boat. How would they find her when she was snowbound with no communication with the outside world?

"Don't you worry, Finn," Isabelle said. "If Mirik come, I promise you Schumann will find way to get in touch with me." The supply of cigarettes fell so drastically, Finn and Isabelle had to share one when they stood out in the snow and smoked, discussing what else they could ration before they walked three miles and called Schumann from a public telephone at the general store to ask him to visit with some supplies.

But when Schumann finally came—by train and taxi—he brought cigarettes and newspapers but no news from overseas.

60

Litter of Leaves

It was torture to be stuck inside for six weeks. The moment the earth was brown, not white, the family (save Vanessa) put on their warmest clothes and, after gulping down their morning coffee and swallowing a hunk of fried bread, stood at attention in front of Isabelle, begging for instructions.

She gave it to them straight, the way she gave everyone everything. Before any wonderful things could be planted in the ground, before the ground could be exposed and tilled and fertilized, before crop rows could be planned and plowed or the irrigation ditches dug, they first had to clear the land. On any farm, the fields became covered with debris over the normal course of fall and winter. Dead leaves, branches, twigs, bushes, all kinds of plant matter, dead animals. On an abandoned farm, the rubble piled up for years, all on top of grass and weeds whose dead roots were fixed in the soil. Walter's fields had been cleared by John Reade in preparation for the sale that never was, but had amassed some serious fallen foliage since then. "In other words, there's heaploaf to do before we can seed," Isabelle told the downcast but determined family.

"The word you're looking for is fuckload," Finn said to her quietly.

"I'm going to say that in front of your father the judge?"

"You think he hasn't heard it?"

Five acres of land was too big an area for ten people to clear, three of them children and three of them near seventy. They agreed to begin their farming life conservatively and to prepare less than an acre—just the part they planned to sow. They put on work gloves, grabbed rakes, and started scraping the field, one square meter at a time, taking special care to rid the soil of weed roots and shrub growth. Afterward, they separated the organic matter into piles for farm use. Rocks in one, twigs and branches in another, and leaves and plant detritus in the third. "What do we do with the dead animals?" said Eleanor, who had found a skeletal skunk.

"That can be job for children," Isabelle said. "In Ukraine, children loved to burn things." The American children were also thrilled at the prospect.

After two weeks of hearty labor, of raking and yanking, collecting and kicking, bending and grumbling, of aching backs and sore shoulders, stiff arms and hurting muscles, wind-chapped faces and frozen fingers, the family (but not Isabelle) confronted Finn about Vanessa one evening after supper when they were all exhausted and their nerves frayed.

"This can't continue, Finn," Eleanor said. "We know she is upset about leaving Boston, but if my Monty can pick up a rake, anyone can do anything."

"Finn, she hasn't even unpacked!" said Lucy. "How can that be? She's been in that room by herself for eight weeks! What has she been doing?"

"Son, I think what Eleanor and Lucy are trying to say, and I don't disagree with them," Olivia said, sounding reluctant to join in, "is that it doesn't seem fair that the rest of us are ready for our marching orders from Isabelle by eight, while Vanessa—"

"Eleanor the dilettante doesn't receive her marching orders until ten," Finn said lightly.

"At least I receive them at ten," Eleanor said. "My sister is not ready to help with anything at *noon*."

"Not ready or not willing?" said Lucy.

"Some fine difference!" said Eleanor.

"You raised her, Lucy," Walter said to his wife. "She is a child of privilege. She had a model upbringing. But she didn't have to complete anything she didn't want to. And now, here we are."

"This isn't *my* doing!" Lucy exclaimed. "Ellie turned out just fine."

Walter bobbed his head. "There's fine and there's fine," he said. "I love Ellie, but the child never stops crabbing."

"I'm only upset because Vanessa does nothing, Daddy!" Eleanor said. "I'm doing the work of two women!"

"Isabelle is doing the work of five. You don't hear her whining."

"She is used to working," Eleanor said philosophically. "There was nothing else to do over there."

"You think she wouldn't like to stay in bed till noon?" Walter looked around the kitchen. "Isabelle, where are you? Come here."

As if by magic, Isabelle appeared out of the shadows. Finn loved when she did that. He smiled.

"Isabelle," Walter said, "do you ever want to stay in bed till noon?"

"I don't know," Isabelle said. "I never been in bed at noon. One time I had pneumonia and overslept. I was up and out by 8:30."

"This impresses no one, Isabelle," said Eleanor.

"It impresses me," Walter said.

"And me," said Earl.

"And me," said Finn.

"What about complaining?" Walter asked. "Do you do some of that? But not as much as Eleanor, right?"

"Daddy!"

"No," Isabelle agreed. "I don't complain as much as Eleanor. But who could?"

"Isabelle!"

Quietly Finn laughed in his corner of the kitchen.

"Isabelle," asked Walter, "You spent a lot of time with Vanessa in Boston. What do you think is ailing her?"

Isabelle glanced at Finn. He shrugged, as if to say, *go ahead, if you must.*

"She can't go outside," Isabelle said. "It's no use trying."

"She's been outside, Isabelle," said Lucy glibly.

"Not much in last five years," Isabelle said. "And not at all in last two."

Olivia lowered her head in somber assent. Mae and Junie lowered theirs. Finn lowered his.

"Vanessa hasn't left the house in *two years*?" said an incredulous Lucy.

"Once," Isabelle said. "When we took train to come here. That was . . . it was . . . what's right word, Finn?"

"Excruciating?" Finn offered helpfully.

Walter was baffled. He stared at Earl, seeking guidance. Earl opened his hands; he had no answers. "But *why*?" said Walter.

"Mommy lost her favorite hat outside," said Junie. "And stopped going out."

"Lost her hat?" Blankly, Walter looked around at the others. "Girls, what are you *talking* about—"

"Mae, Junie!" Finn cut in. "Time for bed. Say goodnight and go on upstairs. Let the adults talk."

After his grumbling daughters trudged upstairs, Finn stepped closer to the conversation he did not want to have. "Look, there's no easy way to say this," he said. "Vanessa is not the woman she once was. And the woman she is now is not going outside. This reason, that reason—it doesn't matter why. It's just how it is." He stared at his hands.

"Why didn't you say something?"

"I was hoping a life emergency would help her cope," Finn replied. "Sometimes you get waylaid by little things, but when important things demand you act, you rise up and act. Right, Isabelle?" Who would know that better than Isabelle? But she didn't even twitch, didn't acknowledge in any way the creation of a new version of herself, a solitary woman with no family.

"Vanessa doesn't like when things are out of her control," was all Isabelle said.

"She's just lazy," Eleanor said.

Isabelle shook her head.

"She is," Eleanor said. "She's always coasted on her beauty. She thinks her pretty face entitles her to things."

"Isabelle is beautiful too," Walter said. "She's not entitled."

"Maybe beautiful in that Ukrainian way," Eleanor said with a scoff.

"Beauty is irrelevant to work," Isabelle said. "My house, my stable, all my land was kept together only because of my labor. I work because I live—and vice virtue."

"*Vice versa*," said Finn.

"That's what I say. But also, Vanessa is not coasting on her looks. Every night, after you go to sleep, she spends hours cleaning house."

"She does not!"

"She does," said Isabelle. "Every night. She cleans candles, dusts, waxes. She washes down counters and puts away every book and plate and glass we left behind. She sweeps and wipes and arranges all items in pantry, so in morning I can't find anything. All labels face out, but all cans of same size are stacked together, no matter what they are. She scrapes down vat of butter, she sifts flour, she washes all rags and napkins by hand in cold water she pumps from cistern. Sometimes she is up until three in morning cleaning." Isabelle folded her hands. "And reason your daughter is not unpacking, Lucy, is because she brought all wrong things. She brought dresses she can't wear and books she doesn't want to read. She brought towels and linens she can't find closets for because there aren't any. At least we're using her fancy napkins while we eat bread off your best china. She's not unpacking because she needs to sell her old clothes to Schumann, not take them out of boxes."

To help Vanessa help the family, Isabelle began leaving Vanessa daily notes written out in her expansive round hand, with ingredients and instructions for some simple things Vanessa could make them for lunch, like sandwiches and soup and casseroles.

Vanessa demurred. Isabelle persisted.

"Leave it alone," Finn said to Isabelle when he overheard their culinary yin and yang one morning. "She won't cook. My mother will do it."

"No," Isabelle said. "I need your mother. Turns out she is good worker.

She needs to finish rutabaga and potato area. I hope she can do it by April. We need, how you say, all heads on deck."

"All *hands* on deck."

"I need your mother's hands outside. I can't have her inside making sandwiches. Walter and Vanessa can be inside. How you say, old and infirm only. But you know, even your father-in-law with his half-working heart is tying up kindling piles. Please tell your wife that. Maybe it will shame her."

"You're wasting your breath," Finn said.

But Isabelle refused to accept defeat.

"Vanessa," she said. "I know you see out your bedroom window. Your mother with garden fork, your children with tills and rakes. Your father picking up sticks and your sister dressed in what I can only describe as her Sunday best, organizing rocks for future firepit and flower beds."

"So?" Vanessa said. "I told you I can't go outside, Isabelle."

"You *telling* me doesn't mean anything," Isabelle said. "So what if you tell me? What does it have to do with our present life? We need help."

"I can't do it."

"No one is asking you to go outside," Isabelle said. "But you can walk out of bedroom and make your family lunch and dinner. You can boil water, can't you? You need to boil our muddy clothes or we will have nothing to wear. Until we get electricity, you must do this."

"I was going to make lunch today," Vanessa said, pulling up the covers, "but I wasn't feeling well."

"Your father has bad ticker," Isabelle said. "Your youngest daughter has eye infection. Your sister is in her monthly. They are also not feeling well, but they're still out there. And now they're hungry. They need you to make them something to eat."

"I was going to do it!" Vanessa said, defensive and truculent.

"But you're *not* doing it."

"Leave me alone. I'm not well."

Finn stood in the hallway, listening in part anger, part incredulity, part something else he didn't want to examine. Isabelle stormed past him.

"I told you," he said, following her into the kitchen.

"Yeah, you told me, your wife told me, everybody told me. Finn, if we don't get circus act together, there won't be any wheat, there won't be nothing. Get into room with your wife and get her to help us. Do whatever you need to do. Use your wiles. You have wiles, don't you, Finn?"

"I don't have wiles to get a woman *out* of bed," he said.

And even though Isabelle was upset, she laughed. She couldn't help it. "You're not funny."

"Then why are you laughing?"

"Are you going or not going?"

"Not going." Isabelle wasn't the only one who was stubborn. In red frustration, Finn said quietly, but not *that* quietly, "I don't want to spend a *fucking second* cajoling anyone to live their life."

"Not even your wife?"

"Especially not my wife," said Finn. "If this is how a woman wishes to live, who am I to stop her?"

"Finn..."

"Don't Finn me. No."

She put both hands on his arm. "Finn, *please*," she said. "This is not good for her. Or you. Not good for farm. I'm asking you—*please* talk to her. No one but you can do it."

With extreme reluctance, Finn stepped inside the bedroom to speak to Vanessa.

He stood at the foot of their bed, raw irritation roiling inside him. Behind him, from the hallway, he heard the call of a corncrake. "*Krek-krek*," sounded Isabelle. Finn managed to keep from laughing, and his hostility dissipated.

"Vanessa..."

Vanessa remained with her back to him, eyes closed, hand over her ear.

He sat on the bed and put his hand on her leg. She buckled away. He came around to sit in front of her, rubbing her hip gently. "Darling," said Finn, "I know it's hard. You're doing wonderfully—"

"Stop it."

"You are. I'm trying to be supportive. Please get up and go into the kitchen. Your sister will help you make lunch."

"No, she won't. She told me an hour ago that she's been working in the field since *ten* and is hungry and tired."

Finn tried to make a joke of it. "Yes, or as Isabelle said earlier, Eleanor's been up since the *crank* of nine."

"I don't care, Finn, not for your frivolity and certainly not for hers."

"Fine." He forced himself to unclench. "Just get up and out."

"Yes, you've told me a thousand times what I *need* to do."

"But you're not doing it, Vee," Finn said, at the end of his patience.

"Can *you* get up and out?" Vanessa said, balking away from his hand. "Let me get dressed. I'll be right there."

Finn left, but Vanessa wasn't right there. She didn't emerge until five in the evening, when they had already made themselves lunch, eaten, and gone back into the fields.

61

Unraveling

Vanessa couldn't face her life. The scrutiny from her own family in her own home was unendurable. Even Isabelle had turned on her. She used to be a comforting presence. Isabelle's solicitous, (mostly) non-judgmental nature and her positive outlook were better than most elixirs. But now even Isabelle was attacking her—Isabelle, who *knew* how hard it was for Vanessa.

Her feelings for Isabelle changed. She began to resent the woman for being up at first light, for being indefatigable, for doing whatever was asked of her, and a thousand things that weren't, for never saying *I can't do it* or *that's too much for me*. For being level-headed, not easily riled, for her competence and her temperance, and for the way the children adored her, even sloth-like Monty who Vanessa thought would be her ally against the farming onslaught. One time she asked Monty why he tolerated Isabelle when he tolerated almost no one else, and he said it was because she was kinder to him than anyone.

"Kinder? All I hear is her yelling at you about what you're doing wrong."

"No one else ever tells me I'm doing anything wrong," Monty said. "I could kill someone and Grandma would still say *nice boy*." He lowered his voice. "Sometimes I do things wrong intentionally to see if Isabelle will notice, and she always does."

"And you like that?" Vanessa was appalled.

"Someone caring what I'm up to? Who wouldn't?"

Vanessa resented Isabelle for playing mind-numbing games with Monty and the girls, play-acting with their dollhouses and the interminable hide-and-seek, for which Isabelle had seemingly infinite patience. She resented Isabelle for shoveling coal and dirt, for having such an easy rapport with her father and an even deeper connection with Finn's parents—oh, how Vanessa resented her for that! For over ten years, Vanessa had tried to establish a relationship with Finn's intimidating father. From their earliest days, she felt that Judge Earl Evans judged Vanessa—for what, she didn't want to know.

Vanessa resented that Isabelle was more attached to Finn's parents than to Vanessa's own. Lucy and Walter were warm and open people, why should a Ukrainian villager care less for them than a stern teacher and a taciturn judge? Now that Vanessa knew they weren't Finn's real parents, she resented Isabelle even more for bonding with them.

But the thing that bothered Vanessa most of all was that Isabelle worked in Vanessa's house ceaselessly and without pay. Most people would slow down, would say *I'm doing this for free, so I don't have to do as much.* If anything, Isabelle tripled her efforts in the fields and in the house. What possible reason could this peculiar and mystifying woman have for working as if it weren't work at all, but a labor of deepest love?

"Finn, why are you quiet with me?" Vanessa said, unable to bear his brusque near-muteness when they were alone together.

"I'm tired," he said. "I've been up since six."

"You worked hard when we lived in Boston, too," she said, "but you still talked to me when you came home."

"That was then and this is now," Finn said. "Now the labor is physical, and my body's exhausted."

"Okay, darling," she said, patting his shoulder. "As long as you're not upset with me."

He tensed under her hand and didn't speak.

For a few moments she also didn't speak. "You know how hard this is for me, Finn," she said. "No one understands."

"Do *you*?"

"Frankly, I didn't appreciate you marching in here last week and badgering me to make food for everyone like they're children—"

Finn jumped out of bed before she could finish.

"*Badger* you? You should be grateful I didn't drag you out of bed in front of your family," he said. "I didn't want to embarrass you by treating you like a spoiled child. You don't want to cook for us like *we're* children? Fine. You don't want to do our laundry? Fine. But do *something*, Vanessa! Anything! You're not an infant! You're not an invalid! You're a grown adult woman. Who do you think you are? Your children and your mother are working while you're lying in bed!"

"Why should I cook when we have a servant who can do it?"

"She is not your fucking servant," Finn said.

"She washes my bedding, doesn't she? She shovels our coal, doesn't she? Sounds like a servant to me." Vanessa knew she was being cruel and didn't care.

"What should I tell your family you're afflicted with, your majesty? How do I explain a sickness that makes you act like Marie Antoinette?"

"Why do you have to explain anything?"

"You've tried to hide it from me our entire marriage," Finn said. "In Boston I was busy at the bank while you had a team of actual paid servants taking care of the house and the girls. Yet I still knew. I didn't want to know, but I *knew*. But here on the farm, all pretense is gone. Explain it to *me*!" He breathed in deeply and lowered his voice. "Tell me what the hell is wrong with you."

"Don't swear. I won't stand for it. This conversation is over until you can talk to me civilly."

"This conversation is over for good until you help me."

"You don't need my help," Vanessa said, turning away from him. "You have all the help you need."

"Good thing, or we'd all be fucking sunk."

"You're the one who sank us!" Vanessa cried. "*You* did this to us! We wouldn't be here if it wasn't for you! I wouldn't be in this hateful, horrible place! I hate it here, and you don't even care. It's *your* fault I'm sick like this!"

"How is that *my* fault?"

"I told you I didn't want any more babies, but you insisted, and look what happened. Look what's happened to me!"

"Oh my God, Vanessa." Finn staggered back from the bed, from her. "What about before that?" he said hoarsely, when he could speak again.

"This isn't about me. It's about *you*. It's *your* fault we're in this ditch. *Your* fault my father had a stroke and a heart attack. Your fault Adder left my sister, your fault we're broke and homeless! It's. All. Your. Fault."

The only thing her shook husband said in response was, "We are not homeless." But his anguished face bore the struggle of what he wanted to say in reply and somehow found the strength not to.

Vanessa didn't care about what he felt. She only cared about what she felt. "I'd rather live in a Hooverville than here with all of you!" she cried. "You think I want to live with my mother in the next room? You think I want to live with my sister, who's always wanted me to fail? Or with your Ukrainian serf sitting at our marble table like she's our equal, like she's one of us! I don't want any of it! But I still don't turn away from you in our bed."

"Oh yes, you do," he said.

"I don't flinch every time you touch me."

"Oh *yes*, you do."

"I don't walk around like I'm the wounded dead!"

"No, you wallow in bed instead like your life's already over."

"Isn't it? I didn't lie to you for ten years of our marriage, pretending to be something I'm not."

"You think *you* didn't lie to me for ten years of our marriage?" Finn said. "*You* didn't pretend to be something you're not?"

"I was better in Boston. I was normal."

"Were you? Were you *really*?" Finn was panting, perspiring, boiling over. "Did you come for a walk in the park with me? Did you visit your father when he was near death? Did you help your sister after her husband ran out on her? What exactly did you do that was normal, Vanessa?"

"At least I'm not a mick and a paddy," she retorted. "I have a malady. What's your excuse?"

"Is it the blaming malady?" Finn yelled, unable to control himself any longer. "You're blaming me for being adopted, blaming me for the stock market crash, for the unemployment. Maybe it's my fault too that I was born to Cora McBride? You have a lot of grievances against me, I get it, but what about your obligations to your own life? You don't like living here? Fine. What are you doing to change it?"

"You're saying all the wrong things," she said. "Don't shout at me and don't swear at me."

"If any conversation warrants a raised voice and swearing, Vanessa, it's this one."

"What's gotten into you?" she hissed. "I don't even know who you are."

"I've been talking to you nicely for ten years. How has *that* worked out?"

"Well, this is definitely *not* going to work out for us," she said, her lips and fingertips trembling.

"I'm sick and tired of this," Finn said. "Never more so than now—when the whole family is asking for you and you refuse to leave the bedroom."

"Fine," she said. "Send me away. You think I'm sick—"

"There's nothing wrong with you!"

"You're not a doctor," Vanessa said. "You don't know. If you want me to get better, then take me to a place where I can be treated."

"Treated for *what*? Do you have TB? Do you have typhus? Pneumonia? The shakes? When you talk to the doctor, what are you going to tell him?"

"I can't function sometimes," she said. "I can't do what other people do."

"Which is what, get out of bed? Give me a fucking break," said Finn. "Then what the hell are you doing at two o'clock in the morning, cleaning and mopping and wiping soot off candles? You're getting out of bed then, aren't you? What were you doing in our Boston house, washing towels every week, dusting the cupboards, putting the towels back, taking them out again, repeat ad nauseam for half a decade? You weren't taking care of the children we still had because you were too busy washing the fucking towels! How are you going to explain *that* to your good doctor? Do they have a pill for that? Do they have a pill to stop beautiful healthy women from scrubbing the floors at three in the morning but not at any other time?"

"You're mocking me."

"You're damn right I am," said Finn. "You need a little mocking. You could've used it earlier, instead of everyone walking on eggshells around you."

"Send me away if you think I'm so deviant," Vanessa repeated. "*Please.*"

"Unless you have a secret stash of cash under that mattress on which you spend your God-given days," Finn said, "we have no fucking money to send you anywhere." He grabbed his pillow and blanket. "No matter how much I want to. And you have no idea how much I want to."

She recoiled from the sting of his words. "Why don't you go get drunk with Lucas again," she said. "Be somewhere else when I need you most."

"Me staying out too late one night was an accident," Finn said. "But your continued injustice toward me is deliberate—like cold and pointless revenge."

"Maybe if you'd come home like you were supposed to, I wouldn't have lost our baby and wouldn't be like this!"

Finn nearly screamed. The guttural sound that came from him was almost too much for her. It certainly seemed like it was too much for him. He barely got the words out when he spoke. "You spending hours looking for a fucking hat in the freezing cold is not my fault or my responsibility," he said. "It's yours. But by all means, add it to your list of things to blame me for."

He slept on the floor that night and for many nights that followed. He barricaded himself with her unpacked boxes, made himself a twin-sized mattress out of cardboard and old blankets and Vanessa's unused but spotless linens and slept in the corner of the room by one of the windows. And all Vanessa could think in reaction was how she couldn't believe he had taken her best table linens, some made of silk, and put his sleeping body on them. They'd all have to be boiled before they could be put on the table again.

And so she boiled them.

62

Absence of Seed

"Isabelle, my dear, here's the part the banker in me doesn't understand," Walter said in mid-March during their nightly post-supper discussion with cigarettes and tea. "We're almost out of what little money we came with. How are we going to get the seeds? They're not free, are they?"

Isabelle acknowledged they weren't free. "But fields are not ready for seed, Walter. We need to plan, measure, dig. Then we'll need seed."

"Right now, our main problem is transportation, not seeds," Finn said, smoking at the table. "We need a truck, family."

Loudly the family objected, citing penury.

"Rend your robes all you want," Finn said. "But a Ford Model B with a closed cab and an open bed must be in our immediate future if we're going to climb out of this penury."

"We need some ammunition, too," Isabelle said. "We're alone on farm with no close neighbors."

"This isn't Ukraine, Isabelle," Lucy said.

"Alone is alone," Isabelle said. "Also, we shoot some rabbits. Make stew."

"I want Isabelle to teach me how to shoot!" said Monty.

"Monty, shh!" said Eleanor, muttering under her breath, "My Lord, does my son need a father."

"Are we just jibber-jabbering, listing off our wishes?" said Vanessa. "Because I'd like to move back to the city."

"Shush, Vanessa," Walter said to his daughter. "The adults are speaking."

"We need electricity, Finn," said Lucy. "We need to plug in our radio. This is no way to live. We need a little diversion."

"Get me balalaika," Isabelle said. "I'll play and sing and tell jokes."

"Balalaika is not the worst idea," Finn said. "If only the rest of us knew what it was." He kept himself from winking at her. "But electricity is coming soon, Lucy. A man came by the other day, said we're on the schedule for post installation in early April."

Walter banged the table. "Can we discuss things in order? Before we get to guns and balalaikas and Ford Model Bs, I would like an answer to my question. Isabelle, how do we get seed?"

Isabelle smiled. "Like Finn said, Walter, we buy truck—before everything. We need it to get seed. Also to drive to town, and to haul things away."

"Like garbage," said Vanessa.

"No, on farm we keep garbage," said Isabelle. "Garbage is precious."

"*Garbage* is precious," Vanessa repeated.

"Garbage is, how you say, compote."

"*Compost*," said Finn, correcting her. "Compote is a tasty beverage."

"Maybe I make us tasty beverage from garbage," said Isabelle. "Then you'll be sorry."

"That does sound like I'll be pretty sorry," said Finn, his eyes twinkling. He turned to the others. "We'll need the truck to sell our vegetables, and to drive to the ocean to fish and swim."

"Oh, I want to go," Monty said.

"Us, too, us too, Daddy!" said Mae and Junie.

"How do you suppose we get this truck, Mr. Big Spender?" said Eleanor.

"There's no talking to him, Ellie," Vanessa said. "I note that Finn was listing off his wishes and no one told him to pipe down."

"Vanessa, pipe down," Walter said.

"First, though," Finn said, "I'll have to go to the post office to get my mail."

"What are you waiting on, Finn, love letters?" Eleanor chuckled.

"A check, actually," Finn replied. "A dividend check from Electric Boat."

"Son, if you sell your shares in that nothing company, you could buy your truck outright," Earl said. It was the first thing he'd said all meeting. "How many did you keep?"

"Whatever you gave me for my graduation present, Father," Finn replied. "How many was that—a thousand half-penny shares? And I'm not selling them. I mean, I could, but after we spend those five hundred bucks, there'll be no more dividends, and the truck will get old. This way, a few times a year, hopefully we'll continue to get a little bit of money."

"Enough for seed?" asked Walter.

"We're not spending Finn's precious dividend check on stupid seed!" Eleanor said, and Vanessa nodded in vigorous agreement.

"Don't say *seed* like it's a dirty word, Eleanor," snapped Walter. "Seed is literally our future. Speak of it reverentially."

"Yes, Ellie," Finn said. "Don't mock Isabelle's seed. But I would like to use the dividend money to put a down payment on the truck."

"Why don't you buy the truck outright as your dad suggested?" Vanessa said. "We don't have the money to make monthly payments on some loan."

"Child, honestly, stop interrupting," Walter said to his daughter. "Let Finn handle the business end and you handle whatever it is you handle."

"We *do* have money for monthly payments," said Finn, his tone polite but cold as he addressed Vanessa. "From the same dividend fund. If I spend it all on the truck, there won't be any money left over. But if I put only a little down, we can afford a small payment each month and we'll be able to buy food with the rest."

Walter nodded in approval. "Spoken like a true banker."

"I still don't see why we need a truck," said Vanessa.

"Just because you won't go anywhere in it," said Finn, "doesn't mean the rest of us don't need it."

"It's a waste of money," Vanessa repeated stubbornly.

"I'm going to put my foot down, Vanessa," said Walter. "Either be nice or leave the meeting. What's gotten into you?"

"You know what *hasn't* gotten into her, Daddy?" said Eleanor. "Industriousness."

Finn said nothing. Vanessa got up and left.

63

Acquisition of Seed

Isabelle was happy Finn bought the truck despite Vanessa's objections because with it, everything became not just easier, it became *possible*.

In their new Model B, she dragged Finn and his girls to a neighboring farm, two miles away on Winnicutt. It was the end of March and still cool out, but she put on a floral dress underneath her coat, brushed out her shoulder-length hazel-colored hair, pinched her cheeks and bit her lips to give them color. She asked Finn to cover up his button-down shirt with a buttoned-*up* winter jacket. "No one is going to trust man in dress shirt who says he's farmer," she told him as they got going. "We talked about this when we were rumrunners, Finn. You dress for part."

"The man is not a farmer," Finn said. "The man is a banker who turned to farming to feed his family."

"Is man banker at heart?"

He didn't answer her. "Girls!" Finn yelled. "Let's go!"

In the truck, with the girls squeezed between them, Finn said to her, "Is the woman a farmer?"

"Woman is also not farmer," Isabelle replied. "Like man, woman farmed to feed family."

"So what is the woman if not a farmer? A horse rider?"

"Not if she doesn't have horse," Isabelle said.

"A mother?" asked Junie.

"Junie!" said Mae, pinching her sister's leg.

"I don't think so," Isabelle said, her voice faltering. "Not if she doesn't have children."

An undaunted Junie said, "But you do have them, Isabelle. You're just waiting for them to come back to you."

"That is true." Isabelle stared ahead.

"June is rarely right," Mae said, "but maybe she's right this time. Once a mother, always a mother."

"Girls, quiet," Finn said, and to Isabelle he added, "I don't know if I should be proud or terrified."

"They're your children," Isabelle said, "so probably both."

"So what's at the neighbors'?"

She smiled. She liked that Finn had agreed to come with her without even asking why. "First we introduce ourselves," she said. "Important to be good neighbors."

"What's second?"

"Seed is second."

The Bryson property was twice the size of the Adams farm. The main house was smaller, but they had two stables, two barns, a silo, a tractor, and a cistern nearly the height of the house.

"Girls," Isabelle said as they got out of the truck, "carry box of cookies, smile, look adults in eye, but don't talk unless they talk to you. Be polite."

"Is that how the horse ranchers behaved in Ispas?" Finn said quietly as they began toward the house. "Polite, with good manners?"

"Yes, if neighbors didn't come to take your land and kill your horses," said Isabelle. "Bryson won't be too polite either if he thinks that's our purpose. Now, Finn, if man open door, you talk. If woman, I talk. Got it?"

"No, I don't got it. What do I say?"

"You don't know what to say to man?"

"For God's sake! A little heads-up would've been nice."

"This is your heads-up."

They knocked three times and waited.

The door was opened by a reserved gentleman farmer in his sixties.

"Hi there," said Finn, business-friendly. "I'm Finn Evans." They shook hands, and the man introduced himself as Chuck Bryson. "We're your new neighbors over at Lovering Road. Just came by to say hello."

Chuck glanced behind Finn, was quiet for a moment. "That's a nice truck you got there. Model B?"

"Yup. Brand new."

"How do you like it?"

"Real swell."

"Four-cylinder engine?" Chuck asked.

"That one's eight," Finn replied. "With a four-speed transmission, instead of three. Got an upgrade."

"Nice, real nice."

"Real workhorse." Finn put his hands on his daughters' heads. "Chuck, these are my daughters, Mae and June. And this—um, this is Isabelle."

The girls offered Chuck their box of cookies and were promptly invited in. Isabelle thought the truck talk alone would've done it.

Shelly Bryson was a large, salt-and-pepper-haired woman, who clearly had a soft spot for girls, herself having raised four sons. They chatted only for a short while. Isabelle, not one to linger, got to the point. "We wanted to talk to you neighbor to neighbor," she said.

"Where are you from, Isabelle?" said Shelly. "You have an accent."

"I'm from Ukraine."

With interest, Chuck and Shelly studied Finn, Isabelle, and the two girls, but manners dictated that they say nothing presumptuous. Speaking on assumptions was bad manners, especially when meeting people for the first time. And reacting to unspoken assumptions was *really* bad manners, especially getting defensive at people whom you were about to ask for a favor. Isabelle could see that Finn, ever the gentleman in front of his girls, was eager to dispel the illusions the Brysons had about the precise nature of their relationship, so she cut in quickly before he could put his foot in it. "You have horses on your farm, Chuck?" Isabelle asked.

"Funny you should mention it," Chuck said. "We did have a stallion, but we had to put him down last year."

"Our mare is fifteen and foaling in June," Shelly said. "Probably for the last time. Why, do you want to buy the foal?"

"Maybe next year," Isabelle said. "We just getting started. Chuck, we don't need horses, but we are little bit short on seeds."

Chuck got up and beckoned her. "Of course. What do you need?"

Isabelle smiled. That's how it was done—here, there, everywhere. In five minutes, she made a deal with the Brysons. In exchange for a supply of seeds, she would help with the foaling of the mare and at harvest time return double what she had borrowed. The Brysons wouldn't hear of it. "I give you all you need, just ask," Chuck said. "But help with the foal will be most welcome, I won't lie. You know horses?"

"Little bit," said Isabelle.

Chuck studied Isabelle keenly. "Is *little bit* a euphemism for everything?"

"Little bit." Isabelle smiled.

"Oh, Chuck, don't bother the poor woman!" Shelly cut in. "But I must say, you coming here, it's a gift from the good Lord. For months, Chuck and I have been praying for help with the foal. We thought we might have to sell or shoot our poor mare."

"No, no. No more shooting," said Isabelle. "I will help you."

"Finn, are you a horseman too like your lovely wife?" asked Chuck.

Mae and Junie giggled.

"No, no. Not a horseman," Finn said. "And Isabelle is not my lovely wife. My wife, Vanessa, the children's mother, is at home. She is a *little bit* under the weather." He coughed. "Isabelle is a friend of the family."

The expressions on Chuck and Shelly's faces were priceless. "Well," Chuck said after he recovered, "I guess everybody could use themselves one of those."

"No kidding," said Finn.

The Brysons gave Isabelle a bushel each of wheat berries and corn kernels. They gave her a glass jar of oat groats and paper bags filled with every vegetable Isabelle wanted, and even some dill. The potatoes in a wicker peck were small and sprouting, and the onions were tiny buds. The Brysons' seed pantry was a well-ordered coldroom, organized like a store. Isabelle remembered their own pantry in Ispas. Her mother took such pride in it. *But then the devil came, ate the berries and the onions and all the tiny buds, and said what are you feeding me tomorrow?*

Chuck offered to lend Finn any tools he needed. Finn nodded his head. Isabelle tried not to laugh. "Isabelle," Finn said, rubbing his face in fake rumination, "what do you think?" Finn was growing out a beard, a trim, blond, fastidiously groomed banker's beard, not a black, bushy, overgrown Cossack beard. It was adorable. "Can we make do with the tools we have?"

"We have armful of equipment," she replied. "But thank you, Chuck."

"*Barnful*," said Finn.

Isabelle tightened her mouth. If he was going to play it like that, she could play it like that too. "What *do* you think of our garden tiller, Finn? You think it's all right or should we borrow one from Chuck just in case?"

"You said we were okay."

"I wasn't sure. What about *adze*?"

"What?"

"You don't know what an *adze* is, Finn?" said Chuck.

"I do, I do, of course. I'm sure we'll be fine."

Quickly they said their goodbyes and were off.

"Why did you do that?" Finn said when they were inside the truck.

"Do what?"

"You know I don't know what an adze is."

"Then maybe keep your public corrections to yourself next time," Isabelle said. "Man living in stone house should not throw glass."

"That doesn't even make sense," Finn said.

"You know what doesn't make sense?" said Isabelle. "Man not knowing what adze is."

They dropped off the girls and the seeds at home and drove to town.

"We need lumber," she said. "I want you to help me build fence."

"Not smoking bench?" He smiled.

"Is that likely to happen? We also need to build enclosure for outdoor shower in back because field work makes you filthy and you don't want to bring dirt into house your wife cleans at two o'clock in morning. But yes, we need to build low fence for support of our raspberry bushes."

"Why do we need raspberries?"

"To make *compost* of course."

"Look at you, trying to be funny."

"I don't need to try. I am naturally humorful."

He and Isabelle spent the rest of the afternoon at the hardware store and the lumberyard and afterward, Finn drove them to the ocean, where they sat huddled up on a bench, smoking and debating how long it would take for the cold water to kill you if you went swimming in it.

64

Sowing

"Finn! Come here, bricks are heavy."
"Isabelle! The hammer is here, I found it under the wood pile."
"Finn! Pipe of water broken! Gushing, gushing!"
"Isabelle! Can the eggplant go next to the cucumbers?"
"Finn, push post in harder. Harder, Finn! Look, it's still wobbling! Whole fence is going to fall."
"Isabelle! How close do we space the zucchini, nine or ten inches apart?"
"Finn! Damn rabbits! Why are there so many rabbits already! Are they multiplying?"
"Yes, like rabbits."
"Finn! Where's gun?"
"Isabelle! Where's the ammunition?"

After her argument with Finn, Vanessa tried to get up earlier, she really did. She struggled out of bed around ten or eleven, forced herself to do it by counting down from a hundred or by naming all the items in her room as she put one foot, then the other, on the wood floor. The house was so blissfully quiet. She would creep to the kitchen, pour herself a cup of coffee that someone else had already made, butter a piece of bread, and then stand by the window in her room and watch them in the fields, to-ing and fro-ing. She couldn't hear what they said to each other, but Finn and Isabelle were constantly discussing something, animatedly shaking their heads, pointing, waving hoes and tillers, measuring the rows with their booted feet. Isabelle would walk it like she was proving a point, and then Finn would walk it like he was proving a different point. They would argue and argue. Sometimes they would laugh.

Isabelle wore a kerchief tied around her hair and was dusty from head to foot, and Finn wore a cap on his dark blond head and suspenders to hold up his trousers and was dusty from head to foot. They would swat flies from each other's heads and adjust one another's head coverings and work and talk and occasionally amble over to the well and drink from the same bucket of water and have a cigarette. He would light hers and then his own, and they would stand and smoke and discuss more things, and just before lunch, Vanessa would watch them pump water from the well for each other, and Finn would wash his arms and neck and face while Isabelle watched him as her hand moved up and down on the pump, pouring water onto his body, and then she would wash her arms and neck and face while he watched her as his hand moved up and down on the pump, pouring water onto her body.

And what Vanessa thought as she watched this day in and day out was: *They're about to come inside, demanding I do this or that for them. I wish it were summer already and hot and they could stay out till sundown and not bother me.*

The utility pole was finally installed on Lovering Road. Lines were run to the service mast and dropped into the electrical box, and at last, the family had power! Vanessa put on the radio to drown out the farming ruckus outside, but the radio turned out to be a mixed blessing. The news stories and discussion hours during the day kept drawing her to the outside world, where she also didn't want to be. Staggering unemployment, dust storms in Oklahoma, the upcoming presidential election, another firefight in Boston Harbor between rumrunners and the Coast Guard, rumblings of a humanitarian catastrophe in Ukraine despite vehement Soviet denials. There was no good place for Vanessa, not there and not here.

After they cleared the ground of stones and debris and dead grass, after they raked and leveled it, Isabelle told the family they had to decide what was going to grow where. Before they divided the rows into sections and dug the trenches, they had to plan and allocate the correct amount of space for each crop. She thought she'd be the only one with an opinion on this. She couldn't have been more wrong.

The debate continued for the better part of a week. Isabelle thought she'd be discussing it only with Finn, but out of all of them, Finn, surprisingly, was the most agreeable. "Grow whatever wherever. I don't care. Just tell man in dress shirt with shovel where to dig." The children wanted corn and cucumbers. Lucy cared nothing for eggplant. No one was familiar with zucchini, so they didn't want to grow it at all. And no one could imagine what a fully grown wheat field might look like in four months, so they kept relegating the wheat to a small bed near the cabbages. No one knew that potatoes didn't grow five feet in the air like oats, or that they didn't require supports like cucumbers.

At the beginning of April, Isabelle showed Finn and Monty how deep to dig the trenches for the plantings and how shallow to make the narrower trenches next to them for irrigation.

Finally, on April 8, the whole family—except Vanessa—went out into the field that was ready at last to receive the seed. Under Isabelle's direction, they dropped the berries and kernels into the open beds. Isabelle thought this part would be easy, but she had a hard time teaching them to drop seeds in a circular motion, and not to drop so many in one spot at once, and not to plant them so close to each other. "Twelve inches apart," Isabelle kept saying. "Little circle of sprinkle, then twelve inches away for next circle."

"Doesn't seem like enough," Walter said. "We want lots of tomatoes."

"And lots of corn!" said Junie.

"We're not planting corn yet, Junebug," Isabelle said. "That's middle of May. We need to make different soil for corn." Corn needed something called loamy earth—soil filled with sand and clay.

"Why so few seeds?" said Lucy. "Walter's right, it doesn't seem enough."

"Walter, think of it like money in your bank," Isabelle said. "Start with little and it will grow—unless there's hurricane or Big Crash. But on field, unlike in bank, if you seed too much, crops will suffocate each other. Roots won't have anywhere to spread."

It took four hours, the entire mild April afternoon. After they were finished and had watered the soil, Isabelle told the family this was a wonderful birthday gift to her. Junie asked when her actual birthday was, and Isabelle said, "Today. That's why I say birthday gift."

"Today is your birthday? Daddy, Daddy! Did you hear? Today is Isabelle's birthday!"

"I heard," Finn said, peering into Isabelle's face. "I can't tell if Isabelle is joking."

"Where is joke here?" Isabelle said. "Do you know what joke is?"

"Why didn't you tell us?"

"You never asked."

"Oh, we should have!" said Mae. "We're so sorry! What can we do for you for your birthday?"

"You did it already," Isabelle said. "We planted what is going to be bountiful harvest."

At night, after everyone had gone to bed, Finn and Isabelle sat on the bench he had finally built for her—just two tree stumps and a long plank of wood nailed into them. They sat under a dark and still-leafless oak on the side of the house by the pantries and sheds, the side that had no windows, where no one could see them, where no one ever went. They had a smoke and a celebratory glass of whisky. The kerosene lamp flickered between them, next to the ashtray, the cigarettes, and the glasses.

The clinked and drank and said *Budmo*.

"Lots of arguments today," he said. "Everyone is usually so fake-polite."

"It's better this way," Isabelle said. "They care what they put in soil. Wait till it starts growing. They're going to feel real ownership of it. You think your father barely cares about planting, but once Earl's tomatoes sprout, just you wait. Your mother too. She wanted eggplant. And Lucy said she didn't like eggplant, and your mother said she wasn't growing it for Lucy. And I have the most delicious recipe for eggplant. What?" Finn was looking at her with an expression she couldn't decipher.

"Nothing."

"Why you looking at me funny?"

"Not funny."

"No, you're right, definitely not funny. But peculiar."

"How long for germination?" he asked.

"A week with good weather."

"You grew all this on your farm?"

"Much less. My mother and all kids grew it mostly. We helped at beginning, and of course at end, when harvest came and all heads or hands on farm had to help. But I didn't do much of actual farming, not like here. I was with horses most of day. And I helped Mirik with milk."

"Should we get a horse?"

"You don't get horse," Isabelle said. "You buy horse. That's expensive. And horse must eat. We barely feeding ourselves."

"But do we need a horse for the farm?"

She shook her head. "Horse big help, but horse is work. Also we are not growing enough crops for horse. This is very small."

"What we planted today is *small*?"

"Tiny. Only forty meters by forty meters."

"Your mother planted more than this?"

"No, I told you, less," Isabelle said. "But when we gave up ten acres of our land to plant wheat for communists, area we sowed was 220 meters long by 180 meters wide."

Finn whistled. "That's nearly 700 square feet. That's colossal."

"*That's what the actress said to the bishop*," said Isabelle in a Mae West voice. "But yes, big field. Definitely needed horses for that. And steel plow."

Finn smoked, listening intently to her every word.

"But wheat didn't grow," she said, her voice growing desolate, as it often did when she talked about her life in Ukraine. "Because of freeze and then flood, but also—we didn't plant all berries they gave us. We sowed only half. Rest we ground into flour. We were hungry. We had no food."

"What if it doesn't grow here either?" Finn said. "What if there's a dust storm?"

"A storm of dust in New Hampshire? Not likely. Too many trees." Smiling, she almost patted him. "Don't worry. I have good feeling."

"Why?"

"I don't know—experience? We had heavy snow. That means ground put to sleep with long freeze. That's good for ground. It renews it. Crops explode after ground asleep."

"I bet." He put away his cigarettes and got ready to leave. "Did you have a silo? Do *we* need a silo?"

"How much wheat you think you're going to reap, Finn Evans, from two rows each hundred feet long?" She laughed. "We don't need silo. Maybe basket." She gazed at him fondly. "If we need to put extra grain somewhere, we have small granary."

"Where's that?"

"Next to corn crib."

"You're just making up words now," he said, mining her face from crown to chin. "I didn't even ask how old you were."

"Thirty-two. What you looking at? Do I look thirty-two?"

"Nope, not a day over thirty-one."

"Thanks, old man. You nearly thirty-four, right?"

"I can't believe you've been with me for almost three years and never told me your date of birth," said Finn.

"I can't believe I've been with you for almost three years and you never asked," said Isabelle.

65

Germinating

"I don't see it."

"Where?"

"What are you talking about? There's nothing there."

"What green sprout?"

"What, *this* little piece of weed?"

"You're telling me this invisible blade of grass is going to be bread? It's going to grow as tall as Finn?"

"That sprig seems very small. If it grows one inch a week, it'll be next year before the stalks are ready to be reaped."

"I best get my strongest glasses if I'm going to inspect this so-called future harvest. You want me to get yours for you, Walter?"

"Maybe wheat is like justice, Earl, it moves slowly through the fields."

"What about carrots, Isabelle, will they grow faster?"

They teased and mocked and were skeptical—just for one day.

And then, just as Isabelle had hoped, a remarkable thing happened.

One day after germination and eight days after planting, Isabelle watched Earl and Olivia, barely dressed, ungroomed and unwashed, walk out of the house together, before they'd had their first coffee, walk into the planting rows, and kneel to examine the progress. They were first. The girls were second, and they even dragged Monty with them. Walter and Lucy were next. Eleanor was last.

Finn was up even before Isabelle. He had already thrown a log onto the low-burning stove and was making a pot of coffee when she walked through the house. "My mother and father are in the fields, and it's not even six am," he said to her. "You must be some kind of sorceress."

The girls woke Vanessa to tell her of their blossoming sugar snap peas, which were about two inches tall. "Why don't you use words to describe the tiny slivers of grass to me, my darlings," said a groggy Vanessa, not lifting her head off the pillows. "It's too early for Mommy to be outside."

The second morning again brought doubt. After two months of moving rocks around and raking and tilling and shoveling and filling, it still didn't seem possible.

But on the third day, it was no longer disbelief that propelled the entire family minus one into the fields at dawn.

It was hope for a brand new life. It was resurrection.

"I want to know what we're going to eat until this holy harvest," said Vanessa in the evening after dinner, sounding peevish and overwhelmed by the relentless excitement around her.

"We're eating now, aren't we?" said Finn.

Below the family's sightline, Isabelle stepped on his foot. He was being rude.

"Then why do we need a harvest?" asked Vanessa.

"So we can eat like kings, not paupers, Vanessa," said Isabelle. "So we can seed penny and harvest dollar. So we can sell our tomatoes and make money to buy other things we need that we don't grow, like milk, and wire for fence, and cistern for outdoor shower, and maybe chickens."

"And I want a boat," Finn said.

"And your husband wants boat," said Isabelle.

"Bite your tongue, girl," said Walter. "We're not selling my beautiful tomatoes."

"They're my tomatoes, too, Walter," said Earl, bristling.

"Why on earth do you need a boat, Finn?" said Vanessa.

"Because the ocean has food in it," Finn said.

"Finn says Cape Cod across ocean has clams to dive for," Isabelle added.

"*To die for*," whispered Finn.

"Finn's not wrong, but boats cost money," said Walter.

"Yes, and without boat, Monty and I can catch lots of fish in brook," said Isabelle. "Trout. Perch. Even pike sometimes, if brook is full. Pike very delicious. Little bony, but tasty."

That's what the actress said to the bishop, Finn mouthed nearly inaudibly next to her ear. Not a muscle on her poker face moved in reaction.

"My goodness, would I love me some of those exquisite clams from the Cape!" Walter said. "Vanessa, too, right, my dear? They used to be your favorite. Fine. Perhaps I will allow some of my future prize-winning tomatoes to be sold if it means Finn can charter a boat and bring home a bucket of quahogs."

Isabelle shook her head. "It's not good for me," she said. "I don't know anything about clamming."

"Wait, what did I just hear?" Walter said. "There's something Isabelle doesn't know how to do? That's impossible! Earl, did you hear this? Why, Isabelle, we thought you knew *everything*!"

"Clearly there is lot I don't—"

"She also can't sew," said Finn.

"Lucky for you," Isabelle returned, "or Schumann would not have supposed me on you."

"*Imposed*," Finn said.

"I'm starting to wish I could sew."

When she and Finn went to town, Isabelle would regularly call Schumann—to say hello, to ask if there was any news, to ask if he had some clothes for her or the children, or shoes for Eleanor who, in her daintiest white Mary Janes, would hobble to the growing crops and gingerly pull out a weed or two with her gloveless hands. Isabelle would commend Eleanor on a job well done and say, "Maybe . . . don't pull out actual cucumbers. Just weeds, Ellie. Also, do you have some brown shoes? With small heel?"

And to Schumann, Isabelle said, "I beg you—help me."

"I am not a cobbler, Isa," Schumann said. "Do you want me to lend you some money so you can buy Eleanor a pair of work shoes?"

"Yes, darling, Schumann, yes, please. And maybe a few more dollars for me?"

"Oh, now I'm a darling. What else do you need? Lucas keeps coming by to say hello, and to ask if I have any work for him."

"Tell him yes, but only if he stops drinking."

"I'm not saying that. He'll deck me! When I come with your clothes, should I bring him for a visit? I'll need his help to carry the suitcases of dresses you're asking me to sew for you."

"Yes, thank you, my dear, thank you."

Schumann came by train, with Lucas in tow—Lucas wearing *his* Sunday best, an ironed shirt! a tie! a felt hat!—and carrying a suitcase, from which the tailor produced comfortable work clothes for the children, work pants and chambray long-sleeve shirts for Finn, and fitted summer dresses for Isabelle—with scooped necklines, embroidered collars, cinched waists, dresses that draped brazenly just to the calf instead of all the way down to the ankle.

Lucas came bearing gifts of his own. He brought cigars for Earl. "I remember you once saying to the court clerk how much you enjoyed them, Your Honor," said Lucas.

"Thank you, Lucas," said Earl, visibly touched. "But call me Earl. Why such formalities? You're not on probation here."

"Actually, I *am* on probation, Your Honor—I mean Earl."

"Oh no, what did you do now, Lucas?"

"Filched these cigars for one."

"Lucas!"

"Just joking, Your Honor, keeping it breezy."

Lucas brought a bouquet of flowers for the lady of the house and her "lovely" sister and four packets of poppy seeds for Isabelle. He handed her the brown bags of seeds as if the red flowers were already fragrant and blooming.

Vanessa grudgingly acknowledged Lucas's flowers, but she was much warmer toward Schumann. He spent hours repairing some of her old clothes while she sat next to him, volleying his questions about how she was feeling.

While Schumann entertained Vanessa, Lucas and Isabelle helped Finn construct a compost box out of heavy pallets. Even Eleanor came out to help—but mainly to flirt with Lucas.

It was a good day.

"Why do you keep telling me how to hold a hammer? Teaching or teasing?" Finn said to Isabelle when they were sitting outside, having a smoke in the cool night air.

"Lifesaving," she replied. "If I don't teach you how to grip hammer, you will break your thumb holding it like baby instead of like growing man."

"*Grown* man."

Her eyes traveled away from him. Finn's arms and chest had *grown* big from chopping wood, carrying lumber, building brick retaining walls. His back had *grown* broad from shoveling dirt. He was *growing* stronger each day. Even his neck had acquired new muscles. His heart pulsed through them when he exerted himself in the field. Every time Isabelle saw his neck throbbing from exertion, she couldn't help but imagine other exertions his muscles might tense through. He was never more exciting to her than when he was panting. Sometimes she had to close her eyes because she couldn't bear to look at him. She was afraid he'd take one glimpse at her and know what she was thinking—and what a disgrace *that* would be.

Soon it would be summer and warm and maybe he would take off his dress shirt with long sleeves—the one he always worked in—and wear a T-shirt instead. He could get tanned and she could gaze at him—but from afar, away from the pulsing veins in his perspiring neck. Maybe in the hot summer they could have a party. They could dress in their nicest clothes and sing and dance—maybe together? That didn't seem likely. But perhaps she could dance and he could watch her. Sometimes, in her other life, when she danced in a red dress with flowers in her hair, she felt sexy. Could she do that here, on the farm in front of him, so he could watch her and perhaps imagine *her* perspiring, pulsing body?

Maybe in the sweltering summer, they could go swimming.

Isabelle couldn't tell where her longing was most intensely fixated: the idea of a day alone with him, the dream of a whole summer with him, swimming in the hot ocean with him, seeing *all* of his body, feeling his hard wet body on hers, touching him—or being touched by him. The carnal part of her had been dormant for so long, and like everything else, it was germinating with every sunrise.

He was talking but she could barely hear him. Outwardly, she smoked and her expression was blank. She hoped her pupils weren't dilated, her breath wasn't shallow.

He nudged her. "Isa . . . where are you? Why do you keep asking Schumann if he's heard from Nate? Don't you believe him when he says no?"

"I just want to make sure," she said. "He likes to keep things from me he thinks might upset me. Nate sends telegram from Brindisi to warn Schumann how many are coming." Isabelle took a breath. "Or who."

Finn smoked silently.

Reluctantly, Isabelle shifted from reveries about hot pulsing bodies to a conversation about black buried things. "Things in Ukraine are not good. Many people flooding out. Makes problem for Nate. Romania and Poland put more soldiers on borders. There is shooting—and worse."

"Worse than shooting?"

"Yes. Sometimes Poles send people back to Soviet Union."

"How do you know?"

"Nate hears stories he doesn't want to believe." She lit another cigarette and smoked tensely. "Good thing Romania hates Soviet Union. Soviets asked Romania to return escapees too, but Romania refused. Nate and Florin's shipping vessel is too small for many who want passage. And America is also in crisis. Different degree, but no less real. Because of unemployment, special visa approvals for refugees have nearly stopped. Sometimes Nate sneaks few in without papers, but this is difficult for them and dangerous for him. If he gets caught, he goes to jail."

"What about the ones he can't get to Boston?"

"Some stay in Romania. Some stay in Italy or go to other places in Europe. But Nate says there's trouble with police in Constanta. Too many hungry people wandering around port with nothing to do." She stared at the ground. "Everyone afraid what's coming next."

Finn smoked and pondered. "Why does Nate keep doing it?"

"You know why. He started for Cici and her mother, Kasia. Why he continue? It's become his life's mission. Like obsession with him now. Trying to find them space on ship, haggling for housing in Brindisi and here, wheeling, dealing, fundraising. At bottom of it, he's still hoping somebody we know might show up. We all are." Isabelle smoked down her cigarette with such intensity, she burned her lip.

He patted her wilting back. "As I see it, Nate has two problems," Finn said, taking the stub out of her hands and passing her his own lit cigarette. "He needs visas for the refugees and Florin needs a bigger ship."

"Finn, you see how both things are inmountstable."

"They're not *insurmountable*."

"If there's no work for Americans, no one's going to let Ukrainians in."

"A little at a time is the best approach," Finn said. "I can't help with the ship. Not yet. But let me see what I can do about the visas."

Finn talked to his father about it. Earl had worked his entire career in the Boston judicial system. He knew people in many departments, including immigration. "Anything for Isabelle," said Earl when he agreed to help.

A week later, Earl and Finn dusted off their suits and took a train to Boston to meet with Franklin Reynolds, an old friend of Earl's from his law school days. Earl had helped Franklin get a job at the District Attorney's office and years later recommended him for a position on the federal bench. Earl's courtroom was in criminal proceedings, while Franklin veered off toward immigration violations.

The three men went to the Parker House Hotel for lunch. Earl brought up Finn's predicament as carefully and hypothetically as he could.

In reply, Franklin explained how difficult it was to alter the number of visas granted, how the restrictive quota didn't allow for Eastern European immigrants to be admitted into the country in the quantities warranted by the crisis in the Soviet republic. He told them the labor department would have to get involved to confer a Special status on new arrivals, apologizing that his hands were tied by the 1924 Immigration Act.

"The only thing I can say in your favor," Franklin said to Earl and Finn, "is that since 1930, we have come well under the annual immigration quota. Must be because of the perceived difficulty in finding employment in this country. But Ukrainian visas?" Franklin shook his head. "Are these people all without passports?"

"To the one," said Finn. "They're running across borders at night, hoping not to get stopped and shot. A passport is the last thing on their minds."

"Franklin," said Earl, "even if they somehow had it, a Soviet passport would hold no quarter here. The United States has not formally recognized the creation of the Soviet Union as a political entity. No embassies, no consulates, no diplomatic relations. A passport is meaningless in that context. The visas would have to be for Ukrainian nationals."

"You're right, Earl, I hadn't thought of that," Franklin said. "It actually might make things easier. Let me see what I can do."

"You did this?" Isabelle said when Finn told her about the outcome of his meeting with Franklin. "Why?"

"Well, *I* didn't do it. My father did it," Finn said. "Technically, Franklin Reynolds is doing it." For a service fee of thirty dollars each, Franklin agreed to produce a small number of Ukrainian visas with Special status, which would allow Nate's immigrants to enter and work in America. "But what do you mean, why?"

"I mean, *why* would you do this?" She looked so emotional.

"To help Nate. To help Schumann. To help you," he said. "If anyone from your family comes to Constanta, I don't want them to be unable to get to you because Nate can't get his hands on a damn visa."

"But we don't have thirty dollars for damn visa," Isabelle said. She couldn't meet his eye.

"Not yet, but we will." He patted her hand. "In the meantime, Franklin said he will spot me for the first hundred visas."

"Hundred visas! Finn, that's . . ." She counted silently. "Three thousand dollars!"

"It sounds a lot when you put it like that."

Agitated, she shook her head. "Please. We can't. We literally can't. We don't have even three *hundred* dollars."

"Isabelle, what are you worried about? Where is your plucky optimism? Look at our blades of grass. They're a foot tall. A few weeks ago they were barely out of the earth."

"If we sowed all five acres we couldn't grow enough to pay for that many visas," Isabelle said. "You keep saying how wheat is only sixty cents bushel."

"We grow more than just wheat. Other crops will yield a bigger return. And we could go clamming for the rest." Finn smiled. "Don't you want to learn how to clam?"

"No." But she contemplated. "I might have way to make small money. When you were in Boston, Bryson came by," she said. "He told me breeder friend of his got delivered some thoroughbreds from overseas. Breeder wants someone to tell him if they're worth four thousand dollars each."

"Four thousand dollars *each*!"

"Crazy, I know. Apparently seller told breeder each Arabian horse fast enough to win Kentucky Derby."

"I may not know horses, but I know a snow job when I hear one," Finn said, shaking his head.

"Breeder wants honest opinion." Isabelle shrugged. "In my experience that is last thing people want. But we'll see."

"For how much?"

"He didn't say. Maybe you can come with me and negotiate money part, like banker?"

"You mean like your top-notch booking agent?" He grinned.

"But we shouldn't borrow money from this Franklin fellow, Finn," Isabelle said. "That's what got you into trouble in first place."

"That's not what got me into trouble, but . . . okay, maybe a little, but Isabelle, Nate needs visas now," Finn said. "You said yourself—he's got a backlog. Of people like you."

"Not like me," Isabelle said. "They gave us Special status for free because of Lavelle. Perhaps shipwreck perfect solution. Maybe Florin can crash ship again—he is good at that—and then we won't have to pay no one nothing."

66

First Fruit

Every morning Isabelle woke up and said hallelujah, and every night she went to sleep and said amen. The excitement and participation of Finn and his family reached extraordinary levels. It was a special point of pride for each of them to keep their crops free of weeds, to water them properly, to inspect for bugs or broken supports. Each day brought something new to look at and something new to do. The peonies and poppies Mae and Junie planted, the raspberry bushes Isabelle and Finn tied to the newly installed horse rail fence, the supports Walter himself learned to hammer together for the cucumbers, the scarecrows they built out of hay and burlap sacks, the tin cans they tied together to keep away the birds, the chicken-wire fence they laid down to stop the raccoons from eating everything. Isabelle began each day with delight and hope—and with other things, too.

Every day, after their morning field work, Finn, Isabelle, and the girls drove to a dairy farm on Winterberry to get milk and eggs, and every morning Junie said, "Isabelle, we drink milk like you, but our boobies aren't growing, and yours are. Why?" And Mae said, "June, don't be ridiculous. Isabelle is a woman, she's not growing anymore, and you are just a baby and it's not time for you yet." And Junie said, "I'm not a baby, you're a blind baby because hers are definitely growing!" And Mae said, "You know nothing!" And they would go back and forth like this unabashedly, as if their father wasn't even there.

But their strapping father was most certainly there, carrying the heavy milk jug, driving the truck, slinging the girls in and out of the cab, offering Isabelle his hand, acting amused and nonchalant.

Acting nonchalant, right? Isabelle would glance down at the top of her dress, where her breasts abounded, covered by flimsy cotton fabric stitched together with lace or held together by barely adequate buttons. He was always proper, mannered, polite, as if nothing of her womanhood reached in to tug at his manhood. That was the way it had to be, needed to be. But still, was he a man? Did he have eyes? Did he see? The more offhand he acted, the more milk Isabelle drank.

The farm was a place for men to be rugged and brawny, but it was not a place for women to be dainty and delicate. This had never mattered to Isabelle before, but it mattered to her now. She bought a full-length mirror at the market so she could see the whole of herself before she went out into the sun with him. She washed extra carefully so she didn't smell of sweat and grime. She changed her clothes before dinner, as they all did, but she took special care to look clean and fresh. She bought something called flip-flops. She even bought some red gloss, but it made her lips look so prominent and sexual that she wiped it off immediately, ashamed of herself. All she could do was drink more milk, brush her hair and teeth, scrub her face, and put her bare feet into the flip-flops for dinner. That would have to be enough, because it was all she had.

It was all they could have.

In mid-May, Finn, Isabelle, Monty, and the girls shoveled wheelbarrows of sand and clay from the riverbed near Cornelius Brook to build up a long row of loam for the corn planting. With half a bushel of dried kernels borrowed from Bryson, Isabelle let Junie and Mae seed the row themselves. She watched the girls, and Finn watched her.

"Junebug," said Isabelle, "do you want your corn sweet and plentiful? Then please, dear girl, stop chewing on kernels. I see you—you can't hide from me. For each one you drop in ground, two go in your mouth. They're not for eating, they're only for planting. Your daddy and I made this loamy earth special just for you. We tilled and turned and raked so you could have what you want. One tiny kernel you throw in ground is going to grow into tall stalk which will make you six or seven huge sweet juicy delicious ears of corn. You want that, right? Sure you do. So please—more in ground, less in teeth, okay, baby girl?"

Was it Finn's imagination or were Isabelle's cotton dresses growing lighter and more snug? Had the dresses always failed to contain her swaying bosom? When she stood in the sun, the diaphanous fabric presented him with silhouettes of her thighs and shadow curves of her hips. There were no more muted prints or pastel hues; the woman was all kaleidoscope, all the time.

Back in Boston, every once in a rare while—when Finn needed comfort during the onslaught of hard, dry times—he sometimes reached for the fleeting image of a dripping Isabelle bouncing her soft, naked body against him on the dark landing. But here on the farm, as the weather got warmer and her dresses sheerer and her neckline lower, he found that more and more often, it was the image that reached out of the night for him.

* * *

One morning, after they washed by the well and were in the kitchen putting together the family breakfast, Finn said, "Would you like some milk, Isabelle?" His blue-green eyes gleamed.

She blinked at him twice in response. "I had some earlier, but thank you," she said slowly. "Why, do I look thirsty to you?"

"No, no," he said, pouring himself a large glass. "But you can never have enough. And *that's* what the actress said to the bishop."

And Isabelle laughed, full-throated—just as Walter walked inside with Eleanor and Junie, and all three wanted to know what was so funny that would make the solemn Isabelle laugh like that.

In May the onions and leeks were ready to be harvested. The onions grew big like baby pumpkins, and the leeks grew tall like corn stalks.

When the carrots came in, at first it was just one or two small ones. They ate those raw in a salad. "I know it's hard to wait," Isabelle said to the family at dinner, when she knew Finn couldn't make an off-color joke about it, "but we must wait to pull carrots from ground until they are much bigger. Longer we wait, bigger they grow." No jokes from Finn, not even a one.

The next day brought five or six adequate-sized carrots, which they boiled with brown sugar. The day after, they numbered large and in the dozens and the day after that, huge and in the hundreds. Finn's father said there was a real danger that the very next morning giant carrots would mutiny by the thousands and attack the farm and there'd be no way of stopping it.

"You're right, Earl," said Isabelle. "Giant carrots cannot be stopped." She nearly laughed out loud at Finn, across from her, unable to utter a single bawdy syllable in response.

At the end of May, Isabelle and the girls got dressed up and took nearly 150 pounds of carrots in two overflowing bushels to the local farmers' market in Rye. Finn of course came to drive and carry. "I also need you to count money," Isabelle said. "I don't want your considerate banking skills to go to waste."

"*Considerable.*"

"You're so desperate, you've resorted to counting giant carrots."

"I'm counting the *yield*, Isabelle."

"There is no quota, Finn. We grow what we grow. We sell what we sell. You count money at end."

They sold all the carrots for fifteen cents a pound and *yielded* twenty-two dollars! They bought ice cream, glass jars for canning, some ribbons for their hair, a vase for Isabelle's lair. They bought coffee, sugar, lemons, they gave half the money they made to Finn, and the girls got a dollar each for their efforts. At the end of the day Mae, not prone to exaggeration, said it was the best day of her life, right before she fell asleep in the truck, at six o'clock, and had to be carried to bed by her father.

Isabelle went to bed early herself, and only after she woke at sunrise on Sunday did she acknowledge that yesterday had marked three years since the day she flashed her Cossack blade and lost her life and found another, a life in which her own children were ghosts and another woman's children clung to her neck and held her hand; a life in which Isabelle's flooding desire for a man who was not her husband, for another woman's husband, crawled out of the water like a silent beast and sat panting, waiting, threatening to devour all there was.

In June, right after Junie turned nine, the house changed and changed again when the sugar snap peas came. The girls collected a plateful of pods, a dozen in all, gave out a single pod to each member of the family like a holy wafer, and took two hours to open their own and eat the three peas inside. The remaining two pods they examined and studied till dinnertime, in between searching the leafy bushes for more. They neglected to do any of their other work. They were concerned these twelve were all there would be, and every few minutes Isabelle had to reassure Finn's heartbreaking, animated children that this was just the beginning of their joys, that soon there would be so many peas, they would get sick of them.

Junie listened to Isabelle, but clearly didn't believe her. When he saw their worries, Finn picked up his daughters, set them both on his lap and promised them that Isabelle would never tell them something that wasn't true. That was simply not Isabelle's way. "If Isabelle says it, you can take it to the bank, girls," Finn said. "Eat your peas, sweet peas, and go to sleep quick, so you can wake up tomorrow and see what new magic has sprung on your vines."

Isabelle hoped she would be worthy of Finn's faith in her.

More and more, Vanessa felt like an observer in her own life. Sometimes, not even an observer, sometimes, just an intruder. Their happy, laughing voices, and chatty, argumentative teasing were down the hall from her, past two doors and a corridor. She'd hear singing, her parents clapping, her children—oh, why were they up so late!—squealing, "Let me! My turn!"

And when Vanessa would step out, down the dark hall and into the open room, under the wooden arch and into the kitchen, where her family congregated around the island or the long dining table, all music, talking, singing, and especially laughing would stop. It would stop as if the plug had been pulled from the radio. The silence would be replaced by a solicitous, near-formal interrogation. "Hi, Vee, how are you, darling?" "Hi, Mommy, how do you feel?" "Are you hungry? We were just about to clean up—do you want a plate?" And Isabelle would say, "I prepared plate for you, Vanessa. I left it on stove and it's still warm. Do you want to sit down with us?"

The girls would tell Vanessa about their day. They lived, and she listened. The scarecrows fell in the wind. They collected two more wheelbarrows full of rocks for their flower garden. They dug up two small taters and ate them raw. Isabelle let them. Next spring they might get a horse and Isabelle would teach them how to ride. Isabelle caught four fish, and they only caught two, and Daddy caught a huge pike so he won.

"Daddy always needs to win, darlings," Vanessa said.

67

Starfire

The Bryson mare foaled in mid-June. When the mare started acting restless one morning, kicking the walls of the stall and burrowing her nose in the hay, Isabelle went to Chuck's stables and stayed there overnight. Bryson dropped her back home the following morning. She walked inside the house as the family was having their second breakfast. Opening her arms, she said, beaming, "It's a boy!" The foal weighed fifty-five pounds at birth, stood on his own legs after an hour, nursed happily, and both mother and baby were now resting. "I don't know why poor Shelly and Chuck were so worried. Mare did all work. I cleaned foal's breathing passage and repositioned his legs—he was tiny bit stuck—but they didn't need me."

The Brysons felt very much otherwise. They kept bringing over eggs and bread. "I don't know why they so grateful," Isabelle said. "They act as if I gave birth to boy horse myself."

But Chuck Bryson told Finn that the foal had been breech and both mare and foal would've died for sure if not for Isabelle's expert handling.

A week later, by way of thanks, Bryson arranged a meeting between Isabelle and his friend the horse breeder. Finn drove Isabelle and his two daughters to Berkshire Valley Farm, half an hour away in Kingston, where they met Michael "call me Mickey" Winslow, a tall, talkative, chain-smoking man. The jittery Mickey was both thrilled and daunted by the championship potential of the steeds he was set on acquiring. Fast upon introduction, Mickey and Isabelle engaged in a conversation that, although in English, was incomprehensible to Finn. When he mentioned this to Isabelle, she said, "Lot like when you and Lionel were going on and on to me about call money and debentures."

Finn watched her at the fence of the paddock studying the movements of the six Arabians as they paced and cantered. "You have tack for me?" she said to Mickey. "And spurs?"

Mickey glanced at her coarse braided leather boots. "You bring those with you from the old country?"

"It's only thing I bring," she said. "You have spurs or not?"

"Of course. But what do you think of the horses, Isabelle?"

"I give you my opinion after I ride. Have you agreed to buy them?"

"That sounds ominous," Mickey said. ". . . Yes?"

"They good horses," she said. "You can give lessons on them."

"You haven't got anywhere near them! You can't possibly tell if they're worthy from this distance!"

"They will be good for training, lessons, regular purpose."

"I told you, that's not what I'm looking for," he said. "I have enough of that kind of horse to open ten facilities in the Northeast. I bought these to be winning racehorses—"

Finn cut him off. "Mickey, she knows. She said she'll give you her opinion after she rides them. But we should agree on compensation."

"She finds me a champion horse, she can name her price," Mickey said. "You want a horse, Isabelle? Take your pick. Hell, have two, if you want to breed them. You want cash later? No problem. You want a job on my ranch? You're welcome here."

Junie yanked on Finn's arm, tugging him down to her. "Daddy," she whispered fiercely, "Isabelle doesn't need a job! She is with us."

"I know, pumpkin, shh."

"Tell him, Daddy!"

Finn straightened out. "It's up to Isabelle," he said to Mickey.

"It's up to Finn," said Isabelle. "Whatever he says is fair."

"If you find me horses that win any race they enter," Mickey said, "heck, if they *place*, I'll give you a cut of the purse. Ten percent."

"Fifteen percent is what we're looking for," said Finn. "But what about for her time today? She gives you her opinion and you don't like it, she still gets paid."

"That's fine."

"Upfront. I don't want any haggling afterward," Finn said. "A hundred per horse."

Mickey whistled. "Too steep. I usually pay five or ten bucks per."

"I don't know what to tell you," Finn said. "That's her rate. Take it or leave it. Is she going to save you more or less than a hundred a horse?"

Mickey's expression read like he couldn't believe the audacity. It remained unchanged even as he took out a wad of cash from his pocket.

Isabelle was barely listening. Stepping away, she watched a stout rider returning to the paddock on a chestnut stallion. "Who is *that*?" she said.

"That's the hostler's son, Bobby," Mickey said, not even glancing at where she was pointing as he counted off the hundreds.

"Not rider," Isabelle said. "Horse."

"I don't know. I think it's my stableman's horse."

"How old is he?"

"Bobby just turned seventeen."

"Not rider," Isabelle said. "*Horse.*"

"Bobby!" Mickey called to the boy. "How old is the stallion?"

"Two in July!" Bobby yelled back.

Isabelle nodded. "Let's get started. One by one. Him last." She pointed to Bobby's steed.

"You want to ride *him*?"

"He's only one I want to ride. But I'll ride rest for you too, as promised."

"How many horses, Isabelle?" asked Finn.

"Seven."

Mickey handed Finn seven hundred-dollar bills. "Do you need gloves?"

She shook her head. "I feel horse with my hands," she said. Before she left she pulled Finn down to her and whispered, "A hundred per horse?! He'll kill us for robbing him."

"The money's in my hand, Isa."

"Yes, Finn Evans, that's what robbery means. His money is in your hand. Where did you get nerve to ask for so much?"

"This isn't worth it for five or ten bucks. We have a field full of carrots we can sell. And how do you think I kept us afloat in Boston for two years?"

"By highway robbery?"

He laughed. "By these kinds of shenanigans."

"But how did you know he'd say yes?"

"I didn't. I named the craziest price I could think of. If he didn't want to pay it, we would've walked away. Though clearly I didn't ask for enough. Did you see how fast he parted with his money?"

They chuckled. She squeezed his arm and ran to the stables.

Finn watched her carry the tack, enter the paddock, and approach the first horse. She threw the saddle over him, bridled him, adjusted the stirrups, the straps, patted the horse with her hands as she circled him, peered at his hindquarters, his hooves, ran her hands up and down each of his legs. She wore a cream blouse and tailored beige trousers. Finn hadn't seen her wear the outfit before. Schumann had made the slacks for her after she told him she might get to ride. She was slim and long-legged, and it had never been more obvious just how slim and long-legged she was than when she was in formfitting riding gear.

Light at Lavelle

Finn watched her leap into the air and bestride the horse. With a pang in his heart, he realized that not when she worked the fields or played with his children—not even when she was with him—did she ever look more at ease, more natural, or happier than she did in the saddle.

Bobby the hostler's son opened the rear gate for her. She yelled something Finn didn't recognize, something that sounded like *"Davai!"* and was off.

She rode with a measured pace at first, in fits and spurts. She would ride, pull up on the reins, release the horse, go again. But then she took off. Lowering her body to the stallion's and her head to his mane, she spurred him and flew over the meadow, her movements in perfect harmony with the steed's, flying up, bearing down, her equestrian prowess on full display. Finn beheld Isabelle unconcealed, her untamed spirit ablaze. He watched her fly, all confidence and grace, her bond with the horse as if she had been raised on the creature's back.

Finally, he understood.

Finally, unequivocally, irrevocably, he understood who Isabelle Martyn Lazar really was.

She cantered back, jumped off, and saddled up the next one. She harnessed and unharnessed seven tacks, mounted and dismounted seven saddles, she rode seven horses, indefatigable to the end. The last one was Bobby's stallion. She rode him the longest, the hardest, and the fastest.

Finn felt a tectonic shift inside himself. He had been watching her for years, but today he saw her through a new lens. She was a force of nature. Her life inside war would've broken a lesser woman. *Here I am*, she seemed to say. *You took this from me, took my family, cast a shadow over my life, but here atop the stallion, I reclaim my identity. I reunite with my true self.*

Keenly aware of her struggle, Finn's heart swelled with turbulent emotion. Through his profound compassion for her, he saw the magnitude of her loss and bore witness to her unmasking—as well as to his own. Her return to the saddle after years of separation became an act of defiance against her fate, a testament to her unyielding spirit.

Mickey stood by Finn and his daughters, pacing and smoking. He must have smoked a pack in the time it took Isabelle to finish.

"Do you *see* her, Daddy?" Junie whispered to him, pulling on his hand.

"I see her, Junebug."

Flushed and perspiring, her hair wild, Isabelle finally hopped off the honey-colored stallion, patted his body, rubbed his legs one last time, ruffled his mane, and then handed the reins to Bobby. She walked up to Finn and Mickey, panting, radiant, joyous. Finn offered her a glass of lemonade. Words were inadequate, so he didn't utter any.

"Isabelle, you were so *good!*" said Junie.

She downed the lemonade before she spoke. "Thanks, Junebug," she said. "But we're not here to see if I can ride. We're here to see if Mickey's horses can race."

"And?" asked Mickey.

"Either return six horses to seller or use them for trail rides," she said. "None of them will win you Kentucky."

Mickey threw down his cigarette. "This is ridiculous!" he said. "Chuck Bryson is a man I deeply respect and he couldn't say enough about you, so I decided to take a chance. I'm going to have to give him a good talking to. No wonder your husband wanted seven bills upfront. What a con."

"Daddy is not her husband," said Junie.

"Shh, Junebug," said Finn. "The adults are arguing."

"You want me to tell you they're excellent?" Isabelle said to Mickey. "That they can win for you? That wouldn't be scam? You'll know what they are as soon as you race them, but you'll be out all your money."

"It's not possible," Mickey said. "They're Arabian stallions, best of the best! You don't know what you're talking about."

"Your guy didn't sell you best of best," said Isabelle. "He sold you third best. Maybe fourth."

"You were against them even before you mounted them. Your mind was made up."

"Sometimes horse can prove me wrong when I ride it," she said. "Not this time. I've been around too many horses not to tell you truth." She smiled brightly. "Cheer up, Mickey, all is not lost. I'm trying to save you $24,000. That's not con, that's good money where I come from. You already have winner on your hands. Bobby's horse. He will do for you what you need."

Mickey laughed. "You're insane, lady. Get the devil out of here."

"Hey," said Finn, frowning.

"It's okay, Finn," said Isabelle, laying her hand on him. "Mickey is upset. People often are when they hear truth. But Mickey, I don't know why you insulted. You wanted me to find you champion. I did. You own your winning horse. He is two, he is eager, he is responsive, he is kind, he wants to please, he listens to commands, but most important, and really, this is *most* important, he is one of fastest horses I've ever been on." She chuckled. "And let me tell you, I have been on *lot* of horses." The smile faded from her eyes.

"What's wrong with the rest of them?" Mickey struggled to light another cigarette. His fingers were shaking. "I'm not going to listen, but you might as well tell me anyway. I'm definitely getting a second opinion."

"Just don't get opinion from guy who wants your money," said Isabelle. "Your other six horses have problems, big and small. One is over three years old, so man is lying to you and you won't be able to race him. One had broken leg some time ago. He limps on left side, do you not see it? One doesn't listen to either whip or spur. I couldn't get him to ride full out until I nearly made him bleed—last thing you want in racehorse. And two of them have, how you say in English, *lamiNEET*."

"Laminitis?"

"Guess so. When hoof wall separates from coffee bone."

"*Coffin* bone," whispered Finn.

"That's what I said," said Isabelle. "They are not racehorses, Mickey. Guy who sold you this bill of goods is trying to, how you said, *con* you. He tries to hide *lamiNEET* by hammering horseshoe too loose into hoof. He's crook, not me."

Finn could see Mickey was wavering. How could he not be? Isabelle was so calm and confident. She didn't say *I think*, or *I guess*, or *perhaps*. She stated everything as fact. It didn't matter to her what he thought. She already had his seven hundred bucks.

"Explain to me what you saw in Bobby's horse," Mickey said. "You saw something right away."

"I liked the way his hindquarters moved."

"Why?"

"He has sloped croup—*croop* same word in my language—that extends down length of his femur. It's source of his power. In full gallop his hind legs reach all way under him, increasing his forward motion. I've seen only two horses in my life that have it, and he is one of them."

Mickey stared at Finn, slack-jawed.

Finn stared at Isabelle, slack-jawed.

Isabelle, however, was staring only at the horse, also slightly slack-jawed.

"He's your horse, Mickey," she said, affection and wonder in her voice. "Plus, he already has perfect name. He is Starfire."

68

Kolomeyka

Electric Boat was good to Finn in June. His dividend check topped $800. He drove to Boston, tried (unsuccessfully) to pay Franklin Reynolds, and called in on Schumann. Guided by the tailor's advice, Finn bought Isabelle a balalaika. He even wrapped it before presenting it to her on their bench.

"Oh my God," she said, hugging it to her chest. "Why did you do this?"

He shrugged. "I thought you might like it."

"It's so expensive. You shouldn't have."

"That can't be right," he said. "You don't think you've done enough to deserve a small gift?"

"This isn't small," she said. "It's little bit priceless." She strummed the three strings. "I'm going to play you such nice Ukrainian songs." She played and sang for him "*Ochi Chernye*" or "Dark Eyes." "*Ochi chernye, ochi strastnye, ochi zhguchie i prekrasnye! Kak lyublyu ya vas . . . kak boyus' ya vas! Znat', uvidel vas, ya v nedobryy chas . . .*"

"Why does that sound so familiar?" Finn said. "Tell me the lyrics."

"*All the best in life God has given us . . .*" she sang in English.

"You sang for ten minutes and recited one line. Where's the rest?"

"Rest unrecitable."

"*Untranslatable*. I'll ask Schumann. He'll translate for me."

"I made song up. He's never heard it before."

"We'll see about that," Finn said. "We should have a summer party, invite him. Lucas, too. The Brysons. Mickey Winslow, maybe?"

"Only if you want him to talk about nothing but horses. No songs, no dance, no fire, no games, just horse talk."

"Uh, no, thanks. Nate? He's supposed to be back at the start of July."

Isabelle chewed her lip. "Did Schumann have any news when you saw him? Telegram from Nate maybe?"

Finn shook his head. Schumann had told him the people coming from

Ukraine carried with them soul-crushing stories. There was no point telling Isabelle that. As if she didn't already know. "Franklin managed to get two hundred visas for Nate," he said.

"Finn, don't say two hundred. *Please*," said Isabelle. "At thirty dollars each? How much do we already owe that man?"

"He refused to take my money."

"He's not giving you any more visas?"

"He is. He just didn't take my money."

"Really?"

"Yes. So don't worry. When is Starfire running his first race?"

"Travers Stakes in August," Isabelle said. "Mickey invited me to Saratoga with him to watch race. But it's harvest season."

"Do you want to go? You can if you want." He didn't mean it.

She shook her head. "*It's harvest season*," she sang, strumming her balalaika.

"How much is first prize?"

"*Twenty thousand dollars*," sang Isabelle.

Finn whistled. "So if he wins, you get three grand." He grinned. "I am exceptional. The banker in me came in quite handy."

"Yes, you did all work." She smiled. "Will that be enough to get new ship for Nate and Florin?"

"No. But don't worry. I'm working on a plan."

"You got plan for everything, don't you." She played a soft sad slow tune. He smoked, watching her hands on the strings, listening to her sing.

"I don't want you to worry about the money, Isa," he said. "I learned the hard way. We all did. *Easy come, easy go.* We'll get more. Or we won't. Now that we're growing our own food, I'm philosophical about it. If it makes you feel better, Franklin told me he's not actually paying for the visas. His INS contact is budgeting it out of his discretionary fund, which hasn't been divested in two years."

"I'm going to start talking about horses if you don't stop."

"What part was financial jargon?" Finn laughed. "Budget? Money?"

"A well-conformed stallion can do live cover one to three times daily," Isabelle said, her eyes twinkling.

"Touché." He twinkled right back at her. "What's live cover?"

"Someday maybe I tell you." She clutched the balalaika. "Thank you."

"I owe you a lot."

"You owe me nothing,"

"But when they ask you"—he pointed to the dark house—"as they inevitably will, don't tell them I bought it for you."

"I won't. But why?"

O, you fool and slow of heart, Finn thought, whether about himself or her, he couldn't say. He wanted to reach out and stroke her face with the back of his fingers. He wanted to lean over and press his bearded cheek to her satin skin to feel her gratitude, but it was too dark and too late at night for caresses and cheek kisses, and they were too alone and had consumed too much of Schumann's celebratory whisky. What he really wanted to do was lean forward and place his lips over hers. He wanted to kiss her. He wanted her to kiss him. And then he wanted them to kiss each other. Without answering her, he said an unwilling goodnight, and she stayed behind, and through his open window he listened to her melancholy strumming as she played him to sleep, singing the same line about *God giving us the best in life* over and over. "*Kak luyblyu ya vas, kak luyblyu ya vas, kak luyblyu ya vas, kak luyblyu ya vas* . . ."

Yes, July was a very good month. Even though on Friday, July 8, 1932, the Dow Jones Industrial Average finished the trading day at a shocking 41.

"You heard that right, Walter, Earl, gracious ladies and children," said Finn, addressing his family as he raised a glass of toothless lemonade. "That wasn't a misprint as my father and father-in-law had reasonably assumed this morning when I brought them the *Boston Globe*. After the infamous, notorious, never before, and possibly never again to be repeated Great Crash of 1929, we all—wise college graduates and business and finance experts alike—fully believed that the hiccup was temporary, that things would improve, that investors would come back to the market, that the economy of this great land would straighten out—for how could it not? The stock market was at a record 381 in September 1929, at 260 on the worst day in the market's history, and since then has not only *not* corrected itself, but has continued to plummet—50 points here, 70 points there, 100 points one year, 100 points the next—until we found ourselves here, on July 8, 1932, at 41! We have lost more than 90 percent of the value of our largest companies in less than three years. That simply beggars belief. No wonder we are suffering an economic depression such as we've never had."

Though things were gloomy in the market, on the Adams farm, it was party time. A little joy had to be found somewhere. They were gathered around the firepit, lounging on the outdoor chairs. With Mae and Junie's help, Isabelle had strung some lights around the patio and arranged flowers and fruit baskets as decorations. Earlier that day, Finn had desperately tried to convince Vanessa to join them. Right before he left to pick up their guests at the station, he came in to change into a clean linen shirt and trousers. "Our neighbors Chuck and Shelly Bryson are coming, with some of their children and grandchildren," he said. "It's going to be the first party we've thrown in a very long time. It would be nice if the beautiful lady of the house came out and said hello to our new friends and old, if she sat and had an iced tea and a conversation. You could fix yourself up, put on one of your fancy dresses. It would be good for us."

"The party isn't good for *me*, Finn," Vanessa said, not looking directly at him. "Why are *my* feelings not taken into *any* consideration?"

"Vanessa, if we planned a party around your moods, we would never have one," Finn said. "One person cannot decide for twenty others. And Lucas, Schumann, and Nate are coming from Boston. You want me to cancel with them because you're not feeling up to it?"

She opened her hands.

"This isn't normal," Finn said. "This isn't right."

"Don't you have a party to attend?" She motioned him out. "Spit-spot."

"You know, I keep asking you to participate in this life, in this marriage," Finn said. "Less and less, it's true, but eventually, I'm going to stop caring whether or not you come outside, whether or not you eat with us, whether or not you lie down with me." Finn paused. "Whether or not you're my wife."

"Do you have somewhere else to be, Finn?"

"Do *you* have somewhere else to be, Vanessa?"

They stared at each other grimly. "We're trapped, with nowhere to go," she said. "Welcome to modern marriage, darling."

"This may not be the bottom yet," Finn said in his State of the Union speech to his family, talking about the market but thinking about his wife. "Even though it feels like the bottom. But we said this about the market at 260, at 200, at 130, at 80. Today we are at 41. Soon we might be at zero. No profits to be earned, no profits to be made, and the country is dancing on the backs of a third of its people out of work—*one-third* of its people! What a calamity. Well, we know why. Because our business giants have lost 90 percent of their value! They're making nothing and employing no one." He glanced toward the windows of his bedroom. "However, despite falling on unprecedented hard times, I'm going to point to some rays of sunshine for our family. Most important—ten of us are not unemployed." He deliberately excluded Vanessa from that figure, hoping she was listening. "We work nonstop, feed ourselves, and make a little money. We've grown zucchinis the size of small submarines, when a month ago we barely knew what a zucchini was. We've sold nine-tenths of our cucumber and carrot harvest and still have too much left for ourselves. Our wheat is already taller than I am, and we're six weeks away from reaping. If our cabbage crop is as good as we hope, we might afford twenty chickens next year.

"Elsewhere, Isabelle's handpicked thoroughbred is running his first big race next month in Saratoga, and if any of you are betting men, I suggest placing a few dollars on him.

"Nate and Florin are doing God's work, sailing back and forth across the seven seas, trying to help the destitute and desperate who have fled their blighted borderlands. We are all working to secure our future. Our cucumbers and eggplant have been canned. We bought strawberries and prepared jams and jellies to last until next year when our own strawberries and raspberries come in.

"To help us along, my graduation gift from my father, which, like a sentimental fool, I refused to part with, has continued to pay us dividends through the toughest times. What's impressive about the barely surviving submarine company Electric Boat is that over the last few years, its shares have split, and though they're not worth very much, the quarterly dividend on what is now three thousand shares allows us to pay our debts and better withstand the vagaries of our intermittent cashflow.

"This fall we are going to buy a car to supplement my truck so the entire family can travel in comfort. And of course, the most important election in our lifetime is right around the corner and with any luck, Franklin Delano Roosevelt will make good on his campaign promise to end the true blight on our country—Prohibition." Finn smiled, raising his glass of virgin lemonade fizz. "And so, with hope for the future, and barring any floods, blizzards, tornadoes, droughts, and enemy invaders, the state of the Adams Evans Lazar Schumann McBride union is good. God bless America."

Vanessa listened to Finn through her open bedroom window. But what she heard even louder than Finn's sermon, or the cheering, or the laughter, was her girls running in and saying, "Mommy, please come outside. We're about to play sack races. Come, Mommy."

"Why do we have to have the party outside, my darlings?" Was it even *that* irrational? Mosquitoes lived outside, bees, flies, spiders. There was dirt and dust everywhere, as evidenced by the dirt and dust the humans brought inside her clean house. Once she had thought she and Finn were the same and hated to be dusty, sandy, gritty. Not anymore. He washed, but he got dirty. There was not a single thing to recommend being outside, not one, save for the incalculable loss Vanessa felt at not being able to share in some of the fun they were having without her.

The adults and children alike played horseshoes and cornhole. They ran three-legged races, blindfolded each other and whacked a piñata, they raced in sacks, played tug of war, they dragged out a radio onto the patio, but instead Schumann offered to play his accordion for the musical chairs game. It simply wasn't fair how much fun they were having—even Vanessa's father. Walter had a bad heart yet was hopping a three-legged race with her mother against Junie and Mae and Lucas and Isabelle!

Lucas and Isabelle won because Isabelle needed to win at everything, even against the young and infirm. Eleanor got upset that Lucas raced with Isabelle and not her, so she harassed Finn to take a break from grilling and pair up with Isabelle against her and Lucas. Eleanor tied herself to Lucas's leg with a bandana, and Finn tied his leg to Isabelle's with rope—"Very securely," Vanessa heard him say, "so we don't get loose." The two pairs raced while everyone else hooted and hollered, and of course Finn and Isabelle won because Finn needed to win at everything, too. But Eleanor didn't care because all she wanted was to be close to Lucas. Vanessa couldn't think of anything worse than Lucas and Eleanor getting together. *He doesn't have a steady job, Ellie!* Vanessa wanted to shout through the window.

She heard Lucas wheedling Schumann for some work in front of Earl sitting next to them, and Schumann, not knowing what to say, trying to get Isabelle's attention with an expression that read *help me!* And Isabelle, flushed and breathy, leaning over Lucas with a warm arm around his shoulder and saying, "Lucas, Schumann wouldn't mind hiring you to drive few of his immigrants to North Carolina. He needs steady driver. But he can't give you work if you can't hold your wheel dry and sober for twelve hours. Those poor Ukrainians, Lucas, they've suffered enough."

"Is that true, Schumann?" Lucas said with hope in his voice. "About the work, not the Ukrainians."

"It's not *not* true, Lucas," Schumann replied, with a grateful glance at Isabelle. "But it's a question only you can answer—*can* you do it?"

"Of course he can, Schumann," said Earl in his no-nonsense judge voice, answering for Lucas. "He can and he will. Only a dead thing cannot go against a stream. And our boy Lucas here is a living thing."

Isabelle put her arm around Earl and kissed his cheek. And he let her with a smile! She flitted away, shouting, "I'm coming, Walter!" because Vanessa's father was calling for her. Vanessa had never seen Isabelle so carefree and happy. No one had. She was laughing and was so out of breath, she was red in the face. It wasn't very becoming, even for a foreign woman, to look that exhilarated because of a little party. Isabelle ran a sack race against Vanessa's father and let him win. And a delighted Walter hugged Isabelle as if this was the Olympics! The whole thing was one level of vexation on top of another.

Finn grilled sausages and hamburgers and chicken. They had a smorgasbord of salads and Isabelle's delectable fried eggplant. They ate while the radio played. For dessert Isabelle made her own whipped cream and ladled it over raspberries and blueberries, and they all oohed and ahhed as if they'd never tasted anything so good. Vanessa harrumphed down on her bed, and a few minutes later Isabelle came in, offering her a bowl of berries with cream.

Vanessa tried it grudgingly and hated that she liked it. When Isabelle asked how it was, Vanessa said she didn't enjoy it. "For shame, Vanessa," Isabelle said, probably meaning *oh, shame,* and ran off, and a moment later Vanessa heard her doing her best Goodman and Ace impression and chortling as if she couldn't care less what Vanessa thought of her raspberries.

"Goodman: *Jane, did you hear about the talking cow on Farmer Brown's farm?*
"Jane: *No, Goodman. What did the talking cow say?*
"Goodman: *I'm udderly fantastic!*"

She was fantastic every which way, including utterly.

When she gave Finn his dessert bowl, he swallowed a spoonful of her whipped cream and said he'd never tasted anything so good, and she replied that he probably hadn't tasted a lot of delicious Ukrainian things, before fluttering away to laugh by the fire.

"The Kolomeyka" was a relentless tune that started at 120 beats per minute and ended at 240. For three minutes Isabelle played it on the balalaika, faster than Finn had ever seen anyone play a stringed instrument. It was fantastic. And then Nate and Schumann played it on the fiddle and the accordion and Isabelle danced to it, faster than Finn had ever seen anyone dance to anything, and that was fantastic too.

She started out fast, but by the end she was twirling like an out-of-control merry-go-round at spin-top speed. Mae and Junie tried to keep up, Lucas tried, Chuck Bryson's thirteen-year-old granddaughter tried, Nate tried, but no one could. Bright and vivacious, she was almost as much in her element dancing in a red dress as she was galloping in ivory on top of Starfire.

Her wraparound necklaces swung from side to side, her hair flew wild, her face was flushed with joy. Romance and poetry were her companions in the dust by the fire, just as they had been out in the broad sunny meadow where she chased the ghosts that haunted her.

Chased or outran?

She was musical, tender, sacred, irreverent.

Quantifiable physical things were being mortared in the crucible inside Finn along with his elemental awe. He took in her body, the perspiration on her neck, the tanned swell in the deep cleft of her cheerful dress, held together with a belt made of dried tulips. He took in her abundant breasts pushed together by a low snug collar, her exposed pulsing throat, her bare neckline. She bobbed and twirled with abandon as if she were still alive in another life, and all that she loved was alive with her.

Made of crimson velvet roses, the tiara crowning her hair kept falling off as she spun to the beat of the music. The heady air where she danced glowed with jasmine and lavender, her body was in a swirling fever, her voice as she sang in Ukrainian was bluesy, potent, chaotic. She was a breathtaking spectacle of all that was beautiful in women.

This is the new world: an exclamation in a red dress, a flame. Welcome to America, Finn whispered to himself, *stunning, heartrending Ukraine.*

"Isa, sing the song you sang to me the other week," he called out to her when she was taking a break, still panting.

"Which one? 'Hopak?' 'Kalinka?' 'Song of Volga Boatmen?'"

"No, the untranslatable one." Finn knew he'd heard it on the radio sometime before she came into his life. "Feodor Chaliapin!" he said, suddenly placing it. "He performed it at the Boston Metropolitan Opera."

"Chaliapin sings hundreds of songs," Isabelle said. "How do I know which one you mean?"

"I went to that concert," Schumann said. "Maybe I can help, Finn. Do you remember any of the words? Or a melody, perhaps?"

"Would you like some more dessert, Schumann?" interrupted Isabelle.

"No, thank you. Finn, how did the song go?"

"Something about the best in life being given to us by God."

Schumann nodded. "Of course!" he said. "It's 'Dark Eyes.' One of the most popular songs. Every Ukrainian knows it by heart. We'll sing it for you. Kids, shall we?" he said to Isabelle and Nate, opening his accordion.

"We shall not," said Isabelle, whooshing the accordion shut. "Lucas! Don't you know any Irish ballads? You must! Please sing them for us—and your brother can join you."

"Now I want to hear 'Dark Eyes' more than anything," Finn said, his ardent gaze trained on Isabelle.

"Lucas!" said Isabelle.

Lucas didn't know if he could. "I've never sung drinking songs without getting hammered first. I can't remember the words without whisky to help me."

"Come on, Lucas," said Earl. "Sing a song with your brother."

Instantly Lucas jumped up and said he would do it.

As the fire burned and the marshmallows melted, Lucas and Finn sang the ditty their brother Travis had taught Finn on the banks of the Piave River, near the Italian Alps, while they waited for the last battle of the Great War to claim them.

"*Too-ra-loo-ra-loo-ral, Too-ra-loo-ra-li, Too-ra-loo-ra-loo-ral, hush now, don't you cry ... Too-ra-loo-ra-loo-ral ... that's an Irish Lullaby ...*"

Perspiring and light-headed, overjoyed and carefree, Isabelle forgot herself utterly for three minutes of "The Kolomeyka." She spun in bliss, and when she opened her eyes, she saw Finn in a chair by the fire, smoking and watching her, his sun-bleached hair brushed back, his trimmed beard neat around his soft mouth, his eyes more familiar to her than her own. He was magnetized to her, his gaze blinkless, his pupils dilated. He looked so casually handsome in his cream linen shirt and trousers, with one leg draped over the other, and so besotted, it took her breath away.

He gawped at her, the soul bond between them the melody, but desire the drumbeat they dared not go near. In his expression she saw that it was pounding through his blood. His eyes said, *I'm a firedrake and I don't care that you know it. I am Dionysus, son of Zeus, and I'm not hiding. Approach me at your peril.*

Late that night, when everyone had gone to bed, and Isabelle cleaned up after one of her happiest days in recent memory, she hummed the full lyric from "Dark Eyes" she hadn't offered Finn. "*All the best in life God has given us, I have sacrificed to your blazing eyes. Kak lyublyu ya vas, kak lyublyu ya vas . . .*"

69

Raspberry Mash

August was many things. One of them was raspberry season.

With their own bushes fruitless till next year, Isabelle had to buy the berries at the farmers' market. She was determined to make something delicious and intoxicating for Finn. She didn't know what his family would think, but she wasn't too worried about it. The family was firmly for change at the top, and Roosevelt was running on employment and *repeal* in the November election—not necessarily in that order.

To get enough raspberries to make a decent amount of moonshine, Isabelle cleaned out the berry sellers at the Rye market, the twins Pug and Mitch. "Are you making jam?" one of the sisters asked her, possibly Pug. "They spoil in three days if you don't eat them or cook them, especially in this heat. You don't plan to eat twenty pounds of raspberries, do ya? They'll give ya a stomachache something wicked."

"Pug is right, that's a fuckload of raspberries, pardon my French," Finn said when he saw her placing the overfilled wicker baskets in the well of the passenger seat and sitting above them with her legs tucked under her.

"Hmm," she said.

"And excuse me, but aren't the tubs you bought for these twenty pounds of berries only five gallons each? Math, anyone?"

"You don't think a five-gallon tub can fit ten *pounds* of berries?" She crossed her arms. "How much does gallon of milk weigh, Mr. Banker?" He looked stumped. She tried not to laugh. "If you don't know answer to such basic thing, math whiz, how can *you* be mocking *me*?" He looked even more stumped. "Instead of trying to be funny, you should think up explanation to tell your family for drink I'm about to make you."

"Do they need an explanation? They're not very observant."

She glanced at him. "Aren't they?"

"Not very, no," Finn said, avoiding her gaze.

* * *

Before they began mashing, she had to make an airlock. She pierced a small hole in the lid, stuffed a cork into the hole so it fit snugly, and snaked in a metal wire through the middle of the cork to make an opening. She inserted the rubber tubing into the cork. One end of the tubing dangled inside the container, and the other end was immersed in a jar of water outside.

"What do we need an airlock for?" asked Finn.

"To release gases in raspberries."

"Raspberries have gases?"

"When they ferment, yes."

His eyes twinkled so brightly Isabelle wanted to kiss him. "We're *fermenting* the raspberries?" he said, his grin from ear to ear. He almost looked as if he wanted to kiss *her*!

"What kind of pointless beverage would it be otherwise?" Isabelle stepped away slightly in case he could read female Ukrainian minds if he stood too close.

Finn rolled up his sleeves. "I'm ready for some mischief," he said.

"Didn't we already make all the jams we need?" said the practical Olivia, who had come out on the patio with her book to see what they were up to.

"In June we made strawberry jam, Mother," Finn said. "This is to make raspberry juice. Or *compost*, as Isabelle likes to say."

"Don't tease the immigrant, darling, it's not polite," said Olivia.

"*Then I am not very polite*," Finn whispered.

Isabelle disagreed. He was very polite. *Exceedingly* so.

"Will it store through the winter, son?" Olivia asked.

"Yes, Mother. Isabelle knows an excellent Ukrainian method for preserving the raspberries."

"Oh, I'd like to hear about it," Olivia said. "But from a distance."

"Yes, it's much messier than making jam," Isabelle said. "We have to use our hands to make mash. Now, who wants to help?"

"Me, me!" said Junie.

"Me, me!" said Mae.

"Me, me!" said Finn.

How could you not laugh?

"No, no," Olivia said. "Not on our back patio. We'll be stepping in loose raspberries for weeks, and they stain. Please take your venture elsewhere." She waved them to the far side of the house. "Do it around the corner in the shed area, Isabelle. You'll be out of the way, and it's right next to the shower in case you need a quick rinse. Back there, you can swim in them for all I care. I'm out on this patio far too often for such a mess."

"You heard your nana, girls," Isabelle said, lifting the heavy berry baskets. "Follow me. Olivia, do you want to come help?"

"Heaven forfend." Grabbing her book, Olivia darted back inside.

Isabelle made Mae, Junie, and Finn wash their arms up to the elbows like they were doctors. She herself wore a sleeveless wraparound dress, but Finn, as always, was enclosed in a linen shirt with long sleeves. "Finn, come on."

"What? I rolled up the sleeves."

"No part of clothing can touch raspberries," she said. "Berries will stain shirt permanently."

"You're asking me to take off my shirt," he said, lowering his voice.

It was the dog days of August. Every day was boiling hot under the blinding sun. It made everybody's language a little hot and dirty because the desires that pushed the words out of throats were hot and dirty also.

"I didn't say *that*," she said, pretending she didn't know what he was talking about. "You do what you like, of course."

"You want me to do what I *like*?"

"I didn't say that. I said do what you like."

"Do you *want* me to do what I like?"

"*Finn.*"

"*Isabelle.*"

The children were still rinsing their little arms under the spigot nearby.

"If you want to help, your arms need to be uncovered to the biceps one way or another, is all I'm saying."

Finn unbuttoned and threw off his shirt and stood before her in a white tank top. His strong, sweltering arms, his chest, his neck all glistened. Six months of outdoor work had done wondrous things to his body. He was a lumberjack and a bricklayer all in one.

"Is that better?" He was all teeth. His light eyes were dancing.

She cleared her throat. "You're not going to get yourself blood-red messy, so yes, I suppose."

"You're wearing a yellow dress, Isa," he said, looking her over up and down. "How clean do you think *you're* going to remain?"

"I'm not going to swim in the raspberries."

"No?"

Isabelle was having a hard time meeting his teasing gaze. He was just teasing, right? The heat was ruinous. It made liquid of her brain.

She poured one basket of berries into the girls' container and the other into her and Finn's. She left the girls' tub on the ground, put theirs on the table, and showed Mae and Junie what to do. "Use your little hands to squeeze the raspberries as hard as you can to release the juices. Don't be afraid to make a mess, girlies."

"Do you want me to use my little hands to make a mess, too?" Finn said.

"Silly Daddy, your hands aren't little, they're yuge!" Junie said.

"Dad is joking, June," said Mae. "Learn what a joke is."

"Your dad is *trying* to joke, girls," said Isabelle. "Important difference."

She stuck her hands inside the container. He stuck his in after her.

Immersed up to their elbows, tilted toward each other across the worktable, they pureed the berries with their occasionally interlocking hands. Isabelle's gaze was aimed down into the soft warm red pulp. She didn't know where his gaze was because she didn't dare raise her eyes to him from this close. His head was less than a foot away! His face, his *mouth* less than a foot away. And what if he could read her mind from this distance? Isabelle fervently hoped not.

"How are we doing?" squealed Junie.

"Yes, how are we doing?" said Finn.

"Go check on your children," Isabelle said, trying in vain to thin out her thickened voice.

"What would I even be looking for?" Finn said. Was it her imagination, or was he working to control his voice too? "I don't know what *I'm* doing. How will I know if my kids are successful?"

"If berries are smooshed together in smooshy smoosh is how you know."

Walking over, he glanced into the girls' container. "Looks pretty smooshy smoosh to me."

Isabelle applauded the girls' efforts and sent them to the well on the other side of the house to thoroughly wash and then go upstairs and change before dinner. But after they ran off, she told Finn they would have to redo the girls' mash. It was still too solid. "They're little, they have no strength."

"Not like me, right?"

"Let's finish ours, we're almost done." She poured in half a jug of sugar and a gallon of water and told Finn to continue mixing the mash with his hands until it was blended.

"It doesn't seem like juice," Finn said. "It's so squishy. You can't drink solid chunks."

"Squish it until there are no chunks left." Their hands circled the tub, blending the sugar and water with the liquified berries.

"You're telling me we're going to put a lid on this thing and in a week it'll be alcohol?" Finn said.

"Depending on how hot it'll be, but yes."

"It's pretty hot, Isa."

She kept her gaze firmly on the raspberries! "It won't be particularly strong alcohol. To make it stronger, I'll need to boil it and then distill it."

After a moment of silence he nudged her head with his.

"What?" she said. But she didn't look up.

"You're going to distill this in our kitchen?"

She was very focused on her hands inside the bucket—and on his big, bare, tanned forearms pressing against her bare arms. "You're right, maybe I should cook it on firepit outside instead."

"Good idea," he said.

"Shame, because boiling mash is one of best smells you'll ever smell."

"But not *the* best, right?"

She mustn't look at him! "I said *one* of the best. Finn, you're not mushing. You're just . . ."

"What am I doing, Isa?"

"Nothing remotely helpful is what you're doing," Isabelle said, lifting her hands out of the bucket and shaking off the excess juice. Some of it landed on Finn's white tank top.

"I wouldn't play that game if I were you," he said, lifting his own hands.

"No, stop!" She grabbed his forearms. "You're going to get me filthy. Put lid on it."

"Excuse me?"

"On tub. Put lid on tub and move into pantry. I'll switch out containers. We need to hurry. We have evening watering to do and eggplant to pick."

"Ah, yes," he said, lifting the heavy container. "Watering. Eggplant. The farmer's work is never done."

They spent extra time methodically pulping the mash in the second container. Isabelle didn't want it to stop. They were quiet until Finn spoke. "When Travis and I were fifteen or so," he said, "I had a mad crush on a girl at the park, and I didn't know how to tell her." His gaze remained lowered.

"Oh yeah? So what did you do?"

"What do you think I should have done?"

"Told her, I suppose. Unless she already knew." Her hands were near his, mixing, mixing. "Did your girl know you were in love with her?" she asked, staring at his lowered blond head.

Finn was silent. His gaze was on the raspberries. Presently he raised his eyes and stared into her face. Their gazes locked. "I don't know, Isabelle," he said in a deep low voice. *"Does she?"*

Isabelle! Your lover stands too close. Yes, the fields are burning, but you haven't yet christened all the stars in the sky with his name. Be brave and run before the scales fall from your eyes. Or does his true heart remind you that you are still alive, that you want to live, that no matter how near the ground you eat and sleep, you still want a fairytale to make you fly through hoops of flame?

She couldn't even raise her raspberry-soaked hands in surrender. "Finn, *please*," she whispered.

He leaned forward and kissed her. Her arms trembled. His hands were still immersed in the raspberry mash, her wrists encircled in his clenched fists. He kissed her until she moaned.

"Finn, we *can't*."

"I'm well aware." His mouth was on her. "But I can't *not*." His panting lips traveled to her throat, to her neckline. He rubbed his face into the swell of her breasts.

She tipped toward him, wobbling. "Don't touch me."

"You don't want me to touch you?"

"With *those* hands?"

"Yes, Isabelle. With these hands." He raised them out of the tub and held them splayed open in front of her, dripping with berry juice.

Everything was forgotten. Her red hands slid around his neck. She pulled him to her and kissed him madly. He threw his arms around her, clutched her, rent her wraparound dress apart, fondled her, her bare breasts cupped in his intense hands drenched with berries. Gripping her ribcage, he lowered his lips to her nipples, sticky with red hot pulpy sweetness. There was no control or order or cleanliness, no pretense or courtesy. There were no manners. There was no civilization. They tore at each other. His tank flew off. He pulled her around to his side of the table and rubbed his sticky chest against her sticky breasts, against her red hard nipples. She fumbled with the drawstring on his trousers, pulling them down, pulling him up into her avid hands. They both groaned. He hoisted her up on the table, sat her at the edge, and opening her hips, tugged her forward. She threw her legs around him. They couldn't stay quiet. "Finn, wait, wait, we *can't!*" They were out in the open. Anyone in the house, old and very young, could walk around back and find them on the worktable, flagrantly exposed.

Still coupled together, his hands under her, he carried her into the shower enclosure, hidden between the outside shed and the root cellar, and pushed her flat against the wooden stall.

"*Bozhe Mii*," was all she could say.

"*Oh my God*," was all he could say.

Her colt legs around him quivered but never faltered. She clasped him into her thighs as they tried desperately to suppress their noises except the panting, and the sloshing pulp of their hands, and their bodies crashing against one another. To dampen the sound and to smother the fire, with one hand still underneath her, Finn spun the lever with the other and forced the pump down to release a few gallons of hot August water from the shower head, drenching them. He pushed the pump down again. And again. And again. There came a flashpoint so extreme, he let go of her, delivering himself to her under a flood, just before she cried out for the world to hear. His hands holding her up lost their strength for a moment. Her legs, wrapped around him, never lost theirs.

The liquid slowed to a trickle, then to a drip. They stayed slammed against the stall with his lips at her throat. The only thing Finn whispered before he set her to the ground was, "Oh, Isabelle."

They washed their red hands, their red steaming bodies, scrubbed soap on their throats, on their faces, between their legs. She was still wearing her yellow dress like a soaked, flung-open robe. He kissed her deeply, kissed her hands, threw on his clothes, still on the ground where they'd left them, and walked away.

Isabelle heard the squealing laughter of his children greeting him as he came around the house. To regain her composure, she pumped out the remaining water and stood under it for a few moments. Everything inside, from her soul to her loins, was on fire. Holding the wet dress to herself, she tiptoed, dripping, to her dusky little room and fell to her knees, pressing her face into her dress.

Afterward she dried herself as best she could and dressed, though it was so humid, her skin was wet before she tied the sash around her waist. She rinsed out the stained yellow dress under a spigot, hung it up, performed other rituals of organization to calm her hands and her nerves, and then stood in the side yard, smoking a cigarette, looking up at the sky, saying *why why why*.

She knew why.

But my God.

It was nearly five on a Saturday afternoon. He planned to grill some chicken and hamburgers, she planned to make a salad with potatoes, they planned to sit with eight other people, two of them his children, one of them his wife, and serve and spoon and sit and socialize, pass the peas, pass the beans, pass the beets, in between their impossible gestures all their dreams and screams smothering their pointless questions. The fields burned and they were left in the dirt. That was the answer.

She tamped out her cigarette and sealed the criminal mash that overrode all reason, that compelled her to negate all sense, that drove her to enter a new dimension of time and space—a realm where she wasn't half destroyed.

She tried so hard to be circumspect and good, to be vigilant and proper, but her love for him poured out, flooding the fields and rivers.

It started with bloodshed, she thought, walking through the pantry to get the cucumbers and tomatoes before entering the kitchen.

Would it end with bloodshed?

Isabelle didn't know how she got through dinner. Through sitting, chatting, smoking, cleaning up, making conversation. It was excruciating. She didn't look at him, nor address him. She spoke no malapropisms and responded to no teasing. That was easy because there was no teasing coming from Finn. She cleaned and wiped and got ready for tomorrow. She wouldn't even go into the fields for her usual last check for fear he would follow her. When it was almost dark, they listened to the *Jack Benny Show*, and she said goodnight and went up with the girls, where she stayed all night on their hard floor. She and Finn didn't even have their ritual evening smoke! She stayed upstairs because she was terrified that he would come into her room, come inside without even knocking.

She was terrified that he wouldn't.

On Sunday she barely dragged herself up and out at eight in the morning, as if she had pneumonia.

He'd already made a pot of coffee and was out in the fields. For reasons unclear, Vanessa sauntered into the kitchen. What was worse, facing Finn or facing Vanessa? Isabelle was about to find out.

"You're up early," Isabelle said.

"I don't know what was wrong with Finn last night," Vanessa said. "He tossed and turned nonstop! Usually he sleeps like a fallen tree. I barely got any rest because of him. I thought if I'm up anyway, I might as well have some breakfast. It is *so* hot, Isabelle."

"I *know*."

"Finn said he wanted to take the girls to the ocean to cool off. Will you go with him?"

Isabelle made some unintelligible noise.

"Maybe my parents and his will want to go too."

"Schumann may be coming today," Isabelle muttered. "And Lucas. I don't know if they'll want to go to beach. They probably don't have any swimwear. I certainly don't."

"They still come only once a month, don't they?" said Vanessa. "They were here just last Sunday. Remember Finn, Earl, Lucas, and you went fishing? I've been picking pike bones out of my teeth all week."

Isabelle grunted.

"By the way, the girls told me you made thirty dollars yesterday selling eggplant—and then spent it all on raspberries?"

"Not all on, um, raspberries."

"Thirty dollars is very good," said Vanessa.

Isabelle shrugged. It was a *lot* of work for thirty dollars. She'd rather appraise a horse for a hundred. "Olivia's eggplant is talk of town. Line was forty people before we even set up at our table."

"Yes, Junie told me. I wouldn't mind having some of those raspberries, though. Maybe with some whipped cream like you made at the party?"

"We don't have any cream. Or raspberries. I'll get you some next week."

"What do you mean we don't have any raspberries? You *ate* them?"

"We used them."

"On what? And who is we?"

"Me—and your girls—and Finn." Isabelle made sure to position two innocent children in the words between herself and her lover. "We're making brew for winter. That compote we've been talking about." Isabelle never looked at Vanessa as they spoke, pretending to search for a frying pan, a log for the fire, an egg. She wasn't hungry, and she could barely drink her coffee. It kept coming up in her throat. The throat he had kissed so forcefully that her breath couldn't escape her lungs. Even now, when his lips were no longer on her and she was chatting with his wife, she still couldn't breathe.

In the fields, she went straight to Eleanor to help her pull the zucchini off the vine without ripping out the entire plant. "Gently, gently," Isabelle said. She talked to Earl about his insect worries. The tin cans and chimes kept away the birds, but the aphids and locusts cared nothing for noise and were eating the leaves off his beloved tomatoes. "They come during day," Isabelle said. "Most bugs are not nocturnal. In summer, we need to remove ripe vegetables at first light, definitely before eight. Bugs won't eat green tomatoes."

"You think I'm not here early enough?" Earl said. "It's Sunday. Is there no day of rest on the farm?"

"Bugs unfortunately do not know Jesus," Isabelle said. "But other thing we used to do in Ispas is leave two or three ripe tomatoes on vine for bugs to feast on. Insects are herd creatures. They follow first offender and leave rest of tomatoes alone." Earl agreed this was a good idea.

Olivia kept digging up potatoes that weren't fully grown. She was using the shovel, but she needed to crouch and feel for the potato with her hands and leave it if it wasn't big enough. "Girls need to help you with this part, Olivia," said Isabelle. "You mustn't dig them yet. They are not ready. Mae, Junebug! Come here! Your nana needs you."

Monty had gone fishing with Walter. They were out by the river, trying to catch another pike for a Sunday feast.

Finn was in the corn.

She pumped the water out of the cistern into the channels by the beds. She hoped it would rain soon. The reservoirs were dangerously low on water. The shower tank was bone empty.

She felt him before she saw him or heard him.

"*Isabelle.*"

"Don't say my name like that." She could hardly look at him, could barely speak, for how could you hide the truth? *I need you inside me* was truth. Everything else was a dirty lie.

"Like what?"

"Please..."

"Where were you last night?" He lowered his voice. "I looked for you."

"Up with your children. I fell asleep." She barely got two hours.

"*Isabelle...*" he whispered.

"We're going to lose everything."

"What's everything?"

She swirled her arm to the field and farm.

"No, we won't," he said. "We'll hide like we've been hiding."

"It's one thing to hide your heart..."

"Is this not also your heart?" He tilted his head to peer into her face. The expression in his eyes was imploring, adoring, overflowing.

"Finn!" Her legs were buckling. "If anyone catches glimpse of us speaking right now, they'll instantly know what it means."

"It can mean a thousand things."

"No," she said. "Some things can only be understood one way because they have only one meaning."

He continued to gaze at her as if the rest of the world had fallen away.

"Finn, don't do that..."

"Don't do what?" he said huskily.

"Someone will see."

"See what?"

"The way you're looking at me."

"How am I looking at you?"

She nearly moaned. "Before yesterday, I had some control over myself."

"Not me."

Her head was down. She took a stumbling step away from him. One more word and he might take her then and there in full sun in the dust by the well.

And what was even worse, one more word—and she would let him.

"I need to go help your mother," she said hoarsely. "She is going to ruin our potato harvest. She needs to wait."

"I *can't* wait."

She took another shaky step back.

He reached for her. His hand circled her wrist and squeezed. "Come with me to the barn."

"Finn, you're crazy!" She didn't even pretend to pull away.

"Crazed, yes. Come with me behind the corn crib. For a cigarette."

"That's what you call it?"

"The hay inside the stables needs fixing. One of the gates broke. It's an emergency. *Come.*"

"Some emergency. We have no horses."

"We do, and they're *all* about to get out. *All* of them, Isabelle."

"My God, what are we going to do?"

"I'll show you. *Come.*"

And so went the scorched-earth dog day afternoon when the world caught on fire.

70

Clams and Stallions

"Aaaand—they're coming down the stretch, ladies and gentlemen! What a sight! Starfire, the dark horse of this race, has taken an astonishing lead! He's leaving the competition in the dust!"

The sound of horses' hooves pounding on the track grew louder.

"As they approach the finish line, Starfire is widening the gap, folks! It's a true spectacle!"

The crowd noise reached a crescendo.

"Starfire crosses the finish line at 2:01 and 3/5ths of a second and wins the Travers Stakes by a *staggering* seven lengths! Ladies and gentlemen, what an incredible victory!"

The crowd erupted in cheers and applause.

"What an *extraordinary* performance by Starfire! Only Man O'War, one of the greatest horses in racing history, has won this race with a faster time! And there you have it, folks! A historic moment in horse racing! Starfire, the dazzling newcomer, has left us all in awe! Who is this remarkable colt that has swept the field in Saratoga in such spectacular fashion?"

Walter and Earl had bet twenty dollars each on Starfire to win.

The odds were 100:1.

When Finn had asked Isabelle how sure she was about her stallion, she told him to bet nothing. "What have you learned from October 29, 1929?"

"So, you have no faith at all is what you're saying?"

He had bet a hundred dollars—the money his girls earned in one full week of selling their vegetables at the market.

But Finn and Isabelle had no idea that Starfire had won. Two days earlier, they'd gone clamming in Truro, a hundred miles across the water.

Bryson's friend Bertie Dunn lent them his boat as a favor, in exchange for a pail of Cape Cod quahogs and an introduction to the "bountylicious" Eleanor.

Finn and Isabelle took with them clam rakes, pails, fishing lines, mesh baskets, and gloves. Isabelle brought two sandwiches and a flask of Schumann's strongest brew.

They set out at first light.

They were gone four days.

71

Return

They returned with a pail of live clams and a hundred dollars. There was a storm, they said. They couldn't dig until the tide went out—and the tide wouldn't go out. Afterward, there was a bounty of clams such as Finn had never seen. They could've dug for a month.

The family didn't care about the clamming, the storm, the four-day absence, and they especially didn't care about the hundred dollars.

Starfire was the only thing they wanted to talk about.

Walter and Earl had won $2000 each!

"How much did you win, son?" Earl asked.

Finn didn't want to tell his father he had risked a hundred dollars of the family's money on a gamble, even if he did end up winning $10,000. "About as much as you and Walter, Father," he said. "Maybe a few dollars more."

While the family recounted every detail of the thrilling race over and over, Isabelle steamed the clams and tossed them with garlic and olive oil and fresh tomatoes and spooned them over handmade pasta. They had fried bread on the side. They opened a bottle of apple cider and Coca-Cola.

"Speaking of drinks," said Olivia, "your raspberry mash is smelling a little off, Isabelle. I was in the outdoor pantry the other day, and the odor from the containers was pungent. Should we compost it?"

"Thanks, Olivia, but no," said Isabelle. "Soon maybe, if I have time, I will make beverage out of it."

"Why wouldn't you have time?"

"It's harvest season," Isabelle said quietly. "And mash takes long time. It needs to be boiled to get rid of impurities and to concentrate flavor."

"Is there a word for that?" asked Walter.

"Yes. It's called distilling."

"No kidding," said Walter, exchanging a glance with Earl and Finn.

Olivia perked up. "Distilling? You mean similar to alcohol?"

"Similar, yes," said Isabelle.

"Is that the compote you and Finn have been going on and on about? Son, what's that joke you and Isabelle make about compote and compost?"

"I don't recall," said Finn, his neutral gaze on his mother.

"Isabelle," said Walter, "after what you did, Mickey Winslow is going to be at your door with flowers and a blanket, begging you to go work for him."

"What did I do?" Isabelle said without humor or a smile.

"You won him the coveted Man O'War trophy! You found him a historic racehorse. He's a businessman. He'll throw money at you until you say yes."

"Isabelle can't work for him," Junie said. "She is ours. Isabelle, while you were digging clams, we were digging tatums, but it was so hard to find good ones without you."

"What are tatums?"

"I said taters!"

"Junie, speak clearly so she can understand you," said Finn.

"*She* is a cat, Daddy," said Mae. "You told us yourself—never say *she* when the person you're talking about is present."

"You're right, Mayflower, bad manners on Daddy's part." But Finn didn't speak Isabelle's name. "Say taters, June. Or potatoes."

"Tatums is a much better word, Daddy," said Junie. "Right, Isabelle?"

"Tatums may be my favorite word, Junebug," Isabelle said. "But it's not time for tatums yet. Right, Olivia? Few more weeks."

"Junie is right, though, Isabelle," said Eleanor. "You were gone too long. Tell me about this Bertie Dunn person. Is he a married fellow?"

"Oh, hush, you all," said Vanessa, spooning seconds onto her plate. "Look at the king's feast we're having. This is the best meal I've had in years. Finn, darling, do you remember how you used to dig clams for us when we had that marvelous house on Cape Cod? You'd return carrying the wire basket and the girls would be jumping up and down. They couldn't wait to see how many you got. We taught our babies to count to twenty on those clams." She sighed wistfully. "Those were happier days."

"I don't know, daughter," Walter said, sparing Finn an answer. "Isabelle just made our family thousands of dollars. We're growing our own wheat and tomatoes, and soon we may make our own raspberry juice." He winked at Isabelle. "I say these times are pretty tootin' good." He raised a glass to happiness and they all clinked with him.

72

Live Cover

Bertie's small sturdy boat had a cuddy at the bow and above it a small deck, where Isabelle reclined while Finn was behind her at the wheel inside the canopied cabin. Propped up on her elbows in a loose summer frock, she lounged in front of him, her long legs stretched out, her head tipped back, her face to the sun.

When she opened her eyes, she saw him watching her.

"Are we there soon?" she said. "Have you even looked at compass?"

"Something is orienting me," he said, turning his gaze to the sea. "I'm heading south. That's all I know. Like you, I will find my way."

"I didn't find my way," she said. "Cici found it for us. And Black Sea coastline hundreds kilometers long. Hard to miss. But narrow Cape Cod? Ten miles wide maybe. Overshoot Provincetown, we're lost at sea until Portugal."

Finn said nothing.

"We're going to run out of fuel before Portugal," he finally said.

"Yes, that's only problem with missing Cape Cod."

And Finn said nothing.

"But seriously, Finn, I don't know how to rake clams."

"I'll teach you. Just like you rake the earth," he said. "But more fun and you're in the water. You hold the handle with both hands and pull toward you." He smiled, she smiled. "You'll hear an unmistakable clink when you find one. I know several good places in the salt marshes near Truro. If the seabed is full, we'll harvest as much as our backs will allow."

After an hour of the sun on her face, Isabelle asked a follow-up question. "How much do clams sell for?"

"I've never sold them before," he said. "Bertie said they go for fifty cents a pound in Hampton. Perhaps more on the Cape. We'll see."

"How many in pound?"

"Five to ten, depending on size."

"*Why does it always depend on size?*" Isabelle said in a Mae West voice. "Um, fifty *cents* for ten clams?" She laughed.

"I didn't say it wasn't going to be work," Finn said. "We might have to be at it for a few days."

She turned her gaze away.

"You don't have a joke for that?" he said.

She put the hat over her face to contain her smile.

There was beauty on the still, flat ocean, salty breeze rustling the ropes, the squawking of seagulls overhead, distant sandpipers, laughter from a passing boat. There was so much to say and they said none of it. It took them five nearly silent hours to get from Hampton to Truro and when they got there, they knew each other better.

She asked him what he wished for. *If you could have anything you wanted.*

He said, raspberry moonshine.

We don't have that kind of time. She was already longing for more.

If I could ask you anything, he said, what would it be?

She said she couldn't hear him over the silence of the salty sea. But she wanted him to ask her to ask him when he first knew she loved him. *When did you first know I loved you, Finn?*

Still some way from shore, near the edge of Cape Cod Bay, he dropped anchor, took off his clothes, and jumped into the water to cool off. She watched him, a rippling, ripped, bobbing fool.

Come into the water with me, he said, slicking his hair back.

She searched the sea for other people. But it was just him and her.

He climbed out to lie by her side, dripping wet and getting her wet too. You asked me what I wanted, he said. It's this. Just you and me.

It was always just you and me. Sitting on our bench side by side, smoking, drinking, talking about our day.

He lowered his soft lips to her shoulder. The beard around his mouth tickled her, prickled her. Now might be good time to ask me what live cover is, she said in a thickening alto.

Raising himself above her on his wet arms, Finn smiled. I *know*, he said. It's when horses are brought together physically to mate.

Live cover is a life bond, she said. We're in the wake now. She placed her palms on his bare chest, tipping, tipping back. Boats will come in. Under her fingers was his thundering heart.

Yes, boats will *also* come in, said Finn. Who are you afraid will see us?

I'm not afraid. *Not of that.*

Show me, he said, caressing her face, his fingers gliding up and down the inside of her arm.

Finn.

Isabelle. Open your dress. Show me.

We are on deck. It's broad daylight.

Yes. I'm not jumping ahead, to tonight, to clams, to tomorrow. This is what we came for, we're in the mystic show.

She rubbed her lips against his damp chest, pressed her cheek to him. *Can I tell you my words of love*, she whispered.

Show me, Isabelle.

She opened her dress for him. She opened her soul, her heart, her all to him.

The deck was good for a picture of love from above, but it wasn't good for actual love. They clambered into the triangular hold below the stern, just wide enough to fit one man and one woman side by side, barely high enough to fit a man and a woman stacked, barely enough for a big man to fit.

He stretched out flat on top of her and she stretched out flat under him.

It was effective, and good enough.

He sat halfway up against the side of the cuddy and she climbed into his lap. And that was good enough too. Naked he wrapped around her like a bear with all his paws. Naked she wrapped around him like a mama bear with all of hers. They kissed as if no man and woman had ever kissed before them, or ever would again.

His large strong hands around her, her slim strong hips around him, they barely had to move. The boat moved, and they moved with it. It bobbed and swayed, back and forth, back and forth, it drifted and rocked, side to side, side to side, it rolled and surged and surged and surged—and finally pitched forward.

His body listed, his head fell back. He was without words. *Finn*, she whispered, kissing him. *Finn* . . . He said he wasn't done. He said he hadn't even begun. *I'm just passed out in my ecstasy*, whispered Finn.

The tide came out.

The tide came in.

In the opaque sun the wind kicked up, the waves got rough, they beat and beat against the boat.

Finally, when they couldn't breathe, they fell into the sea in flames.

I'm burning my hands on you, he whispered. There was no inside and no outside, no Finn, no Isabelle, no his, no hers, no separate wishes, no separate dreams.

Their impassioned cries skipped across the water like flat stones.

I can't believe I'm kissing you, he whispered, kissing her, *caressing you*, he whispered, caressing her, *making love to you*, he whispered, making love to her, *holding you.* Actually *holding you, wet and soft and naked, not on a landing, not for a moment, not in an accident, not with eyes closed. Maybe a little bit with eyes closed.* She wrapped her legs around him in response and drew him in, and he groaned, *help,* and she said, *help is on the way.*

I can't believe I'm holding you, she whispered, holding him wet and hard and naked, *I'm kissing you,* she whispered, kissing him, *caressing you,* she whispered, caressing him, *making love to you,* she said, her mouth a gift to him and to herself.

Tell truth, she murmured in the glow, *tell me you weren't casing your house on all landings for days afterward hoping for another wet run-in.*

Oh, every night, he said, and she laughed, and he said, you think I'm joking? And she said, of *course* not, my love.

He made love to her face to face, held her down, roped them together. But she was an acrobat, a phantasmagorical funambulist. No face to face could contain her. Their famished bodies stretched out on a rack, they tumbled and rolled. She was face down, he was behind her, he covered her with himself from head to foot and she cried out his name, passed out in her own ecstasy.

They never slept.

Isa, tell me, what do Ukrainian girls like best? Is it this?
Tak.
Or this?
Tak.
And this?
Tak.
Best, Isabelle, what do you like best?
I like you best, she said.
After a while, she murmured, *anything you do is good with me.*
Anything?
Anything. Dream, Finn, dream big, and let me dream with you.

They forgot the clams, missed another tide. He raised anchor, took them closer to shore, hid them in the reeds and the marshes from all but the tingling stars, their hearts soaring above the fork-tailed woodnymphs and the violet-fronted brilliants. He said they'd clam doubly hard tomorrow. Her arms were tossed above her head. What are clams, she said. And what is tomorrow?

They dragged their boat onto the sandy bank and stood side by side in four feet of water. They pulled their rakes until they heard a clink or two, but most of the clams were gone. They got scorched by wind, by sun, and the sea washed over them and another night and another briny breathless morning.

At dawn they drank whisky that went straight to their heads and made them lose all sense; the whisky, right? We forgot to eat, she said when drenched hours swam by and they still weren't sober.

We forgot a lot, he said.

They crawled out of the sea and remembered the clams. They won't care if we don't find them, she said. But they tried again. Barely clad and hungover, they stood half submerged, they raked and clanked, crawled on the sand, kept tumbling over. I think these clams you speak of may just be pigment of your imagination, she said. He laughed and didn't correct her. The clams fell into their basket one by one. Slowly they counted them, as if they had just learned to count. Are there only *twenty*? she muttered. So we made *one dollar*? That can't be right. We've been clamming for days.

Is *that* what you call it, said Finn, kicking over the basket of the freed and fortunate clams, lifting her and carrying her through the shallow waters to their cuddy cave on the bay.

They lay on the hard narrow bed of their rebirth and flew through the minutes, fleeting and everlasting, the boat rocking, rocking, the lulling sound of the Truro tide splashing near. They were soaked, conjoined, hot.

You have *undone* me, he said.

I've undone *you*?

Isabelle . . . He fondled her breasts, kissed her nipples. His warm fingers caressed her. *I have nothing to say*, he whispered. *I just wanted to hear your exquisite name on my lips. Even before raspberries, before* this, *I could hardly speak your name without tremor. Your three syllables hold the storied volumes of everything I feel for you.* Your name, he said, is where I hide my love.

It's not where you hide it, she said. It's where you carry it.

No one had ever held him closer, loved him harder, kissed him with more tenderness or abandon.

Isa, what's *laska*?

What you're doing to me right now, that's *laska*. What we've been doing on the swaying water, that's *laska*.

Isa . . . what's *miy kohanyi*?

You, Finn Esmond Evans, my beloved lover, are miy kohanyi, whispered Isabelle.

She was helpless and in thrall, famished and filled up, emptied and overflowing. Am I ashes or fire? Am I the moon or the stars, am I dreams or terror, broken or put together? Am I fragile or flint, made of straw or of brick? Do I swim? Do I drown?

Do I fly? Do I fall?

Yes. Yes to all these things.

His lips charred her flesh from the nape of her neck, down the length of her spine. His mouth was motionless between her thighs, as if he had forgotten where he was or was maybe praying. He raised her up to him with the palms of his hands like she was holy water. She started to cry and he said why and she said it's right to weep when grace is offered you, grace you don't deserve.

That's why they call it grace. He was on his knees when he said it.

If only she could tell him of the long ago forfeit of her life and what she had recovered here with him in these breathless days. She hadn't been touched in so long. She hadn't been loved in so long. Hadn't been wanted, valued, beloved.

Yes, you were, Isabelle. My God, every day you were, and every night. Just without live cover.

Do you know how long it's been since somebody held me? she said. I didn't realize how lonely I was until I started spending my days with you.

You're not the only one, he said. I lived my life, but I had no one to share my life. I forgot who I was. I don't know if I ever knew. And then you came.

They whispered each other's names. They shouted them from mountains of heaven.

All words were spoken, all feats laid bare. She gave him herself. He gave her himself. He took from her. He received from her. She took from him. She received from him. She worshipped him. She adored him. She offered him all he wanted. She offered him all she had.

And he took it.

When did you first know I loved you, Finn?

When you told me to leave you, he said. In the street that cold January when we fought in the rain and you told me to go.

That's when you knew I *loved* you?

I don't know if that's when *you* first knew it, he said. Only when I did.

She laughed. Why, because I told you to say goodbye and go?

Tak, he said. You told me to go because you knew I never would.

She nearly wept.

I loved you long before then, said Isabelle.

How many pink suns were in their future? Why did it feel that one of these gold dawns would be their last, and she would never know which one until it was already behind her?

Finn, what's our story going to be? What has it been before this? This is the part where I serve out my sorrow, where I tell you what I truly hope for, what I wish for, what I'm waiting for. What do *you* hope for, my sweetest friend, my heart, my life, my fire? She held him in her mighty limbs, on her mighty wings. *We are thunderbirds*, she whispered. *We are flying so high, I can see the cranes below us, below the clouds. Eventually, even we must ground.*

What the romantics told them to do, they did. What the poets wrote for them, they said. They bounced and bounded, they let the overflowing tide pull them back into the deepest water. They roped their boat to the shore and lay on the sandbar on their backs, they held hands and popped with joy in their snapshot of found life. *We will stay here*, he whispered, *and dream upon our dreams and wish upon our wishes and love upon our love and cry upon our cries. We are not worn out by life, we are not blackened, we are not old. Nothing has failed. I reached out and said help me and you were near my hand, you never left me. You think you are a ghost, Isabelle, but if so, you are a ghost aflame. In my secret life with you, you have never known savagery. No matter what fate has made of you, you have made of yourself an immortal priestess and crowned yourself and me with triumph and promise.*

They had to either run—and keep running—or return.

Like clams, we crawled outside ourselves and got caught, she said as their time grew short. We should've continued to hide in shelled silence between our breaths and our cigarettes.

No, he said. Three years is all I had of the other me.

To save us, we should've kept to just part of us. Part we could show.

Is that what you want?

What do *you* want, Finn?

Let's not go back.

Is *that* what you want? To be man who doesn't go back?

Finn didn't reply. *Let's lie on our backs and dream the impossible dream for just one more moment, Isabelle.*

Finally they lurched back, shut down as if in mourning. "How many days has it been?" She put her face in her hands. They had caught no clams, not even a one. They walked to a monger in Truro and from him bought enough small and tender quahogs to fill two pails' worth, one for the house and one for Bertie. It cost them a hundred dollars. Good thing they'd brought some cash with them. They arranged the clams in the buckets filled with wet sand and layers of newspaper and wordlessly set out for home. In the middle of the ocean, they dropped anchor and made mute furious love, like they were underwater, gasping for life, their lungs filling up with death.

I'm a warrior who wants to serve a queen.

I'm no queen. I'm also a warrior, who wants to serve a king.

"We are glittering and insatiable," he said. "Every time we kiss, we are back in red pulp up to our hearts."

In Hampton, after they tied up Bertie's boat and returned to their truck, for a long time he embraced her, held her to him without speaking, caressed her face. *Isabelle*, he whispered.

Finn, she whispered back.

73

Reaping

Here is how you hide when there's nowhere to hide: you work until your hands fall off. You work until you fall into bed and are asleep before your head hits the pillow. You steady your gaze on the job ahead, and you don't look up. And at the end of the night, when everyone else has gone to bed and the world is still, you sit beside the gorgeous smoking man and ask him to give you your heart back. And he says he will never. And then you go your separate ways, he to his bed and you to yours.

But before another hard day dawns, he opens the door to your chamber, and for a few minutes before the house rises you remind each other why it can't be any other way. In the earliest morning, you go to church. You lower your heads, you fold your hands, and with your palms up you receive communion. You kneel and say thank you and kiss the cup in your abandon.

September was a time for reaping. There was more work in September than during any other month, and all of it had to be done by the hands that held his steadfast love, held his love until the hands couldn't close into fists.

They cut the wheat down with their nineteenth-century scythes, even though Walter didn't want to. He said the ripe stalks looked too majestic, swaying golden in the breeze at sunset. Walter and Earl both said that next year they would sow a whole field of wheat, not just two long rows.

Finn agreed. There was never enough beauty. But sometimes if you were lucky, he said, there was just enough.

Isabelle, there are tools in this barn I've never seen. Come inside for a second and tell me what they are. What's a grain cradle scythe? Is that what you're using? Look at these serrated edges, the long fingers, the curved blades. No wonder you are so much faster than the rest of us. Look at your weapon. Put it down for a second, Isabelle. Put down the scythe and come here.

She smiled all day as she swept the heavy cutter against the base of the plants.

They stuffed the bundled stalks into large burlap sacks and threshed them against the walls of the barn and the stable and the corn crib, they flailed them until the wheat berries separated from the shafts and fell to the bottom of the bags.

They poured the berries onto clean sheets spread out on the ground and winnowed them with large pieces of cardboard until the chaff flew away. Finn and Isabelle threw the berries up in the air like confetti, like rice at a wedding, like their hearts. The children imitated them, the light husks quivering like dandelion fluff, the heavy grain falling onto the white sheets. They gathered the wheat berries into bins and brought them inside for Vanessa.

Finally, a job Vanessa was born to do. For many September days she sat at the dining table and painstakingly cleaned the wheat of debris. She sifted the berries through her fingers or ran them through a sieve. She threw out the blackened and the cracked and filled bushel after bushel with gorgeous, oval, beige-colored, perfect grain.

Up in the empty barn which smells like dry grass and hot sun and earth, there's a loft with a ladder, and this loft has windows and a view. Isabelle, you can see past the trees to the river, to other meadows, to the very sea. Climb up on me, let me show you.

When September was over and done, the family had harvested six bushels of wheat, totaling 360 pounds of grain, equaling 360 pounds of milled flour. They were amazed. It seemed so much. Isabelle had to gently explain that two loaves of bread used a pound and a half of flour, and their large family of eleven ate two loaves of bread a day. Not including cookies, cakes, pies, pastries, the thickening of sauces, and the formation of dumplings. Six bushels wouldn't last them until next harvest.

That was even more astonishing.

Isabelle, why do you enjoy shocking the hell out of everyone? I saw it on your face. You rejoice in their exclamations. Come inside the granary, quick.

Why, Finn, do you want to shock hell out of me?

Next spring they could plant one additional row, Isabelle said. Three rows would yield them 540 pounds of wheat, Finn said. "Meantime, it's not as if we don't have money to buy flour. Starfire took care of that." He grinned.

"Starfire and Electric Boat," said Isabelle, grinning back.

"I want to plant a whole field more, not one *row* more!" said Walter.

"Walter, calm yourself," cried Lucy. "How on God's green earth are we going to reap a *field* of wheat? Two lousy rows almost killed this family!"

September. Two bushels of oats, a *thousand* ears of corn. For days the children sat cross-legged on the ground inside the corn maze, surrounded by hills of silks and husks, eating the sugar-sweet ears raw, and singing with joy.

Are you singing with joy too, Isa?

You know it. No, ne grustna ya, ne pechalna ya, uteshitelna mne sudjba moya . . .

To Olivia's delight, the "tatums" were finally so plentiful, Isabelle feared they might need to build another root cellar to store them. When one massive root cellar wasn't enough, you knew you had a good harvest.

The family agreed. It was a spectacular one.

It was a harvest like I've never ever seen.

Nor me, Finn.

It was abundant and unexpected.

Not unexpected. As we always say where I come from—you reap what you sow.

In October they picked and carved out pumpkins, decorated them into jack-o'-lanterns, and canned the puree. They turned over the fields and prepared them for the winter. The wood supports were taken down, the rows were tilled and cleared of old roots. Isabelle planted oats as cover crops in some of the beds to improve the soil's richness. They repaired their equipment, bought new rakes and rotary tillers, fixed doors and fence gates, and chopped enough wood to last two winters.

Isabelle, are you coming into the woods with me? I brought my axe.

Always, Finn. Want to play hide-and-seek? You can be woodsman.

They insulated the windows and bought a gasoline-powered snow blower to make it easier for the truck and the newly bought car to get out. The new Ford V8 sedan was a remarkable model with an innovative flathead engine, which greatly increased the performance and power of the vehicle.

"Performance and power are key," said Finn, who liked his cars.

Isabelle agreed.

Isa, take a drive with me to the ocean in our new spacious Ford to catch first light. Let's climb in the back seat. We can see the sunrise better from there.

Finn, I can't see anything at all.

Can't you, Isabelle?

Not the sunrise!

They stored the scarecrows in the barn, in the hay under the ladder, under the loft, under the windows that faced the fields and the river, and the sea.

Isa, let me kiss the palms of your hands. Let me kiss the backs of your legs, let me fall asleep with you again, just once. Let me wake with you again, just once.

They figured out that part too. When there was no more field work, she went to Boston to spend a few days with Schumann. Finn drove her, and spent the day with Lucas. They left together and came back separately. He drove back one day and she took a train the next. And while they were there, they spent one sleepless torrential night at the Parker House Hotel on the Boston Common, in the largest bed their money could buy.

In November 1932, Franklin Roosevelt clobbered Herbert Hoover in the presidential election, winning by 479 electoral votes to Hoover's 59. The Adams farm celebrated with the rest of America. Isabelle doled out small glasses of her awe-inspiring raspberry moonshine. She had distilled eight quarts back in September, and a quart was all that was left. She and Finn had partaken quite a bit of the fiery potion after hours.

It's communion wine, Finn said. *It's communion time.*

It was, it was.

"Isabelle, is this what you and the girls mashed together in August?" exclaimed Olivia, running her finger around the inside of the glass, scraping out the last of the red sticky liquid. "How did you make it so sweet and delicious?"

Good question, Isabelle.

"I fermented it for long time and boiled it to make it stronger."

"I didn't smell this being cooked inside the house," Olivia said. "The scent is hard to hide." She stuck her face into the empty glass and inhaled deeply. "Impossible, I'd say."

"Nothing is impossible to hide, Mother," said Finn. Olivia clearly thought he was referring to her. She looked wounded. And he could have said, I wasn't talking about you, Mom, but couldn't and didn't.

I couldn't apologize to her, Isa, without explaining what I really meant.

"I cooked it outside over firepit, Olivia," Isabelle said hastily. "I didn't want to upset anyone."

And right on cue—Vanessa glared at Finn. "Homemade moonshine is against the law," Vanessa said, dour as all that.

"That's why I didn't make it inside," said Isabelle.

"Vanessa!" Walter said to his daughter. "What's the point of finger wagging now? Roosevelt won!"

"But she didn't know Roosevelt would win, Daddy."

"You'd have to be simple-minded to think otherwise," said Walter. "Bottle up, girl. It's over. Prohibition is as good as dead."

"And good riddance," said Earl, Finn, and even Eleanor.

"Isabelle, is this all you got from those huge vats of red mash?" Olivia said. "That can't be right."

We got a lot from that red mash, Isa, didn't we?

"Some of it was lost in the distilling process, Mother," Finn said smoothly. "Don't worry. We have *plenty*." He smiled.

"Then perhaps there's a tiny bit more for your mother, darling?" said Olivia, sliding her glass to him.

Isabelle poured everyone seconds except herself, because she was conserving it, and Vanessa, because she was Vanessa.

In December, when it snowed and they were snowed in, they had daily debriefings about their failures and successes. Tomatoes, eggplant, and wheat were their superstars. Did they plant too many potatoes and not enough cabbage? They definitely sowed too many carrots. Never again. Should they buy some chickens to have fresh eggs, or were chickens more trouble than they were worth? Was a cow? What was the most profitable crop to sell and should they plant more of it? Should they plant other crops they hadn't yet considered? Finn and Walter, ever the number crunchers, spent joyful days figuring out what and how much they needed to grow to yield the best return, both on the field and in the pocket.

The next harvest would be even better, they all agreed. The apple trees would produce fruit. The blueberries would bloom, the strawberry patch would grow berries for Mae and June. And the raspberry bushes would allow Isabelle to make moonshine practically on tap.

Honestly nothing sounds better to me than moonshine on tap, Isa.

It's already on tap, Finn. Anytime you want.

"My dear, never tell anyone your secret," said Olivia.

"As if I would," said Isabelle.

"The secret of the moonshine."

"Ah—that. Yes."

"Or you'll have a line down Lovering Road, begging you for more."

"And we wouldn't want that, would we, Mother?" said Finn, his arm around Olivia's shoulder, looking back at Isabelle and smiling.

"I must say, though, had the girl made it during Prohibition, we might not have fallen on the hard times we did."

"Oh I *know*, Olivia," said Isabelle. "Believe me, I tried. Alas, it was like casting pearls before swine."

"Look at you," said Olivia with an approving chuckle, not seeing Finn's long, adoring glance at Isabelle.

"Finn, are you enjoying my English idiots?" She almost beamed at him.

"*Idioms.*"

"That's what I said."

Never tell anyone the secret of your shine, Isabelle.

Beg me for more, miy kohanyi.

There was radio in the snowed-in days and nights, there was light. They bought some games—chess and Parcheesi and backgammon and a new game on the market called Monopoly. They played Monopoly all winter. Finn always won, but Walter gave him a run for his money.

In December, Electric Boat sent Finn a dividend check for $2000 and a bonus of $500. Mickey Winslow sent Isabelle a basket of fresh fruit and flowers, cashmere blankets, and a check for $1000. They had a lavish, generous Christmas, almost like days of yore. As a gift to themselves, they bought the largest refrigerator they could afford. It was pretty damn large.

They went sledding down to the frozen riverbanks. They rolled in the snow.

Every atom of your flesh is as dear to me as my own, Miss Eyre...

All my heart is yours, Mr. Rochester. It belongs to you, and with you it will remain.

To ring in 1933, they raised a glass and sang a song. Schumann and Lucas shared in the common pot of good wishes, no longer needing to hide their own bottles. But Lucas did not get blotto! He was Schumann's driver now, he said, and he had to keep his head. Schumann looked pleased, but no one looked prouder than Earl.

With Olivia's new camera, Isabelle snapped a picture of Finn, Lucas, and Earl together, Earl's arms around the younger men—one of them his son, one of them his son's brother—and Lucas was just tipsy enough to tear up.

So was Earl.

The grandiose toasts poured in, one after another. To life, to health, to happiness, to prosperity, to Ukraine—*Budmo!*—to Isabelle's husband and children returning to her, to Eleanor's husband never returning to her, to another fruitful harvest, to Nate and his tempest-tossed refugees finding calm seas and safe harbors. They sang "Auld Lang Syne," and when the clock struck midnight, they hugged and kissed.

Everyone kissed except Finn and Isabelle.

The two of them rang in the New Year alone, hours later at dawn, with Bengal lights, the balalaika, an open silk robe, and the very last of the moonshine, together lustily singing, *And here's a hand, my trusty friend, and give a hand of thine, we'll take a right good-willie waught for the sake of auld lang syne...*

The bells rang late, but loudly. They did, they did.

74

Plain Sight

Something was wrong in Vanessa's house.

She didn't know when she first noticed it, but somewhere between first tomatoes and the Cape Cod clams, the call and response between her husband and Isabelle stopped. Others still yelled out questions, called her name, and there was still "Daddy! Daddy," but the incessant back and forth that drove Vanessa crazy was no more. At first, all Vanessa could think was, what a blessing. Not *why?* but *thank God*.

But something was wrong in her house.

Vanessa couldn't put her finger on it.

No matter how hard she tried, she couldn't pinpoint what gnawed at her. Over the course of her life she had become so adept at turning away from the things that made her anxious, so skilled at engaging her mind and her hands with other thoughts and tasks, that when she suddenly found herself wanting to examine a question, she didn't know how. She didn't have the tools.

It was uncharted tides: how to plow through the anxiety to unearth the reason for it.

She kept coming back to it, though. The more she thought about not thinking about it, the more she thought about it. On the surface, everything was right. Yet just underneath the serenity was a circling black drain. What was it?

It came to her one night in late February. Finn was too nice to her.

The question was why.

He had been very good to her the first years of their marriage. Never a cross word between them, never a raised voice. But recently they had developed a new, unpleasant way of talking to each other—in stroppy monosyllables, punctuated with ironic remarks and snide comments.

Suddenly, all that stopped as if her husband had turned off that part of himself. Another Finn emerged, like the old Finn—but not quite. This new husband never asked Vanessa to come out of her room anymore. He never asked her to do a single thing, even if it meant having Olivia do it.

The new Finn would rather ask his mother than Vanessa!

On the one hand, commendable.

On the other hand, why?

The new Finn had been in a remarkably good mood for months. She couldn't determine when she first noticed it, but she'd never seen him with such a smile on his face and a spring in his step. He literally walked around humming all day. The best you could say about the former Finn was written by Yeats, that *being Irish, he had an abiding sense of tragedy, which sustained him through temporary periods of joy*. But that wasn't the constantly whistling man currently living in her house.

On the one hand, a pleasant change from the gloom of the last few years.

On the other hand, why?

The new Finn turned to her in bed, said *goodnight darling*, gave her a warm husbandly pat and was asleep in minutes. And in the morning, he was gone hours before Vanessa woke up. She never heard him leave.

The pat and the kiss and the *goodnight darling* was what was left. Gone was even a pretense of him reaching for her before she could say she was tired or her head hurt or her body ached or she wasn't at peace or the world wasn't at peace. He never asked for anything and was perfectly nice about it.

She remembered how last summer, during one of their ugliest arguments—their new normal—he said, "You know Vanessa, I keep asking and you keep saying no, but there will come a day when I will stop asking, and after that will come a day when I will stop caring that I've stopped asking, and after that will come a day when I won't give it to you even if you ask it of me."

Was that what was happening now? Was that what was wrong?

But to ask her own husband for something that no woman should have to ask for was beneath Vanessa. That wasn't how she was raised and she was incapable of it. Some things were simply not done in an Evans marriage or in any marriage she had ever heard of. The man asked, and the woman gave, that was all.

Vanessa might not have initiated marital coition but she did say a few coquettish things to Finn in bed to see where the dust settled. She did put on his favorite nightgown. She dabbed on some of his favorite perfume. She scooted over one or two inches closer to him in bed.

Was it her imagination, or did he inch away from her in response? No nightgown or perfume or flirting carried her nearer to him.

Yet he was so delightfully good to her!

Since there was no one to talk to about this, Vanessa dismissed it—mostly. They had been married twelve years. They had gone through difficult times. This was simply the next stage in their marriage. At least they still slept in the same bed, unlike her mother and father, who'd had separate bedrooms for decades. Did Walter and Lucy have separate rooms since the twelfth year of *their* marriage?

One time—just once—Vanessa asked Finn if anything was the matter.

He hugged and kissed her. "Absolutely nothing, darling. Everything is *wonderful*."

"You don't get as upset with me for my little bouts of nerves," she said with a small chuckle.

"I've learned to accept you as you are," he said. "There's no point in getting worked up about it. I know how hard it's been for you. You're doing your best, and that's all I want from you, nothing more."

And then he turned his back to her.

Was there a finality in the way he said *nothing more*? Was there a veil over his eyes when he looked at her? A curtain that fell and didn't rise again.

Nothing rose again.

She tried to remember the last time she and Finn had been together. Admittedly, it was difficult, with Vanessa's mother sleeping in the room next to them, and all the fights they'd been having.

Could it have been over a *year*?

That seemed impossible.

Yet Vanessa couldn't remember their last moment of real intimacy.

But what was *most* fascinating about the debate within herself regarding the reasons for Finn's outward warmth and inner reserve was that it wasn't the thing that was wrong.

Something *else* was wrong.

It wasn't her husband not touching her, it wasn't her husband being caring toward her. It wasn't his turned back, his bright and early jumping out of bed, his late turning in, his carefree whistling. It wasn't any of those things.

It was something else.

Something that was adjacent to their lack of physical closeness, yet utterly removed from it.

After months of trying to pretend these thoughts didn't exist, after months of trying to think about other things, in April 1933, Vanessa realized that since New Year's Eve, from the moment she woke up to the moment she went to sleep, the intrusive thoughts had replaced all other things. Something had happened on New Year's Eve that made her unable to concentrate or read or teach the children or process jokes or understand recipes. It almost made her unable to clean! Something happened—but she didn't know what it was.

If the problem isn't him not making love to me, if the problem isn't him smiling and joking all day, if the problem isn't him being considerate of me for no good reason—then what is the problem?

75

Revelation

Vanessa was having breakfast. It was around noon. She was chatting with her mother and sister, who had come in from the fields and were relaxing for a few minutes before making lunch, when the front door was flung open without a knock and a stranger entered.

He was a young man in rags and a torn hat. He was dirty and overgrown, missing his teeth and his manners. He stank, and he was in Vanessa's house.

When Vanessa saw him, she dropped the hot cup of coffee she'd been holding. The cup broke and the coffee splashed over her legs. In her shock, what Vanessa thought was, oh no, I bet the coffee got on my housedress. Dang it, and I just washed it. Now I'll have to wash it again—but it's Monday and the washing machine is always backed up after Sunday's day of rest. Why didn't they just wash on Sundays? Then her favorite covering wouldn't remain stained. Could you even get coffee stains out of light cotton fabric? She'd have to ask her mother. Lucy was an expert in getting stains out. Was now a good time to ask?

But Lucy spoke first. "Excuse me," Lucy said to the intruder. She stood from her chair. "We don't know who you are. Please leave."

"Sit down, old woman, and relax," the man said. "I'm not here for you." He cast an insolent gaze over the braless Vanessa. "But I would like something to eat, gentle lady."

Lucy slid back into the chair. Vanessa glanced at the floor. Should she bend down and clean up the coffee mess before people started walking in it? The ceramic shards could cut someone. Good thing she was wearing slippers or she'd be bleeding for sure.

"We have some food on the table near the road," said Eleanor, who didn't get up from her chair. "We leave it there for people like you."

"I'm not a dog," the man said. "So no thanks."

"Then go out back and ask the woman there to give you something to eat," said Vanessa. "There is plenty."

"It's too hot out there, and I've been walking too long." In his filthy boots the man strolled into the kitchen area where Vanessa was.

Fear broke through. Where was Finn! Where were her father and Earl! She had just told Junie and Mae to go outside to wash their hands and feet. They would be back any minute. Her children!

"Go out back," Vanessa repeated, and thought, *am I sending him out there where my children are?* She peered through the front window but couldn't see Finn's truck. He must have gone to town.

"You're trespassing," said Eleanor. "You're on our property without our permission. We do not allow you to be in our house."

"I am sure I heard you invite me in." The man smirked, exposing his rotting teeth. "You said you would feed me."

Vanessa's eyes darted from the front window to the rear. Her father and Earl were out in the onions. Isabelle was even farther away, fixing the scarecrow in the wheat rows. She was two green fields away, a world away. Monty was by her side. There was no way to alert her.

"We'll give you some food," Vanessa said, "but first get out. Step out onto the porch, and I'll get something for you."

"I can get food anywhere," he said.

"You said you wanted food!"

"It's not *just* food I want." He glanced around the room, at Vanessa, at Eleanor, at Lucy. His eyes found a silent Olivia in the corner. She had been reading but now put down the newspaper and sat motionlessly.

"You four lovely ladies live alone in this awfully big place?" he asked. "Doors wide open, no one to protect you." He tutted. "You ought to be more careful. I'm a nice man, but you get all kinds walking past here. You look like you could really use a male pair of hands." He leered. Perhaps he thought he was being witty. "It's plantin' season."

"We have all the help we need," Vanessa said. "My husband will be back any minute."

"If he was really coming back any minute, y'all wouldn't be acting like jittery ferrets." Lewdly he grinned, black holes for teeth in his crumbly mouth.

From the corner of her eye, Vanessa saw her young daughters, bouncy and chatty, begin walking from the water pump to the back door. They were about to come inside!

"Please get out!" Vanessa cried in her loudest, most piercing voice, hoping, *praying*, her children would hear. "You're not welcome here! You heard my sister—you're trespassing! You're committing a crime!"

Unperturbed, the man shook his head. "I'm not leavin' till I get done all the things I come to do," he said. "Food's well and good, but I need me a few dollars.

You got some? I'm trying to get out west." He snorted. "I been in prison a while and I'm hungerin' for some fine female company." He clucked his tongue. "Oh, don't worry. It was for nothing bad. Some robbing. A little fighting." He took a step toward Vanessa. "Maybe some other things."

Isabelle was out in the fields when she saw Junie running flat out, flailing her arms in mute desperation. "Someone's in the house!" Junie was gasping. "Someone—"

Before June was finished speaking, Isabelle had thrown off her work gloves and was striding with all deliberate speed to the house. Not running. Striding. "Go get your grandfather, Monty," she said to the boy following her. "Tell him there's trouble."

"I want to go with you—"

"Did you hear what I said? *Now*."

Without stopping, barely even leaning down, she scooped up the twelve-gauge shotgun standing upright by the back door, checked that it was loaded, and stormed inside. She walked through the kitchen, not slowing, raised her arms above her head, and hit the man on the side of his skull with the butt of her gun.

He staggered, almost losing his balance and falling, but not quite. Righting himself, he sprang to his feet, wiping the blood off his ear. "Ow! Why did you do that?" His back was to the open front door, his malevolent face to Isabelle. He was stupefied, bleeding, but still grinning idiotically. "Look at you, little lady," he said, edging away—but only a step.

"I'm not little lady," Isabelle said. "I'm punishment with shotgun."

Behind her, Eleanor hissed, "*Isabelle! Get away from him!*"

"Now, now, that's not very hospitable of you," the man said. "The lovely woman of the house offered a hungry fella some food, and the ladies and I, we been havin' us a conversation. They're much nicer than you."

"I've done enough talking to build barn," said Isabelle, pointing the muzzle of the shotgun at his face. She depressed the trigger block lever. "There's only one way this will go. If you want different way, you will turn around and walk out of this house on your own two feet—while you still can. Not sentence from now, not meal from now, not minute from now. *Now*."

"Isabelle, stop antagonizing him!" whispered Eleanor from behind her.

"Oh, I ain't leavin'," the man said, reaching into his jacket and pulling out a Colt Magnum pistol. Four women gasped, even though no part of the Colt firing mechanism had been engaged. "Not unless you make me. And you don't want to mess up your shiny floor with dirty old me, do you?"

Isabelle was done talking. Lowering her weapon slightly and aiming at his ribcage, she took two long strides forward and pulled the trigger. She wanted to be as close as possible to him when the shotgun went off.

The chamber had only one slug in it, but the force of the shell, discharged from two meters away, propelled the man out of the house like a projectile through a cannon. He flew backwards through the open door and crashed halfway on the porch, halfway down the steps.

Everybody screamed. Everybody but Isabelle. Monty was jumping up and down, clapping and hollering.

Moments later, Finn pulled up. He bolted toward the house, up the steps past the man's ruined body and inside. Isabelle was still holding the gun to her shoulder. She sprang the catch, hard-pumped the shotgun to release the expended shell, slammed it shut, and stood it on its muzzle against the dining room chair.

Finn walked straight to her. "What happened?" His voice was calm.

"I asked him to get out. He refused." Her voice was calm too.

"You didn't give him a chance!" cried Vanessa. "He was about to leave!"

"I don't think so," said Isabelle. "And once he shoots one of us, it's too late for could've, should've."

"He was leaving! He was!"

Walter and Earl rushed through the back door, both panting. Mae and Junie were with them. The family stood in shock in the middle of their living space, Lucy and Eleanor shrieking, Vanessa crying. Earl went to Olivia, Walter to Lucy, the girls to their father and Isabelle.

"Are you all right, Mother?" asked Finn.

"I'm fine, darling," Olivia said quietly, her hands shaking. She never rose from her reading chair. She took Earl's hand.

"Mayflower, Junebug, you did well to warn me," said Isabelle.

Vanessa ran to Finn and buried her face in his chest. Mae and Junie huddled next to Isabelle. "You okay, girls?" Finn said to his daughters. "Go help your grandmothers."

"Don't look, darlings, don't look," Lucy said. But they were children. All they wanted to do was look. The adults were loud and emotional, asking questions, speaking all at once.

Except Isabelle. She went to the fridge and poured herself a glass of cold orange juice. "Either we clean it up or we get the police," she said, gulping down the drink. "I have work to do. This is no time for dilly-dally."

"Dilly-dally! You just shot a man!" Vanessa cried.

"If anyone deserved little shooting, Vanessa, it was him," said Isabelle.

"Why did you do it!"

"He came in uninvited, demanding your food," said Isabelle. "You asked him to leave. That should have been enough. Appeasement never solution, trust me."

"He was turning to go!"

"Is that before or after he pulled out Colt and said he wasn't leaving? When trespassers with evil intent tell me who they are, I believe them."

"Vanessa, darling," Walter said, shaken but calm, "it's a horror, but Isabelle's right."

"You always take her side, Daddy!"

"There was no talking to that man, Vee. If Isabelle wasn't here, I don't know what we would've done."

"She killed a man in our *house*!" Vanessa shrieked.

"Not quite," Isabelle said, "I made sure he died *out* of our house."

"It's not your house, don't you dare say *our*!"

Finn prodded his wife toward the bedroom, "Go lie down, Vee. I will go get the police."

Vanessa sobbed. "Is he really dead? What if he gets up?"

"I think that's not very likely," said Isabelle.

"Don't leave me, Finn, please!"

"Would you like to come to the police station with me?" Finn said.

"Don't worry, Aunt Vanessa," said Monty, "you'll be safe here. Isabelle will protect you."

Vanessa wailed.

"We can bury him out back and leave police out of it," Isabelle said, her arm around Monty's shoulder. "He didn't seem like kind of guy other people will miss. Vanessa, would you prefer that?"

"Is that how you do it in your country?" cried Vanessa.

"You don't want to know how we do it in my country," replied Isabelle.

"Oh, please let's bury him!" exclaimed Monty. "We could be like real-life vigilantes! Or let's burn him on the pyre with the dead raccoons."

"Monty, pipe down!" snapped Eleanor.

Vanessa ran to her room, sobbing.

"We need to decide," Isabelle said. "Because you don't want blood to dry into wood. It's hard to get stains out once blood dries."

Finn and Earl left and returned forty minutes later with the police and the coroner's truck. The cops took a statement, inspected the shotgun and the single shell left on the living room floor, and seemed satisfied. The coroner carted the body away. After they left, Finn, Monty, and Isabelle scrubbed the porch with soap and cold water. Because it had taken over three hours for the body to be removed, the blood did settle into the boards. Isabelle was quite irritated by that.

After she was done with her field work, she used the adze to remove the top layer of discolored wood, and then a plane to level out the slight indentations left on the steps. The smoothed-out porch looked good.

"Look at that—like new," said a smiling Isabelle that evening, admiring her work. "Maybe we should paint it light blue, glossy. Vanessa, Finn, don't you think that would look pretty? Glossy blue porch for house?"

The intruder with his sinister intentions may have been dealt with, but Vanessa could not be dealt with. She stayed in her room with the curtains drawn and didn't come out, not even to eat.

"I feel like a trespasser in my own home," she said to Finn. "She shot him, but it's as if I'm the one who was shot."

He tried to pacify her.

"She committed murder in our home!"

"Not murder, Vanessa, let's calm—"

"How can you be all right with that?"

"I prefer it to the alternative."

"Who is she that she can do that and not bat an eyelash?"

"She's lived through a lot, seen a lot," Finn said. "Like me, she's been at war. But what's really bothering you? That she killed him or that she is all right with it?"

"Where do I start, my darling, to enumerate the things that are *really* bothering me?"

"At the beginning," Finn said, his unblinking gaze directly on her. "Tell me the first thing, the last thing, anything. You want a conversation? Let's have it."

A daunted Vanessa backed away. "We're living with someone who can kill a man and mop the porch afterward. Why doesn't that terrify you?"

"I'm also someone like that," Finn said.

"You're a man!"

"I'm unclear—does that mean less is expected of me or more?" said Finn. "And what about you? Because you're a woman, is less expected of you—or more?"

"This isn't about me or you! It's about her!"

"Armed men came inside her home to take away the things she loved most," Finn said. "This is what happens when you live on the borderlands. You learn to defend yourself."

"Finn, you sound as if you admire her for this!"

"For being able to defend herself? Who wouldn't?"

"*I* wouldn't! This is not who we are. This is not how we live."

"It *is*!" said Finn. "We live on a farm with no close neighbors."

"You were pulling into the driveway!" Vanessa cried.

"Vanessa, what do you think *I* would've done," Finn said, "if I'd come in and seen that animal threatening you and my mother and my children? I would've killed him too, except I wouldn't have had the presence of mind to blow him out into the yard first. His blood would've been seeping into our living room floorboards, not our porch."

"She didn't move, Finn!" Vanessa whispered. "She didn't flinch."

"Good thing, too."

"*I* couldn't have done it."

"I guess we all act differently in times of trouble," Finn said, his voice cold. "But someone has to do what must be done."

"You want someone like *her* in your corner?" Vanessa said incredulously.

Finn didn't reply.

"I'm in prison here, Finn," she whispered. "Can't you see I'm in a cage!"

"You're not the only one," said Finn. "Every person who tries to help you, who's rebuffed by you, who begs you to put yourself right is in the cage with you too. You think you're the only one with no way out?"

A hole opened inside Vanessa and tar poured in. Her mouth opening, her eyes closing, she fell back against the pillows, raking and raking the single thought in her head. She'd been coming at it all wrong.

Finn didn't want Isabelle in *his* corner. He wanted to be in *hers*.

Somewhere in the silence between the words, near the memory of the killing blast and the minutes before and the seconds after, Vanessa came upon a midnight clear, and in the solemn stillness finally grasped good and proper what was wrong in her house.

PART V
Cri Du Coeur

"What need of question, what of your replying?
Oh! well I know that you
Would toss the world away to be but lying
Again in my canoe,
In listless indolence entranced and lost,
Wave-rocked, and passion tossed."

Emily Pauline Johnson

76

Austen Riggs

At the end of her rope and harboring terrible thoughts of self-harm, Vanessa cornered her father in the hallway one morning.

"Daddy, I need your help," she said. She knew how her father would react. Vanessa had never directly asked her father for anything. Since she was seventeen, she had made her wishes known to him only through Finn.

Her father reeled. They sat down in the quiet house.

"Daddy, I haven't wanted to admit it to anyone," Vanessa said, "not you or Mommy, or even Finn, but I'm afraid there is something wrong with me."

"What is it, my darling?" said Walter, his gruffness gone. "How can I help you? Your mother and I have been so worried about you."

"I know, and I'm sorry. I've wanted to fix it myself and believe me I've tried. I don't know what it is. I've talked to Schumann about it. If I had an open wound, he'd be able to help me better. But the latest incident proved to me I cannot go on."

"What do you mean, cannot go on?"

"I don't want to live anymore, Daddy," whispered Vanessa.

"Darling, darling, no! What are you talking about?" Walter looked and sounded unmoored. "We should get your mother in here—"

"No." Vanessa blew her nose. "I can't talk to anyone else about this."

"It's just a bout of nerves, my angel. Is this about the man in the house?"

"The murdered man in the house, yes." Vanessa forced her fingers to bend backwards, wishing she were brave enough to break them. "Other things, too, I don't want to go into. I want to be better, Daddy, I promise you, I really do. But I'm convinced I can't do it without help."

"Schumann is a doctor."

"Another kind of doctor."

"You mean like a sanatorium?"

"Yes, Daddy. Yes." She breathed out.

He sat back and breathed out too. "You want to leave your family, leave your husband, your children, and go to live in another place?" he said, his brow curving away from compassion. "How long for?"

"As long as it takes," said Vanessa. "Isn't my health worth it?"

Walter sat quietly, his hands folded, studying his daughter through his glasses, twisting his mouth. "Vanessa, I don't quite know how to say this, my dear, but... do you think that's a good idea?" He looked deeply uncomfortable. "You leaving, I mean." It was as if Walter couldn't say out loud what he didn't even want to think. "Maybe to stay would be better. Talk to Schumann. Maybe—"

"Daddy, with all my heart I'm telling you this is the last resort," Vanessa said. "I *have* stayed. I *have* tried not to leave. But I can't right this ship without external correction."

"You mean like electric shock treatment?" Walter was aghast. "I heard they do that in some places. Sometimes they lobotomize women who have maladies they don't know how to treat."

"I don't want to be lobotomized!" Vanessa was aghast herself. "I'm not being involuntarily committed. But before I get to a point where I need to be—and unfortunately I'm close to that point now—I need to convalesce somewhere... somewhere else."

"Convalescence means recovery and rest," Walter said.

"Like from tuberculosis! Yes, exactly, Daddy."

"Isn't there a step missing?" said Walter. "Isn't there something between injury and convalescence? Like treatment, maybe?"

"I might need that too," said Vanessa in a dull, numb voice.

"Darling, you well know we don't have the money for long-term rehabilitation," Walter said. "We have more than last year but sanatoriums are expensive. My friend Ralph Wheeler, do you remember him? He had emphysema and had to be on oxygen someplace in Maine. It cost $600 a month, Vee! Can you get better in two months? I have enough to pay for that. Finn too, we can scrape together six months possibly. Maybe we can ask Isabelle—"

"No, no, no, Daddy, that's not what I want. Never—please."

Walter fell silent, sad.

"I don't know if six months will be enough time," said Vanessa.

"Six *months* won't be enough time? Ralph was only gone four months and he couldn't breathe!"

"Sometimes I also can't breathe," Vanessa said. "You know professional people. You've had business relationships. Isn't there *anyone* you can call on my behalf and plead for a favor? Isn't there anyone at all who can help me?" She wrung her hands. "No one hears me anymore. I have no words left to speak to anyone. And even when I do speak, no one is listening."

"I'm sorry, dear girl." Walter sounded as helpless as Vanessa felt. "You should've come to me earlier. Let me think on it. Let me see what I can do."

After a few days of pondering, Walter called his old friend and former investment client Percival Ford, who was the current president of Austen Riggs Sanatorium in Stockbridge, Massachusetts, 150 miles away. Austen Riggs had an exclusive clientele and specialized in nervous maladies. The fees were outrageous—$1000 a month. But Percival said he would waive them for Walter if it meant his friend's daughter could get the help she needed.

"Mommy is leaving us?" said Junie.

Mae yanked on her sister's arm as they stood at the bedroom door and watched their father help their mother with her suitcase. "Not forever, June!" said Mae.

"That's right, my darlings," Vanessa said, distracted and remorseless. "You know I've been having a hard time, but I'm going to a wonderful place that will make me better."

"Yes, June," Mae said. "Mommy is going to a wonderful place that's not this place. A different wonderful place."

"Away from us?"

"Maybe that's what makes it so wonderful," said Mae, a grim shell of her former self.

Neither Finn nor Vanessa addressed their children. Finn said he would talk to the girls when he returned. Vanessa couldn't offer even that much. "I'll see you soon, darlings. Don't forget to come visit me with your daddy."

"Let's go," Finn said to her. "We're scheduled for a noon check-in and it's after nine."

Vanessa forced herself to say goodbye to Isabelle because she didn't want any gossip or questions about why she hadn't.

"Goodbye, Vanessa," said Isabelle. "I hope you get better soon. And don't worry about anything. Everything will be taken care of."

Somehow, saying a fake goodbye made it even more degrading. That things would be taken care of by *her* of all people! Frankly, Vanessa wasn't in the least worried about things *not* being taken care of, and she suspected that Isabelle knew it.

During the three-hour ride to Stockbridge, she and Finn chatted about the girls, her sister, her father, how often Finn might be able to visit, how pleasant the weather was, how green the hills, how smoothly paved the country roads. Vanessa drifted out of the conversation when she realized that Finn—sitting behind the wheel, steering confidently, brushed, shaved, light, smiling, more handsome than ever, acting in other words as if what was happening wasn't happening—believed with near-total certainty that Vanessa would never ask the question that was a hard one for healthy women and an impossible one for a woman in Vanessa's condition. Her husband believed that the woman who didn't ask about the stock market crash or about the failure of her father's bank would never ask him if he was in love with someone else.

And he was right.

Vanessa felt like a dying bird in the open yard in darkness.

77

Omelian Marchenko

A month after Vanessa left, in May 1933, there was a knock on the door.
On the porch stood Schumann.
Isabelle's legs went numb. She swayed.
"It's okay, Isa," he said. "I have no bad news."
"Then why are you at my door!" she yelled.
"I have no other way of getting in touch with you," he said. "May I come in?"
She dragged him inside, ran out back, and shouted for Finn. She couldn't listen to Schumann, no matter what he had to say, without Finn by her side. Earl and Walter sat at the table with them.
"Nate is docking in the next few days," Schumann said. "But he sent me a telegram from Brindisi."
"Schumann, don't beat bush! Just come out with it!"

WHO IS OMELIAN MARCHENKO. ASK ISABELLE. FORMER OGPU. BARELY ALIVE. KNOWS ISPAS WELL. BRINGING HIM IN.

They studied the telegram, passed it around between their unsteady fingers. And then they stared at Isabelle.
"What you looking at me for? I don't know Omelian Marchenko!"
"Maybe you forgot?"
Isabelle wondered if Omelian was in the black hole with her husband and children. She didn't want it to be true.
"Why would Nate bring someone like that to America?" Earl said. "We don't know what his intentions are."
"What could his intentions possibly be, Dad?" said Finn.
"Former OGPU? Who knows. But why would you give a man like that a visa to the United States, when actual refugees are literally *dying* to get here?"

"Earl is not wrong," Schumann said. "But Nate did it only because of Ispas. Maybe this man knows something about Isabelle's family, can give us some answers."

Isabelle didn't know what she looked like at that moment, but inside she was a crumbling volcano, erupting, yet being destroyed in the process. She wasn't ready. She would never be ready. She couldn't imagine such a man could have good news about her brothers, Cici, her husband, and her—

There was no sweet fruit from a poisonous tree. "Let's go, Schumann," Isabelle said in a voice that said *let's never go*. "We'll get ready for him, figure out how to deal with it." She wouldn't allow herself a concrete thought, a nebulous hope. She wished she could say no. "I'll come back as soon as I can," she said. "Walter, watch for aphids on tomatoes. And Finn, keep eye on wheat. Don't water it if it rains. Tell Junie we'll plant corn when I come back."

"I'll take care of the wheat," Earl said. "Finn, go with Isabelle."

"Yes, yes, your father is right," said Walter. "Go with her, dear boy. We'll be fine, don't worry. Monty will handle it if there's any trouble. Isabelle taught him well. Take the truck. Bring weapons."

"Walter, *what*?" Earl exclaimed.

"Earl, you and I are on different sides of the law on this issue," Walter said. "Your son was a soldier. I don't know why you forget that. Once a soldier, always a soldier. He needs to protect the woman, the tailor, and the sailor. What are they going to do if this Soviet has evil intentions? The man was a member of Stalin's secret police. Maybe he still is."

Finn also got up. "I will go, of course," he said. "And I'll even bring a pistol just in case. But I assure you, Walter, you have it upside down. The woman doesn't need protection from the OGPU. Omelian Marchenko needs protection from the woman."

Two days later, when the ship finally docked at Long Wharf and thirty people disembarked for immigration processing, Marchenko wasn't among them. Nate said he had been taken off the ship at Gallops Island and confined to three months of quarantine because after five days at sea, he'd entered United States waters with undefined open sores all over his body. The medical officer at Gallops, the quarantine area for the City of Boston, had no idea if the sores were contagious. "He told me they looked like the plague," Nate said. "But they also could be scurvy or dystrophy."

Marchenko was not being released until he either healed or died. If Isabelle wanted to talk to the man, they would have to ferry out to him. But when Nate, shuffling from foot to foot, suggested the boat trip, he said it to the ground, not to anyone's face. Schumann and Isabelle also stared elsewhere—the sea, the docks, the ships, the crying gulls. Isabelle pressed herself into Finn's arm. Her body tilted toward him, a twig listing.

"What do you mean, *if* we want to talk to him?" Finn said. "Isn't that what we came for?"

No one replied.

"Isa, tell me—what? What am I missing?"

Nothing, my love, nothing, she whispered so only he could hear.

Nate, who for years worked closely with officials at Gallops, got the quarantine supervisor to arrange a small boat to ferry them three miles out into Boston Harbor, to the isolation facility on a remote hunk of rocky grass between the city and the sea.

On the ferry, Isabelle was deeply unwell. Her wintry porcelain features looked as if blood had drained away from her skin. Schumann hovered over her, talking to her in Ukrainian as she clung to the rail. Nate pulled Finn away. They had just passed Battery Hitchcock, a fortification defense post jutting out from Castle Island, and entered the narrows. Nate pointed to a small landmass in front of Finn. "That's Gallops."

"You needed to speak to me privately about that?"

Nate pointed to an island on the left, four hundred yards across the narrows. "And *that's* Lovell's Island," he said.

Ah. Finn exhaled. Now he understood.

"I didn't know Marchenko was going to turn into a leper overnight," Nate said. "Otherwise I would've waited till we got here to tell my father about him. I wouldn't have brought her out here had I known. I know how she feels about the shipwreck—and about me."

Finn stared at the granite sea, at Lovell with its two squat white lighthouses, and at Isabelle. She looked so fragile, standing at the rail in her dark coat. He felt a portent of he didn't know what.

It was a gray May morning, the sky overcast, the temperature chilly. Lovell's Island was rocky in the narrows, a glacial bedrock full of crags and moraines. A ship at night in a storm, having lost its bearings, would be thrown against Appalachian granite. Wood could not do battle with igneous rock.

By what providential hand was the quarantine island that held a ghoul from Isabelle's past life a mere stormy throw away from the place where she had fallen into the black water? She was passing over the inferno, guided by Nate's hand, the man she held—justly or unjustly—responsible for her crisis and her involuntary salvation.

Finn walked back to stand next to Isabelle. An icy gloom sprayed his face and neck. Nate was right. It was a bad idea to come here. No good would come from it. He finally understood what he was feeling, and what Isabelle must have been feeling too.

It was dread.

Omelian was half a corpse. It was shocking to see. In Finn's entire life, in all the books he'd read, all the pictures he'd seen, all the stories Isabelle had told him of her wars and her struggles, in all the brutality he had witnessed firsthand in his only battle on the Piave River front, Finn had never seen a human being look how Omelian Marchenko looked as he slowly rose from the bed, his clothes hanging off him, and stood in front of them as they stared at him bleakly from the corridor. Isabelle said she did not recognize him and Finn wanted to ask how she would even know.

He looked withered and old and was the color of dust. He was a skeleton with swollen lumps on his neck and face and arms. The lumps had burst and the sores festered. He looked as if his skin was breaking off in pieces. His pupils were dilated into his irises. The man's huge black eyes bulged, and his breathing was rapid and shallow even though he was barely mobile. He hobbled past them into the interview room down the hall, and sat across from them at a metal table. Isabelle sat next to Finn. Schumann and Nate stood behind them.

"Omelian," Nate said, "what's going on with you? Why aren't you eating? You were doing all right in Brindisi. What happened?"

Omelian said something in Russian. Schumann asked him to speak in Ukrainian. The man refused. "I speak in the language of my Revolution," he said. Standing behind Finn, Schumann translated for him.

Nate supplied some of the known details about Marchenko's past. He was born in Poltava in 1890, raised in Kiev, educated in Moscow, and joined the Bolshevik security ranks in Petrograd in April 1917 after Lenin returned from Switzerland to overthrow Kerensky's Provisional government. During the Russian Civil War he was sent to Vinnitsa in Ukraine as a lieutenant in the internal security forces that was first CHEKA, then became the GPU, and then the OGPU. After the war, he was transferred to Kammenets, a dozen kilometers from Ispas, where for a decade he shuffled through the middle ranks, a commissar of this, a chairman of that. His main responsibility was to assign procurement and requisition units to various villages in southwest Ukraine to confiscate food, assist with collectivization, and suppress opposition.

Omelian Marchenko was the one who sent Zhuk and Efros to Ispas.

After Isabelle learned this, it took her a few minutes to gather herself to speak to the man in Russian since he refused to answer questions posed to him in another language. Omelian spoke in a weak mechanical monotone, though his words were clear. His body may have been consuming itself, but his mind was sharp.

"Since 1929, the region I had authority over has turned into a lawless nightmare," Omelian said. "And it all started with Ispas. But we have bigger problems in the Soviet Union than one ruined village. Soon weeds will grow over it. Unless the people eat the weeds. Then nothing will grow."

"What happened in 1929 in Ispas?" she asked. She wanted from him only one thing, no matter how determined he was to give her another.

"Who cares?" Omelian said. "What's happening now is the slow but sure destruction of Carthage." *Razrusheniye Karfagena* is how Marchenko put it.

"What happened in 1929 in Ispas?" repeated Isabelle.

"Anarchy and murder," he replied. "But it doesn't matter anymore, don't you understand that?"

"We're looking for people who lived—"

"The people are dead."

"We're looking for the Kovalenkos," she said, barreling through his words. "Dairy farmers. Father, brother, sons, other children. Do you have any information about them? Or the Lazars—"

When he heard the name Lazar, Omelian's nostrils flared. An animating force ignited a spark throughout his body. He sat up. His round coal eyes fixed on Isabelle. "And you are?" he said.

"No longer questioned by you is who I am," said Isabelle. Leaning forward, Schumann translated their back and forth into Finn's ear. "We three are from Ispas. My father and brother—and I—left in 1919."

"Left in 1919 but want to know about the Lazars in 1929." It wasn't a question.

"Yes. And the Kovalenkos."

"You want to lift the coffin lid and peek inside?" Omelian said. "You won't like what you see."

"Just tell it."

"In other parts of Ukraine, the farms weren't armed," Omelian said, "or if they were, their weapons had been seized. But where I was stationed, the land changed hands ten times in five years before, during, and after the Revolution. From Poland, to Romania, to Russia, to Austria-Hungary, to Bessarabia, back to Poland, back to Russia. And each time men fought, they took weapons from the vanquished and hoarded them like they hoarded their grain. Owning rifles and shotguns was forbidden in all of Ukraine, but the farmers in my region considered themselves to be outside the law. They unearthed their buried rifles and grenades, they sharpened their sabers, and they waited for us to come."

"Maybe you shouldn't have come."

"We tried to reason with them! We explained as politely as we could that there was no theirs, only ours. All farms, all land, all cattle, all grain belonged to the Communist Party. Theft of any crop was punishable by five to ten years' hard labor. And their answer to that? To burn down their homes and burn us down along with them!"

"Is that what happened to your procurement operative Kondraty Zhuk?" said Isabelle. "Or was he spared being burned alive by being shot first?"

Omelian stopped speaking. He stared at her for a long time with a dark gaze. Isabelle stared back at him with her own dark gaze.

"Comrade Zhuk was one of my best men," he said. "Who *are* you?"

"Who are *you*?" she said. "Tell me—was there trouble on the Lazar farm?"

"That's where the trouble began," said Omelian, speaking slowly and breathing rapidly. "But it didn't end there. We suffered some casualties, yes. But we believed, after the battle on the farm and in the nearby fields, that all the Lazars had been killed."

"As with all things," said Isabelle, "your beliefs were wrong."

"And then, out of nowhere, a few weeks later," Marchenko continued, "four lawless vigilantes on horses—three men and one woman—rode through Ispas at night and murdered the guards on duty."

"What woman?"

"What woman indeed," Omelian said. "We were certain it was Isabelle Lazar with her Kazak brothers." His black stare bored into her. "But if it wasn't Isabelle, who was it?"

"Just tell it." *Oh, Cici.*

"They invaded the Party Headquarters in Ispas and killed the men sleeping in their beds. They woke them, dragged them into the public square, tied them to their chairs and cut off their heads. They rode off yelling *Urrah!* and left them sitting headless with rifles in their hands."

Isabelle's hands were clenched, as if around a rifle.

"After word got around, this utterly pointless rebellion spread like wildfire throughout the countryside. When farmers in other villages heard what was possible, they also took up arms against us. But the Lazar handiwork was different. No matter how many men we put up as sentries, it wasn't enough. They would behead the entire house guard and then line up their bodies with weapons in their hands as if ready for battle. They came at night, and you could barely hear them. They came on foot, in stealth and under cover of darkness. None of my men wanted to be on night duty because it was a death sentence. The men couldn't shoot what they couldn't see.

"Needless to say, with so many problems of law enforcement, my grain quota wasn't met in 1929 despite forced collectivization. In 1930, we increased the quota and started arresting anyone caught in possession of hand mills—to stop people from stealing the wheat and making their own bread. By decree, all grinding of wheat in Ukraine was to be performed only in nationalized mills operated by the Party. In other parts of Ukraine that stood as law. But in my part? They burned the collectives and Soviet property. They beat us to death with the hand mills and then slaughtered their cattle and set their own homes on fire!"

"They wouldn't yield their lives without a fight," said Isabelle.

"We would send ten men, and ten men would be dead. We would send twenty men, and they too would be dead, tied up and burned alive with potatoes stuffed in their charred mouths. We came into their homes to feed the Revolution and they took our lives. We came for the grain, but they came for our heads."

Her body in a knot, Isabelle sat and listened.

"Did the commissars in Kiev care about these added pressures in my region?" said Omelian. "Not in the least. They stopped sending me new men and told me to do a better job of keeping the men I had. You want to know what I had? Beheaded soldiers clutching rifles in their dead hands, with the words YOU REAP WHAT YOU SOW written above their corpses in their own blood.

"The Lazar bandits added more and more to their ranks. It was no longer an isolated skirmish in southwest Ukraine. It was a peasant rebellion, just like the one in 1919 that killed their father Martyn Lazar."

He glared at her.

She glared back.

"The brothers trained others to ride horses and to fight with *shashkas*. They trained them to steal the crops from the collectives and distribute it to the starving farmers. And each time they killed my men, they seized our weapons. Their revolution against us was being supplied by the Soviet Union itself!"

"How infuriating that must have been for you," said Isabelle.

"Oh, we took measures. Like everywhere in Ukraine, we erected watchtowers in the middle of the fields to shoot anyone who took any crops for themselves. During the day we could see the thieves, but the outlaws learned to raid from the collectives at night.

"In the fall of 1931, in complete darkness, they somehow picked off an entire *hectare* of wheat! It's an outrage! They took it brazenly to say, fuck your quota. From that point, we regarded anyone who didn't look starved or half-dead as guilty of being a malicious hoarder of state grain. We upended their houses to find their secret stash and arrested them and their families."

Schumann was struggling to translate for Finn, so fast and bitter came Marchenko's words. He had his own story to tell. "When the first Five-Year

Plan began in 1928, we believed that collectivization was the best solution to procure the requisite grain from Ukraine," he said.

"As with all things," Isabelle said, "your beliefs were wrong."

"It wasn't our choice. These were our orders! The country had to be industrialized. The miners in Siberia and the workers in the cities had to be fed. The quota was necessary. The wheat was the only way to buy heavy equipment from the West to modernize the Soviet Union. If we didn't deliver, the Five-Year Plan would fail, and if it failed, the great Soviet experiment, the first of its kind in the history of man, would fail. That could never happen."

"Yes, yes," said Isabelle. "What happened to the Lazars?"

"The grain quota wasn't met. So Stalin accused the Ukrainian Bolsheviks of being too lenient with the farmers forced to work the collectives. He said there were many ways other than stealing and hoarding by which some people, spurred on by irrational nationalist pride, could hurt grain production. Yes, I wanted to reply, one way was beheading my fucking men! Stalin said the farmers sowed the collective land partially, cultivated it poorly, only half reaped it—and the Ukrainian Bolsheviks like me allowed it to happen."

Everyone in the room stayed quiet. Even Isabelle held off asking her questions.

"For four years in a row, from '29 to '32, the quota, increasing each year, was not met. And of course, the punishment for failing to deliver the grain also increased. We arrested tens of thousands of farmers and sent them out east into the mines. With less and less to eat, the ones left behind started going hungry in '29, were starving in 1930, and dying in '31. But at least in '31, I was finally given more men, and we came into their homes with rifles and shotguns to take the grain that didn't exist."

"You did this in '29, too," Isabelle said. "What happened to the Lazars?" She couldn't stop her hands from trembling. Omelian saw it, and Isabelle willed her hands to be still.

"Their suffering was a direct result of their own stubbornness," Omelian said. "Their due punishment for starving *us* was their own starvation. They believed they knew how to live best, how to farm best, how to sow best. We came into their homes and turned them upside down looking for hidden produce. In '30 and '31, we still found kilos of hidden crops, but by the spring of '32, in house after house, we found nothing but starving families. And still, in the summer of each year, we sent these skeletons out into the fields to reap the harvest and fulfil the quota. Stalin called it deliberate disruption on their part. But it was famine. They couldn't work as they were supposed to because they were dying in their boots, right in the wheat."

"What happened to the Lazars?"

"We stopped paying the workers on the collectives until the entire grain quota from their farms had been delivered. If they fell short, we levied all additional wheat from the farmers' own supplies. If they resisted, we killed them. Those were our orders. It was us or them."

"Just answer my question!" Isabelle said. "What happened to the Lazars?"

"The woman was ambushed and shot in 1931, finally," Omelian said. "Is that the answer you were looking for?"

Behind Isabelle, Schumann and Nate cried out. She heard their sobbing.

"You want more? One of the younger Lazar brothers was killed in 1932."

Isabelle forced herself not to cry out. She barely moved, barely breathed.

"The other two brothers disappeared, the way everyone disappeared," Omelian said. "The beheadings stopped, praise be to the Communist Party. They were either killed or died of hunger. Famine made their defiance impossible."

Isabelle hung her head. Behind her, Schumann was still sobbing.

"At the end of 1932, less than 5 million tons of grain had been collected, three-quarters of the total requirement for Ukraine. Personally, 75 percent seemed like a spectacular success to me. In my region, I couldn't reach even 40 percent of the annual goal." He appeared deeply pained by his own failures.

"Moscow was clear about who was to blame. We were—for being too soft. The harvest was poor, we were told, because we allowed the farmers to eat the brand new plantings right out of the ground. It was true, to feed themselves, they ate the seeded potatoes and onions. They ate the tomato stalks before they had a chance to bear fruit, they ate the plant matter and the leaves of every living thing they put in the earth. The weeds came up first and they ate them. Even the beetroot seeds were eaten, and those, as I'm sure you know, are inedible. But nothing was deemed inedible."

Schumann got up and left the room. Half-able, Nate continued to translate for Finn in his father's place.

Marchenko continued. "We quadrupled our efforts to stop them from feeding themselves. First you deliver to the state what's demanded of you, we said, then you eat. We shot peasants eating buried horses they had dug up. We forbade farmers to catch fish in the rivers near their villages and arrested them if they did. We watched people eat meat off mice and rats and grind the rodent bones into a flour they mixed with nettles and sorrel for food. Their desperation was revolting."

"Ask him," Finn said, "when he's going to get to the part where he learned the error of his ways."

But before Isabelle could ask, Omelian spoke. "I fully believed," he said, "as did all who belonged to the Party, that the end justified the means."

"And when you realized that everything you believed was wrong, is that when you ran?" said Isabelle.

"You are the one who doesn't understand," Omelian said. "It *wasn't* wrong. It was right! Everything was permitted because our cause was just. Our goal was the victory of communism over the whole world—the Soviet Union first. It was our moral duty to wipe out anything that stood in our way. Shooting small children wandering the countryside digging for onions—"

Isabelle pushed away from the table with such ferocity, her chair fell over and the table pitched to the side. She slid it out of the way and lunged toward Marchenko. Finn jumped up, certain the man was about to lose his life.

Incredibly, Nate stood back to let her do it.

"Isa!" Finn exclaimed, grabbing her arms from behind and pulling her away. "Come on, Isa . . ."

"Will you ever ever *ever* stop talking?" said Isabelle in a gutted voice.

As if she hadn't spoken, Omelian went on. ". . . It was our duty to kill pregnant mothers picking off wheat from the fields. All of it was allowed and encouraged and right. We believed the Ukrainian farmer was trying to deliberately starve us to sabotage the Revolution, to upend our fight for fairness for all mankind, which was a most noble cause, the most valiant struggle. Therefore, his suffering was necessary. You may call us thugs, but we called ourselves idealists."

"When you sold us the bill of goods on your glorious revolution," Isabelle said, "we didn't realize it meant we would be left penniless and starving."

Finn picked up the chairs and the table and moved them against the window. Isabelle looked as if she might throw one or both at Marchenko's head. Omelian remained sitting in a lone chair in the middle of the room, still talking. Isabelle stood with her back against the wall, next to Finn who stood next to Nate, who continued to translate.

"This past fall and winter there was no food for the farmers, nothing, nothing," Omelian said. "From our towers we watched the villagers send their children to dig for acorns in the fields. They mashed the insides, cooked them, and ate them as a kind of bread. We arrested their mothers and fathers for this and sent them to the work camps. Look what they would rather do instead of working for the Soviet state, we said. They make their children dig acorns in the dirt like pigs."

"Isabelle, come on," Finn whispered, reaching for her twisted hands. "We've heard enough. Do you want to go? Let's go."

"But here is the thing you don't know, *Isabelle Lazar*," said Omelian Marchenko. "There *was* wheat to feed the Ukrainian farmer! And plenty of it. Beets and potatoes too. The OGPU was more or less fed, the army was well fed, our chairmen, commissars, propagandists, apparatchiks, land reorganization facilitators, procurement coordinators, and people's welfare officers were all very well fed. Four months ago in January 1933, when my delegation and I took the train to attend the All-Party Conference in Kharkov, we passed by mounds of unthreshed wheat, each pile as big as this island! We passed mountains of churned butter the size of the boat I arrived on. They called it surplus and placed it near the train tracks for photographers and journalists and international correspondents to view, right next to the functioning collective farms where the workers were smiling and *not* emaciated, to prove to the world that talk of famine was a blatant lie, that there was abundance, not scarcity!

"That's when I knew for sure: Ukraine was being starved to death systematically and deliberately, with the full support and cooperation of people like me. Ukraine had to be rendered powerless the way the Lazars had been rendered powerless, and the *kulaks*. At the Conference, not one word was spoken about our recent enemies. The *kulaks* didn't exist anymore. They had been exterminated. The Ukrainian people were now enemies of the state."

Isabelle's arms hung at her sides. "I get it now," she said. "Earlier, when you said *Carthage*, you meant the Soviet Union. A state that slaughters its children, literally, as ritual sacrifice in service of their ideals."

"Yes, that is what I meant," Omelian said. "And I would have continued anyway because I was a true believer. But I knew that my days were numbered—"

"Your days *are* numbered."

"—when Comrade Stalin told my delegation from Kammenets that we were personally responsible for the failure to satisfy the regional quota because of our refusal to contain the anti-Soviet forces. We had allowed them to form into a rebellion that caused our procurement disaster.

"That's when I knew I would be next. Already I'd been regularly demoted. Since 1931, I had no standing and no rank. My ration was barely above the informers'. When we returned from Kharkov, I grabbed my rifle, my pistol, and I fled. It was February and freezing and there was no food. I ate bark off the trees to survive—like an animal. I didn't know where I was going. South maybe, trying to get to Romania. Near the river at Zhvanets, I stopped a family trying to cross at night. They were from Rykhta, a village a few kilometers from Ispas. At gunpoint I demanded food from them, but they told me about a passing rumor that if only they could get to some port on the Black Sea, they could buy passage on a ship that would take them to Italy and beyond. It sounded like a fable, frankly. They didn't know I was a deserter. I showed them my credentials and told them they had a choice: either I shot them or they let me come with them."

He stopped talking—to take a breath, not because he was done. "Out of seven in that family, only two made it to Constanta, the mother and the aunt. The father and the children died during the journey. That was always the case in Ukraine, by the way," said Omelian Marchenko. "Men died first. Children second. And women last—"

78

Men Died First

Finn didn't know what happened. One moment Isabelle stood against the wall, grimly listening, and the next she was down on the floor and making the most terrible sounds, half crying, half dying. "Isabelle?" he said, but she didn't answer. She was crawling away, retching. She kept trying to cover her ears to stop Omelian's voice from getting through. And he kept on talking, indifferent to what was happening in front of him.

Finn dropped on the floor by her side. "Isa," he whispered in alarm, his hand on her back. "Oh my God, what's wrong?"

Isabelle was vomiting blood.

Panicking as he hadn't panicked since the Great War, Finn ripped off his dress shirt and held it to her face. She was gasping in agony, choking on her every breath.

Nate ran from the room and a moment later, Schumann ran in. He crouched beside Isabelle, one hand on her back, the other in her mouth. He pushed her head down to her chest and held Finn's shirt to her. He whispered in Ukrainian, words Finn wished he knew so he could say them to her too. But he could see from Schumann's expression that the doctor had no idea what was ailing her. "She needs a hospital," Schumann said, his face deeply fearful.

"We're on a fucking island in the middle of the ocean!" Finn said.

"I don't know what happened, Papa," said Nate, glaring at Marchenko. "I was in the room when it happened, and I can't tell you."

"What did he say?"

"He was yammering away like now!" Nate paused, listening to Omelian. A dark expression crossed his face.

"*I told her she wouldn't like what she sees when she lifts the lid on the coffin,*" Nate translated Marchenko's words, sending a chill down Finn's spine.

"Help me tilt down her head, Finn," said Schumann. "She is choking on her own blood." The three men labored to help her.

Omelian stopped his incantation, skulked to the opposite corner of the room, and with lifeless eyes observed the struggle in front of him.

Finn tried to lift Isabelle into his arms to get her out of the room, but she crawled away from them and fell to her side, her face to the wall. When they leaned over her, she covered her head with Finn's bloodied shirt. In a stifled voice she said, "I'm okay. I need a minute."

Nate rounded on Omelian and snapped harshly in Ukrainian, "*What did you do?!*"

The man answered in Russian. Later, Schumann told Finn what he said. "*I do what I've always done. Destroy life in the name of the Revolution.*"

It took a while for her to stop shaking, to stop heaving, to sit up. Finn's bloodied shirt remained in her hands. He was without words, but his presence was enough for her.

"I'm okay," she said, patting him. "Where is he?"

"They took him back to his room."

"Can you help me up?"

After he lifted her to her feet, she gave him his shirt back and asked him to wait. She said she needed to go get cleaned up. He offered to walk her to the washroom but she declined and staggered out on her own two feet.

He waited.

She was gone only a few minutes, but when she came back, she had washed her face, re-tied her hair, got herself together. Nate and Schumann were waiting in the corridor. They put on their coats and left.

In silence they stood in the cold, waiting for the ferry. In silence they rode back through the narrows. It was getting dark, and the lighthouses were dimly lit up. *Look, Isabelle,* Finn wanted to say. *Your lights at Lavelle.* But her expression of dismal hopelessness didn't allow for diversion or distraction, so he said nothing.

The cold wind revived her a little. She buttoned up her coat and leaned into him, and he put his arm around her. Their walk to the Parker House Hotel was long and icy. By the time they got to the lobby and received their keys, she had some of her color back.

"Check-out is at noon," the front desk clerk said.

"We'll be staying at least one more day," Finn said.

She had a hot bath while he lay on the bed, watching the half-open door and drifting in and out of sleep. It was dark and quiet, and the shades were drawn. Did he hear her crying? Every now and then he'd call out to her, "*Isabelle, Isabelle,*" and she would respond, "*I'm all right, Finn, my love, I'm okay. Just sleep, I'll be out soon.*"

When he woke up, he was covered by a wool throw and she was asleep under the covers, naked and warm and clean. Awful sounds came from her as she slept.

She was out twelve hours.

And then, soundlessly, she wept.

She went into the bathroom to brush her teeth and wash her face. They sat together in bed, their backs against the headboard. He gave her some tea, some bread. For a long while she stared at his shirt, stained with her dried blood.

"Why didn't I stay and fall with my brothers, with Cici, the rest of my countrymen?" she said in a numb voice. "Be wiped out, starved, absorbed into our black soil."

"Please don't say that, Isabelle. *Please.*"

He laid her down, cradling her in his arms. "You don't want your family scattered into the diaspora to be unwept and forgotten," Finn said, pressing his lips to her head. "You don't want to cut their lives even shorter. If you were struck down, who would mourn them, Isa? You are witness to their fate. As long as you are here, your motherland is not empty. By their stories, you raise them up again, and their holiness is resurrected on this earth."

She lay in his arms, leafless with pain, long enough for comfort, but not long enough to forget.

"I don't know what happened to me yesterday," she said, eventually. "It *was* only yesterday, wasn't it?"

"You looked like you went into some kind of trance, Isabelle," Finn said. "It was really frightening."

"For me too. I don't remember that part"—she emitted a strangled cry—"I don't know what to say about it. The answers are not in me. I think listening to him talk about Roman, Cici, my country became too much for me."

"I get it. But he didn't say anything about your husband and sons, right?"

"He did not."

"Doesn't that give you a little bit of hope?"

She said nothing.

"He said some of the Ukrainian labor camps were emptied this year, and the prisoners were let out."

"Because the Soviets didn't want to feed them."

"Still, that's a little encouraging. There's a chance if they'd been arrested and were in one of those places, they could have been released."

"Absolutely."

"Isa, if *that* man, a skeletal monster, could make it to Constanta, angels could fly there too. They can make it to the Black Sea even better. Nate and I are going to triple our efforts to keep the special visas coming."

She kissed him, hid herself deep in his consoling embrace. "Thank you," she whispered. "With all my heart, *myi milyi, myi kohanyi*, thank you."

They stayed together at Parker House a few more days. As always, he drove back first while she remained with Schumann.

When she returned home to the overjoyed Junie and anxious Walter and Earl, she behaved as if neither Lavelle nor Ukraine nor her decimated family were anywhere near the things she was thinking about. She talked about corn and wheat and the loamy earth.

Earl told her to keep the faith, to stay resolute. "*The sacred rights of mankind,*" he said, "*are written, as with a sunbeam, in the whole volume of human nature, by the hand of divinity itself; and can never be erased.*"

Isabelle embraced him.

"Don't thank me," the honorable judge said. "Alexander Hamilton wrote it."

"I'm thanking you, Earl, because you are so pure and good. Like your son. Clearly sacred rights of mankind can be obliterated—and are, even as we speak."

She didn't talk about it afterward except to say it was a good thing they met the man when they did. An hour after they left, Omelian Marchenko was found dead in his isolation cell.

"Probably extreme starvation right?" Finn said slowly, mining her expression for a shade of truth.

"Probably," said Isabelle. No truth could be mined from her inscrutable face.

For Finn, three indelible memories remained burned into his mind's eye from those awful days. Isabelle, on her knees, vomiting blood into his white shirt. Isabelle looming over the neutered Omelian as if she were about to behead him with her bare hands.

And the third was the last words Omelian Marchenko spoke before Isabelle lost her legendary control over herself.

Men died first.

79

Crawford

It was weeks before the sanatorium finally put Vanessa in a room with a therapist in a lab coat. Until then she saw only nurses who wasted Vanessa's time combing through her medical history. They harassed her daily about going outside. Finally, she got on a doctor's schedule—but only to discuss her aversion to the outdoors! Everyone spent time in the gardens, apparently, especially during sunny and fragrant May. Why didn't *she*?

At first Homer Crawford seemed like a decent man with a friendly enough demeanor. He was slight and neat with Golden Retriever eyes. But Vanessa soon realized it was a ruse, a disguise to hide what he really was—a tyrannical tormenter. He wasn't a Golden, he was a Doberman.

He didn't even have a notebook on his lap! He didn't sit behind a desk like a proper doctor. He sat in the plush wingback chair by the tall open window, while he directed her to a hardwood bench in a nearby corner by the wall. "You're not going outside why?" Crawford said.

"I don't want to talk about it."

"What *do* you want to talk about?"

Did she have the nerve to tell this man? "I believe my husband is in love with another woman." Vanessa was proud of herself for being forthright, but Crawford wasn't the least impressed.

"Before you tell me your theories, I need to know some hard facts about you."

"Like why I'm not outside?"

"Sure, let's start with that."

Vanessa didn't want to start with that. They delved into her background instead, but Crawford wasn't particularly interested in that either, other than to ask if she had been outside since childhood. He probed and probed until he goaded Vanessa into the Story of the Lost Hat. He sat befuddled.

"I don't want to explain what I don't want to explain," Vanessa said.

"Explain what you want, then."

"I have a real crisis in my house and you keep trying to pick apart something from ten years ago that doesn't matter anymore."

"Sounds like there's been a crisis in your house for ten years." Crawford appeared to be barely paying attention. His gaze was on the lawns below. "Has your marriage been sound before this latest. . . ?"

"Absolutely," Vanessa said. "We have a wonderful marriage."

"*Wonderful*. I see. Then I'd say your suspicions are unfounded. Let's get back to this lost hat. What is the hat a stand-in for?"

"No! I said *no*."

"Suit yourself." Crawford sat and stared out the window, absorbed in the activities below.

Vanessa shifted from side to side in the silence. "Is there anyone else I can talk to? A woman perhaps?"

"You want to talk to a woman, do you?" Crawford said. "I'm the psychiatrist in residence. We have a cardiologist, an infectious diseases specialist, and an ear and nose doctor. All men. The thirty nurses on staff take care of a hundred patients and don't have an hour in their day to talk only to you. You're welcome to try—with any one of them. But here's the issue I have. You're not at home. You're in a sanatorium. This isn't a pensione where you can spend your days fiddling with your hands like you're doing now. Sick people come here to get better. And you know what happens after they get better? They go home. What you're proposing—to use Austen Riggs as a permanent hotel—isn't going to work for us, not even if your benefactor is our president. When Percival and I have our weekly review and I explain to him what you're trying to do, he'll be on the phone with your father posthaste, demanding you leave immediately."

"Threats don't work on me," Vanessa said. "I just retreat further."

"By all means retreat—back to Hampton. I have thirteen other patients I need to see today."

Sometime later, Crawford introduced Vanessa to Shiba Miata, a nurse of indeterminate ethnic background. "Shiba said she's willing to talk to you," Crawford said. "She knows your history. Fill her in on the details if you wish. Good luck, Shiba. I'll be on rounds."

He left the two women alone. Vanessa hated to admit it, but Crawford was right. Vanessa was more wary of Shiba than she was of Crawford, even though Shiba let her sit in the comfy chair by the window.

"What else happened when you lost your hat?" Shiba said.

"I don't want to talk about it!" Vanessa said. "Didn't you hear me? I told you, my husband is in love with another woman."

"Impossible," said Shiba. "You are beautiful and elegant. You have a lovely smile, a genteel demeanor, graceful gestures. You came here well dressed, and the man who dropped you off was solicitous and caring toward you. He clearly wants you to be better, so whatever is ailing you, let's get to it."

"You're looking at the problem from the outside," Vanessa said. "You see only the visible, what you can observe with your myopic eye."

Here is what ailed Vanessa:

After Isabelle shot the intruder and Finn leaped across the porch and into the house, the person he rushed to first was Isabelle, still violently expelling the shotgun shell from her smoking weapon. He stepped up to her as in a *pas de deux*, a dance for two. He didn't speak to her, he merely came close and peered into her face. Only after that momentary lapse did Finn seek out Vanessa. Before that, no one else existed for him.

When Finn cast his brief gaze on Isabelle, he gazed upon her as the *most* familiar thing, not the least familiar thing.

And that didn't make *any* sense, because in recent months, Vanessa had observed Finn and Isabelle having almost zero connection. Their old banter was gone, their arguing, their joking. *Obviously* Vanessa didn't know how they were with each other out in the fields, but during family meals they talked almost exclusively to others. Vanessa remembered one afternoon when Isabelle was by the stove, and Finn walked close behind her and didn't say a word. Now that Vanessa thought about it, perhaps he passed *too close* behind her. Like he could brush against her if she moved. But he ignored her as if she weren't even there, and she ignored him! She ladled out soup in a bowl for him and placed it on the counter, and he took it from the counter—not her hands. They never even glanced at each other.

He stopped speaking her name. Not just to call for her across the growing greenery, but even inside the house.

They didn't sit next to each other anymore, not even outside by the fire, where Vanessa was not.

From the outside, if you were to observe Finn and Isabelle without knowing anything about them, you would think they were strangers.

But it wasn't always that way. Vanessa was certain about *that*. Their previous nonstop repartee had been so irritating to her. She remembered the feeling it provoked within her, the churlishness. Now it was the absence of churlishness that was the glaring wrong.

Had they flirted, had they touched, or said inappropriate things, it would have been easier to deal with. This—it was like a slow deadly poison. By the time it killed you, you hardly knew you were dying.

And when you looked at the two of them from the outside, you could never tell.

Eventually, in broken passages, Vanessa managed to convey this to Shiba.

Like Crawford, Shiba was deeply unimpressed with Vanessa's assessments. "I don't know your husband," she said, "and I don't know the woman who lives with you. But I do know something about love. Love is the animating force in all life. It's something you cannot hide. You would see it instantly between them, every time they looked at each other."

"Exactly," said Vanessa. "And they made sure they *never* looked at each other." Except when she killed a man.

"You're saying the absence of love is proof of love?" said Shiba. "That doesn't seem right."

"I'm telling you how it is. The external is not real."

"Very good," said Shiba. "But you're speaking about yourself right now, correct? Earlier, I described you from the outside, and you just confessed to me that you are not what you appear to be. The external is not real. So who is the real Vanessa?"

After that, Vanessa sheepishly crawled back to Crawford, gladly sat on the hard bench while he lounged in comfort by his open window, and didn't ask to speak to anyone else.

When she told Crawford again about her suspicions, he also shrugged. "It doesn't seem likely. They live surrounded by nine other people. It doesn't sound as if there's a gap in their day for what you're proposing. He sleeps at night with you, yes?"

"Yes."

"And during the day they labor alongside your parents, his parents, your sister, and your children, yes?"

"Yes."

"Every meal you have, you have together. And during those meals they don't speak. Every evening you have, you have together. And during the radio hour they don't speak. So when exactly does this breathless love affair take place? Only in their hearts? Only deep within themselves?"

Vanessa chewed her lip. In the winter months Isabelle had horse things to do for Mickey, and Finn drove her because she didn't drive. The stables were in Virginia or Vermont, so they were gone a few days at a time. But often they took Mae and Junie with them and once even Earl and Walter! It seemed so harmless. And once a month, they went to Boston together—without the girls. Isabelle had things to do for Schumann and stayed with him while Finn visited Lucas and stayed with him. Finn drove home without her, and she returned later by train.

Why didn't Vanessa want to disclose this little charade to the good doctor?

Maybe because it made her seem like an idiot for not noticing and not even caring.

"Have you ever seen them acting inappropriately with one another?"

"Like how?" She was glad to veer off in another direction.

"Anything. Passing a private joke. Discussing things a man and woman who are not intimate should not discuss. Touching each other, perhaps."

"No, never!" But Vanessa chewed her lip even worse than before. And there she'd been, thinking this was a good direction to veer off in!

They played in the snow when they were supposed to be shoveling. Sometimes they hosed each other with water. They fought like angry children when they tried to build a rail fence and the posts broke. Isabelle even shoved him. "I told you they weren't strong enough, and you never listen!" Once she fell off a ladder. Maybe Finn caught her. Did she fall or jump? Vanessa couldn't see past the raspberry bushes. Once he cut himself and she bandaged his arm. She did a *very* thorough job. Once they jumped from a high ledge in the barn into the hay below. They did it for hours with the kids. Vanessa rocked back and forth, wishing she could run over her memories with a concrete spreader.

There were other things, too. How united Finn and Isabelle were in trying to get Vanessa to function better, how often they cajoled her and appealed to her, how often they spoke to her as if they were well versed in their separate interactions with her. How relieved Vanessa had been to send Isabelle across Boston to bring Finn his dinner, so she herself wouldn't have to do it. How after the bank closed, Finn and Isabelle ran the entire household, and how grateful Vanessa was that she herself didn't have to do it. How often during that last year in Beacon Hill, Finn came late to bed, smelling of cigarettes and liquor and denying the liquor.

Vanessa didn't tell Crawford how they raced down to the river together, and went to town and the market and the ocean together. How Isabelle played the balalaika and sang in a foreign language and how he sat and listened as if he understood the words. Her heart hurt.

"Here's my proof," Vanessa said to the doctor. "A dozen people are celebrating New Year's Eve. At midnight, we all hug and kiss one another. My God, I even hugged and air-kissed Finn's brother, and I can't stand that man!"

"Why?"

"Why did I kiss him or why can't I stand him? No—he's not the point of my story! Everyone kissed, yet neither Finn nor Isabelle came anywhere near each other."

"Did you want them to?"

"They *didn't* is the point."

"How do you know," said Crawford, "unless you were already watching them? They could have."

"You think I'm imagining the whole thing?"

"I don't know. Tell me about this Isabelle."

Vanessa told him.

Crawford listened intently. It was the first time he turned his head away from the window.

"Do you think she's attractive?"

Vanessa shrugged. "In my view, not really. She used to be a horse rider, so she's trim and toned in the legs and hips, like a gymnast."

"Or a rider."

"Do men like that sort of thing?"

"They don't *not* like it," said Crawford.

"She does have an ample bosom, but she wears peasant dresses, how attractive is that?"

Crawford didn't reply.

"She's always perspiring and dusty from field work. It's disagreeable to a man like my husband." Or so Vanessa thought. "He has a strong distaste for dirt and germs."

"What else?"

"She's got a direct, open face. Unswerving eyes, well-formed lips. Her eyebrows are too thick. She doesn't pluck them. She doesn't do anything with her long hair either, all she does is brush it and leave it down. Or she braids it in two and looks like Heidi. She wears almost no makeup except when we have summer parties. She kind of dresses up then. Puts flowers in her hair—who does that? And she dances and sings and plays the balalaika and tells jokes like a jester. I didn't think any of that would be particularly appealing to a serious professional like my husband."

Crawford shrugged. "It's not *un*appealing," he said. "I've seen your husband when he comes to visit you. He is a handsome, hale and hearty man. I can't speak for his taste in women."

"His taste in women is me," Vanessa said. "Refined, made up, neat, delicate, put together."

"Except you are here, and he is there. With her."

"By my choice, not theirs," Vanessa said loftily.

Crawford was silent, as if figuring out what to say or how to say it. "During the months and years this was happening, and your husband and this woman lived and worked together side by side, what were *you* doing?"

"How is this about me?" she exclaimed, flustered and unhappy.

"Because this is your story," said Crawford. "You are the center of your own narrative. If I were talking to your husband or to Isabelle, I suspect you would not be the focus of *their* story. I'll ask you again—what are *you*, Vanessa Evans, doing in the middle of your days?"

"I'm in the house," Vanessa said. "I'm in my bedroom."

"What are you doing in your bedroom?"

"In the mornings, sleeping. Sometimes I clean at night, and I go to bed late. So I sleep late."

"And then?"

"It takes me a while to get out of bed."

"And then?"

"It takes me a while to get myself together, to get dressed, ready for the day."

"And then?"

"I clean my room, or scrub the washbasin, or dust the wood blinds or the windowsills, or I wipe the floor where Finn has been. He tries to be careful but he always drags in dirt from outside. I wash the floor with rags, and then I wash the rags."

"And then?"

"I make the bed, tidy my nightstand, dust my lamps, underneath the trays, the inside of the wardrobe and the dressers, wipe the mirror, do my makeup again. Normal things."

"You put your makeup on twice. Why? Why even once?"

"Same reason I put it on here," she said. "To look put together."

"Yes, it's important to *look* put together," the doctor echoed. "By this time, I imagine it's evening?"

"Yes. And the girls come in, and tell me what they've been doing, and then Isabelle comes in and tells me about dinner."

"And then you go out and cook?"

"No," Vanessa said. "I have a hard time cooking. Not because I don't like it. But the act makes such a mess of my clean kitchen that it gives me tremendous anxiety."

He studied her pensively. "I suspect there are many activities you probably find messy and distasteful."

"Yes—such as cooking," said Vanessa, averting her gaze. "So I remove myself from the process. I set the table, and after dinner I clear the table and wash the dishes and wipe the counters and make it spotless."

"And then?"

"After dinner, they listen to a program, while I continue tidying up," Vanessa said. "Or I wipe the floor under their feet, or I go clean the bathroom, because with so many muddy farm people washing before dinner, the bathroom is always a dire mess."

Crawford was quiet. "You are dusting under your family's feet while they're relaxing at the end of their long day listening to Lone Ranger?"

"No!" Vanessa exclaimed. "Sometimes it's Fibber McGee and Molly."

"Let's say it's true about your husband and this Isabelle," Crawford said. "Why are you here?"

"What do you mean why? It's not obvious?"

"Not in the slightest."

"I needed to remove myself from that incredibly stressful situation. Is that really hard to understand?"

Crawford stared at Vanessa for so long she became uncomfortable. "Isn't that what you've been doing your whole life?" he said at last. "Removing yourself utterly from any situation that made you the least bit uneasy? Even something as anodyne and virtuous as cooking for your family. You couldn't participate in it. Field work? Not for you. Educating your own children? Sounds like your mother-in-law is performing that task."

"She is an actual teacher! It's the role she was born to play."

"There's always a reason, isn't there, why someone else does what you don't want to do. Tending to your father? Your mother has that in hand. Where are you, Vanessa Evans, while another woman lives your life and takes care of your husband?"

Vanessa got up and left.

"I see where you are," the doctor called after her. "Missing."

It was a long time before she appeared again in Crawford's office.

She sat quietly at first, mulling her words.

"I came to Austen Riggs," she said, "because when I realized he was in love with her, I didn't know what else to do."

"Of course," Crawford said. "You did the only thing you ever do. Bolt and run. But why didn't you first ask your husband if it was true?"

"Why would I?"

"If you didn't want to know, why are you talking to *me* about it? For rhetorical exercise?"

"I'm talking to you about it because I thought you could help me."

"Help you do what?"

Vanessa didn't reply.

"Why didn't you stay and fight?"

"How could I?" whispered Vanessa, her voice breaking. "I didn't ask him because I couldn't bear to have him look into my face and lie." She raised her hand to stop Crawford from speaking again. "I didn't ask him," she said in a collapsing, deadened voice, "because I couldn't bear to have him look into my face and tell me the truth." She burst into tears.

Crawford sat and waited for her to stop crying. He didn't even offer her a napkin, she had to get her own!

"You're afraid of the truth," he said.

"Who wouldn't be!"

"Why are you afraid?"

"Because then what?" whispered Vanessa.

"*Finally*," Crawford said with great emphasis. "After many months, we are finally getting somewhere." He folded his hands. "You haven't asked my opinion but I'm going to give it to you anyway. What you've described to me cannot continue."

"I agree!"

"What you are doing cannot continue."

"What? No—it's not me! It's them!"

"No, Vanessa. I know you feel as if you had no choice but to come here, but while you're here, what do you think is happening there? Now that they don't have *you* to worry about, do you think they're growing *less* intimate, falling *less* in love, becoming *less* committed to each other?"

"I don't think about it," half a Vanessa said in half a voice.

"Your marriage is going to end," Crawford said. "And then what will you do? Sounds like the farm life can't succeed without Isabelle. In the scenario you've painted for me, *she* is the indispensable one. You have been sidelined. Not only is life going on without you, but it's going on *swimmingly*. How does that make you feel? If you go back and give your husband an ultimatum—it's either her or me, darling—what kind of response do you think you'll get?"

"You don't think *I* know this?" Vanessa exclaimed. "That's why I didn't ask him."

"What do you plan to do about it after you leave here?"

"You're the doctor. I was hoping you'd tell me."

"I'm a doctor, not a magician," Crawford said. "You have been a non-existent wife. You have not helped him, not even in the smallest way, to carry the burden that was placed on him."

"What about the burden on *me*?" Vanessa said, insulted.

"While your husband seeks a way to feed his family, your parents, his parents, and your sister, what are *you* burdened by? The country is facing challenging times. The pressures on him are enormous. And what have you done? I would be more surprised if you told me he was still faithful to you, frankly."

"How dare you!"

"I'll tell you how you can begin another life," Crawford went on, ignoring her outburst, her outraged glare, her frazzled hands. "First, acknowledge your own failures."

"You sound like Finn, not like my doctor," she said.

"You mean your husband has discussed this with you?"

"Many times. We do communicate, you know. We are married."

"You've communicated with your husband about all the ways in which you refuse to participate in the marriage?" Crawford stared at her coolly. "Vanessa, let him go. You clearly don't love him. Leave him be."

"What are you talking about?" she cried. "Of course I love him."

"Not one thing you've told me comes from the mouth of a wife who loves her husband. I've heard a lot about what he did wrong. He doesn't understand, he doesn't care, he works too hard, he drinks illegally, he brought you to the farm, he keeps asking you to go outside. That's what I'm hearing. Anger. Contempt. Disrespect. Resentment. Not even between the lines do I hear love."

"The love is there. It's just covered with those other things."

"Not covered. Buried. As in dead."

"That's not true!"

"Listen to me," said Crawford, a little louder, as if Vanessa was having trouble hearing him. "It doesn't exist. *Let him be.* Let him make a better life with someone else."

"You're insane," said a horrified Vanessa. "I'm the one who should be treating *you* for nervous maladies. I didn't come here to let him go, you fool. Do you even have a degree? I came here to get him back."

"You're here because you ran away, the same reason you hid in your bunker on the farm. It's why you mindlessly dust your drawers and don't go outside with your children."

"I went outside with my children—and look what happened!"

Crawford couldn't hide his astonishment. "You blame your children for losing your baby?"

"It was so slippery out, and we have such steep hills! *Take us to the park, take us to the park*, they said. I relented, I tried to be a good mother. I took them, and I lost my favorite hat! Had I not gone out with them, I'd still have it, and I'd still have my child, and we wouldn't have *this* to deal with."

"It's the *children's* fault you slipped on a curb?"

"It happened because I went looking for my hat and couldn't find it. And Finn was out drinking with Lucas! He wasn't home where he was supposed to be, to help me, to go with me! I was all alone, and I slipped." She put her face into her hands. "And when Lucas finally brought him home, he was so toasted, he didn't even know what was happening to me." She couldn't speak about it anymore. She left. It was a long time before she returned.

"If our governess hadn't taken the day off because her husband was sick, I wouldn't have had to go to the park in the first place," said Vanessa after she sat down on her hard bench.

"You wouldn't have had to go to the park with *your children*," Crawford repeated.

"Yes."

"Vanessa, I'm unclear—is it the governess's fault for taking a day off, or the children's fault for wanting to play, or your husband's fault for having a drink, or this Lucas person's fault? Is any of it your fault?"

"It's my fault for trying to be a good mother, for trying to be a good wife."

"Is that why you've stopped trying to be either?"

"I haven't stop—"

"Enough." He regrouped. "Did you consider the possibility that perhaps the baby wasn't meant to be?" Crawford said. "Millions of mothers have walked in the snow, taken their children to the park, slipped off curbs, lost hats even—and they didn't lose their babies. I know there is grief. I know that what happened is unfair. But instead of blaming your entire family and the great outdoors, and this Lucas character, couldn't you—solely for comfort—entertain the possibility that maybe the child wasn't meant to survive? Maybe there was some abnormality that would have made life difficult for him? Why didn't you try to have another one? Nothing like the birth of a healthy child to make you forget your anguish."

"I couldn't risk it," said Vanessa. "What if I miscarried again? A scalded cat doesn't jump on a hot stove again."

"Yes, but it won't jump on a cold stove either," returned Crawford. "You'd rather live inside your anger and pain than try for another baby your husband desperately wanted?"

"Why should he get to have what he wants?"

"Yes, spoken like a woman in love."

"I didn't get to have what I wanted."

"And what is that, Vanessa?"

"A living baby," she barely mouthed, struggling up and staggering from Crawford's office.

She had come to the sanatorium hoping that she could get better, and maybe she could offer herself to Finn and her girls as the woman she was always meant to be, instead of the woman she had become, nothing but an irrational fraction divided again and again. But this was going so poorly.

When she and Crawford met again, she was quiet. "The next time you provoke me, I may not come back at all," she said, trying to be funny.

"And who would that be a punishment for?" said Crawford.

They sat. He stared out the window.

"I think you're right," she said.

"I'm right about so many things. What specifically?"

"It could be my imagination," she said. "I'm in a room alone with my thoughts all day. Some of them are bound to be irrational."

"Which part is either imagination or irrational?"

"The part about Isabelle and my husband," said Vanessa. "I get too worked up about things. I've blown the whole thing out of proportion."

Crawford nodded.

"You agree?" She was excited.

"Only that you are using another one of your tricks to stop yourself from dealing with your terrible situation, to stop yourself from fixing yourself and your life. If it's all someone else's fault, if it's all in your head, you don't have to do anything."

"Okay, yes, maybe—but also," said Vanessa, "then I can go back home and pretend like nothing's happened."

"Is that what you want?"

"Everything else is too unbearable," Vanessa said, looking at her hands with shame. "I have nowhere else to go. And we as a family have nowhere else to go. Your way, my entire world explodes. My way, everything stays the same."

"You'd rather live a life in which your husband continues an intimate relationship with another woman in your house?"

"Nothing else seems possible," Vanessa said.

"No other solution presents itself to you?"

"Like what, some kind of pill? Electric shock treatment? A lobotomy?"

"There is no pill that will make you love your husband," Crawford said. "No treatment that will make you stop being angry at others for your own failings. No lobotomy is going to help you cope with your anxiety."

"So what are we talking about then?" She said it as if she wanted a lobotomy, preferred it to this.

"If I asked you what you want, what would you tell me?"

"What I want from what?"

"From this day forward. From the moment you leave here. When you return home. What do you *want*, Vanessa?"

"I want things to go back to the way they were," Vanessa said weakly. "Before she came into our lives. We were managing. We were happy, more or less. We had a house, servants, money. Everything ran smoothly."

"Except you couldn't go outside, and you didn't want to be touched by your husband."

"Only because I was afraid of having a child!"

"And that life is something you'd want again?"

"Yes, it was wonderful."

"If Finn was here with you, and I asked him the same question, what would he say?"

"I can't speak for him."

"Of course you can. You can give an opinion, can't you? What do you *think* he would say? Would he tell me it was wonderful? Would he tell me he would like that life back?" Crawford paused. "Or would he say that despite the endless toil, the unceasing labor, the absence of financial security, the lack of material comforts, he would still take his present life over any other life he's ever had?"

It took Vanessa a very long time to reply. "That is what I'm most afraid of," she said.

"You keep telling me all the things I've done wrong," Vanessa said to Crawford.

"I'm not. I'm like a recording. I repeat to you what you say to me."

"But you're not telling me how to fix it."

"I can't fix it."

"So what good are you?"

"Only you can fix it."

"How?"

"Ask yourself what you want," Crawford said. "Ask yourself what you can't live without. I don't think you've suffered enough. Until you answer those questions, you can't know what to work toward. Roosevelt wanted to be president and not even a potentially life-ending illness would stop him. First and foremost, you need to know your order of desire."

"I don't want to go outside," she said.

"First and foremost?" said Crawford. "Because if you can't go outside, you cannot be a wife and mother. It's one thing or the other thing. Are you a paralytic or are you the President of the United States? That's the choice you must make, Vanessa."

"It's all well and good for us to sit and speculate on the president's choices," Vanessa said. "But I can't live on my own, and I don't want to be forced to do what I don't want to do."

"Okay, this is progress," Crawford exclaimed dryly. "You're admitting that you're resigned to living out your days in a wheelchair, an invalid by choice whom other healthy people—including your husband and his sensual, charismatic, inexhaustible woman—must care for. And that this lamentable existence is enough for you. Better that than a future in which you rediscover your purpose. This is an important breakthrough you've made about yourself, Vanessa. I hope you're proud."

"Do you have any idea how infuriating you are?" she said, standing and turning toward the door. "How mind-bogglingly vexatious?"

"No, but do tell. I have a half-hour before my next patient."

Weeks and weeks of crying and eating in her room, while outside was sunny and bright and the yellow-bellied tanagers chirped and fairytales were read to visiting children.

Or was it months and months?

Or was it years?

Who wrote that fairytales did not tell children that dragons existed? Children already knew that dragons existed. Fairytales told children that dragons could be killed.

"Vanessa, from my window, I saw you out on the patio yesterday," Crawford said. "Were my eyes deceiving me?"

"I wish they were deceiving you," she said. "It was dreadful. As soon as I dared set one foot on the concrete, something flew into my eye. I had to be sedated."

"Shiba told me it was fluff from a dandelion."

"It was a bumblebee," Vanessa said. "It was huge like a bumblebee."

"Vanessa, did you tell your husband when he came to visit you that you've been going outside?"

"I didn't need to. We sat outside and had our tea."

"Was he impressed? Were your daughters impressed? They're lovely young ladies, by the way. They look like their mother."

"Are you being forward with me, Dr. Crawford?" said Vanessa.

"I'm being observant."

"They were moderately impressed, I suppose, by my single step into the fresh air," Vanessa said. "And thank you."

"All great things begin with a single step. How is everything at home?"

"Good. We have a tractor. It was a gift for Isabelle from a horse breeder."

"That is *some* gift," Crawford said. "What does Isabelle do for this man?"

"Like I pay attention. Evaluates his horses, I think." Vanessa shrugged. "One of her horses won the Kentucky Derby."

Crawford whooped. "That's an extraordinary achievement!"

"I suppose. We also bought a combine. The girls love all that, but the farming talk is debilitating for me."

"It's important for mothers to pay attention to the interests of their children," Crawford said. "What else? How is your sister's new husband?"

"I don't know. Bertie is a fisherman. When he comes, I have nothing to say to him. Neither does Eleanor. I think she only married him to have an extra pair of hands in the fields."

"Extra hands are important. Most of your family came last month?"

"Yes. Everyone but Isabelle."

"Yes." Crawford was quiet. "She never comes."

Vanessa was quiet. "I suppose that's how you know what I fear is true. If it wasn't true, she'd be here."

"Yes." Crawford sighed. "Did you and your husband have a few minutes alone?"

"Of course not. We never do. His design, not mine. He comes once a month, brings gifts, stays the afternoon, but there's always someone by his side. The girls always—"

"You're happy to see your daughters, no?"

"Of course. But he brings my sister, whom I'm less happy to see, and Eleanor drags her son with her, and now her new husband, too. Finn often brings my parents. My father looks a little frail." Vanessa shuddered. "He's lost weight. His hands tremble. I don't know."

"What would you say to Finn if he came alone?"

Vanessa stammered.

"Why don't you ask him to come by himself next time and we can work on what you can say to him."

"You're just making things worse, Crawford, with your damn words. Where did you get your degree, the School of Ruin Everything?"

"You're upset with your husband for not coming by himself, yet the thought of being alone with him is an unimaginable terror?"

"Somewhere in there I know you're trying to catch me in something."

"Yes, in your maddening inconsistency." Crawford looked out the window and smoked.

"I see you didn't ask Finn to come alone. Who was that with him?"

"His father."

"The retired judge?"

"Yes. He scares me. But apparently Finn and Earl drove down to Connecticut some months back and sweet-talked the CEO of a submarine company into donating one of their decommissioned boats to charity."

"A submarine to charity?"

Vanessa chuckled. "No, Crawford," she said. "They make ferry boats and other ships. But that's pretty good, right? As good as the Kentucky Derby?" She smiled. "They talked the CEO into repurposing an old unused ship into a merchant vessel."

"Always good to repurpose old unused things. For what charity?"

"My husband helps people who bring in refugees from Ukraine every few months."

"What an unending disaster that part of the world is," Crawford said.

"Tell me about it. That's the main dinner talk at my table."

"But a great act of charity on the part of the boat company. And your husband is involved in this because of Isabelle?"

"Yes," Vanessa said. "To help her husband and sons get to America."

"Isabelle has a husband and sons? Why have you not mentioned them?"

"They're missing," Vanessa said. "But every boat that comes in, she prays they're on it."

Crawford began to say something.

"You asked me a while back what I hope for, do you remember?" said Vanessa. "I guess in the half of an imperfect life that's still left for me to live, I'm hoping that Finn's herculean efforts on her behalf will not be in vain, and that her family will find their way to America and be reunited with her, and then they can go off and live their own imperfect life, and my husband will return to me."

"That sounds almost like a plan, or a dream," said Crawford. "In which case, we're going to have to work harder, Vanessa, to give Finn something real to come back to."

"Do I have too many problems to be a good wife?" she asked Crawford, when her progress seemed too insignificant to warrant a change in her marital circumstances.

"No," Crawford said. "You're doing well."

"Seems sort of pathetic. Outside for thirty minutes. It's hardly a triumph. It's hardly the sacking of Troy."

"Are you Troy or Greece in your analogy?" asked Crawford.

"Jury's still out on that," she said.

"Because it took Greece over ten years to achieve victory."

"Yes, yes, I know, Troy wasn't sacked in a day," Vanessa said, and Crawford laughed.

"We've been working on two areas," he said. "One you can heal by relatively simple therapies just as you've been doing. Going outside, for example. Since you've separated the loss of your child from being outdoors, you have been slowly regaining your sense of the world by venturing out onto our gorgeous lawns. Carry on, and success will be yours. Just remember, if you are outside thirty minutes on Monday, you must sit by yourself at least forty minutes on Tuesday. If you took forty steps on Wednesday, you must take fifty steps on

Thursday. Every day push yourself a little farther, a little harder. And when you feel uncomfortable—"

"Stop immediately!"

Crawford smiled. "When you feel stressed or anxious, push yourself another minute or two into that anxiety. Then stop if you want, but don't let the stress control you. Learn how to walk through it. Remind yourself you are a strong, attractive, capable woman."

"Yes, a strong, attractive, capable woman who doesn't like to get dirty or endure mess, and are you being forward with me again, Crawford?"

"Merely observant," he said. "So what if you get dirty? That's what soap is for. So what if the kitchen is a mess? That's what a sponge is for."

"What about the other problem? Not so easy, that one."

He sat by the window and breathed in the air. "Your second habit is admittedly more difficult because you've trained yourself to give in to it instead of to overcome it. It's a nasty lifetime pattern to break."

"And that is?"

"Coping by way of distraction," Crawford said. "It started with the lemons and continued right into your husband's love affair. A direct line from lemons to Ukrainian lovers."

"Are you making fun of me?"

"No, Vanessa," Crawford said. "Unfortunately our time is growing short. It took us a while to get here. You were one tough nut. However, you've had some major steps forward. I've given you the tools. The rest is up to you."

"I don't see any tools," said Vanessa, "and I certainly don't know how to use them."

"The lemons have ruined you," Crawford said. "You distracted yourself from them at an early age by planting flowers or organizing your wardrobe."

"Yes, Crawford, I'm the one who told you this."

"The next time you faced a new anxiety—like your sister's jealousy or your mother's unrealistic expectations of you—you again coped the only way you knew how, by busying yourself with mindless physical tasks. No matter how small the problem, you turned away from it. You sponged or dusted or scrubbed or mopped. And then you added another impediment by inserting excuses into the busyness. You stopped saying, I'm distracting myself with cleaning because I know Finn is keeping something from me and I'm afraid to ask what it is, and started saying, I'm cleaning because the house or the nursery or the kitchen is a dire mess and I must deal with this new problem at once to the exclusion of all else."

"Crawford, sometimes things are messy," Vanessa said. "Closets really are dusty and windows *are* disgusting."

"A lot less often than you think," Crawford said. "And even when the windows are clean, the other, much more serious problems persist."

"Yes, but the windows are clean," said Vanessa. She was teasing.

"Your defense mechanism against anxiety is infinitely regressive," said Crawford. "You became so proficient with the compulsion that you lost your ability to deal with any situation. And losing a child is an *enormous* ordeal. If you turned away from the lemons, think about how far you ran from the grief. And in 1929 when your family endured another genuine crisis, you had no ability to meet it or to support your husband through it other than to hide inside your rags and your sponges."

"Someone had to wash the towels," Vanessa muttered, less jovially.

"You created for yourself and in yourself an untenable make-believe world in which all reality was blocked and all that was left was a chaos of your own invention. You kept saying if only the books got alphabetized, if only the children didn't lose their mittens, if only the immigrant woman stopped placing jars on shelves and cans in cupboards, everything would be all right again."

"In my defense, Crawford, the books have *never* gotten alphabetized."

Crawford drummed on the window ledge. "How are you going to confront the very real crisis inside your marriage?"

"I guess I'll have to scrub harder."

"When you find yourself reaching for a rag or a duster instead of confronting Finn, when you feel yourself unable to leave your room, say to yourself: I know the floor is not dusty. I know his clothes on the floor is not why I'm upset. I need to talk to him, and I'm afraid."

"Sometimes his clothes *are* on the floor. Both things can be true."

"Vanessa."

"Oh, fine. But I've had a lot to be afraid of," she said. "The loss of my father's bank. His heart attack. Adder's abandonment of my sister. Our sudden calamitous poverty. Our moving to an awful remote place in the middle of nowhere. My husband's love for another woman."

"Every one of the things you listed except the last one has already happened and been dealt with by people other than you. You were nowhere to be found. You left your husband adrift and alone. He is responsible for his actions, but if you cast the one you say you love into a storm, you can't blame *only* him for finding a life raft. Some of that, you must own."

"I'm confused—do I clean or not?"

"You don't clean *first*. You clean last. You don't clean for coping. You clean for reward. This is your chance to do something about the thing you can still do something about, Vanessa. You want to save your marriage? Talk to Finn and *then* dust. Stop postponing the confrontation. Stalling only adds to your burdens. Say instead, I will mop as a gift to myself—for facing the most difficult thing. Because to face a hard thing deserves applause, deserves reward. First you speak to him, and then you scrub, knowing you have faced him. Sponge to your heart's content knowing you have earned it."

"Sounds like another trick of the mind." But she leaned back on her bench feeling more hopeful. "Live first, then run from living? Are you *sure* changing the order of operations will help?"

"Has your way made your life livable?" Crawford said. "For years, you've been dusting the corners while your marriage fell apart. Now try dusting your marriage while your corners fall apart. I fully expect that by the time you finish with the marriage and the fields and the cooking and the children, you will have so little energy for scraping wax off candles that you will listen to Jack Benny, laugh a few times, and be out like a light."

As Vanessa was about to leave, she turned around. Crawford was still by the window, looking longingly at the green sloping lawns and the lengthening shadows.

"Are you all right, Homer?" she said, seeing him suddenly. His hair had thinned. He had lost weight, had trouble taking a deep breath.

He turned to her and smiled. "I'm fine," he said. "Thank you for asking. By the way, did you ever find out if you were allergic to lemons?"

"I did," said Vanessa. "And I'm not."

He laughed.

She laughed too.

"You are a lovely woman, Vanessa," he said.

"Okay, you're definitely being forward now."

"Maybe," Homer Crawford said. "But also a little bit observant."

80

Fireman's Fair

"Daddy, please!"

"Dad, we're going to miss it!"

"Uncle Finn!"

"Isabelle, please go see what's holding Dad up. We don't want to be late. We've been waiting all year."

It was Saturday night during the Fourth of July weekend, and they were about to go to the Fireman's Fair on the ocean boardwalk in Rye. They had worked hard, got cleaned up and dressed up, and now were sitting in the truck waiting. "Hold on, Junebug," said Isabelle, wearing a bias-cut floral dress with a bare neckline and white flowers in her hair. "Daddy's on the phone, I think." She got out of the truck and stepped inside the house. The screen door slammed. Finn was on the phone, his back turned to her, talking quietly. She waited. When he replaced the receiver by slamming it down, she knew instantly whom he'd been speaking to. "Vanessa?"

Grabbing his keys, he nodded. "Let's go."

"Everything all right?"

"Fine, but we ain't talking about it now," he said. "Let's go have fun."

The third annual Fireman's Fair was a joyous occasion. People came from miles around for the three-day event. Saturday night especially was mobbed. If you didn't get there early enough, they ran out of tickets. There was a Ferris wheel and a tilt-a-whirl and a merry-go-round and a haunted house and funhouse mirrors and funnel cake. The girls went on rides, Monty went off to hang out with some friends, and Finn and Isabelle, like two blissed-out old chaperones, paced Mae and Junie. The night was warm and loud, and they stood close, eating hot dogs and fried clams and ice cream and donuts and cotton candy. It was hard to hear each other, and every time they spoke, he had to lean down to her ear, tickling her neck with his breath. The fair was held on the boardwalk, and the salt night wind blew off the ocean and mottled her hair and made her smell like the sea, which she knew Finn loved—when she was briny and windswept and warm. They stood by a chain-link fence watching the girls on the Wild West swings. He was behind her, just off to the side, pressing his body lightly against her hips. One of his big arms rested atop the chest-high fence, and the other hand lay on the small of her back.

"It's almost over," she said with a wistful sigh, ripping off the cotton candy and sucking it into her mouth.

"We've been here three hours," he said. "Is that not long enough for you . . . said the bishop to the actress?"

"Please don't try to be funny."

Moving her hair aside, he bent down and kissed the back of her neck. *You are so beautiful, Isa*, he whispered. *You are so, so beautiful.*

She murmured something back, like *what's gotten into you*, tremulous and delighted. Facing him, she stared into his face, filling her eyes with everything she felt for him, and then turned back to the Wild West swings. They resumed their semi-casual, deeply intimate pose.

"We didn't even get to do our favorite thing," she said.

"Right here?"

"Finn."

"Yes, Isabelle?"

"I meant the shooting gallery."

"Oh."

"The line is still too long." She squinted at the amusement tents down the boardwalk. "We'll try again before we go. The kids love it when we do it."

"Yeah, yeah." He leaned in close. "Don't eat all the cotton candy," he whispered. "Save some for later. You know how much I like to lick it off your—"

The girls ran up. Finn moved away. They found Monty and together stood in line for another half-hour, waiting for their turn at the shooting range. The fair was almost closing. As always, Isabelle made Finn go first. "I want to see what I'm up against." He picked up the rifle, aimed, and shot five out of seven scrolling ducks. Isabelle shot six out of seven. The next round, he got seven out of seven and she got six. "Daddy won! Daddy won!" That was Finn jumping up and down, not his mortified daughters.

They won a prize for the girls, and then Finn picked up the rifle again, and shot enough ducks to win a prize for Isabelle. The girls picked out two huge bears, and she chose a gibbon with extra-long arms which Finn wrapped around her neck. She carried the ape to the truck until Junie said, "Isa, did you carry your boys like this when they were little?"

"I did, Junebug," Isabelle said, taking off the gibbon. She stopped smiling. "I carried one in front and one on my back. It was their favorite game."

"Did Mom carry us like that?" Mae asked. "I don't think so, right, Dad?"

"I don't think she did, Mae," Finn said. "Maybe we can ask her when we see her."

"Are we going there again tomorrow, Daddy?" asked Junie with a little whine. "I really don't want to."

"Not tomorrow, Junebug," Finn said. "I'm going to drive there by myself next week." Before the girl could emit a sound of relief, he quickly said, "That was Mom on the phone earlier. She said she is ready to come home to us."

He looked at the truck when he spoke, not at Isabelle. She knew he couldn't face her in front of his children. A hush fell over the family. "When you say come home," Mae said, "you mean like *forever*?"

"Yes. She told me she wanted to come home tomorrow."

"Tomorrow!" both girls exclaimed. Isabelle couldn't tell what was in their voices, but she knew what would have been in hers had she not been rendered mute.

"I told her we wanted to welcome her with a clean house, and this was rather short notice. So she's coming home next Sunday."

Out of them all only the sainted Junie mustered a response. "Mommy's coming home! I can't believe it. That's great, Daddy, right?"

"It's great, Junebug. It's been a long time."

"Yes, I'll say," said Mae. "But are you sure it's a good idea, Dad?"

"You think we're rushing things, Mayflower?" Finn smiled.

"I mean, she was so unhappy when she was here," Mae said.

"I'm not a doctor," said Finn, his arm around his daughter's shoulder, "but an actual doctor supposedly wrote in her report that she is much better."

"But Isabelle taught us, Dad," said Mae, "that much better from zero is still zero."

"That is true," said Finn, "but I think that applies more to counting Communists and less to assessing your mother."

"What was wrong with her anyway?" Mae asked as they piled into the truck. It was a brand-new Chevy with a second bench seat in the back.

"Not sure," Finn said.

"The report didn't say what was wrong with Mom?"

"Don't know, haven't read it. You can ask her about it when you see her."

"Mommy is not going to believe how much has changed," Junie said.

"With any luck, June, she won't notice," said Mae.

At night in her soft pink silk bed, after feats and acts and miracles of love, they lay together and breathed heavily. "We knew this day would come," Isabelle said, breaking the pained silence between them.

"But why did it have to come so fast?" said Finn, sounding despondent.

"It's been more than two years." Two years and three months, but who was counting.

"In some places you could sue for divorce on grounds of abandonment after two years," he said.

"We're not going to be doing that," she said gently.

"Oh? And what is your plan?"

"My plans are limited to the next twenty minutes." She reached for him, softly caressing him.

"Eventually she is going to ask me about it."

Isabelle contemplated mutely, feeling pretty desolate herself. "Every story has a journey through the desert," she said. "Your wife just had hers."

"You think spending two years in a sanatorium, not having to work, not having to lift a finger for yourself or anyone else, having your three squares brought to you by cooks, having your room cleaned and your bed made, lounging around all day near open windows with white curtains is a journey through the desert?" he said incredulously. "Yes, walking fifteen feet outside your front door is an achievement on par with Christ spending forty days with the devil."

"Oh, your wife has been in the desert with the devil for a lot longer than forty days," said Isabelle.

"Clearly you and I have very different ideas of what adversity is."

"Maybe she has found her way," Isabelle whispered, wrapping her legs around him, pulling him into her naked body. "Maybe she's found her way back to you."

"For her sake, I hope not." He was on top of her, but he couldn't look at her.

"Don't you want her to be better, like she was before?"

No, he whispered.

They could barely breathe. Other things overtook them and carried them away, their bodies shivering, shimmering like falling starlings.

"Nothing has to change," he said when they were spent but still as one.

"Except everything is going to. She left because she finally saw the truth and couldn't accept it. She's coming back to deal with it."

"Whatever happens, I'm not going to lose you. I will not live without you. *I cannot live without you.*"

"Finn . . ." She held his beloved face between her hands. "Don't you feel we're endangered?" She kissed him. "Soon you and I will be extinct. There'll be nothing left of us."

"Comfort me, Isabelle, don't hurt me with your words."

She stopped speaking. Both of them increasingly mute in their shared solitary pain, they spent an agonizing week picking the ripe and overripe vegetables off the vines, never moving fast enough, driving the girls to the market, selling, despairing, canning the last of the cucumbers, making jam, making wordless love, all of it nonstop. Despite the shadow of her children ever at her feet, Isabelle had found paradise here with Finn. They covered slightly, for some outward pretense. But the open fields were abundant to make them free, as was the barn with layers of hay in the loft, and the shady trees in the distance by the brook that invited blankets and wine. They found bliss on the rocks in the water where they cast their lines, in the truck they parked by the ocean like two kids sneaking out at night, and in her little hidden haven where he slept with her and woke up with her and loved her like no one had ever loved her.

After the shooting of the intruder, they were loath to both leave the house overnight. But they'd installed a phone, built a fence with a car gate along the front of the property, and snaked a tripwire on the ground across the drive so a bell would trill inside the house and near the barn if anyone drove or walked through. They taught Monty how to shoot. And once Eleanor married Bertie, they felt even more secure. They took some time, because they had the time. They traveled down to Kentucky and Saratoga for the daily races. They must have disturbed the drapes in all the rooms at the Parker House Hotel with their cries.

The night before Vanessa came home, they barely slept, aflutter and in the dirt. In her bed, she lay kissing him, rubbing her body against his back. He was turned away from her, bad-tempered, almost wanting to fight. *You don't even care*, he whispered.

She kissed his neck, caressed him, pressed her breasts into his shoulder blades so he could feel her beating heart. *Does my heart feel to you like it doesn't care? We're not giving up, not yet. Turn around, let me see your face.*

"Is there any scenario in which someone doesn't get butchered?" Finn said in a dead voice, turning to her. "I didn't think this through. I didn't think ahead to this day."

"We've been given so much." Isabelle touched his downcast mouth. "We've been so blessed."

He made love to her to oblivion—as if he wanted to forget her.

"*You have been given every gift,*" she whispered to him, holding his head in her hands.

"Except the gift of time," Finn said, pressing his face into her bare stomach. *And though the world shall fall, I will love you through all my dark bright days.*

On Sunday morning, they dragged themselves out at dawn and drove to a Catholic church in Rye, and then to a silent breakfast in town. He dropped her off at the farm and then, still in his church clothes, left to get Vanessa.

Isabelle stood in the road, watching him drive away, her arms crossed over her chest, as if she were headed into battle. The only thing missing were her sabers. She knew it was going to be one of the longest rides of Finn's life. But even harder would be what followed. *What would it look like, if you got everything you wanted?* she asked him once in the dead of night. And he had no answers. He pretended he didn't hear her.

Isabelle, woman, warrior, lover.

She barely kept herself from crying out.

Go, Finn, she whispered after him. *Go, and take your fate.*

81

A Wife, Her Husband, and His Lover

Vanessa was waiting for him in the front lobby of the sanatorium, her two suitcases packed. Finn carried her bags to the truck, loaded them in the back seat, helped her inside. When he was by her door, she turned to hug him, and he had to force himself, literally and physically, not to stagger back from her.

"I'm so happy to be coming back, darling," she said as they got going.

"Yes, everyone's excited to have you home," said Finn, his eyes on the traffic signs ahead, on the road, on the trees. "But tell me what happened. When I saw you last month, you didn't even mention this was a possibility."

"I didn't think it was," she said. "But my doctor died." She burst into tears.

That was awkward. "Oh, I'm so sorry to hear that, darling. Very sorry." She sniffled for a few minutes. It seemed to Finn like a lot of emotion to feel for the passing of a doctor. Perhaps he was excellent. Perhaps she was cured. She did manage to walk out of the building and to the parking lot without clutching him—very different from when Finn first brought her there. "My sympathies. He must have been quite good."

"He was the best doctor. He had lung cancer. He was sick for a year and never told me."

"Perhaps because you were not his doctor?"

Vanessa wiped her face. "Shiba told me only after he was already gone. That wasn't right. He should've told me. I would have liked to see him one more time, to thank him. He helped me so much."

Finn didn't know what to say next.

"With Crawford gone and his last report on me so optimistic, Shiba and I agreed it was time for me to return to my life," Vanessa said. "You probably could use another pair of hands. Harvest season is coming up. Has it helped to have Bertie around?"

"He's fine. He never shuts up, though, and unfortunately he can't do more than one thing at a time. It's either talk or work with him."

"Are they planning to move out on their own?"

"I don't know," said Finn. "Your sister wants to move back to the city. But she married a fisherman, so we'll see how *that* goes."

"Mother and Daddy are well?"

"Your dad is hanging in there, the old critter."

"And your parents?"

"Very good. Dad's stronger than ever. He's in the fields before I am."

"And the girls? Are they excited I'm coming home?"

"Yes, they helped me clean our room." Finn smiled. "I don't think I'd mopped once since you've been gone."

"Finn!"

"I'm joking, joking. Of course I have—once."

He didn't need to mop. He was never in there. Finn gripped the wheel.

They didn't chat as much on the way back as they had on the way to Austen Riggs two years earlier. Finn ran out of things to say, even small things. The big things were too loud. Just before they got to the house, Vanessa put her hand on his leg.

"Darling, I'm sorry," she said. "I know I did a lot of things wrong, and I want you to know I acknowledge it. I wasn't a very good wife, and for that I deeply apologize. I know now how much you needed me and how I let you down. I couldn't see it before. I hope you can forgive me."

"There's nothing to forgive," Finn said.

"There is," she said. "I was selfish and unkind. I was so busy feeling sorry for myself, I forgot to think about you."

Even when I reminded you of me for years? Finn wanted to say, but what he said was, "I hear what you're saying."

"I'm apologizing now, darling," she said.

"And I hear you, I said."

"No point in being testy, is there? In reopening old wounds?"

"The wounds are not as closed as you think, Vanessa."

He pulled through the open gate into their drive, stopped the truck, and turned off the ignition.

"The house looks nice," she said. "Freshly painted?"

"Yes. We planted new apple and peach trees in front."

"And put up a fence and a gate, I see. That must have been expensive."

"Your father is growing enough wheat to compete with Iowa."

"What are all these vehicles in our front yard? Are we having a party?"

"No, they're ours," Finn replied. "You're in my new truck. Bertie's got one too, and we have two sedans."

"What about our old Model B over there?"

"I gave it to Isabelle. That way she can drive herself to Mickey's stables."
"She drives now?"
"Yeah, since last year."
"Did you teach her how to drive?"
"She practically taught herself," Finn said. "But yes, I taught her the rest."
They both clammed up.
Through the front windshield, he saw commotion in the house, heard Junie's excited voice.
"I did what I could with myself, my darling," Vanessa said. "I hope this can be a fresh start for us."
Finn couldn't say a word. "Look, the girls," he said.
Junie ran out of the house. Mae followed more slowly. They embraced their mother, held her hands as they guided her up the porch steps, now painted in glossy blue. Finn trudged behind them carrying the suitcases.
Dinner was on. They were having a sunset cookout—chicken and steak and salads galore, apple pie and beer and wine and Isabelle's raspberry moonshine. The radio played. The family greeted her warmly, Bertie the warmest of all. That man was always trying too hard.
Isabelle came forward to the center of the room, almost precisely to the spot where she blew the vagabond out the front door and blew Vanessa all the way out to Stockbridge, Massachusetts. "Hello, Vanessa," said Isabelle with a smile, a dishtowel, and spatula in her hands. "Welcome home."
"Hello, Isabelle," said Vanessa.
It was a good thing music was playing on the radio, Finn thought, as he pushed past them to carry the suitcases into the bedroom. Because a hush fell over ten people, a hush like a collective held breath, as if everyone in the room tried to stop making all noise so that they might hear better what happened next.
What happened next was nothing. Isabelle brought Vanessa an iced tea, asked if she wanted anything stronger. Vanessa declined—with a whiff of disapproval, as if just because it was legal to drink didn't mean it was a good idea. While Olivia and Isabelle got dinner ready, everyone else crowded around Vanessa.
"Vanessa," Isabelle called from the kitchen, "we set the outdoor table for dinner, I hope that's all right."
"Yes, that's absolutely fine," Vanessa said. "There's no problem with that whatsoever. I see someone is using definite articles now?"
"Hit and miss," said Isabelle.
"*Hit or miss*," Finn said, sweeping by her.
"Unlike your shooting, Isabelle," said Monty. "You never miss."
"Monty!" Lucy exclaimed.
"I meant at the Fireman's Fair, Grandma!" Monty said defensively. "I didn't

mean the other thing. Yeesh." But to Isabelle he whispered, "Maybe a little bit the other thing."

"Monty, shh, please go get more wood for me," Isabelle said, squeezing the boy's arm.

"Monty seems to be doing well," said Vanessa. "He's lost weight, grown tall."

It was Isabelle who answered instead of Eleanor. "Yes, he's turning into a fine young man," she said with a whiff of pride.

While she mixed the potato salad, Finn walked by her to get himself a drink from the fridge. His body brushed against her dress, his bare arm bumped hers. "You okay?" he said quietly.

I'm fine, my love, she whispered.

When Finn looked across the house, he saw Vanessa watching them.

The family filtered outside, arranged themselves around the table and poured the drinks. There was some awkwardness about where Vanessa would sit. In their old house in Beacon Hill, Finn and Vanessa had sat at opposite ends of their long dining table, but here on the farm, Finn asked Vanessa to sit by his side. "I haven't had you by my side for so long, my dear," he said to her, hoping to make her feel better about the fact that Isabelle would be sitting across from him, in the spot Vanessa once occupied.

And because Vanessa didn't immediately say it was fine, because she said nothing for a moment or two, Isabelle stepped in as she carried a tray of toasted buns to the table. "I get up a thousand times," Isabelle said, "which is why I sit where I sit, but Vanessa, of course you're welcome to take whichever seat you prefer. You decide. Next to Finn or across from him." She said it so calmly, so directly that Finn didn't have a chance even to shake his head.

But somehow Isabelle managed to checkmate Vanessa in view of everyone without saying a single improper word. *Either you sit by your husband's side or you sit at the head of the table as the lady of the house. Either way, I take the seat you don't want. What will you choose, Vanessa?*

"By Finn's side is fine," Vanessa said, planting herself on the bench.

The sun was going down, but the overflowing fields in the back looked so full and lush and green that even Vanessa, who had cared nothing for these things, noticed. "Look at that!" she said. "You almost can't see to the tree line by the river. It's all growing so beautifully. Must be hard to irrigate."

"Easier than ever," Finn said. "We got connected to the town main last year. We have running water now."

Many improvements had been made. They'd rebuilt the corn crib to make it bigger, and bought a small metal granary to store their wheat. The fields were divided into separate areas and each crop was fenced in with tall chicken wire and a little gate.

"How is Nate's new ship?" asked Vanessa. "My doctor was impressed you got Electric Boat to donate a whole vessel for your cause, darling. That's an extraordinary gesture."

"They're a real good company," Earl said. "Their president impressed us. Walter, you would've liked him. He ran a tight ship, pardon the pun, during the worst years when there was no money, slashed the budget, and is now coming out of it with new contracts to build ships and submarines for the U.S. Navy. And they were so impressed with my boy, they even offered him a job!"

"They did?" Fake-casually, Vanessa put her hand on Finn's arm. "Oh, that's wonderful, darling!"

Finn pretended to reach for something at the table to extricate himself from her touch. "It would've been a terrible fit. I know nothing about the financial health of a shipbuilding company or how to grow that business."

"But you've always liked the submarines," said Vanessa. "It's very encouraging." She paused. "I guess there's been no news about Isabelle's husband and children?"

"Not yet," Finn said. "But Nate just left Constanta for Brindisi with a new manifest, so we'll see. With every ship we get a few more from that part of Ukraine. We're still hoping."

"Of course we are," said Vanessa. "Most certainly are."

Finn sat with a drink in one hand and a cigarette in the other and stared across the table at Isabelle with a drink in her hand and a cigarette in the other. They blinked at each other in silence.

Vanessa helped clean up and wipe down the tables and counters, excusing herself around ten. "It's been a fulfilling but long day for me," she said. "Thank you all. It's good to be home. Finn, are you coming?"

"I've got some work outside," he said. "I'll be in soon."

Finn and Isabelle sat outside on their bench and shared a cigarette.

"Mae is reserved with her mother," Isabelle said. "Not like Junie."

"Well, Mae is thirteen now," Finn said. "She feels things keenly—like the absence of her mother." Lightly he smiled. "You were practically married at thirteen."

"Hold your horses right there, mister. Whoa to all of them. I was a very old nineteen." She inhaled deeply. "Probably better for everyone to be like Junie. Like a puppy. Loves everyone and everything."

Drawing her close, Finn kissed her, stroked her hair, her face. "Are you worried about Vanessa?"

"I'm not *not* worried."

"It'll be okay," he whispered. "I'll take care of it."

She pinched his arm, held on to him for a moment. "Look at you, big guy, taking care of things," she said fondly, deep tenderness in her weary voice. Her gray eyes glistened. They kissed, open and true, before he left to go inside.

In the bedroom, Vanessa was sitting up in the bed, in a negligee, the covers in her lap. He nodded to her with a tight and twisted mouth, stared at the empty space next to her. His heart aching, he undressed and got into bed.

"Are you tired?" she said, reaching for his hand.

"Very," he said. "And tomorrow we must clear the eggplant before eight. We made a deal with a local supplier; he buys nearly all of it from us for a good price, but he's coming early." He squeezed her hand and forced himself to lean over and kiss her goodnight.

In response she leaned back against the pillows invitingly. "Anything else?" she whispered.

"It's been a long day," he said, patting her and turning away.

After a few minutes, he heard Vanessa's tremulous voice. "Do you want to talk about—anything?"

"We can talk tomorrow."

"But tomorrow you're going to be in the fields all day," she said.

"You can come outside," he said. "Like you said, we could use the help."

"It's not about whether I can help. It's about us having some private time. To talk. To—whatever."

"We're going to take this one step at a time," Finn said.

"Isn't the first step some private time?"

Finn remained silent until the light went off, and he heard her turn away. Sleeplessly he lay, facing his open window, through which he heard the soft sad sounds of Isabelle's trilling balalaika, and her whispering alto singing his song for him. *Take me to a faraway land . . . where love reigns . . . where peace reigns . . . where there is no suffering . . . where there is no pain . . . kak lyublyu ya vas, kak lyublyu ya vas . . .*

82

Last Stand

Finn wasn't going to broach the subject himself—a difficult one in any marriage. If Vanessa didn't feel they needed to talk yet, so be it. But he also wasn't going to touch her, not with so much water under their bridge. How could he tell her his fingers went numb when she reached for his hand?

"It's not even sunrise," she said, when he was quietly milling around. "You're up already?"

"A lot to do. Why are you awake?"

"Because I went to bed at a reasonable hour. Come on, stay in for a few minutes. The eggplant will keep."

"Can't. But you rest up," Finn said. "No need for you to jump out of bed."

Another day, another, and another.

A tortuous week went by like this, a *week*! Finn kissed Vanessa in the morning and at night, talked to her about the day and the children, made little jokes, asked questions about dinner and lunch, if she wanted to go to town or if she needed anything, but otherwise exchanged no intimate words with her.

More worryingly for Finn, there was something pale about Isabelle. Not physically; she was as robust and healthy as ever; she was blooming, soft, warm, but there was something pale in the way she embraced him, how she responded to him, the way she touched him, the way her fingers stroked his bearded face. There was something almost ghostlike in her caress. She wouldn't say, and Finn couldn't define it. It gnawed at him.

On the eighth day after Vanessa's return, on a Monday morning around nine, a dusty and sweaty Finn came inside to grab a glass of orange juice. The rest of the family were still outside. He and the girls were getting ready to drive to the market. Vanessa came out of the bedroom, dressed, made up, brushed out, smiling. Almost smiling. There was something anemic in her smile, too. What an effect Finn was having on the women in his life. Her arms were full of folded towels. Was she washing towels again?

"You're up and about," he said. "It's so early."

"It's not early," she said. "It's late." She put down the towels and walked to the island.

He downed the orange juice. "Well, best I return to it," he said.

"Finn," said Vanessa. "I know this is hard for you. I understand."

"It's not that hard for me."

"You've done the best you can—"

"I appreciate that."

"No, wait. You've done the best you can. I want you to know that I forgive you."

The glass hovered in Finn's hand.

"You forgive me?" he repeated.

"Yes. I know you've been afraid to talk to me, afraid to face me. It's a terrible situation. I take some responsibility. You needed me and I wasn't there for you. I was unwell."

"Yes, I suppose I forgive you for that," he said.

"It's very important to forgive each other," she said. "So we can move forward."

Finn's thumping heart was drowning out his thoughts. "I don't know what moving forward means for you, Vanessa. Or even what it is you forgive me for. I haven't asked for your forgiveness."

"You don't need to. I give it to you unbidden. I haven't been myself the last few years, but I am much better now. I have the tools now, and I'm using them, and I will continue to improve. I want to be a good wife to you. I want to be a good mother." She was businesslike and non-inflecting, as if she thought that's what he admired, that's what he wanted. But because he knew her, he saw by her clenched jaw and quivering fingers how fraught and wound up she was just under the surface.

He opened his mouth to speak, but she stopped him.

"I know you can't admit to things," she said. "We both know what it is."

"You might need to spell out what it is I can't admit," said Finn. He steadied himself. His hand clenched the glass hard enough to break it. He relaxed his hold on it, breathed deeply, set it slowly on the table. "If we are going to have this conversation, let's have it. But don't minimize it."

"I know you've found comfort in the arms of another woman," Vanessa said in a monotone, as if she were reciting the grocery list. "There was a time in my life when that discovery would have destroyed me. I once thought I would never be able to live through that kind of betrayal or forgive you for it. But I don't think like that anymore. I don't feel that way anymore. Because I know that I have betrayed *you* by not being there when you needed me—in every sense, not just the physical one. I don't want to reduce our whole marriage to one small mistake on your part. I have made mistakes myself and as I said already, for them I am deeply sorry. I went away because I wanted to make myself better. I didn't want to issue you an ultimatum. That is so childish, and we are adults."

"You're well enough to issue me an ultimatum, Vanessa? By all means, issue away."

"They don't work. If two years ago, or three, you had given me one, if you'd said, Vanessa, be the way I need you to be or else, I don't know if I could've done it."

"I did ask you to be how I needed you to be," he said. "And you most certainly didn't do it."

"I couldn't! But now I can. Because I want to save our marriage. That's the most important thing to me. But there is no way to do that—"

"You can stop right there," Finn said. "There is no way to save it."

"That's not true. Of course there is."

"There is not."

"I want to save our marriage," Vanessa repeated, her voice faltering but dogged, "and there is no way to do that if she remains in our house. Even if you stop your dalliance with her."

Finn was merciless in his response. "You're saying that to save our marriage she must leave?"

"That's what I'm saying."

"Sounds like an ultimatum to me, Vanessa. I thought you were too grown up for that?"

"It's not an ultimatum, darling. It's a path forward."

"That's what an ultimatum is!"

"No, no, no," said Vanessa. "A path forward is a reasonable and rational course for two people with a shared history to proceed down, along one common road."

"It's no use arguing about the *definitions of words*," said Finn. "What you're proposing, I cannot do. It's neither reasonable nor rational."

"Of course you can!" Vanessa chose to misunderstand him, though this time with a white face. "She taught us everything we need to know." Vanessa spoke fake-brightly. "She gave us the tools and taught us how to use them. We can do the rest. No, no, darling, *please* let me finish. We can hire help, we are not broke anymore—we have five vehicles and a tractor! We can hire people to work for us while we enjoy the fruits of this wonderful farm. And she is always going to land on her feet. She makes money doing her horse things, doesn't she? And if you really feel we can't make the farm work without her"—her hands were spasming—"then maybe you can meet with that nice man at Electric Boat who offered you a job you turned down and say you'd like to reconsider."

"I will not do that. But even if I did reconsider, you don't seem to—"

"Where is that company based?"

"Connecticut," he replied dully.

"Connecticut! Well, there you go! We don't know Connecticut, but I hear it's lovely. Can't be that different from Massachusetts. We'll move."

"And your family?"

"We're not responsible for them permanently, are we, my dear?"

"Your parents and *my* parents? Yes, Vanessa, we are."

She moved toward him. He backed away. "Vanessa, I—"

"Finn," she interrupted, folding her hands in prayer. "We are husband and wife. You're the father of my babies. And Finn . . ." Vanessa took another step toward him. "I want us to have more babies. I want us to try again. I know how much you wanted it, how broken you were when we lost him and how sad that I didn't want to try again. I wasn't well then, darling. But I'm better now. I want to have more children with you. I want you to have what you want. I love you. I want to make you happy. I know it hasn't always been easy for us, but I promise you, I'm going to build us a different life. I'm going to do my best. I'm not going to stay shut in. You'll be able to tell me things."

"You want me to tell you things?" Finn said.

"Yes—*please!*"

"I can't stay with you, Vanessa," said Finn. "That's what I'm telling you."

"Of course you can! We hit a rough patch—"

"A rough patch that's lasted eleven years," he said. "We've been married not even fifteen. Some rough patch. More like rough road through and through."

"Finn, I wasn't well! You must forgive me for that. I forgive you for her."

"I don't want your forgiveness for her," he said. "I don't want it and I don't need it."

"Well, I don't know what you're thinking," Vanessa said, her calm demeanor faltering.

"I think you do."

She was biting her lip furiously. "You're Catholic!" she said. "Catholics don't get divorced."

"Now I'm suddenly a Catholic."

"Through and through."

"We have ourselves a problem," Finn said.

"No..."

"Vanessa, I don't know if I can be any clearer. I will try. There is no path forward for me without her. I need you to hear me because I don't think you've been listening. She is my present and my future. I'm sorry."

A thin bitter pause hung between them. Vanessa's eyes were frantic, desperate, like a drowning woman looking for a lifeline.

"How is your brother, Finn? How is Lucas?"

"Swell. He got married and moved to Florida. I'm sure you're very broken up about missing his wedding. But then, you missed your own sister's wedding, so my brother's would hardly have been a priority. Do you want to make more small talk about Lucas, your favorite person? I have work to do."

"Do you remember what happened to you?" she blurted. "Do you remember why? Your mother was broke! She gave you up, she sold you because she couldn't pay her bills."

"Who are you planning to sell, Vanessa, Mae or Junie?"

"That's not what I'm saying—"

"Oh, I know what you're saying, and I know exactly what you're trying to do," Finn said, putting his palms up to protect himself. "Stop it."

"Lucas is your proof, Finn, that the very core of who you are has been grown around a dissolving vine," said Vanessa. "All your life you've tried to reorder yourself into a different man. I've witnessed your struggle firsthand. But how can you reorder yourself if deep in your heart you know you're altering yourself around a lie?"

"Olivia and Earl raised me," Finn said. "And they have nothing to do with this."

"You're right about that—they most certainly don't," Vanessa said. "Because they're still married, forty-five years and counting. But you know who *does* have something to do with what's happening here?"

"Stop." Finn wanted to slam his hands over his ears. It was only through a supreme act of will that he didn't.

"Tadhg McBride, your real father, the man whose genes you carry, whose legacy presses down on your shoulders. The man who left your mother and his children to pursue whatever it was that moved his heart. It was hard to stay, hard to make money, hard to raise a family, hard to make the right choice. So he up and ran. He pulled up anchor and sailed away, la-di-da! Sick and dying babies, penniless pregnant wife, desperate need, nothing mattered to Tadhg except his own desires."

"Vanessa!"

"You wanted to talk? I'm talking. Let me say what I have to say and then you can think whatever you want about it."

"I am not going to be defined by my non-existent relationship with my vanished father," Finn said, his fists clenched, his teeth gritted, not looking at her. "I don't know him. I've never met him. He is nothing to me." He couldn't stand to look at her. She couldn't help what she was doing. It was venal but effective. She wanted to go out with guns blazing.

"Yes, I know," she said. "Your whole adult life—consciously and subconsciously—you have tried with all your formidable, intimidating, extraordinary strength to be the exact opposite of everything Tadhg was—an indigent, an alcoholic, a non-provider, a degenerate gambler. You have carried him inside you like a stone. Your heart was so full of secrets you managed to weigh me down with them too. I knew you were hiding something, and my own heart drowned under your unshared burdens."

"Still blaming me for your old troubles, new Vanessa?"

"Are you still blaming Tadhg for yours?"

"Nope. I never think of him."

"Bullshit," she said. "You know what else? In my list of paternal curses, I forgot to mention the most important of all. Yes, Tadhg was all those things. But you know the main thing he was, Finn?"

"Vanessa, for fuck's sake, *stop it!*"

"He was a man who deserted his family. That's the flag your real father carries through life. Through his own, and Lucas's—and yours." With tears in her eyes, she stood back and glared at him defiantly. "So as you contemplate throwing me out of my house—and by the way, does this include just me or my children, too?"

"Just you." Finn could barely form the words.

"Think about what kind of man you really are. Are you your father? Or are you a different kind of man? Where is your place, Finn Esmond Evans McBride? Is it with the Tadhgs or the Earls of this world?"

83

A Lake Full of Longing

Isabelle was sitting on the stones of the patio, her back against the house, when a shaken Finn stormed outside and turned his head to find her there.

He crouched next to her, trying to calm down, still extremely upset. "Did you hear any of it?"

"All of it." She made a sound like a crane falling out of the sky.

Late that night when he came to see her, he found her on her knees, her head pressed into the floor. "*Isabelle*," he whispered, closing the door, his hand shaking.

With her back to him, she wiped her face before she rose to her feet and turned around. With his questioning arms he enveloped her, peering into her miserable face. "What's the matter, Isa?"

"It's nothing, my love," she said with a forced smile, willing her voice not to crack. "It's just my heartbreak making a little noise."

"I'm going to fix it," he said, gliding his hands up and down her hair, her back, her hips. "I told you I will, and I will."

"You told me, you told me. Shh," she said. "How are you here?"

"Where else should I be? My place is with you."

"Then come lie down with me and stop making such a ruckus. All these words. You know what you need to do. Rub all the parts that are sore. Kiss all the parts that are tender. Then I will kiss all your parts that are sore. I will rub all your parts that are tender. And face to face we will fall asleep like lovers. Unless you are going back."

"I'm not."

"Then shh and come. Come, my love."

They were barely finished, still in each other's arms, when there was a timid knock on the door.

Another one, a little louder.

"Is it Junie?" Finn whispered.

"Even Junie doesn't knock this shyly," Isabelle whispered back.

A voice sounded. "Isabelle? Is Finn there? Isabelle?" It was Vanessa.

"Definitely *not* Junie," Isabelle said.

"This is what happens when she thinks she is cured," Finn said. "She starts roaming all over the property."

"Well, go answer it!"

"She's not calling for *me*!"

"Finn!"

"Ugh."

He threw on his trousers. She threw on her dress and went to sit in a chair by the window. Finn opened the door.

"Finn?" Vanessa said, in a pale voice. "What are you doing? Aren't you coming to bed?"

"No, Vanessa," Finn said, his frame filling the doorway so Vanessa wouldn't see the unmade bed behind him. "Go back inside the house."

"Finn..."

He started to close the door.

"Please, can you just... just come outside and talk to me."

"You've talked today already," he said. "I think you're finished with talking."

"Please..."

"Go, Finn," said Isabelle from the chair. "Go talk to your wife."

Grabbing his shirt, an aggravated Finn followed Vanessa through the house into their bedroom.

"I don't understand why you're doing this," she said. "I was honest with you, I told you how I felt, I told you what I wanted. I told you we could put the past behind us and start fresh. I was hoping you would take my olive branch and extend one of your own."

"Vanessa, this is an unexpected turn of events for me," said Finn. "I didn't know how our discussion was going to go, but I must admit I didn't think it would go like this. You've taken a different approach than I expected. But just because you said some words, Vanessa, doesn't change how I feel about your behavior—toward me, toward our children, toward our life, and toward this house. It doesn't change how you behaved toward me in Boston. You had your reasons, I accept that, but two thousand days of your indifference and cruelty is not erased just because you said today you forgive *me*. I don't forgive *you*."

"That's why I said we could have a fresh start."

"I would like nothing more than a fresh start," Finn said. "But you and I have *very* different ideas about what that means."

"We need to try together," she said. "I'm willing to try."

"Not me."

"What about all the things I said to you?"

"Yes, yes, you brought out the big guns," he said dismissively and impatiently. "First babies, then my faith, then my father. I got it. Heard you loud and clear. I'm thinking on it. I'm contemplating your words. I've had seven lousy years with you, and now I'm going to take my time to consider what you said. I promise it will be less than seven years. But in the meantime, I'm going to continue my life. The life I've been living since you abandoned your family—you know, *that* life."

"I wasn't well!"

"There's always a reason to justify your bad behavior."

"Don't go. Stay and think on it."

"No."

"How often have you been—how often have you—"

"In this room? Not once since you left," Finn said.

A speechless Vanessa fought to control herself.

"Does my family know? How could they not!"

"We don't speak about it at the dinner table if that's what you mean."

"That's why they've been so awkward with me."

"Probably a thousand reasons for that."

"I don't care. What's past is past," she croaked, waving her hands in conciliation.

"It hasn't passed. It's not even *the* past. It is the eternal present." Finn grabbed some clothes, a hat, a shirt.

"This isn't right."

"I agree. I suggest not wandering around knocking on any more doors." He was about to leave when she spoke again.

"In a subconscious way I must have known," she said brokenly. "I didn't *know it* know it. But I knew. I just couldn't face it. I hid it from myself. I turned away, retreated into my shell. I turned away because I knew I couldn't change it."

"Bullshit," Finn said.

"I couldn't do so many things myself, and she could do all of them," Vanessa said. "I was helpless, but I loved you. I still do. I love you so much."

"Wow, you'll say anything, won't you? First Tadhg, now love."

"I want to save our marriage," she said. "That's all I want. It's worth saving. It has value. But also—yes, to save it, I'll say anything."

He didn't want to say it to her, but Finn had seen what real love looked like, and nothing Vanessa had shown him in the last ten years, and even now, looked like love to him. He left, but the following night, to avoid another scene, he and Isabelle slept in the loft in the barn. Finn didn't think even the new and improved Vanessa would dare go to the barn at night, and he was right.

They still heard her knocking on Isabelle's door, calling out Finn's name, and Isabelle's. Then the knocking stopped. For a few minutes there was nothing. Then the shadow of Vanessa stumbled across the back patio, stood at the edge of the yard looking out onto the inky barn and the dark fields, turned around and slowly walked back into the house.

"I left my door unlocked," Isabelle said, "so she could come in if she wanted and not wake the house with her cries."

"Wise."

"Was it? I don't know. She saw my room."

Finn knew: Vanessa saw the bed with the soft pillows and the pink-and-gray bedspread and the down quilt all in white. She saw the embroidered Ukrainian-style tablecloth and on it a vase with fresh pink peonies and amaryllis, two glasses, the decanter of raspberry wine, the summer dresses hanging on hooks on the walls like decorations, Finn's second pair of boots in the corner, his belt, his suspenders, his linen shirts all cleaned and ironed hanging next to Isabelle's dresses. She saw a bowl of lavender in water, the room smelling of florals and strong liquor, the walls painted with large purple blossoms and gray clamshells, the ivory silk robe Finn bought for Isabelle years ago hanging near the bed. She saw the place where Isabelle lived with Finn. It can't have been easy.

But the next morning, Vanessa, giving no indication that she had seen anything to upset her, asked Finn if he had thought about their previous conversation.

"No, Vanessa," Finn said. "But if I had known you'd be this cavalier about things, I wouldn't have expended so much effort trying to hide it."

"How well did you hide it if everyone knows? And I'm not cavalier," Vanessa said. "I want you back. I'm willing to do whatever it takes. I know you need a little time. If you need me to be patient with you, then that's what I'll be. Anything—as long as you come back to me."

Something wasn't right with Isabelle. The following night, Finn pried and prodded her in the barn until she opened up to him.

"Are we bringing an irrational amount of misery to her?" Isabelle said at last. "She has not been good, for sure. But she doesn't deserve this, does she?"

"Nobody deserves anything," Finn said. "You didn't deserve what you've been given."

"Okay, but look what I've been given," murmured Isabelle. They lay in the hay in the loft in the barn. She was in his arms. After a hard and heavy silence, she took a deep breath and spoke. "Finn, did I ever tell you about the Lake Full of Longing?"

"No, but I already don't like the sound of it."

"In Poland, near Lvov, there is a lake," Isabelle said. "My mother told me and my brothers about it. Roman loved this story best because he was insane. Lvov is an ancient city where countless battles have been won and lost, heroes made and heroes felled. It's a medieval town full of fables about knights and kings and unrescued damsels."

"Did you say *un*rescued? I love you." He kissed her face.

Her eyes were closed as she received his caress. "Near Lvov there is a lake which the Russians, who've been trying to make Lvov their own for centuries, called *Ozero Toski*. The Poles called it *Jezioro Tesknoty*. And we called it *Ozero Tuhi*. But the meaning is the same. The lake is supposed to have mystical powers. Legend has it that you swim out into the lake at night to heal your suffering, your wounds, your grief. You give the lake your fear and your burdens. You give the lake your sins. But the lake was deep and cold and had dangerous rip currents. People would swim out to heal and never come back."

"I knew it. The worst lake in the world."

"You'd think so." She nuzzled his shoulder, patted his stomach. "Here's where the story takes flight though. The people who *didn't* die and managed to return to shore said their wounds indeed had been healed, both physical and eternal."

"Eternal or *internal*?"

"*Eternal*, Finn. They were restored and mended. Their hearts were lighter, their stony griefs released. As lore of that spread, the lake became a pilgrimage. People traveled from all over to give the lake their suffering. But there were so many casualties that the Lvov government had to close it, put up a barbed-wire fence around it with signs telling people the lake had crocodiles in it and sharks and flesh-eating creatures."

Finn squeezed her. "Let me guess—people being people, they climbed over the barbed wire and continued to drown en masse."

"They did. The rising deaths only added to the lake's power. With every death, people believed that another life had been healed. Every unfinished life was someone else's answered prayer. We heard about this lake throughout my childhood, but after my father was murdered, my mother, usually the most practical of women, actually considered going to Lvov to cleanse herself of the hate and the pain."

"She didn't, I hope?"

"She didn't," said Isabelle, wrapping her arms around him, pressing her warm full breasts into him, trying to surround his hulking body with her soft sad body. "When she was in jail, days from being vanished, she told me that what bothered her most about the lake wasn't that people would be dumb enough to swim in its deadly waters, hoping for a different outcome, but why anyone would create such a lake in the first place."

84

Nate

One morning in late July, unwilling to have yet another scene, Finn grabbed his keys and left the house, slamming the front door behind him. In the distance, on Lovering Road, he saw Schumann, slightly stooped, turning into their long drive—on his own two feet.

Schumann had taken the train and walked to the farm only once before—when he'd brought news of Omelian Marchenko. Finn stood on the porch and did not want to walk toward the tailor, the doctor, his friend.

Schumann wasn't smiling. The men greeted each other near the road, shook hands. "You look like you walked here from Boston, Schumann."

"Just from the station," the older man said, out of breath.

"Let's go inside, I'll get you a cold drink. It's too hot for you to be wandering the countryside. You should've called me, I would've picked you up as always."

"It's a beautiful day. I wanted to stretch my legs after a long train ride."

Something behind Finn's eye began to throb.

"Where's Isabelle?" said Schumann.

"She's not here." Finn didn't want to go into it. "She's at Berkshire, helping one of Mickey's broodmares." He didn't ask why Schumann was asking. He didn't want to step over the minute now into the minute then, when one way or another her life—and his—might be irrevocably changed.

"I have news for her," Schumann said, pulling out a telegram.

Finn stood motionless and soundless.

"Her husband and sons are on their way to Boston from Brindisi," Schumann said, simply and directly. "I got word from Nate." In his hands, he held a telegram.

Finn's keys fell to the ground. He didn't want to take the piece of paper from Schumann's hands, the written side open to him, random uppercase words filling his vision.

HER FAMILY FOUND-MIRIK. SLAVA. MAXIM-SAFE-LEAVING BRINDISI-

"Oh my God." Finn's voice was hoarse. He didn't know what to say. "She will be happy, so happy." That was a good thing to start with. "When you said news, I didn't know what to expect. For a moment I thought it might be the worst news. But it's not." His voice was failing him. "Why didn't you call?"

"I did. This morning before I left," Schumann said. "No one picked up. Besides, some things are probably best told in person. I wanted her to see it to believe it. Do you want to drive me to the stables?"

"Yes—of course." Finn breathed deeply. "I just need a minute. One second." With his back to the tailor, he walked to the side of the drive and grabbed the gate post for support. For a few minutes he couldn't turn around, couldn't speak. He was trying to find his heart, all the way by his feet in the dust. Finn searched for the thing inside him that would help him get through it. The wind whistled softly through the rustling leaves; the meadowlarks chirped; the summer song of a sunny countryside. Long ago he had a dream. He said to her, kiss me. And she did. He stared at his boots, his hands, the fence rail. He brushed some dirt off the white paint and forced himself to breathe and not break.

"If you want, you can go tell her," Schumann said quietly, coming up behind Finn. "If that's easier."

Finn whirled around. "Her husband and sons are on their way to her!" he said. "What do you mean, easier?" He frowned.

"I meant easier for you," Schumann said.

"Oh. Yes, well, it's a shock, no question. You have no details?"

"It's a telegram. Just facts. I suppose we'll get the details in a few days. But Nate sent it days ago, and I picked it up just yesterday. They're going to be here soon. A day or two at most."

"Well, that's something. Isn't that something? That's really something." Finn got stuck. He didn't know what to say, what to do. "I'll take you. I was on my way to see her when you walked up." He retrieved the dropped keys, dangled them in his limp hands.

The front door opened. Vanessa stepped out onto the porch. "Hello, Schumann. Nice to see you again."

"Nice to see you, too, Vanessa. How have you been?"

"Can't complain, can't complain." Holding on to the rails, gingerly she navigated the three short stairs. "Is everything all right?"

"Yes." Schumann waved the telegram. "I have good news for Isabelle. Her husband and children have finally been found."

Vanessa gasped. "Oh, that is the most *wonderful* news!" she exclaimed, raising her disbelieving gaze to the sky. "Thank you, *God.*" There were tears in Vanessa's eyes. "Isabelle is going to weep from joy. I couldn't be happier for her. We both couldn't, right, Finn?" With a racked sob, she turned and rushed back into the house.

Finn ushered Schumann inside, got him a drink, excused himself for a moment, and stepped into the bedroom.

She sat on the bed, crying.

"Don't cry," Finn said. But he knew how she felt.

"Oh, Finn," Vanessa said. "She's wanted this for so long." She blew her nose. "I'm hoping this means a happy ending for all of us, yes?" But glancing at the expression on his face made her feel worse for some reason. "Happy ending eventually, I mean," Vanessa said with a stifled howl. "Of course not now."

"Of course not now."

"I'm perplexed by your face, darling. Are you and she planning to—I don't even know how to say this—to make a *different* choice?" How brave of Vanessa to ask this. Her body shook as she spoke the words.

"Of course not now," said Finn.

85

Another Life

Isabelle. I called your name across the field and you heard me and came.
    At Berkshire Stables, Finn stood apart from them, near the paddock fence, under his own tree, near his own bench, smoking down his own cigarettes, far enough away that he wouldn't hear them. All he could do was watch her read the telegram. The first thing she did after she read it was spin in his direction.
    And the only thing he did in return was stretch his mouth in a lopsided smile. *We will straighten out the crooked lives of those who love us and wish us well.*
    Who said that once? He, she?
    Schumann kept patting her back paternally. He gave her a handkerchief before they walked toward Finn with tearful smiles damp on their faces.

Their bodies trembled under the sycamore, her hands on his back, his arms around her. It was Schumann's turn to stand apart from them near the paddock fence.
    It's okay, he whispered. *Everything is going to be okay.*
    It's okay, she whispered back. *Everything's going to be okay.*
    But it's incredible news—finally. It's what you've been waiting for.
    It is, my love, absolutely.
    I have to stay with Vanessa, Isabelle, Finn said.
    Of course you do.
    I really wish I could make a different choice.
    It's the only choice.
    I'm sorry.
    Don't be sorry.
    But your family is coming back, that's a miracle.
    It *is* a miracle, absolutely.

So you couldn't have stayed with me anyway.

I couldn't have stayed with you anyway.

It's the only way.

It's the only way.

Then why did he want to rip his windpipe out of his throat?

Was the choice taken from us? Finn said. I can't think straight.

I know you can't, she said, her love for him running down her face. You've been reeling these past few weeks, you hardly knew what to say or do. But no, the choice has *not* been taken from us. And if it has, it's been taken from us by grace.

How can we go our separate ways, he said. How can you walk away into another life?

She didn't speak or couldn't.

We have so much land, he said. Why can't we build you and Mirik a house?

And you and I live separately but together? She almost smiled.

Yes. Why not?

She said nothing.

Are you silent because you're thinking about it?

I'm silent because I'm listening to you dream an impossible dream, she said.

I don't want to be half-alive, Isabelle.

You will never be half anything.

If you are happy, why are tears falling from your eyes? You hardly ever cry.

It's not obvious why?

But where will you go?

There's a wide world to choose from. We'll figure it out. Montana? She smiled. I will ride horses and plant tulips. I'll wear my white hat and every so often recall what you once said when I asked you what you wanted and you replied that you wanted to follow me into a time inside a time when all our dreams came true.

Your dreams *have* come true, Finn said. Your children have been found.

Isabelle breathed low and shallow. I said *all* our dreams, Finn.

Their silence fell on summer flowers.

Perhaps in another life, Isa.

Yes, perhaps in another life.

Language was inadequate for what was too hard to put into words. But he tried again. Why don't you stay on the farm with Mirik and the boys? We'll leave. I'll go to Connecticut, get that job. You can have the farm. Walter has signed the deed over to me, and I'll sign it over to you, like I did with the truck. So easy. And I wouldn't mind working with submarines. You know I like wearing a suit, nice shoes, being clean.

Just say banker, Finn, one word to mean all others.

He smiled. Once a year you can bring me your prize-winning tomatoes.

Myi kohanyi, she whispered. Thank you. But the savior farm is also not where my heart is. I was there because you were there. But I need a riding life.

You can't ride on Loving Lane?

I need a limitless plain. *Kazak* means free man.

But where?

Why, do you want to follow me? She smiled.

Forever.

I'm not kidding. Montana boundless.

That's so far. A world apart.

We can have a ranch there, some acres. Little by little heal, plant, breed horses. The children would like it. Mirik too. Helena has a wonderful university if they want to go. Mirik can have his cows. He's always liked cows.

What's Mickey Winslow going to do without you? That's not what Finn wanted to ask. He used the wrong name. He could hardly speak.

She threaded her fingers through his. *You're going to do great, you'll see.*

They're going to come to you from all over and beg you to do for them what you did with Starfire.

Some gift, she said. I can recognize greatness in others. She held his face in her hands. I suppose it *is* a little bit of a gift. You are beautiful and precious. I saw it from the start. She kissed him. He kissed her. I can't believe we weren't meant to be, she said.

We were meant to be, Isabelle, he said. We just weren't meant to last.

It's okay, she whispered, her arms around him. *Everything is going to be okay.*

It's okay, he whispered, his arms around her. *Everything is going to be okay.*

The three of them returned to the farm so she could say goodbye to his family, to the children who had spent half their lives with her. Junie was inconsolable.

And so was Walter. "What are we going to do without you, Isabelle?" It was too sudden for everyone. "Harvest season is coming."

"Yes, Walter," she said. "It's my favorite season."

Walter tried to get himself together. "Don't worry, my dear," he said, "we'll manage, we promise. You've been a marvel for us, an absolute marvel. Don't listen to me, I'm just an old fool. Your children are coming back, that's everything—" But he couldn't finish speaking before he had to rush tearfully from the room. Olivia, ever the practical one, asked what Isabelle and her family were going to live on.

"The horses have taken care of a lot," Isabelle said. "And your son took care of the rest."

"If you ever need anything, Isabelle..." Earl said.

"I know where to find you, Your Honor." She smiled.

"Finn's been working for years to make this happen," Earl said. "All his efforts have been for this."

"Yes, your son has been very good to me. You all have."

"Why can't you just bring them here? They can help us, they can stay here." It wasn't Junie who said this, it was Walter, trying again.

Junie pitched in. "Mae and I will give up our room, why can't they live with us here?" Junie kept repeating over and over.

"Shut up, June," said Mae. "You don't understand *anything*. They can't!"

"But *why*?" Junie cried.

"They can't, that's all! No use going on about why."

Vanessa cornered Isabelle in the pantry. "Isabelle," she said in her best Beacon Hill mistress tone, "Finn and I are so happy your family is finally returning. We both know how much that means to you. And now that Finn knows you're going to be all right, he is *so* relieved. It's been very hard for him . . . He wanted to make the right choice but he was so worried about you . . ." She trailed off.

Isabelle kept her tongue.

"Thank you for all you've done for Finn and me, for your many years of helping us."

"Vanessa," Isabelle said, "it was an act of service. Do you even know what that is?"

Vanessa stammered.

"This isn't the time to be unkind—to me or to him—when you and I both know that a mere shadow can overthrow you."

"Isabelle, I didn't mean anything—"

Isabelle was no longer listening. She was already in the kitchen. "Finn? Ah, there you are. Ready? It's time to go."

"Do you have what you need?" Finn managed to ask her out on the porch. Her balalaika and small suitcase were in her hands. They stood with their downcast faces.

"I have what I need."

Unable to meet each other's gaze or speak one more word, they nodded into the glossy blue planks. She turned and walked to the truck, where Schumann sat waiting, his hat in his lap. She got in and started the engine.

"Did you say goodbye to her, Daddy?" said Junie, standing in the drive pressed into Finn's side, clutching his sleeve, weeping, her shoulders heaving. "I didn't see you say goodbye to her."

"I said goodbye to her, Junie," said Finn.

"Say goodbye to Daddy, Isabelle!" Junie cried, ripping away from him, sobbing, and running toward the reversing truck. "You forgot to say goodbye to him!"

Isabelle stopped the Model B, opened the door, and hopped out. She walked toward him and his daughter. "Junebug, I would never forget to say goodbye to your dad," she said. "But here, I'll say it one more time so you can hear, all right, pumpkin?" Putting on her bravest face, she hugged him, she kissed him on the lips. With clenched fists she crossed both arms over her chest in a gesture of strength and tribute and stepped away. "Goodbye, Finn."

"Godspeed. Be well, Isabelle."

She got back into the truck with Schumann, they waved, and took off.

It's short, Finn whispered. *It's really quite . . . quite short.*

He and Junie stood at the end of the drive and watched them until the truck reached the end of Loving Lane, made a right, and disappeared.

86

The Box

Finn accepted Henry Barrett's job offer at Electric Boat and the family moved to Groton, Connecticut, a seaside town near Mystic. They stayed on the farm until the end of the harvest in October, until the last of the wheat had been reaped and the potatoes were in the root cellar and the corn was in the crib. Finn was initially hired as their business operations manager, but soon got promoted to vice president and chief strategy officer. They bought a house in the center of Mystic and a summer home on nearby Mason's Island. Finn's office windows in Groton overlooked the water, and every day at lunch he took a walk on the marina.

Like Finn, the country slowly but surely got to its feet, even before the war. Though the Dow Jones continued to hover around the lowly 120, employment was up, production was up, consumer confidence, retail sales, house values were all on the rise.

Walter never made it out of Hampton. He died of congestive heart failure a month before they moved. "I want my tombstone to say, *I bought the farm*," Walter said on his deathbed. "I've never been happier in my life than the four years I spent here."

Finn kept the property in his family and rented it out to tenant farmers who took good care of it. They cultivated all five acres, feeding themselves and selling their produce to the surrounding towns, and bred their own animals: cows, chickens, goats, even horses.

Eleanor and Bertie's marriage lasted all of five minutes. Eleanor moved to Mystic with Monty and they lived with Lucy in Finn and Vanessa's guest cottage. After Eleanor divorced in Hampton, she remarried in Groton, divorced in Portland, Maine, and got engaged again in Providence, Rhode Island. Monty went to Harvard and then to war—command sergeant major, designation: sharpshooter, in the Big Red One. He died in Okinawa in 1945.

Finn bought his mother and father a house a block from him, so they could come over any time they wanted. The house had a small yard where they grew eggplant and tomatoes. A few times a week, Earl biked five miles to Groton to meet Finn for lunch, and together father and son enjoyed a walk along the water.

Slowly, Finn and Vanessa adapted to their new life. Finn liked the submarines and the sea. He and Vanessa made new friends, had cookouts, spent their anniversaries in New York City. They had two more children, both girls, Charlotte born in 1937, and Emily in 1939. Mae was nearly seventeen and Junie sixteen when their last sister arrived. Vanessa was forty.

When World War II broke out, Electric Boat, the only company to build submarines for the United States Navy since 1899, went from a small struggling business that built a few submersible ships and some merchant vessels to a multi-billion-dollar corporation. The Electric Boat shares Earl Evans had given his son as a graduation present jumped in price by 5000 percent through the Depression years and the war.

Lucas remained in Florida from where he wrote and called, begging Finn to move down south. "What a wonderful life it is here," he wrote at the end of every letter, said at the end of every phone call.

After the family left for Connecticut, Finn lost touch with Schumann and Nate.

For many years he mourned her. He walked around the edges of his life as what he was, a man who had suffered a loss from which he could not recover. He felt removed from everything. Nothing had any meaning.

Little by little Finn took hold of himself. He couldn't stand to see the disenchantment on Vanessa's face when she looked at him. That's not what Finn wanted to be—a disappointment to his wife. He found the relief inside himself: he remembered the war. From a box among his personal belongings, he pulled out a bundled sheaf of Vanessa's old letters, the ones she wrote to him when he was convalescing in Italy, and re-read them. They were emotional, funny, deeply loving. He remembered how much they had meant to him, how they revived him when he had been at his lowest. They had the same effect on him now. She had scented every paper with her delicate perfume, and though faint, it was still there, and each time he inhaled, he remembered the love he had felt for her then. She was his only comfort after losing Travis. And so Finn set about rebuilding his life on the faded memory of the love he once felt for Vanessa. He brought her letters out into the open, and into the small wooden box where the letters had been he set down his grief everlasting and closed the lid and buried it in a far-away corner of his house.

We are hard-pressed on every side, but not crushed; perplexed, but not in despair; persecuted, but not abandoned; struck down, but not destroyed.

Eleven years passed.

In the middle of one night in the summer of 1946 Finn opened his eyes, awakened by unbearable dreams. He was in a winter field and came upon Isabelle's children buried up to their chests in the frozen earth. They reached out their arms to him and he stretched out his hand and woke up touching nothing but thawed-out air.

He sat bolt upright in bed and gasped.

"Oh my God!" Finn said. "She *lied.*"

Epilogue

Finn took a few days off work and drove to Boston. He needed to find Schumann. The tailor would know the truth. He wouldn't lie to a direct question. He stopped on the way to re-read Nate's telegram to Schumann that Isabelle had left for him. The telegram was seared into his memory—yet he read it again, to search for the part he might have missed.

> STOP EVERYTHING. TELL ISABELLE HER FAMILY FOUND. MIRIK. SLAVA. MAXIM. STORY TO FOLLOW. BUT ALL WELL. ON BOAT AND SAFE. LEAVING BRINDISI TOMORROW. BOSTON FIVE DAYS.

Where did it go wrong? What didn't he see? Finn was so sure now that it wasn't true, yet there was nothing specific he could point to, no detail that was glaringly out of place. The date was right. The name was right. It had the look of a real telegram. It was an authentic bill of lading, it wasn't backdated, there was no mistaking it, no translating it wrong.

Yet it was false.

Did the truth lie in the words Schumann spoke to Finn many years ago when Isabelle was still brand new and he was mystified by her?

Define tough.

She will do whatever needs to be done.

Finn hadn't been to Boston in many years. It looked different, yet the same. Perhaps like him. In North End he couldn't find parking as usual. Nice to see some things never changed.

Schumann's old tailor shop was gone, replaced by a tiny lunch joint. Next to it was a coffee shop and a shoe repair. Finn tried the shoe guy. Perhaps all tailors and cobblers knew each other. Apparently not. He spoke to the owner of the lunch place. The man didn't take over the spot from a tailor, he bought the place from a brush maker. Where was the brush maker now? Dead, as it turned out.

There was a new saloon nearby. He tried there.

Finn walked up and down Salem Street searching for a business that was around in 1930. The neighborhood had really changed. Finally he found a small butcher around the corner on Prince Street. The old man remembered Schumann! But after that, the trail went cold. Schumann had left North End years ago, sold his shop, moved somewhere, no one knew where.

"What about Nate?"

"Nate Schumann?"

"Yes, his son, Nate."

"Oh, sure. Everybody around here knows Nate. Half the kids in North End were born to the people he brought here. You can't spit without running into one of them. He had to stop when the war started, and then fell on hard times, had to sell his beautiful ship, but I heard he started sailing again."

"Is he still in Boston?"

"Last I heard Nate's been docking in Provincetown. You could try there. Maybe the old doctor is with his son."

"Provincetown on Cape Cod? Why?"

"The port fees are cheaper. You got a car? It's a bit of a drive."

"I know where Provincetown is," Finn said. It was next to Truro.

It took him nearly three hours to drive to the Canal Causeway and down the two-lane Mid-Cape Highway that ran like a spine through Cape Cod. Unlike North End, not much had changed here. The dune conservationists had made sure of that. Bourne, Sandwich, Barnstable, Yarmouth, Dennis, Brewster; the towns could barely be seen from the road, flanked by tall sandy grasses that hid the cliffs and the rolling ocean. Only when he neared Orleans, Eastham, and Wellfleet did the dunes shorten, the hills flatten, and the sea became prominent and visible on both sides—the Atlantic and the salty Cape Cod Bay. Shops, hotels, private houses, and little restaurants lined the road.

After Wellfleet was Truro. After Truro, Provincetown.

Truro was slightly more built out. Finn didn't recall there being quite as many restaurants and hotels. He drove slowly through the familiar landscape, remembering the many golden days he had spent on these shores with his young babies, and less long ago with the woman who changed his life.

His heart stopped. He nearly drove off the road. He pulled onto the shoulder and sat stunned for a few minutes trying to collect himself.

Were his eyes deceiving him? Across the highway, on the bay side, half covered by dunes and trees, behind a white picket fence, stood a little white clapboard cottage. It was a restaurant with a menu board out in front, and its name high across the gray cedar shakes roof read: *Isabelle's*.

For many minutes Finn sat, kneading the wheel, deciding what to do. He would look so foolish. But he couldn't *not* go inside and check.

Why did it feel like the thing it was? It had the aura of truth around it.

The real truth.

He got out of his car, straightened his tie, pulled back his graying blond hair, ran his hand through his neatly trimmed beard. After another minute of staring at the sign on the house—literally a sign—he headed inside.

It was four o'clock and the restaurant was empty. The bell trilled as he came in. It was a small, clean place with white tablecloths and silver candlesticks. There was a dining patio in the back with a view of the bay. It was dusky inside. Clanging noises and an occasional *fuck!* came from the kitchen. Presently, a man walked out, dressed all in black, and headed toward Finn at the hostess podium. The man was olive-skinned, curly-haired, black-eyed, soccer-player thin. He smiled a big friendly smile and in a Portuguese accent said, "Sorry, we don't open till 5:30."

Finn shook his head. "No, no," he said. "I just wanted to ask a question."

"Shoot, fella, ask away."

"The name of your restaurant . . . Is it named after someone? Your mother, perhaps?"

The man offered a wide grin. "It's named after someone, all right, but she's definitely not my mother."

"Who is Isabelle?" Finn said.

"And who are you?" asked the Portuguese man. There was a blink, a double take, a deep stare up and down. "Oh my God—are you *Finn*?"

Finn didn't know what he wanted to hear until he heard it.

But after he heard it, he knew that wasn't it.

He wished the man didn't know who he was. He wished it wasn't the same Isabelle. He wished for no one in Truro to speak his name.

I wish this Isabelle wasn't *you*, Isabelle.

I wish what you had told me was true, and I wasn't just a fool.

But I was a fool.

And I wish I didn't know that.

The man stuck out his hand and pumped Finn's, amiably, confidently. "I'm Adao Diaz," he said. "Everyone calls me Dio, even she."

"Where is—she?"

"Out back. Picking some stuff for me to cook. Go ahead. She'll be happy to see you." Adao Diaz smiled, pointing Finn to the side exit, raised his hand in farewell, and returned to the kitchen.

Finn stood at the door with his hand on the handle and waited. No, he wasn't waiting. He was praying. *Please—keep me together.* He stared at his shoes. He didn't think he would ever see her again.

Did he have enough of the old him left to open the door?

He closed his eyes.

But isn't this what he came for? If not for this, for what?

He took the deepest breath, in case he couldn't breathe again, and stepped out into the blinding sunshine.

Wide wooden steps led down to a small vegetable garden, full of supports and little dividing fences and lush growth. Beyond the garden lay the achingly familiar beach and bay.

Below his sightline in the verdant bushes he saw a glimpse of a cream dress, a wave of honey hair. He heard a familiar robust alto say, "Dio! I'm not ready yet—two minutes."

Isabelle, he said, or thought he said. *Isabelle.*

She rose to her feet and raised her eyes to the cottage.

The basket dangled in her hands, fell to the ground. She put her hands on her heart. *Finn!*

He stepped to her. She rushed up the stairs to him. They embraced. She was in his arms a long time.

After they disengaged, a big smile lit up her face. "I knew it—once a banker, always a banker." She touched his tie, brushed dandelion fuzz off the lapel of his jacket, lightly ran her fingers across the edge of his trimmed beard.

She looked older but the same. She was tanned, and her bare arms were toned and smooth as if she still rode horses. Her gray eyes had lines around them, her mouth too. She was still slim, still busty, still spilling out of her peasant dress. On her feet were flip-flops and her toenails were painted red.

"Hello, Isabelle."

"Hello, Finn." Her smile was as effervescent as ever.

"Montana, Isabelle? *Really?*"

"I hope you're not a detective in your new life." The accent was there but her words were fluent.

"What happened to Montana, to a ranch, to horses?"

"I have ranch. I have horses," she said with a cheerful shrug. "Just not in Montana. Finn, come on, I don't even know where Montana is. You know how bad I am with maps. That should've been your clue. I could've said Montevideo or Mauritania."

"You're just naming M words now."

"Yes! Like Montana."

"They have stables in Truro?"

"All over Cape Cod, yes. And mine's right across the road, on the ocean."

"Are you breeding horses?"

"Like rabbits. Though dang it, I still can't get them to foal more than once a year." She grinned.

"You're just not trying hard enough, Isabelle."

"Ha. Working on it."

"Still giving people horse advice they don't want to hear?"

She rolled her eyes. "No one likes the truth, Finn. They all want their horses to be Triple Crown caliber. I tell them, if you want me to lie to you, you'll have to pay me double."

Finn let her words hang in the air. "Is that what I did—pay you double?"

"You," she said lightly, "still owe me six years of back pay. But how are you? How's Vanessa?"

"She's fine. Better." He shrugged. "Two steps forward, one step back."

"Sounds like one step forward to me," Isabelle said. "And your girls?"

"Good. Junie just got married—to a naval officer of all things."

"Little Junebug! Good for her. Of course, now Army man has Navy son-in-law. Yikes. And Mayflower?"

"Mae is in med school. She wants to be a doctor."

"A doctor is a wonderful thing for a woman to be." They caught up on all the rest. She told him about the many things she was doing.

"So, you're still a whirling dervish, I see," he said.

"Well, you know what you Americans say," said Isabelle. "A rolling stone gathers no moths."

They both laughed. "Thank you for that," Finn said.

"You're welcome. I'm here all week."

"And who's Adao Diaz?"

"Dio? He owns this place."

"Owns a place called *Isabelle's*?"

She chuckled. "He likes how it sounds. I guess we co-own it. He's a fantastic chef. I just grow the food. Help him out on the weekends when it's busy. Mostly I'm with the horses. Gallop right through the ocean tides." She smiled.

"Did you come here after you left me?"

"Yes."

"And stayed here?"

"And stayed here."

"What about Schumann? Nate?" *Where are your husband and children, Isabelle?* Finn wanted to ask, but couldn't bear to ask.

"Nate is still sailing the world like a maniac," Isabelle said. "Doing less of the other thing, now that the Soviet Union expanded into Poland and Romania and surrounded itself with Communists on all sides." She sighed. "Schumann is here with me. He retired a few years ago." She rolled her eyes. "When I say retired, I mean, he was going blind so he packed up shop and came here, supposedly out to pasture, but instead continued tailoring and doctoring in Provincetown. There are few things more concerning than a blind doctor with a needle and thread. We are not allowed to tell him he's blind."

"He doesn't know?"

"He thinks his lenses are dirty."

Finn stood. She stood.

"Well, is that it?" he said finally. "Have you told me everything?" He paused. "Have you told me everything—but the truth?"

She drew in her breath—almost imperceptibly. "Oh, Finn. Do you really want one more story?"

"From your tone, I'm guessing not."

"Do you even remember the things I told you so long ago about Ispas, Ukraine, my family?"

He remembered everything. It was all he had left of her.

"Do you have a few minutes? Want to go sit?" She pointed to the bench in the garden that overlooked the sea. They sat next to each other. He pulled out two cigarettes, one for him and one for her. He lit hers, then his own. They inhaled and smoked silently for a few moments amid the daisies and the wild roses.

A burning cigarette in his mouth, Finn retrieved Nate's telegram from his pocket.

"Why do you still have that old thing!" She unfolded the browning paper, read the words, folded it carefully, and handed it back to him. "Did you come to Truro for your lake full of longing, Finn Evans?" she said quietly, becoming momentarily grayed out by a trace of the old life.

He supposed he did. "Where's your family, Isabelle? Where are the husband and children the telegram said were on their way to you?"

And then she spoke the words he dreaded to hear. "Long dead and gone," she said, inhaling the nicotine, the hand in her lap tightening into a fist.

Mama, Mama!

Isabelle was on Boyko, in the saddle with Cici, as they zigzagged through the trees and the boulders toward the hill before the Dniester, so close to Romania, so close to freedom.

Wait, do you hear that?

Hear what?

Behind her, below her, to the side of her, unmistakably, Isabelle heard her children's voices. At first she thought she was imagining them.

A man's coarse voice yelled, *Woman, turn around! Behold your children.*

But Isabelle heard another voice, telling her to never turn around. It was shouting to her through the trees and across the plain, and it was Mirik's. *No, Isabelle, go, Isabelle!*

Whatever you do, Mirik, run, run, and don't turn around.

Go, Isabelle! Don't look back!

A shot rang out. Mirik's voice ceased shouting.

Isabelle couldn't not look back. Through the trees, in the distance behind her, Mirik lay lifeless at her sons' feet. Slava and Maxim stood shoulder to shoulder over the body of their father, their desperate faces to her, their small backs to the machine guns trained on them.

Isabelle thought she said, *Stop, Cici, my children!* but Cici was spurring, struggling uphill, and didn't stop.

No, Mama, go, Mama! Don't stop!

In horror, Isabelle saw her children pull from their jackets the stick grenades that Roman had given them. She had time to open her mouth in a suffocating NO but it came out as a silent O. They pulled out the detonating pins, in unison yelled, *Go, go, go!* yelled *Urrah!* spun around and smashed their grenades as hard as they could against the ground at the feet of their captors, at their own feet.

Isabelle screamed or thought she screamed.

An explosion, a rising blast of flame, a torrent of fire.

She fainted and fell off the horse sideways. Her feet got tangled in the stirrups and straps and sidebags. While Cici barreled upward and onward, Isabelle hung upside down. Up the hill, down the hill, across the river.

Cici never turned around.

The shock of it was merciless. The details were erased, and in that was small mercy, but the agony remained. Savage children born of a savage mother, pounded into savage dust.

"Like this, I brought my boys with me to America," Isabelle said, "and in the saddle we stayed, bound in our terror, strapped to each other and unburied together. My inner life was the waters of Lavelle over my head and Nate saying to me *they're alive, they're alive*. And they were. For so long I refused to accept that the black void inside me sprang from the same well as my light." She took a breath. "Such was the requiem for my fallen children. I gave it to the lake, and the lake took it. I didn't die. Eventually I crawled out, like a crippled thing. I wasn't helpless—but I wasn't blameless either, do you know what I mean? I had all that broken love that had nowhere to go until I gave it to you and learned to fly."

They sat lost in thought, their legs touching. They smoked one more cigarette before Finn spoke. "When did you know it?" he asked. "It was that awful afternoon at Gallops, wasn't it, when we met Omelian Marchenko. That's why you fell to the floor weeping blood from your lungs."

Isabelle didn't answer immediately, as if even after all the years she still didn't want to think about the devastation, or talk about it. "Yes." She smoked. "The flesh-eating creature said, *Men died first*. And I saw Mirik's body on the ground. And then the rest of it. It poured in."

"Oh, Isabelle." He was so sad for her.

"You know, I still believe I'm going to see them again one day," she said.

You will, he whispered.

"Right." She nodded, as if grateful he knew exactly what she meant. "But I'm so afraid—what if they won't know who I am? What if they don't recognize me? What if they've forgotten the one who loves them and who mourns them to this day?"

Finn shook his head. *That can never happen.*

You don't know. Maybe that's what happens. "I didn't tell you," she said, finding her voice, "because I didn't want you to feel you were tethered to me by anything but your heart and free will. I didn't want you to think of me as alone in the world."

But you were alone in the world, he wanted to say but didn't for fear he would weep.

He fidgeted with the telegram in his hands. She nudged him lightly. "What did I tell you about Nate? Don't trust a word he says. The man lies for a living. If he weren't a sailor he'd be an actor or a writer. All he does is lie."

How could you do it, Isabelle? Finn whispered. *Why did you do it?*

"You know how. You know why." She took his hand, held it for a moment, put her fist into it. "All I did was destroy life. I created life, and then I destroyed it. That could not be my purpose, especially not in your life. There was pain enough. And we were all bloodied."

He didn't speak.

"The things Vanessa said to you, Finn, that morning on the farm, the things you didn't want to hear, that you were so angry at her for saying. They were manipulative and calculating. But they were true."

Finn couldn't see the ground in front of his black dress shoes. He shook his head. "I came to you that day at the stables and said I was staying with her because I thought your husband and sons were finally coming back. I didn't want you to make the impossible choice. I did it for you."

"And I knew what it meant for you not to be another Tadhg McBride. It was the strongest, most ardent imperative of your life." Her eyes were soft on him. "I didn't want you to make the impossible choice either. I did it for you."

"But yours wasn't true!"

"Was yours true? Did you *want* to leave your family, abandon your blameless daughters?"

His soul was burning.

Reaching out, she put her hand on his arm. "I forgave Nate when I finally understood," she said. "You lie to save a life."

He tried hard to stay composed, to sit straight.

"Finn . . . look at me. I bestowed on you grace for grace. You took me in when I was wounded, and in return I gave you back the life I nearly took from you." Her voice was a whisper. "I was the crane wife. Out of my falling-out silk feathers I stitched you a beautiful woman who loved you, and it turned out she was already living in your house. She was your wife."

With shaking hands, Finn lit another cigarette for her and him, and they both pitched forward, their elbows on their knees, smoking, wordless.

Mama, Mama, a voice cried from the sea.

She lifted her gaze. Finn lifted his. Near the water, a young boy was jumping up and down and waving to get her attention. Finn peered into the quivering sun glare. He stood up to see better. He sat down.

"You have a son." It wasn't a question.

"Yes."

The boy was skipping up and down the shore.

"How old is he?"

There was an interminable pause.

Ten, she breathed out.

In ineffable silence, Finn stared at Isabelle. Unable to take the expression in his eyes, she turned her face toward the water.

He tried to make out the boy's features, but there was something in his eye preventing him from seeing clearly, a glassy occlusion, an opaque, bottomless sorrow. *How could you do it, Isabelle?*

"Finn, forgive me," she whispered. "You would have never *ever* left me if you found out I was carrying your baby."

He knew that was true.

His throat made an uncontrolled guttural sound. *It's nothing, my love,* Finn thought he said. *It's just my heartbreak making a little noise.*

"Come, let's go meet him." She stubbed out her cigarette and stood up.

Finn shook his head.

She laid her hand on his forearm, like she used to, to steady him. "It's all right. It's right. Come and meet him."

They opened the wooden gate and started toward the water.

"What's his name?"

"Tatum."

"*Tatum?*"

"Yes. I wanted him to have a free name. Not Roman, or Mirik, or Travis. I didn't want to flinch every time I called for him. But you know what?" Isabelle smiled. "I do *smile* every time I call for him—remembering your lovely Junebug and you. How you laughed at my speakings, how you loved to correct me."

"Does the boy know he's named after a mispronounced potato?"

"No, and more important, does he need to?"

They neared the shoreline. Truro, a strip of windblown land between the ocean and the sea, a mythical land of cold mist and hot make-believe. The child ran up, blond-haired and gray-eyed. He was skinny, tanned, smiling. He had strong, developed legs, perhaps was a rider like his mother.

"Tatum, I want you to meet my dear friend Finn. He's the one who gave your mom a place to live when I came to America from Ukraine."

Tatum, his gaze unwavering, stuck out his little hand. "Nice to finally meet you! My mom's told me so much about you. I'm Tatum Evans Lazar. How did you know we were here?"

Mutely, Finn shook the boy's outstretched hand. "I was passing by," he said, "and there you were."

"Neat! Mama, I wanted to show you how many clams I found. Finn, do you want to see too? Dio can put them on the menu tonight. I caught like four hundred. They practically crawled into my rake basket."

"Yes, in a minute, son," Isabelle said, ruffling the boy's salt-dried hair.

"Do you know clamming, Finn?" Tatum asked.

"I do," Finn said. "Many years ago, I taught your mother how to clam."

"You did?" The boy was excited. "Did you teach her how to ride horses?"

"No," Finn said. "That she learned before her time with me. Tell me about the clams. Are they good sized?"

"Oh, some are too big, good for chowder and not much else, but most are little necks and quahogs! Mama said when I'm older, she'll get me a proper boat."

"You like boats?"

"Very much," the boy said. "I like them more than I like horses." He twinkled. "But neither as much as I like baseball." He was teasing her.

"How is *that* an inherited trait?" Isabelle said quietly.

"Are you a good boy for your mother, Tatum?"

Tatum shrugged. "Not always. I try. Mom says it's the wildfire in my blood. I can't help it. Sometimes, I just want to do what I like."

"Don't we all," said Finn.

The boy ran off to find more clams in the departing tide, and they were left on the beach, just the two of them.

It was warm and mild in the late afternoon. There was no wind, and the sun lit up the water like razzle dazzle. Everywhere you looked there was beauty.

"I haven't been in this neck of the woods for so many years," Finn said. "Still magical here at this hour."

"Magic here morning, noon, and night," Isabelle said, straightening out her spine. "The world swells with tyrants, more each passing day. But here is a place of the just—a spot on this earth where happiness is allowed me forevermore. Despite the loud birds overhead." She lifted her eyes to the sky. "Sometimes I imagine my sons are white cranes, flying over me, noisy like they used to be, to remind me they're still here. *My crane sons,*" Isabelle whispered, blinking once, twice, and casting her gaze on Finn. "I work with my hands. I ride the animals of my heart and my youth. Our boy canters along without memories of evil, and I know that just downstream from us you are whole and true, walking the same great ocean, breathing the same hallowed air."

He formed his words, tried to make them leave his throat without breaking. "Yes, the poetess was wrong, and you are, as always, right," Finn said at last. "There isn't another beach in all the world like the one in Truro."

"And there never will be," said Isabelle. Her mouth trembling, she faced the sea. And when you looked at her from the outside, self-possessed, graceful, good-humored, smiling, you'd never suspect that anything inside had ever been broken.

"Wherever you were, Isabelle, I hoped you were in sunshine," he said.

"I am. You see that I am."

Divided by a life of time, of value, of place, of space, for one more moment Finn and Isabelle stood side by side as they watched Tatum wade and splash in Truro's shallow waters, his young voice carrying joy up and down the shoreline, fading, fading.

Mama, Mama.

Acknowledgments

Heartfelt gratitude to the men, women, and dog who have helped bring this book to life.

Alex Lloyd, my publisher, for believing in the book's potential, for his invaluable first reactions, and for never taking no for an answer. Without him, this book would not be.

Ingrid Ohlsson for her love of *Tully* and her warm enthusiasm in welcoming me to my new home at Pan Macmillan, this book's original publisher.

Brianne Collins, the Brienne of Tarth of the publishing world and my Evenstar, for keeping me level and grounded and for her stoic can-do attitude worthy of Marcus Aurelius at the first hour and the eleventh hour, on all matters great and small. Your patience and attention to detail are unmatched.

Vanessa Lanaway, my meticulous copy editor, for her keen eye and steadfast commitment to elevating the quality of my words.

Jo Pilgrim, the inexhaustible proofreader, for finding crazy things a minute before we were about to go to print. Well done!

Rufus Cuthbert and Ellen Kirkness, the marketing and publicity gurus, for their stellar efforts in promoting my book.

Jacinta di Mase and Danielle Binks, my agents, for their hard work on my behalf.

Thanks to Dr. Jeffrey Martin, who kept me from going blind. Book deadline was April 4th, and he advised surgery on both eyes on March 14th and 28th. My publisher said, "Of *course* it's good to be able to see what you're writing, but you'll still be able to deliver the manuscript by the due date, right?" That's *some* faith from all concerned.

To Sandra Noakes, my old friend, my erstwhile publicist and travel companion, for her lifelong passion for horses that proved to be so inspiring.

Thanks to my family, especially those who were with me during the final insane months of finishing *Light at Lavelle*: namely my husband Kevin, always by my side, my sounding board and support, and my youngest child Tatiana, who called herself my "stay at home daughter" and who brought me food and drink and reminded me as only she can that after being holed up for sixteen hours, it was time for her mother to leave the lair to watch the Yankees lose and play beer pong.

Finally, thanks to Santino Corleone, "Sonny," the Golden Retriever who brought me his ball a thousand times an hour during my writing life, even when I didn't ask for it.

About the Author

Paullina Simons is the author of sixteen internationally acclaimed, bestselling novels, including *Tully* and the Bronze Horseman Saga. Born and raised in the former Soviet Union, Paullina immigrated to the United States with her family in the mid-seventies. She has lived in Rome, London, and Dallas, and now resides in New York with her husband, one child, one dog, and a one-eyed cat.

PAULLINA SIMONS

FROM OPEN ROAD MEDIA

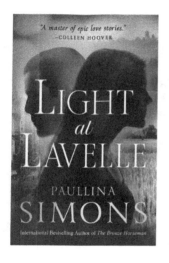 

Find a full list of our authors and titles at www.openroadmedia.com

FOLLOW US
@OpenRoadMedia